Grace Livingston Hill

Finding Love in Wild West

OK Publishing 2021

Grace Livingston Hill
Finding Love in Wild West

3 Western Romance Novels

Published by
MUSAICUM
Books

- Advanced Digital Solutions & High-Quality book Formatting -

musaicumbooks@okpublishing.info

2021 OK Publishing

ISBN 978-80-272-7439-0

Contents

THE GIRL FROM MONTANA	13
CHAPTER I THE GIRL, AND A GREAT PERIL	16
CHAPTER II THE FLIGHT	20
CHAPTER III THE PURSUIT	26
CHAPTER IV THE TWO FUGITIVES	31
CHAPTER V A NIGHT RIDE	35
CHAPTER VI A CHRISTIAN ENDEAVOR MEETING IN THE WILDERNESS	39
CHAPTER VII BAD NEWS	46
CHAPTER VIII THE PARTING	50
CHAPTER IX IN A TRAP	55
CHAPTER X PHILADELPHIA AT LAST	60
CHAPTER XI IN FLIGHT AGAIN	66
CHAPTER XII ELIZABETH'S DECLARATION OF INDEPENDENCE	69
CHAPTER XIII ANOTHER GRANDMOTHER	73
CHAPTER XIV IN A NEW WORLD	79
CHAPTER XV AN EVENTFUL PICNIC	83
CHAPTER XVI ALONE AGAIN	89
CHAPTER XVII A FINAL FLIGHT AND PURSUIT	93
THE MAN OF THE DESERT	103
I. PROSPECTING	104
II. THE MAN	109
III. THE DESERT	115
IV. THE QUEST	121
V. THE TRAIL	127
VI. CAMP	131
VII. REVELATION	136
VIII. RENUNCIATION	140
IX. "FOR REMEMBRANCE"	145
X. HIS MOTHER	149
XI. REFUGE	154
XII. QUALIFYING FOR SERVICE	159
XIII. THE CALL OF THE DESERT	165
XIV. HOME	169
XV. THE WAY OF THE CROSS	175
XVI. THE LETTER	179
XVII. DEDICATION	184
A VOICE IN THE WILDERNESS	187
CHAPTER I	188

CHAPTER II	192
CHAPTER III	196
CHAPTER IV	199
CHAPTER V	203
CHAPTER VI	206
CHAPTER VII	210
CHAPTER VIII	214
CHAPTER IX	218
CHAPTER X	222
CHAPTER XI	225
CHAPTER XII	230
CHAPTER XIII	234
CHAPTER XIV	240
CHAPTER XV	243
CHAPTER XVI	246
CHAPTER XVII	251
CHAPTER XVIII	258
CHAPTER XIX	262
CHAPTER XX	266
CHAPTER XXI	270
CHAPTER XXII	275
CHAPTER XXIII	280
CHAPTER XXIV	284
CHAPTER XXV	288
CHAPTER XXVI	294
CHAPTER XXVII	300
CHAPTER XXVIII	305
CHAPTER XXIX	310
CHAPTER XXX	316
CHAPTER XXXI	320
CHAPTER XXXII	323
CHAPTER XXXIII	326
CHAPTER XXXIV	331

THE GIRL FROM MONTANA

Dedicated to

MISS VIRGINIA COWAN

OF COWAN, MONTANA, WHOSE BRIGHT, BREEZY LETTERS AIDED
ME IN WRITING OF ELIZABETH'S EXPERIENCES IN THE WEST

CHAPTER I
THE GIRL, AND A GREAT PERIL

The late afternoon sun was streaming in across the cabin floor as the girl stole around the corner and looked cautiously in at the door.

There was a kind of tremulous courage in her face. She had a duty to perform, and she was resolved to do it without delay. She shaded her eyes with her hand from the glare of the sun, set a firm foot upon the threshold, and, with one wild glance around to see whether all was as she had left it, entered her home and stood for a moment shuddering in the middle of the floor.

A long procession of funerals seemed to come out of the past and meet her eye as she looked about upon the signs of the primitive, unhallowed one which had just gone out from there a little while before.

The girl closed her eyes, and pressed their hot, dry lids hard with her cold fingers; but the vision was clearer even than with her eyes open.

She could see the tiny baby sister lying there in the middle of the room, so little and white and pitiful; and her handsome, careless father sitting at the head of the rude home-made coffin, sober for the moment; and her tired, disheartened mother, faded before her time, dry-eyed and haggard, beside him. But that was long ago, almost at the beginning of things for the girl.

There had been other funerals, the little brother who had been drowned while playing in a forbidden stream, and the older brother who had gone off in search of gold or his own way, and had crawled back parched with fever to die in his mother's arms. But those, too, seemed long ago to the girl as she stood in the empty cabin and looked fearfully about her. They seemed almost blotted out by the last three that had crowded so close within the year. The father, who even at his worst had a kind word for her and her mother, had been brought home mortally hurt-an encounter with wild cattle, a fall from his horse in a treacherous place-and had never roused to consciousness again.

At all these funerals there had been a solemn service, conducted by a travelling preacher when one happened to be within reach, and, when there was none, by the trembling, determined, untaught lips of the white-faced mother. The mother had always insisted upon it, especially upon a prayer. It had seemed like a charm to help the departed one into some kind of a pitiful heaven.

And when, a few months after the father, the mother had drooped and grown whiter and whiter, till one day she clutched at her heart and lay down gasping, and said: "Good-by, Bess! Mother's good girl! Don't forget!" and was gone from her life of burden and disappointment forever, the girl had prepared the funeral with the assistance of the one brother left. The girl's voice had uttered the prayer, "Our Father," just as her mother had taught her, because there was no one else to do it; and she was afraid to send the wild young brother off after a preacher, lest he should not return in time.

It was six months now since the sad funeral train had wound its way among sage-brush and greasewood, and the body of the mother had been laid to rest beside her husband. For six months the girl had kept the cabin in order, and held as far as possible the wayward brother to his work and home. But within the last few weeks he had more and more left her alone, for a day, and sometimes more, and had come home in a sad condition and with bold, merry companions who made her life a constant terror. And now, but two short days ago, they had brought home his body lying across his own faithful horse, with two shots through his heart. It was a drunken quarrel, they told her; and all were sorry, but no one seemed responsible.

They had been kind in their rough way, those companions of her brother. They had stayed and done all that was necessary, had dug the grave, and stood about their comrade in good-natured grimness, marching in order about him to give the last look; but, when the sister tried to utter the prayer she knew her mother would have spoken, her throat refused to make a sound, and her tongue cleaved to the roof of her mouth. She had taken sudden refuge in the little shed that was her own room, and there had stayed till the rough companions had taken away the still form of the only one left in the family circle.

In silence the funeral train wound its way to the spot where the others were buried. They respected her tearless grief, these great, passionate, uncontrolled young men. They held in the rude jokes with which they would have taken the awesomeness from the occasion for themselves, and for the most part kept the way silently and gravely, now and then looking back with admiration to the slim girl with the stony face and unblinking eyes who followed them mechanically. They had felt that some one ought to do something; but no one knew exactly what, and so they walked silently.

Only one, the hardest and boldest, the ringleader of the company, ventured back to ask whether there was anything he could do for her, anything she would like to have done; but she answered him coldly with a "No!" that cut him to the quick. It had been a good deal for him to do, this touch of gentleness he had forced himself into. He turned from her with a wicked gleam of intent in his eyes, but she did not see it.

When the rude ceremony was over, the last clod was heaped upon the pitiful mound, and the relentless words, "dust to dust," had been murmured by one more daring than the rest, they turned and looked at the girl, who had all the time stood upon a mound of earth and watched them, as a statue of Misery might look down upon the world. They could not make her out, this silent, marble girl. They hoped now she would change. It was over. They felt an untold relief themselves from the fact that their reckless, gay comrade was no longer lying cold and still among them. They were done with him. They had paid their last tribute, and wished to forget. He must settle his own account with the hereafter now; they had enough in their own lives without the burden of his.

Then there had swept up into the girl's face one gleam of life that made her beautiful for the instant, and she had bowed to them with a slow, almost haughty, inclination of her head, and spread out her hands like one who would like to bless but dared not, and said clearly, "I thank you-all!" There had been just a slight hesitation before that last word "all," as if she were not quite sure, as her eyes rested upon the ringleader with doubt and dislike; then her lips had hardened as if justice must be done, and she had spoken it, "all!" and, turning, sped away to her cabin alone.

They were taken by surprise, those men who feared nothing in the wild and primitive West, and for a moment they watched her go in silence. Then the words that broke upon the air were not all pleasant to hear; and, if the girl could have known, she would have sped far faster, and her cheeks would have burned a brighter red than they did.

But one, the boldest, the ringleader, said nothing. His brows darkened, and the wicked gleam came and sat in his hard eyes with a green light. He drew a little apart from the rest, and walked on more rapidly. When he came to the place where they had left their horses, he took his and went on toward the cabin with a look that did not invite the others to follow. As their voices died away in the distance, and he drew nearer to the cabin, his eyes gleamed with cunning.

The girl in the cabin worked rapidly. One by one she took the boxes on which the rude coffin of her brother had rested, and threw them far out the back door. She straightened the furniture around fiercely, as if by erasing every sign she would force from memory the thought of the scenes that had just passed. She took her brother's coat that hung against the wall, and an old pipe from the mantle, and hid them in the room that was hers. Then she looked about for something else to be done.

A shadow darkened the sunny doorway. Looking up, she saw the man she believed to be her brother's murderer.

"I came back, Bess, to see if I could do anything for you."

The tone was kind; but the girl involuntarily put her hand to her throat, and caught her breath. She would like to speak out and tell him what she thought, but she dared not. She did not even dare let her thought appear in her eyes. The dull, statue-like look came over her face that she had worn at the grave. The man thought it was the stupefaction of grief.

"I told you I didn't want any help," she said, trying to speak in the same tone she had used when she thanked the men.

"Yes, but you're all alone," said the man insinuatingly; she felt a menace in the thought, "and I am sorry for you!"

He came nearer, but her face was cold. Instinctively she glanced to the cupboard door behind which lay her brother's belt with two pistols.

"You're very kind," she forced herself to say; "but I'd rather be alone now." It was hard to speak so when she would have liked to dash on him, and call down curses for the death of her brother; but she looked into his evil face, and a fear for herself worse than death stole into her heart.

He took encouragement from her gentle dignity. Where did she get that manner so imperial, she, born in a mountain cabin and bred on the wilds? How could she speak with an accent so different from those about her? The brother was not so, not so much so; the mother had been plain and quiet. He had not known her father, for he had lately come to this State in hiding from another. He wondered, with his wide knowledge of the world, over her wild, haughty beauty, and gloated over it. He liked to think just what worth was within his easy grasp. A prize for the taking, and here alone, unprotected.

"But it ain't good for you to be alone, you know, and I've come to protect you. Besides, you need cheering up, little girl." He came closer. "I love you, Bess, you know, and I'm going to take care of you now. You're all alone. Poor little girl."

He was so near that she almost felt his breath against her cheek. She faced him desperately, growing white to the lips. Was there nothing on earth or in heaven to save her? Mother! Father! Brother! All gone! Ah! Could she but have known that the quarrel which ended her wild young brother's life had been about her, perhaps pride in him would have salved her grief, and choked her horror.

While she watched the green lights play in the evil eyes above her, she gathered all the strength of her young life into one effort, and schooled herself to be calm. She controlled her involuntary shrinking from the man, only drew herself back gently, as a woman with wider experience and gentler breeding might have done.

"Remember," she said, "that my brother just lay there dead!" and she pointed to the empty centre of the room. The dramatic attitude was almost a condemnation to the guilty man before her. He drew back as if the sheriff had entered the room, and looked instinctively to where the coffin had been but a short time before, then laughed nervously and drew himself together.

The girl caught her breath, and took courage. She had held him for a minute; could she not hold him longer?

"Think!" said she. "He is but just buried. It is not right to talk of such things as love in this room where he has just gone out. You must leave me alone for a little while. I cannot talk and think now. We must respect the dead, you know." She looked appealingly at him, acting her part desperately, but well. It was as if she were trying to charm a lion or an insane man.

He stood admiring her. She argued well. He was half minded to humor her, for somehow when she spoke of the dead he could see the gleam in her brother's eyes just before he shot him. Then there was promise in this wooing. She was no girl to be lightly won, after all. She could hold her own, and perhaps she would be the better for having her way for a little. At any rate, there was more excitement in such game.

She saw that she was gaining, and her breath came freer.

"Go!" she said with a flickering smile. "Go! For—a little while," and then she tried to smile again.

He made a motion to take her in his arms and kiss her; but she drew back suddenly, and spread her hands before her, motioning him back.

"I tell you you must not now. Go! Go! or I will never speak to you again."

He looked into her eyes, and seemed to feel a power that he must obey. Half sullenly he drew back toward the door.

"But, Bess, this ain't the way to treat a fellow," he whined. "I came way back here to take care of you. I tell you I love you, and I'm going to have you. There ain't any other fellow going to run off with you—"

"Stop!" she cried tragically. "Don't you see you're not doing right? My brother is just dead. I must have some time to mourn. It is only decent." She was standing now with her back to the little cupboard behind whose door lay the two pistols. Her hand was behind her on the wooden latch.

"You don't respect my trouble!" she said, catching her breath, and putting her hand to her eyes. "I don't believe you care for me when you don't do what I say."

The man was held at bay. He was almost conquered by her sign of tears. It was a new phase of her to see her melt into weakness so. He was charmed.

"How long must I stay away?" he faltered.

She could scarcely speak, so desperate she felt. O if she dared but say, "Forever," and shout it at him! She was desperate enough to try her chances at shooting him if she but had the pistols, and was sure they were loaded—a desperate chance indeed against the best shot on the Pacific coast, and a desperado at that.

She pressed her hands to her throbbing temples, and tried to think. At last she faltered out, "Three days!"

He swore beneath his breath, and his brows drew down in heavy frowns that were not good to see. She shuddered at what it would be to be in his power forever. How he would play with her and toss her aside! Or kill her, perhaps, when he was tired of her! Her life on the mountain had made her familiar with evil characters.

He came a step nearer, and she felt she was losing ground.

Straightening up, she said coolly:

"You must go away at once, and not think of coming back at least until to-morrow night. Go!" With wonderful control she smiled at him, one frantic, brilliant smile; and to her great wonder he drew back. At the door he paused, a softened look upon his face.

"Mayn't I kiss you before I go?"

She shuddered involuntarily, but put out her hands in protest again. "Not to-night!" She shook her head, and tried to smile.

He thought he understood her, but turned away half satisfied. Then she heard his step coming back to the door again, and she went to meet him. He must not come in. She had gained in sending him out, if she could but close the door fast. It was in the doorway that she faced him as he stood with one foot ready to enter again. The crafty look was out upon his face plainly now, and in the sunlight she could see it.

"You will be all alone to-night."

"I am not afraid," calmly. "And no one will trouble me. Don't you know what they say about the spirit of a man—" she stopped; she had almost said "a man who has been murdered"—"coming back to his home the first night after he is buried?" It was her last frantic effort.

The man before her trembled, and looked around nervously.

"You better come away to-night with me," he said, edging away from the door.

"See, the sun is going down! You must go now," she said imperiously; and reluctantly the man mounted his restless horse, and rode away down the mountain.

She watched him silhouetted against the blood-red globe of the sun as it sank lower and lower. She could see every outline of his slouch-hat and muscular shoulders as he turned now and then and saw her standing still alone at her cabin door. Why he was going he could not tell; but he went, and he frowned as he rode away, with the wicked gleam still in his eye; for he meant to return.

At last he disappeared; and the girl, turning, looked up, and there rode the white ghost of the moon overhead. She was alone.

CHAPTER II
THE FLIGHT

A great fear settled down upon the girl as she realized that she was alone and, for a few hours at least, free. It was a marvellous escape. Even now she could hear the echo of the man's last words, and see his hateful smile as he waved his good-by and promised to come back for her to-morrow.

She felt sure he would not wait until the night. It might be he would return even yet. She cast another reassuring look down the darkening road, and strained her ear; but she could no longer hear hoof-beats. Nevertheless, it behooved her to hasten. He had blanched at her suggestion of walking spirits; but, after all, his courage might arise. She shuddered to think of his returning later, in the night. She must fly somewhere at once.

Instantly her dormant senses seemed to be on the alert. Fully fledged plans flashed through her brain. She went into the cabin, and barred the door. She made every movement swiftly, as if she had not an instant to spare. Who could tell? He might return even before dark. He had been hard to baffle, and she did not feel at all secure. It was her one chance of safety to get away speedily, whither it mattered little, only so she was away and hidden.

Her first act inside the cottage was to get the belt from the cupboard and buckle it around her waist. She examined and loaded the pistols. Her throat seemed seized with sudden constriction when she discovered that the barrels had been empty and the weapons would have done her no good even if she could have reached them.

She put into her belt the sharp little knife her brother used to carry, and then began to gather together everything eatable that she could carry with her. There was not much that could be easily carried-some dried beef, a piece of cheese, some corn-meal, a piece of pork, a handful of cheap coffee-berries, and some pieces of hard corn bread. She hesitated over a pan half full of baked beans, and finally added them to the store. They were bulky, but she ought to take them if she could. There was nothing else in the house that seemed advisable to take in the way of eatables. Their stores had been running low, and the trouble of the last day or two had put housekeeping entirely out of her mind. She had not cared to eat, and now it occurred to her that food had not passed her lips that day. With strong self-control she forced herself to eat a few of the dry pieces of corn bread, and to drink some cold coffee that stood in the little coffee-pot. This she did while she worked, wasting not one minute.

There were some old flour-sacks in the house. She put the eatables into two of them, with the pan of beans on the top, adding a tin cup, and tied them securely together. Then she went into her little shed room, and put on the few extra garments in her wardrobe. They were not many, and that was the easiest way to carry them. Her mother's wedding-ring, sacredly kept in a box since the mother's death, she slipped upon her finger. It seemed the closing act of her life in the cabin, and she paused and bent her head as if to ask the mother's permission that she might wear the ring. It seemed a kind of protection to her in her lonely situation.

There were a few papers and an old letter or two yellow with years, which the mother had always guarded sacredly. One was the certificate of her mother's marriage. The girl did not know what the others were. She had never looked into them closely, but she knew that her mother had counted them precious. These she pinned into the bosom of her calico gown. Then she was ready.

She gave one swift glance of farewell about the cabin where she had spent nearly all of her life that she could remember, gathered up the two flour-sacks and an old coat of her father's that hung on the wall, remembering at the last minute to put into its pocket the few matches and the single candle left in the house, and went out from the cabin, closing the door behind her.

She paused, looking down the road, and listened again; but no sound came to her save a distant howl of a wolf. The moon rode high and clear by this time; and it seemed not so lonely here, with everything bathed in soft silver, as it had in the darkening cabin with its flickering candle.

The girl stole out from the cabin and stealthily across the patch of moonlight into the shadow of the shackly barn where stamped the poor, ill-fed, faithful horse that her brother had ridden to his death upon. All her movements were stealthy as a cat's.

She laid the old coat over the horse's back, swung her brother's saddle into place,—she had none of her own, and could ride his, or without any; it made no difference, for she was perfectly at home on horseback,—and strapped the girths with trembling fingers that were icy cold with excitement. Across the saddle-bows she hung the two flour-sacks containing her provisions. Then with added caution she tied some old burlap about each of the horse's feet. She must make no sound and leave no track as she stole forth into the great world.

The horse looked curiously down and whinnied at her, as she tied his feet up clumsily. He did not seem to like his new habiliments, but he suffered anything at her hand.

"Hush!" she murmured softly, laying her cold hands across his nostrils; and he put his muzzle into her palm, and seemed to understand.

She led him out into the clear moonlight then, and paused a second, looking once more down the road that led away in front of the cabin; but no one was coming yet, though her heart beat high as she listened, fancying every falling bough or rolling stone was a horse's hoof-beat.

There were three trails leading away from the cabin, for they could hardly be dignified by the name of road. One led down the mountain toward the west, and was the way they took to the nearest clearing five or six miles beyond and to the supply store some three miles further. One led off to the east, and was less travelled, being the way to the great world; and the third led down behind the cabin, and was desolate and barren under the moon. It led down, back, and away to desolation, where five graves lay stark and ugly at the end. It was the way they had taken that afternoon.

She paused just an instant as if hesitating which way to take. Not the way to the west-ah, any but that! To the east? Yes, surely, that must be the trail she would eventually strike; but she had a duty yet to perform. That prayer was as yet unsaid, and before she was free to seek safety-if safety there were for her in the wide world-she must take her way down the lonely path. She walked, leading the horse, which followed her with muffled tread and arched neck as if he felt he were doing homage to the dead. Slowly, silently, she moved along into the river of moonlight and dreariness; for the moonlight here seemed cold, like the graves it shone upon, and the girl, as she walked with bowed head, almost fancied she saw strange misty forms flit past her in the night.

As they came in sight of the graves, something dark and wild with plumy tail slunk away into the shadows, and seemed a part of the place. The girl stopped a moment to gain courage in full sight of the graves, and the horse snorted, and stopped too, with his ears a-quiver, and a half-fright in his eyes.

She patted his neck and soothed him incoherently, as she buried her face in his mane for a moment, and let the first tears that had dimmed her eyes since the blow had fallen come smarting their way out. Then, leaving the horse to stand curiously watching her, she went down and stood at the head of the new-heaped mound. She tried to kneel, but a shudder passed through her. It was as if she were descending into the place of the dead herself; so she stood up and raised her eyes to the wide white night and the moon riding so high and far away.

"Our Father," she said in a voice that sounded miles away to herself. Was there any Father, and could He hear her? And did He care? "Which art in heaven —" but heaven was so far away and looked so cruelly serene to her in her desolateness and danger! "hallowed be thy name. Thy kingdom come —" whatever that might mean. "Thy will be done in earth, as it is in heaven." It was a long prayer to pray, alone with the pale moon-rain and the graves, and a distant wolf, but it was her mother's wish. Her will being done here over the dead-was that anything like the will of the Father being done in heaven? Her untrained thoughts hovered on the verge of great questions, and then slipped back into her pathetic self and its fear, while her tongue hurried on through the words of the prayer.

Once the horse stirred and breathed a soft protest. He could not understand why they were stopping so long in this desolate place, for nothing apparently. He had looked and looked at the shapeless mound before which the girl was standing; but he saw no sign of his lost master, and his instincts warned him that there were wild animals about. Anyhow, this was no place for a horse and a maid to stop in the night.

A few loose stones rattled from the horse's motion. The girl started, and looked hastily about, listening for a possible pursuer; but everywhere in the white sea of moonlight there was empty, desolate space. On to the "Amen" she finished then, and with one last look at the lonely graves she turned to the horse. Now they might go, for the duty was done, and there was no time to be lost.

Somewhere over toward the east across that untravelled wilderness of white light was the trail that started to the great world from the little cabin she had left. She dared not go back to the cabin to take it, lest she find herself already followed. She did not know the way across this lonely plain, and neither did the horse. In fact, there was no way, for it was all one arid plain so situated that human traveller seldom came near it, so large and so barren that one might wander for hours and gain no goal, so dry that nothing would grow.

With another glance back on the way she had come, the girl mounted the horse and urged him down into the valley. He stepped cautiously into the sandy plain, as if he were going into a river and must try its depth. He did not like the going here, but he plodded on with his burdens. The girl was light; he did not mind her weight; but he felt this place uncanny, and now and then would start on a little spurt of haste, to get into a better way. He liked the high mountain trails, where he could step firmly and hear the twigs crackle under his feet, not this muffled, velvet way where one made so little progress and had to work so hard.

The girl's heart sank as they went on, for the sand seemed deep and drifted in places. She felt she was losing time. The way ahead looked endless, as if they were but treading sand behind them which only returned in front to be trodden over again. It was to her like the valley of the dead, and she longed to get out of it. A great fear lest the moon should go down and leave her in this low valley alone in the dark took hold upon her. She felt she must get away, up higher. She turned the horse a little more to the right, and he paused, and seemed to survey the new direction and to like it. He stepped up more briskly, with a courage that could come only from an intelligent hope for better things. And at last they were rewarded by finding the sand shallower, and now and then a bit of rock cropping out for a firmer footing.

The young rider dismounted, and untied the burlap from the horse's feet. He seemed to understand, and to thank her as he nosed about her neck. He thought, perhaps, that their mission was over and they were going to strike out for home now.

The ground rose steadily before them now, and at times grew quite steep; but the horse was fresh as yet, and clambered upward with good heart; and the rider was used to rough places, and felt no discomfort from her position. The fear of being followed had succeeded to the fear of being lost, for the time being; and instead of straining her ears on the track behind she was straining her eyes to the wilderness before. The growth of sage-brush was dense now, and trees were ahead.

After that the way seemed steep, and the rider's heart stood still with fear lest she could never get up and over to the trail which she knew must be somewhere in that direction, though she had never been far out on its course herself. That it led straight east into all the great cities she never doubted, and she must find it before she was pursued. That man would be angry, *angry* if he came and found her gone! He was not beyond shooting her for giving him the slip in this way.

The more she thought over it, the more frightened she became, till every bit of rough way, and every barrier that kept her from going forward quickly, seemed terrible to her. A bob-cat shot across the way just ahead, and the green gleam of its eyes as it turned one swift glance at this strange intruder in its chosen haunts made her catch her breath and put her hand on the pistols.

They were climbing a long time-it seemed hours to the girl-when at last they came to a space where a better view of the land was possible. It was high, and sloped away on three sides. To her looking now in the clear night the outline of a mountain ahead of her became distinct, and the lay of the land was not what she had supposed. It brought her a furious sense of being lost. Over there ought to be the familiar way where the cabin stood, but there was no sign of anything she had ever seen before, though she searched eagerly for landmarks. The course she had chosen, and which had seemed the only one, would take her straight up, up over the mountain, a way well-nigh impossible, and terrible even if it were possible.

It was plain she must change her course, but which way should she go? She was completely turned around. After all, what mattered it? One way might be as good as another, so it led not home to the cabin which could never be home again. Why not give the horse his head, and let him pick out a safe path? Was there danger that he might carry her back to the cabin again, after all? Horses did that sometimes. But at least he could guide through this maze of perplexity till some surer place was reached. She gave him a sign, and he moved on, nimbly picking a way for his feet.

They entered a forest growth where weird branches let the pale moon through in splashes and patches, and grim moving figures seemed to chase them from every shadowy tree-trunk. It was a terrible experience to the girl. Sometimes she shut her eyes and held to the saddle, that she might not see and be filled with this frenzy of things, living or dead, following her. Sometimes a real black shadow crept across the path, and slipped into the engulfing darkness of the undergrowth to gleam with yellow-lighted eyes upon the intruders.

But the forest did not last forever, and the moon was not yet gone when they emerged presently upon the rough mountain-side. The girl studied the moon then, and saw by the way it was setting that after all they were going in the right general direction. That gave a little comfort until she made herself believe that in some way she might have made a mistake and gone the wrong way from the graves, and so be coming up to the cabin after all.

It was a terrible night. Every step of the way some new horror was presented to her imagination. Once she had to cross a wild little stream, rocky and uncertain in its bed, with slippery, precipitous banks; and twice in climbing a steep incline she came sharp upon sheer precipices down into a rocky gorge, where the moonlight seemed repelled by dark, bristling evergreen trees growing half-way up the sides. She could hear the rush and clamor of a tumbling mountain stream in the depths below. Once she fancied she heard a distant shot, and the horse pricked up his ears, and went forward excitedly.

But at last the dawn contended with the night, and in the east a faint pink flush crept up. Down in the valley a mist like a white feather rose gently into a white cloud, and obscured everything. She wished she might carry the wall of white with her to shield her. She had longed for the dawn; and now, as it came with sudden light and clear revealing of the things about her, it was almost worse than night, so dreadful were the dangers when clearly seen, so dangerous the chasms, so angry the mountain torrents.

With the dawn came the new terror of being followed. The man would have no fear to come to her in the morning, for murdered men were not supposed to haunt their homes after the sun was up, and murderers were always courageous in the day. He might the sooner come, and find her gone, and perhaps follow; for she felt that he was not one easily to give up an object he coveted, and she had seen in his evil face that which made her fear unspeakably.

As the day grew clearer, she began to study the surroundings. All seemed utter desolation. There was no sign that any one had ever passed that way before; and yet, just as she had thought that, the horse stopped and snorted, and there in the rocks before them lay a man's hat riddled with shot. Peering fearfully around, the girl saw a sight which made her turn icy cold and begin to tremble; for there, below them, as if he had fallen from his horse and rolled down the incline, lay a man on his face.

For the instant fear held her riveted, with the horse, one figure like a statue, girl and beast; the next, sudden panic took hold upon her. Whether the man were dead or not, she must make haste. It might be he would come to himself and pursue her, though there was that in the rigid attitude of the figure down below that made her sure he had been dead some time. But how had he died? Scarcely by his own hand. Who had killed him? Were there fiends lurking in the fastnesses of the mountain growth above her?

With guarded motion she urged her horse forward, and for miles beyond the horse scrambled breathlessly, the girl holding on with shut eyes, not daring to look ahead for fear of seeing more terrible sights, not daring to look behind for fear of-what she did not know.

At last the way sloped downward, and they reached more level ground, with wide stretches of open plain, dotted here and there with sage-brush and greasewood.

She had been hungry back there before she came upon the dead man; but now the hunger had gone from her, and in its place was only faintness. Still, she dared not stop long to eat. She must make as much time as possible here in this open space, and now she was where she could be seen more easily if any one were in pursuit.

But the horse had decided that it was time for breakfast. He had had one or two drinks of water on the mountain, but there had been no time for him to eat. He was decidedly hungry, and the plain offered nothing in the shape of breakfast. He halted, lingered, and came to a neighing stop, looking around at his mistress. She roused from her lethargy of trouble, and realized that his wants-if not her own-must be attended to.

She must sacrifice some of her own store of eatables, for by and by they would come to a good grazing-place perhaps, but now there was nothing.

The corn-meal seemed the best for the horse. She had more of it than of anything else. She poured a scanty portion out on a paper, and the beast smacked his lips appreciatively over it, carefully licking every grain from the paper, as the girl guarded it lest his breath should blow any away. He snuffed hungrily at the empty paper, and she gave him a little more meal, while she ate some of the cold beans, and scanned the horizon anxiously. There was nothing but sage-brush in sight ahead of her, and more hills farther on where dim outlines of trees could be seen. If she could but get up higher where she could see farther, and perhaps reach a bench where there would be grass and some shelter.

It was only a brief rest she allowed; and then, hastily packing up her stores, and retaining some dry corn bread and a few beans in her pocket, she mounted and rode on.

The morning grew hot, and the way was long. As the ground rose again, it was stony and overgrown with cactus. A great desolation took possession of the girl. She felt as if she were in an endless flight from an unseen pursuer, who would never give up until he had her.

It was high noon by the glaring sun when she suddenly saw another human being. At first she was not quite sure whether he were human. It was only a distant view of a moving speck; but it was coming toward her, though separated by a wide valley that had stretched already for miles. He was moving along against the sky-line on a high bench on one side of the valley, and she mounting as fast as her weary beast would go to the top of another, hoping to find a grassy stretch and a chance to rest.

But the sight of the moving speck startled her. She watched it breathlessly as they neared each other. Could it be a wild beast? No, it must be a horse and rider. A moment later there came a puff of smoke as from a rifle discharged, followed by the distant echo of the discharge. It was a man, and he was yet a great way off. Should she turn and flee before she was discovered? But where? Should she go back? No, a thousand times, no! Her enemy was there. This could not be the one from whom she fled. He was coming from the opposite direction, but he might be just as bad. Her experience taught her that men were to be shunned. Even fathers and brothers were terribly uncertain, sorrow-bringing creatures.

She could not go back to the place where the dead man lay. She must not go back. And forward she was taking the only course that seemed at all possible through the natural obstructions of the region. She shrank to her saddle, and urged the patient horse on. Perhaps she could reach the bench and get away out of sight before the newcomer saw her.

But the way was longer to the top, and steeper than it had seemed at first, and the horse was tired. Sometimes he stopped of his own accord, and snorted appealingly to her with his head turned inquiringly as if to know how long and how far this strange ride was to continue. Then the man in the distance seemed to ride faster. The valley between them was not so wide here. He was quite distinctly a man now, and his horse was going rapidly. Once it seemed as if he waved his arms; but she turned her head, and urged her horse with sudden fright. They were almost to the top now. She dismounted and clambered alongside of the animal up the steep incline, her breath coming in quick gasps, with the horse's breath hot upon her cheek as they climbed together.

At last! They were at the top! Ten feet more and they would be on a level, where they might disappear from view. She turned to look across the valley, and the man was directly opposite. He must have ridden hard to get there so soon. Oh, horror! He was waving his hands and calling. She could distinctly hear a cry! It chilled her senses, and brought a frantic, unreasoning fear. Somehow she felt he was connected with the one from whom she fled. Some emissary of his sent out to foil her in her attempt for safety, perhaps.

She clutched the bridle wildly, and urged the horse up with one last effort; and just as they reached high ground she heard the wild cry ring clear and distinct, "Hello! Hello!" and then something else. It sounded like "Help!" but she could not tell. Was he trying to deceive her? Pretending he would help her?

She flung herself into the saddle, giving the horse the signal to run; and, as the animal obeyed and broke into his prairie run, she cast one fearful glance behind her. The man was pursuing her at a gallop! He was crossing the valley. There was a stream to cross, but he would cross it. He had determination in every line of his flying figure. His voice was pursuing her, too. It seemed as if the sound reached out and clutched her heart, and tried to draw her back as she fled. And now her pursuers were three: her enemy, the dead man upon the mountain, and the voice.

CHAPTER III
THE PURSUIT

Straight across the prairie she galloped, not daring to stop for an instant, with the voice pursuing her. For hours it seemed to ring in her ears, and even after she was far beyond any possibility of hearing it she could not be sure but there was now and then a faint echo of it ringing yet, "Hello!" —ringing like some strange bird amid the silence of the world.

There were cattle and sheep grazing on the bench, and the horse would fain have stopped to dine with them; but the girl urged him on, seeming to make him understand the danger that might be pursuing them.

It was hours before she dared stop for the much-needed rest. Her brain had grown confused with the fright and weariness. She felt that she could not much longer stay in the saddle. She might fall asleep. The afternoon sun would soon be slipping down behind the mountains. When and where dared she rest? Not in the night, for that would be almost certain death, with wild beasts about.

A little group of greasewood offered a scanty shelter. As if the beast understood her thoughts he stopped with a neigh, and looked around at her. She scanned the surroundings. There were cattle all about. They had looked up curiously from their grazing as the horse flew by, but were now going quietly on about their business. They would serve as a screen if any should be still pursuing her. One horse among the other animals in a landscape would not be so noticeable as one alone against the sky. The greasewood was not far from sloping ground where she might easily flee for hiding if danger approached.

The horse had already begun to crop the tender grass at his feet as if his life depended upon a good meal. The girl took some more beans from the pack she carried, and mechanically ate them, though she felt no appetite, and her dry throat almost refused to swallow. She found her eyes shutting even against her will; and in desperation she folded the old coat into a pillow, and with the horse's bridle fastened in her belt she lay down.

The sun went away; the horse ate his supper; and the girl slept. By and by the horse drowsed off too, and the bleating sheep in the distance, the lowing of the cattle, the sound of night-birds, came now and again from the distance; but still the girl slept on. The moon rose full and round, shining with flickering light through the cottonwoods; and the girl stirred in a dream and thought some one was pursuing her, but slept on again. Then out through the night rang a vivid human voice, "Hello! Hello!" The horse roused from his sleep, and stamped his feet nervously, twitching at his bridle; but the relaxed hand that lay across the leather strap did not quicken, and the girl slept on. The horse listened, and thought he heard a sound good to his ear. He neighed, and neighed again; but the girl slept on.

The first ray of the rising sun at last shot through the gray of dawning, and touched the girl full in the face as it slid under the branches of her sheltering tree. The light brought her acutely to her senses. Before she opened her eyes she seemed to be keenly and painfully aware of much that had gone on during her sleep. With another flash her eyes flew open. Not because she willed it, but rather as if the springs that held the lids shut had unexpectedly been touched and they sprang back because they had to.

She shrank, as her eyes opened, from a new day, and the memory of the old one. Then before her she saw something which kept her motionless, and almost froze the blood in her veins. She could not stir nor breathe, and for a moment even thought was paralyzed. There before her but a few feet away stood a man! Beyond him, a few feet from her own horse, stood his horse. She could not see it without turning her head, and that she dared not do; but she knew it was there, felt it even before she noticed the double stamping and breathing of the animals. Her keen senses seemed to make the whole surrounding landscape visible to her without the moving of a muscle. She knew to a nicety exactly how her weapons lay, and what movement would bring her hand to the trigger of her pistol; yet she stirred not.

Gradually she grew calm enough to study the man before her. He stood almost with his back turned toward her, his face just half turned so that one cheek and a part of his brow were visible. He was broad-shouldered and well built. There was strength in every line of his body. She felt how powerless she would be in his grasp. Her only hope would be in taking him unaware. Yet she moved not one atom.

He wore a brown flannel shirt, open at the throat, brown leather belt and boots; in short, his whole costume was in harmonious shades of brown, and looked new as if it had been worn but a few days. His soft felt sombrero was rolled back from his face, and the young red sun tinged the short brown curls to a ruddy gold. He was looking toward the rising sun. The gleam of it shot across his brace of pistols in his belt, and flashed twin rays into her eyes. Then all at once the man turned and looked at her.

Instantly the girl sprang to her feet, her hands upon her pistol, her eyes meeting with calm, desperate defiance the blue ones that were turned to her. She was braced against a tree, and her senses were measuring the distance between her horse and herself, and deciding whether escape were possible.

"Good morning," said the man politely. "I hope I haven't disturbed your nap."

The girl eyed him solemnly, and said nothing. This was a new kind of man. He was not like the one from whom she had fled, nor like any she had ever seen; but he might be a great deal worse. She had heard that the world was full of wickedness.

"You see," went on the man with an apologetic smile, which lit up his eyes in a wonderfully winning way, "you led me such a desperate race nearly all day yesterday that I was obliged to keep you in sight when I finally caught you."

He looked for an answering smile, but there was none. Instead, the girl's dark eyes grew wide and purple with fear. He was the same one, then, that she had seen in the afternoon, the voice who had cried to her; and he had been pursuing her. He was an enemy, perhaps, sent by the man from whom she fled. She grasped her pistol with trembling fingers, and tried to think what to say or do.

The young man wondered at the formalities of the plains. Were all these Western maidens so reticent?

"Why did you follow me? Who did you think I was?" she asked breathlessly at last.

"Well, I thought you were a man," he said; "at least, you appeared to be a human being, and not a wild animal. I hadn't seen anything but wild animals for six hours, and very few of those; so I followed you."

The girl was silent. She was not reassured. It did not seem to her that her question was directly answered. The young man was playing with her.

"What right had you to follow me?" she demanded fiercely.

"Well, now that you put it in that light, I'm not sure that I had any right at all, unless it may be the claim that every human being has upon all creation."

His arms were folded now across his broad brown flannel chest, and the pistols gleamed in his belt below like fine ornaments. He wore a philosophical expression, and looked at his companion as if she were a new specimen of the human kind, and he was studying her variety, quite impersonally, it is true, but interestedly. There was something in his look that angered the girl.

"What do you want?" She had never heard of the divine claims of all the human family. Her one instinct at present was fear.

An expression that was almost bitter flitted over the young man's face, as of an unpleasant memory forgotten for the instant.

"It really wasn't of much consequence when you think of it," he said with a shrug of his fine shoulders. "I was merely lost, and was wanting to inquire where I was-and possibly the way to somewhere. But I don't know as 'twas worth the trouble."

The girl was puzzled. She had never seen a man like this before. He was not like her wild, reckless brother, nor any of his associates.

"This is Montana," she said, "or was, when I started," she added with sudden thought.

"Yes? Well, it was Montana when I started, too; but it's as likely to be the Desert of Sahara as anything else. I'm sure I've come far enough, and found it barren enough."

"I never heard of that place," said the girl seriously; "is it in Canada?"

"I believe not," said the man with sudden gravity; "at least, not that I know of. When I went to school, it was generally located somewhere in Africa."

"I never went to school," said the girl wistfully; "but —" with a sudden resolve —"I'll go now."

"Do!" said the man. "I'll go with you. Let's start at once; for, now that I think of it, I haven't had anything to eat for over a day, and there might be something in that line near a schoolhouse. Do you know the way?"

"No," said the girl, slowly studying him-she began to feel he was making fun of her; "but I can give you something to eat."

"Thank you!" said the man. "I assure you I shall appreciate anything from hardtack to bisque ice-cream."

"I haven't any of those," said the girl, "but there are plenty of beans left; and, if you will get some wood for a fire, I'll make some coffee."

"Agreed," said the man. "That sounds better than anything I've heard for forty-eight hours."

The girl watched him as he strode away to find wood, and frowned for an instant; but his face was perfectly sober, and she turned to the business of getting breakfast. For a little her fears were allayed. At least, he would do her no immediate harm. Of course she might fly from him now while his back was turned; but then of course he would pursue her again, and she had little chance of getting away. Besides, he was hungry. She could not leave him without something to eat.

"We can't make coffee without water," she said as he came back with a bundle of sticks.

He whistled.

"Could you inform me where to look for water?" he asked.

She looked into his face, and saw how worn and gray he was about his eyes; and a sudden compassion came upon her.

"You'd better eat something first," she said, "and then we'll go and hunt for water. There's sure to be some in the valley. We'll cook some meat."

She took the sticks from him, and made the fire in a businesslike way. He watched her, and wondered at her grace. Who was she, and how had she wandered out into this waste place? Her face was both beautiful and interesting. She would make a fine study if he were not so weary of all human nature, and especially woman. He sighed as he thought again of himself.

The girl caught the sound, and, turning with the quickness of a wild creature, caught the sadness in his face. It seemed to drive away much of her fear and resentment. A half-flicker of a smile came to her lips as their eyes met. It seemed to recognize a comradeship in sorrow. But her face hardened again almost at once into disapproval as he answered her look.

The man felt a passing disappointment. After a minute, during which the girl had dropped her eyes to her work again, he said: "Now, why did you look at me in that way? Ought I to be helping you in some way? I'm awkward, I know, but I can obey if you'll just tell me how."

The girl seemed puzzled; then she replied almost sullenly:

"There's nothing more to do. It's ready to eat."

She gave him a piece of the meat and the last of the corn bread in the tin cup, and placed the pan of beans beside him; but she did not attempt to eat anything herself.

He took a hungry bite or two, and looked furtively at her.

"I insist upon knowing why you looked —" he paused and eyed her —"why you look at me in that way. I'm not a wolf if I am hungry, and I'm not going to eat you up."

The look of displeasure deepened on the girl's brow. In spite of his hunger the man was compelled to watch her. She seemed to be looking at a flock of birds in the sky. Her hand rested lightly at her belt. The birds were coming towards them, flying almost over their heads.

Suddenly the girl's hand was raised with a quick motion, and something gleamed in the sun across his sight. There was a loud report, and one of the birds fell almost at his feet, dead. It was a sage-hen. Then the girl turned and walked towards him with as haughty a carriage as ever a society belle could boast.

"You were laughing at me," she said quietly.

It had all happened so suddenly that the man had not time to think. Several distinct sensations of surprise passed over his countenance. Then, as the meaning of the girl's act dawned upon him, and the full intention of her rebuke, the color mounted in his nice, tanned face. He set down the tin cup, and balanced the bit of corn bread on the rim, and arose.

"I beg your pardon," he said. "I never will do it again. I couldn't have shot that bird to save my life," and he touched it with the tip of his tan leather boot as if to make sure it was a real bird.

The girl was sitting on the ground, indifferently eating some of the cooked pork. She did not answer. Somehow the young man felt uncomfortable. He sat down, and took up his tin cup, and went at his breakfast again; but his appetite seemed in abeyance.

"I've been trying myself to learn to shoot during the last week," he began soberly. "I haven't been able yet to hit anything but the side of a barn. Say, I'm wondering, suppose I had tried to shoot at those birds just now and had missed, whether you wouldn't have laughed at me-quietly, all to yourself, you know. Are you quite sure?"

The girl looked up at him solemnly without saying a word for a full minute.

"Was what I said as bad as that?" she asked slowly.

"I'm afraid it was," he answered thoughtfully; "but I was a blamed idiot for laughing at you. A girl that shoots like that may locate the Desert of Sahara in Canada if she likes, and Canada ought to be proud of the honor."

She looked into his face for an instant, and noted his earnestness; and all at once she broke into a clear ripple of laughter. The young man was astonished anew that she had understood him enough to laugh. She must be unusually keen-witted, this lady of the desert.

"If 'twas as bad as that," she said in quite another tone, "you c'n laugh."

They looked at each other then in mutual understanding, and each fell to eating his portion in silence. Suddenly the man spoke.

"I am eating your food that you had prepared for your journey, and I have not even said, 'Thank you' yet, nor asked if you have enough to carry you to a place where there is more. Where are you going?"

The girl did not answer at once; but, when she did, she spoke thoughtfully, as if the words were a newly made vow from an impulse just received.

"I am going to school," she said in her slow way, "to learn to 'sight' the Desert of Sahara."

He looked at her, and his eyes gave her the homage he felt was her due; but he said nothing. Here evidently was an indomitable spirit, but how did she get out into the wilderness? Where did she come from, and why was she alone? He had heard of the freedom of Western women, but surely such girls as this did not frequent so vast a waste of uninhabited territory as his experience led him to believe this was. He sat studying her.

The brow was sweet and thoughtful, with a certain keen inquisitiveness about the eyes. The mouth was firm; yet there were gentle lines of grace about it. In spite of her coarse, dark calico garb, made in no particular fashion except with an eye to covering with the least possible fuss and trouble, she was graceful. Every movement was alert and clean-cut. When she turned to look full in his face, he decided that she had almost beautiful eyes.

She had arisen while he was watching her, and seemed to be looking off with sudden apprehension. He followed her gaze, and saw several dark figures moving against the sky.

"It's a herd of antelope," she said with relief; "but it's time we hit the trail." She turned, and put her things together with incredible swiftness, giving him very little opportunity to help, and mounted her pony without more words.

For an hour he followed her at high speed as she rode full tilt over rough and smooth, casting furtive, anxious glances behind her now and then, which only half included him. She seemed to know that he was there and was following; that was all.

The young man felt rather amused and flattered. He reflected that most women he knew would have ridden by his side, and tried to make him talk. But this girl of the wilderness rode straight ahead as if her life depended upon it. She seemed to have nothing to say to him, and to be anxious neither to impart her own history nor to know his.

Well, that suited his mood. He had come out into the wilderness to think and to forget. Here was ample opportunity. There had been a little too much of it yesterday, when he wandered from the rest of his party who had come out to hunt; and for a time he had felt that he would rather be back in his native city with a good breakfast and all his troubles than to be alone in the vast waste forever. But now there was human company, and a possibility of getting somewhere sometime. He was content.

The lithe, slender figure of the girl ahead seemed one with the horse it rode. He tried to think what this ride would be if another woman he knew were riding on that horse ahead, but there was very small satisfaction in that. In the first place, it was highly improbable, and the young man was of an intensely practical turn of mind. It was impossible to imagine the haughty beauty in a brown calico riding a high-spirited horse of the wilds. There was but one parallel. If she had been there, she would, in her present state of mind, likely be riding imperiously and indifferently ahead instead of by his side where he wanted her. Besides, he came out to the plains to forget her. Why think of her?

The sky was exceedingly bright and wide. Why had he never noticed this wideness in skies at home? There was another flock of birds. What if he should try to shoot one? Idle talk. He would probably hit anything but the birds. Why had that girl shot that bird, anyway? Was it entirely because she might need it for food? She had picked it up significantly with the other things, and fastened it to her saddle-bow without a word. He was too ignorant to know whether it was an edible bird or not, or she was merely carrying it to remind him of her skill.

And what sort of a girl was she? Perhaps she was escaping from justice. She ran from him yesterday, and apparently stopped only when utterly exhausted. She seemed startled and anxious when the antelopes came into sight. There was no knowing whether her company meant safety, after all. Yet his interest was so thoroughly aroused in her that he was willing to risk it.

Of course he might go more slowly and gradually, let her get ahead, and he slip out of sight. It was not likely he had wandered so many miles away from human habitation but that he would reach one sometime; and, now that he was re-enforced by food, perhaps it would be the part of wisdom to part with this strange maiden. As he thought, he unconsciously slackened his horse's pace. The girl was a rod or more ahead, and just vanishing behind a clump of sage-brush. She vanished, and he stopped for an instant, and looked about him on the desolation; and a great loneliness settled upon him like a frenzy. He was glad to see the girl riding back toward him with a smile of good fellowship on her face.

"What's the matter?" she called. "Come on! There's water in the valley."

The sound of water was good; and life seemed suddenly good for no reason whatever but that the morning was bright, and the sky was wide, and there was water in the valley. He rode forward, keeping close beside her now, and in a moment there gleamed below in the hot sunshine the shining of a sparkling stream.

"You seem to be running away from some one," he explained. "I thought you wanted to get rid of me, and I would give you a chance."

She looked at him surprised.

"I am running away," she said, "but not from you."

"From whom, then, may I ask? It might be convenient to know, if we are to travel in the same company."

She looked at him keenly.

"Who are you, and where do you belong?"

CHAPTER IV
THE TWO FUGITIVES

"I'm not anybody in particular," he answered, "and I'm not just sure where I belong. I live in Pennsylvania, but I didn't seem to belong there exactly, at least not just now, and so I came out here to see if I belonged anywhere else. I concluded yesterday that I didn't. At least, not until I came in sight of you. But I suspect I am running away myself. In fact, that is just what I am doing, running away from a woman!"

He looked at her with his honest hazel eyes, and she liked him. She felt he was telling her the truth, but it seemed to be a truth he was just finding out for himself as he talked.

"Why do you run away from a woman? How could a woman hurt you? Can she shoot?"

He flashed her a look of amusement and pain mingled.

"She uses other weapons," he said. "Her words are darts, and her looks are swords."

"What a queer woman! Does she ride well?"

"Yes, in an automobile!"

"What is that?" She asked the question shyly as if she feared he might laugh again; and he looked down, and perceived that he was talking far above her. In fact, he was talking to himself more than to the girl.

There was a bitter pleasure in speaking of his lost lady to this wild creature who almost seemed of another kind, more like an intelligent bird or flower.

"An automobile is a carriage that moves about without horses," he answered her gravely. "It moves by machinery."

"I should not like it," said the girl decidedly. "Horses are better than machines. I saw a machine once. It was to cut wheat. It made a noise, and did not go fast. It frightened me."

"But automobiles go very fast, faster than any horses And they do not all make a noise."

The girl looked around apprehensively.

"My horse can go very fast. You do not know how fast. If you see her coming, I will change horses with you. You must ride to the nearest bench and over, and then turn backward on your tracks. She will never find you that way. And I am not afraid of a woman."

The man broke into a hearty laugh, loud and long. He laughed until the tears rolled down his cheeks; and the girl, offended, rode haughtily beside him. Then all in a moment he grew quite grave.

"Excuse me," he said; "I am not laughing at you now, though it looks that way. I am laughing out of the bitterness of my soul at the picture you put before me. Although I am running away from her, the lady will not come out in her automobile to look for me. She does not want me!"

"She does not want you! And yet you ran away from her?"

"That's exactly it," he said. "You see, *I* wanted *her*!"

"Oh!" She gave a sharp, quick gasp of intelligence, and was silent. After a full minute she rode quite close to his horse, and laid her small brown hand on the animal's mane.

"I am sorry," she said simply.

"Thank you," he answered. "I'm sure I don't know why I told you. I never told any one before."

There was a long silence between them. The man seemed to have forgotten her as he rode with his eyes upon his horse's neck, and his thoughts apparently far away.

At last the girl said softly, as if she were rendering return for the confidence given her, "I ran away from a man."

The man lifted his eyes courteously, questioningly, and waited.

"He is big and dark and handsome. He shoots to kill. He killed my brother. I hate him. He wants me, and I ran away from him. But he is a coward. I frightened him away. He is afraid of dead men that he has killed."

The young man gave his attention now to the extraordinary story which the girl told as if it were a common occurrence.

"But where are your people, your family and friends? Why do they not send the man away?"

"They're all back there in the sand," she said with a sad little flicker of a smile and a gesture that told of tragedy. "I said the prayer over them. Mother always wanted it when we died. There wasn't anybody left but me. I said it, and then I came away. It was cold moonlight, and there were noises. The horse was afraid. But I said it. Do you suppose it will do any good?"

She fastened her eyes upon the young man with her last words as if demanding an answer. The color came up to his cheeks. He felt embarrassed at such a question before her trouble.

"Why, I should think it ought to," he stammered. "Of course it will," he added with more confident comfort.

"Did you ever say the prayer?"

"Why,—I—yes, I believe I have," he answered somewhat uncertainly.

"Did it do any good?" She hung upon his words.

"Why, I—believe-yes, I suppose it did. That is, praying is always a good thing. The fact is, it's a long time since I've tried it. But of course it's all right."

A curious topic for conversation between a young man and woman on a ride through the wilderness. The man had never thought about prayer for so many minutes consecutively in the whole of his life; at least, not since the days when his nurse tried to teach him "Now I lay me."

"Why don't you try it about the lady?" asked the girl suddenly.

"Well, the fact is, I never thought of it."

"Don't you believe it will do any good?"

"Well, I suppose it might."

"Then let's try it. Let's get off now, quick, and both say it. Maybe it will help us both. Do you know it all through? Can't you say it?" This last anxiously, as he hesitated and looked doubtful.

The color came into the man's face. Somehow this girl put him in a very bad light. He couldn't shoot; and, if he couldn't pray, what would she think of him?

"Why, I think I could manage to say it with help," he answered uneasily. "But what if that man should suddenly appear on the scene?"

"You don't think the prayer is any good, or you wouldn't say that." She said it sadly, hopelessly.

"O, why, certainly," he said, "only I thought there might be some better time to try it; but, if you say so, we'll stop right here." He sprang to the ground, and offered to assist her; but she was beside him before he could get around his horse's head.

Down she dropped, and clasped her hands as a little child might have done, and closed her eyes.

"Our Father," she repeated slowly, precisely, as if every word belonged to a charm and must be repeated just right or it would not work. The man's mumbling words halted after hers. He was reflecting upon the curious tableau they would make to the chance passer-by on the desert if there were any passers-by. It was strange, this aloneness. There was a wideness here that made praying seem more natural than it would have been at home in the open country.

The prayer, by reason of the unaccustomed lips, went slowly; but, when it was finished, the girl sprang to her saddle again with a businesslike expression.

"I feel better," she said with a winning smile. "Don't you? Don't you think He heard?"

"Who heard?"

"Why, 'our Father.'"

"O, certainly! That is, I've always been taught to suppose He did. I haven't much experimental knowledge in this line, but I dare say it'll do some good some where. Now do you suppose we could get some of that very sparkling water? I feel exceedingly thirsty."

They spurred their horses, and were soon beside the stream, refreshing themselves.

"Did you ride all night?" asked the girl.

"Pretty much," answered the man. "I stopped once to rest a few minutes; but a sound in the distance stirred me up again, and I was afraid to lose my chance of catching you, lest I should be hopelessly lost. You see, I went out with a party hunting, and I sulked behind. They went off up a steep climb, and I said I'd wander around below till they got back, or perhaps ride back to camp; but, when I tried to find the camp, it wasn't where I had left it."

"Well, you've got to lie down and sleep awhile," said the girl decidedly. "You can't keep going like that. It'll kill you. You lie down, and I'll watch, and get dinner. I'm going to cook that bird."

He demurred, but in the end she had her way; for he was exceedingly weary, and she saw it. So he let her spread the old coat down for him while he gathered some wood for a fire, and then he lay down and watched her simple preparations for the meal. Before he knew it he was asleep.

When he came to himself, there was a curious blending of dream and reality. He thought his lady was coming to him across the rough plains in an automobile, with gray wings like those of the bird the girl had shot, and his prayer as he knelt in the sand was drawing her, while overhead the air was full of a wild, sweet music from strange birds that mocked and called and trilled. But, when the automobile reached him and stopped, the lady withered into a little, old, dried-up creature of ashes; and the girl of the plains was sitting in her place radiant and beautiful.

He opened his eyes, and saw the rude little dinner set, and smelt the delicious odor of the roasted bird. The girl was standing on the other side of the fire, gravely whistling a most extraordinary song, like unto all the birds of the air at once.

She had made a little cake out of the corn-meal, and they feasted royally.

"I caught two fishes in the brook. We'll take them along for supper," she said as they packed the things again for starting. He tried to get her to take a rest also, and let him watch; but she insisted that they must go on, and promised to rest just before dark. "For we must travel hard at night, you know," she added fearfully.

He questioned her more about the man who might be pursuing, and came to understand her fears.

"The scoundrel!" he muttered, looking at the delicate features and clear, lovely profile of the girl. He felt a strong desire to throttle the evil man.

He asked a good many questions about her life, and was filled with wonder over the flower-like girl who seemed to have blossomed in the wilderness with no hand to cultivate her save a lazy, clever, drunken father, and a kind but ignorant mother. How could she have escaped being coarsened amid such surroundings. How was it, with such brothers as she had, that she had come forth as lovely and unhurt as she seemed? He somehow began to feel a great anxiety for her lonely future and a desire to put her in the way of protection. But at present they were still in the wilderness; and he began to be glad that he was here too, and might have the privilege of protecting her now, if there should be need.

As it grew toward evening, they came upon a little grassy spot in a coulee where the horses might rest and eat. Here they stopped, and the girl threw herself under a shelter of trees, with the old coat for a pillow, and rested, while the man paced up and down at a distance, gathering wood for a fire, and watching the horizon. As night came on, the city-bred man longed for shelter. He was by no means a coward where known quantities were concerned, but to face wild animals and drunken brigands in a strange, wild plain with no help near was anything but an enlivening prospect. He could not understand why they had not come upon some human habitation by this time. He had never realized how vast this country was before. When he came westward on the train he did not remember to have traversed such long stretches of country without a sign of civilization, though of course a train went so much faster than a horse that he had no adequate means of judging. Then, besides, they were on no trail now, and had probably gone in a most roundabout way to anywhere. In reality they had twice come within five miles of little homesteads, tucked away beside a stream in a fertile spot; but they had not known it. A mile further to the right at one spot would have put them on the trail and made their way easier and shorter, but that they could not know.

The girl did not rest long. She seemed to feel her pursuit more as the darkness crept on, and kept anxiously looking for the moon.

33

"We must go toward the moon," she said as she watched the bright spot coming in the east.

They ate their supper of fish and corn-bread with the appetite that grows on horseback, and by the time they had started on their way again the moon spread a path of silver before them, and they went forward feeling as if they had known each other a long time. For a while their fears and hopes were blended in one.

Meantime, as the sun sank and the moon rose, a traveller rode up the steep ascent to the little lonely cabin which the girl had left. He was handsome and dark and strong, with a scarlet kerchief knotted at his throat; and he rode slowly, cautiously, looking furtively about and ahead of him. He was doubly armed, and his pistols gleamed in the moonlight, while an ugly knife nestled keenly in a secret sheath.

He was wicked, for the look upon his face was not good to see; and he was a coward, for he started at the flutter of a night-bird hurrying late to its home in a rock by the wayside. The mist rising from the valley in wreaths of silver gauze startled him again as he rounded the trail to the cabin, and for an instant he stopped and drew his dagger, thinking the ghost he feared was walking thus early. A draught from the bottle he carried in his pocket steadied his nerves, and he went on, but stopped again in front of the cabin; for there stood another horse, and there in the doorway stood a figure in the darkness! His curses rang through the still air and smote the moonlight. His pistol flashed forth a volley of fire to second him.

In answer to his demand who was there came another torrent of profanity. It was one of his comrades of the day before. He explained that he and two others had come up to pay a visit to the pretty girl. They had had a wager as to who could win her, and they had come to try; but she was not here. The door was fastened. They had forced it. There was no sign of her about. The other two had gone down to the place where her brother was buried to see whether she was there. Women were known to be sentimental. She might be that kind. He had agreed to wait here, but he was getting uneasy. Perhaps, if the other two found her, they might not be fair.

The last comer with a mighty oath explained that the girl belonged to him, and that no one had a right to her. He demanded that the other come with him to the grave, and see what had become of the girl; and then they would all go and drink together-but the girl belonged to him.

They rode to the place of the graves, and met the two others returning; but there was no sign of the girl, and the three taunted the one, saying that the girl had given him the slip. Amid much argument as to whose she was and where she was, they rode on cursing through God's beauty. They passed the bottle continually, that their nerves might be the steadier; and, when they came to the deserted cabin once more, they paused and discussed what to do.

At last it was agreed that they should start on a quest after her, and with oaths, and coarse jests, and drinking, they started down the trail of which the girl had gone in search by her roundabout way.

CHAPTER V
A NIGHT RIDE

It was a wonderful night that the two spent wading the sea of moonlight together on the plain. The almost unearthly beauty of the scene grew upon them. They had none of the loneliness that had possessed each the night before, and might now discover all the wonders of the way.

Early in the way they came upon a prairie-dogs' village, and the man would have lingered watching with curiosity, had not the girl urged him on. It was the time of night when she had started to run away, and the same apprehension that filled her then came upon her with the evening. She longed to be out of the land which held the man she feared. She would rather bury herself in the earth and smother to death than be caught by him. But, as they rode on, she told her companion much of the habits of the curious little creatures they had seen; and then, as the night settled down upon them, she pointed out the dark, stealing creatures that slipped from their way now and then, or gleamed with a fearsome green eye from some temporary refuge.

At first the cold shivers kept running up and down the young man as he realized that here before him in the sage-brush was a real live animal about which he had read so much, and which he had come out bravely to hunt. He kept his hand upon his revolver, and was constantly on the alert, nervously looking behind lest a troop of coyotes or wolves should be quietly stealing upon him. But, as the girl talked fearlessly of them in much the same way as we talk of a neighbor's fierce dog, he grew gradually calmer, and was able to watch a dark, velvet-footed moving object ahead without starting.

By and by he pointed to the heavens, and talked of the stars. Did she know that constellation? No? Then he explained. Such and such stars were so many miles from the earth. He told their names, and a bit of mythology connected with the name, and then went on to speak of the moon, and the possibility of its once having been inhabited.

The girl listened amazed. She knew certain stars as landmarks, telling east from west and north from south; and she had often watched them one by one coming out, and counted them her friends; but that they were worlds, and that the inhabitants of this earth knew anything whatever about the heavenly bodies, she had never heard. Question after question she plied him with, some of them showing extraordinary intelligence and thought, and others showing deeper ignorance than a little child in our kindergartens would show.

He wondered more and more as their talk went on. He grew deeply interested in unfolding the wonders of the heavens to her; and, as he studied her pure profile in the moonlight with eager, searching, wistful gaze, her beauty impressed him more and more. In the East the man had a friend, an artist. He thought how wonderful a theme for a painting this scene would make. The girl in picturesque hat of soft felt, riding with careless ease and grace; horse, maiden, plain, bathed in a sea of silver.

More and more as she talked the man wondered how this girl reared in the wilds had acquired a speech so free from grammatical errors. She was apparently deeply ignorant, and yet with a very few exceptions she made no serious errors in English. How was it to be accounted for?

He began to ply her with questions about herself, but could not find that she had ever come into contact with people who were educated. She had not even lived in any of the miserable little towns that flourish in the wildest of the West, and not within several hundred miles of a city. Their nearest neighbors in one direction had been forty miles away, she said, and said it as if that were an everyday distance for a neighbor to live.

Mail? They had had a letter once that she could remember, when she was a little girl. It was just a few lines in pencil to say that her mother's father had died. He had been killed in an accident of some sort, working in the city where he lived. Her mother had kept the letter and cried over it till almost all the pencil marks were gone.

No, they had no mail on the mountain where their homestead was.

Yes, her father went there first because he thought he had discovered gold, but it turned out to be a mistake; so, as they had no other place to go to, and no money to go with, they had just stayed there; and her father and brothers had been cow-punchers, but she and her mother had scarcely ever gone away from home. There were the little children to care for; and, when they died, her mother did not care to go, and would not let her go far alone.

O, yes, she had ridden a great deal, sometimes with her brothers, but not often. They went with rough men, and her mother felt afraid to have her go. The men all drank. Her brothers drank. Her father drank too. She stated it as if it were a sad fact common to all mankind, and ended with the statement which was almost, not quite, a question, "I guess you drink too."

"Well," said the young man hesitatingly, "not that way. I take a glass of wine now and then in company, you know —"

"Yes, I know," sighed the girl. "Men are all alike. Mother used to say so. She said men were different from women. They had to drink. She said they all did it. Only she said her father never did; but he was very good, though he had to work hard."

"Indeed," said the young man, his color rising in the moonlight, "indeed, you make a mistake. I don't drink at all, not that way. I'm not like them. I —why, I only-well, the fact is, I don't care a red cent about the stuff anyway; and I don't want you to think I'm like them. If it will do you any good, I'll never touch it again, not a drop."

He said it earnestly. He was trying to vindicate himself. Just why he should care to do so he did not know, only that all at once it was very necessary that he should appear different in the eyes of this girl from, the other men she had known.

"Will you really?" she asked, turning to look in his face. "Will you promise that?"

"Why, certainly I will," he said, a trifle embarrassed that she had taken him at his word. "Of course I will. I tell you it's nothing to me. I only took a glass at the club occasionally when the other men were drinking, and sometimes when I went to banquets, class banquets, you know, and dinners —"

Now the girl had never heard of class banquets, but to take a glass occasionally when the other men were drinking was what her brothers did; and so she sighed, and said: "Yes, you may promise, but I know you won't keep it. Father promised too; but, when he got with the other men, it did no good. Men are all alike."

"But I'm not," he insisted stoutly. "I tell you I'm not. I don't drink, and I won't drink. I promise you solemnly here under God's sky that I'll never drink another drop of intoxicating liquor again if I know it as long as I live."

He put out his hand toward her, and she put her own into it with a quick grasp for just an instant.

"Then you're not like other men, after all," she said with a glad ring in her voice. "That must be why I wasn't so very much afraid of you when I woke up and found you standing there."

A distinct sense of pleasure came over him at her words. Why it should make him glad that she had not been afraid of him when she had first seen him in the wilderness he did not know. He forgot all about his own troubles. He forgot the lady in the automobile. Right then and there he dropped her out of his thoughts. He did not know it; but she was forgotten, and he did not think about her any more during that journey. Something had erased her. He had run away from her, and he had succeeded most effectually, more so than he knew.

There in the desert the man took his first temperance pledge, urged thereto by a girl who had never heard of a temperance pledge in her life, had never joined a woman's temperance society, and knew nothing about women's crusades. Her own heart had taught her out of a bitter experience just how to use her God-given influence.

They came to a long stretch of level ground then, smooth and hard; and the horses as with common consent set out to gallop shoulder to shoulder in a wild, exhilarating skim across the plain. Talking was impossible. The man reflected that he was making great strides in experience, first a prayer and then a pledge, all in the wilderness. If any one had told him he was going into the West for this, he would have laughed him to scorn.

Towards morning they rode more slowly. Their horses were growing jaded. They talked in lower tones as they looked toward the east. It was as if they feared they might waken some one too soon. There is something awesome about the dawning of a new day, and especially when one has been sailing a sea of silver all night. It is like coming back from an unreal world into a sad, real one. Each was almost sorry that the night was over. The new day might hold so much of hardship or relief, so much of trouble or surprise; and this night had been perfect, a jewel cut to set in memory with every facet flashing to the light. They did not like to get back to reality from the converse they had held together. It was an experience for each which would never be forgotten.

Once there came the distant sound of shots and shouts. The two shrank nearer each other, and the man laid his strong hand protectingly on the mane of the girl's horse; but he did not touch her hand. The lady of his thoughts had sometimes let him hold her jewelled hand, and smiled with drooping lashes when he fondled it; and, when she had tired of him, other admirers might claim the same privilege. But this woman of the wilderness-he would not even in his thoughts presume to touch her little brown, firm hand. Somehow she had commanded his honor and respect from the first minute, even before she shot the bird.

Once a bob-cat shot across their path but a few feet in front of them, and later a kit-fox ran growling up with ruffled fur; but the girl's quick shot soon put it to flight, and they passed on through the dawning morning of the first real Sabbath day the girl had ever known.

"It is Sunday morning at home," said the man gravely as he watched the sun lift its rosy head from the mist of mountain and valley outspread before them. "Do you have such an institution out here?"

The girl grew white about the lips. "Awful things happen on Sunday," she said with a shudder.

He felt a great pity rising in his heart for her, and strove to turn her thoughts in other directions. Evidently there was a recent sorrow connected with the Sabbath.

"You are tired," said he, "and the horses are tired. See! We ought to stop and rest. The daylight has come, and nothing can hurt us. Here is a good place, and sheltered. We can fasten the horses behind these bushes, and no one will guess we are here."

She assented, and they dismounted. The man cut an opening into a clump of thick growth with his knife, and there they fastened the weary horses, well hidden from sight if any one chanced that way. The girl lay down a few feet away in a spot almost entirely surrounded by sage-brush which had reached an unusual height and made a fine hiding-place. Just outside the entrance of this natural chamber the man lay down on a fragrant bed of sage-brush. He had gathered enough for the girl first, and spread out the old coat over it; and she had dropped asleep almost as soon as she lay down. But, although his own bed of sage-brush was tolerably comfortable, even to one accustomed all his life to the finest springs and hair mattress that money could buy, and although the girl had insisted that he must rest too, for he was weary and there was no need to watch, sleep would not come to his eyelids.

He lay there resting and thinking. How strange was the experience through which he was passing! Came ever a wealthy, college-bred, society man into the like before? What did it all mean? His being lost, his wandering for a day, the sight of this girl and his pursuit, the prayer under the open sky, and that night of splendor under the moonlight riding side by side. It was like some marvellous tale.

And this girl! Where was she going? What was to become of her? Out in the world where he came from, were they ever to reach it, she would be nothing. Her station in life was beneath his so far that the only recognition she could have would be one which would degrade her. This solitary journey they were taking, how the world would lift up its hands in horror at it! A girl without a chaperon! She was impossible! And yet it all seemed right and good, and the girl was evidently recognized by the angels; else how had she escaped from degradation thus far?

Ah! How did he know she had? But he smiled at that. No one could look into that pure, sweet face, and doubt that she was as good as she was beautiful. If it was not so, he hoped he would never find it out. She seemed to him a woman yet unspoiled, and he shrank from the thought of what the world might do for her-the world and its cultivation, which would not be for her, because she was friendless and without money or home. The world would have nothing but toil to give her, with a meagre living.

Where was she going, and what was she proposing to do? Must he not try to help her in some way? Did not the fact that she had saved his life demand so much from him? If he had not found her, he must surely have starved before he got out of this wild place. Even yet starvation was not an impossibility; for they had not reached any signs of habitation yet, and there was but one more portion of corn-meal and a little coffee left. They had but two matches now, and there had been no more flights of birds, nor brooks with fishes.

In fact, the man found a great deal to worry about as he lay there, too weary with the unaccustomed exercise and experiences to sleep.

He reflected that the girl had told him very little, after all, about her plans. He must ask her. He wished he knew more of her family. If he were only older and she younger, or if he had the right kind of a woman friend to whom he might take her, or send her! How horrible that that scoundrel was after her! Such men were not men, but beasts, and should be shot down.

Far off in the distance, it might have been in the air or in his imagination, there sometimes floated a sound as of faint voices or shouts; but they came and went, and he listened, and by and by heard no more. The horses breathed heavily behind their sage-brush stable, and the sun rose higher and hotter. At last sleep came, troubled, fitful, but sleep, oblivion. This time there was no lady in an automobile.

It was high noon when he awoke, for the sun had reached around the sage-brush, and was pouring full into his face. He was very uncomfortable, and moreover an uneasy sense of something wrong pervaded his mind. Had he or had he not, heard a strange, low, sibilant, writhing sound just as he came to consciousness? Why did he feel that something, some one, had passed him but a moment before?

He rubbed his eyes open, and fanned himself with his hat. There was not a sound to be heard save a distant hawk in the heavens, and the breathing of the horses. He stepped over, and made sure that they were all right, and then came back. Was the girl still sleeping? Should he call her? But what should he call her? She had no name to him as yet. He could not say, "My dear madam" in the wilderness, nor yet "mademoiselle."

Perhaps it was she who had passed him. Perhaps she was looking about for water, or for fire-wood. He cast his eyes about, but the thick growth of sage-brush everywhere prevented his seeing much. He stepped to the right and then to the left of the little enclosure where she had gone to sleep, but there was no sign of life.

At last the sense of uneasiness grew upon him until he spoke.

"Are you awake yet?" he ventured; but the words somehow stuck in his throat, and would not sound out clearly. He ventured the question again, but it seemed to go no further than the gray-green foliage in front of him. Did he catch an alert movement, the sound of attention, alarm? Had he perhaps frightened her?

His flesh grew creepy, and he was angry with himself that he stood here actually trembling and for no reason. He felt that there was danger in the air. What could it mean? He had never been a believer in premonitions or superstitions of any kind. But the thought came to him that perhaps that evil man had come softly while he slept, and had stolen the girl away. Then all at once a horror seized him, and he made up his mind to end this suspense and venture in to see whether she were safe.

CHAPTER VI
A CHRISTIAN ENDEAVOR MEETING IN THE WILDERNESS

He stepped boldly around the green barrier, and his first glance told him she was lying there still asleep; but the consciousness of another presence held him from going away. There, coiled on the ground with venomous fangs extended and eyes glittering like slimy jewels, was a rattlesnake, close beside her.

For a second he gazed with a kind of fascinated horror, and his brain refused to act. Then he knew he must do something, and at once. He had read of serpents and travellers' encounters with them, but no memory of what was to be done under such circumstances came. Shoot? He dared not. He would be more likely to kill the girl than the serpent, and in any event would precipitate the calamity. Neither was there any way to awaken the girl and drag her from peril, for the slightest movement upon her part would bring the poisoned fangs upon her.

He cast his eyes about for some weapon, but there was not a stick or a stone in sight. He was a good golf-player; if he had a loaded stick, he could easily take the serpent's head off, he thought; but there was no stick. There was only one hope, he felt, and that would be to attract the creature to himself; and he hardly dared move lest the fascinated gaze should close upon the victim as she lay there sweetly sleeping, unaware of her new peril.

Suddenly he knew what to do. Silently he stepped back out of sight, tore off his coat, and then cautiously approached the snake again, holding the coat up before him. There was an instant's pause when he calculated whether the coat could drop between the snake and the smooth brown arm in front before the terrible fangs would get there; and then the coat dropped, the man bravely holding one end of it as a wall between the serpent and the girl, crying to her in an agony of frenzy to awaken and run.

There was a terrible moment in which he realized that the girl was saved and he himself was in peril of death, while he held to the coat till the girl was on her feet in safety. Then he saw the writhing coil at his feet turn and fasten its eyes of fury upon him. He was conscious of being uncertain whether his fingers could let go the coat, and whether his trembling knees could carry him away before the serpent struck; then it was all over, and he and the girl were standing outside the sage-brush, with the sound of the pistol dying away among the echoes, and the fine ache of his arm where her fingers had grasped him to drag him from danger.

The serpent was dead. She had shot it. She took that as coolly as she had taken the bird in its flight. But she stood looking at him with great eyes of gratitude, and he looked at her amazed that they were both alive, and scarcely understanding all that had happened.

The girl broke the stillness.

"You are what they call a 'tenderfoot,'" she said significantly.

"Yes," he assented humbly, "I guess I am. I couldn't have shot it to save anybody's life."

"You are a tenderfoot, and you couldn't shoot," she continued eulogistically, as if it were necessary to have it all stated plainly, "but you—you are what my brother used to call 'a white man.' You couldn't shoot; but you could risk your life, and hold that coat, and look death in the face. *You* are no tenderfoot."

There was eloquence in her eyes, and in her voice there were tears. She turned away to hide if any were in her eyes. But the man put out his hand on her sure little brown one, and took it firmly in his own, looking down upon her with his own eyes filled with tears of which he was not ashamed.

"And what am I to say to you for saving my life?" he said.

"I? O, that was easy," said the girl, rousing to the commonplace. "I can always shoot. Only you were hard to drag away. You seemed to want to stay there and die with your coat."

"They laughed at me for wearing that coat when we started away. They said a hunter never bothered himself with extra clothing," he mused as they walked away from the terrible spot.

"Do you think it was the prayer?" asked the girl suddenly.

"It may be!" said the man with wondering accent.

Then quietly, thoughtfully, they mounted and rode onward.

Their way, due east, led them around the shoulder of a hill. It was tolerably smooth, but they were obliged to go single file, so there was very little talking done.

It was nearly the middle of the afternoon when all at once a sound reached them from below, a sound so new that it was startling. They stopped their horses, and looked at each other. It was the faint sound of singing wafted on the light breeze, singing that came in whiffs like a perfume, and then died out. Cautiously they guided their horses on around the hill, keeping close together now. It was plain they were approaching some human being or beings. No bird could sing like that. There were indistinct words to the music.

They rounded the hillside, and stopped again side by side. There below them lay the trail for which they had been searching, and just beneath them, nestled against the hill, was a little schoolhouse of logs, weather-boarded, its windows open; and behind it and around it were horses tied, some of them hitched to wagons, but most of them with saddles.

The singing was clear and distinct now. They could hear the words. "O, that will be glory for me, glory for me, glory for me —"

"What is it?" she whispered.

"Why, I suspect it is a Sunday school or something of the kind."

"O! A school! Could we go in?"

"If you like," said the man, enjoying her simplicity. "We can tie out horses here behind the building, and they can rest. There is fresh grass in this sheltered place; see?"

He led her down behind the schoolhouse to a spot where the horses could not be seen from the trail. The girl peered curiously around the corner into the window. There sat two young girls about her own age, and one of them smiled at her. It seemed an invitation. She smiled back, and went on to the doorway reassured. When she entered the room, she found them pointing to a seat near a window, behind a small desk.

There were desks all over the room at regular intervals, and a larger desk up in front. Almost all the people sat at desks.

There was a curious wooden box in front at one side of, the big desk, and a girl sat before it pushing down some black and white strips that looked like sticks, and making her feet go, and singing with all her might. The curious box made music, the same music the people were singing. Was it a piano? she wondered. She had heard of pianos. Her father used to talk about them. O, and what was that her mother used to want? A "cab'net-organ." Perhaps this was a cab'net-organ. At any rate, she was entranced with the music.

Up behind the man who sat at the big desk was a large board painted black with some white marks on it. The sunlight glinted across it, and she could not tell what they were; but, when she moved a little, she saw quite clearly it was a large cross with words underneath it —"He will hide me."

It was a strange place. The girl looked around shyly, and felt submerged in the volume of song that rolled around her, from voices untrained, perhaps, but hearts that knew whereof they sang. To her it was heavenly music, if she had the least conception of what such music was like. "Glory," "glory," "glory!" The words seemed to fit the day, and the sunshine, and the deliverance that had come to her so recently. She looked around for her companion and deliverer to enjoy it with him, but he had not come in yet.

The two girls were handing her a book now and pointing to the place. She could read. Her mother had taught her just a little before the other children were born, but not much in the way of literature had ever come in her way. She grasped the book eagerly, hungrily, and looked where the finger pointed. Yes, there were the words. "Glory for me!" "Glory for me!" Did that mean her? Was there glory for her anywhere in the world? She sighed with the joy of the possibility, as the "Glory Song" rolled along, led by the enthusiasm of one who had recently come from a big city where it had been sung in a great revival service. Some kind friend had given some copies of a leaflet containing it and a few other new songs to this little handful of Christians, and they were singing them as if they had been a thousand strong.

The singing ceased and the man at the big desk said, "Let us have the verses."

"'The eternal God is thy refuge, and underneath are the everlasting arms,'" said a careworn woman in the front seat.

"'He shall cover thee with his feathers, and under his wings shalt thou trust,'" said a young man next.

"'In the time of trouble he shall hide me in his pavilion; in the secret of his tabernacle shall he hide me,'" read the girl who had handed the book. The slip of paper she had written it on fluttered to the floor at the feet of the stranger, and the stranger stooped and picked it up, offering it back; but the other girl shook her head, and the stranger kept it, looking wonderingly at the words, trying to puzzle out a meaning.

There were other verses repeated, but just then a sound smote upon the girl's ear which deadened all others. In spite of herself she began to tremble. Even her lips seemed to her to move with the weakness of her fear. She looked up, and the man was just coming toward the door; but her eyes grew dizzy, and a faintness seemed to come over her.

Up the trail on horseback, with shouts and ribald songs, rode four rough men, too drunk to know where they were going. The little schoolhouse seemed to attract their attention as they passed, and just for deviltry they shouted out a volley of oaths and vile talk to the worshippers within. One in particular, the leader, looked straight into the face of the young man as he returned from fastening the horses and was about to enter the schoolhouse, and pretended to point his pistol at him, discharging it immediately into the air. This was the signal for some wild firing as the men rode on past the schoolhouse, leaving a train of curses behind them to haunt the air and struggle with the "Glory Song" in the memories of those who heard.

The girl looked out from her seat beside the window, and saw the evil face of the man from whom she had fled. She thought for a terrible minute, which seemed ages long to her, that she was cornered now. She began to look about on the people there helplessly, and wonder whether they would save her, would help her, in her time of need. Would they be able to fight and prevail against those four terrible men mad with liquor?

Suppose he said she was his-his wife, perhaps, or sister, who had run away. What could they do? Would they believe her? Would the man who had saved her life a few minutes ago believe her? Would anybody help her?

The party passed, and the man came in and sat down beside her quietly enough; but without a word or a look he knew at once who the man was he had just seen. His soul trembled for the girl, and his anger rose hot. He felt that a man like that ought to be wiped off the face of the earth in some way, or placed in solitary confinement the rest of his life.

He looked down at the girl, trembling, brave, white, beside him; and he felt like gathering her in his arms and hiding her himself, such a frail, brave, courageous little soul she seemed. But the calm nerve with which she had shot the serpent was gone now. He saw she was trembling and ready to cry. Then he smiled upon her, a smile the like of which he had never given to human being before; at least, not since he was a tiny baby and smiled confidingly into his mother's face. Something in that smile was like sunshine to a nervous chill.

The girl felt the comfort of it, though she still trembled. Down her eyes drooped to the paper in her shaking hands. Then gradually, letter by letter, word by word, the verse spoke to her. Not all the meaning she gathered, for "pavilion" and "tabernacle" were unknown words to her, but the hiding she could understand. She had been hidden in her time of trouble. Some one had done it. "He"—the word would fit the man by her side, for he had helped to hide her, and to save her more than once; but just now there came a dim perception that it was some other He, some One greater who had worked this miracle and saved her once more to go on perhaps to better things.

There were many things said in that meeting, good and wise and true. They might have been helpful to the girl if she had understood, but her thoughts had much to do. One grain of truth she had gathered for her future use. There was a "hiding" somewhere in this world, and she had had it in a time of trouble. One moment more out upon the open, and the terrible man might have seen her.

There came a time of prayer in which all heads were bowed, and a voice here and there murmured a few soft little words which she did not comprehend; but at the close they all joined in "the prayer"; and, when she heard the words, "Our Father," she closed her eyes, which had been curiously open and watching, and joined her voice softly with the rest. Somehow it seemed to connect her safety with "our Father," and she felt a stronger faith than ever in her prayer.

The young man listened intently to all he heard. There was something strangely impressive to him in this simple worship out in what to him was a vast wilderness. He felt more of the true spirit of worship than he had ever felt at home sitting in the handsomely upholstered pew beside his mother and sister while the choir-boys chanted the processional and the light filtered through costly windows of many colors over the large and cultivated congregation. There was something about the words of these people that went straight to the heart more than all the intonings of the cultured voices he had ever heard. Truly they meant what they said, and God had been a reality to them in many a time of trouble. That seemed to be the theme of the afternoon, the saving power of the eternal God, made perfect through the need and the trust of His people. He was reminded more than once of the incident of the morning and the miraculous saving of his own and his companion's life.

When the meeting was over, the people gathered in groups and talked with one another. The girl who had handed the book came over and spoke to the strangers, putting out her hand pleasantly. She was the missionary's daughter.

"What is this? School?" asked the stranger eagerly.

"Yes, this is the schoolhouse," said the missionary's daughter; "but this meeting is Christian Endeavor. Do you live near here? Can't you come every time?"

"No. I live a long way off," said the girl sadly. "That is, I did. I don't live anywhere now. I'm going away."

"I wish you lived here. Then you could come to our meeting. Did you have a Christian Endeavor where you lived?"

"No. I never saw one before. It's nice. I like it."

Another girl came up now, and put out her hand in greeting. "You must come again," she said politely.

"I don't know," said the visitor. "I sha'n't be coming back soon."

"Are you going far?"

"As far as I can. I'm going East."

"O," said the inquisitor; and then, seeing the missionary's daughter was talking to some one else, she whispered, nodding toward the man, "Is he your husband?"

The girl looked startled, while a slow color mounted into her cheeks.

"No," said she gravely, thoughtfully. "But-he saved my life a little while ago."

"Oh!" said the other, awestruck. "My! And ain't he handsome? How did he do it?"

But the girl could not talk about it. She shuddered.

"It was a dreadful snake," she said, "and I was—I didn't see it. It was awful! I can't tell you about it."

"My!" said the girl. "How terrible!"

The people were passing out now. The man was talking with the missionary, asking the road to somewhere. The girl suddenly realized that this hour of preciousness was over, and life was to be faced again. Those men, those terrible men! She had recognized the others as having been among her brother's funeral train. Where were they, and why had they gone that way? Were they on her track? Had they any clue to her whereabouts? Would they turn back pretty soon, and catch her when the people were gone home?

It appeared that the nearest town was Malta, sixteen miles away, down in the direction where the party of men had passed. There were only four houses near the schoolhouse, and they were scattered in different directions along the stream in the valley. The two stood still near the door after the congregation had scattered. The girl suddenly shivered. As she looked down the road, she seemed again to see the coarse face of the man she feared, and to hear his loud laughter and oaths. What if he should come back again? "I cannot go that way!" she said, pointing down the trail toward Malta. "I would rather die with wild beasts."

"No!" said the man with decision. "On no account can we go that way. Was that the man you ran away from?"

"Yes." She looked up at him, her eyes filled with wonder over the way in which he had coupled his lot with hers.

"Poor little girl!" he said with deep feeling. "You would be better off with the beasts. Come, let us hurry away from here!"

They turned sharply away from the trail, and followed down behind a family who were almost out of sight around the hill. There would be a chance of getting some provisions, the man thought. The girl thought of nothing except to get away. They rode hard, and soon came within hailing-distance of the people ahead of them, and asked a few questions.

No, there were no houses to the north until you were over the Canadian line, and the trail was hard to follow. Few people went that way. Most went down to Malta. Why didn't they go to Malta? There was a road there, and stores. It was by all means the best way. Yes, there was another house about twenty miles away on this trail. It was a large ranch, and was near to another town that had a railroad. The people seldom came this way, as there were other places more accessible to them. The trail was little used, and might be hard to find in some places; but, if they kept the Cottonwood Creek in sight, and followed on to the end of the valley, and then crossed the bench to the right, they would be in sight of it, and couldn't miss it. It was a good twenty miles beyond their house; but, if the travellers didn't miss the way, they might reach it before dark. Yes, the people could supply a few provisions at their house if the strangers didn't mind taking what was at hand.

The man in the wagon tried his best to find out where the two were going and what they were going for; but the man from the East baffled his curiosity in a most dexterous manner, so that, when the two rode away from the two-roomed log house where the kind-hearted people lived, they left no clue to their identity or mission beyond the fact that they were going quite a journey, and had got a little off their trail and run out of provisions.

They felt comparatively safe from pursuit for a few hours at least, for the men could scarcely return and trace them very soon. They had not stopped to eat anything; but all the milk they could drink had been given to them, and its refreshing strength was racing through their veins. They started upon their long ride with the pleasure of their companionship strong upon them.

"What was it all about?" asked the girl as they settled into a steady gait after a long gallop across a smooth level place.

He looked at her questioningly.

"The school. What did it mean? She said it was a Christian Endeavor. What is that?"

"Why, some sort of a religious meeting, or something of that kind, I suppose," he answered lamely. "Did you enjoy it?"

"Yes," she answered solemnly, "I liked it. I never went to such a thing before. The girl said they had one everywhere all over the world. What do you think she meant?"

"Why, I don't know, I'm sure, unless it's some kind of a society. But it looked to me like a prayer meeting. I've heard about prayer meetings, but I never went to one, though I never supposed they were so interesting. That was a remarkable story that old man told of how he was taken care of that night among the Indians. He evidently believes that prayer helps people."

"Don't you?" she asked quickly.

"O, certainly!" he said, "but there was something so genuine about the way the old man told it that it made you feel it in a new way."

"It is all new to me," said the girl. "But mother used to go to Sunday school and church and prayer meeting. She's often told me about it. She used to sing sometimes. One song was 'Rock of Ages.' Did you ever hear that?

"'Rock of Ages, cleft for me.
Let me hide myself in Thee.'"

She said it slowly and in a singsong voice, as if she were measuring the words off to imaginary notes. "I thought about that the night I started. I wished I knew where that rock was. Is there a rock anywhere that they call the Rock of Ages?"

The young man was visibly embarrassed. He wanted to laugh, but he would not hurt her in that way again. He was not accustomed to talking religion; yet here by this strange girl's side it seemed perfectly natural that he, who knew so very little experimentally himself about it, should be trying to explain the Rock of Ages to a soul in need. All at once it flashed upon him that it was for just such souls in need as this one that the Rock of Ages came into the world.

"I've heard the song. Yes, I think they sing it in all churches. It's quite common. No, there isn't any place called Rock of Ages. It refers-that is, I believe-why, you see the thing is figurative-that is, a kind of picture of things. It refers to the Deity."

"O! Who is that?" asked the girt.

"Why-God." He tried to say it as if he had been telling her it was Mr. Smith or Mr. Jones, but somehow the sound of the word on his lips thus shocked him. He did not know how to go on. "It just means God will take care of people."

"O!" she said, and this time a light of understanding broke over her face. "But," she added, "I wish I knew what it meant, the meeting, and why they did it. There must be some reason. They wouldn't do it for nothing. And how do they know it's all so? Where did they find it out?"

The man felt he was beyond his depth; so he sought to change the subject. "I wish you would tell me about yourself," he said gently. "I should like to understand you better. We have travelled together for a good many hours now, and we ought to know more about each other."

"What do you want to know?" She asked it gravely. "There isn't much to tell but what I've told you. I've lived on a mountain all my life, and helped mother. The rest all died. The baby first, and my two brothers, and father, and mother, and then John. I said the prayer for John, and ran away."

"Yes, but I want to know about your life. You know I live in the East where everything is different. It's all new to me out here. I want to know, for instance, how you came to talk so well. You don't talk like a girl that never went to school. You speak as if you had read and studied. You make so few mistakes in your English. You speak quite correctly. That is not usual, I believe, when people have lived all their lives away from school, you know. You don't talk like the girls I have met since I came out here."

"Father always made me speak right. He kept at every one of us children when we said a word wrong, and made us say it over again. It made him angry to hear words said wrong. He made mother cry once when she said 'done' when she ought to have said 'did.' Father went to school once, but mother only went a little while. Father knew a great deal, and when he was sober he used to teach us things once in a while. He taught me to read. I can read anything I ever saw."

"Did you have many books and magazines?" he asked innocently.

"We had three books!" she answered proudly, as if that were a great many. "One was a grammar. Father bought it for mother before they were married, and she always kept it wrapped up in paper carefully. She used to get it out for me to read in sometimes; but she was very careful with it, and when she died I put it in her hands. I thought she would like to have it close to her, because it always seemed so much to her. You see father bought it. Then there was an almanac, and a book about stones and earth. A man who was hunting for gold left that. He stopped over night at our house, and asked for some, thing to eat. He hadn't any money to pay for it; so he left that book with us, and said when he found the gold he would come and buy it back again. But he never came back."

"Is that all that you have ever read?" he asked compassionately.

"O, no! We got papers sometimes. Father would come home with a whole paper wrapped around some bundle. Once there was a beautiful story about a girl; but the paper was torn in the middle, and I never knew how it came out."

There was great wistfulness in her voice. It seemed to be one of the regrets of her girlhood that she did not know how that other girl in the story fared. All at once she turned to him.

"Now tell me about your life," she said. "I'm sure you have a great deal to tell."

His face darkened in a way that made her sorry.

"O, well," said he as if it mattered very little about his life, "I had a nice home-have yet, for the matter of that. Father died when I was little, and mother let me do just about as I pleased. I went to school because the other fellows did, and because that was the thing to do. After I grew up I liked it. That is, I liked some studies; so I went to a university."

"What is that?"

"O, just a higher school where you learn grown-up things. Then I travelled. When I came home, I went into society a good deal. But" —and his face darkened again —"I got tired of it all, and thought I would come out here for a while and hunt, and I got lost, and I found you!" He smiled into her face. "Now you know the rest."

Something passed between them in that smile and glance, a flash of the recognition of souls, and a gladness in each other's company, that made the heart warm. They said no more for some time, but rode quietly side by side.

They had come to the end of the valley, and were crossing the bench. The distant ranch could quite distinctly be seen. The silver moon had come up, for they had not been hurrying, and a great beauty pervaded everything. They almost shrank from approaching the buildings and people. They had enjoyed the ride and the companionship. Every step brought them nearer to what they had known all the time was an indistinct future from which they had been joyously shut away for a little time till they might know each other.

CHAPTER VII
BAD NEWS

They found rest for the night at the ranch house. The place was wide and hospitable. The girl looked about her with wonder on the comfortable arrangements for work. If only her mother had had such a kitchen to work in, and such a pleasant, happy home, she might have been living yet. There was a pleasant-faced, sweet-voiced woman with gray hair whom the men called "mother." She gave the girl a kindly welcome, and made her sit down to a nice warm supper, and, when it was over, led her to a little room where her own bed was, and told her she might sleep with her. The girl lay down in a maze of wonder, but was too weary with the long ride to keep awake and think about it.

They slept, the two travellers, a sound and dreamless sleep, wherein seemed peace and moonlight, and a forgetting of sorrows.

Early the next morning the girl awoke. The woman by her side was already stirring. There was breakfast to get for the men. The woman asked her a few questions about her journey.

"He's your brother, ain't he, dearie?" asked the woman as she was about to leave the room.

"No," said the girl.

"O," said the woman, puzzled, "then you and he's goin' to be married in the town."

"O, no!" said the girl with scarlet cheeks, thinking of the lady in the automobile.

"Not goin' to be married, dearie? Now that's too bad. Ain't he any kind of relation to you? Not an uncle nor cousin nor nothin'?"

"No."

"Then how be's you travellin' 'lone with him? It don't seem just right. You's a sweet, good girl; an' he's a fine man. But harm's come to more'n one. Where'd you take up with each other? Be he a neighbor? He looks like a man from way off, not hereabouts. You sure he ain't deceivin' you, dearie?"

The girl flashed her eyes in answer.

"Yes, I'm sure. He's a good man. He prays to our Father. No, he's not a neighbor, nor an uncle, nor a cousin. He's just a man that got lost. We were both lost on the prairie in the night; and he's from the East, and got lost from his party of hunters. He had nothing to eat, but I had; so I gave him some. Then he saved my life when a snake almost stung me. He's been good to me."

The woman looked relieved.

"And where you goin', dearie, all 'lone? What your folks thinkin' 'bout to let you go 'lone this way?"

"They're dead," said the girl with great tears in her eyes.

"Dearie me! And you so young! Say, dearie, s'pose you stay here with me. I'm lonesome, an' there's no women near by here. You could help me and be comp'ny. The men would like to have a girl round. There's plenty likely men on this ranch could make a good home fer a girl sometime. Stay here with me, dearie."

Had this refuge been offered the girl during her first flight in the wilderness, with what joy and thankfulness she would have accepted! Now it suddenly seemed a great impossibility for her to stay. She must go on. She had a pleasant ride before her, and delightful companionship; and she was going to school. The world was wide, and she had entered it. She had no mind to pause thus on the threshold, and never see further than Montana. Moreover, the closing words of the woman did not please her.

"I cannot stay," she said decidedly. "I'm going to school. And I do not want a man. I have just run away from a man, a dreadful one. I am going to school in the East. I have some relations there, and perhaps I can find them."

"You don't say so!" said the woman, looking disappointed. She had taken a great fancy to the sweet young face. "Well, dearie, why not stay here a little while, and write to your folks, and then go on with some one who is going your way? I don't like to see you go off with that man. It ain't the proper thing. He knows it himself. I'm afraid he's deceivin' you. I can see by his clo'es he's one of the fine young fellows that does as they please. He won't think any good of you if you keep travellin' 'lone with him. It's all well 'nough when you get lost, an' he was nice to help you out and save you from snakes; but he knows he ain't no business travellin' 'lone with you, you pretty little creature!"

"You must not talk so!" said the girl, rising and flashing her eyes again. "He's a good man. He's what my brother called 'a white man all through.' Besides, he's got a lady, a beautiful lady, in the East. She rides in some kind of a grand carriage that goes of itself, and he thinks a great deal of her."

The woman looked as if she were but half convinced.

"It may seem all right to you, dearie," she said sadly; "but I'm old, and I've seen things happen. You'd find his fine lady wouldn't go jantin' round the world 'lone with him unless she's married. I've lived East, and I know; and what's more, he knows it too. He may mean all right, but you never can trust folks."

The woman went away to prepare breakfast then, and left the girl feeling as if the whole world was against her, trying to hold her. She was glad when the man suggested that they hurry their breakfast and get away as quickly as possible. She did not smile when the old woman came out to bid her good-by, and put a detaining hand on the horse's bridle, saying, "You better stay with me, after all, hadn't you, dearie?"

The man looked inquiringly at the two women, and saw like a flash the suspicion of the older woman, read the trust and haughty anger in the beautiful younger face, and then smiled down on the old woman whose kindly hospitality had saved them for a while from the terrors of the open night, and said:

"Don't you worry about her, auntie. I'm going to take good care of her, and perhaps she'll write you a letter some day, and tell you where she is and what she's doing."

Half reassured, the old woman gave him her name and address; and he wrote them down in a little red notebook.

When they were well started on their way, the man explained that he had hurried because from conversation with the men he had learned that this ranch where they had spent the night was on the direct trail from Malta to another small town. It might be that the pursuers would go further than Malta. Did she think they would go so far? They must have come almost a hundred miles already. Would they not be discouraged?

But the girl looked surprised. A hundred miles on horseback was not far. Her brother often used to ride a hundred miles just to see a fight or have a good time. She felt sure the men would not hesitate to follow a long distance if something else did not turn them aside.

The man's face looked sternly out from under his wide hat. He felt a great responsibility for the girl since he had seen the face of the man who was pursuing her.

Their horses were fresh, and the day was fine. They rode hard as long as the road was smooth, and did little talking. The girl was turning over in her mind the words the woman had spoken to her. But the thing that stuck there and troubled her was, "And he knows it is so."

Was she doing something for which this man by her side would not respect her? Was she overstepping some unwritten law of which she had never heard, and did he know it, and yet encourage her in it?

That she need fear him in the least she would not believe. Had she not watched the look of utmost respect on his face as he stood quietly waiting for her to awake the first morning they had met? Had he not had opportunity again and again to show her dishonor by word or look? Yet he had never been anything but gentle and courteous to her. She did not call things by these names, but she felt the gentleman in him.

Besides, there was the lady. He had told about her at the beginning. He evidently honored the lady. The woman had said that the lady would not ride with him alone. Was it true? Would he not like to have the lady ride alone with him when she was not his relative in any way? Then was there a difference between his thought of the lady and of herself? Of course, there was some; he loved the lady, but he should not think less honorably of her than of any lady in the land.

She sat straight and proudly in her man's saddle, and tried to make him feel that she was worthy of respect. She had tried to show him this when she had shot the bird. Now she recognized that there was a fine something, higher than shooting or prowess of any kind, which would command respect. It was something she felt belonged to her, yet she was not sure she commanded it. What did she lack, and how could she secure it?

He watched her quiet, thoughtful face, and the lady of his former troubled thoughts was as utterly forgotten by him as if she had never existed. He was unconsciously absorbed in the study of eye and lip and brow. His eyes were growing accustomed to the form and feature of this girl beside him, and he took pleasure in watching her.

They stopped for lunch in a coulee under a pretty cluster of cedar-trees a little back from the trail, where they might look over the way they had come and be warned against pursuers. About three o'clock they reached a town. Here the railroad came directly from Malta, but there was but one train a day each way.

The man went to the public stopping-place and asked for a room, and boldly demanded a private place for his "sister" to rest for a while. "She is my little sister," he told himself in excuse for the word. "She is my sister to care for. That is, if she were my sister, this is what I should want some good man to do for her."

He smiled as he went on his way after leaving the girl to rest. The thought of a sister pleased him. The old woman at the ranch had made him careful for the girl who was thus thrown in his company.

He rode down through the rough town to the railway station, but a short distance from the rude stopping-place; and there he made inquiries concerning roads, towns, etc., in the neighboring locality, and sent a telegram to the friends with whom he had been hunting when he got lost. He said he would be at the next town about twenty miles away. He knew that by this time they would be back home and anxious about him, if they were not already sending out searching parties for him. His message read:

> "Hit the trail all right.
> Am taking a trip for my health.
> Send mail to me at —— —"

Then after careful inquiry as to directions, and learning that there was more than one route to the town he had mentioned in his telegram, he went back to his companion. She was ready to go, for the presence of other people about her made her uneasy. She feared again there would be objection to their further progress together. Somehow the old woman's words had grown into a shadow which hovered over her. She mounted her horse gladly, and they went forward. He told her what he had just done, and how he expected to get his mail the next morning when they reached the next town. He explained that there was a ranch half-way there where they might stop all night.

She was troubled at the thought of another ranch. She knew there would be more questions, and perhaps other disagreeable words said; but she held her peace, listening to his plans. Her wonder was great over the telegram. She knew little or nothing about modern discoveries. It was a mystery to her how he could receive word by morning from a place that it had taken them nearly two days to leave behind, and how had he sent a message over a wire? Yes, she had heard of telegrams, but had never been quite sure they were true. When he saw that she was interested, he went on to tell her of other wonderful triumphs of science, the telephone, the electric light, gas, and the modern system of water-works. She listened as if it were all a fairy tale. Sometimes she looked at him, and wondered whether it could be true, or whether he were not making fun of her; but his earnest, honest eyes forbade doubt.

At the ranch they found two women, a mother and her daughter. The man asked frankly whether they could take care of this young friend of his overnight, saying that she was going on to the town in the morning, and was in his care for the journey. This seemed to relieve all suspicion. The two girls eyed each other, and then smiled.

"I'm Myrtle Baker," said the ranch-owner's daughter. "Come; I'll take you where you can wash your hands and face, and then we'll have some supper."

Myrtle Baker was a chatterer by nature. She talked incessantly; and, though she asked many questions, she did not wait for half of them to be answered. Besides, the traveller had grown wary. She did not intend to talk about the relationship between herself and her travelling companion. There was a charm in Myrtle's company which made the girl half regret leaving the next morning, as they did quite early, amid protests from Myrtle and her mother, who enjoyed a visitor in their isolated home.

But the ride that morning was constrained. Each felt in some subtle way that their pleasant companionship was coming to a crisis. Ahead in that town would be letters, communications from the outside world of friends, people who did not know or care what these two had been through together, and who would not hesitate to separate them with a firm hand. Neither put this thought into words, but it was there in their hearts, in the form of a vague fear. They talked very little, but each was feeling how pleasant the journey had been, and dreading what might be before.

They wanted to stay in this Utopia of the plains, forever journeying together, and never reaching any troublesome futures where were laws and opinions by which they must abide.

But the morning grew bright, and the road was not half long enough. Though at the last they walked their horses, they reached the town before the daily train had passed through. They went straight to the station, and found that the train was an hour late; but a telegram had arrived for the man. He took it nervously, his fingers trembling. He felt a premonition that it contained something unpleasant.

The girl sat on her horse by the platform, watching him through the open station door where he was standing as he tore open the envelope. She saw a deathly pallor overspread his face, and a look of anguish as if an arrow had pierced his heart. She felt as if the arrow had gone on into her own heart, and then she sat and waited. It seemed hours before he glanced up, with an old, weary look in his eyes. The message read:

"Your mother seriously ill. Wants you immediately. Will send your baggage on morning train. Have wired you are coming."

It was signed by his cousin with whom he had been taking his hunting-trip, and who was bound by business to go further West within a few days more.

The strong young man was almost bowed under this sudden stroke. His mother was very dear to him. He had left her well and happy. He must go to her at once, of course; but what should he do with the girl who had within the last two days taken so strong a hold upon his—he hesitated, and called it "protection." That word would do in the present emergency.

Then he looked, and saw her own face pale under the tan, and stepped out to the platform to tell her.

CHAPTER VIII
THE PARTING

She took the news like a Spartan. Her gentle pity was simply expressed, and then she held her peace. He must go. He must leave her. She knew that the train would carry him to his mother's bedside quicker than a horse could go. She felt by the look in his eyes and the set of his mouth that he had already decided that. Of course he must go. And the lady was there too! His mother and the lady! The lady would be sorry by this time, and would love him. Well, it was all right. He had been good to her. He had been a strong, bright angel God had sent to help her out of the wilderness; and now that she was safe the angel must return to his heaven. This was what she thought.

He had gone into the station to inquire about the train. It was an hour late. He had one short hour in which to do a great deal. He had very little money with him. Naturally men do not carry a fortune when they go out into the wilderness for a day's shooting. Fortunately he had his railroad return ticket to Philadelphia. That would carry him safely. But the girl. She of course had no money. And where was she going? He realized that he had failed to ask her many important questions. He hurried out, and explained to her.

"The train is an hour late. We must sell our horses, and try to get money enough to take us East. It is the only way. Where do you intend going?"

But the girl stiffened in her seat. She knew it was her opportunity to show that she was worthy of his honor and respect.

"I cannot go with you," she said very quietly.

"But you must," said he impatiently. "Don't you see there is no other way? I must take this train and get to my mother as soon as possible. She may not be living when I reach her if I don't." Something caught in his throat as he uttered the horrible thought that kept coming to his mind.

"I know," said the girl quietly. "You must go, but I must ride on."

"And why? I should like to know. Don't you see that I cannot leave you here alone? Those villains may be upon us at any minute. In fact, it is a good thing for us to board the train and get out of their miserable country as fast as steam can carry us. I am sorry you must part with your horse, for I know you are attached to it; but perhaps we can arrange to sell it to some one who will let us redeem it when we send the money out. You see I have not money enough with me to buy you a ticket. I couldn't get home myself if I hadn't my return ticket with me in my pocket. But surely the sale of both horses will bring enough to pay your way."

"You are very kind, but I must not go." The red lips were firm, and the girl was sitting very erect. She looked as she had done after she had shot the bird.

"But why?"

"I cannot travel alone with you. It is not your custom where you come from. The woman on the ranch told me. She said you knew girls did not do that, and that you did not respect me for going alone with you. She said it was not right, and that you knew it."

He looked at her impatient, angry, half ashamed that she should face him with these words.

"Nonsense!" said he. "This is a case of necessity. You are to be taken care of, and I am the one to do it."

"But it is not the custom among people where you live, is it?"

The clear eyes faced him down, and he had to admit that it was not.

"Then I can't go," she said decidedly.

"But you must. If you don't, I won't go."

"But you must," said the girl, "and I mustn't. If you talk that way, I'll run away from you. I've run away from one man, and I guess I can from another. Besides, you're forgetting the lady."

"What lady?"

"Your lady. The lady who rides in a carriage without horses."

"Hang the lady!" he said inelegantly. "Do you know that the train will be along here in less than an hour, and we have a great deal to do before we can get on board? There's no use stopping to talk about this matter. We haven't time. If you will just trust things to me, I'll attend to them all, and I'll answer your questions when we get safely on the train. Every instant is precious. Those men might come around that corner ever there any minute. That's all bosh about respect. I respect you more than any woman I ever met. And it's my business to take care of you."

"No, it's not your business," said the girl bravely, "and I can't let you. I'm nothing to you, you know."

"You're every-that is-why, you surely know you're a great deal to me. Why, you saved my life, you know!"

"Yes, and you saved mine. That was beautiful, but that's all."

"Isn't that enough? What are you made of, anyway, to sit there when there's so much to be done, and those villains on our track, and insist that you won't be saved?' Respect you! Why, a lion in the wilderness would have to respect you. You're made of iron and steel and precious stones. You've the courage of a —a —I was going to say a man but I mean an angel. You're pure as snow, and true as the heavenly blue, and firm as a rock; and, if I had never respected you before, I would have to now. I respect, I honor, I —I —I —pray for you!" he finished fiercely.

He turned his back to hide his emotion.

She lifted her eyes to his when he turned again, and her own were full of tears.

"Thank you!" She said it very simply. "That makes me-very-glad! But I cannot go with you."

"Do you mean that?" he asked her desperately.

"Yes," steadily.

"Then I shall have to stay too."

"But you can't! You must go to your mother. I won't be stayed with. And what would she think? Mothers are-everything!" she finished. "You must go quick and get ready. What can I do to help?"

He gave her a look which she remembered long years afterward. It seemed to burn and sear its way into her soul. How was it that a stranger had the power to scorch her with anguish this way? And she him?

He turned, still with that desperate, half-frantic look in his face, and accosted two men who stood at the other end of the platform. They were not in particular need of a horse at present; but they were always ready to look at a bargain, and they walked speculatively down the uneven boards of the platform with him to where his horse stood, and inspected it.

The girl watched the whole proceeding with eyes that saw not but into the future. She put in a word about the worth of the saddle once when she saw it was going lower than it should. Three other men gathered about before the bargain was concluded, and the horse and its equipments sold for about half its value.

That done, the man turned toward the girl and motioned to her to lead her horse away to a more quiet place, and set him down to plead steadily against her decision. But the talk and the horse-selling had taken more time than he realized. The girl was more decided than ever in her determination not to go with him. She spoke of the lady again. She spoke of his mother, and mothers in general, and finished by reminding him that God would take care of her, and of him, too.

Then they heard the whistle of the train, and saw it growing from a speck to a large black object across the plain. To the girl the sight of this strange machine, that seemed more like a creature rushing toward her to snatch all beauty and hope and safety from her, sent a thrill of horror. To the man it seemed like a dreaded fate that was tearing him asunder. He had barely time to divest himself of his powder-horn, and a few little things that might be helpful to the girl in her journey, before the train was halting at the station. Then he took from his pocket the money that had been paid him for his horse; and, selecting a five-dollar bill for himself, he wrapped the rest in an envelope bearing his own name and address. The envelope was one addressed by the lady at home. It had contained some gracefully worded refusal of a request. But he did not notice now what envelope he gave her.

"Take this," he said. "It will help a little. Yes, you must! I cannot leave you —I *will* not-unless you do," when he saw that she hesitated and looked doubtful. "I owe you all and more for saving my life. I can never repay you. Take it. You may return it sometime when you get plenty more of your own, if it hurts your pride to keep it. Take it, please. Yes, I have plenty for myself. You will need it, and you must stop at nice places overnight. You will be very careful, won't you? My name is on that envelope. You must write to me and let me know that you are safe."

"Some one is calling you, and that thing is beginning to move again," said the girl, an awesome wonder in her face. "You will be left behind! O, hurry! Quick! Your mother!"

He half turned toward the train, and then came back.

"You haven't told me your name!" he gasped. "Tell me quick!"

She caught her breath.

"Elizabeth!" she answered, and waved him from her.

The conductor of the train was shouting to him, and two men shoved him toward the platform. He swung himself aboard with the accustomed ease of a man who has travelled; but he stood on the platform, and shouted, "Where are you going?" as the train swung noisily off.

She did not hear him, but waved her hand, and gave him a bright smile that was brimming with unshed tears. It seemed like instant, daring suicide in him to stand on that swaying, clattering house as it moved off irresponsibly down the plane of vision. She watched him till he was out of sight, a mere speck on the horizon of the prairie; and then she turned her horse slowly into the road, and went her way into the world alone.

The man stood on the platform, and watched her as he whirled away —a little brown girl on a little brown horse, so stanch and firm and stubborn and good. Her eyes were dear, and her lips as she smiled; and her hand was beautiful as it waved him good-by. She was dear, dear, dear! Why had he not known it? Why had he left her? Yet how could he stay? His mother was dying perhaps. He must not fail her in what might be her last summons. Life and death were pulling at his heart, tearing him asunder.

The vision of the little brown girl and the little brown horse blurred and faded. He tried to look, but could not see. He brought his eyes to nearer vision to fix their focus for another look, and straight before him whirled a shackly old saloon, rough and tumble, its character apparent from the men who were grouped about its doorway and from the barrels and kegs in profusion outside. From the doorway issued four men, wiping their mouths and shouting hilariously. Four horses stood tied to a fence near by. They were so instantly passed, and so vaguely seen, that he could not be sure in the least, but those four men reminded him strongly of the four who had passed the schoolhouse on Sunday.

He shuddered, and looked back. The little brown horse and the little brown girl were one with the little brown station so far away, and presently the saloon and men were blotted out in one blur of green and brown and yellow.

He looked to the ground in his despair. He *must* go back. He could not leave her in such peril. She was his to care for by all the rights of manhood and womanhood. She had been put in his way. It was his duty.

But the ground whirled by under his madness, and showed him plainly that to jump off would be instant death. Then the thought of his mother came again, and the girl's words, "I am nothing to you, you know."

The train whirled its way between two mountains and the valley, and the green and brown and yellow blur were gone from sight. He felt as if he had just seen the coffin close over the girl's sweet face, and he had done it.

By and by he crawled into the car, pulled his slouch hat down over his eyes, and settled down in a seat; but all the time he was trying to see over again that old saloon and those four men, and to make out their passing identity. Sometimes the agony of thinking it all over, and trying to make out whether those men had been the pursuers, made him feel frantic; and it seemed as if he must pull the bell-cord, and make the train stop, and get off to walk back. Then the utter hopelessness of ever finding her would come over him, and he would settle back in his seat again and try to sleep. But the least drowsiness would bring a vision of the girl galloping alone over the prairie with the four men in full pursuit behind. "Elizabeth, Elizabeth, Elizabeth!" the car-wheels seemed to say.

Elizabeth-that was all he had of her. He did not know the rest of her name, nor where she was going. He did not even know where she had come from, just "Elizabeth" and "Montana." If anything happened to her, he would never know. Oh! why had he left her? Why had he not *made* her go with him? In a case like that a man should assert his authority. But, then, it was true he had none, and she had said she would run away. She would have done it too. O, if it had been anything but sickness and possible death at the other end-and his mother, his own little mother! Nothing else would have kept him from staying to protect Elizabeth.

What a fool he had been! There were questions he might have asked, and plans they might have made, all those beautiful days and those moon-silvered nights. If any other man had done the same, he would have thought him lacking mentally. But here he had maundered on, and never found out the all-important things about her. Yet how did he know then how important they were to be? It had seemed as if they had all the world before them in the brilliant sunlight. How could he know that modern improvements were to seize him in the midst of a prairie waste, and whirl him off from her when he had just begun to know what she was, and to prize her company as a most precious gift dropped down from heaven at his feet?

By degrees he came out of his hysterical frenzy, and returned to a somewhat normal state of mind. He reasoned himself several times into the belief that those men were not in the least like the men he had seen Sunday. He knew that one could not recognize one's own brother at that distance and that rate of passing speed. He tried to think that Elizabeth would be cared for. She had come through many a danger, and was it likely that the God in whom she trusted, who had guarded her so many times in her great peril, would desert her now in her dire need? Would He not raise up help for her somewhere? Perhaps another man as good as he, and as trustworthy as he had tried to be, would find her and help her.

But that thought was not pleasant. He put it away impatiently. It cut him. Why had she talked so much about the lady? The lady! Ah! How was it the lady came no more into his thoughts? The memory of her haughty face no more quickened his heart-beats. Was he fickle that he could lose what he had supposed was a lifelong passion in a few days?

The darkness was creeping on. Where was Elizabeth? Had she found a refuge for the night? Or was she wandering on an unknown trail, hearing voices and oaths through the darkness, and seeing the gleaming of wild eyes low in the bushes ahead? How could he have left her? How could he? He must go back even yet. He must, he must, *he must*!

And so it went on through the long night.

The train stopped at several places to take on water; but there seemed to be no human habitation near, or else his eyes were dim with his trouble. Once, when they stopped longer than the other times, he got up and walked the length of the car and down the steps to the ground. He even stood there, and let the train start jerkily on till his car had passed him, and the steps were just sliding by, and tried to think whether he would not stay, and go back in some way to find her. Then the impossibility of the search, and of his getting back in time to do any good, helped him to spring on board just before it was too late. He walked back to his seat saying to himself, "Fool! Fool!"

It was not till morning that he remembered his baggage and went in search of it. There he found a letter from his cousin, with other letters and telegrams explaining the state of affairs at home. He came back to his seat laden with a large leather grip and a suitcase. He sat down to read his letters, and these took his mind away from his troubled thoughts for a little while. There was a letter from his mother, sweet, graceful, half wistfully offering her sympathy. He saw she guessed the reason why he had left her and gone to this far place. Dear little mother!

What would she say if she knew his trouble now? And then would return his heart-frenzy over Elizabeth's peril. O to know that she was protected, hidden!

Fumbling in his pocket, he came upon a slip of paper, the slip the girl had given Elizabeth in the schoolhouse on Sunday afternoon. "For in the time of trouble he shall hide me in his pavilion; in the secret of his tabernacle shall he hide me."

Ah! God had hidden her then. Why not again? And what was that he had said to her himself, when searching for a word to cover his emotion? "I pray for you!" Why could he not pray? She had made him pray in the wilderness. Should he not pray for her who was in peril now? He leaned back in the hot, uncomfortable car-seat, pulling his hat down closer over his eyes, and prayed as he had never prayed before. "Our Father" he stumbled through as far as he could remember, and tried to think how her sweet voice had filled in the places where he had not known it the other time. Then, when he was done, he waited and prayed, "Our Father, care for Elizabeth," and added, "For Jesus' sake. Amen." Thereafter through the rest of his journey, and for days and weeks stretching ahead, he prayed that prayer, and sometimes found in it his only solace from the terrible fear that possessed him lest some harm had come to the girl, whom it seemed to him now he had deserted in cold blood.

CHAPTER IX
IN A TRAP

Elizabeth rode straight out to the east, crossing the town as rapidly as possible, going full gallop where the streets were empty. On the edge of the town she crossed another trail running back the way that they had come; but without swerving she turned out toward the world, and soon passed into a thick growth of trees, around a hill.

Not three minutes elapsed after she had passed the crossing of the trails before the four men rode across from the other direction, and, pausing, called to one another, looking this way and that:

"What d'ye think, Bill? Shall we risk the right hand 'r the left?"

"Take the left hand fer luck," answered Bill. "Let's go over to the ranch and ask. Ef she's been hereabouts, she's likely there. The old woman'll know. Come on, boys!"

And who shall say that the angel of the Lord did not stand within the crossing of the ways and turn aside the evil men?

Elizabeth did not stop her fierce ride until about noon. The frenzy of her fear of pursuit had come upon her with renewed force. Now that she was alone and desolate she dared not look behind her. She had been strong enough as she smiled her farewell; but, when the train had dwindled into a mere speck in the distance, her eyes were dropping tears thick and fast upon the horse's mane. So in the first heaviness of her loneliness she rode as if pursued by enemies close at hand.

But the horse must rest if she did not, for he was her only dependence now. So she sat her down in the shade of a tree, and tried to eat some dinner. The tears came again as she opened the pack which the man's strong hands had bound together for her. How little she had thought at breakfast-time that she would eat the next meal alone!

It was all well enough to tell him he must go, and say she was nothing to him; but it was different now to face the world without a single friend when one had learned to know how good a friend could be. Almost it would have been better if he had never found her, never saved her from the serpent, never ridden beside her and talked of wonderful new things to her; for now that he was gone the emptiness and loneliness were so much harder to bear; and now she was filled with a longing for things that could not be hers.

It was well he had gone so soon, well she had no longer to grow into the charm of his society; for he belonged to the lady, and was not hers. Thus she ate her dinner with the indifference of sorrow.

Then she took out the envelope, and counted over the money. Forty dollars he had given her. She knew he had kept but five for himself. How wonderful that he should have done all that for her! It seemed a very great wealth in her possession. Well, she would use it as sparingly as possible, and thus be able the sooner to return it all to him. Some she must use, she supposed, to buy food; but she would do with as little as she could. She might sometimes shoot a bird, or catch a fish; or there might be berries fit for food by the way. Nights she must stop by the way at a respectable house. That she had promised. He had told her of awful things that might happen to her if she lay down in the wilderness alone. Her lodging would sometimes cost her something. Yet often they would take her in for nothing. She would be careful of the money.

She studied the name on the envelope. George Trescott Benedict, 2 — — Walnut Street, Philadelphia, Penn. The letters were large and angular, not easy to read; but she puzzled them out. It did not look like his writing. She had watched him as he wrote the old woman's address in his little red book. He wrote small, round letters, slanting backwards, plain as print, pleasant writing to read. Now the old woman's address would never be of any use, and her wish that Elizabeth should travel alone was fulfilled.

There was a faint perfume from the envelope like Weldwood flowers. She breathed it in, and wondered at it. Was it perfume from something he carried in his pocket, some flower his lady had once given him? But this was not a pleasant thought. She put the envelope into her bosom after studying it again carefully until she knew the words by heart.

Then she drew forth the papers of her mother's that she had brought from home, and for the first time read them over.

The first was the marriage certificate. That she had seen before, and had studied with awe; but the others had been kept in a box that was never opened by the children. The mother kept them sacredly, always with the certificate on the top.

The largest paper she could not understand. It was something about a mine. There were a great many "herebys" and "whereases" and "agreements" in it. She put it back into the wrapper as of little account, probably something belonging to her father, which her mother had treasured for old time's sake.

Then came a paper which related to the claim where their little log home had stood, and upon the extreme edge of which the graves were. That, too, she laid reverently within its wrapper.

Next came a bit of pasteboard whereon was inscribed, "Mrs. Merrill Wilton Bailey, Rittenhouse Square, Tuesdays." That she knew was her grandmother's name, though she had never seen the card before-her father's mother. She looked at the card in wonder. It was almost like a distant view of the lady in question. What kind of a place might Rittenhouse Square be, and where was it? There was no telling. It might be near that wonderful Desert of Sahara that the man had talked about. She laid it down with a sigh.

There was only one paper left, and that was a letter written in pale pencil lines. It said:

> "*My dear Bessie:* Your pa died last week. He was killed falling from a scaffold. He was buried on Monday with five carriages and everything nice. We all got new black dresses, and have enough for a stone. If it don't cost too much, we'll have an angle on the top. I always thought an angle pointing to heaven was nice. We wish you was here. We miss you very much. I hope your husband is good to you. Why don't you write to us? You haven't wrote since your little girl was born. I s'pose you call her Bessie like you. If anything ever happens to you, you can send her to me. I'd kind of like her to fill your place. Your sister has got a baby girl too. She calls her Lizzie. We couldn't somehow have it natural to call her 'Lizabeth, and Nan wanted her called for me. I was always Lizzie, you know. Now you must write soon.
>
> "Your loving mother,
>
> ELIZABETH BRADY."

There was no date nor address to the letter, but an address had been penciled on the outside in her mother's cramped school-girl hand. It was dim but still readable, "Mrs. Elizabeth Brady, 18 — — Flora Street, Philadelphia."

Elizabeth studied the last word, then drew out the envelope again, and looked at that. Yes, the two names were the same. How wonderful! Perhaps she would sometime, sometime, see him again, though of course he belonged to the lady. But perhaps, if she went to school and learned very fast, she might sometime meet him at church-he went to church, she was sure-and then he might smile, and not be ashamed of his friend who had saved his life. Saved his life! Nonsense! She had not done much. He would not feel any such ridiculous indebtedness to her when he got back to home and friends and safety. He had saved her much more than she had saved him.

She put the papers all back in safety, and after having prepared her few belongings for taking up the journey, she knelt down. She would say the prayer before she went on. It might be that would keep the terrible pursuers away.

She said it once, and then with eyes still closed she waited a moment. Might she say it for him, who was gone away from her? Perhaps it would help him, and keep him from falling from that terrible machine he was riding on. Hitherto in her mind prayers had been only for the dead, but now they seemed also to belong to all who were in danger or trouble. She said the prayer over once more, slowly, then paused a moment, and added: "Our Father, hide him from trouble. Hide George Trescott Benedict. And hide me, please, too."

Then she mounted her horse, and went on her way.

It was a long and weary way. It reached over mountains and through valleys, across winding, turbulent streams and broad rivers that had few bridges. The rivers twice led her further south than she meant to go, in her ignorance. She had always felt that Philadelphia was straight ahead east, as straight as one could go to the heart of the sun.

Night after night she lay down in strange homes, some poorer and more forlorn than others; and day after day she took up her lonely travel again.

Gradually, as the days lengthened, and mountains piled themselves behind her, and rivers stretched like barriers between, she grew less and less to dread her pursuers, and more and more to look forward to the future. It seemed so long a way! Would it never end?

Once she asked a man whether he knew where Philadelphia was. She had been travelling then for weeks, and thought she must be almost there. But he said "Philadelphia? O, Philadelphia is in the East. That's a long way off. I saw a man once who came from there."

She set her firm little chin then, and travelled on. Her clothes were much worn, and her skin was brown as a berry. The horse plodded on with a dejected air. He would have liked to stop at a number of places they passed, and remain for life, what there was left of it; but he obediently walked on over any kind of an old road that came in his way, and solaced himself with whatever kind of a bite the roadside afforded. He was becoming a much-travelled horse. He knew a threshing-machine by sight now, and considered it no more than a prairie bob-cat.

At one stopping-place a good woman advised Elizabeth to rest on Sundays. She told her God didn't like people to do the same on His day as on other days, and it would bring her bad luck if she kept up her incessant riding. It was bad for the horse too. So, the night being Saturday, Elizabeth remained with the woman over the Sabbath, and heard read aloud the fourteenth chapter of John. It was a wonderful revelation to her. She did not altogether understand it. In fact, the Bible was an unknown book. She had never known that it was different from other books. She had heard it spoken of by her mother, but only as a book. She did not know it was a book of books.

She carried the beautiful thoughts with her on the way, and pondered them. She wished she might have the book. She remembered the name of it, Bible, the Book of God. Then God had written a book! Some day she would try to find it and read it.

"Let not your heart be troubled"; so much of the message drifted into her lonesome, ignorant soul, and settled down to stay. She said it over nights when she found a shelter in some unpleasant place or days when the road was rough or a storm came up and she was compelled to seek shelter by the roadside under a haystack or in a friendly but deserted shack. She thought of it the day there was no shelter and she was drenched to the skin. She wondered afterward when the sun came out and dried her nicely whether God had really been speaking the words to her troubled heart, "Let not your heart be troubled."

Every night and every morning she said "Our Father" twice, once for herself and once for the friend who had gone out into the world, it seemed about a hundred years ago.

But one day she came across a railroad track. It made her heart beat wildly. It seemed now that she must be almost there. Railroads were things belonging to the East and civilization. But the way was lonely still for days, and then she crossed more railroads, becoming more and more frequent, and came into the line of towns that stretched along beside the snake-like tracks.

She fell into the habit of staying overnight in a town, and then riding on to the next in the morning; but now her clothes were becoming so dirty and ragged that she felt ashamed to go to nice-looking places lest they should turn her out; so she sought shelter in barns and small, mean houses. But the people in these houses were distressingly dirty, and she found no place to wash.

She had lost track of the weeks or the months when she reached her first great city, the only one she had come near in her uncharted wanderings.

Into the outskirts of Chicago she rode undaunted, her head erect, with the carriage of a queen. She had passed Indians and cowboys in her journeying; why should she mind Chicago? Miles and miles of houses and people. There seemed to be no end to it. Nothing but houses everywhere and hurried-looking people, many of them working hard. Surely this must be Philadelphia.

A large, beautiful building attracted her attention. There were handsome grounds about it, and girls playing some game with a ball and curious webbed implements across a net of cords. Elizabeth drew her horse to the side of the road, and watched a few minutes. One girl was skilful, and hit the ball back every time. Elizabeth almost exclaimed out loud once when a particularly fine ball was played. She rode reluctantly on when the game was finished, and saw over the arched gateway the words, "Janeway School for Girls."

Ah! This was Philadelphia at last, and here was her school. She would go in at once before she went to her grandmother's. It might be better.

She dismounted, and tied the horse to an iron ring in a post by the sidewalk. Then she went slowly, shyly up the steps into the charmed circles of learning. She knew she was shabby, but her long journey would explain that. Would they be kind to her, and let her study?

She stood some time before the door, with a group of laughing girls not far away whispering about her. She smiled at them; but they did not return the salutation, and their actions made her more shy. At last she stepped into the open door, and a maid in cap and apron came forward. "You must not come in here, miss," she said imperiously. "This is a school."

"Yes," said Elizabeth gravely, smiling. "I want to see the teacher."

"She's busy. You can't see her," snapped the maid.

"Then I will wait till she is ready. I've come a great many miles, and I must see her."

The maid retreated at this, and an elegant woman in trailing black silk and gold-rimmed glasses approached threateningly. This was a new kind of beggar, of course, and must be dealt with at once.

"What do you want?" she asked frigidly.

"I've come to school," said Elizabeth confidingly. "I know I don't look very nice, but I've had to come all the way from Montana on horseback. If you could let me go where I can have some water and a thread and needle, I can make myself look better."

The woman eyed the girl incredulously.

"You have come to school!" she said; and her voice was large, and frightened Elizabeth. "You have come all the way from Montana! Impossible! You must be crazy."

"No, ma'am, I'm not crazy," said Elizabeth. "I just want to go to school."

The woman perceived that this might be an interesting case for benevolently inclined people. It was nothing but an annoyance to herself. "My dear girl," —her tone was bland and disagreeable now, —"are you aware that it takes money to come to school?"

"Does it?" said Elizabeth. "No, I didn't know it, but I have some money. I could give you ten dollars right now; and, if that is not enough, I might work some way, and earn more."

The woman laughed disagreeably.

"It is impossible," she said. "The yearly tuition here is five hundred dollars. Besides, we do not take girls of your class. This is a finishing school for young ladies. You will have to inquire further," and the woman swept away to laugh with her colleagues over the queer character, the new kind of tramp, she had just been called to interview. The maid came pertly forward, and said that Elizabeth could not longer stand where she was.

Bewilderment and bitter disappointment in her face, Elizabeth went slowly down to her horse, the great tears welling up into her eyes. As she rode away, she kept turning back to the school grounds wistfully. She did not notice the passers-by, nor know that they were commenting upon her appearance. She made a striking picture in her rough garments, with her wealth of hair, her tanned skin, and tear-filled eyes. An artist noticed it, and watched her down the street, half thinking he would follow and secure her as a model for his next picture.

A woman, gaudily bedecked in soiled finery, her face giving evidence of the frequent use of rouge and powder, watched her, and followed, pondering. At last she called, "My dear, my dear, wait a minute." She had to speak several times before Elizabeth saw that she was talking to her. Then the horse was halted by the sidewalk.

"My dear," said the woman, "you look tired and disappointed. Don't you want to come home with me for a little while, and rest?"

"Thank you," said Elizabeth, "but I am afraid I must go on. I only stop on Sundays."

"But just come home with me for a little while," coaxed the wheedling tones. "You look so tired, and I've some girls of my own. I know you would enjoy resting and talking with them."

The kindness in her tones touched the weary girl. Her pride had been stung to the quick by the haughty woman in the school. This woman would soothe her with kindness.

"Do you live far from here?" asked Elizabeth.

"Only two or three blocks," said the woman. "You ride along by the sidewalk, and we can talk. Where are you going? You look as if you had come a long distance."

"Yes," said the girl wearily, "from Montana. I am going to school. Is this Philadelphia?"

"This is Chicago," said the woman. "There are finer schools here than in Philadelphia. If you like to come and stay at my house awhile, I will see about getting you into a school."

"Is it hard work to get people into schools?" asked the girl wonderingly. "I thought they would want people to teach."

"No, it's very hard," said the lying woman; "but I think I know a school where I can get you in. Where are your folks? Are they in Montana?"

"They are all dead," said Elizabeth, "and I have come away to school."

"Poor child!" said the woman glibly. "Come right home with me, and I'll take care of you. I know a nice way you can earn your living, and then you can study if you like. But you're quite big to go to school. It seems to me you could have a good time without that. You are a very pretty girl; do you know it? You only need pretty clothes to make you a beauty. If you come with me, I will let you earn some beautiful new clothes."

"You are very kind," said the girl gravely. "I do need new clothes; and, if I could earn them, that would be all the better." She did not quite like the woman; yet of course that was foolish.

After a few more turns they stopped in front of a tall brick building with a number of windows. It seemed to be a good deal like other buildings; in fact, as she looked up the street, Elizabeth thought there were miles of them just alike. She tied her horse in front of the door, and went in with the woman. The woman told her to sit down a minute until she called the lady of the house, who would tell her more about the school. There were a number of pretty girls in the room, and they made very free to speak to her. They twitted her about her clothes, and in a way reminded Elizabeth of the girls in the school she had just interviewed.

Suddenly she spoke up to the group. An idea had occurred to her. This was the school, and the woman had not liked to say so until she spoke to the teacher about her.

"Is this a school?" she asked shyly.

Her question was met with a shout of derisive laughter.

"School!" cried the boldest, prettiest one. "School for scandal! School for morals!"

There was one, a thin, pale girl with dark circles under her eyes, a sad droop to her mouth, and bright scarlet spots in her cheeks. She came over to Elizabeth, and whispered something to her. Elizabeth started forward, unspeakable horror in her face.

She fled to the door where she had come in, but found it fastened. Then she turned as if she had been brought to bay by a pack of lions.

CHAPTER X
PHILADELPHIA AT LAST

"Open this door!" she commanded. "Let me out of here at once."

The pale girl started to do so, but the pretty one held her back. "No, Nellie; Madam will be angry with us all if you open that door." Then she turned to Elizabeth, and said:

"Whoever enters that door never goes out again. You are nicely caught, my dear."

There was a sting of bitterness and self-pity in the taunt at the end of the words. Elizabeth felt it, as she seized her pistol from her belt, and pointed it at the astonished group. They were not accustomed to girls with pistols. "Open that door, or I will shoot you all!" she cried.

Then, as she heard some one descending the stairs, she rushed again into the room where she remembered the windows were open. They were guarded by wire screens; but she caught up a chair, and dashed it through one, plunging out into the street in spite of detaining hands that reached for her, hands much hindered by the gleam of the pistol and the fear that it might go off in their midst.

It took but an instant to wrench the bridle from its fastening and mount her horse; then she rode forward through the city at a pace that only millionaires and automobiles are allowed to take. She met and passed her first automobile without a quiver. Her eyes were dilated, her lips set; angry, frightened tears were streaming down her cheeks, and she urged her poor horse forward until a policeman here and there thought it his duty to make a feeble effort to detain her. But nothing impeded her way. She fled through a maze of wagons, carriages, automobiles, and trolley-cars, until she passed the whirl of the great city, and at last was free again and out in the open country.

She came toward evening to a little cottage on the edge of a pretty suburb. The cottage was covered with roses, and the front yard was full of great old-fashioned flowers. On the porch sat a plain little old lady in a rocking-chair, knitting. There was a little gate with a path leading up to the door, and at the side another open gate with a road leading around to the back of the cottage.

Elizabeth saw, and murmuring, "O 'our Father,' please hide me!" she dashed into the driveway, and tore up to the side of the piazza at a full gallop. She jumped from the horse; and, leaving him standing panting with his nose to the fence, and a tempting strip of clover in front of him where he could graze when he should get his breath, she ran up the steps, and flung herself in a miserable little heap at the feet of the astonished old lady.

"O, please, please, won't you let me stay here a few minutes, and tell me what to do? I am so tired, and I have had such a dreadful, awful time!"

"Why, dearie me!" said the old lady. "Of course I will. Poor child; sit right down in this rocking-chair, and have a good cry. I'll get you a glass of water and something to eat, and then you shall tell me all about it."

She brought the water, and a tray with nice broad slices of brown bread and butter, a generous piece of apple pie, some cheese, and a glass pitcher of creamy milk.

Elizabeth drank the water, but before she could eat she told the terrible tale of her last adventure. It seemed awful for her to believe, and she felt she must have help somewhere. She had heard there were bad people in the world. In fact, she had seen men who were bad, and once a woman had passed their ranch whose character was said to be questionable. She wore a hard face, and could drink and swear like the men. But that sin should be in this form, with pretty girls and pleasant, wheedling women for agents, she had never dreamed; and this in the great, civilized East! Almost better would it have been to remain in the desert alone, and risk the pursuit of that awful man, than to come all this way to find the world gone wrong.

The old lady was horrified, too. She had heard more than the girl of licensed evil; but she had read it in the paper as she had read about the evils of the slave-traffic in Africa, and it had never really seemed true to her. Now she lifted up her hands in horror, and looked at the beautiful girl before her with something akin to awe that she had been in one of those dens of iniquity and escaped. Over and over she made the girl tell what was said, and how it looked, and how she pointed her pistol, and how she got out; and then she exclaimed in wonder, and called her escape a miracle.

They were both weary from excitement when the tale was told. Elizabeth ate her lunch; then the old lady showed her where to put the horse, and made her go to bed. It was only a wee little room with a cot-bed white as snow where she put her; but the roses peeped in at the window, and the box covered with an old white curtain contained a large pitcher of fresh water and a bowl and soap and towels. The old lady brought her a clean white nightgown, coarse and mended in many places, but smelling of rose leaves; and in the morning she tapped at the door quite early before the girl was up, and came in with an armful of clothes.

"I had some boarders last summer," she explained, "and, when they went away, they left these things and said I might put them into the home-mission box. But I was sick when they sent it off this winter; and, if you ain't a home mission, then I never saw one. You put 'em on. I guess they'll fit. They may be a mite large, but she was about your size. I guess your clothes are about wore out; so you jest leave 'em here fer the next one, and use these. There's a couple of extra shirt-waists you can put in a bundle for a change. I guess folks won't dare fool with you if you have some clean, nice clothes on."

Elizabeth looked at her gratefully, and wrote her down in the list of saints with the woman who read the fourteenth chapter of John. The old lady had neglected to mention that from her own meagre wardrobe she had supplied some under-garments, which were not included in those the boarders had left.

Bathed and clothed in clean, sweet garments, with a white shirt-waist and a dark-blue serge skirt and coat, Elizabeth looked a different girl. She surveyed herself in the little glass over the box-washstand and wondered. All at once vanity was born within her, and an ambition to be always thus clothed, with a horrible remembrance of the woman of the day before, who had promised to show her how to earn some pretty clothes. It flashed across her mind that pretty clothes might be a snare. Perhaps they had been to those girls she had seen in that house.

With much good advice and kindly blessings from the old lady, Elizabeth fared forth upon her journey once more, sadly wise in the wisdom of the world, and less sweetly credulous than she had been, but better fitted to fight her way.

The story of her journey from Chicago to Philadelphia would fill a volume if it were written, but it might pall upon the reader from the very variety of its experiences. It was made slowly and painfully, with many haltings and much lessening of the scanty store of money that had seemed so much when she received it in the wilderness. The horse went lame, and had to be watched over and petted, and finally, by the advice of a kindly farmer, taken to a veterinary surgeon, who doctored him for a week before he finally said it was safe to let him hobble on again. After that the girl was more careful of the horse. If he should die, what would she do?

One dismal morning, late in November, Elizabeth, wearing the old overcoat to keep her from freezing, rode into Philadelphia.

Armed with instructions from the old lady in Chicago, she rode boldly up to a policeman, and showed him the address of the grandmother to whom she had decided to go first, her mother's mother. He sent her on in the right direction, and in due time with the help of other policemen she reached the right number on Flora Street.

It was a narrow street, banked on either side by small, narrow brick houses of the older type. Here and there gleamed out a scrap of a white marble door-step, but most of the houses were approached by steps of dull stone or of painted wood. There was a dejected and dreary air about the place. The street was swarming with children in various stages of the soiled condition.

Elizabeth timidly knocked at the door after being assured by the interested urchins who surrounded her that Mrs. Brady really lived there, and had not moved away or anything. It did not seem wonderful to the girl, who had lived her life thus far in a mountain shack, to find her grandmother still in the place from which she had written fifteen years before. She did not yet know what a floating population most cities contain.

Mrs. Brady was washing when the knock sounded through the house. She was a broad woman, with a face on which the cares and sorrows of the years had left a not too heavy impress. She still enjoyed life, oven though a good part of it was spent at the wash-tub, washing other people's fine clothes. She had some fine ones of her own up-stairs in her clothes-press; and, when she went out, it was in shiny satin, with a bonnet bobbing with jet and a red rose, though of late years, strictly speaking, the bonnet had become a hat again, and Mrs. Brady was in style with the other old ladies.

The perspiration was in little beads on her forehead and trickling down the creases in her well-cushioned neck toward her ample bosom. Her gray hair was neatly combed, and her calico wrapper was open at the throat even on this cold day. She wiped on her apron the soap-suds from her plump arms steaming pink from the hot suds, and went to the door.

She looked with disfavor upon the peculiar person on the door-step attired in a man's overcoat. She was prepared to refuse the demands of the Salvation Army for a nickel for Christmas dinners; or to silence the banana-man, or the fish-man, or the man with shoe-strings and pins and pencils for sale; or to send the photograph-agent on his way; yes, even the man who sold albums for post-cards. She had no time to bother with anybody this morning.

But the young person in the rusty overcoat, with the dark-blue serge Eton jacket under it, which might have come from Wanamaker's two years ago, who yet wore a leather belt with gleaming pistols under the Eton jacket, was a new species. Mrs. Brady was taken off her guard; else Elizabeth might have found entrance to her grandmother's home as difficult as she had found entrance to the finishing school of Madame Janeway.

"Are you Mrs. Brady?" asked the girl. She was searching the forbidding face before her for some sign of likeness to her mother, but found none. The cares of Elizabeth Brady's daughter had outweighed those of the mother, or else they sat upon a nature more sensitive.

"I am," said Mrs. Brady, imposingly.

"Grandmother, I am the baby you talked about in that letter," she announced, handing Mrs. Brady the letter she had written nearly eighteen years before.

The woman took the envelope gingerly in the wet thumb and finger that still grasped a bit of the gingham apron. She held it at arm's length, and squinted up her eyes, trying to read it without her glasses. It was some new kind of beggar, of course. She hated to touch these dirty envelopes, and this one looked old and worn. She stepped back to the parlor table where her glasses were lying, and, adjusting them, began to read the letter.

"For the land sakes! Where'd you find this?" she said, looking up suspiciously. "It's against the law to open letters that ain't your own. Didn't me daughter ever get it? I wrote it to her meself. How come you by it?"

"Mother read it to me long ago when I was little," answered the girl, the slow hope fading from her lips as she spoke. Was every one, was even her grandmother, going to be cold and harsh with her? "Our Father, hide me!" her heart murmured, because it had become a habit; and her listening thought caught the answer, "Let not your heart be troubled."

"Well, who are you?" said the uncordial grandmother, still puzzled. "You ain't Bessie, me Bessie. Fer one thing, you're 'bout as young as she was when she went off 'n' got married, against me 'dvice, to that drunken, lazy dude." Her brow was lowering, and she proceeded to finish her letter.

"I am Elizabeth," said the girl with a trembling voice, "the baby you talked about in that letter. But please don't call father that. He wasn't ever bad to us. He was always good to mother, even when he was drunk. If you talk like that about him, I shall have to go away."

"Fer the land sakes! You don't say," said Mrs. Brady, sitting down hard in astonishment on the biscuit upholstery of her best parlor chair. "Now you ain't Bessie's child! Well, I *am clear* beat. And growed up so big! You look strong, but you're kind of thin. What makes your skin so black? Your ma never was dark, ner your pa, neither."

"I've been riding a long way in the wind and sun and rain."

"Fer the land sakes!" as she looked through the window to the street. "Not on a horse?"

"Yes."

"H'm! What was your ma thinkin' about to let you do that?"

"My mother is dead. There was no one left to care what I did. I had to come. There were dreadful people out there, and I was afraid."

"Fer the land sakes!" That seemed the only remark that the capable Mrs. Brady could make. She looked at her new granddaughter in bewilderment, as if a strange sort of creature had suddenly laid claim to relationship.

"Well, I'm right glad to see you," she said stiffly, wiping her hand again on her apron and putting it out formally for a greeting.

Elizabeth accepted her reception gravely, and sat down. She sat down suddenly, as if her strength had given way and a great strain was at an end. As she sat down, she drooped her head back against the wall; and a gray look spread about her lips.

"You're tired," said the grandmother, energetically. "Come far this morning?"

"No," said Elizabeth, weakly, "not many miles; but I hadn't any more bread. I used it all up yesterday, and there wasn't much money left. I thought I could wait till I got here, but I guess I'm hungry."

"Fer the land sakes!" ejaculated Mrs. Brady as she hustled out to the kitchen, and clattered the frying-pan onto the stove, shoving the boiler hastily aside. She came in presently with a steaming cup of tea, and made the girl drink it hot and strong. Then she established her in the big rocking-chair in the kitchen with a plate of appetizing things to eat, and went on with her washing, punctuating every rub with a question.

Elizabeth felt better after her meal, and offered to help, but the grandmother would not hear to her lifting a finger.

"You must rest first," she said. "It beats me how you ever got here. I'd sooner crawl on me hands and knees than ride a great, scary horse."

Elizabeth sprang to her feet.

"The horse!" she said. "Poor fellow! He needs something to eat worse than I did. He hasn't had a bite of grass all this morning. There was nothing but hard roads and pavements. The grass is all brown, anyway, now. I found some cornstalks by the road, and once a man dropped a big bundle of hay out of his load. If it hadn't been for Robin, I'd never have got here; and here I've sat enjoying my breakfast, and Robin out there hungry!"

"Fer the land sakes!" said the grandmother, taking her arms out of the suds and looked troubled. "Poor fellow! What would he like? I haven't got any hay, but there's some mashed potatoes left, and what is there? Why, there's some excelsior the lamp-shade come packed in. You don't suppose he'd think it was hay, do you? No, I guess it wouldn't taste very good."

"Where can I put him, grandmother?"

"Fer the land sakes! I don't know," said the grandmother, looking around the room in alarm. "We haven't any place fer horses. Perhaps you might get him into the back yard fer a while till we think what to do. There's a stable, but they charge high to board horses. Lizzie knows one of the fellers that works there. Mebbe he'll tell us what to do. Anyway, you lead him round to the alleyway, and we'll see if we can't get him in the little ash-gate. You don't suppose he'd try to get in the house, do you? I shouldn't like him to come in the kitchen when I was getting supper."

"O no!" said Elizabeth. "He's very good. Where is the back yard?"

This arrangement was finally made, and the two women stood in the kitchen door, watching Robin drink a bucketful of water and eat heartily of the various viands that Mrs. Brady set forth for him, with the exception of the excelsior, which he snuffed at in disgust.

"Now, ain't he smart?" said Mrs. Brady, watching fearfully from the door-step, where she might retreat if the animal showed any tendency to step nearer to the kitchen. "But don't you think he's cold? Wouldn't he like a —a —shawl or something?"

The girl drew the old coat from her shoulders, and threw it over him, her grandmother watching her fearless handling of the horse with pride and awe.

"We're used to sharing this together," said the girl simply.

"Nan sews in an up-town dressmaker's place," explained Mrs. Brady by and by, when the wash was hung out in fearsome proximity to the weary horse's heels, and the two had returned to the warm kitchen to clean up and get supper. "Nan's your ma's sister, you know, older'n her by two year; and Lizzie, that's her girl, she's about 's old 's you. She's got a good place in the ten-cent store. Nan's husband died four years ago, and her and me've been livin' together ever since. It'll be nice fer you and Lizzie to be together. She'll make it lively fer you right away. Prob'ly she can get you a place at the same store. She'll be here at half past six to-night. This is her week to get out early."

The aunt came in first. She was a tall, thin woman with faded brown hair and a faint resemblance to Elizabeth's mother. Her shoulders stooped slightly, and her voice was nasal. Her mouth looked as if it was used to holding pins in one corner and gossiping out of the other. She was one of the kind who always get into a rocking-chair to sew if they can, and rock as they sew. Nevertheless, she was skilful in her way, and commanded good wages. She welcomed the new niece reluctantly, more excited over her remarkable appearance among her relatives after so long a silence than pleased, Elizabeth felt. But after she had satisfied her curiosity she was kind, beginning to talk about Lizzie, and mentally compared this thin, brown girl with rough hair and dowdy clothes to her own stylish daughter. Then Lizzie burst in. They could hear her calling to a young man who had walked home with her, even before she entered the house.

"It's just fierce out, ma!" she exclaimed. "Grandma, ain't supper ready yet? I never was so hungry in all my life. I could eat a house afire."

She stopped short at sight of Elizabeth. She had been chewing gum-Lizzie was always chewing gum-but her jaws ceased action in sheer astonishment.

"This is your cousin Bessie, come all the way from Montana on horseback, Lizzie. She's your aunt Bessie's child. Her folks is dead now, and she's come to live with us. You must see ef you can't get her a place in the ten-cent store 'long with you," said the grandmother.

Lizzie came airily forward, and grasped her cousin's hand in mid-air, giving it a lateral shake that bewildered Elizabeth.

"Pleased to meet you," she chattered glibly, and set her jaws to work again. One could not embarrass Lizzie long. But she kept her eyes on the stranger, and let them wander disapprovingly over her apparel in a pointed way as she took out the long hat-pins from the cumbersome hat she wore and adjusted her ponderous pompadour.

"Lizzie'll have to help fix you up," said the aunt noting Lizzie's glance. "You're all out of style. I suppose they get behind times out in Montana. Lizzie, can't you show her how to fix her hair pompadour?"

Lizzie brightened. If there was a prospect of changing things, she was not averse to a cousin of her own age; but she never could take such a dowdy-looking girl into society, not the society of the ten-cent store.

"O, cert!" answered Lizzie affably. "I'll fix you fine. Don't you worry. How'd you get so awful tanned? I s'pose riding. You look like you'd been to the seashore, and lay out on the beach in the sun. But 'tain't the right time o' year quite. It must be great to ride horseback!"

"I'll teach you how if you want to learn," said Elizabeth, endeavoring to show a return of the kindly offer.

"Me? What would I ride? Have to ride a counter, I guess. I guess you won't find much to ride here in the city, 'cept trolley-cars."

"Bessie's got a horse. He's out in the yard now," said the grandmother with pride.

"A horse! All your own? Gee whiz! Won't the girls stare when I tell them? Say, we can borrow a rig at the livery some night, and take a ride. Dan'll go with us, and get the rig for us. Won't that be great?"

Elizabeth smiled. She felt the glow of at last contributing something to the family pleasure. She did not wish her coming to be so entirely a wet blanket as it had seemed at first; for, to tell the truth, she had seen blank dismay on the face of each separate relative as her identity had been made known. Her heart was lonely, and she hungered for some one who "belonged" and loved her.

Supper was put on the table, and the two girls began to get a little acquainted, chattering over clothes and the arrangement of hair.

"Do you know whether there is anything in Philadelphia called 'Christian Endeavor'?" asked Elizabeth after the supper-table was cleared off.

"O, Chrishun'deavor! Yes, I used t' b'long," answered Lizzie. She had removed the gum from her mouth while she ate her supper, but now it was busy again between sentences. "Yes, we have one down to our church. It was real interesting, too; but I got mad at one of the members, and quit. She was a stuck-up old maid, anyway. She was always turning round and scowling at us girls if we just whispered the least little bit, or smiled; and one night she was leading the meeting, and Jim Forbes got in a corner behind a post, and made mouths at her behind his book. He looked awful funny. It was something fierce the way she always screwed her face up when she sang, and he looked just like her. We girls, Hetty and Em'line and I, got to laughing, and we just couldn't stop; and didn't that old thing stop the singing after one verse, and look right at us, and say she thought Christian Endeavor members should remember whose house they were in, and that the owner was there, and all that rot. I nearly died, I was so mad. Everybody looked around, and we girls choked, and got up and went out. I haven't been down since. The lookout committee came to see us 'bout it; but I said I wouldn't go back where I'd been insulted, and I've never been inside the doors since. But she's moved away now. I wouldn't mind going back if you want to go."

"Whose house did she mean it was? Was it her house?"

"O, no, it wasn't her house," laughed Lizzie. "It was the church. She meant it was God's house, I s'pose, but she needn't have been so pernickety. We weren't doing any harm."

"Does God have a house?"

"Why, yes; didn't you know that? Why, you talk like a heathen, Bessie. Didn't you have churches in Montana?"

"Yes, there was a church fifty miles away. I heard about it once, but I never saw it," answered Elizabeth. "But what did the woman mean? Who did she say was there? God? Was God in the church? Did you see Him, and know He was there when you laughed?"

"O, you silly!" giggled Lizzie. "Wouldn't the girls laugh at you, though, if they could hear you talk? Why, of course God was there. He's everywhere, you know," with superior knowledge; "but I didn't see Him. You can't see God."

"Why not?"

"Why, because you can't!" answered her cousin with final logic. "Say, haven't you got any other clothes with you at all? I'd take you down with me in the morning if you was fixed up."

CHAPTER XI
IN FLIGHT AGAIN

When Elizabeth lay down to rest that night, with Lizzie still chattering by her side, she found that there was one source of intense pleasure in anticipation, and that was the prospect of going to God's house to Christian Endeavor. Now perhaps she would be able to find out what it all had meant, and whether it were true that God took care of people and hid them in time of trouble. She felt almost certain in her own little experience that He had cared for her, and she wanted to be quite sure, so that she might grasp this precious truth to her heart and keep it forever. No one could be quite alone in the world if there was a God who cared and loved and hid.

The aunt and the grandmother were up betimes the next morning, looking over some meagre stores of old clothing, and there was found an old dress which it was thought could be furbished over for Elizabeth. They were hard-working people with little money to spare, and everything had to be utilized; but they made a great deal of appearance, and Lizzie was proud as a young peacock. She would not take Elizabeth to the store to face the head man without having her fixed up according to the most approved style.

So the aunt cut and fitted before she went off for the day, and Elizabeth was ordered to sew while she was gone. The grandmother presided at the rattling old sewing-machine, and in two or three days Elizabeth was pronounced to be fixed up enough to do for the present till she could earn some new clothes. With her fine hair snarled into a cushion and puffed out into an enormous pompadour that did not suit her face in the least, and with an old hat and jacket of Lizzie's which did not become her nor fit her exactly, she started out to make her way in the world as a saleswoman. Lizzie had already secured her a place if she suited.

The store was a maze of wonder to the girl from the mountains-so many bright, bewildering things, ribbons and tin pans, glassware and toys, cheap jewelry and candies. She looked about with the dazed eyes of a creature from another world.

But the manager looked upon her with eyes of favor. He saw that her eyes were bright and keen. He was used to judging faces. He saw that she was as yet unspoiled, with a face of refinement far beyond the general run of the girls who applied to him for positions. And he was not beyond a friendly flirtation with a pretty new girl himself; so she was engaged at once, and put on duty at the notion-counter.

The girls flocked around her during the intervals of custom. Lizzie had told of her cousin's long ride, embellished, wherever her knowledge failed, by her extremely wild notions of Western life. She had told how Elizabeth arrived wearing a belt with two pistols, and this gave Elizabeth standing at once among all the people in the store. A girl who could shoot, and who wore pistols in a belt like a real cowboy, had a social distinction all her own.

The novel-reading, theatre-going girls rallied around her to a girl; and the young men in the store were not far behind. Elizabeth was popular from the first. Moreover, as she settled down into the routine of life, and had three meals every day, her cheeks began to round out just a little; and it became apparent that she was unusually beautiful in spite of her dark skin, which whitened gradually under the electric light and high-pressure life of the store.

They went to Christian Endeavor, Elizabeth and her cousin; and Elizabeth felt as if heaven had suddenly dropped down about her. She lived from week to week for that Christian Endeavor.

The store, which had been a surprise and a novelty at first, began to be a trial to her. It wore upon her nerves. The air was bad, and the crowds were great. It was coming on toward Christmas time, and the store was crammed to bursting day after day and night after night, for they kept open evenings now until Christmas. Elizabeth longed for a breath from the mountains, and grew whiter and thinner. Sometimes she felt as if she must break away from it all, and take Robin, and ride into the wilderness again. If it were not for the Christian Endeavor, she would have done so, perhaps.

Robin, poor beast, was well housed and well fed; but he worked for his living as did his mistress. He was a grocer's delivery horse, worked from Monday morning early till Saturday night at ten o'clock, subject to curses and kicks from the grocery boy, expected to stand meekly at the curbstones, snuffing the dusty brick pavements while the boy delivered a box of goods, and while trolleys and beer-wagons and automobiles slammed and rumbled and tooted by him, and then to start on the double-quick to the next stopping-place.

He to be thus under the rod who had trod the plains with a free foot and snuffed the mountain air! It was a great come-down, and his life became a weariness to him. But he earned his mistress a dollar a week besides his board. There would have been some consolation in that to his faithful heart if he only could have known it. Albeit she would have gladly gone without the dollar if Robin could have been free and happy.

One day, one dreadful day, the manager of the ten-cent store came to Elizabeth with a look in his eyes that reminded her of the man in Montana from whom she had fled. He was smiling, and his words were unduly pleasant. He wanted her to go with him to the theatre that evening, and he complimented her on her appearance. He stated that he admired her exceedingly, and wanted to give her pleasure. But somehow Elizabeth had fallen into the habit ever since she left the prairies of comparing all men with George Trescott Benedict; and this man, although he dressed well, and was every bit as handsome, did not compare well. There was a sinister, selfish glitter in his eyes that made Elizabeth think of the serpent on the plain just before she shot it. Therefore Elizabeth declined the invitation.

It happened that there was a missionary meeting at the church that evening. All the Christian Endeavorers had been urged to attend. Elizabeth gave this as an excuse; but the manager quickly swept that away, saying she could go to church any night, but she could not go to this particular play with him always. The girl eyed him calmly with much the same attitude with which she might have pointed her pistol at his head, and said gravely,

"But I do not want to go with you."

After that the manager hated her. He always hated girls who resisted him. He hated her, and wanted to do her harm. But he fairly persecuted her to receive his attentions. He was a young fellow, extremely young to be occupying so responsible a position. He undoubtedly had business ability. He showed it in his management of Elizabeth. The girl's life became a torment to her. In proportion as she appeared to be the manager's favorite the other girls became jealous of her. They taunted her with the manager's attentions on every possible occasion. When they found anything wrong, they charged it upon her; and so she was kept constantly going to the manager, which was perhaps just what he wanted.

She grew paler and paler, and more and more desperate. She had run away from one man; she had run away from a woman; but here was a man from whom she could not run away unless she gave up her position. If it had not been for her grandmother, she would have done so at once; but, if she gave up her position, she would be thrown upon her grandmother for support, and that must not be. She understood from the family talk that they were having just as much as they could do already to make both ends meet and keep the all-important god of Fashion satisfied. This god of Fashion had come to seem to Elizabeth an enemy of the living God. It seemed to occupy all people's thoughts, and everything else had to be sacrificed to meet its demands.

She had broached the subject of school one evening soon after she arrived, but was completely squelched by her aunt and cousin.

"You're too old!" sneered Lizzie. "School is for children."

"Lizzie went through grammar school, and we talked about high for her," said the grandmother proudly.

"But I just hated school," grinned Lizzie. "It ain't so nice as it's cracked up to be. Just sit and study all day long. Why, they were always keeping me after school for talking or laughing. I was glad enough when I got through. You may thank your stars you didn't have to go, Bess."

"People who have to earn their bread can't lie around and go to school," remarked Aunt Nan dryly, and Elizabeth said no more.

But later she heard of a night-school, and then she took up the subject once more. Lizzie scoffed at this. She said night-school was only for very poor people, and it was a sort of disgrace to go. But Elizabeth stuck to her point, until one day Lizzie came home with a tale about Temple College. She had heard it was very cheap. You could go for ten cents a night, or something like that. Things that were ten cents appealed to her. She was used to bargain-counters.

She heard it was quite respectable to go there, and they had classes in the evening. You could study gymnastics, and it would make you graceful. She wanted to be graceful. And she heard they had a course in millinery. If it was so, she believed she would go herself, and learn to make the new kind of bows they were having on hats this winter. She could not seem to get the right twist to the ribbon.

Elizabeth wanted to study geography. At least, that was the study Lizzie said would tell her where the Desert of Sahara was. She wanted to know things, all kinds of things; but Lizzie said such things were only for children, and she didn't believe they taught such baby studies in a college. But she would inquire. It was silly of Bessie to want to know, she thought, and she was half ashamed to ask. But she would find out.

It was about this time that Elizabeth's life at the store grew intolerable.

One morning-it was little more than a week before Christmas-Elizabeth had been sent to the cellar to get seven little red tin pails and shovels for a woman who wanted them for Christmas gifts for some Sunday-school class. She had just counted out the requisite number and turned to go up-stairs when she heard some one step near her, and, as she looked up in the dim light, there stood the manager.

"At last I've got you alone, Bessie, my dear!" He said it with suave triumph in his tones. He caught Elizabeth by the wrists, and before she could wrench herself away he had kissed her.

With a scream Elizabeth dropped the seven tin pails and the seven tin shovels, and with one mighty wrench took her hands from his grasp. Instinctively her hand went to her belt, where were now no pistols. If one had been there she certainly would have shot him in her horror and fury. But, as she had no other weapon, she seized a little shovel, and struck him in the face. Then with the frenzy of the desert back upon her she rushed up the stairs, out through the crowded store, and into the street, hatless and coatless in the cold December air. The passers-by made way for her, thinking she had been sent out on some hurried errand.

She had left her pocketbook, with its pitifully few nickels for car-fare and lunch, in the cloak-room with her coat and hat. But she did not stop to think of that. She was fleeing again, this time on foot, from a man. She half expected he might pursue her, and make her come back to the hated work in the stifling store with his wicked face moving everywhere above the crowds. But she turned not to look back. On over the slushy pavements, under the leaden sky, with a few busy flakes floating about her.

The day seemed pitiless as the world. Where could she go and what should she do? There seemed no refuge for her in the wide world. Instinctively she felt her grandmother would feel that a calamity had befallen them in losing the patronage of the manager of the ten-cent store. Perhaps Lizzie would get into trouble. What should she do?

She had reached the corner where she and Lizzie usually took the car for home. The car was coming now; but she had no hat nor coat, and no money to pay for a ride. She must walk. She paused not, but fled on in a steady run, for which her years on the mountain had given her breath. Three miles it was to Flora Street, and she scarcely slackened her pace after she had settled into that steady half-run, half-walk. Only at the corner of Flora Street she paused, and allowed herself to glance back once. No, the manager had not pursued her. She was safe. She might go in and tell her grandmother without fearing he would come behind her as soon as her back was turned.

CHAPTER XII
ELIZABETH'S DECLARATION OF INDEPENDENCE

Mrs. Brady was at the wash-tub again when her most uncommon and unexpected grandchild burst into the room.

She wiped her hands on her apron, and sat down with her usual exclamation, "Fer the land sakes! What's happened? Bessie, tell me quick. Is anything the matter with Lizzie? Where is she?"

But Elizabeth was on the floor at her feet in tears. She was shaking with sobs, and could scarcely manage to stammer out that Lizzie was all right. Mrs. Brady settled back with a relieved sigh. Lizzie was the first grandchild, and therefore the idol of her heart. If Lizzie was all right, she could afford to be patient and find out by degrees.

"It's that awful man, grandmother!" Elizabeth sobbed out.

"What man? That feller in Montana you run away from?" The grandmother sat up with snapping eyes. She was not afraid of a man, even if he did shoot people. She would call in the police and protect her own flesh and blood. Let him come. Mrs. Brady was ready for him.

"No, no, grandmother, the man-man-manager at the ten-cent store," sobbed the girl; "he kissed me! Oh!" and she shuddered as if the memory was the most terrible thing that ever came to her.

"Fer the land sakes! Is that all?" said the woman with much relief and a degree of satisfaction. "Why, that's nothing. You ought to be proud. Many a girl would go boasting round about that. What are you crying for? He didn't hurt you, did he? Why, Lizzie seems to think he's fine. I tell you Lizzie wouldn't cry if he was to kiss her, I'm sure. She'd just laugh, and ask him fer a holiday. Here, sit up, child, and wash your face, and go back to your work. You've evidently struck the manager on the right side, and you're bound to get a rise in your wages. Every girl he takes a notion to gets up and does well. Perhaps you'll get money enough to go to school. Goodness knows what you want to go for. I s'pose it's in the blood, though Bess used to say your pa wa'n't any great at study. But, if you've struck the manager the right way, no telling what he might do. He might even want to marry you."

"Grandmother!"

Mrs. Brady was favored with the flashing of the Bailey eyes. She viewed it in astonishment not unmixed with admiration.

"Well, you certainly have got spirit," she ejaculated. "I don't wonder he liked you. I didn't know you was so pretty, Bessie; you look like your mother when she was eighteen; you really do. I never saw the resemblance before. I believe you'll get on all right. Don't you be afraid. I wish you had your chance if you're so anxious to go to school. I shouldn't wonder ef you'd turn out to be something and marry rich. Well, I must be getting back to me tub. Land sakes, but you did give me a turn. I thought Lizzie had been run over. I couldn't think what else'd make you run off way here without your coat. Come, get up, child, and go back to your work. It's too bad you don't like to be kissed, but don't let that worry you. You'll have lots worse than that to come up against. When you've lived as long as I have and worked as hard, you'll be pleased to have some one admire you. You better wash your face, and eat a bite of lunch, and hustle back. You needn't be afraid. If he's fond of you, he won't bother about your running away a little. He'll excuse you ef 'tis busy times, and not dock your pay neither."

"Grandmother!" said Elizabeth. "Don't! I can never go back to that awful place and that man. I would rather go back to Montana. I would rather be dead."

"Hoity-toity!" said the easy-going grandmother, sitting down to her task, for she perceived some wholesome discipline was necessary. "You can't talk that way, Bess. You got to go to your work. We ain't got money to keep you in idleness, and land knows where you'd get another place as good's this one. Ef you stay home all day, you might make him awful mad; and then it would be no use goin' back, and you might lose Lizzie her place too."

But, though the grandmother talked and argued and soothed by turns, Elizabeth was firm. She would not go back. She would never go back. She would go to Montana if her grandmother said any more about it.

With a sigh at last Mrs. Brady gave up. She had given up once before nearly twenty years ago. Bessie, her oldest daughter, had a will like that, and tastes far above her station. Mrs. Brady wondered where she got them.

"You're fer all the world like yer ma," she said as she thumped the clothes in the wash-tub. "She was jest that way, when she would marry your pa. She could 'a' had Jim Stokes, the groceryman, or Lodge, the milkman, or her choice of three railroad men, all of 'em doing well, and ready to let her walk over 'em; but she would have your pa, the drunken, good-for-nothing, slippery dude. The only thing I'm surprised at was that he ever married her. I never expected it. I s'posed they'd run off, and he'd leave her when he got tired of her; but it seems he stuck to her. It's the only good thing he ever done, and I'm not sure but she'd 'a' been better off ef he hadn't 'a' done that."

"Grandmother!" Elizabeth's face blazed.

"Yes, *gran'*mother!" snapped Mrs. Brady. "It's all true, and you might's well face it. He met her in church. She used to go reg'lar. Some boys used to come and set in the back seat behind the girls, and then go home with them. They was all nice enough boys 'cept him. I never had a bit a use fer him. He belonged to the swells and the stuck-ups; and he knowed it, and presumed upon it. He jest thought he could wind Bessie round his finger, and he did. If he said, 'Go,' she went, no matter what I'd do. So, when his ma found it out, she was hoppin' mad. She jest came driving round here to me house, and presumed to talk to me. She said Bessie was a designing snip, and a bad girl, and a whole lot of things. Said she was leading her son astray, and would come to no good end, and a whole lot of stuff; and told me to look after her. It wasn't so. Bess got John Bailey to quit smoking fer a whole week at a time, and he said if she'd marry him he'd quit drinking too. His ma couldn't 'a' got him to promise that. She wouldn't even believe he got drunk. I told her a few things about her precious son, but she curled her fine, aristocratic lip up, and said, 'Gentlemen never get drunk.' Humph! Gentlemen! That's all she knowed about it. He got drunk all right, and stayed drunk, too. So after that, when I tried to keep Bess at home, she slipped away one night; said she was going to church; and she did too; went to the minister's study in a strange church, and got married, her and John; and then they up and off West. John, he'd sold his watch and his fine diamond stud his ma had give him; and he borrowed some money from some friends of his father's, and he off with three hundred dollars and Bess; and that's all I ever saw more of me Bessie."

The poor woman sat down in her chair, and wept into her apron regardless for once of the soap-suds that rolled down her red, wet arms.

"Is my grandmother living yet?" asked Elizabeth. She was sorry for this grandmother, but did not know what to say. She was afraid to comfort her lest she take it for yielding.

"Yes, they say she is," said Mrs. Brady, sitting up with a show of interest. She was always ready for a bit of gossip. "Her husband's dead, and her other son's dead, and she's all alone. She lives in a big house on Rittenhouse Square. If she was any 'count, she'd ought to provide fer you. I never thought about it. But I don't suppose it would be any use to try. You might ask her. Perhaps she'd help you go to school. You've got a claim on her. She ought to give you her son's share of his father's property, though I've heard she disowned him when he married our Bess. You might fix up in some of Lizzie's best things, and go up there and try. She might give you some money."

"I don't want her money," said Elizabeth stiffly. "I guess there's work somewhere in the world I can do without begging even of grandmothers. But I think I ought to go and see her. She might want to know about father."

Mrs. Brady looked at her granddaughter wonderingly. This was a view of things she had never taken.

"Well," said she resignedly, "go your own gait. I don't know where you'll come up at. All I say is, ef you're going through the world with such high and mighty fine notions, you'll have a hard time. You can't pick out roses and cream and a bed of down every day. You have to put up with life as you find it."

Elizabeth went to her room, the room she shared with Lizzie. She wanted to get away from her grandmother's disapproval. It lay on her heart like lead. Was there no refuge in the world? If grandmothers were not refuges, where should one flee? The old lady in Chicago had understood; why had not Grandmother Brady?

Then came the sweet old words, "Let not your heart be troubled." "In the time of trouble he shall hide me in his pavilion; in the secret of his tabernacle shall he hide me." She knelt down by the bed and said "Our Father." She was beginning to add some words of her own now. She had heard them pray so in Christian Endeavor in the sentence prayers. She wished she knew more about God, and His Book. She had had so little time to ask or think about it. Life seemed all one rush for clothes and position.

At supper-time Lizzie came home much excited. She had been in hot water all the afternoon. The girls had said at lunch-time that the manager was angry with Bessie, and had discharged her. She found her coat and hat, and had brought them home. The pocketbook was missing. There was only fifteen cents in it; but Lizzie was much disturbed, and so was the grandmother. They had a quiet consultation in the kitchen; and, when the aunt came, there was another whispered conversation among the three.

Elizabeth felt disapproval in the air. Aunt Nan came, and sat down beside her, and talked very coldly about expenses and being dependent upon one's relatives, and let her understand thoroughly that she could not sit around and do nothing; but Elizabeth answered by telling her how the manager had been treating her. The aunt then gave her a dose of worldly wisdom, which made the girl shrink into herself. It needed only Lizzie's loud-voiced exhortations to add to her misery and make her feel ready to do anything. Supper was a most unpleasant meal. At last the grandmother spoke up.

"Well, Bessie," she said firmly, "we've decided, all of us, that, if you are going to be stubborn about this, something will have to be done; and I think the best thing is for you to go to Mrs. Bailey and see what she'll do for you. It's her business, anyway."

Elizabeth's cheeks were very red. She said nothing. She let them go on with the arrangements. Lizzie went and got her best hat, and tried it on Elizabeth to see how she would look, and produced a silk waist from her store of garments, and a spring jacket. It wasn't very warm, it is true; but Lizzie explained that the occasion demanded strenuous measures, and the jacket was undoubtedly stylish, which was the main thing to be considered. One could afford to be cold if one was stylish.

Lizzie was up early the next morning. She had agreed to put Elizabeth in battle-array for her visit to Rittenhouse Square. Elizabeth submitted meekly to her borrowed adornings. Her hair was brushed over her face, and curled on a hot iron, and brushed backward in a perfect mat, and then puffed out in a bigger pompadour than usual. The silk waist was put on with Lizzie's best skirt, and she was adjured not to let that drag. Then the best hat with the cheap pink plumes was set atop the elaborate coiffure; the jacket was put on; and a pair of Lizzie's long silk gloves were struggled into. They were a trite large when on, but to the hands unaccustomed to gloves they were like being run into a mould.

Elizabeth stood it all until she was pronounced complete. Then she came and stood in front of the cheap little glass, and surveyed herself. There were blisters in the glass that twisted her head into a grotesque shape. The hairpins stuck into her head. Lizzie had tied a spotted veil tight over her nose and eyes. The collar of the silk waist was frayed, and cut her neck. The skirt-band was too tight, and the gloves were torture. Elizabeth turned slowly, and went down-stairs, past the admiring aunt and grandmother, who exclaimed at the girl's beauty, now that she was attired to their mind, and encouraged her by saying they were sure her grandmother would want to do something for so pretty a girl.

Lizzie called out to her not to worry, as she flew for her car. She said she had heard there was a variety show in town where they wanted a girl who could shoot. If she didn't succeed with her grandmother, they would try and get her in at the show. The girls at the store knew a man who had charge of it. They said he liked pretty girls, and they thought would be glad to get her. Indeed, Mary James had promised to speak to him last night, and would let her know to-day about it. It would likely be a job more suited to her cousin's liking.

Elizabeth shuddered. Another man! Would he be like all the rest? —all the rest save one!

She walked a few steps in the direction she had been told to go, and then turned resolutely around, and came back. The watching grandmother felt her heart sink. What was this headstrong girl going to do next? Rebel again?

"What's the matter, Bessie?" she asked, meeting her anxiously at the door. "It's bad luck to turn back when you've started."

"I can't go this way," said the girl excitedly. "It's all a cheat. I'm not like this. It isn't mine, and I'm not going in it. I must have my own clothes and be myself when I go to see her. If she doesn't like me and want me, then I can take Robin and go back." And like another David burdened with Saul's armor she came back to get her little sling and stones.

She tore off the veil, and the sticky gloves from her cold hands, and all the finery of silk waist and belt, and donned her old plain blue coat and skirt in which she had arrived in Philadelphia. They had been frugally brushed and sponged, and made neat for a working dress. Elizabeth felt that they belonged to her. Under the jacket, which fortunately was long enough to hide her waist, she buckled her belt with the two pistols. Then she took the battered old felt hat from the closet, and tried to fasten it on; but the pompadour interfered. Relentlessly she pulled down the work of art that Lizzie had created, and brushed and combed her long, thick hair into subjection again, and put it in its long braid down her back. Her grandmother should see her just as she was. She should know what kind of a girl belonged to her. Then, if she chose to be a real grandmother, well and good.

Mrs. Brady was much disturbed in mind when Elizabeth came down-stairs. She exclaimed in horror, and tried to force the girl to go back, telling her it was a shame and disgrace to go in such garments into the sacred precincts of Rittenhouse Square; but the girl was not to be turned back. She would not even wait till her aunt and Lizzie came home. She would go now, at once.

Mrs. Brady sat down in her rocking-chair in despair for full five minutes after she had watched the reprehensible girl go down the street. She had not been so completely beaten since the day when her own Bessie left the house and went away to a wild West to die in her own time and way. The grandmother shed a few tears. This girl was like her own Bessie, and she could not help loving her, though there was a streak of something else about her that made her seem above them all; and that was hard to bear. It must be the Bailey streak, of course. Mrs. Brady did not admire the Baileys, but she was obliged to reverence them.

If she had watched or followed Elizabeth, she would have been still more horrified. The girl went straight to the corner grocery, and demanded her own horse, handing back to the man the dollar he had paid her last Saturday night, and saying she had need of the horse at once. After some parley, in which she showed her ability to stand her own ground, the boy unhitched the horse from the wagon, and got her own old saddle for her from the stable. Then Elizabeth mounted her horse and rode away to Rittenhouse Square.

CHAPTER XIII
ANOTHER GRANDMOTHER

Elizabeth's idea in taking the horse along with her was to have all her armor on, as a warrior goes out to meet the foe. If this grandmother proved impossible, why, then so long as she had life and breath and a horse she could flee. The world was wide, and the West was still open to her. She could flee back to the wilderness that gave her breath.

The old horse stopped gravely and disappointedly before the tall, aristocratic house in Rittenhouse Square. He had hoped that city life was now to end, and that he and his dear mistress were to travel back to their beloved prairies. No amount of oats could ever make up to him for his freedom, and the quiet, and the hills. He had a feeling that he should like to go back home and die. He had seen enough of the world.

She fastened the halter to a ring in the sidewalk, which surprised him. The grocer's boy never fastened him. He looked up questioningly at the house, but saw no reason why his mistress should go in there. It was not familiar ground. Koffee and Sons never came up this way.

Elizabeth, as she crossed the sidewalk and mounted the steps before the formidable carved doors, felt that here was the last hope of finding an earthly habitation. If this failed her, then there was the desert, and starvation, and a long, long sleep. But while the echo of the cell still sounded through the high-ceiled hall there came to her the words: "Let not your heart be troubled....In my Father's house are many mansions; if it were not so, I would have told you. I go to prepare a place for you....I will come again and receive you." How sweet that was! Then, even if she died on the desert, there was a home prepared for her. So much she had learned in Christian Endeavor meeting.

The stately butler let her in. He eyed her questioningly at first, and said madam was not up yet; but Elizabeth told him she would wait.

"Is she sick?" asked Elizabeth with a strange constriction about her heart.

"O no, she is not up yet, miss," said the kind old butler; "she never gets up before this. You're from Mrs. Sands, I suppose." Poor soul, for once his butler eyes had been mistaken. He thought she was the little errand-girl from Madam Bailey's modiste.

"No, I'm just Elizabeth," said the girl, smiling. She felt that this man, whoever he was, was not against her. He was old, and he had a kind look.

He still thought she meant she was not the modiste, just her errand-girl. Her quaint dress and the long braid down her back made her look like a child.

"I'll tell her you've come. Be seated," said the butler, and gave her a chair in the dim hall just opposite the parlor door, where she had a glimpse of elegance such as she had never dreamed existed. She tried to think how it must be to live in such a room and walk on velvet. The carpet was deep and rich. She did not know it was a rug nor that it was woven in some poor peasant's home and then was brought here years afterward at a fabulous price. She only knew it was beautiful in its silvery sheen with gleaming colors through it like jewels in the dew.

On through another open doorway she caught a glimpse of a painting on the wall. It was a man as large as life, sitting in a chair; and the face and attitude were her father's—her father at his best. She was fairly startled. Who was it? Could it be her father? And how had they made this picture of him? He must be changed in those twenty years he had been gone from home.

Then the butler came back, and before he could speak she pointed toward the picture. "Who is it?" she asked.

"That, miss? That's Mr. John, Madam's husband that's dead a good many years now. But I remember him well."

"Could I look at it? He is so much like my father." She walked rapidly over the ancient rug, unheeding its beauties, while the wondering butler followed a trifle anxiously. This was unprecedented. Mrs. Sands's errand-girls usually knew their place.

"Madam said you was to come right up to her room," said the butler pointedly. But Elizabeth stood rooted to the ground, studying the picture. The butler had to repeat the message. She smiled and turned to follow him, and as she did so saw on a side wall the portraits of two boys.

"Who are they?" she pointed swiftly. They were much like her own two brothers.

"Them are Mr. John and Mr. James, Madam's two sons. They's both of them dead now," said the butler. "At least, Mr. James is, I'm sure. He died two years ago. But you better come right up. Madam will be wondering."

She followed the old man up the velvet-shod stairs that gave back no sound from footfall, and pondered as she went. Then that was her father, that boy with the beautiful face and the heavy wavy hair tossed back from his forehead, and the haughty, imperious, don't-care look. And here was where he had lived. Here amid all this luxury.

Like a flash came the quick contrast of the home in which he had died, and a great wave of reverence for her father rolled over her. From such a home and such surroundings it would not have been strange if he had grown weary of the rough life out West, and deserted his wife, who was beneath him in station. But he had not. He had stayed by her all the years. True, he had not been of much use to her, and much of the time had been but a burden and anxiety; but he had stayed and loved her-when he was sober. She forgave him his many trying ways, his faultfindings with her mother's many little blunders-no wonder, when he came from this place.

The butler tapped on a door at the head of the stairs, and a maid swung it open.

"Why, you're not the girl Mrs. Sands sent the other day," said a querulous voice from a mass of lace-ruffled pillows on the great bed.

"I am Elizabeth," said the girl, as if that were full explanation.

"Elizabeth? Elizabeth who? I don't see why she sent another girl. Are you sure you will understand the directions? They're very particular, for I want my frock ready for to-night without fail." The woman sat up, leaning on one elbow. Her lace nightgown and pale-blue silk dressing-sack fell away from a round white arm that did not look as if it belonged to a very old lady. Her gray hair was becomingly arranged, and she was extremely pretty, with small features. Elizabeth looked and marvelled. Like a flash came the vision of the other grandmother at the wash-tub. The contrast was startling.

"I am Elizabeth Bailey," said the girl quietly, as if she would break a piece of hard news gently. "My father was your son John."

"The idea!" said the new grandmother, and promptly fell back upon her pillows with her hand upon her heart. "John, John, my little John. No one has mentioned his name to me for years and years. He never writes to me." She put up a lace-trimmed handkerchief, and sobbed.

"Father died five years ago," said Elizabeth.

"You wicked girl!" said the maid. "Can't you see that Madam can't bear such talk? Go right out of the room!" The maid rushed up with smelling-salts and a glass of water, and Elizabeth in distress came and stood by the bed.

"I'm sorry I made you feel bad, grandmother," she said when she saw that the fragile, childish creature on the bed was recovering somewhat.

"What right have you to call me that? Grandmother, indeed! I'm not so old as that. Besides, how do I know you belong to me? If John is dead, your mother better look after you. I'm sure I'm not responsible for you. It's her business. She wheedled John away from his home, and carried him off to that awful West, and never let him write to me. She has done it all, and now she may bear the consequences. I suppose she has sent you here to beg, but she has made a mistake. I shall not have a thing to do with her of her children."

"Grandmother!" Elizabeth's eyes flashed as they had done to the other grandmother a few hours before. "You must not talk so. I won't hear it. I wouldn't let Grandmother Brady talk about my father, and you can't talk so about mother. She was my mother, and I loved her, and so did father love her; and she worked hard to keep him and take care of him when he drank years and years, and didn't have any money to help her. Mother was only eighteen when she married father, and you ought not to blame her. She didn't have a nice home like this. But she was good and dear, and now she is dead. Father and mother are both dead, and all the other children. A man killed my brother, and then as soon as he was buried he came and wanted me to go with him. He was an awful man, and I was afraid, and took my brother's horse and ran away. I rode all this long way because I was afraid of that man, and I wanted to get to some of my own folks, who would love me, and let me work for them, and let me go to school and learn something. But I wish now I had stayed out there and died. I could have lain down in the sage-brush, and a wild beast would have killed me perhaps, and that would be a great deal better than this; for Grandmother Brady does not understand, and you do not want me; but in my Father's house in heaven there are many mansions, and He went to prepare a place for me; so I guess I will go back to the desert, and perhaps He will send for me. Good-by, grandmother."

Then before the astonished woman in the bed could recover her senses from this remarkable speech Elizabeth turned and walked majestically from the room. She was slight and not very tall, but in the strength of her pride and purity she looked almost majestic to the awestruck maid and the bewildered woman.

* * * * *

Down the stairs walked the girl, feeling that all the wide world was against her. She would never again try to get a friend. She had not met a friend except in the desert. One man had been good to her, and she had let him go away; but he belonged to another woman, and she might not let him stay. There was just one thing to be thankful for. She had knowledge of her Father in heaven, and she knew what Christian Endeavor meant. She could take that with her out into the desert, and no one could take it from her. One wish she had, but maybe that was too much to hope for. If she could have had a Bible of her own! She had no money left. Nothing but her mother's wedding-ring, the papers, and the envelope that had contained the money the man had given her when he left. She could not part with them, unless perhaps some one would take the ring and keep it until she could buy it back. But she would wait and hope.

She walked by the old butler with her hand on her pistol. She did not intend to let any one detain her now. He bowed pleasantly, and opened the door for her, however; and she marched down the steps to her horse. But just as she was about to mount and ride away into the unknown where no grandmother, be she Brady or Bailey, would ever be able to search her out, no matter how hard she tried, the door suddenly opened again, and there was a great commotion. The maid and the old butler both flew out, and laid hands upon her. She dropped the bridle, and seized her pistol, covering them both with its black, forbidding nozzle.

They stopped, trembling, but the butler bravely stood his ground. He did not know why he was to detain this extraordinary young person, but he felt sure something wrong. Probably she was a thief, and had taken some of Madam's jewels. He could call the police. He opened his mouth to do so when the maid explained.

"Madam wants you to come back. She didn't understand. She wants to see you and ask about her son. You must come, or you will kill her. She has heart trouble, and you must not excite her."

Elizabeth put the pistol back into its holster and, picking up the bridle again, fastened it in the ring, saying simply, "I will come back."

"What do you want?" she asked abruptly when she returned to the bedroom.

"Don't you know that's a disrespectful way to speak?" asked the woman querulously. "What did you have to get into a temper for, and go off like that without telling me anything about my son? Sit down, and tell me all about it."

"I'm sorry, grandmother," said Elizabeth, sitting down. "I thought you didn't want me and I better go."

"Well, the next time wait until I send you. What kind of a thing have you got on, anyway? That's a queer sort of a hat for a girl to wear. Take it off. You look like a rough boy with that on. You make me think of John when he had been out disobeying me."

Elizabeth took off the offending headgear, and revealed her smoothly parted, thick brown hair in its long braid down her back.

"Why, you're rather a pretty girl if you were fixed up," said the old lady, sitting up with interest now. "I can't remember your mother, but I don't think she had fine features like that."

"They said I looked like father," said Elizabeth.

"Did they? Well, I believe it's true," with satisfaction. "I couldn't bear you if you looked like those lowdown — —"

"Grandmother!" Elizabeth stood up, and flashed her Bailey eyes.

"You needn't 'grandmother' me all the time," said the lady petulantly. "But you look quite handsome when you say it. Take off that ill-fitting coat. It isn't thick enough for winter, anyway. What in the world have you got round your waist? A belt? Why, that's a man's belt! And what have you got in it? Pistols? Horrors! Marie, take them away quick! I shall faint! I never could bear to be in a room with one. My husband used to have one on his closet shelf, and I never went near it, and always locked the room when he was out. You must put them out in the hall. I cannot breathe where pistols are. Now sit down and tell me all about it, how old you are, and how you got here."

Elizabeth surrendered her pistols with hesitation. She felt that she must obey her grandmother, but was not altogether certain whether it was safe for her to be weaponless until she was sure this was friendly ground.

At the demand she began back as far as she could remember, and told the story of her life, pathetically, simply, without a single claim to pity, yet so earnestly and vividly that the grandmother, lying with her eyes closed, forgot herself completely, and let the tears trickle unbidden and unheeded down her well-preserved cheeks.

When Elizabeth came to the graves in the moonlight, she gasped, and sobbed: "O, Johnny, Johnny, my little Johnny! Why did you always be such a bad, bad boy?" and when the ride in the desert was described, and the man from whom she fled, the grandmother held her breath, and said, "O, how fearful!" Her interest in the girl was growing, and kept at white heat during the whole of the story.

There was one part of her experience, however, that Elizabeth passed over lightly, and that was the meeting with George Trescott Benedict. Instinctively she felt that this experience would not find a sympathetic listener. She passed it over by merely saying that she had met a kind gentleman from the East who was lost, and that they had ridden together for a few miles until they reached a town; and he had telegraphed to his friends, and gone on his way. She said nothing about the money he had lent to her, for she shrank from speaking about him more than was necessary. She felt that her grandmother might feel as the old woman of the ranch had felt about their travelling together. She left it to be inferred that she might have had a little money with her from home. At least, the older woman asked no questions about how she secured provisions for the way.

When Elizabeth came to her Chicago experience, her grandmother clasped her hands as if a serpent had been mentioned, and said: "How degrading! You certainly would have been justified in shooting the whole company. I wonder such places are allowed to exist!" But Marie sat with large eyes of wonder, and retailed the story over again in the kitchen afterwards for the benefit of the cook and the butler, so that Elizabeth became henceforth a heroine among them.

Elizabeth passed on to her Philadelphia experience, and found that here her grandmother was roused to blazing indignation, but the thing that roused her was the fact that a Bailey should serve behind a counter in a ten-cent Store. She lifted her hands, and uttered a moan of real pain, and went on at such a rate that the smelling-salts had to be brought into requisition again.

When Elizabeth told of her encounter with the manager in the cellar, the grandmother said: "How disgusting! The impertinent creature! He ought to be sued. I will consult the lawyer about the matter. What did you say his name was? Marie, write that down. And so, dear, you did quite right to come to me. I've been looking at you while you talked, and I believe you'll be a pretty girl if you are fixed up. Marie, go to the telephone, and call up Blandeaux, and tell him to send up a hair-dresser at once. I want to see how Miss Elizabeth will look with her hair done low in one of those new coils. I believe it will be becoming. I should have tried it long ago myself; only it seems a trifle too youthful for hair that is beginning to turn gray."

Elizabeth watched her grandmother in wonder. Here truly was a new phase of woman. She did not care about great facts, but only about little things. Her life was made up of the great pursuit of fashion, just like Lizzie's. Were people in cities all alike? No, for he, the one man she had met in the wilderness, had not seemed to care. Maybe, though, when he got back to the city he did care. She sighed and turned toward the new grandmother.

"Now I have told you everything, grandmother. Shall I go away? I wanted to go to school; but I see that it costs a great deal of money, and I don't want to be a burden on any one. I came here, not to ask you to take me in, because I did not want to trouble you; but I thought before I went away I ought to see you once because-because you are my grandmother."

"I've never been a grandmother," said the little woman of the world reflectively, "but I don't know but it would be rather nice. I'd like to make you into a pretty girl, and take you out into society. That would be something new to live for. I'm not very pretty myself any more, but I can see that you will be. Do you wear blue or pink? I used to wear pink myself, but I believe you could wear either when you get your complexion in shape. You've tanned it horribly, but it may come out all right. I think you'll take. You say you want to go to school. Why, certainly, I suppose that will be necessary; living out in that barbarous, uncivilized region, of course you don't know much. You seem to speak correctly, but John always was particular about his speech. He had a tutor when he was little who tripped him up every mistake he made. That was the only thing that tutor was good for; he was a linguist. We found out afterwards he was terribly wild, and drank. He did John more harm than good, Marie, I shall want Elizabeth to have the rooms next mine. Ring for Martha to see that everything is in order. Elizabeth, did you ever have your hands manicured? You have a pretty-shaped hand. I'll have the woman attend to it when she comes to shampoo your hair and put it up. Did you bring any clothes along? Of course not. You couldn't on horseback. I suppose you had your trunk sent by express. No trunk? No express? No railroad? How barbarous! How John must have suffered, poor fellow! He, so used to every luxury! Well, I don't see that it was my fault. I gave him everything he wanted except his wife, and he took her without my leave. Poor fellow, poor fellow!"

Mrs. Bailey in due time sent Elizabeth off to the suite of rooms that she said were to be hers exclusively, and arose to bedeck herself for another day. Elizabeth was a new toy, and she anticipated playing with her. It put new zest into a life that had grown monotonous.

Elizabeth, meanwhile, was surveying her quarters, and wondering what Lizzie would think if she could see her. According to orders, the coachman had taken Robin to the stable, and he was already rolling in all the luxuries of a horse of the aristocracy, and congratulating himself on the good taste of his mistress to select such a stopping-place. For his part he was now satisfied not to move further. This was better than the wilderness any day. Oats like these, and hay such as this, were not to be found on the plains.

Toward evening the grave butler, with many a deprecatory glance at the neighborhood, arrived at the door of Mrs. Brady, and delivered himself of the following message to that astonished lady, backed by her daughter and her granddaughter, with their ears stretched to the utmost to hear every syllable:

"Mrs. Merrill Wilton Bailey sends word that her granddaughter, Miss Elizabeth, has reached her home safely, and will remain with her. Miss Elizabeth will come sometime to see Mrs. Brady, and thank her for her kindness during her stay with her."

The butler bowed, and turned away with relief. His dignity and social standing had not been so taxed by the family demands in years. He was glad he might shake off the dust of Flora Street forever. He felt for the coachman. He would probably have to drive the young lady down here sometime, according to that message.

Mrs. Brady, her daughter, and Lizzie stuck their heads out into the lamplighted street, and watched the dignified butler out of sight. Then they went in and sat down in three separate stages of relief and astonishment.

"Fer the land sakes!" ejaculated the grandmother. "Wall, now, if that don't beat all!" then after a minute: "The impertinent fellow! And the impidence of the woman! Thank me fer my kindness to me own grandchild! I'd thank her to mind her business, but then that's just like her."

"Her nest is certainly well feathered," said Aunt Nan enviously. "I only wish Lizzie had such a chance."

Said Lizzie: "It's awful queer, her looking like that, too, in that crazy rig! Well, I'm glad she's gone, fer she was so awful queer it was jest fierce. She talked religion a lot to the girls, and then they laughed at her behind her back; and they kep' a telling me I'd be a missionary 'fore long if she stayed with us. I went to Mr. Wray, the manager, and told him my cousin was awfully shy, and she sent word she wanted to be excused fer running away like that. He kind of colored up, and said 'twas all right, and she might come back and have her old place if she wanted, and he'd say no more about it. I told him I'd tell her. But I guess her acting up won't do me a bit of harm. The girls say he'll make up to me now. Wish he would. I'd have a fine time. It's me turn to have me wages raised, anyway. He said if Bess and I would come to-morrow ready to stay in the evening, he'd take us to a show that beat everything he ever saw in Philadelphia. I mean to make him take me, anyway. I'm just glad she's out of the way. She wasn't like the rest of us."

Said Mrs. Brady: "It's the Bailey in her. But she said she'd come back and see me, didn't she?" and the grandmother in her meditated over that fact for several minutes.

CHAPTER XIV
IN A NEW WORLD

Meantime the panorama of Elizabeth's life passed on into more peaceful scenes. By means of the telephone and the maid a lot of new and beautiful garments were provided for her, which fitted perfectly, and which bewildered her not a little until they were explained by Marie. Elizabeth had her meals up-stairs until these things had arrived and she had put them on. The texture of the garments was fine and soft, and they were rich with embroidery and lace. The flannels were as soft as the down in a milkweed pod, and everything was of the best. Elizabeth found herself wishing she might share them with Lizzie, —Lizzie who adored rich and beautiful things, and who had shared her meagre outfit with her. She mentioned this wistfully to her grandmother, and in a fit of childish generosity that lady said: "Certainly, get her what you wish. I'll take you downtown some day, and you can pick out some nice things for them all. I hate to be under obligations."

A dozen ready-made dresses had been sent out before the first afternoon was over, and Elizabeth spent the rest of the day in trying on and walking back and forth in front of her grandmother. At last two or three were selected which it was thought would "do" until the dressmaker could be called in to help, and Elizabeth was clothed and allowed to come down into the life of the household.

It was not a large household. It consisted of the grandmother, her dog, and the servants. Elizabeth fitted into it better than she had feared. It seemed pleasanter to her than the house on Flora Street. There was more room, and more air, and more quiet. With her mountain breeding she could not get her breath in a crowd.

She was presently taken in a luxurious carriage, drawn by two beautiful horses, to a large department store, where she sat by the hour and watched her grandmother choose things for her. Another girl might have gone half wild over the delightful experience of being able to have anything in the shops. Not so Elizabeth. She watched it all apathetically, as if the goods displayed about had been the leaves upon the trees set forth for her admiration. She could wear but one dress at once, and one hat. Why were so many necessary? Her main hope lay in the words her grandmother had spoken about sending her to school.

The third day of her stay in Rittenhouse Square, Elizabeth had reminded her of it, and the grandmother had said half impatiently: "Yes, yes, child; you shall go of course to a finishing school. That will be necessary. But first I must get you fixed up. You have scarcely anything to put on." So Elizabeth subsided.

At last there dawned a beautiful Sabbath when, the wardrobe seemingly complete, Elizabeth was told to array herself for church, as they were going that morning. With great delight and thanksgiving she put on what she was told; and, when she looked into the great French plate mirror after Marie had put on the finishing touches, she was astonished at herself. It was all true, after all. She was a pretty girl.

She looked down at the beautiful gown of finest broadcloth, with the exquisite finish that only the best tailors can put on a garment, and wondered at herself. The very folds of dark-green cloth seemed to bring a grace into her movements. The green velvet hat with its long curling plumes of green and cream-color seemed to be resting lovingly above the beautiful hair that was arranged so naturally and becomingly.

Elizabeth wore her lovely ermine collar and muff without ever knowing they were costly. They all seemed so fitting and quiet and simple, so much less obtrusive than Lizzie's pink silk waist and cheap pink plumes. Elizabeth liked it, and walked to church beside her grandmother with a happy feeling in her heart.

The church was just across the Square. Its tall brown stone spire and arched doorways attracted Elizabeth when she first came to the place. Now she entered with a kind of delight.

It was the first time she had ever been to a Sabbath morning regular service in church. The Christian Endeavor had been as much as Lizzie had been able to stand. She said she had to work too hard during the week to waste so much time on Sunday in church. "The Sabbath was made for man" and "for rest," she had quoted glibly. For the first time in her life since she left Montana Elizabeth felt as if she had a real home and was like other people. She looked around shyly to see whether perchance her friend of the desert might be sitting near, but no familiar face met her gaze. Then she settled back, and gave herself up to delight in the service.

The organ was playing softly, low, tender music. She learned afterward that the music was Handel's "Largo." She did not know that the organ was one of the finest in the city, nor that the organist was one of the most skilful to be had; she knew only that the music seemed to take her soul and lift it up above the earth so that heaven was all around her, and the very clouds seemed singing to her. Then came the processional, with the wonderful voices of the choir-boys sounding far off, and then nearer. It would be impossible for any one who had been accustomed all his life to these things to know how it affected Elizabeth.

It seemed as though the Lord Himself was leading the girl in a very special way. At scarcely any other church in a fashionable quarter of the great city would Elizabeth have heard preaching so exactly suited to her needs. The minister was one of those rare men who lived with God, and talked with Him daily. He had one peculiarity which marked him from all other preachers, Elizabeth heard afterward. He would turn and talk with God in a gentle, sweet, conversational tone right in the midst of his sermon. It made the Lord seem very real and very near.

If he had not been the great and brilliant preacher of an old established church, and revered by all denominations as well as his own, the minister would have been called eccentric and have been asked to resign, because his religion was so very personal that it became embarrassing to some. However, his rare gifts, and his remarkable consecration and independence in doing what he thought right, had produced a most unusual church for a fashionable neighborhood.

Most of his church-members were in sympathy with him, and a wonderful work was going forward right in the heart of Sodom, unhampered by fashion or form or class distinctions. It is true there were some who, like Madam Bailey sat calmly in their seats, and let the minister attend to the preaching end of the service without ever bothering their thoughts as to what he was saying. It was all one to them whether he prayed three times or once, so the service got done at the usual hour. But the majority were being led to see that there is such a thing as a close and intimate walk with God upon this earth.

Into this church came Elizabeth, the sweet heathen, eager to learn all that could be learned about the things of the soul. She sat beside her grandmother, and drank in the sermon, and bowed her lovely, reverent head when she became aware that God was in the room and was being spoken to by His servant. After the last echo of the recessional had died away, and the bowed hush of the congregation had grown into a quiet, well-bred commotion of the putting on of wraps and the low Sabbath greetings, Elizabeth turned to her grandmother.

"Grandmother, may I please go and ask that man some questions? He said just what I have been longing and longing to know, and I must ask him more. Nobody else ever told me these things. Who is he? How does he know it is all true?"

The elder woman watched the eager, flushed face of the girl; and her heart throbbed with pride that this beautiful young thing belonged to her. She smiled indulgently.

"The rector, you mean? Why, I'll invite him to dinner if you wish to talk with him. It's perfectly proper that a young girl should understand about religion. It has a most refining influence, and the Doctor is a charming man. I'll invite his wife and daughter too. They move in the best circles, and I have been meaning to ask them for a long time. You might like to be confirmed. Some do. It's a very pretty service. I was confirmed myself when I was about your age. My mother thought it a good thing for a girl before she went into society. Now, just as you are a schoolgirl, is the proper time. I'll send for him this week. He'll be pleased to know you are interested in these things. He has some kind of a young people's club that meets on Sunday. 'Christian Something' he calls it; I don't know just what, but he talks a great deal about it, and wants every young person to join. You might pay the dues, whatever they are, anyway. I suppose it's for charity. It wouldn't be necessary for you to attend the meetings, but it would please the Doctor."

"Is it Christian Endeavor?" asked Elizabeth, with her eyes sparkling.

"Something like that, I believe. Good morning, Mrs. Schuyler. Lovely day, isn't it? for December. No, I haven't been very well. No, I haven't been out for several weeks. Charming service, wasn't it? The Doctor grows more and more brilliant, I think. Mrs. Schuyler, this is my granddaughter, Elizabeth. She has just come from the West to live with me and complete her education. I want her to know your daughter."

Elizabeth passed through the introduction as a necessary interruption to her train of thought. As soon as they were out upon the street again she began.

"Grandmother, was God in that church?"

"Dear me, child! What strange questions you do ask! Why, yes, I suppose He was, in a way. God is everywhere, they say. Elizabeth, you had better wait until you can talk these things over with a person whose business it is. I never understood much about such questions. You look very nice in that shade of green, and your hat is most becoming."

So was the question closed for the time, but not put out of the girl's thoughts.

The Christmas time had come and passed without much notice on the part of Elizabeth, to whom it was an unfamiliar festival. Mrs. Bailey had suggested that she select some gifts for her "relatives on her mother's side," as she always spoke of the Bradys; and Elizabeth had done so with alacrity, showing good sense and good taste in her choice of gifts, as well as deference to the wishes of the one to whom they were to be given. Lizzie, it is true, was a trifle disappointed that her present was not a gold watch or a diamond ring; but on the whole she was pleased.

A new world opened before the feet of Elizabeth. School was filled with wonder and delight. She absorbed knowledge like a sponge in the water, and rushed eagerly from one study to another, showing marvellous aptitude, and bringing to every task the enthusiasm of a pleasure-seeker.

Her growing intimacy with Jesus Christ through the influence of the pastor who knew Him so well caused her joy in life to blossom into loveliness.

The Bible she studied with the zest of a novel-reader, for it was a novel to her; and daily, as she took her rides in the park on Robin, now groomed into self-respecting sleekness, and wearing a saddle of the latest approved style, she marvelled over God's wonderful goodness to her, just a maid of the wilderness.

So passed three beautiful years in peace and quietness. Every month Elizabeth went to see her Grandmother Brady, and to take some charming little gifts; and every summer she and her Grandmother Bailey spent at some of the fashionable watering-places or in the Catskills, the girl always dressed in most exquisite taste, and as sweetly indifferent to her clothes as a bird of the air or a flower of the field.

The first pocket-money she had been given she saved up, and before long had enough to send the forty dollars to the address the man in the wilderness had given her. But with it she sent no word. It was like her to think she had no right.

She went out more and more with her grandmother among the fashionable old families in Philadelphia society, though as yet she was not supposed to be "out," being still in school; but in all her goings she neither saw nor heard of George Trescott Benedict.

Often she looked about upon the beautiful women that came to her grandmother's house, who smiled and talked to her, and wondered which of them might be the lady to whom his heart was bound. She fancied she must be most sweet and lovely in every way, else such as he could not care for her; so she would pick out this one and that one; and then, as some disagreeableness or glaring fault would appear, she would drop that one for another. There were only a few, after all, that she felt were good enough for the man who had become her ideal.

But sometimes in her dreams he would come and talk with her, and smile as he used to do when they rode together; and he would lay his hand on the mane of her horse-there were always the horses in her dreams. She liked to think of it when she rode in the park, and to

81

think how pleasant it would be if he could be riding there beside her, and they might talk of a great many things that had happened since he left her alone. She felt she would like to tell him of how she had found a friend in Jesus Christ. He would be glad to know about it, she was sure. He seemed to be one who was interested in such things, not like other people who were all engaged in the world.

Sometimes she felt afraid something had happened to him. He might have been thrown from that terrible train and killed, perhaps; and no one know anything about it. But as her experience grew wider, and she travelled on the trains herself, of course this fear grew less. She came to understand that the world was wide, and many things might have taken him away from his home.

Perhaps the money she had sent reached him safely, but she had put in no address. It had not seemed right that she should. It would seem to draw his attention to her, and she felt "the lady" would not like that. Perhaps they were married by this time, and had gone far away to some charmed land to live. Perhaps—a great many things. Only this fact remained; he never came any more into the horizon of her life; and therefore she must try to forget him, and be glad that God had given her a friend in him for her time of need. Some day in the eternal home perhaps she would meet him and thank him for his kindness to her, and then they might tell each other all about the journey through the great wilderness of earth after they had parted. The links in Elizabeth's theology had been well supplied by this time, and her belief in the hereafter was strong and simple like a child's.

She had one great longing, however, that he, her friend, who had in a way been the first to help her toward higher things, and to save her from the wilderness, might know Jesus Christ as he had not known Him when they were together. And so in her daily prayer she often talked with her heavenly Father about him, until she came to have an abiding faith that some day, somehow, he would learn the truth about his Christ.

During the third season of Elizabeth's life in Philadelphia her grandmother decided that it was high time to bring out this bud of promise, who was by this time developing into a more beautiful girl than even her fondest hopes had pictured.

So Elizabeth "came out," and Grandmother Brady read her doings and sayings in the society columns with her morning coffee and an air of deep satisfaction. Aunt Nan listened with her nose in the air. She could never understand why Elizabeth should have privileges beyond her Lizzie. It was the Bailey in her, of course, and mother ought not to think well of it. But Grandmother Brady felt that, while Elizabeth's success was doubtless due in large part to the Bailey in her, still, she was a Brady, and the Brady had not hindered her. It was a step upward for the Bradys.

Lizzie listened, and with pride retailed at the ten-cent store the doings of "my cousin, Elizabeth Bailey," and the other girls listened with awe.

And so it came on to be the springtime of the third year that Elizabeth had spent in Philadelphia.

CHAPTER XV
AN EVENTFUL PICNIC

It was summer and it was June. There was to be a picnic, and Elizabeth was going.

Grandmother Brady had managed it. It seemed to her that, if Elizabeth could go, her cup of pride would be full to overflowing; so after much argument, pro and con, with her daughter and Lizzie, she set herself down to pen the invitation. Aunt Nan was decidedly against it. She did not wish to have Lizzie outshone. She had been working nights for two weeks on an elaborate organdie, with pink roses all over it, for Lizzie to wear. It had yards and yards of cheap lace and insertion, and a whole bolt of pink ribbons of various widths. The hat was a marvel of impossible roses, just calculated for the worst kind of a wreck if a thunder-shower should come up at a Sunday-school picnic. Lizzie's mother was even thinking of getting her a pink chiffon parasol to carry; but the family treasury was well-nigh depleted, and it was doubtful whether that would be possible. After all that, it did not seem pleasant to have Lizzie put in the shade by a fine-lady cousin in silks and jewels.

But Grandmother Brady had waited long for her triumph. She desired above all things to walk among her friends, and introduce her granddaughter, Elizabeth Bailey, and inadvertently remark: "You must have seen me granddaughter's name in the paper often, Mrs. Babcock. She was giving a party in Rittenhouse Square the other day."

Elizabeth would likely be married soon, and perhaps go off somewhere away from Philadelphia-New York or Europe, there was no telling what great fortune might come to her. Now the time was ripe for triumph if ever, and when things are ripe they must be picked. Mrs. Brady proceeded to pick.

She gathered together at great pains pen, paper, and ink. A pencil would be inadequate when the note was going to Rittenhouse Square. She sat down when Nan and Lizzie had left for their day's work, and constructed her sentences with great care.

"*Dear Bessie* —" Elizabeth had never asked her not to call her that, although she fairly detested the name. But still it had been her mother's name, and was likely dear to her grandmother. It seemed disloyalty to her mother to suggest that she be called "Elizabeth." So Grandmother Brady serenely continued to call her "Bessie" to the end of her days. Elizabeth decided that to care much about such little things, in a world where there were so many great things, would be as bad as to give one's mind entirely over to the pursuit of fashion.

The letter proceeded laboriously:

> "Our Sunday school is going to have a picnic out to Willow Grove. It's on Tuesday. We're going in the trolley. I'd be pleased if you would go 'long with us. We will spend the day, and take our dinner and supper along, and wouldn't get home till late; so you could stay overnight here with us, and not go back home till after breakfast. You needn't bring no lunch; fer we've got a lot of things planned, and it ain't worth while. But if you wanted to bring some candy, you might. I ain't got time to make any, and what you buy at our grocery might not be fine enough fer you. I want you to go real bad. I've never took my two granddaughters off to anything yet, and your Grandmother Bailey has you to things all the time. I hope you can manage to come. I am going to pay all the expenses. Your old Christian Deaver you used to 'tend is going to be there; so you'll have a good time. Lizzie has a new pink organdie, with roses on her hat; and we're thinking of getting her a pink umbreller if it don't cost too much. The kind with chiffon flounces on it. You'll have a good time, fer there's lots of side-shows out to Willow Grove, and we're going to see everything there is to see. There's going to be some music too. A man with a name that sounds like swearing is going to make it. I don't remember it just now, but you can see it advertised round on the trolley-cars. He comes to Willow Grove every year. Now please let me hear if you will go at once, as I want to know how much cake to make.

"Your loving grandmother,

ELIZABETH BRADY."

Elizabeth laughed and cried over this note. It pleased her to have her grandmother show kindness to her. She felt that whatever she did for Grandmother Brady was in a sense showing her love to her own mother; so she brushed aside several engagements, much to the annoyance of her Grandmother Bailey, who could not understand why she wanted to go down to Flora Street for two days and a night just in the beginning of warm weather. True, there was not much going on just now between seasons, and Elizabeth could do as she pleased; but she might get a fever in such a crowded neighborhood. It wasn't in the least wise. However, if she must, she must. Grandmother Bailey was on the whole lenient. Elizabeth was too much of a success, and too willing to please her in all things, for her to care to cross her wishes. So Elizabeth wrote on her fine note-paper bearing the Bailey crest in silver:

> *"Dear Grandmother:* I shall be delighted to go to the picnic with you, and I'll bring a nice big box of candy, Huyler's best. I'm sure you'll think it's the best you ever tasted. Don't get Lizzie a parasol; I'm going to bring her one to surprise her. I'll be at the house by eight o'clock.
>
> "Your loving granddaughter,
>
> ELIZABETH."

Mrs. Brady read this note with satisfaction and handed it over to her daughter to read with a gleam of triumph in her eyes at the supper-table. She knew the gift of the pink parasol would go far toward reconciling Aunt Nan to the addition to their party. Elizabeth never did things by halves, and the parasol would be all that could possibly be desired without straining the family pocketbook any further.

So Elizabeth went to the picnic in a cool white dimity, plainly made, with tiny frills of itself, edged with narrow lace that did not shout to the unknowing multitude, "I am real!" but was content with being so; and with a white Panama hat adorned with only a white silken scarf, but whose texture was possible only at a fabulous price. The shape reminded Elizabeth of the old felt hat belonging to her brother, which she had worn on her long trip across the continent. She had put it on in the hat-store one day; and her grandmother, when she found how exquisite a piece of weaving the hat was, at once purchased it for her. It was stylish to wear those soft hats in all sorts of odd shapes. Madam Bailey thought it would be just the thing for the seashore.

Her hair was worn in a low coil in her neck, making the general appearance and contour of her head much as it had been three years before. She wore no jewelry, save the unobtrusive gold buckle at her belt and the plain gold hatpin which fastened her hat. There was nothing about her which marked her as one of the "four hundred." She did not even wear her gloves, but carried them in her hand, and threw them carelessly upon the table when she arrived in Flora Street. Long, soft white ones, they lay there in their costly elegance beside Lizzie's post-card album that the livery-stable man gave her on her birthday, all the long day while Elizabeth was at Willow Grove, and Lizzie sweltered around under her pink parasol in long white silk gloves.

Grandmother Brady surveyed Elizabeth with decided disapproval. It seemed too bad on this her day of triumph, and after she had given a hint, as it were, about Lizzie's fine clothes, that the girl should be so blind or stubborn or both as to come around in that plain rig. Just a common white dress, and an old hat that might have been worn about a livery-stable. It was mortifying in the extreme. She expected a light silk, and kid gloves, and a beflowered hat. Why, Lizzie looked a great deal finer. Did Mrs. Bailey rig her out this way for spite? she wondered.

But, as it was too late to send Elizabeth back for more fitting garments, the old lady resigned herself to her disappointment. The pink parasol was lovely, and Lizzie was wild over it. Even

84

Aunt Nan seemed mollified. It gave her great satisfaction to look the two girls over. Her own outshone the one from Rittenhouse Square by many counts, so thought the mother; but all day long, as she walked behind them or viewed them from afar, she could not understand why it was that the people who passed them always looked twice at Elizabeth and only once at Lizzie. It seemed, after all, that clothes did not make the girl. It was disappointing.

The box of candy was all that could possibly be desired. It was ample for the needs of them all, including the two youths from the livery-stable who had attached themselves to their party from the early morning. In fact, it was two boxes, one of the most delectable chocolates of all imaginable kinds, and the other of mixed candies and candied fruit. Both boxes bore the magic name "Huyler's" on the covers. Lizzie had often passed Huyler's, taking her noon walk on Chestnut Street, and looked enviously at the girls who walked in and out with white square bundles tied with gold cord as if it were an everyday affair. And now she was actually eating all she pleased of those renowned candies. It was almost like belonging to the great élite.

It was a long day and a pleasant one even to Elizabeth. She had never been to Willow Grove before, and the strange blending of sweet nature and Vanity Fair charmed her. It was a rest after the winter's round of monotonous engagements. Even the loud-voiced awkward youths from the livery-stable did not annoy her extremely. She took them as a part of the whole, and did not pay much attention to them. They were rather shy of her, giving the most of their attention to Lizzie, much to the satisfaction of Aunt Nan.

They mounted the horses in the merry-go-rounds, and tried each one several times. Elizabeth wondered why anybody desired this sort of amusement, and after her first trip would have been glad to sit with her grandmother and watch the others, only that the old lady seemed so much to desire to have her get on with the rest. She would not do anything to spoil the pleasure of the others if she could help it; so she obediently seated herself in a great sea-shell drawn by a soiled plaster nymph, and whirled on till Lizzie declared it was time to go to something else.

They went into the Old Mill, and down into the Mimic Mine, and sailed through the painted Venice, eating candy and chewing gum and shouting. All but Elizabeth. Elizabeth would not chew gum nor talk loud. It was not her way. But she smiled serenely on the rest, and did not let it worry her that some one might recognize the popular Miss Bailey in so ill-bred a crowd. She knew that it was their way, and they could have no other. They were having a good time, and she was a part of it for to-day. They weighed one another on the scales with many jokes and much laughter, and went to see all the moving pictures in the place. They ate their lunch under the trees, and then at last the music began.

They seated themselves on the outskirts of the company, for Lizzie declared that was the only pleasant place to be. She did not want to go "way up front." She had a boy on either side of her, and she kept the seat shaking with laughter. Now and then a weary guard would look distressedly down the line, and motion for less noise; but they giggled on. Elizabeth was glad they were so far back that they might not annoy more people than was necessary.

But the music was good, and she watched the leader with great satisfaction. She noticed that there were many people given up to the pleasure of it. The melody went to her soul, and thrilled through it. She had not had much good music in her life. The last three years, of course, she had been occasionally to the Academy of Music; but, though her grandmother had a box there, she very seldom had time or cared to attend concerts. Sometimes, when Melba, or Caruso, or some world-renowned favorite was there, she would take Elizabeth for an hour, usually slipping out just after the favorite solo with noticeable loftiness, as if the orchestra were the common dust of the earth, and she only condescended to come for the soloist. So Elizabeth had scarcely known the delight of a whole concert of fine orchestral music.

She heard Lizzie talking.

"Yes, that's Walter Damrosch! Ain't that name fierce? Grandma thinks it's kind of wicked to pernounce it that way. They say he's fine, but I must say I liked the band they had last year better. It played a whole lot of lively things, and once they had a rattle-box and a squeaking thing that cried like a baby right out in the music, and everybody just roared laughing. I tell you that was great. I don't care much for this here kind of music myself. Do you?" And Jim and Joe both agreed that they didn't, either. Elizabeth smiled, and kept on enjoying it.

Peanuts were the order of the day, and their assertive crackle broke in upon the finest passages. Elizabeth wished her cousin would take a walk; and by and by she did, politely inviting Elizabeth to go along; but she declined, and they were left to sit through the remainder of the afternoon concert.

After supper they watched the lights come out, Elizabeth thinking about the description of the heavenly city as one after another the buildings blazed out against the darkening blue of the June night. The music was about to begin. Indeed, it could be heard already in the distance, and drew the girl irresistibly. For the first time that day she made a move, and the others followed, half wearied of their dissipations, and not knowing exactly what to do next.

They stood the first half of the concert very well, but at the intermission they wandered out to view the electric fountain with its many-colored fluctuations, and to take a row on the tiny sheet of water. Elizabeth remained sitting where she was, and watched the fountain. Even her grandmother and aunt grew restless, and wanted to walk again. They said they had had enough music, and did not want to hear any more. They could hear it well enough, anyway, from further off. They believed they would have some ice-cream. Didn't Elizabeth want some?

She smiled sweetly. Would grandmother mind if she sat right there and heard the second part of the concert? She loved music, and this was fine. She didn't feel like eating another thing to-night. So the two ladies, thinking the girl queer that she didn't want ice-cream, went off to enjoy theirs with a clear conscience; and Elizabeth drew a long breath, and sat back with her eyes closed, to test and breathe in the sweet sounds that were beginning to float out delicately as if to feel whether the atmosphere were right for what was to come after.

It was just at the close of this wonderful music, which the programme said was Mendelssohn's "Spring Song," when Elizabeth looked up to meet the eyes of some one who stood near in the aisle watching her, and there beside her stood the man of the wilderness!

He was looking at her face, drinking in the beauty of the profile and wondering whether he were right. Could it be that this was his little brown friend, the maid of the wilderness? This girl with the lovely, refined face, the intellectual brow, the dainty fineness of manner? She looked like some white angel dropped down into that motley company of Sunday-school picknickers and city pleasure-seekers. The noise and clatter of the place seemed far away from her. She was absorbed utterly in the sweet sounds.

When she looked up and saw him, the smile that flashed out upon her face was like the sunshine upon a day that has hitherto been still and almost sad. The eyes said, "You are come at last!" The curve of the lips said, "I am glad you are here!"

He went to her like one who had been hungry for the sight of her for a long time, and after he had grasped her hand they stood so for a moment while the hum and gentle clatter of talk that always starts between numbers seethed around them and hid the few words they spoke at first.

"O, I have so longed to know if you were safe!" said the man as soon as he could speak.

Then straightway the girl forgot all her three years of training, and her success as a débutante, and became the grave, shy thing she had been to him when he first saw her, looking up with awed delight into the face she had seen in her dreams for so long, and yet might not long for.

The orchestra began again, and they sat in silence listening. But yet their souls seemed to speak to each other through the medium of the music, as if the intervening years were being bridged and brought together in the space of those few waves of melody.

"I have found out," said Elizabeth, looking up shyly with a great light in her eyes. "I have found what it all means. Have you? O, I have wanted so much to know whether you had found out too!"

"Found out what?" he asked half sadly that he did not understand.

"Found out how God hides us. Found what a friend Jesus Christ can be."

"You are just the same," said the man with satisfaction in his eyes. "You have not been changed nor spoiled. They could not spoil you."

"Have you found out too?" she asked softly. She looked up into his eyes with wistful longing. She wanted this thing so very much. It had been in her prayers for so long.

He could not withdraw his own glance. He did not wish to. He longed to be able to answer what she wished.

"A little, perhaps," he said doubtfully. "Not so much as I would like to. Will you help me?"

"*He* will help you. You will find Him if you search for Him with all your heart," she said earnestly. "It says so in His book."

Then came more music, wistful, searching, tender. Did it speak of the things of heaven to other souls there than those two?

He stooped down, and said in a low tone that somehow seemed to blend with the music like the words that fitted it,

"I will try with all my heart if you will help me."

She smiled her answer, brimming back with deep delight.

Into the final lingering notes of an andante from one of Beethoven's sublime symphonies clashed the loud voice of Lizzie:

"O Bess! Bess! B-es-see! I say, Bessie! Ma says we'll have to go over by the cars now if we want to get a seat. The concert's most out, and there'll be a fierce rush. Come on! And grandma says, bring your friend along with you if you want." This last with a smirking recognition of the man, who had turned around wonderingly to see who was speaking.

With a quick, searching glance that took in bedraggled organdie, rose hat, and pink parasol, and set them aside for what they were worth, George Benedict observed and classified Lizzie.

"Will you excuse yourself, and let me take you home a little later?" he asked in a low tone. "The crowd will be very great, and I have my automobile here."

She looked at him gratefully, and assented. She had much to tell him. She leaned across the seats, and spoke in a clear tone to her cousin.

"I will come a little later," she said, smiling with her Rittenhouse Square look that always made Lizzie a little afraid of her. "Tell grandmother I have found an old friend I have not seen for a long time. I will be there almost as soon as you are."

They waited while Lizzie explained, and the grandmother and aunt nodded a reluctant assent. Aunt Nan frowned. Elizabeth might have brought her friend along, and introduced him to Lizzie. Did Elizabeth think Lizzie wasn't good enough to be introduced?

He wrapped her in a great soft rug that was in the automobile, and tucked her in beside him; and she felt as if the long, hard days that had passed since they had met were all forgotten and obliterated in this night of delight. Not all the attentions of all the fine men she had met in society had ever been like his, so gentle, so perfect. She had forgotten the lady as completely as if she had never heard of her. She wanted now to tell her friend about her heavenly Friend.

He let her talk, and watched her glowing, earnest face by the dim light of the sky; for the moon had come out to crown the night with beauty, and the unnatural brilliance of electric blaze, with all the glitter and noise of Willow Grove, died into the dim, sweet night as those two sped onward toward the city. The heart of the man kept singing, singing, singing: "I have found her at last! She is safe!"

"I have prayed for you always," he said in one of the pauses. It was just as they were coming into Flora Street. The urchins were all out on the sidewalk yet, for the night was hot; and they gathered about, and ran hooting after the car as it slowed up at the door. "I am sure He did hide you safely, and I shall thank Him for answering my prayer. And now I am coming to see you. May I come to-morrow?"

There was a great gladness in her eyes. "Yes," she said.

The Bradys had arrived from the corner trolley, and were hovering about the door self-assertively. It was most apparent to an onlooker that this was a good opportunity for an introduction, but the two young people were entirely oblivious. The man touched his hat gravely, a look of great admiration in his eyes, and said, "Good night" like a benediction. Then the girl turned and went into the plain little home and to her belligerent relatives with a light in her eyes and a joy in her steps that had not been there earlier in the day. The dreams that visited her hard pillow that night were heavenly and sweet.

CHAPTER XVI
ALONE AGAIN

"Now we're goin' to see ef the paper says anythin' about our Bessie," said Grandmother Brady the next morning, settling her spectacles over her nose comfortably and crossing one fat gingham knee over the other. "I always read the society notes, Bess."

Elizabeth smiled, and her grandmother read down, the column:

"Mr. George Trescott Benedict and his mother, Mrs. Vincent Benedict, have arrived home after an extended tower of Europe," read Mrs. Brady. "Mrs. Benedict is much improved in health. It is rumored they will spend the summer at their country seat on Wissahickon Heights."

"My!" interrupted Lizzie with her mouth full of fried potatoes. "That's that fellow that was engaged to that Miss What's-her-Name Loring. Don't you 'member? They had his picture in the papers, and her; and then all at once she threw him over for some dook or something, and this feller went off. I heard about it from Mame. Her sister works in a department-store, and she knows Miss Loring. She says she's an awfully handsome girl, and George Benedict was just gone on her. He had a fearful case. Mame says Miss Loring-what is her name? —O, Geraldine-Geraldine Loring bought some lace of her. She heard her say it was for the gown she was going to wear at the horse-show. They had her picture in the paper just after the horse-show, and it was all over lace, I saw it. It cost a whole lot. I forget how many dollars a yard. But there was something the matter with the dook. She didn't marry him, after all. In her picture she was driving four horses. Don't you remember it, grandma? She sat up tall and high on a seat, holding a whole lot of ribbons and whips and things. She has an elegant figger. I guess mebbe the dook wasn't rich enough. She hasn't been engaged to anybody else, and I shouldn't wonder now but she'd take George Benedict back. He was so awful stuck on her!"

Lizzie rattled on, and the grandmother read more society notes, but Elizabeth heard no more. Her hear had suddenly frozen, and dropped down like lead into her being. She felt as if she never would be able to raise it again. The lady! Surely she had forgotten the lady. But Geraldine Loring! Of all women! Could it be possible? Geraldine Loring was almost-well, fast, at least, as nearly so as one who was really of a fine old family, and still held her own in society, could be. She was beautiful as a picture; but her face, to Elizabeth's mind, was lacking in fine feeling and intellect. A great pity went out from her heart to the man whose fate was in that doll-girl's hands. True, she had heard that Miss Loring's family were unquestionable, and she knew her mother was a most charming woman. Perhaps she had misjudged her. She must have done so if he cared for her, for it could not be otherwise.

The joy had gone out of the morning when Elizabeth went home. She went up to her Grandmother Bailey at once, and after she had read her letters for her, and performed the little services that were her habit, she said:

"Grandmother, I'm expecting a man to call upon me to-day. I thought I had better tell you."

"A man!" said Madam Bailey, alarmed at once. She wanted to look over and portion out the right man when the time came. "What man?"

"Why, a man I met in Montana," said Elizabeth, wondering how much she ought to tell.

"A man you met in Montana! Horrors!" exclaimed the now thoroughly aroused grandmother. "Not that dreadful creature you ran away from?"

"O no!" said Elizabeth, smiling. "Not that man. A man who was very kind to me, and whom I like very much."

So much the worse. Immediate action was necessary.

"Well, Elizabeth," said Madam Bailey in her stiffest tones, "I really do not care to have any of your Montana friends visit you. You will have to excuse yourself. It will lead to embarrassing entanglements. You do not in the least realize your position in society. It is all well enough to please your relatives, although I think you often overdo that. You could just as well send them a present now and then, and please them more than to go yourself. But as for any outsiders, it is impossible. I draw the line there."

"But grandmother——"

"Don't interrupt me, Elizabeth; I have something more to say. I had word this morning from the steamship company. They can give us our staterooms on the Deutschland on Saturday, and I have decided to take them. I have telegraphed, and we shall leave here to-day for New York. I have one or two matters of business I wish to attend to in New York. We shall go to the Waldorf for a few days, and you will have more opportunity to see New York than you have had yet. It will not be too warm to enjoy going about a little, I fancy; and a number of our friends are going to be at the Waldorf, too. The Craigs sail on Saturday with us. You will have young company on the voyage."

Elizabeth's heart sank lower than she had known it could go, and she grew white to the lips. The observant grandmother decided that she had done well to be so prompt. The man from Montana was by no means to be admitted. She gave orders to that effect, unknown to Elizabeth.

The girl went slowly to her room. All at once it had dawned upon her that she had not given her address to the man the night before, nor told him by so much as a word what were her circumstances. An hour's meditation brought her to the unpleasant decision that perhaps even now in this hard spot God was only hiding her from worse trouble. Mr. George Benedict belonged to Geraldine Loring. He had declared as much when he was in Montana. It would not be well for her to renew the acquaintance. Her heart told her by its great ache that she would be crushed under a friendship that could not be lasting.

Very sadly she sat down to write a note.

> "*My dear Friend*," she wrote on plain paper with no crest. It was like her to choose that. She would not flaunt her good fortune in his face. She was a plain Montana girl to him, and so she would remain.
>
> "My grandmother has been very ill, and is obliged to go away for her health. Unexpectedly I find that we are to go to-day. I supposed it would not be for a week yet. I am so sorry not to see you again, but I send you a little book that has helped me to get acquainted with Jesus Christ. Perhaps it will help you too. It is called 'My Best Friend.' I shall not forget to pray always that you may find Him. He is so precious to me! I must thank you in words, though I never can say it as it should be said, for your very great kindness to me when I was in trouble. God sent you to me, I am sure. Always gratefully your friend,
>
> "ELIZABETH."

That was all, no date, no address. He was not hers, and she would hang out no clues for him to find her, even if he wished. It was better so.

She sent the note and the little book to his address on Walnut Street; and then after writing a note to her Grandmother Brady, saying that she was going away for a long trip with Grandmother Bailey, she gave herself into the hands of the future like a submissive but weary child.

The noon train to New York carried in its drawing-room-car Madam Bailey, her granddaughter, her maid, and her dog, bound for Europe. The society columns so stated; and so read Grandmother Brady a few days afterward. So also read George Benedict, but it meant nothing to him.

When he received the note, his mind was almost as much excited as when he saw the little brown girl and the little brown horse vanishing behind the little brown station on the prairie. He went to the telephone, and reflected that he knew no names. He called up his automobile, and tore up to Flora Street; but in his bewilderment of the night before he had not noticed which block the house was in, nor which number. He thought he knew where to find it, but in broad daylight the houses were all alike for three blocks, and for the life of him he could not remember whether he had turned up to the right or the left when he came to Flora Street. He tried both, but saw no sign of the people he had but casually noticed at Willow Grove.

He could not ask where she lived, for he did not know her name. Nothing but Elizabeth, and they had called her Bessie. He could not go from house to house asking for a girl named Bessie. They would think him a fool, as he was, for not finding out her name, her precious name, at once. How could he let her slip from him again when he had just found her?

At last he hit upon a bright idea. He asked some children along the street whether they knew of any young woman named Bessie or Elizabeth living there, but they all with one accord shook their heads, though one volunteered the information that "Lizzie Smith lives there." It was most distracting and unsatisfying. There was nothing for it but for him to go home and wait in patience for her return. She would come back sometime probably. She had not said so, but she had not said she would not. He had found her once; he might find her again. And he could pray. She had found comfort in that; so would he. He would learn what her secret was. He would get acquainted with her "best Friend." Diligently did he study that little book, and then he went and hunted up the man of God who had written it, and who had been the one to lead Elizabeth into the path of light by his earnest preaching every Sabbath, though this fact he did not know.

The days passed, and the Saturday came. Elizabeth, heavy-hearted, stood on the deck of the Deutschland, and watched her native land disappear from view. So again George Benedict had lost her from sight.

It struck Elizabeth, as she stood straining her eyes to see the last of the shore through tears that would burn to the surface and fall down her white cheeks, that again she was running away from a man, only this time not of her own free will. She was being taken away. But perhaps it was better.

And it never once entered her mind that, if she had told her grandmother who the friend in Montana was, and where he lived in Philadelphia, it would have made all the difference in the world.

From the first of the voyage Grandmother Bailey grew steadily worse, and when they landed on the other side they went from one place to another seeking health. Carlsbad waters did not agree with her, and they went to the south of France to try the climate. At each move the little old lady grew weaker and more querulous. She finally made no further resistance, and gave up to the rôle of invalid. Then Elizabeth must be in constant attendance. Madam Bailey demanded reading, and no voice was so soothing as Elizabeth's.

Gradually Elizabeth substituted books of her own choice as her grandmother seemed not to mind, and now and then she would read a page of some book that told of the best Friend. At first because it was written by the dear pastor at home it commanded her attention, and finally because some dormant chord in her heart had been touched, she allowed Elizabeth to speak of these things. But it was not until they had been away from home for three months, and she had been growing daily weaker and weaker, that she allowed Elizabeth to read in the Bible.

The girl chose the fourteenth chapter of John, and over and over again, whenever the restless nerves tormented their victim, she would read those words, "Let not your heart be troubled" until the selfish soul, who had lived all her life to please the world and do her own pleasure, came at last to hear the words, and feel that perhaps she did believe in God, and might accept that invitation, "Believe also in me."

One day Elizabeth had been reading a psalm, and thought her grandmother was asleep. She was sitting back with weary heart, thinking what would happen if her grandmother should not get well. The old lady opened her eyes.

"Elizabeth," she said abruptly, just as when she was well, "you've been a good girl. I'm glad you came. I couldn't have died right without you. I never thought much about these things before, but it really is worth while. In my Father's house. He is my Father, Elizabeth."

She went to sleep then, and Elizabeth tiptoed out and left her with the nurse. By and by Marie came crying in, and told her that the Madam was dead.

Elizabeth was used to having people die. She was not shocked; only it seemed lonely again to find herself facing the world, in a foreign land. And when she came to face the arrangements that had to be made, which, after all, money and servants made easy, she found herself dreading her own land. What must she do after her grandmother was laid to rest? She could not live in the great house in Rittenhouse Square, and neither could she very well go and live in Flora Street. O, well, her Father would hide her. She need not plan; He would plan for her. The mansions on the earth were His too, as well as those in heaven.

And so resting she passed through the weary voyage and the day when the body was laid to rest in the Bailey lot in the cemetery, and she went back to the empty house alone. It was not until after the funeral that she went to see Grandmother Brady. She had not thought it wise or fitting to invite the hostile grandmother to the other one's funeral. She had thought Grandmother Bailey would not like it.

She rode to Flora Street in the carriage. She felt too weary to walk or go in the trolley. She was taking account of stock in the way of friends, thinking over whom she cared to see. One of the first bits of news she had heard on arriving in this country had been that Miss Loring's wedding was to come off in a few days. It seemed to strike her like a thunderbolt, and she was trying to arraign herself for this as she rode along. It was therefore not helpful to her state of mind to have her grandmother remark grimly:

"That feller o' yours 'n his oughtymobble has been goin' up an' down this street, day in, day out, this whole blessed summer. Ain't been a day he didn't pass, sometimes once, sometimes twicet. I felt sorry fer him sometimes. Ef he hadn't been so high an' mighty stuck up that he couldn't recognize me, I'd 'a' spoke to him. It was plain ez the nose on your face he was lookin' fer you. Don't he know where you live?"

"I don't believe he does," said Elizabeth languidly. "Say, grandmother, would you care to come up to Rittenhouse Square and live?"

"Me? In Rittenhouse Square? Fer the land sakes, child, no. That's flat. I've lived me days out in me own sp'ere, and I don't intend to change now at me time o' life. Ef you want to do somethin' nice fer me, child, now you've got all that money, I'd like real well to live in a house that hed white marble steps. It's been me one aim all me life. There's some round on the next street that don't come high. There'd be plenty room fer us all, an' a nice place fer Lizzie to get married when the time comes. The parlor's real big, and you would send her some roses, couldn't you?"

"All right, grandmother. You shall have it," said Elizabeth with a relieved sigh, and in a few minutes she went home. Some day pretty soon she must think what to do, but there was no immediate hurry. She was glad that Grandmother Brady did not want to come to Rittenhouse Square. Things would be more congenial without her.

But the house seemed great and empty when she entered, and she was glad to hear the friendly telephone bell ringing. It was the wife of her pastor, asking her to come to them for a quiet dinner.

This was the one home in the great city where she felt like going in her loneliness. There would be no form nor ceremony. Just a friend with them. It was good. The doctor would give her some helpful words. She was glad they had asked her.

CHAPTER XVII
A FINAL FLIGHT AND PURSUIT

"George," said Mrs. Vincent Benedict, "I want you to do something for me."

"Certainly, mother, anything I can."

"Well, it's only to go to dinner with me to-night. Our pastor's wife has telephoned me that she wants us very much. She especially emphasized you. She said she absolutely needed you. It was a case of charity, and she would be so grateful to you if you would come. She has a young friend with her who is very sad, and she wants to cheer her up. Now don't frown. I won't bother you again this week. I know you hate dinners and girls. But really, George, this is an unusual case. The girl is just home from Europe, and buried her grandmother yesterday. She hasn't a soul in the world belonging to her that can be with her, and the pastor's wife has asked her over to dinner quietly. Of course she isn't going out. She must be in mourning. And you know you're fond of the doctor."

"Yes, I'm fond of the doctor," said George, frowning discouragedly; "but I'd rather take him alone, and not with a girl flung at me everlastingly. I'm tired of it. I didn't think it of Christian people, though; I thought she was above such things."

"Now, George," said his mother severely, "that's a real insult to the girl, and to our friend too. She hasn't an idea of doing any such thing. It seems this girl is quite unusual, very religious, and our friend thought you would be just the one to cheer her. She apologized several times for presuming to ask you to help her. You really will have to go."

"Well, who is this paragon, anyway? Any one I know? I s'pose I've got to go."

"Why, she's a Miss Bailey," said the mother, relieved. "Mrs. Wilton Merrill Bailey's granddaughter. Did you ever happen to meet her? I never did."

"Never heard of her," growled George. "Wish I hadn't now."

"George!"

"Well, mother, go on. I'll be good. What does she do? Dance, and play bridge, and sing?"

"I haven't heard anything that she does," said his mother, laughing.

"Well, of course she's a paragon; they all are, mother. I'll be ready in half an hour. Let's go and get it done. We can come home early, can't we?"

Mrs. Benedict sighed. If only George would settle down on some suitable girl of good family! But he was so queer and restless. She was afraid for him. Ever since she had taken him away to Europe, when she was so ill, she had been afraid for him. He seemed so moody and absent-minded then and afterwards. Now this Miss Bailey was said to be as beautiful as she was good. If only George would take a notion to her!

Elizabeth was sitting in a great arm-chair by the open fire when he entered the room. He had not expected to find any one there. He heard voices up-stairs, and supposed Miss Bailey was talking with her hostess. His mother followed the servant to remove her wraps, and he entered the drawing-room alone. She stirred, looked up, and saw him.

"Elizabeth!" he said, and came forward to grasp her hand. "I have found you again. How came you here?"

But she had no opportunity to answer, for the ladies entered almost at once, and there stood the two smiling at each other.

"Why, you have met before!" exclaimed the hostess. "How delighted I am! I knew you two would enjoy meeting. Elizabeth, child, you never told me you knew George."

George Benedict kept looking around for Miss Bailey to enter the room; but to his relief she did not come, and, when they went out to the dining-room, there was no place set for her. She must have preferred to remain at home. He forgot her, and settled down to the joy of having Elizabeth by his side. His mother, opposite, watched his face blossom into the old-time joy as he handed this new girl the olives, and had eyes for no one else.

It was to Elizabeth a blessed evening. They held sweet converse one with another as children of the King. For a little time under the old influence of the restful, helpful talk she forgot "the lady," and all the perplexing questions that had vexed her soul. She knew only that she had entered into an atmosphere of peace and love and joy.

It was not until the evening was over, and the guests were about to leave, that Mrs. Benedict addressed Elizabeth as Miss Bailey. Up to that moment it had not entered her son's mind that Miss Bailey was present at all. He turned with a start, and looked into Elizabeth's eyes; and she smiled back to him as if to acknowledge the name. Could she read his thoughts? he wondered.

It was only a few steps across the Square, and Mrs. Benedict and her son walked to Elizabeth's door with her. He had no opportunity to speak to Elizabeth alone, but he said as he bade her good-night, "I shall see you to-morrow, then, in the morning?"

The inflection was almost a question; but Elizabeth only said, "Good night," and vanished into the house.

"Then you have met her before, George?" asked his mother wonderingly.

"Yes," he answered hurriedly, as if to stop her further question. "Yes, I have met her before. She is very beautiful, mother."

And because the mother was afraid she might say too much she assented, and held her peace. It was the first time in years that George had called a girl beautiful.

Meantime Elizabeth had gone to her own room and locked the door. She hardly knew what to think, her heart was so happy. Yet beneath it all was the troubled thought of the lady, the haunting lady for whom they had prayed together on the prairie. And as if to add to the thought she found a bit of newspaper lying on the floor beside her dressing-table. Marie must have dropped it as she came in to turn up the lights. It was nothing but the corner torn from a newspaper, and should be consigned to the waste-basket; yet her eye caught the words in large head-lines as she picked it up idly, "Miss Geraldine Loring's Wedding to Be an Elaborate Affair." There was nothing more readable. The paper was torn in a zigzag line just beneath. Yet that was enough. It reminded her of her duty.

Down beside the bed she knelt, and prayed: "O my Father, hide me now; hide me! I am in trouble; hide me!" Over and over she prayed till her heart grew calm and she could think.

Then she sat down quietly, and put the matter before her.

This man whom she loved with her whole soul was to be married in a few days. The world of society would be at the wedding. He was pledged to another, and he was not hers. Yet he was her old friend, and was coming to see her. If he came and looked into her face with those clear eyes of his, he might read in hers that she loved him. How dreadful that would be!

Yes, she must search yet deeper. She had heard the glad ring in his voice when he met her, and said, "Elizabeth!" She had seen his eyes. He was in danger himself. She knew it; she might not hide it from herself. She must help him to be true to the woman to whom he was pledged, whom now he would have to marry.

She must go away from it all. She would run away, now at once. It seemed that she was always running away from some one. She would go back to the mountains where she had started. She was not afraid now of the man from whom she had fled. Culture and education had done their work. Religion had set her upon a rock. She could go back with the protection that her money would put about her, with the companionship of some good, elderly woman, and be safe from harm in that way; but she could not stay here and meet George Benedict in the morning, nor face Geraldine Loring on her wedding-day. It would be all the same the facing whether she were in the wedding-party or not. Her days of mourning for her grandmother would of course protect her from this public facing. It was the thought she could not bear. She must get away from it all forever.

Her lawyers should arrange the business. They would purchase the house that Grandmother Brady desired, and then give her her money to build a church. She would go back, and teach among the lonely wastes of mountain and prairie what Jesus Christ longed to be to the people made in His image. She would go back and place above the graves of her father and mother and brothers stones that should bear the words of life to all who should pass by in that desolate region. And that should be her excuse to the world for going, if she needed any excuse-she had gone to see about placing a monument over her father's grave. But the monument should be a church somewhere where it was most needed. She was resolved upon that.

That was a busy night. Marie was called upon to pack a few things for a hurried journey. The telephone rang, and the sleepy night-operator answered crossly. But Elizabeth found out all she wanted to know about the early Chicago trains, and then lay down to rest.

Early the next morning George Benedict telephoned for some flowers from the florist; and, when they arrived, he pleased himself by taking them to Elizabeth's door.

He did not expect to find her up, but it would be a pleasure to have them reach her by his own hand. They would be sent up to her room, and she would know in her first waking thought that he remembered her. He smiled as he touched the bell and stood waiting.

The old butler opened the door. He looked as if he had not fully finished his night's sleep. He listened mechanically to the message, "For Miss Bailey with Mr. Benedict's good-morning," and then his face took on a deprecatory expression.

"I'm sorry, Mr. Benedict," he said, as if in the matter he were personally to blame; "but she's just gone. Miss Elizabeth's mighty quick in her ways, and last night after she come home she decided to go to Chicago on the early train. She's just gone to the station not ten minutes ago. They was late, and had to hurry. I'm expecting the footman back every minute."

"Gone?" said George Benedict, standing blankly on the door-step and looking down the street as if that should bring her. "Gone? To Chicago, did you say?"

"Yes, sir, she's gone to Chicago. That is, she's going further, but she took the Chicago Limited. She's gone to see about a monument for Madam's son John, Miss 'Lizabuth's father. She said she must go at once, and she went."

"What time does that train leave?" asked the young man. It was a thread of hope. He was stung into a superhuman effort as he had been on the prairie when he had caught the flying vision of the girl and horse, and he had shouted, and she would not stop for him.

"Nine-fifty, sir," said the butler. He wished this excited young man would go after her. She needed some one. His heart had often stirred against fate that this pearl among young mistresses should have no intimate friend or lover now in her loneliness.

"Nine-fifty!" He looked at his watch. No chance! "Broad Street?" he asked sharply.

"Yes, sir."

Would there be a chance if he had his automobile? Possibly, but hardly unless the train was late. There would be a trifle more chance of catching the train at West Philadelphia. O for his automobile! He turned to the butler in despair.

"Telephone her!" he said. "Stop her if you possibly can on board the train, and I will try to get there. I must see her. It is important." He started down the steps, his mind in a whirl of trouble. How should he go? The trolley would be the only available way, and yet the trolley would be useless; it would take too long. Nevertheless, he sped down toward Chestnut Street blindly, and now in his despair his new habit came to him. "O my Father, help me! Help me! Save her for me!"

Up Walnut Street at a breakneck pace came a flaming red automobile, sounding its taunting menace, "Honk-honk! Honk-honk!" but George Benedict stopped not for automobiles. Straight into the jaws of death he rushed, and was saved only by the timely grasp of a policeman, who rolled him over on the ground. The machine came to a halt, and a familiar voice shouted: "Conscience alive, George, is that you? What are you trying to do? Say, but that was a close shave! Where you going in such a hurry, anyway? Hustle in, and I'll take you there."

The young man sprang into the seat, and gasped: "West Philadelphia station, Chicago Limited! Hurry! Train leaves Broad Street station at nine-fifty. Get me there if you can, Billy. I'll be your friend forever."

By this time they were speeding fast. Neither of the two had time to consider which station was the easier to make; and, as the machine was headed toward West Philadelphia, on they went, regardless of laws or vainly shouting policemen.

George Benedict sprang from the car before it had stopped, and nearly fell again. His nerves were not steady from his other fall yet. He tore into the station and out through the passageway past the beckoning hand of the ticket-man who sat in the booth at the staircase, and strode up three steps at a time. The guard shouted: "Hurry! You may get it; she's just starting!" and a friendly hand reached out, and hauled him up on the platform of the last car.

For an instant after he was safely in the car he was too dazed to think. It seemed as if he must keep on blindly rushing through that train all the way to Chicago, or she would get away from him. He sat down in an empty seat for a minute to get his senses. He was actually on the train! It had not gone without him!

Now the next question was, Was she on it herself, or had she in some way slipped from his grasp even yet? The old butler might have caught her by telephone. He doubted it. He knew her stubborn determination, and all at once he began to suspect that she was with intention running away from him, and perhaps had been doing so before! It was an astonishing thought and a grave one, yet, if it were true, what had meant that welcoming smile in her eyes that had been like dear sunshine to his heart?

But there was no time to consider such questions now. He had started on this quest, and he must continue it until he found her. Then she should be made to explain once and for all most fully. He would live through no more torturing agonies of separation without a full understanding of the matter. He got upon his shaking feet, and started to hunt for Elizabeth.

Then all at once he became aware that he was still carrying the box of flowers. Battered and out of shape it was, but he was holding it as if it held the very hope of life for him. He smiled grimly as he tottered shakily down the aisle, grasping his floral offering with determination. This was not exactly the morning call he had planned, nor the way he had expected to present his flowers; but it seemed to be the best he could do. Then, at last, in the very furthest car from the end, in the drawing-room he found her, sitting gray and sorrowful, looking at the fast-flying landscape.

"Elizabeth!" He stood in the open door and called to her; and she started as from a deep sleep, her face blazing into glad sunshine at sight of him. She put her hand to her heart, and smiled.

"I have brought you some flowers," he said grimly. "I am afraid there isn't much left of them now; but, such as they are, they are here. I hope you will accept them."

"Oh!" gasped Elizabeth, reaching out for the poor crushed roses as if they had been a little child in danger. She drew them from the battered box and to her arms with a delicious movement of caressing, as if she would make up to them for all they had come through. He watched her, half pleased, half savagely. Why should all that tenderness be wasted on mere fading flowers?

At last he spoke, interrupting her brooding over his roses.

"You are running away from me!" he charged.

"Well, and what if I am?" She looked at him with a loving defiance in her eyes.

"Don't you know I love you?" he asked, sitting down beside her and talking low and almost fiercely. "Don't you know I've been torn away from you, or you from me, twice before now, and that I cannot stand it any more? Say, don't you know it? Answer, please," The demand was kind, but peremptory.

"I was afraid so," she murmured with drooping eyes, and cheeks from which all color had fled.

"Well, why do you do it? Why did you run away? Don't you care for me? Tell me that. If you can't ever love me, you are excusable; but I must know it all now."

"Yes, I care as much as you," she faltered, "but——"

"But what?" sharply.

"But you are going to be married this week," she said in desperation, raising her miserable eyes to his.

He looked at her in astonishment.

"Am I?" said he. "Well, that's news to me; but it's the best news I've heard in a long time. When does the ceremony come off? I wish it was this morning. Make it this morning, will you? Let's stop this blessed old train and go back to the Doctor. He'll fix it so we can't ever run away from each other again. Elizabeth, look at me!"

But Elizabeth hid her eyes now. They were full of tears.

"But the lady —" she gasped out, struggling with the sobs. She was so weary, and the thought of what he had suggested was so precious.

"What lady? There is no lady but you, Elizabeth, and never has been. Haven't you known that for a long time? I have. That was all a hallucination of my foolish brain. I had to go out on the plains to get rid of it, but I left it there forever. She was nothing to me after I saw you."

"But-but people said-and it was in the paper, I saw it. You cannot desert her now; it would be dishonorable."

"Thunder!" ejaculated the distracted young man. "In the paper! What lady?"

"Why, Miss Loring! Geraldine Loring. I saw that the preparations were all made for her wedding, and I was told she was to marry you."

In sheer relief he began to laugh.

At last he stopped, as the old hurt look spread over her face.

"Excuse me, dear," he said gently, "There was a little acquaintance between Miss Loring and myself. It only amounted to a flirtation on her part, one of many. It was a great distress to my mother, and I went out West, as you know, to get away from her. I knew she would only bring me unhappiness, and she was not willing to give up some of her ways that were impossible. I am glad and thankful that God saved me from her. I believe she is going to marry a distant relative of mine by the name of Benedict, but I thank the kind Father that I am not going to marry her. There is only one woman in the whole wide world that I am willing to marry, or ever will be; and she is sitting beside me now."

The train was going rapidly now. It would not be long before the conductor would reach them. The man leaned over, and clasped the little gloved hand that lay in the girl's lap; and Elizabeth felt the great joy that had tantalized her for these three years in dreams and visions settle down about her in beautiful reality. She was his now forever. She need never run away again.

The conductor was not long in coming to them, and the matter-of-fact world had to be faced once more. The young man produced his card, and said a few words to the conductor, mentioning the name of his uncle, who, by the way, happened to be a director of the road; and then he explained the situation. It was very necessary that the young lady be recalled at once to her home because of a change in the circumstances. He had caught the train at West Philadelphia by automobile, coming as he was in his morning clothes, without baggage and with little money. Would the conductor be so kind as to put them off that they might return to the city by the shortest possible route?

The conductor glared and scolded, and said people "didn't know their own minds," and "wanted to move the earth." Then he eyed Elizabeth, and she smiled. He let a grim glimmer of what might have been a sour smile years ago peep out for an instant, and-he let them off.

They wandered delightedly about from one trolley to another until they found an automobile garage, and soon were speeding back to Philadelphia.

They waited for no ceremony, these two who had met and loved by the way in the wilderness. They went straight to Mrs. Benedict for her blessing, and then to the minister to arrange for his services; and within the week a quiet wedding-party entered the arched doors of the placid brown church with the lofty spire, and Elizabeth Bailey and George Benedict were united in the sacred bonds of matrimony.

There were present Mrs. Benedict and one or two intimate friends of the family, besides Grandmother Brady, Aunt Nan, and Lizzie.

Lizzie brought a dozen bread-and-butter-plates from the ten-cent store. They were adorned with cupids and roses and much gilt. But Lizzie was disappointed. No display, no pomp and ceremony. Just a simple white dress and white veil. Lizzie did not understand that the veil had been in the Bailey family for generations, and that the dress was an heirloom also. It was worn because Grandmother Bailey had given it to her, and told her she wanted her to wear it on her wedding-day. Sweet and beautiful she looked as she turned to walk down the aisle on her husband's arm, and she smiled at Grandmother Brady in a way that filled the grandmother's heart with pride and triumph. Elizabeth was not ashamed of the Bradys even among her fine friends. But Lizzie grumbled all the way home at the plainness of the ceremony, and the lack of bridesmaids and fuss and feathers.

The social column of the daily papers stated that young Mr. and Mrs. George Benedict were spending their honeymoon in an extended tour of the West, and Grandmother Brady so read it aloud at the breakfast table to the admiring family. Only Lizzie looked discontented:

"She just wore a dark blue tricotine one-piece dress and a little plain dark hat. She ain't got a bit of taste. Oh *Boy*! If I just had her pocket book wouldn't I show the world? But anyhow I'm glad she went in a private car. There was a *little* class to her, though if t'had been mine I'd uv preferred ridin' in the parlor coach an' havin' folks see me and my fine husband. He's some looker, George Benedict is! Everybody turns to watch 'em as they go by, and they just sail along and never seem to notice. It's all perfectly throwed away on 'em. Gosh! I'd hate to be such a nut!"

"Now, Lizzie, you know you hadn't oughtta talk like that!" reproved her grandmother, "After her giving you all that money fer your own wedding. A thousand dollars just to spend as you please on your cloes and a blow out, and house linens. Jest because she don't care for gewgaws like you do, you think she's a fool. But she's no fool. She's got a good head on her, and she'll get more in the long run out of life than you will. She's been real loving and kind to us all, and she didn't have any reason to neither. We never did much fer her. And look at how nice and common she's been with us all, not a bit high headed. I declare, Lizzie, I should think you'd be ashamed!"

"Oh, well," said Lizzie shrugging her shoulders indifferently, "She's all right in her way, only 'taint my way. And I'm thankful t'goodness that I had the nerve to speak up when she offered to give me my trousseau. She askt me would I druther hav her buy it for me, or have the money and pick it out m'self, and I spoke up right quick and says, 'Oh, cousin Bessie, I wouldn't *think* of givin' ya all that trouble. I'd take the *money* ef it's all the same t'you,' and she jest smiled and said all right, she expected I knew what I wanted better'n she did. So yes'teddy when I went down to the station to see her off she handed me a bank book. And-Oh, say, I fergot! She said there was a good-bye note inside. I ain't had time to look at it since. I went right to the movies on the dead run to get there 'fore the first show begun, and it's in my coat pocket. Wait 'till I get it. I spose it's some of her old *religion*! She's always preaching at me. It ain't that she says so much as that she's always *meanin'* it underneath, everything, that gets my goat! It's sorta like having a piece of God round with you all the time watching you. You kinda hate to be enjoyin' yerself fer fear she won't think yer doin' it accordin' to the Bible."

Lizzie hurtled into the hall and brought back her coat, fumbling in the pocket.

"Yes, here 'tis ma! Wanta see the figgers? You never had a whole thousand dollars in the bank t'woncet yerself, did ya?"

Mrs. Brady put on her spectacles and reached for the book, while Lizzie's mother got up and came behind her mother's chair to look over at the magic figures. Lizzie stooped for the little white note that had fluttered to her feet as she opened the book, but she had little interest to see what it said. She was more intent upon the new bank book.

It was Grandmother Brady that discovered it:

"Why, Lizzie! It ain't *one* thousand, it's *five* thousand, the book says! You don't 'spose she's made a mistake, do you?"

Lizzie seized the book and gazed, her jaw dropping open in amaze. "Let me have it!" demanded Lizzie's mother, reaching for the book.

"Where's yer note, Lizzie, mebbe it'll explain," said the excited Grandmother.

Lizzie recovered the note which again had fluttered to the floor in the confusion and opening it began to read:

"Dear Lizzie," it read

"I've made it five thousand so you will have some over for furnishing your home, and if you still think you want the little bungalow out on the Pike you will find the deed at my lawyer's, all made out in your name. It's my wedding gift to you, so you can go to work and buy your furniture at once, and not wait till Dan gets a raise. And here's wishing you a great deal of happiness,

"Your loving cousin,

ELIZABETH."

"There!" said Grandmother Brady sitting back with satisfaction and holding her hands composedly, "Whadd' I tell ya?"

"Mercy!" said Lizzie's mother, "Let me see that note! The idea of her *giving* all that money when she didn't have to!"

But Lizzie's face was a picture of joy. For once she lost her hard little worldly screwed-up expression and was wreathed in smiles of genuine eagerness:

"Oh *Boy!*" she exclaimed delightedly, dancing around the room, "Now we can have a victrola, an' a player-piano, and Dan'll get a Ford, one o' those limousine-kind! Won't I be some swell? What'll the girls at the store think now?"

"H'm! You'd much better get a washing machine and a 'lectric iron!" grumbled Grandmother Brady practically.

"Well, all I got to say about it is, she was an awful fool to trust *you* with so much money," said Lizzie's mother discontentedly, albeit with a pleased pride as she watched her giddy daughter fling on hat and coat to go down and tell Dan.

"I sh'll work in the store fer the rest of the week, jest to 'commodate 'em," she announced putting her head back in the door as she went out, "but not a day longer. I got a lot t'do. Say, won't I be some lady in the five-an'-ten the rest o' the week? Oh *Boy! I'll tell the world!*"

Meantime in their own private car the bride and groom were whirled on their way to the west, but they saw little of the scenery, being engaged in the all-absorbing story of each other's lives since they had parted.

And one bright morning, they stepped down from the train at Malta and gazed about them.

The sun was shining clear and wonderful, and the little brown station stood drearily against the brightness of the day like a picture that has long hung on the wall of one's memory and is suddenly brought out and the dust wiped away.

They purchased a couple of horses, and with camp accoutrements following began their real wedding trip, over the road they had come together when they first met. Elizabeth had to show her husband where she had hidden while the men went by, and he drew her close in his arms and thanked God that she had escaped so miraculously.

It seemed so wonderful to be in the same places again, for nothing out here in the wilderness seemed much to have changed, and yet they two were so changed that the people they met did not seem to recognize them as ever having been that way before.

They dined sumptuously in the same coulee, and recalled little things they had said and done, and Elizabeth now worldly wise, laughed at her own former ignorance as her husband reminded her of some questions she had asked him on that memorable journey. And ever through the beautiful journey he was telling her how wonderful she seemed to him, both then and now.

Not however, till they reached the old ranchhouse, where the woman had tried to persuade her to stay, did they stop for long.

Elizabeth had a tender feeling in her heart for that motherly woman who had sought to protect her, and felt a longing to let her know how safely she had been kept through the long journey and how good the Lord had been to her through the years. Also they both desired to reward these kind people for their hospitality in the time of need. So, in the early evening they rode up just as they did before to the little old log house. But no friendly door flung open wide as they came near, and at first they thought the cabin deserted, till a candle flare suddenly shone forth in the bedroom, and then Benedict dismounted and knocked.

After some waiting the old man came to the door holding a candle high above his head. His face was haggard and worn, and the whole place looked dishevelled. His eyes had a weary look as he peered into the night and it was evident that he had no thought of ever having seen them before:

"I can't do much fer ya, strangers," he said, his voice sounding tired and discouraged. "If it's a woman ye have with ye, ye better ride on to the next ranch. My woman is sick. Very sick. There's nobody here with her but me, and I have all I can tend to. The house ain't kept very tidy. It's six weeks since she took to bed."

Elizabeth had sprung lightly to the ground and was now at the threshold:

"Oh, is she sick? I'm so sorry? Couldn't I do something for her? She was good to me once several years ago!"

The old man peered at her blinkingly, noting her slender beauty, the exquisite eager face, the dress that showed her of another world-and shook his head:

"I guess you made a mistake, lady. I don't remember ever seeing you before —"

"But I remember you," she said eagerly stepping into the room, "Won't you please let me go to her?"

"Why, shore, lady, go right in ef you want to. She's layin' there in the bed. She ain't likely to get out of it again' I'm feared. The doctor says nothin' but a 'noperation will ever get her up, and we can't pay fer 'noperations. It's a long ways to the hospital in Chicago where he wants her sent, and M'ria and I, we ain't allowin' to part. It can't be many years —"

But Elizabeth was not waiting to hear. She had slipped into the old bedroom that she remembered now so well and was kneeling beside the bed talking to the white faced woman on the thin pillow:

"Don't you remember me," she asked, "I'm the girl you tried to get to stay with you once. The girl that came here with a man she had met in the wilderness. You told me things that I didn't know, and you were kind and wanted me to stay here with you? Don't you remember me? I'm Elizabeth!"

The woman reached out a bony hand and touched the fair young face that she could see but dimly in the flare of the candle that the old man now brought into the room:

"Why, yes, I remember," the woman said, her voice sounded alive yet in spite of her illness, "Yes, I remember you. You were a dear little girl, and I was so worried about you. I would have kept you for my own-but you wouldn't stay. And he was a nice looking young man, but I was afraid for you-You can't always tell about them-You *mostly* can't —!"

"But he was all right Mother!" Elizabeth's voice rang joyously through the cabin, "He took care of me and got me safely started toward my people, and now he's my husband. I want you to see him. George come here!"

The old woman half raised herself from the pillow and looked toward the young man in the doorway:

"You don't say! He's your *husband*! Well, now isn't that grand! Well, I certainly am glad! I was that worried —!"

They sat around the bed talking, Elizabeth telling briefly of her own experiences and her wedding trip which they were taking back over the old trail, and the old man and woman speaking of their trouble, the woman's breakdown and how the doctor at Malta said there was a chance she could get well if she went to a great doctor in Chicago, but how they had no money unless they sold the ranch and that nobody wanted to buy it.

"Oh, but we have money," laughed Elizabeth joyously, "and it is our turn now to help you. You helped us when we were in trouble. How soon can you start? I'm going to play you are my own father and mother. We can send them both, can't we George?"

It was a long time before they settled themselves to sleep that night because there was so much planning to be done, and then Elizabeth and her husband had to get out their stores and cook a good supper for the two old people who had been living mostly on corn meal mush, for several weeks.

And after the others were all asleep the old woman lay praying and thanking God for the two angels who had dropped down to help them in their distress.

The next morning George Benedict with one of the men who looked after their camping outfit went to Malta and got in touch with the Chicago doctor and hospital, and before he came back to the ranch that night everything was arranged for the immediate start of the two old people He had even planned for an automobile and the Malta doctor to be in attendance in a couple of days to get the invalid to the station.

Meantime Elizabeth had been going over the old woman's wardrobe which was scanty and coarse, and selecting garments from her own baggage that would do for the journey.

The old woman looked glorified as she touched the delicate white garments with their embroidery and ribbons:

"Oh, dear child! Why, I couldn't wear a thing like that on my old worn-out body. Those look like angels' clothes." She put a work-worn finger on the delicate tracery of embroidery and smoothed a pink satin ribbon bow.

But Elizabeth overruled her. It was nothing but a plain little garment she had bought for the trip. If the friend thought it was pretty she was glad, but nothing was too pretty for the woman who had taken her in in her distress and tried to help her and keep her safe.

The invalid was thin with her illness, and it was found that she could easily wear the girl's simple dress of dark blue with a white collar, and little dark hat, and Elizabeth donned a khaki skirt and brown cap and sweater herself and gladly arrayed her old friend in her own bridal travelling gown for her journey. She had not brought a lot of things for her journey because she did not want to be bothered, but she could easily get more when she got to a large city, and what was money for but to cloth the naked and feed the hungry? She rejoiced in her ability to help this woman of the wilderness.

On the third day, garbed in Elizabeth's clothes, her husband fitted out for the east in some of George Benedict's extra things, they started. They carried a bag containing some necessary changes, and some wonderful toilet accessories with silver monograms, enough to puzzle the most snobbish nurse, also there was a luscious silk kimona of Elizabeth's in the bag. The two old people were settled in the Benedict private car, and in due time hitched on to the Chicago express and hurried on their way. Before the younger pair went back to their pilgrimage they sent a series of telegrams arranging for every detail of the journey for the old couple, so that they would be met with cars and nurses and looked after most carefully.

And the thanksgiving and praise of the old people seemed to follow them like music as they rode happily on their way.

They paused at the little old school house where they had attended the Christian Endeavor meeting, and Elizabeth looked half fearfully up the road where her evil pursuers had ridden by, and rode closer to her husband's side. So they passed on the way as nearly as Elizabeth could remember every step back as she had come, telling her husband all the details of the journey.

That night they camped in the little shelter where Benedict had come upon the girl that first time they met, and under the clear stars that seemed so near they knelt together and thanked God for His leading.

They went to the lonely cabin on the mountain, shut up and going to ruin now, and Benedict gazing at the surroundings and then looking at the delicate face of his lovely wife was reminded of a white flower he had once seen growing out of the blackness down in a coal mine, pure and clean without a smirch of soil.

They visited the seven graves in the wilderness, and standing reverently beside the sand-blown mounds she told him much of her early life that she had not told him before, and introduced him to her family, telling a bit about each that would make him see the loveable side of them. And then they planned for seven simple white stones to be set up, bearing words from the book they both loved. Over the care worn mother was to be written "Come unto me all ye that labor and are heavy laden and I will give you rest."

It was on that trip that they planned what came to pass in due time. The little cabin was made over into a simple, pretty home, with vines planted about the garden, and a garage with a sturdy little car; and not far away a church nestled into the side of the hill, built out of the stones that were native, with many sunny windows and a belfry in which bells rang out to the whole region round.

At first it had seemed impractical to put a church out there away from the town, but Elizabeth said that it was centrally located, and high up where it could be seen from the settlements in the valleys, and was moreover on a main trail that was much travelled. She longed to have some such spot in the wilderness that could be a refuge for any who longed for better things.

When they went back they sent out two consecrated missionaries to occupy the new house and use the sturdy little car. They were to ring the bells, preach the gospel and play the organ and piano in the little church.

Over the pulpit there was a beautiful window bearing a picture of Christ, the Good Shepherd, and in clear letters above were the words: "And thou shalt remember all the way which the Lord thy God led thee these forty years in the wilderness, to humble thee, and to prove thee, to know what was in thine heart, whether thou wouldst keep his commandments, or no."

And underneath the picture were the words:

"'In the time of trouble He shall hide me in His pavilion; in the secret of his tabernacle shall he hide me.' In memory of His hidings,

"George and Elizabeth Benedict."

But in the beautiful home in Philadelphia, in an inner intimate room these words are exquisitely graven on the wall, "Let not your heart be troubled."

THE MAN OF THE DESERT

I. PROSPECTING

It was morning, high and clear as Arizona counts weather, and around the little railroad station were gathered a crowd of curious onlookers; seven Indians, three women from nearby shacks-drawn thither by the sight of the great private car that the night express had left on a side track-the usual number of loungers, a swarm of children, besides the station agent who had come out to watch proceedings.

All the morning the private car had been an object of deep interest to those who lived within sight, and that was everybody on the plateau; and many and various had been the errands and excuses to go to the station that perchance the occupants of that car might be seen, or a glimpse of the interior of the moving palace; but the silken curtains had remained drawn until after nine o'clock.

Within the last half hour, however, a change had taken place in the silent inscrutable car. The curtains had parted here and there, revealing dim flitting faces, a table spread with a snowy cloth and flowers in a vase, wild flowers they were, too, like those that grew all along the track, just weeds. Strange that one who could afford a private car cared for weeds in a glass on their dining-table, but then perhaps they didn't know.

A fat cook with ebony skin and white linen attire had appeared on the rear platform beating eggs, and half whistling, half singing:

> "Be my little baby Bumble-bee —
> Buzz around, buzz around — —"

He seemed in no wise affected or embarrassed by the natives who gradually encircled the end of the car, and the audience grew.

They could dimly see the table where the inmates of the car were-dining? —it couldn't be breakfast at that hour surely. They heard the discussion about horses going on amid laughter and merry conversation, and they gathered that the car was to remain here for the day at least while some of the party went off on a horseback trip. It was nothing very unusual of course. Such things occasionally occurred in that region, but not often enough to lose their interest. Besides, to watch the tourists who chanced to stop in their tiny settlement was the only way for them to learn the fashions.

Not that all the watchers stood and stared around the car. No, indeed. They made their headquarters around the station platform from whence they took brief and comprehensive excursions down to the freight station and back, going always on one side of the car and returning by way of the other. Even the station agent felt the importance of the occasion, and stood around with all the self-consciousness of an usher at a grand wedding, considering himself master of ceremonies.

"Sure! They come from the East last night. Limited dropped 'em! Going down to prospect some mine, I reckon. They ordered horses an' a outfit, and Shag Bunce is goin' with 'em. He got a letter 'bout a week ago tellin' what they wanted of him. Yes, I knowed all about it. He brung the letter to me to cipher out fer him. You know Shag ain't no great at readin' ef he is the best judge of a mine anywheres about."

Thus the station agent explained in low thrilling tones; and even the Indians watched and grunted their interest.

At eleven o'clock the horses arrived, four besides Shag's, and the rest of the outfit. The onlookers regarded Shag with the mournful interest due to the undertaker at a funeral. Shag felt it and acted accordingly. He gave short, gruff orders to his men; called attention to straps and buckles that every one knew were in as perfect order as they could be; criticized the horses and his men; and every one, even the horses, bore it with perfect composure. They were all showing off and felt the importance of the moment.

Presently the car door opened and Mr. Radcliffe came out on the platform accompanied by his son —a handsome reckless looking fellow-his daughter Hazel, and Mr. Hamar, a thick-set, heavy-featured man with dark hair, jaunty black moustache and handsome black eyes. In the background stood an erect elderly woman in tailor-made attire and with a severe expression, Mr. Radcliffe's elder sister who was taking the trip with them expecting to remain in California with her son; and behind her hovered Hazel's maid. These two were not to be of the riding party, it appeared.

There was a pleasant stir while the horses were brought forward and the riders were mounting. The spectators remained breathlessly unconscious of anything save the scene being enacted before them. Their eyes lingered with special interest on the girl of the party.

Miss Radcliffe was small and graceful, with a head set on her pretty shoulders like a flower on its stem. Moreover she was fair, so fair that she almost dazzled the eyes of the men and women accustomed to brown cheeks kissed by the sun and wind of the plain. There was a wild-rose pink in her cheeks to enhance the whiteness, which made it but the more dazzling. She had masses of golden hair wreathed round her dainty head in a bewilderment of waves and braids. She had great dark eyes of blue set off by long curling lashes, and delicately pencilled dark brows which gave the eyes a pansy softness and made you feel when she looked at you that she meant a great deal more by the look than you had at first suspected. They were wonderful, beautiful eyes, and the little company of idlers at the station were promptly bewitched by them. Moreover there was a fantastic little dimple in her right cheek that flashed into view at the same time with the gleam of pearly teeth when she smiled. She certainly was a picture. The station looked its fill and rejoiced in her young beauty.

She was garbed in a dark green riding habit, the same that she wore when she rode attended by her groom in Central Park. It made a sensation among the onlookers, as did the little riding cap of dark green velvet and the pretty riding gloves. She sat her pony well, daintily, as though she had alighted briefly, but to their eyes strangely, and not as the women out there rode. On the whole the station saw little else but the girl; all the others were mere accessories to the picture.

They noticed indeed that the young man, whose close cropped golden curls, and dark lashed blue eyes were so like the girl's that he could be none other than her brother, rode beside the older man who was presumably the father; and that the dark, handsome stranger rode away beside the girl. Not a man of them but resented it. Not a woman of them but regretted it.

Then Shag Bunce, with a parting word to his small but complete outfit that rode behind, put spurs to his horse, lifted his sombrero in homage to the lady, and shot to the front of the line, his shaggy mane by which came his name floating over his shoulders. Out into the sunshine of a perfect day the riders went, and the group around the platform stood silently and watched until they were a speck in the distance blurring with the sunny plain and occasional ash and cottonwood trees.

"I seen the missionary go by early this mornin'," speculated the station agent meditatively, deliberately, as though he only had a right to break the silence. "I wonder whar he could 'a' bin goin'. He passed on t'other side the track er I'd 'a' ast 'im. He 'peared in a turrible hurry. Anybody sick over towards the canyon way?"

"Buck's papoose heap sick!" muttered an immobile Indian, and shuffled off the platform with a stolid face. The women heaved a sigh of disappointment and turned to go. The show was out and they must return to the monotony of their lives. They wondered what it would be like to ride off like that into the sunshine with cheeks like roses and eyes that saw nothing but pleasure ahead. What would a life like that be? Awed, speculative, they went back to their sturdy children and their ill-kempt houses, to sit in the sun on the door-steps and muse a while.

Into the sunshine rode Hazel Radcliffe well content with the world, herself, and her escort.

Milton Hamar was good company. He was keen of wit and a past-master in the delicate art of flattery. That he was fabulously wealthy and popular in New York society; that he was her father's friend both socially and financially, and had been much of late in their home on account of some vast mining enterprise in which both were interested; and that his wife was said to be uncongenial and always interested in other men rather than her husband, were all facts that combined to give Hazel a pleasant, half-romantic interest in the man by her side. She had been conscious of a sense of satisfaction and pleasant anticipation when her father told her that he was to be of their party. His wit and gallantry would make up for the necessity of having her Aunt Maria along. Aunt Maria was always a damper to anything she came near. She was the personification of propriety. She had tried to make Hazel think she must remain in the car and rest that day instead of going off on a wild goose chase after a mine. No lady did such things, she told her niece.

Hazel's laugh rang out like the notes of a bird as the two rode slowly down the trail, not hurrying, for there was plenty of time. They could meet the others on their way back if they did not get to the mine so soon, and the morning was lovely.

Milton Hamar could appreciate the beauties of nature now and then. He called attention to the line of hills in the distance, and the sharp steep peak of a mountain piercing the sunlight. Then skillfully he led his speech around to his companion, and showed how lovelier than the morning she was.

He had been indulging in such delicate flattery since they first started from New York, whenever the indefatigable aunt left them alone long enough, but this morning there was a note of something closer and more intimate in his words; a warmth of tenderness that implied unspeakable joy in her beauty, such as he had never dared to use before. It flattered her pride deliciously. It was beautiful to be young and charming and have a man say such things with a look like that in his eyes-eyes that had suffered, and appealed to her to pity. With her young, innocent heart she did pity, and was glad she might solace his sadness a little while.

With consummate skill the man led her to talk of himself, his hopes in youth, his disappointments, his bitter sadness, his heart loneliness. He suddenly asked her to call him Milton, and the girl with rosy cheeks and dewy eyes declared shyly that she never could, it would seem so queer, but she finally compromised after much urging on "Cousin Milton."

"That will do for a while," he succumbed, smiling as he looked at her with impatient eyes. Then with growing intimacy in his tones he laid a detaining hand upon hers that held the bridle, and the horses both slackened their gait, though they had been far behind the rest of the party for over an hour now.

"Listen, little girl," he said, "I'm going to open my heart to you. I'm going to tell you a secret."

Hazel sat very still, half alarmed at his tone, not daring to withdraw her hand, for she felt the occasion was momentous and she must be ready with her sympathy as any true friend would be. Her heart swelled with pride that it was to her he came in his trouble. Then she looked up into the face that was bending over hers, and she saw triumph, not trouble, in his eyes. Even then she did not understand.

"What is it?" she asked trustingly.

"Dear child!" said the man of the world impressively, "I knew you would be interested. Well, I will tell you. I have told you of my sorrow, now I will tell you of my joy. It is this: When I return to New York I shall be a free man. Everything is complete at last. I have been granted a divorce from Ellen, and there remain only a few technicalities to be attended to. Then we shall be free to go our ways and do as we choose."

"A divorce!" gasped Hazel appalled. "Not you-divorced!"

"Yes," affirmed the happy man gaily, "I knew you'd be surprised. It's almost too good to be true, isn't it, after all my trouble to get Ellen to consent?"

"But she-your wife-where will she go? What will she do?" Hazel looked up at him with troubled eyes, half bewildered with the thought.

She did not realize that the horses had stopped and that he still held her hand which grasped the bridle.

"Oh, Ellen will be married at once," he answered flippantly. "That's the reason she's consented at last. She's going to marry Walling Stacy, you know, and from being stubborn about it, she's quite in a hurry to make any arrangement to fix things up now."

"She's going to be married!" gasped Hazel as if she had not heard of such things often. Somehow it had never come quite so close to her list of friendships before and it shocked her inexpressibly.

"Yes, she's going to be married at once, so you see there's no need to think of her ever again. But why don't you ask me what I am going to do?"

"Oh, yes!" said Hazel recalling her lack of sympathy at once. "You startled me so. What are you going to do? You poor man-what can you do? Oh, I am so sorry for you!" and the pansy-eyes became suffused with tears.

"No need to feel sorry for me, little one," said the exultant voice, and he looked at her now with an expression she had never seen in his face before. "I shall be happy as I have never dreamed of before," he said. "I am going to be married too. I am going to marry some one who loves me with all her heart, I am sure of that, though she has never told me so. I am going to marry you, little sweetheart!" He stooped suddenly before she could take in the meaning of his words, and flinging his free arm about her pressed his lips upon hers.

With a wild cry like some terrified creature Hazel tried to draw herself away, and finding herself held fast her quick anger rose and she lifted the hand which held the whip and blindly slashed the air about her; her eyes closed, her heart swelling with horror and fear. A great repulsion for the man whom hitherto she had regarded with deep respect surged over her. To get away from him at once was her greatest desire. She lashed out again with her whip, blindly, not seeing what she struck, almost beside herself with wrath and fear.

Hamar's horse reared and plunged, almost unseating his rider, and as he struggled to keep his seat, having necessarily released the girl from his embrace, the second cut of the whip took him stingingly across the eyes, causing him to cry out with the pain. The horse reared again and sent him sprawling upon the ground, his hands to his face, his senses one blank of pain for the moment.

Hazel, knowing only that she was free, followed an instinct of fear and struck her own pony on the flank, causing the little beast to turn sharply to right angles with the trail he had been following and dart like a streak across the level plateau. Thereafter the girl had all she could do to keep her seat.

She had been wont to enjoy a run in the Park with her groom at safe distance behind her. She was proud of her ability to ride, and could take fences as well as her young brother; but a run like this across an illimitable space, on a creature of speed like the wind, goaded by fear and knowing the limitations of his rider, was a different matter. The swift flight took her breath away, and unnerved her. She tried to hold on to the saddle with her shaking hands, for the bridle was already flying loose to the breeze, but her hold seemed so slight that each moment she expected to find herself lying huddled on the plain with the pony far in the distance.

Her lips grew white and cold; her breath came short and painfully; her eyes were strained with trying to look ahead at the constantly receding horizon. Was there no end? Would they never come to a human habitation? Would no one ever come to her rescue? How long could a pony stand a pace like this? And how long could she hope to hold on to the furious flying creature?

Off to the right at last she thought she saw a building. It seemed hours they had been flying through space. In a second they were close by it. It was a cabin, standing alone upon the great plain with sage-brush in patches about the door and a neat rail fence around it.

She could see one window at the end, and a tiny chimney at the back. Could it be that any one lived in such a forlorn spot?

Summoning all her strength as they neared the spot she flung her voice out in a wild appeal while the pony hurled on, but the wind caught the feeble effort and flung it away into the vast spaces like a little torn worthless fragment of sound.

Tears stung their way into her wide dry eyes. The last hairpin left its mooring and slipped down to earth. The loosened golden hair streamed back on the wind like hands of despair wildly clutching for help, and the jaunty green riding cap was snatched by the breeze and hung upon a sage-bush not fifty feet from the cabin gate, but the pony rushed on with the frightened girl still clinging to the saddle.

II. THE MAN

About noon of the same day the missionary halted his horse on the edge of a great flat-topped mesa and looked away to the clear blue mountains in the distance.

John Brownleigh had been in Arizona for nearly three years, yet the wonder of the desert had not ceased to charm him, and now as he stopped his horse to rest, his eyes sought the vast distances stretched in every direction, and revelled in the splendour of the scene.

Those mountains at which he was gazing were more than a hundred miles from him, and yet they stood out clear and distinct in the wonderful air, and seemed but a short journey away.

Below him were ledges of rock in marvellous colours, yellow and gray, crimson and green piled one upon another, with the strange light of the noonday sun playing over them and turning their colours into a blaze of glory. Beyond was a stretch of sand, broken here and there by sage-brush, greasewood, or cactus rearing its prickly spines grotesquely.

Off to the left were pink tinted cliffs and a little farther dark cone-like buttes. On the other hand low brown and white hills stretched away to the wonderful petrified forest, where great tracts of fallen tree trunks and chips lay locked in glistening stone.

To the south he could see the familiar water-hole, and farther the entrance to the canyon, fringed with cedars and pines. The grandeur of the scene impressed him anew.

"Beautiful, beautiful!" he murmured, "and a grand God to have it so!" Then a shadow of sadness passed over his face, and he spoke again aloud as had come to be his habit in this vast loneliness.

"I guess it is worth it," he said, "worth all the lonely days and discouraging months and disappointments, just to be alone with a wonderful Father like mine!"

He had just come from a three days' trip in company with another missionary whose station was a two days' journey by horseback from his own, and whose cheery little home was presided over by a sweet-faced woman, come recently from the East to share his fortunes. The delicious dinner prepared for her husband and his guests, the air of comfort in the three-roomed shack, the dainty touches that showed a woman's hand, had filled Brownleigh with a noble envy. Not until this visit had he realized how very much alone his life was.

He was busy of course from morning till night, and his enthusiasm for his work was even greater than when nearly three years before he had been sent out by the Board to minister to the needs of the Indians. Friends he had by the score. Wherever a white man or trader lived in the region he was always welcome; and the Indians knew and loved his coming. He had come around this way now to visit an Indian hogan where the shadow of death was hovering over a little Indian maiden beloved of her father. It had been a long way around and the missionary was weary with many days in the saddle, but he was glad he had come. The little maid had smiled to see him, and felt that the dark valley of death seemed more to her now like one of her own flower-lit canyons that led out to a brighter, wider day, since she had heard the message of life he brought her.

But as he looked afar over the long way he had come, and thought of the bright little home where he had dined the day before, the sadness still lingered in his face.

"It would be good to have somebody like that," he said, aloud again, "somebody to expect me, and be glad,—but then"—thoughtfully—"I suppose there are not many girls who are willing to give up their homes and go out to rough it as she has done. It is a hard life for a woman-for that kind of a woman!" A pause, then, "And I wouldn't want any other kind!"

His eyes grew large with wistfulness. It was not often thus that the cheery missionary stopped to think upon his own lot in life. His heart was in his work, and he could turn his hand to anything. There was always plenty to be done. Yet to-day for some inexplicable reason, for the first time since he had really got into the work and outgrown his first homesickness, he was hungry for companionship. He had seen a light in the eyes of his fellow-missionary that spoke eloquently of the comfort and joy he himself had missed and it struck deep into his heart.

He had stopped here on this mesa, with the vast panorama of the desert spread before him, to have it out with himself.

The horse breathed restfully, drooping his head and closing his eyes to make the most of the brief respite, and the man sat thinking, trying to fill his soul with the beauty of the scene and crowd out the longings that had pressed upon him. Suddenly he raised his head with a quiet upward motion and said reverently:

"Oh, my Christ, you knew what this loneliness was! You were lonely too! It is the way you went, and I will walk with you! That will be good."

He sat for a moment with uplifted face towards the vast sky, his fine strong features touched with a tender light, their sadness changing into peace. Then with the old cheery brightness coming into his face again he returned to the earth and its duties.

"Billy, it's time we were getting on," he remarked to his horse chummily. "Do you see that sun in the heavens? It'll get there before we do if we don't look out, and we're due at the fort to-night if we can possibly make it. We had too much vacation, that's about the size of it, and we're spoiled! We're lazy, Billy! We'll have to get down to work. Now how about it? Can we get to that water-hole in half an hour? Let's try for it, old fellow, and then we'll have a good drink, and a bite to eat, and maybe ten minutes for a nap before we take the short trail home. There's some of the corn chop left for you, Billy, so hustle up, old boy, and get there."

Billy, with an answering snort, responded to his master's words, and carefully picked his way over boulders and rocks down to the valley below.

But within a half mile of the water-hole the young man suddenly halted his horse and sprang from the saddle, stooping in the sand beside a tall yucca to pick up something that gleamed like fire in the sunlight. In all that brilliant glowing landscape a bit of brightness had caught his eye and insistently flung itself upon his notice as worthy of investigation. There was something about the sharp light it flung that spoke of another world than the desert. John Brownleigh could not pass it by. It might be only a bit of broken glass from an empty flask flung carelessly aside, but it did not look like that. He must see.

Wondering he stooped and picked it up, a bit of bright gold on the handle of a handsome riding whip. It was not such a whip as people in this region carried; it was dainty, costly, elegant, a lady's riding whip! It spoke of a world of wealth and attention to expensive details, as far removed from this scene as possible. Brownleigh stood still in wonder and turned the pretty trinket over in his hand. Now how did that whip come to be lying in a bunch of sage-brush on the desert? Jewelled, too, and that must have given the final keen point of light to the flame which made him stop short in the sand to pick it up. It was a single clear stone of transparent yellow, a topaz likely, he thought, but wonderfully alive with light, set in the end of the handle, and looking closely he saw a handsome monogram engraved on the side, and made out the letters H. R. But that told him nothing.

With knit brows he pondered, one foot in the stirrup, the other still upon the desert, looking at the elegant toy. Now who, *who* would be so foolish as to bring a thing like that into the desert? There were no lady riders anywhere about that he knew, save the major's sister at the military station, and she was most plain in all her appointments. This frivolous implement of horsemanship never belonged to the major's sister. Tourists seldom came this way. What did it mean?

He sprang into the saddle and shading his eyes with his hand scanned the plain, but only the warm shimmer of sun-heated earth appeared. Nothing living could be seen. What ought he to do about it? Was there any way he might find out the owner and restore the lost property?

Pondering thus, his eyes divided between the distance and the glittering whip-handle, they came to the water-hole; and Brownleigh dismounted, his thoughts still upon the little whip.

"It's very strange, Billy. I can't make out a theory that suits me," he mused aloud. "If any one has been riding out this way and lost it, will they perhaps return and look for it? Yet if I leave it where I found it the sand might drift over it at any time. And surely, in this sparsely settled country, I shall be able to at least hear of any strangers who might have carried such a foolish little thing. Then, too, if I leave it where I found it some one might steal it. Well, I guess we'll take it with us, Billy; we'll hear of the owner somewhere some time no doubt."

The horse answered with a snort of satisfaction as he lifted his moist muzzle from the edge of the water and looked contentedly about.

The missionary unstrapped his saddle and flung it on the ground, unfastening the bag of "corn chop" and spreading it conveniently before his dumb companion. Then he set about gathering a few sticks from near at hand and started a little blaze. In a few minutes the water was bubbling cheerfully in his little folding tin cup for a cup of tea, and a bit of bacon was frying in a diminutive skillet beside it. Corn bread and tea and sugar came from the capacious pockets of the saddle. Billy and his missionary made a good meal beneath the wide bright quiet of the sky.

When the corn chop was finished Billy let his long lashes droop lower and lower, and his nose go down and down until it almost touched the ground, dreaming of more corn chop, and happy in having his wants supplied. But his master, stretched at full length upon the ground with hat drawn over his eyes, could not lose himself in sleep for a second. His thoughts were upon the jewelled whip, and by and by he reached his hand out for it, and shoving back his hat lay watching the glinting of lights within the precious heart of the topaz, as the sun caught and tangled its beams in the sharp facets of the cutting. He puzzled his mind to know how the whip came to be in the desert, and what was meant by it. One reads life by details in that wide and lonely land. This whip might mean something. But what?

At last he dropped his hand and sitting up with his upward glance he said aloud:

"Father, if there's any reason why I ought to look for the owner, guide me."

He spoke as if the One he addressed were always present in his consciousness, and they were on terms of the closest intimacy.

He sprang up then and began putting the things together, as if the burden of the responsibility were upon One fully able to bear it.

They were soon on their way again, Billy swinging along with the full realization of the nearness of home.

The way now led towards hazy blue lines of mesas with crags and ridges here and there. Across the valley, looking like a cloud-shadow, miles distant lay a long black streak, the line of the gorge of the canyon. Its dim presence seemed to grow on the missionary's thought as he drew nearer. He had not been to that canyon for more than a month. There were a few scattered Indians living with their families here and there in corners where there was a little soil. The thought of them drew him now. He must make out to go to them soon. If it were not that Billy had been so far he would go up there this afternoon. But the horse needed rest if the man did not, and there was of course no real hurry about the matter. He would go perhaps in the morning. Meantime it would be good to get to his own fireside once more and attend to a few letters that should be written. He was invited to the fort that night for dinner. There was to be some kind of a frolic, some visitors from the East. He had said he would come if he reached home in time. He probably would, but the idea was not attractive just now. He would rather rest and read and go to sleep early. But then, of course he would go. Such opportunities were none too frequent in this lonely land, though in his present mood the gay doings at the fort did not appeal to him strongly; besides it meant a ride of ten miles further. However, of course he would go. He fell to musing over the whip again, and in due time he arrived at his own home, a little one-roomed shanty with a chimney at the back and four big windows. At the extreme end of the fenced enclosure about the structure was a little shed for Billy, and all about was the vast plain dotted with bushes and weeds, with its panorama of mountain and hill, valley and gorge. It was beautiful, but it was desolate. There were neighbours, a few, but they lived at magnificent distances.

"We ought to have a dog, Billy! Why don't we get a dog to welcome us home?" said Brownleigh, slapping the horse's neck affectionately as he sprang from the saddle; "but then a dog would go along with us, wouldn't he, so there'd be three of us to come home instead of two, and that wouldn't do any good. Chickens? How would that do? But the coyotes would steal them. I guess we'll have to get along with each other, old fellow."

The horse, relieved of his saddle, gave a shake of comfort as a man might stretch himself after a weary journey, and trotted into his shed. Brownleigh made him comfortable and turned to go to the house.

As he walked along by the fence he caught sight of a small dark object hanging on a sage-bush a short distance from the front of his house. It seemed to move slightly, and he stopped and watched it a second thinking it might be some animal caught in the bush, or in hiding. It seemed to stir again as objects watched intently often will, and springing over the rail fence Brownleigh went to investigate. Nothing in that country was left to uncertainty. Men liked to know what was about them.

As he neared the bush, however, the object took on a tangible form and colour, and coming closer he picked it up and turned it over clumsily in his hand. A little velvet riding cap, undoubtedly a lady's, with the name of a famous New York costumer wrought in silk letters in the lining. Yes, there was no question about its being a lady's cap, for a long gleaming golden hair, with an undoubted tendency to curl, still clung to the velvet. A sudden embarrassment filled him, as though he had been handling too intimately another's property unawares. He raised his eyes and shaded them with his hand to look across the landscape, if perchance the owner might be at hand, though even as he did so he felt a conviction that the little velvet cap belonged to the owner of the whip which he still held in his other hand. H. R. Where was H. R., and who could she be?

For some minutes he stood thinking it out, locating the exact spot in his memory where he had found the whip. It had not been on any regular trail. That was strange. He stooped to see if there were any further evidences of passers-by, but the slight breeze had softly covered all definite marks. He was satisfied, however, after examining the ground about for some distance either way, that there could have been but one horse. He was wise in the lore of the trail. By certain little things that he saw or did not see he came to this conclusion.

Just as he was turning to go back to his cabin he came to a halt again with an exclamation of wonder, for there close at his feet, half hidden under a bit of sage, lay a small shell comb. He stooped and picked it up in triumph.

"I declare, I have quite a collection," he said aloud. "Are there any more? By these tokens I may be able to find her after all." And he started with a definite purpose and searched the ground for several rods ahead, then going back and taking a slightly different direction, he searched again and yet again, looking back each time to get his bearings from the direction where he had found the whip, arguing that the horse must likely have taken a pretty straight line and gone at a rapid pace.

He was rewarded at last by finding two shell hairpins, and near them a single hoof print, that, sheltered by a heavy growth of sage, had escaped the obliteration of the wind. This he knelt and studied carefully, taking in all the details of size and shape and direction; then, finding no more hairpins or combs, he carefully put his booty into his pocket and hurried back to the cabin, his brow knit in deep thought.

"Father, is this Thy leading?" He paused at the door and looked up. He opened the door and stepped within. The restfulness of the place called to him to stay.

There was the wide fireplace with a fire laid all ready for the touch of a match that would bring the pleasant blaze to dispel the loneliness of the place. There was the easy chair, his one luxury, with its leather cushions and reclining back; his slippers on the floor close by; the little table with its well-trimmed student lamp, his college paper and the one magazine that kept him in touch with the world freshly arrived before he left for his recent trip, and still unopened. How they called to him! Yet when he laid the whip upon the magazine the slanting ray of sun that entered by the door caught the glory of the topaz and sent it scintillating, and somehow the magazine lost its power to hold him.

One by one he laid his trophies down beside the whip; the velvet cap, the hairpins and the little comb, and then stood back startled with the wonder of it and looked about his bachelor quarters.

It was a pleasant spot, far lovelier than its weather-stained exterior would lead one to suppose. A Navajo blanket hung upon one wall above the bed, and another enwrapped and completely covered the bed itself, making a spot of colour in the room, and giving an air of luxury. Two quaint rugs of Indian workmanship upon the floor, one in front of the bed, the other before the fireplace where one's feet would rest when sitting in the big chair, did much to hide the discrepancies of the ugly floor. A rough set of shelves at the side of the fireplace handy to reach from the easy chair were filled with treasures of great minds, the books he loved well, all he could afford to bring with him, a few commentaries, not many, an encyclopedia, a little biography, a few classics, botany, biology, astronomy and a much worn Bible. On the wall above was a large card catalogue of Indian words; and around the room were some of his own pencil drawings of plants and animals.

Over in the opposite end of the room from the bed was a table covered with white oilcloth; and on the wall behind, the cupboard which held his dishes, and his stock of provisions. It was a pleasant spot and well ordered, for he never liked to leave his quarters in disarray lest some one might enter during his absence, or come back with him. Besides, it was pleasanter so to return to it. A rough closet of goodly proportions held his clothes, his trunk, and any other stores.

He stood and looked about it now and then let his eyes travel back to those small feminine articles on the little table beside him. It gave him a strange sensation. What if they belonged there? What if the owner of them lived there, was coming in in a minute now to meet him? How would it seem? What would she be like? For just an instant he let himself dream, and reaching out touched the velvet of the cap, then took it in his hand and smoothed its silken surface. A faint perfume of another world seemed to steal from its texture, and to linger on his hands. He drew a breath of wonder and laid it down; then with a start he came to himself. Suppose she did belong, and were out somewhere and he did not know where? Suppose something had happened to her-the horse run away, thrown her somewhere perhaps, —or she might have strayed away from a camp and lost her way-or been frightened?

These might be all foolish fantasies of a weary brain, but the man knew he could not rest until he had at least made an attempt to find out. He sank down in the big chair for a moment to think it out and closed his eyes, making swift plans.

Billy must have a chance to rest a little; a fagged horse could not accomplish much if the journey were far and the need for haste. He could not go for an hour yet. And there would be preparations to make. He must repack the saddle-bags with feed for Billy, food for himself and a possible stranger, restoratives, and a simple remedy or two in case of accident. These were articles he always took with him on long journeys. He considered taking his camping tent but that would mean the wagon, and they could not go so rapidly with that. He must not load Billy heavily, after the miles he had already come. But he could take a bit of canvas strapped to the saddle, and a small blanket. Of course it might be but a wild goose chase after all-yet he could not let his impression go unheeded.

Then there was the fort. In case he found the lady and restored her property in time he might be able to reach the fort by evening. He must take that into consideration also.

With alacrity he arose and went about his preparations, soon having his small baggage in array. His own toilet came next. A bath and fresh clothing; then, clean shaven and ready, all but his coat, he flung himself upon his bed for ten minutes of absolute relaxation, after which he felt himself quite fit for the expedition. Springing up he put on coat and hat, gathered up with reverent touch the bits of things he had found, locked his cabin and went out to Billy, a lump of sugar in his hand.

"Billy, old fellow, we're under orders to march again," he said apologetically, and Billy answered with a neigh of pleasure, submitting to the saddle as though he were quite ready for anything required of him.

"Now, Father," said the missionary with his upward look, "show us the way."

So, taking the direction from the hoof print in the sand, Billy and his master sped away once more into the westering light of the desert towards the long black shadowed entrance of the canyon.

III. THE DESERT

Hazel, as she was borne along, her lovely hair streaming in the wind and lashing her across the face and eyes now and again, breath coming painfully, eyes smarting, fingers aching in the vise-like hold she was compelled to keep upon the saddle, began to wonder just how long she could hold out. It seemed to her it was a matter of minutes only when she must let go and be whirled into space while the tempestuous steed sped on and left her.

Nothing like this motion had ever come into her experience before. She had been run away with once, but that was like a cradle to this tornado of motion. She had been frightened before, but never like this. The blood pounded in her head and eyes until it seemed it would burst forth, and now and again the surging of it through her ears gave the sensation of drowning, yet on and on she went. It was horrible to have no bridle, and nothing to say about where she should go, no chance to control her horse. It was like being on an express train with the engineer dead in his cab and no way to get to the brakes. They must stop some time and what then? Death seemed inevitable, and yet as the mad rush continued she almost wished it might come and end the horror of this ride.

It seemed hours before she began to realize that the horse was no longer going at quite such a breakneck speed, or else she was growing accustomed to the motion and getting her breath, she could not quite be sure which. But little by little she perceived that the mad flying had settled into a long lope. The pony evidently had no intention of stopping and it was plain that he had some distinct place in mind to which he was going as straight and determinedly as any human being ever laid out a course and forged ahead in it. There was that about his whole beastly contour that showed it was perfectly useless to try to deter him from it or to turn him aside.

When her breath came less painfully, Hazel made a fitful little attempt to drop a quiet word of reason into his ear.

"Nice pony, nice, good pony——!" she soothed, but the wind caught her voice and flung it aside as it had flung her cap a few moments before, and the pony only laid his ears back and fled stolidly on.

She gathered her forces again.

"Nice pony! Whoa, sir!" she cried, a little louder than the last time and trying to make her voice sound firm and commanding.

But the pony had no intention of "whoa-ing," and though she repeated the command many times, her voice growing each time more firm and normal, he only showed the whites of his eyes at her and continued doggedly on his way.

She saw it was useless; and the tears, usually with her under fine control, came streaming down her white cheeks.

"Pony, good horse, *dear* pony, won't you stop!" she cried and her words ended with a sob. But still the pony kept on.

The desert fled about her yet seemed to grow no shorter ahead, and the dark line of cloud mystery, with the towering mountains beyond, were no nearer than when she first started. It seemed much like riding on a rocking-horse, one never got anywhere, only no rocking-horse flew at such a speed.

Yet she realized now that the pace was much modified from what it had been at first, and the pony's motion was not hard. If she had not been so stiff and sore in every joint and muscle with the terrible tension she had kept up the riding would not have been at all bad. But she was conscious of most terrible weariness, a longing to drop down on the sand of the desert and rest, not caring whether she ever went on again or not. She had never felt such terrible weariness in her life.

She could hold on now with one hand, and relax the muscles of the other a little. She tried with one hand presently to do something with that sweeping pennant of hair that lashed her in the face so unexpectedly now and then, but could only succeed in twisting it about her neck and tucking the ends into the neck of her riding habit; and from this frail binding it soon slipped free again.

She was conscious of the heat of the sun on her bare head, the smarting of her eyes. The pain in her chest was subsiding, and she could breathe freely again, but her heart felt tired, so tired, and she wanted to lie down and cry. Would she never get anywhere and be helped?

How soon would her father and brother miss her and come after her? When she dared she looked timidly behind, and then again more lingeringly, but there was nothing to be seen but the same awful stretch of distance with mountains of bright colour in the boundaries everywhere; not a living thing but herself and the pony to be seen. It was awful. Somewhere between herself and the mountains behind was the place she had started from, but the bright sun shone steadily, hotly down and shimmered back again from the bright earth, and nothing broke the awful repose of the lonely space. It was as if she had suddenly been caught up and flung out into a world where was no other living being.

Why did they not come after her? Surely, surely, pretty soon she would see them coming. They would spur their horses on when they found she had been run away with. Her father and brother would not leave her long in this horrible plight.

Then it occurred to her that her father and brother had been for some time out of sight ahead before she began her race. They would not know she was gone, at once; but of course Mr. Hamar would do something. He would not leave her helpless. The habit of years of trusting him assured her of that. For the instant she had forgotten the cause of her flight. Then suddenly she remembered it with sickening thought. He who had been to her a brave fine hero, suffering daily through the carelessness of a wife who did not understand him, had stepped down from his pedestal and become the lowest of the low. He had dared to kiss her! He had said he would marry her-he,—a married man! Her whole soul revolted against him again, and now she was glad she had run away-glad the horse had taken her so far-glad she had shown him how terrible the whole thing looked to her. She was even glad that her father and brother were far away too, for the present, until she should adjust herself to life once more. How could she have faced them after what happened? How could she ever live in the same world with that man again,—that fallen hero? How could she ever have thought so much of him? She had almost worshipped him, and had been so pleased when he had seemed to enjoy her company, and complimented her by telling her she had whiled away a weary hour for him! And he? He had been meaning—*this*—all the time! He had looked at her with that thought in his mind! Oh-awful degradation!

There was something so revolting in the memory of his voice and face as he had told her that she closed her eyes and shuddered as she recalled it, and once more the tears went coursing down her cheeks and she sobbed aloud, piteously, her head bowing lower and lower over the pony's neck, her bright hair falling down about her shoulders and beating against the animal's breast and knees as he ran, her stiffened fingers clutching his mane to keep her balance, her whole weary little form drooping over his neck in a growing exhaustion, her entire being swept by alternate waves of anger, revulsion and fear.

Perhaps all this had its effect on the beast; perhaps somewhere in his make-up there lay a spot, call it instinct or what you please, that vibrated in response to the distress of the human creature he carried. Perhaps the fact that she was in trouble drew his sympathy, wicked little willful imp though he usually was. Certain it is that he began to slacken his pace decidedly, until at last he was walking, and finally stopped short and turned his head about with a troubled neigh as if to ask her what was the matter.

The sudden cessation of the motion almost threw her from her seat; and with new fear gripping her heart she clutched the pony's mane the tighter and looked about her trembling. She was conscious more than anything else of the vast spaces about her in every direction, of the loneliness of the spot, and her own desolate condition. She had wanted the horse to stop and let her get down to solid ground, and now that he had done so and she might dismount a great horror filled her and she dared not. But with the lessening of the need for keeping up the tense strain of nerve and muscle, she suddenly began to feel that she could not sit up any longer, that she must lie down, let go this awful strain, stop this uncontrollable trembling which was quivering all over her body.

The pony, too, seemed wondering, impatient that she did not dismount at once. He turned his nose towards her again with a questioning snuff and snort, and showed the wicked whites of his eyes in wild perplexity. Then a panic seized her. What if he should start to run again? She would surely be thrown this time, for her strength was almost gone. She must get down and in some way gain possession of the bridle. With the bridle she might perhaps hope to guide his movements, and make further wild riding impossible.

Slowly, painfully, guardedly, she took her foot from the stirrup and slipped to the ground. Her cramped feet refused to hold her weight for the moment and she tottered and went into a little heap on the ground. The pony, feeling his duty for the present done, sidled away from her and began cropping the grass hungrily.

The girl sank down wearily at full length upon the ground and for a moment it seemed to her she could never rise again. She was too weary to lift her hand or to move the foot that was twisted under her into a more comfortable position, too weary to even think. Then suddenly the sound of the animal moving steadily away from her roused her to the necessity of securing him. If he should get away in this wide desolation she would be helpless indeed.

She gathered her flagging energy and got painfully upon her feet. The horse was nearly a rod away, and moving slowly, steadily, as he ate, with now and then a restless lifting of his head to look off into the distance and take a few determined steps before he stopped for another bite. That horse had something on his mind and was going straight towards it. She felt that he cared little what became of her. She must look out for herself. This was something she had never had to do before; but the instinct came with the need.

Slowly, tremblingly, feeling her weakness, she stole towards him, a bunch of grass in her hand she had plucked as she came, holding it obviously as she had fed a lump of sugar or an apple to her finely groomed mare in New York. But the grass she held was like all the grass about him, and the pony had not been raised a pet. He tossed his nose energetically and scornfully as she drew near and hastened on a pace or two.

Cautiously she came on again talking to him gently, pleadingly, complimentarily: "Nice good horsey! Pretty pony so he was!" But he only edged away again.

And so they went on for some little way until Hazel almost despaired of catching him at all, and was becoming more and more aware of the vastness of the universe about her, and the smallness of her own being.

At last, however, her fingers touched the bridle, she felt the pony's quick jerk, strained every muscle to hold on, and found she had conquered. He was in her hands. For how long was a question, for he was strong enough to walk away and drag her by the bridle perhaps, and she knew little about tricks of management. Moreover her muscles were so flabby and sore with the long ride that she was ill-fitted to cope with the wise and wicked little beast. She dreaded to get upon his back again, and doubted if she could if she tried, but it seemed the only way to get anywhere, or to keep company with the pony, for she could not hope to detain him by mere physical force if he decided otherwise.

She stood beside him for a moment, looking about her over the wide distance. Everything looked alike, and different from anything she had ever seen before. She must certainly get on that pony's back, for her fear of the desert became constantly greater. It was almost as if it would snatch her away in a moment more if she stayed there longer, and carry her into vaster realms of space where her soul would be lost in infinitude. She had never been possessed by any such feeling before and it frightened her unreasoningly.

Turning to the pony, she measured the space from the ground to the queer saddle and wondered how people mounted such things without a groom. When she had mounted that morning it had been Milton Hamar's strong arm that swung her into the saddle, and his hand that held her foot for the instant of her spring. The memory of it now sent a shudder of dislike over her whole body. If she had known, he never should have touched her! The blood mounted uncomfortably into her tired face, and made her conscious of the heat of the day, and of a burning thirst. She must go on and get to some water somewhere. She could not stand this much longer.

Carefully securing the bridle over her arm she reached up and took hold of the saddle, doubtfully at first, and then desperately; tried to reach the stirrup with one foot, failed and tried again; and then wildly struggling, jumping, kicking, she vainly sought to climb back to the saddle. But the pony was not accustomed to such a demonstration at mounting and he strongly objected. Tossing his head he reared and dashed off, almost throwing the girl to the ground and frightening her terribly.

Nevertheless the desperation of her situation gave her strength for a fresh trial, and she struggled up again, and almost gained her seat, when the pony began a series of circles which threw her down and made her dizzy with trying to keep up with him.

Thus they played the desperate game for half an hour more. Twice the girl lost the bridle and had to get it again by stealthy wiles, and once she was almost on the point of giving up, so utterly exhausted was she.

But the pony was thirsty too, and he must have decided that the quickest way to water would be to let her mount; for finally with lifted head he stood stock still and let her struggle up his side; and at last, well-nigh falling from sheer weariness, she sat astonished that she had accomplished it. She was on his back, and she would never dare to get down again, she thought, until she got somewhere to safety. But now the animal, his courage renewed by the bite he had taken, started snorting off at a rapid pace once more, very nearly upsetting his rider at the start, and almost losing her the bridle once more. She sat trembling, and gripping bridle and saddle for some time, having enough to do to keep her seat without trying to direct her bearer, and then she saw before her a sudden descent, steep but not very long, and at its bottom a great puddle of dirty water. The pony paused only an instant on the brink and then began the descent. The girl cried out with fear, but managed to keep her seat, and the impatient animal was soon ankle deep in the water drinking long and blissfully.

Hazel sat looking in dismay about her. The water-hole seemed to be entirely surrounded by steep banks like that they had descended, and there was no way out except to return. Could the horse climb up with her on his back? And could she keep her seat? She grew cold with fear at the thought, for all her riding experience had been on the level, and she had become more and more conscious of her flagging strength.

Besides, the growing thirst was becoming awful. Oh, for just one drop of that water that the pony was enjoying! Black and dirty as it was she felt she could drink it. But it was out of her reach and she dared not get down. Suddenly a thought came to her. She would wet her handkerchief and moisten her lips with that. If she stooped over quite carefully she might be able to let it down far enough to touch the water.

She pulled the small bit of linen from the tiny pocket of her habit and the pony, as if to help her, waded into the water farther until her skirt almost touched it. Now she found that by putting her arm about the pony's neck she could dip most of her handkerchief in the water, and dirty as it was it was most refreshing to bathe her face and hands and wrists and moisten her lips.

But the pony when he had his fill had no mind to tarry, and with a splash, a plunge and a wallow that gave the girl an unexpected shower bath, he picked his way out of the hole and up the rocky side of the descent, while she clung frightened to the saddle and wondered if she could possibly hang on until they were up on the mesa again. The dainty handkerchief dropped in the flight floated pitifully on the muddy water, another bit of comfort left behind.

But when they were up and away again, what with the fright, and the fact that they had come out of the hole on the opposite side from that which they had entered it, the girl had lost all sense of direction, and everywhere stretched away one vast emptiness edged with mountains that stood out clear, cold and unfriendly.

The whole atmosphere of the earth seemed to have changed while they were down at the drinking hole, for now the shadows were long and had almost a menacing attitude as they crept along or leaped sideways after the travellers. Hazel noticed with a startled glance at the sky that the sun was low and would soon be down. And that of course where the sun hung like a great burning opal must be the west, but that told her nothing, for the sun had been high in the heavens when they had started, and she had taken no note of direction. East, west, north or south were all one to her in her happy care-free life that she had hitherto led. She tried to puzzle it out and remember which way they had turned from the railroad but grew more bewildered, and the brilliant display in the west flamed alarmingly as she realized that night was coming on and she was lost on a great desert with only a wild tired little pony for company, hungry and thirsty and weary beyond anything she had ever dreamed before.

They had been going down into a broad valley for some little time, which made the night seem even nearer. Hazel would have turned her horse back and tried to retrace her steps, but that he would not, for try as she might, and turn him as she would he circled about and soon was in the same course again, so that now the tired hands could only hold the reins stiffly and submit to be carried where the pony willed. It was quite evident he had a destination in view, and knew the way thereto. Hazel had read of the instinct of animals. She began to hope that he would presently bring her to a human habitation where she would find help to get to her father once more.

But suddenly even the glory of the dying sun was lost as the horse entered the dimness of the canyon opening, whose high walls of red stone, rising solemnly on either hand, were serrated here and there with long transverse lines of grasses and tree-ferns growing in the crevices, and higher up appeared the black openings of caves mysterious and fearsome in the twilight gloom. The way ahead loomed darkly. Somewhere from out the memories of her childhood came a phrase from the church-service to which she had never given conscious attention, but which flashed vividly to mind now: "Though I walk through the valley of the shadow-the Valley of the Shadow!" Surely this must be it. She wished she could remember the rest of it. What could it have meant? She shivered visibly, and looked about her with wild eyes.

The cottonwoods and oaks grew thickly at the base of the cliffs, almost concealing them sometimes, and above the walls rose dark and towering. The way was rough and slippery, filled with great boulders and rocks, around which the pony picked his way without regard to the branches of trees that swept her face and caught in her long hair as they went by.

Vainly she strove to guide him back, but he turned only to whirl again, determinedly. Somewhere in the deep gloom ahead he had a destination and no mere girl was to deter him from reaching it as soon as possible. It was plain to his horse-mind that his rider did not know what she wanted, and he did, so there were no two ways about it. He intended to go back to his old master as straight and as fast as he could get there. This canyon was the shortest cut and through this canyon he meant to walk whether she liked it or not.

Further and further into the gloom they penetrated, and the girl, frenzied with fear, cried out with the wild hope that some one might be near and come to her rescue. But the gloomy aisle of the canyon caught up her voice and echoed it far and high, until it came back to her in a volume of sepulchral sound that filled her with a nameless dread and made her fear to open her lips again. It was as if she had by her cry awakened the evil spirit who inhabited the canyon and set it searching for the intruder. "Help! Help!" How the words rolled and returned upon her trembling senses until she quaked and quivered with their echoes!

On went the pony into the deepening shadows, and each moment the darkness shut down more impenetrably, until the girl could only close her eyes, lower her head as much as possible to escape the branches-and pray.

Then suddenly, from above where the distant sky gave a line of light and a single star had appeared to pierce the dusk like a great jewel on a lady's gown, there arose a sound; bloodcurdling and hideous, high, hollow, far-echoing, chilling her soul with horror and causing her heart to stand still with fear. She had heard it once before, a night or two ago, when their train had stopped in a wide desert for water or repairs or something and the porter of the car had told her it was coyotes. It had been distant then, and weird and interesting to think of being so near real live wild animals. She had peered from the safety of her berth behind the silken curtains and fancied she saw shadowy forms steal over the plain under the moonlight. But it was a very different thing to hear the sound now, out alone among their haunts, with no weapon and none to protect her. The awfulness of her situation almost took away her senses.

Still she held to the saddle, weak and trembling, expecting every minute to be her last; and the horrid howling of the coyotes continued.

Down below the trail somewhere she could hear the soft trickling of water with maddening distinctness now and then. Oh, if she could but quench this terrible thirst! The pony was somewhat refreshed with his grass and his drink of water, but the girl, whose life up to this day had never known a want unsatisfied, was faint with hunger and burning with thirst, and this unaccustomed demand upon her strength was fast bringing it to its limit.

The darkness in the canyon grew deeper, and more stars clustered out overhead; but far, so very far away! The coyotes seemed just a shadow removed all about and above. Her senses were swimming. She could not be sure just where they were. The horse slipped and stumbled on in the darkness, and she forgot to try to turn him from his purpose.

By and by she grew conscious that the way was leading upward again. They were scrambling over rough places, large rocks in the way, trees growing close to the trail, and the pony seemed not to be able to avoid them, or perhaps he didn't care. The howling of the coyotes was growing clearer every minute but somehow her fear of them was deadened, as her fear of all else. She was lying low upon the pony, clinging to his neck, too faint to cry out, too weak to stop the tears that slowly wet his mane. Then suddenly she was caught in the embrace of a low hanging branch, her hair tangled about its roughness. The pony struggled to gain his uncertain footing, the branch held her fast and the pony scrambled on, leaving his helpless rider behind him in a little huddled heap upon the rocky trail, swept from the saddle by the tough old branch.

The pony stopped a moment upon a bit of shelving rock he had with difficulty gained, and looked back with a troubled snort, but the huddled heap in the darkness below him gave forth no sign of life, and after another snort and a half neigh of warning the pony turned and scrambled on, up and up till he gained the mesa above.

The late moon rose and hunted its way through the canyon till it found the gold of her hair spread about on the rocky way, and touched her sweet unconscious face with the light of cold beauty; the coyotes howled on in solemn chorus, and still the little figure lay quiet and unconscious of her situation.

IV. THE QUEST

John Brownleigh reached the water-hole at sunset, and while he waited for his horse to drink he meditated on what he would do next. If he intended to go to the fort for dinner he should turn at once sharply to the right and ride hard, unless he was willing to be late. The lady at the fort liked to have her guests on hand promptly, he knew.

The sun was down. It had left long splashes of crimson and gold in the west, and their reflection was shimmering over the muddy water below him so that Billy looked as if he quaffed the richest wine from a golden cup, as he satisfied his thirst contentedly.

But as the missionary watched the painted water and tried to decide his course, suddenly his eye caught a bit of white something floating, half clinging to a twig at the edge of the water, a bit of thin transparentness, with delicate lacy edge. It startled him in that desert place much as the jewel in its golden setting in the sand had startled him that morning.

With an exclamation of surprise he stooped over, picked up the little wet handkerchief and held it out-dainty, white and fine, and in spite of its wet condition sending forth its violet breath to the senses of a man who had been in the wilds of the desert for three years. It spoke of refinement and culture and a world he had left behind him in the East.

There was a tiny letter embroidered in the corner, but already the light was growing too dim to read it, and though he held it up and looked through it and felt the embroidery with his finger-tip he could not be sure that it was either of the letters that had been engraved on the whip.

Nevertheless, the little white messenger determined his course. He searched the edge of the water-hole for hoof prints as well as the dying light would reveal, then mounted Billy with decision at once and took up his quest where he had almost abandoned it. He was convinced that a lady was out alone in the desert somewhere.

It was long past midnight when Billy and the missionary came upon the pony, high on the mesa, grazing. The animal had evidently felt the need for food and rest before proceeding further, and was perhaps a little uneasy about that huddled form in the darkness he had left.

Billy and the pony were soon hobbled and left to feed together while the missionary, all thought of his own need of rest forgotten, began a systematic search for the missing rider. He first carefully examined the pony and saddle. The saddle somehow reminded him of Shag Bunce, but the pony was a stranger to him; neither could he make out the letter of the brand in the pale moonlight. However, it might be a new animal, just purchased and not yet branded-or there might be a thousand explanations. The thought of Shag Bunce reminded him of the handsome private car he had seen upon the track that morning. But even if a party had gone out to ride how would one of them get separated? Surely no lady would venture over the desert alone, not a stranger at any rate.

Still in the silver and black of the shadowed night he searched on, and not until the rosy light of dawning began to flush and grow in the east did he come to stand at the top of the canyon where he could look down and see the girl, her green riding habit blending darkly with the dark forms of the trees still in shadow, the gold of her hair glinted with the early light, and her white, white face turned upward.

He lost no time in climbing down to her side, dreading what he might find. Was she dead? What had happened to her? It was a perilous spot where she lay, and the dangers that might have harmed her had been many. The sky grew pink, and tinted all the clouds with rose as he knelt beside the still form.

A moment served to convince him that she was still alive; even in the half darkness he could see the drawn, weary look of her face. Poor child! Poor little girl, lost on the desert! He was glad, glad he had come to find her.

He gathered her in his strong arms and bore her upward to the light.

Laying her in a sheltered spot he quickly brought water, bathed her face and forced a stimulant between the white lips. He chafed her cold little hands, blistered with the bridle, gave her more stimulant, and was rewarded by seeing a faint colour steal into the lips and cheeks. Finally the white lids fluttered open for a second and gave him a glimpse of great dark eyes in which was still mirrored the horror and fright of the night.

He gave her another draught, and hastened to prepare a more comfortable resting place, bringing the canvas from Billy's pack, and one or two other little articles that might make for comfort, among them a small hot water bottle. When he had her settled on the canvas with sweet ferns and grass underneath for a pillow and his own blanket spread over her he set about gathering wood for a fire, and soon he had water boiling in his tin cup, enough to fill the rubber bottle. When he put it in her cold hands she opened her eyes again wonderingly. He smiled reassuringly and she nestled down contentedly with the comfort of the warmth. She was too weary to question or know aught save that relief from a terrible horror was come at last.

The next time he came to her it was with a cup of strong beef tea which he held to her lips and coaxed her to swallow. When it was finished she lay back and slept again with a long drawn trembling sigh that was almost like a sob, and the heart of the young man was shaken to its depths over the agony through which she must have passed. Poor child, poor little child!

He busied himself with making their temporary camp as comfortable as possible, and looking after the needs of the horses, then coming back to his patient he stood looking down at her as she slept, wondering what he ought to do next.

They were a long distance from any human habitation. Whatever made the pony take this lonely trail was a puzzle. It led to a distant Indian settlement, and doubtless the animal was returning to his former master, but how had it come that the rider had not turned him back?

Then he looked down at the frail girl asleep on the ground and grew grave as he thought of the perils through which she had passed alone and unguarded. The exquisite delicacy of her face touched him as the vision of an angelic being might have done, and for an instant he forgot everything in the wonder with which her beauty filled him; the lovely outline of the profile as it rested lightly against her raised arm, the fineness and length of her wealth of hair, like spun gold in the glint of the sunshine that was just peering over the rim of the mountain, the clearness of her skin, so white and different from the women in that region, the pitiful droop of the sweet lips showing utter exhaustion. His heart went out from him with longing to comfort her, guard her, and bring her back to happiness. A strange, joyful tenderness for her filled him as he looked, so that he could scarcely draw his gaze from her face. Then all at once it came over him that she would not like a stranger thus to stand and gaze upon her helplessness, and with quick reverence he turned his eyes away towards the sky.

It was a peculiar morning, wonderfully beautiful. The clouds were tinted pink almost like a sunset and lasted so for over an hour, as if the dawn were coming gently that it might not waken her who slept.

Brownleigh, with one more glance to see if his patient was comfortable, went softly away to gather wood, bring more water, and make various little preparations for a breakfast later when she should waken. In an hour he tiptoed back to see if all was going well, and stooping laid a practiced finger on the delicate wrist to note the flutter of her pulse. He could count it with care, feeble, as if the heart had been under heavy strain, but still growing steadier on the whole. She was doing well to sleep. It was better than any medicine he could administer.

Meantime, he must keep a sharp lookout for travellers. They were quite off the trail here, and the trail was an old one anyway and almost disused. There was little likelihood of many passers. It might be days before any one came that way. There was no human habitation within call, and he dared not leave his charge to go in search of help to carry her back to civilization again. He must just wait here till she was able to travel.

It occurred to him to wonder where she belonged and how she came to be thus alone, and whether it was not altogether probable that a party of searchers might be out soon with some kind of a conveyance to carry her home. He must keep a sharp lookout and signal any passing rider.

To this end he moved away from the sleeping girl as far as he dared leave her, and uttered a long, clear call occasionally, but no answer came.

He dared not use his rifle for signalling lest he run out of ammunition which he might need before he got back with his charge. However, he felt it wise to combine hunting with signalling, and when a rabbit hurried across his path not far away he shot it, and the sound echoed out in the clear morning, but no answering signal came.

After he had shot two rabbits and dressed them ready for dinner when his guest should wake, he replenished the fire, set the rabbits to roasting on a curious little device of his own, and lay down on the opposite side of the fire. He was weary beyond expression himself, but he never thought of it once. The excitement of the occasion kept him up. He lay still marvelling at the strangeness of his position, and wondering what would be revealed when the girl should wake. He almost dreaded to have her do so lest she should not be as perfect as she looked asleep. His heart was in a tumult of wonder over her, and of thankfulness that he had found her before some terrible fate had overtaken her.

As he lay there resting, filled with an exalted joy, his mind wandered to the longings of the day before, the little adobe home of his co-labourer which he had left, its homeyness and joy; his own loneliness and longing for companionship. Then he looked shyly towards the tree shade where the glint of golden hair and the dark line of his blanket were all he could see of the girl he had found in the wilderness. What if his Father had answered his prayer and sent her to him! What miracle of joy! A thrill of tenderness passed through him and he pressed his hands over his closed eyes in a kind of ecstasy.

What foolishness! Dreams, of course! He tried to sober himself but he could not keep from thinking how it would seem to have this lovely girl enthroned in his little shack, ready to share his joys and comfort his sorrows; to be beloved and guarded and tenderly cared for by him.

A stir of the old blanket and a softly drawn sigh brought this delicious reverie to a close, and himself to his feet flushing cold and hot at thought of facing her awake.

She had turned over towards him slightly, her cheeks flushed with sleep. One hand was thrown back over her head, and the sun caught and flashed the sparkle of jewels into his eyes, great glory-clear gems like drops of morning dew when the sun is new upon them, and the flash of the jewels told him once more what he had known before, that here was a daughter of another world than his. They seemed to hurt him as he looked, those costly gems, for they pierced to his heart and told him they were set on a wall of separation which might rise forever between her and himself.

Then suddenly he came to himself and was the missionary again, with his senses all on the alert, and a keen realization that it was high noon and his patient was waking up. He must have slept himself although he thought he had been broad awake all the time. The hour had come for action and he must put aside the foolish thoughts that had crowded in when his weary brain was unable to cope with the cool facts of life. Of course all this was stuff and nonsense that he had been dreaming. He must do his duty by this needy one now.

Stepping softly he brought a cup of water that he had placed in the shade to keep cool, and stood beside the girl, speaking quietly, as though he had been her nurse for years.

"Wouldn't you like a drink of water?" he asked.

The girl opened her eyes and looked up at him bewildered.

"Oh, yes," she said eagerly, though her voice was very weak. "Oh, yes, —I'm so thirsty. —I thought we never would get anywhere!"

She let him lift her head, and drank eagerly, then sank back exhausted and closed her eyes. He almost thought she was going to sleep again.

"Wouldn't you like something to eat?" he asked. "Dinner is almost ready. Do you think you can sit up to eat or would you rather lie still?"

"Dinner!" she said languidly; "but I thought it was night. Did I dream it all, and how did I get here? I don't remember this place."

She looked around curiously and then closed her eyes as if the effort were almost too much.

"Oh, I feel so queer and tired, as if I never wanted to move again," she murmured.

"Don't move," he commanded. "Wait until you've had something to eat. I'll bring it at once."

He brought a cup of steaming hot beef extract with little broken bits of biscuit from a small tin box in the pack, and fed it to her a spoonful at a time.

"Who are you?" she asked as she swallowed the last spoonful, and opened her eyes, which had been closed most of the time, while he fed her, as if she were too tired to keep them open.

"Oh, I'm just the missionary. Brownleigh's my name. Now don't talk until you've had the rest of your dinner. I'll bring it in a minute. I want to make you a cup of tea, but you see I have to wash this cup first. The supply of dishes is limited." His genial smile and hearty words reassured her and she smiled and submitted.

"A missionary!" she mused and opened her eyes furtively to watch him as he went about his task. A missionary! She had never seen a missionary before, to her knowledge. She had fancied them always quite a different species, plain old maids with hair tightly drawn behind their ears and a poke bonnet with little white lawn strings.

This was a man, young, strong, engaging, and handsome as a fine piece of bronze. The brown flannel shirt he wore fitted easily over well knit muscles and exactly matched the brown of the abundant wavy hair in which the morning sun was setting glints of gold as he knelt before the fire and deftly completed his cookery. His soft wide-brimmed felt hat pushed far back on the head, the corduroy trousers, leather chaps and belt with brace of pistols all fitted into the picture and made the girl feel that she had suddenly left the earth where she had heretofore lived and been dropped into an unknown land with a strong kind angel to look after her.

A missionary! Then of course she needn't be afraid of him. As she studied his face she knew that she couldn't possibly have been afraid of that face anyway, unless, perhaps, she had ventured to disobey its owner's orders. He had a strong, firm chin, and his lips though kindly in their curve looked decided as though they were not to be trifled with. On the whole if this was a missionary then she must change her ideas of missionaries from this time forth.

She watched his light, free movements, now sitting back upon his heels to hold the cup of boiling water over the blaze by a curiously contrived handle, now rising and going to the saddle pack for some needed article. There was something graceful as well as powerful about his every motion. He gave one a sense of strength and almost infinite resource. Then suddenly her imagination conjured there beside him the man from whom she had fled, and in the light of this fine face the other face darkened and weakened and she had a swift revelation of his true character, and wondered that she had never known before. A shudder passed over her, and a gray pallor came into her face at the memory. She felt a great distaste for thinking or the necessity for even living at that moment.

Then at once he was beside her with a tin plate and the cup of steaming tea, and began to feed her, as if she had been a baby, roast rabbit and toasted corn bread. She ate unquestioningly, and drank her tea, finding all delicious after her long fast, and gaining new strength with every mouthful.

"How did I get here?" she asked suddenly, rising to one elbow and looking around. "I don't seem to remember a place like this."

"I found you hanging on a bush in the moonlight," he said gravely, "and brought you here."

Hazel lay back and reflected on this. He had brought her here. Then he must have carried her! Well, his arms looked strong enough to lift a heavier person than herself-but he had brought her here!

A faint colour stole into her pale cheeks.

"Thank you," she said at last. "I suppose I wasn't just able to come myself." There was a droll little pucker at the corner of her mouth.

"Not exactly," he answered as he gathered up the dishes.

"I remember that crazy little steed of mine began to climb straight up the side of a terrible wall in the dark, and finally decided to wipe me off with a tree. That is the last I can recall. I felt myself slipping and couldn't hold on any longer. Then it all got dark and I let go."

"Where were you going?" asked the young man.

"Going? I wasn't going anywhere," said the girl; "the pony was doing that. He was running away, I suppose. He ran miles and hours with me and I couldn't stop him. I lost hold on the bridle, you see, and he had ideas about what he wanted to do. I was almost frightened to death, and there wasn't a soul in sight all day. I never saw such an empty place in my life. It can't be this is still Arizona, we came so far."

"When did you start?" the missionary questioned gravely.

"Why, this morning, —that is-why, it must have been yesterday. I'm sure I don't know when. It was Wednesday morning about eleven o'clock that we left the car on horseback to visit a mine papa had heard about. It seems about a year since we started."

"How many were in your party?" asked the young man.

"Just papa and my brother, and Mr. Hamar, a friend of my father's," answered the girl, her cheeks reddening at the memory of the name.

"But was there no guide, no native with you at all?" There was anxiety in the young man's tone. He had visions of other lost people who would have to be looked after.

"Oh, yes, there was the man my father had written to, who brought the horses, and two or three men with him, some of them Indians, I think. His name was Bunce, Mr. Bunce. He was a queer man with a lot of wild looking hair."

"Shag Bunce," said the missionary thoughtfully. "But if Shag was along I cannot understand how you came to get so widely separated from your party. He rides the fastest horse in this region. No pony of his outfit, be he ever so fleet, could get far ahead of Shag Bunce. He would have caught you within a few minutes. What happened? Was there an accident?"

He looked at her keenly, feeling sure there was some mystery behind her wanderings that he ought to unravel for the sake of the girl and her friends. Hazel's cheeks grew rosy.

"Why, nothing really happened," she said evasively. "Mr. Bunce was ahead with my father. In fact he was out of sight when my pony started to run. I was riding with Mr. Hamar, and as we didn't care anything about the mine we didn't hurry. Before we realized it the others were far ahead over a hill or something, I forget what was ahead, only they couldn't be seen. Then we —I —that is-well, I must have touched my pony pretty hard with my whip and he wheeled and started to run. I'm not sure but I touched Mr. Hamar's horse, too, and he was behaving badly. I really hadn't time to see. I don't know what became of Mr. Hamar. He isn't much of a horseman. I don't believe he had ever ridden before. He may have had some trouble with his horse. Anyway before I knew it I was out of sight of everything but wide empty stretches with mountains and clouds at the end everywhere, and going on and on and not getting any nearer to any thing."

"This Mr. Hamar must have been a fool not to have given an alarm to your friends at once if he could do nothing himself," said Brownleigh sternly. "I cannot understand how it could happen that no one found you sooner. It was the merest chance that I came upon your whip and other little things and so grew anxious lest some one was lost. It is very strange that no one found you before this. Your father will have been very anxious."

Hazel sat up with flaming cheeks and began to gather her hair in a knot. A sudden realization of her position had come upon her and given her strength.

"Well, you see," she stumbled, trying to explain without telling anything, "Mr. Hamar might have thought I had gone back to the car, or he might have thought I would turn back in a few minutes. I do not think he would have wanted to follow me just then. I was-angry with him!"

The young missionary looked at the beautiful girl sitting upright on the canvas he had spread for her bed, trying vainly to reduce her bright hair to something like order, her cheeks glowing, her eyes shining now, half with anger, half with embarrassment, and for a second he pitied the one who had incurred her wrath. A strange unreasoning anger towards the unknown man took possession of him, and his face grew tender as he watched the girl.

"That was no excuse for letting you go alone into the perils of the desert," he said severely. "He could not have known. It was impossible that he could have understood or he would have risked his life to save you from what you have been through. No man could do otherwise!"

Hazel looked up, surprised at the vehemence of the words, and again the contrast between the two men struck her forcibly.

"I am afraid," she murmured looking off towards the distant mountains thoughtfully, "that he isn't much of a man."

And somehow the young missionary was relieved to hear her say so. There was a moment's embarrassed silence and then Brownleigh began to search in his pocket, as he saw the golden coil of hair beginning to slip loose from its knot again.

"Will these help you any?" he asked handing out the comb and hairpins he had found, a sudden awkwardness coming upon him.

"Oh, my own comb!" she exclaimed. "And hairpins! Where did you find them? Indeed they will help," and she seized upon them eagerly.

He turned away embarrassed, marvelling at the touch of her fingers as she took the bits of shell from his hand. No woman's hand like that had touched his own, even in greeting, since he bade good-bye to his invalid mother and came out to these wilds to do his work. It thrilled him to the very soul and he was minded of the sweet awe that had come upon him in his own cabin as he looked upon the little articles of woman's toilet lying upon his table as if they were at home. He could not understand his own mood. It seemed like weakness. He turned aside and frowned at himself for his foolish sentimentality towards a stranger whom he had found upon the desert. He laid it to the weariness of the long journey and the sleepless night.

"I found them in the sand. They showed me the way to find you," he said, trying vainly to speak in a commonplace tone. But somehow his voice seemed to take on a deep significance. He looked at her shyly, half fearing she must feel it, and then murmuring something about looking after the horses he hurried away.

When he came back she had mastered the rebellious hair, and it lay shining and beautiful, braided and coiled about her shapely head. She was standing now, having shaken down and smoothed out the rumpled riding habit, and had made herself look quite fresh and lovely in spite of the limited toilet conveniences.

He caught his breath as he saw her. The two regarded one another intensely for just an instant, each startlingly conscious of the other's personality, as men and women will sometimes get a glimpse beyond mere body and sight the soul. Each was aware of a thrilling pleasure in the presence of the other. It was something new and wonderful that could not be expressed nor even put into thoughts as yet but something none the less real that flashed along their consciousness like the song of the native bird, the scent of the violet, the breath of the morning.

The instant of soul recognition passed and then each recovered self-possession, but it was the woman who spoke first.

"I feel very much more respectable," she laughed pleasantly. "Where is my vicious little horse? Isn't it time we were getting back?"

Then a cloud of anxiety came over the brightness of the man's face.

"That is what I was coming to tell you," he said in a troubled tone. "The wicked little beast has eaten off his hobble and fled. There isn't a sight of him to be seen far or wide. He must have cleared out while we were at dinner, for he was munching grass peaceably enough before you woke up. It was careless of me not to make him more secure. The hobble was an old one and worn, but the best I had. I came back to tell you that I must ride after him at once. You won't be afraid to stay alone for a little while, will you? My horse has had a rest. I think I ought to be able to catch him."

V. THE TRAIL

But the look of horror in the eyes of the girl stopped him.

She gave a quick frightened glance around and then her eyes besought him. All the terror of the night alone in the wideness returned upon her. She heard again the howl of the coyotes, and saw the long dark shadows in the canyon. She was white to the lips with the thought of it.

"Oh, don't leave me alone!" she said trying to speak bravely. "I don't feel as if I could stand it. There are wild beasts around"—she glanced furtively behind her as if even now one was slyly tracking her—"it was awful-awful! Their howls! And it is so alone here!—I never was alone before!"

There was that in her appealing helplessness that gave him a wild desire to stoop and fold her in his arms and tell her he would never leave her while she wanted him. The colour came and went in his fine bronzed face, and his eyes grew tender with feeling.

"I won't leave you," he said gently, "not if you feel that way, though there is really no danger here in daytime. The wild creatures are very shy and only show themselves at night. But if I do not find your horse how are you to get speedily back to your friends? It is a long distance you have come, and you could not ride alone."

Her face grew troubled.

"Couldn't I walk?" she suggested. "I'm a good walker. I've walked five miles at once many a time."

"We are at least forty miles from the railroad," he smiled back at her, "and the road is rough, over a mountain by the nearest way. Your horse must have been determined indeed to take you so far in one day. He is evidently a new purchase of Shag's and bent on returning to his native heath. Horses do that sometimes. It is their instinct. I'll tell you what I'll do. It may be that he has only gone down in the valley to the water-hole. There is one not far away, I think. I'll go to the edge of the mesa and get a view. If he is not far away you can come with me after him. Just sit here and watch me. I'll not go out of your sight or hearing, and I'll not be gone five minutes. You'll not be afraid?"

She sat down obediently where he bade her, her eyes large with fear, for she dreaded the loneliness of the desert more than any fear that had ever visited her before.

"I promise I'll not go beyond your sight and call," he reassured her and with a smile turned towards his own horse, and swinging himself into the saddle galloped rapidly away to the edge of the mesa.

She watched him riding away, her fears almost forgotten in her admiration of him, her heart beating strangely with the memory of his smile. The protection of it seemed to linger behind him, and quiet her anxiety.

He rode straight to the east, and then more slowly turned and skirted the horizon, riding north along the edge of the mesa. She saw him shade his eyes with his hand and look away in all directions. At last after a prolonged gaze straight north he wheeled his horse and came quickly back to her.

His face was grave as he dismounted.

"I've sighted him," he said, "but it's no use. He has three or four miles start, and a steep hill climbed. When he reaches the top of the next mesa he has a straight course before him, and probably down-hill after that. It might take me three or four hours to catch him and it's a question if I could do it then. We'll have to dismiss him from our arrangements and get along with Billy. Do you feel equal to riding now? Or ought you to rest again?"

"Oh, I can ride, but—I cannot take your horse. What will you do?"

"I shall do nicely," he answered smiling again; "only our progress will be slower than if we had both horses. What a pity that I had not taken off his saddle! It would have been more comfortable for you than this. But I was searching so anxiously for the rider that I took little heed to the horse except to hastily hobble him. And when I found you you needed all my attention. Now I advise you to lie down and rest until I get packed up. It won't take me long."

She curled down obediently to rest until he was ready to fold up the canvas on which she lay, and watched his easy movements as he put together the few articles of the pack, and arranged the saddle for her comfort. Then he strode over to her.

"With your permission," he said and stooping picked her up lightly in his arms and placed her on the horse.

"I beg your pardon," he said, "but you are not equal to the exertion of mounting in the ordinary way. You will need every bit of strength for the ride. You are weaker than you realize."

Her laugh rippled out faintly.

"You make me feel like an insignificant baby. I didn't know what was happening until you had me here. You must have the strength of a giant. I never felt so little before."

"You are not a heavy burden," he said smiling. "Now are you quite comfortable? If so we'll start."

Billy arched his neck and turned his head proudly to survey his new rider, a look of friendliness on his bay face and in his kindly eye.

"Oh, isn't he a beauty!" exclaimed the girl reaching out a timid hand to pat his neck. The horse bowed and almost seemed to smile. Brownleigh noticed the gleam of a splendid jewel on the little hand.

"Billy is my good friend and constant companion," said the missionary. "We've faced some long, hard days together. He is wanting me to tell you now that he is proud to carry you back to your friends."

Billy bowed up and down and smiled again, and Hazel laughed out with pleasure. Then her face grew sober again.

"But you will have to walk," she said. "I cannot take your horse and let you walk. I won't do that. I'm going to walk with you."

"And use up what strength you have so that you could not even ride?" he said pleasantly. "No, I couldn't allow that, you know, and I am pleased to walk with a companion. A missionary's life is pretty lonesome sometimes, you know. Come, Billy, we must be starting, for we want to make a good ten miles before we stop to rest if our guest can stand the journey."

With stately steppings as if he knew he bore a princess Billy started; and with long, easy strides Brownleigh walked by his side, ever watchful of the way, and furtively observing the face of the girl, whose strength he well knew must be extremely limited after her ride of the day before.

Out on the top of the mesa looking off towards the great mountains and the wide expanse of seemingly infinite shades and colourings Hazel drew her breath in wonder at the beauty of the scene. Her companion called her attention to this and that point of interest. The slender dark line across the plain was mesquite. He told her how when once they had entered it it would seem to spread out vastly as though it filled the whole valley, and that then looking back the grassy slope below them would seem to be an insignificant streak of yellow. He told her it was always so in this land, that the kind of landscape through which one was passing filled the whole view and seemed the only thing in life. He said he supposed it was so in all our lives, that the immediate present filled the whole view of the future until we came to something else; and the look in his eyes made her turn from the landscape and wonder about him and his life.

Then he stooped and pointed to a clump of soapweed, and idly broke off a bit of another bush, handing it to her.

"The Indians call it 'the weed that was not scared,'" he said. "Isn't it an odd suggestive name?"

"It must be a brave little weed indeed to live out here all alone under this terribly big sky. I wouldn't like it even if I were only a weed," and she looked around and shivered with the thought of her fearful ride alone in the night. But she tucked the little spray of brave green into the buttonhole of her riding habit and it looked of prouder lineage than any weed as it rested against the handsome darkness of the rich green cloth. For an instant the missionary studied the picture of the lovely girl on the horse and forgot that he was only a missionary. Then with a start he came to himself. They must be getting on, for the sun had already passed its zenith, and the way was long before them. His eyes lingered wistfully on the gleam of her hair where the sun touched it into burnished gold. Then he remembered.

"By the way, is this yours?" he asked, and brought out of his pocket the little velvet cap.

"Oh, where did you find it?" she cried, settling it on her head like a touch of velvet in a crown. "I dropped it in front of a tiny little cabin when my last hope vanished. I called and called but the wind threw my voice back into my throat and no one came out to answer me."

"It was my house," he said. "I found it on a sage-bush a few feet from my own door. Would that I had been at home to answer your call!"

"Your house!" she exclaimed, in wonder. "Oh, why, it couldn't have been. It wasn't big enough for anybody-not anybody like you-to live in. Why, it wasn't anything more than a—a shed,—just a little board shanty."

"Exactly; my shack!" he said half apologetically, half comically. "You should see the inside. It's not so bad as it looks. I only wish I could take you that way, but the fact is it's somewhat out of the way to the railroad, and we must take the short cut if we want to shorten your father's anxiety. Do you feel able to go on further now?"

"Oh, yes, quite," she said with sudden trouble in her face. "Papa will be very much worried, and Aunt Maria-oh, Aunt Maria will be wild with anxiety. She will tell me that this is just what she expected from my going out riding in this heathen land. She warned me not to go. She said it wasn't ladylike."

As they went on gradually she told him all about her people, describing their little idiosyncrasies; her aunt, her brother, her father, her maid and even the fat man cook. The young man soon had the picture of the private car with all its luxuries, and the story of the days of travel that had been one long fairy tale of pleasure. Only the man Hamar was not mentioned; but the missionary had not forgotten him. Somehow he had taken a dislike to him from the first mention of his name. He blamed him fiercely for not having come after the maiden, yet blessed the fortune that had given himself that honour.

They were descending into the canyon now, but not by the steep trail up which the pony had taken her the night before. However it was rough enough and the descent, though it was into the very heart of nature's beauty storehouse, yet frightened Hazel. She started at every steep place, and clutched at the saddle wildly, pressing her white teeth hard into her under lip until it grew white and tense. Her face was white also, and a sudden faintness seemed to come upon her. Brownleigh noticed instantly, and walking close beside the horse, guiding carefully his every step, he put his free arm about her to steady her, and bade her lean towards him and not be afraid.

His strength steadied her and gave her confidence; and his pleasant voice pointing out the beauties of the way helped her to forget her fright. He made her look up and showed her how the great ferns were hanging over in a fringe of green at the top of the bare rocks above, their delicate lacery standing out like green fretwork against the blue of the sky. He pointed to a cave in the rocks far above, and told her of the dwellers of old who had hollowed it out for a home; of the stone axes and jars of clay, the corn mills and sandals woven of yucca that were found there; and of other curious cave-houses in this part of the country; giving in answer to her wondering questions much curious information, the like of which she had never heard before.

Then when they were fairly down in the shadows of the canyon he brought her a cooling draught of spring water in the tin cup, and lifting her unexpectedly from the horse made her sit in a mossy spot where sweet flowers clustered about, and rest for a few minutes, for he knew the ride down the steep path had been terribly trying to her nerves.

Yet all his attentions to her, whether lifting her to and from the saddle, or putting his arm about her to support her on the way, were performed with such grace of courtesy as to remove all personality from his touch, and she marvelled at it while she sat and rested and watched him from the distance watering Billy at a noisy little stream that chattered through the canyon.

He put her on the horse again and they took their way through the coolness and beauty of the canyon winding along the edge of the little stream, threading their way among the trees, and over boulders and rough places until at last in the late afternoon they came out again upon the plain.

The missionary looked anxiously at the sun. It had taken longer to come through the canyon than he had anticipated. The day was waning. He quickened Billy into a trot and settled into a long athletic run beside him, while the girl's cheeks flushed with the exercise and wind, and her admiration of her escort grew.

"But aren't you very tired?" she asked at last when he slowed down and made Billy walk again. Billy, by the way, had enjoyed the race immensely. He thought he was having a grand time with a princess on his back and his beloved master keeping pace with him. He was confident by this time that they were bringing the princess home to be there to welcome them on all returns hereafter. His horse-sense had jumped to a conclusion and approved most heartily.

"Tired!" answered Brownleigh and laughed; "not consciously. I'm good for several miles yet myself. I haven't had such a good time in three years, not since I left home-and mother," he added softly, reverently.

There was a look in his eyes that made the girl long to know more. She watched him keenly and asked:

"Oh, then you have a mother!"

"Yes, I have a mother,—a wonderful mother!" He breathed the words like a blessing. The girl looked at him in awe. She had no mother. Her own had died before she could remember. Aunt Maria was her only idea of mothers.

"Is she out here?" she asked.

"No, she is at home up in New Hampshire in a little quiet country town, but she is a wonderful mother."

"And have you no one else, no other family out here with you?"

Hazel did not realize how anxiously she awaited the answer to that question. Somehow she felt a jealous dislike of any one who might belong to him, even a mother-and a sudden thought of sister or wife who might share the little shanty cabin with him made her watch his face narrowly. But the answer was quick, with almost a shadow like deep longing on his face:

"Oh, no, I have no one. I'm all alone. And sometimes if it were not for mother's letters it would seem a great way from home."

The girl did not know why it was so pleasant to know this, and why her heart went out in instant sympathy for him.

"O-oo!" she said gently. "Tell me about your mother, please!"

And so he told her, as he walked beside her, of his invalid mother whose frail body and its needs bound her to a couch in her old New England home, helpless and carefully tended by a devoted nurse whom she loved and who loved her. Her great spirit had risen to the sacrifice of sending her only son out to the desert on his chosen commission.

They had been climbing a long sloping hill, and at the climax of the story had reached the top and could look abroad again over a wide expanse of country. It seemed to Hazel's city bred eyes as though the kingdoms of the whole world lay spread before her awed gaze. A brilliant sunset was spreading a great silver light behind the purple mountains in the west, red and blue in flaming lavishness, with billows of white clouds floating above, and over that in sharp contrast the sky was velvet black with storm. To the south the rain was falling in a brilliant shower like yellow gold, and to the east two more patches of rain were rosy pink as petals of some wondrous flowers, and arching over them a half rainbow. Turning slightly towards the north one saw the rain falling from dark blue clouds in great streaks of white light.

"Oh-oo!" breathed the girl; "how wonderful! I never saw anything like that before."

But the missionary had no time for answer. He began quickly to unstrap the canvas from behind the saddle, watching the clouds as he did so.

"We are going to get a wetting, I'm afraid," he said and looked anxiously at his companion.

VI. CAMP

It came indeed before he was quite ready for it, but he managed to throw the canvas over horse and lady, bidding her hold it on one side while he, standing close under the extemporized tent, held the other side, leaving an opening in front for air, and so they managed to keep tolerably dry, while two storms met overhead and poured down a torrent upon them.

The girl laughed out merrily as the first great splashes struck her face, then retreated into the shelter as she was bidden and sat quietly watching, and wondering over it all.

Here was she, a carefully nurtured daughter of society, until now never daring to step one inch beyond the line of conventionality, sitting afar from all her friends and kindred on a wide desert plain, under a bit of canvas with a strange missionary's arm about her, and sitting as securely and contentedly, nay happily, as if she had been in her own cushioned chair in her New York boudoir. It is true the arm was about her for the purpose of holding down the canvas and keeping out the rain, but there was a wonderful security and sense of strength in it that filled her with a strange new joy and made her wish that the elements of the universe might continue to rage in brilliant display about her head a little longer, if thereby she might continue to feel the strength of that fine presence near her and about her. A great weariness was upon her and this was rest and content, so she put all other thoughts out of her mind for the time and rested back against the strong arm in full realization of her safety amidst the disturbance of the elements.

The missionary wore his upward look. No word passed between them as the panorama of the storm swept by. Only God knew what was passing in his soul, and how out of that dear nearness of the beautiful girl a great longing was born to have her always near him, his right to ever protect her from the storms of life.

But he was a man of marked self-control. He held even his thoughts in obedience to a higher power, and while the wild wish of his heart swept exquisitely over him he stood calmly, and handed it back to heaven as though he knew it were a wandering wish, a testing of his true self.

At the first instant of relief from necessity he took his arm away. He did not presume a single second to hold the canvas after the wind had subsided, and she liked him the better for it, and felt her trust in him grow deeper as he gently shook the raindrops from their temporary shelter.

The rain had lasted but a few minutes, and as the clouds cleared the earth grew lighter for a space. Gently melting into the silver and amethyst and emerald of the sky the rainbow faded and now they hurried on, for Brownleigh wished to reach a certain spot where he hoped to find dry shelter for the night. He saw that the excitement of travel and the storm had sorely spent the strength of the girl, and that she needed rest, so he urged the horse forward, and hurried along by his side.

But suddenly he halted the horse and looked keenly into the face of his companion in the dying light.

"You are very tired," he said. "You can hardly sit up any longer."

She smiled faintly.

Her whole body was drooping with weariness and a strange sick faintness had come upon her.

"We must stop here," he said and cast about him for a suitable spot. "Well, this will do. Here is a dry place, the shelter of that big rock. The rain was from the other direction, and the ground around here did not even get sprinkled. That group of trees will do for a private room for you. We'll soon have a fire and some supper and then you'll feel better."

With that he stripped off his coat and, spreading it upon the ground in the dry shelter of a great rock, lifted the drooping girl from the saddle and laid her gently on the coat.

She closed her eyes wearily and sank back. In truth she was nearer to fainting than she had ever been in her life, and the young man hastened to administer a restorative which brought the colour back to her pale cheeks.

"It is nothing," she murmured, opening her eyes and trying to smile. "I was just tired, and my back ached with so much riding."

"Don't talk!" he said gently. "I'll give you something to hearten you up in a minute."

He quickly gathered sticks and soon had a blazing fire not far from where she lay, and the glow of it played over her face and her golden hair, while he prepared a second cup of beef extract, and blessed the fortune that had made him fill his canteen with water at the spring in the canyon, for water might not be very near, and he felt that to have to move the girl further along that night would be a disaster. He could see that she was about used up. But while he was making preparations for supper, Billy, who was hobbled but entirely able to edge about slowly, had discovered a water-hole for himself, and settled that difficulty. Brownleigh drew a sigh of relief, and smiled happily as he saw his patient revive under the influence of the hot drink and a few minutes' rest.

"I'm quite able to go on a little further," she said, sitting up with an effort, "if you think we should go further to-night. I really don't feel bad at all any more."

He smiled with relief.

"I'm so glad," he said; "I was afraid I had made you travel too far. No, we'll not go further till daylight, I think. This is as good a place to camp as any, and water not far away. You will find your boudoir just inside that group of trees, and in half an hour or so the canvas will be quite dry for your bed. I've got it spread out, you see, close to the fire on the other side there. And it wasn't wet through. The blanket was sheltered. It will be warm and dry. I think we can make you comfortable. Have you ever slept out under the stars before-that is, of course, with the exception of last night? I don't suppose you really enjoyed that experience."

Hazel shuddered at the thought.

"I don't remember much, only awful darkness and howling. Will those creatures come this way, do you think? I feel as if I should die with fright if I have to hear them again."

"You may hear them in the distance, but not nearby," he answered reassuringly; "they do not like the fire. They will not come near nor disturb you. Besides, I shall be close at hand all night. I am used to listening and waking in the night. I shall keep a bright fire blazing."

"But you-you-what will you do? You are planning to give me the canvas and the blanket, and stay awake yourself keeping watch. You have walked all day while I have ridden, and you have been nurse and cook as well, while I have been good for nothing. And now you want me to rest comfortably all night while you sit up."

There was a ring in the young man's voice as he answered her that thrilled her to the heart.

"I shall be all right," he said, and his voice was positively joyous, "and I shall have the greatest night of my life taking care of you. I count it a privilege. Many a night have I slept alone under the stars with no one to guard, and felt the loneliness. Now I shall always have this to remember. Besides, I shall not sit up. I am used to throwing myself down anywhere. My clothing is warm, and my saddle is used to acting as a pillow. I shall sleep and rest, and yet be always on the alert to keep up the fire and hear any sound that comes near." He talked as though he were recounting the plan of some delightful recreation, and the girl lay and watched his handsome face in the play of the firelight and rejoiced in it. Somehow there was something very sweet in companionship alone in the vast silence with this stranger friend. She found herself glad of the wideness of the desert and the stillness of the night that shut out the world and made their most unusual relationship possible for a little while. A great longing possessed her to know more and understand better the fine personality of this man who was a man among men, she was convinced.

Suddenly as he came and sat down by the fire not far from her after attending to the few supper dishes, she burst forth with a question:

"Why did you do it?"

He turned to her eyes that were filled with a deep content and asked, "Do what?"

"Come here! Be a missionary! Why did you do it? You are fitted for better things. You could fill a large city church, or-even do other things in the world. Why did you do it?"

The firelight flickered on his face and showed his features fine and strong in an expression of deep feeling that gave it an exalted look. There seemed a light in his eyes that was more than firelight as he raised them upward in a swift glance and said quietly, as though it were the simplest matter in the universe:

"Because my Father called me to this work. And —I doubt if there can be any better. Listen!"

And then he told her of his work while the fire burned cheerfully, and the dusk grew deeper, till the moon showed clear her silver orb riding high in starry heavens.

The mournful voice of the coyotes echoed distantly, but the girl was not frightened, for her thoughts were held by the story of the strange childlike race for whom this man among men was giving his life.

He told her of the Indian hogans, little round huts built of logs on end, and slanting to a common centre thatched with turf and straw, an opening for a door and another in the top to let out the smoke of the fire, a dirt floor, no furniture but a few blankets, sheepskins, and some tin dishes. He carried her in imagination to one such hogan where lay the little dying Indian maiden and made the picture of their barren lives so vivid that tears stood in her eyes as she listened. He told of the medicine-men, the ignorance and superstition, the snake dances and heathen rites; the wild, poetic, conservative man of the desert with his distrust, his great loving heart, his broken hopes and blind aspirations; until Hazel began to see that he really loved them, that he had seen the possibility of greatness in them, and longed to help develop it.

He told her of the Sabbath just past, when in company with his distant neighbour missionary he had gone on an evangelistic tour among the tribes far away from the mission station. He pictured the Indians sitting on rocks and stones amid the long shadows of the cedar trees, just before the sundown, listening to a sermon. He had reminded them of their Indian god Begochiddi and of Nilhchii whom the Indians believe to have made all things, the same whom white men call God; and showed them a book called the Bible which told the story of God, and of Jesus His Son who came to save men from their sin. Not one of the Indians had ever heard the name of Jesus before, nor knew anything of the great story of salvation.

Hazel found herself wondering why it made so very much difference whether these poor ignorant creatures knew all this or not, and yet she saw from the face of the man before her that it did matter, infinitely. To him it mattered more than anything else. A passing wish that she were an Indian to thus hold his interest flashed through her mind, but he was speaking yet of his work, and his rapt look filled her with awe. She was overwhelmed with the greatness and the fineness of the man before her. Sitting there in the fitful firelight, with its ruddy glow upon his face, his hat off and the moon laying a silver crown upon his head, he seemed half angel, half god. She had never before been so filled with the joy of beholding another soul. She had no room for thoughts of anything else.

Then suddenly he remembered that it was late.

"I have kept you awake far too long," he said penitently, looking at her with a smile that seemed all tenderness. "We ought to get on our way as soon as it is light, and I have made you listen to me when you ought to have been sleeping. But I always like to have a word with my Father before retiring. Shall we have our worship together?"

Hazel, overcome by wonder and embarrassment, assented and lay still in her sheltered spot watching him as he drew a small leather book from his breast pocket and opened to the place marked by a tiny silken cord. Then stirring up the fire to brightness he began to read and the majestic words of the ninety-first psalm came to her unaccustomed ears as a charmed page.

"He that dwelleth in the secret place of the Most High shall abide under the shadow of the Almighty."

"He shall cover thee with His feathers and under His wings shalt thou trust." The words were uttered with a ringing tone of trust. The listener knew little of birds and their ways, but the phrasing reminded her of the way she had been sheltered from the storm a little while before and her heart thrilled anew with the thought of it.

"Thou shalt not be afraid for the terror by night!"

Ah! Terror by night! She knew what that meant. That awful night of darkness, steep riding, howling beasts and black oblivion! She shuddered involuntarily at the remembrance. Not afraid!

What confidence the voice had as it rang on, and all at once she knew that this night was free from terror for her because of the man whose confidence was in the Unseen.

"He shall give His angels charge over thee," and looking at him she half expected to see flitting wings in the moonlit background. How strong and true the face! How tender the lines about the mouth! What a glow of inner quietness and power in the eyes as he raised them now and again to her face across the firelight! What a thing it would be to have a friend like that always to guard one! Her eyes glowed softly at the thought and once again there flashed across her mind the contrast between this man and the one from whom she had fled in horror the day before.

The reading ended, he replaced the little marker, and dropping upon one knee on the desert with his face lifted to the sky and all the radiance of the moon flooding over him he spoke to God as a man speaks with his friend, face to face.

Hazel lay with open, wondering eyes and watched him, awe growing within her. The sense of an unseen Presence close at hand was so strong that once she lifted half frightened eyes to the wide clear sky. The light on the face of the missionary seemed like glory from another world.

She felt herself enfolded and upborne into the Presence of the infinite by his words, and he did not forget to commend her loved ones to the care of the Almighty. A great peace came upon her as she listened to the simple, earnest words and a sense of security such as she had never known before.

After the brief prayer he turned to her with a smile and a few words of assurance about the night. There was her dressing-room behind those trees, and she need not be afraid; he would not be far away. He would keep the fire bright all night so that she would not be annoyed by the near howling of the coyotes. Then he moved away to gather more wood, and she heard him singing, softly at first, and then gathering volume as he got further away, his rich tenor voice ringing clear upon the night in an old hymn. The words floated back distinctly to her listening ears:

> "My God, is any hour so sweet
> From flush of dawn to evening star,
> As that which calls me to Thy feet,
> The hour of prayer?
>
> "Then is my strength by Thee renewed;
> Then are my sins by Thee forgiven;
> Then dost Thou cheer my solitude
> With hopes of heaven.
>
> "No words can tell what sweet relief
> There for my every want I find;
> What strength for warfare, balm for grief,
> What peace of mind!"

She lay down for the night marvelling still over the man. He was singing those words as if he meant every one, and she knew that he possessed something that made him different from other men. What was it? It seemed to her that he was the one man of all the earth, and how was it that she had found him away out here alone in the desert?

The great stars burned sharply in the heavens over her, the white radiance of the moon lay all about her, the firelight played at her feet. Far away she could hear the howling of the coyotes, but she was not afraid.

She could see the broad shoulders of the man as he stooped over on the other side of the fire to throw on more wood. Presently she knew he had thrown himself down with his head on the saddle, but she could hear him still humming softly something that sounded like a lullaby. When the firelight flared up it showed his fine profile.

Not far away she could hear Billy cropping the grass, and throughout the vast open universe there seemed to brood a great and peaceful silence. She was very tired and her eyelids drooped shut. The last thing she remembered was a line he had read from the little book, "He shall give His angels charge ——" and she wondered if they were somewhere about now.

That was all until she awoke suddenly with the consciousness that she was alone, and that in the near distance a conversation in a low tone was being carried on.

VII. REVELATION

The moon was gone, and the luminous silver atmosphere was turned into a clear dark blue, with shadows of the blackness of velvet; but the stars burned redder now, and nearer to the earth.

The fire still flickered brightly, with a glow the moon had paled before she went to sleep, but there was no protecting figure on the other side of the flames, and the angels seemed all to have forgotten.

Off at a little distance, where a group of sage-brush made dense darkness, she heard the talking. One speaking in low tones, now pleading, now explaining, deeply earnest, with a mingling of anxiety and trouble. She could not hear any words. She seemed to know the voice was low that she might not hear; yet it filled her with a great fear. What had happened? Had some one come to harm them, and was he pleading for her life? Strange to say it never entered her head to doubt his loyalty, stranger though he was. Her only feeling was that he might have been overpowered in his sleep, and be even now in need of help himself. What could she do?

After the first instant of frozen horror she was on the alert. He had saved her, she must help him. She could not hear any other voice than his. Probably the enemy spoke in whispers, but she knew that she must go at once and find out what was the matter. The distance from her pleasant couch beside the fire was but a few steps, yet it seemed to her frightened heart and trembling limbs, as she crept softly over towards the sage-brush, that it was miles.

At last she was close to the bush, could part it with her cold hand and look into the little shelter.

There was a faint light in the east beyond the mountains that showed the coming dawn, and silhouetted against this she saw the figure of her rescuer, dropped upon one knee, his elbow on the other and his face bowed in his hand. She could hear his words distinctly now, but there was no man else present, though she searched the darkness carefully.

"I found her lost out here in the wilderness," he was saying in low, earnest tones, "so beautiful, so dear! But I know she cannot be for me. Her life has been all luxury and I would not be a man to ask her to share the desert! I know too that she is not fitted for the work. I know it would be all wrong, and I must not wish it, but I love her, though I may not tell her so! I must be resolute and strong, and not show her what I feel. I must face my Gethsemane, for this girl is as dear to me as my own soul! God bless and guard her, for I may not."

The girl had stood rooted to the spot unable to move as the low voice went on with its revelation, but when the plea for a blessing upon her came with all the mighty longing of a soul who loved absorbingly, it was as if she were unable to bear it, and she turned and fled silently back to her couch, creeping under the canvas, thrilled, frightened, shamed and glad all in one. She closed her eyes and the swift tears of joy came. He loved her! He loved her! How the thought thrilled her. How her own heart leaped up to meet his love. The fact of it was all she could contain for the time and it filled her with an ecstasy such as she had never known before. She opened her eyes to the stars and they shone back a great radiance of joy to her. The quiet darkness of the vast earth all about her seemed suddenly to have become the sweetest spot she had known. She had never thought there could be joy like this.

Gradually she quieted the wild throbbing of her heart and tried to set her thoughts in order. Perhaps she was taking too much for granted. Perhaps he was talking of another girl, some one he had met the day before. But yet it seemed as if there could be no doubt. There would not be two girls lost out in that desert. There could not-and her heart told her that he loved her. Could she trust her heart? Oh, the dearness of it if it were true!

Her face was burning too, with the sweet shame of having heard what was not meant for her ears.

Then came the flash of pain in the joy. He did not intend to tell her. He meant to hide his love-and for her sake! And he was great enough to do so. The man who could sacrifice the things that other men hold dear to come out to the wilderness for the sake of a forgotten, half-savage people, could sacrifice anything for what he considered right. This fact loomed like a wall of adamant across the lovely way that joy had revealed to her. Her heart fell with the thought that he was not to speak of this to her, —and she knew that more than for anything else in life, more than anything she had ever known, she longed to hear him speak those words to her. A half resentment filled her that he had told his secret to Another-what concerned her-and would not let her know.

The heart searching went on, and now she came to the thorn-fact of the whole revelation. There had been another reason besides care for herself why he could not tell her of his love, — why he could not ask her to share his life. She had not been accounted worthy. He had put it in pleasant words and said she was unfitted, but he might as well have made it plain and said how useless she would be in his life.

The tears came now, tears of mortification, for Hazel Radcliffe had never before in all her petted life been accounted unworthy for any position. It was not that she considered at all the possibility of accepting the position that was not to be offered her. Her startled mind had not even reached so far; but her pride was hurt to think that any one should think her unworthy.

Then over the whole tumultuous state of mind would come the memory of his voice throbbing with feeling as he said, "She is dear to me as my own soul," and the joy of it would sweep everything else away.

There was no more sleep to be had for her.

The stars grew pale, and the rose dawn grew in the east. She presently heard her companion return and replenish the fire, stirring about softly among the dishes, and move away again, but she had turned her head away that he might not see her face, and he evidently thought her still sleeping.

So she lay and tried to reason things out; tried to scold herself for thinking his words applied to her; tried to recall her city life and friends, and how utterly alien this man and his work would be to them; tried to think of the new day when she would probably reach her friends again and this new friend would be lost sight of; felt a sharp twinge of pain at the thought; wondered if she could meet Milton Hamar and what they would say to one another, and if any sort of comfortable relations could ever be established between them again; and knew they could not. Once again the great horror rolled over her at thought of his kiss. Then came the startling thought that he had used almost the same words to her that this man of the desert had used about her, and yet how infinitely different! How tender and deep and true, and pure and high his face in contrast to the look she had seen upon that handsome, evil face bent over her! She covered her eyes and shuddered again, and entertained a fleeting wish that she might stay forever here and not return to his hated presence.

Then back like a flood-tide of sunshine would come the thought of the missionary and his love for her, and everything else would be obliterated in the rapture it brought.

And thus on rosy wings the morning dawned, a clean, straight sunrise.

Hazel could hear the missionary stepping softly here and there preparing breakfast, and knew he felt it time to be on the move. She must bestir herself and speak, but her cheeks grew pink over the thought of it. She kept waiting and trying to think how to say good-morning without a look of guilty knowledge in her eyes. Presently she heard him call to Billy and move away in the direction where the horse was eating his breakfast. Then snatching her opportunity she slipped from under the canvas into her green boudoir.

But even here she found evidences of her wise guide's care, for standing in front of the largest cedar were two tin cups of clear water and beside them a small pocket soap-case and a clean folded handkerchief, fine and white. He had done his best to supply her with toilet articles.

Her heart leaped up again at his thoughtfulness. She dashed the water into her glowing face, and buried it in the clean folds of the handkerchief-his handkerchief. How wonderful that it should be so! How had a mere commonplace bit of linen become so invested with the currents of life as to give such joyful refreshment with a touch? The wonder of it all was like a miracle. She had not known anything in life could be like that.

The great red cliff across the valley was touched with the morning sun when she emerged from her green shelter, shyly conscious of the secret that lay unrevealed between them.

Their little camp was still in the shadow. The last star had disappeared as if a hand had turned the lights low with a flash and revealed the morning.

She stood for an instant in the parting of the cedars, a hand on each side holding back the boughs, looking forth from her retreat; and the man advancing saw her and waited with bared head to do her reverence, a great light of love in his eyes which he knew not was visible, but which blinded the eyes of the watching girl, and made her cheeks grow rosier.

The very air about them seemed charged with an electrical current. The little commonplaces which they spoke sank deep into the heart of each and lingered to bless the future. The glances of their eyes had many meetings and lingered shyly on more intimate ground than the day before, yet each had grown more silent. The tenderness of his voice was like a benediction as he greeted her.

He seated her on the canvas he had arranged freshly beside a bit of green grass, and prepared to serve her like a queen. Indeed she wore a queenly bearing, small and slender though she was, her golden hair shining in the morning, and her eyes bright as the stars that had just been paled by day.

There were fried rabbits cooking in the tiny saucepan and corn bread was toasting before the fire on two sharp sticks. She found to her surprise that she was hungry, and that the breakfast he had prepared seemed a most delicious feast.

She grew secure in her consciousness that he did not know she had guessed his secret, and let the joy of it all flow over her and envelop her. Her laugh rang out musically over the plain, and he watched her hungrily, delightedly, enjoying every minute of the companionship with a kind of double joy because of the barren days that he was sure were to come.

Finally he broke away from the pleasant lingering with an exclamation, for the sun was hastening upward and it was time they were on their way. Hastily he packed away the things, she trying in her bungling unaccustomedness to help and only giving sweet hindrance, with the little white hands that thrilled him so wonderfully as they came near with a plate or a cup, or a bit of corn bread that had been left out.

He put her on the horse and they started on their way. Yet not once in all the pleasant contact had he betrayed his secret, and Hazel began to feel the burden of what she had found out weighing guiltily upon her like a thing stolen which she would gladly replace but dared not. Sometimes, as they rode along, he quietly talking as the day before, pointing out some object of interest, or telling her some remarkable story of his experiences, she would wonder if she had not been entirely mistaken; heard wrong, maybe, or made more of the words than she should have done. She grew to feel that he could not have meant her at all. And then turning suddenly she would find his eyes upon her with a light in them so tender, so yearning, that she would droop her own in confusion and feel her heart beating wildly with the pleasure and the pain of it.

About noon they came to a rain-water hole near which were three Indian hogans. Brownleigh explained that he had come this way, a little out of the shortest trail, hoping to get another horse so that they might travel faster and reach the railroad before sundown.

The girl's heart went suddenly heavy as he left her sitting on Billy under a cottonwood tree while he went forward to find out if any one was at home and whether they had a horse to spare. Of course she wanted to find her friends and relieve their anxiety as soon as possible, but there was something in the voice of the young missionary as he spoke of hastening onward that seemed to build a wall between them. The pleasant intercourse of the morning seemed drawing so quickly to a close: the wonderful sympathy and interest between them pushed with a violent hand out of her reach. She felt a choking sensation in her throat as if she would like to put her head down on Billy's rough neck-locks and sob.

She tried to reason with herself. It was but a little over twenty-four hours since she first looked upon this stranger, and yet her heart was bound to him in such a way that she was dreading their separation. How could it be? Such things were not real. People always laughed at sudden love affairs as if they were impossible, but her heart told her that it was not merely hours by which they numbered their acquaintance. The soul of this man had been revealed to her in that brief space of time as another's might not have been in years. She dreaded the ending of this companionship. It would be the end, of course. He had said it, and she knew his words were true. His world was not her world, more the pity! He would never give up his world, and he had said she was unfitted for his. It was all too true-this world of rough, uncouth strangers, and wild emptiness of beauty. But how she longed to have this day with him beside her prolonged indefinitely!

The vision would fade of course when she got back into the world again, and things would assume their normal proportions very likely. But just now she admitted to herself that she did not want to get back. She would be entirely content if she might wander thus with him in the desert for the rest of her natural life.

He came back to her presently accompanied by an Indian boy carrying an iron pot and some fresh mutton. Hazel watched them as they built a fire, arranged the pot full of water to boil, and placed the meat to roast. The missionary was making corn cake which presently was baking in the ashes, and giving forth a savoury odour.

An Indian squaw appeared in the doorway of one of the hogans, her baby strapped to her back, and watched her with great round wondering eyes. Hazel smiled at the little papoose, and it soon dimpled into an answering smile. Then she discovered that the missionary was watching them both, his heart in his eyes, a strange wonderful joy in his face, and her heart-beats quickened. She was pleasing him! It was then as she smiled back at the child of the forest that she discovered an interest of her own in these neglected people of his. She could not know that the little dark-skinned baby whom she had noticed would from this time forth become the special tender object of care from the missionary, just because she had noticed it.

They had a merry meal, though not so intimate as the others had been; for a group of Indian women and children huddled outside the nearest hogan watching their every move with wide staring eyes, and stolid but interested countenances; and the little boy hovered not far away to bring anything they might need. It was all pleasant but Hazel felt impatient of the interruption when their time together was now so short. She was glad when, mounted on Billy again, and her companion on a rough little Indian pony with wicked eyes, they rode away together into the sunshine of the afternoon.

But now it seemed but a breathless space before they would come into the presence of people, for the two horses made rapid time, and the distances flew past them mile by mile, the girl feeling each moment more shy and embarrassed, and conscious of the words she had overheard in the early morning.

It seemed to her a burden she could not carry away unknown upon her soul and yet how could she let him know?

VIII. RENUNCIATION

They had entered a strip of silvery sand, about two miles wide, and rode almost in silence, for a singular shyness had settled upon them.

The girl was conscious of his eyes upon her with a kind of tender yearning as if he would impress the image on his mind for the time when she would be with him no more. Each had a curious sense of understanding the other's thoughts, and needing no words. But as they neared a great rustling stretch of corn he looked at her keenly again and spoke:

"You are very tired, I'm sure." It was not a question but she lifted her eyes to deny it, and a flood-tide of sweet colour swept over the cheeks. "I knew it," he said, searching her raised eyes. "We must stop and rest after we have passed through this corn. There is a spot under some trees where you will be sheltered from the sun. This corn lasts only a mile or so more, and after you have rested we will have only a short distance to go"—he caught his breath as though the words hurt him—"our journey is almost over!" They rode in silence through the corn, but when it was passed and they were seated beneath the trees the girl lifted her eyes to him filled with unspeakable things.

"I haven't known how to thank you," she said earnestly, the tears almost in evidence.

"Don't, please!" he said gently. "It has been good to me to be with you. How good you never can know." He paused and then looked keenly at her.

"Did you rest well last night, your first night under the stars? Did you hear the coyotes, or feel at all afraid?"

Her colour fled, and she dropped her glance to Billy's neck, while her heart throbbed painfully.

He saw how disturbed she was.

"You were afraid," he charged gently. "Why didn't you call? I was close at hand all the time. What frightened you?"

"Oh, it was nothing!" she said evasively. "It was only for a minute."

"Tell me, please!" his voice compelled her.

"It was just for a minute," she said again, speaking rapidly and trying to hide her embarrassment. "I woke and thought I heard talking and you were not in sight; but it was not long before you came back with an armful of wood, and I saw it was almost morning."

Her cheeks were rosy, as she lifted her clear eyes to meet his searching gaze and tried to face him steadily, but he looked into the very depths of her soul and saw the truth. She felt her courage going from her, and tried to turn her gaze carelessly away, but could not.

At last he said in a low voice full of feeling:

"You heard me?"

Her eyes, which he had held with his look, wavered, faltered, and drooped. "I was afraid," he said as her silence confirmed his conviction. "I heard some one stirring. I looked and thought I saw you going back to your couch." There was grave self-reproach in his tone, but no reproach for her. Nevertheless her heart burned with shame and her eyes filled with tears. She hid her glowing face in her hands and cried out:

"I am so sorry. I did not mean to be listening. I thought from the tone of your voice you were in trouble. I was afraid some one had attacked you, and perhaps I could do something to help——"

"You poor child!" he said deeply moved. "How unpardonable of me to frighten you. It is my habit of talking aloud when I am alone. The great loneliness out here has cultivated it. I did not realize that I might disturb you. What must you think of me? What *can* you think?"

"Think!" she burst forth softly. "I think you are all wrong to try to keep a thing like that to yourself!"

And then the full meaning of what she had said broke upon her, and her face crimsoned with embarrassment.

But he was looking at her with an eager light in his eyes.

"What do you mean?" he asked. "Won't you please explain?"

Hazel was sitting now with her face entirely turned away, and the soft hair blowing concealingly about her burning cheeks. She felt as if she must get up and run away into the desert and end this terrible conversation. She was getting in deeper and deeper every minute.

"Please!" said the gentle, firm voice.

"Why, I —think —a —a —woman-has a right-to know—a thing like that!" she faltered desperately.

"Why?" asked the voice again after a pause.

"Because-she-she-might not ever-she might not ever know there was such a love for a woman in the world!" she stammered, still with her head turned quite away from him. She felt that she could never turn around and face this wonderful man of the desert again. She wished the ground would open and show her some comfortable way of escape.

The pause this time was long, so long that it frightened her, but she dared not turn and look at him. If she had done so she would have seen that he was sitting with bowed head for some time, in deep meditation, and that at last he lifted his glance to the sky again as if to ask a swift permission. Then he spoke.

"A man has no right to tell a woman he loves her when he cannot ask her to marry him."

"That," said the girl, her throat throbbing painfully, "*that* has nothing to do with it. I —was-not talking about-marrying! But I think she has a right to know. It would-make a difference all her life!" Her throat was dry and throbbing. The words seemed to stick as she tried to utter them, yet they would be said. She longed to hide her burning face in some cool shelter and get away from this terrible talk, but she could only sit rigidly quiet, her fingers fastened tensely in the coarse grass at her side.

There was a longer silence now, and still she dared not look at the man.

A great eagle appeared in the heaven above and sailed swiftly and strongly towards a mountain peak. Hazel had a sense of her own smallness, and of the fact that her words had made an exquisite anguish for the soul of her companion, yet she could not think of anything to say that would better matters. At last he spoke, and his voice was like one performing a sad and sacred rite for one tenderly beloved:

"And now that you know I love you can it possibly make any difference to you?"

Hazel tried three times to answer, but every time her trembling lips would frame no words. Then suddenly her face went into her hands and the tears came. She felt as if a benediction had been laid upon her head, and the glory of it was greater than she could bear.

The man watched her, his arms longing to enfold her and soothe her agitation, but he would not. His heart was on fire with the sweetness and the pain of the present moment, yet he could not take advantage of their situation upon the lonely plain, and desecrate the beauty of the trust she had put upon him.

Then her strength came again, and she raised her head and looked into his waiting eyes with a trembling, shy glance, yet true and earnest.

"It will make a difference-to me!" she said. "I shall never feel quite the same towards life again because I know there is such a wonderful man in the world."

She had fine control of her voice now, and was holding back the tears. Her manner of the world was coming to her aid. He must not see how much this was to her, how very much. She put out a little cold hand and laid it timidly in his big brown one, and he held it a moment and looked down at it in great tenderness, closed his fingers over it in a strong clasp, then laid it gently back in her lap as though it were too precious to keep. Her heart thrilled and thrilled again at his touch.

"Thank you," he said simply, a great withdrawing in his tone. "But I cannot see how you can think well of me. I am an utter stranger to you. I have no right to talk of such things to you."

"You did not tell me," answered Hazel. "You told-God." Her voice was slow and low with awe. "I only overheard. It was my fault-but —I am not-sorry. It was a great-thing to hear!"

He watched her shy dignity as she talked, her face drooping and half turned away. She was exquisitely beautiful in her confusion. His whole spirit yearned towards hers.

"I feel like a monster," he said suddenly. "You know I love you, but you do not understand how, in this short time even, you have filled my life, my whole being. And yet I may not ever try or hope to win your love in return. It must seem strange to you———"

"I think I understand," she said in a low voice; "you spoke of all that in the night-you know." It seemed as if she shrank from hearing it again.

"Will you let me explain it thoroughly to you?"

"If-you think best." She turned her face away and watched the eagle, now a mere speck in the distance.

"You see it is this way. I am not free to do as I might wish-as other men are free. I have consecrated my life to the service of God in this place. I know—I knew when I came here-that it was no place to bring a woman. There are few who could stand the life. It is filled with privations and hardships. They are inevitable. You are used to tender care and luxury. No man could ask a sacrifice like that of a woman he loved. He would not be a man if he did. It is not like marrying a girl who has felt the call herself, and loves to give her life to the work. That would be a different matter. But a man has no right to expect it of a woman——" he paused to find the right words and Hazel in a small still voice of dignity reminded him:

"You are forgetting one of the reasons."

"Forgetting?" he turned towards her wonderingly and their eyes met for just an instant, then hers were turned away again.

"Yes," she went on inscrutably. "You thought I—was not-fit!"

She was pulling up bits of green from the ground beside her. She felt a frightened flutter in her throat. It was the point of the thorn that had remained in her heart. It was not in nature for her not to speak of it, yet when it was spoken she felt how it might be misunderstood.

But the missionary made answer in a kind of cry like some hurt creature.

"Not fit! Oh, my dear! You do not understand——"

There was that in his tone that extracted the last bit of rankling thorn from Hazel's heart and brought the quick blood to her cheeks again.

With a light laugh that echoed with relief and a deep new joy which she dared not face as yet, she sprang to her feet.

"Oh, yes, I understand," she said gaily, "and it's all true. I'm not a bit fit for a missionary. But oughtn't we to be moving on? I'm quite rested now."

With a face that was grave to sadness he acquiesced, fastening the canvas in place on the saddle, and putting her on her horse with swift, silent movements. Then as she gathered up the reins he lingered for an instant and taking the hem of her gown in his fingers he stooped and touched his lips lightly, reverently to the cloth.

There was something so humble, so pathetic, so self-forgetful in the homage that the tears sprang to the girl's eyes and she longed to put her arms about his neck and draw his face close to hers and tell him how her heart was throbbing in sympathy.

But he had not even asked for her love, and there must be silence between them. He had shown that it was the only way. Her own reserve closed her lips and commanded that she show no sign.

And now they rode on silently for the most part, the horses' hoofs beating rapidly in unison. Now and then a rabbit scuttled on ahead of them or a horned toad hopped out of their path. Short brown lizards palpitated on bits of wood along the way; now and then a bright green one showed itself and disappeared. Once they came upon a village of prairie dogs and paused to watch their antics for a moment. It was then as they turned away that she noticed the bit of green he had stuck in his buttonhole and recognized it for the same that she had played with as they talked by the wayside. Her eyes charged him with having picked it up afterwards and his eyes replied with the truth, but they said no words about it. They did not need words.

It was not until they reached the top of a sloping hill, and suddenly came upon the view of the valley with its winding track gleaming in the late afternoon sun, the little wooden station and few cabins dotted here and there, that she suddenly realized that their journey together was at an end, for this was the place from which she had started two days before.

He had no need to tell her. She saw the smug red gleam of their own private car standing on the track not far away. She was brought face to face with the fact that her friends were down there in the valley and all the stiff conventionalities of her life stood ready to build a wall between this man and herself. They would sweep him out of her life as if she had never met him, never been found and saved by him, and carry her away to their tiresome round of parties and pleasure excursions again.

She lifted her eyes with a frightened, almost pleading glance as if for a moment she would ask him to turn with her back to the desert again. She found his eyes upon her in a long deep gaze of farewell, as one looks upon the face of a beloved soon to be parted from earth. She could not bear the blinding of the love she saw there, and her own heart leaped up anew to meet it in answering love.

But it was only this one flash of a glance they had, when they were aware of voices and the sound of horses' hoofs, and almost instantly around the clump of sage-brush below the trail there swept into sight three horsemen, Shag Bunce, an Indian, and Hazel's brother. They were talking excitedly, and evidently starting out on a new search.

The missionary with quick presence of mind started the horses on, shouting out a greeting, and was answered with instant cheers from the approaching party, followed by shots from Shag Bunce in signal that the lost was found; shots which immediately seemed to echo from the valley and swell into shouting and rejoicing.

Then all was confusion at once.

The handsome, reckless brother with gold hair like Hazel's embraced her, talking loud and eagerly; showing how he had done this and that to find her; blaming the country, the horses, the guides, the roads; and paying little heed to the missionary who instantly dropped behind to give him his place. It seemed but a second more before they were surrounded with eager people all talking at once, and Hazel, distressed that her brother gave so little attention to the man who had saved her, sought thrice to make some sort of an introduction, but the brother was too much taken up with excitement, and with scolding his sister for having gotten herself lost, to take it in.

Then out came the father, who, it appeared, had been up two nights on the search, and had been taking a brief nap. His face was pale and haggard. Brownleigh liked the look of his eyes as he caught sight of his daughter, and his face lighted as he saw her spring into his arms, crying: "Daddy! Daddy! I'm so sorry I frightened you!"

Behind him, tall and disapproving, with an I-told-you-so in her eye, stood Aunt Maria.

"Headstrong girl," she murmured severely. "You have given us all two terrible days!" and she pecked Hazel's cheek stiffly. But no one heard her in the excitement.

Behind Aunt Maria Hazel's maid wrung her hands and wept in a kind of hysterical joy over her mistress' return, and back of her in the gloom of the car vestibule loomed the dark countenance of Hamar with an angry, red mark across one cheek. He did not look particularly anxious to be there. The missionary turned from his evil face with repulsion.

In the confusion and delight over the return of the lost one the man of the desert prepared to slip away, but just as he was about to mount his pony Hazel turned and saw him.

"Daddy, come over here and speak to the man who found me and brought me safely back again," she said, dragging her father eagerly across the platform to where the missionary stood.

The father came readily enough and Hazel talked rapidly, her eyes shining, her cheeks like twin roses, telling in a breath of the horrors and darkness and rescue, and the thoughtfulness of her stranger-rescuer.

Mr. Radcliffe came forward with outstretched hand to greet him, and the missionary took off his hat and stood with easy grace to shake hands. He was not conscious then of the fire of eyes upon him, cold society stares from Aunt Maria, Hamar and young Radcliffe, as if to say, How dared he presume to expect recognition for doing what was a simple duty! He noted only the genuine heartiness in the face of the father as he thanked him for what he had done. Then, like the practical man of the world that he was, Mr. Radcliffe reached his hand into his pocket and drew out his check book remarking, as if it were a matter of course, that he wished to reward his daughter's rescuer handsomely, and inquiring his name as he pulled off the cap from his fountain pen.

Brownleigh stood back stiffly with a heightened colour, and an almost haughty look upon his face.

"Thank you," he said coldly, "I could not think of taking anything for a mere act of humanity. It was a pleasure to be able to serve your daughter," and he swung himself easily into the saddle.

But Mr. Radcliffe was unaccustomed to such independence in those who served him and he began to bluster. Hazel, however, her cheeks fairly blazing, her eyes filled with mortification, put a hand upon her father's arm.

"Daddy, you don't understand," she said earnestly; "my new friend is a clergyman-he is a missionary, daddy!"

"Nonsense, daughter! You don't understand these matters. Just wait until I am through. I cannot let a deed like this go unrewarded. A missionary, did you say? Then if you won't take anything for yourself take it for your church; it's all the same in the end," and he gave a knowing wink towards the missionary whose anger was rising rapidly, and who was having much ado to keep a meek and quiet spirit.

"Thank you!" he said again coldly, "not for any such service."

"But I mean it!" grumbled the elder man much annoyed. "I want to donate something to a cause that employs a man like you. It is a good to the country at large to have such men patrolling the deserts. I never thought there was much excuse for Home Missions, but after this I shall give it my hearty approval. It makes the country safer for tourists. Come, tell me your name and I'll write out a check. I'm in earnest."

"Send any contribution you wish to make to the general fund," said Brownleigh with dignity, mentioning the address of the New York Board under whose auspices he was sent out, "but don't mention me, please." Then he lifted his hat once more and would have ridden away but for the distress in Hazel's eyes.

Just then the brother created a digression by rushing up to his father. "Dad, Aunt Maria wants to know if we can't go on, with this train. It's in sight now, and she is nearly crazy to get on the move. There's nothing to hinder our being hitched on, is there? The agent has the order. Do, dad, let's get out of this. I'm sick of it, and Aunt Maria is unbearable!"

"Yes, certainly, certainly, Arthur, speak to the agent. We'll go on at once. Excuse me, Mr. — — Ah, what did you say was the name? I'm sorry you feel that way about it; though it's very commendable, very commendable, I'm sure. I'll send to New York at once. Fifth Avenue, did you say? I'll speak a good word for you. Excuse me, the agent is beckoning me. Well, good-bye, and thank you again! Daughter, you better get right into the car. The train is almost here, and they may have no time to spare," and Mr. Radcliffe hastened up the platform after his son and the agent.

IX. "FOR REMEMBRANCE"

Hazel turned her troubled eyes to the face of the man pleadingly. "My father does not understand," she said apologetically. "He is very grateful and he is used to thinking that money can always show gratitude."

Brownleigh was off his horse beside her, his hat off, before she had finished speaking.

"Don't, I beg of you, think of it again," he pleaded, his eyes devouring her face. "It is all right. I quite understand. And you understand too, I am sure."

"Yes, I understand," she said, lifting her eyes full of the love she had not dared to let him see. She was fidgeting with her rings as she spoke and looked back anxiously at the onrushing train. Her brother, hurrying down the platform to their car, called to her to hasten as he passed her, and she knew she would be allowed but a moment more. She caught her breath and looked at the tall missionary wistfully.

"You will let me leave something of my own with you, just for remembrance?" she asked eagerly.

His eyes grew tender and misty.

"Of course," he said, his voice suddenly husky, "though I shall need nothing to remember you by. I can never forget you." The memory of that look of his eyes was meat and drink to her soul during many days that followed, but she met it now steadily, not even flushing at her open recognition of his love.

"This is mine," she said. "My father bought it for me when I was sixteen. I have worn it ever since. He will never care." She slipped a ring from her finger and dropped it in his palm.

"Hurry up there, sister!" called young Radcliffe once more from the car window, and looking up, Brownleigh saw the evil face of Hamar peering from another window.

Hazel turned, struggling to keep back the rising tears. "I must go," she gasped.

Brownleigh flung the reins of the pony to a young Indian who stood near and turning walked beside her, conscious the while of the frowning faces watching them from the car windows.

"And I have nothing to give you," he said to her in a low tone, deeply moved at what she had done.

"Will you let me have the little book?" she asked shyly.

His eyes lit with a kind of glory as he felt in his pocket for his Bible.

"It is the best thing I own," he said. "May it bring you the same joy and comfort it has often brought to me." And he put the little book in her hand.

The train backed crashing up and jarred into the private car with a snarling, grating sound. Brownleigh put Hazel on the steps and helped her up. Her father was hurrying towards them and some train hands were making a great fuss shouting directions. There was just an instant for a hand-clasp, and then he stepped back to the platform, and her father swung himself on, as the train moved off. She stood on the top step of the car, her eyes upon his face, and his upon hers, his hat lifted in homage, and renunciation upon his brow as though it were a crown.

It was the voice of her Aunt Maria that recalled her to herself, while the little station with its primitive setting, its straggling onlookers and its one great man, slipped past and was blurred into the landscape by the tears which she could not keep back.

"Hazel! For pity's sake! Don't stand mooning and gazing at that rude creature any longer. We'll have you falling off the train and being dramatically rescued again for the delectation of the natives. I'm sure you've made disturbance enough for one trip, and you'd better come in and try to make amends to poor Mr. Hamar for what you have made him suffer with your foolish persistence in going off on a wild western pony that ran away. You haven't spoken to Mr. Hamar yet. Perhaps you don't know that he risked his life for you trying to catch your horse and was thrown and kicked in the face by his own wretched little beast, and left lying unconscious for hours on the desert, until an Indian came along and picked him up and helped him back to the station." (As a matter of fact Milton Hamar had planned and enacted this touching drama with the help of a passing Indian, when he found that Hazel was gone, leaving an ugly whip

145

mark on his cheek which must be explained to the family.) "He may bear that dreadful scar for life! He will think you an ungrateful girl if you don't go at once and make your apologies."

For answer Hazel, surreptitiously brushing away the tears, swept past her aunt and locked herself into her own little private stateroom.

She rushed eagerly to the window which was partly open, guarded with a screen, and pressed her face against the upper part of the glass. The train had described a curve across the prairie, and the station was still visible, though far away. She was sure she could see the tall figure of her lover standing with hat in hand watching her as she passed from his sight.

With quick impulse she caught up a long white crepe scarf that lay on her berth, and snatching the screen from the window fluttered the scarf out to the wind. Almost instantly a flutter of white came from the figure on the platform, and her heart quickened with joy. They had sent a message from heart to heart across the wide space of the plains, and the wireless telegraphy of hearts was established. Great tears rushed to blot the last flutter of white from the receding landscape, and then a hill loomed brilliant and shifting, and in a moment more shut out the sight of station and dim group and Hazel knew that she was back in the world of commonplace things once more, with only a memory for her company, amid a background of unsympathetic relatives.

She made her toilet in a leisurely way, for she dreaded to have to talk as she knew she would, and dreaded still more to meet Hamar. But she knew she must go and tell her father of her experiences, and presently she came out to them fresh and beautiful, with eyes but the brighter for her tears, and a soft wild-rose flush on her wind-browned cheeks that made her beauty all the sweeter.

They clamoured at once, of course, for all the details of her experience, and began by rehearsing once more how hard Mr. Hamar had tried to save her from her terrible plight, risking his life to stop her horse. Hazel said nothing to this, but one steady clear look at the disfigured face of the man who had made them believe all this was the only recognition she gave of his would-be heroism. In that look she managed to show her utter disbelief and contempt, though her Aunt Maria and perhaps even her father and brother thought her gratitude too deep for utterance before them all.

The girl passed over the matter of the runaway with a brief word, saying that the pony had made up his mind to run, and she had lost the bridle, which of course explained her inability to control him. She made light of her ride, however, before her aunt, and told the whole story most briefly until she came to the canyon and the howl of the coyotes. She was most warm in praise of her rescuer, though here too she used few words and avoided any description of the ride back, merely saying that the missionary had shown himself a gentleman in every particular, and had given her every care and attention that her own family could have done under the circumstances, making the way pleasant with stories of the country and the people. She said that he was a man of unusual culture and refinement, she thought, and yet most earnestly devoted to his work, and then she abruptly changed the subject by asking about certain plans for their further trip and seeming to have no further interest in what had befallen her; but all the while she was conscious of the piercing glance and frowning visage of Milton Hamar watching her, and she knew that as soon as opportunity offered itself he would continue the hateful interview begun on the plain. She decided mentally that she would avoid any such interview if possible, and to that end excused herself immediately after lunch had been served, saying she needed a good sleep to make up for the long ride she had taken.

But it was not to sleep that she gave herself when she was at last able to take refuge in her little apartment again. She looked out at the passing landscape, beautiful with varied scenery, all blurred with tears as she thought of how she had but a little while before been out in its wide free distance with one who loved her. How that thought thrilled and thrilled her, and brought her a fresh joy each time it repeated itself! She wondered over the miracle of it. She never had dreamed that love was like this. She scarce believed it now. She was excited, stirred to the depths by her unusual experience, put beyond the normal by the strangeness of the surroundings that had brought this man into her acquaintance; so said common sense, and warned her that to-morrow, or the next day, or at most next week, the thrill would all be gone and she would think of the stranger missionary as one curious detail of her Western trip. But her heart resented this, and down, deep down, something else told her this strange new joy would not vanish, that it would live throughout her life, and that whatever in the years came to her, she would always know underneath all that this had been the real thing, the highest fullness of a perfect love for her.

As the miles lengthened and her thoughts grew sad with the distance, she drew from its hiding place the little book he had given her at parting. She had slipped it into the breast pocket of her riding habit as she received it, for she shrank from having her aunt's keen eyes detect it and question her. She had been too much engrossed with the thought of separation to remember it till now.

She touched it tenderly, shyly, as though it were a part of himself; the limp, worn covers, the look of constant use, all made it inexpressibly dear. She had not known before that an inanimate object, not beautiful in itself, could bring such tender love.

Opening to the flyleaf, there in clear, bold writing was his name, "John Chadwick Brownleigh," and for the first time she realized that there had passed between them no word of her name. Strange that they two should have come so close as to need no names one with the other. But her heart leaped up with joy that she knew his name, and her eyes dwelt yearningly upon the written characters. John! How well the name fitted him. It seemed that she would have known it was his even if she had not seen it written first in one of his possessions. Then she fell to meditating whether he would have any way of discovering her name. Perhaps her father had given it to him, or the station agent might have known to whom their car belonged. Of course he would when he received the orders, — or did they give orders about cars only by numbers? She wished she dared ask some one. Perhaps she could find out in some way how those orders were written. And yet all the time she had an instinctive feeling that had he known her name a thousand times he would not have communicated with her. She knew by that exalted look of renunciation upon his face that no longing whatsoever could make him overstep the bounds which he had laid down between her soul and his.

With a sigh she opened the little book, and it fell apart of itself to the place where he had read the night before, the page still marked by the little silk cord he had placed so carefully. She could see him now with the firelight flickering on his face, and the moonlight silvering his head, that strong tender look upon his face. How wonderful he had been!

She read the psalm over now herself, the first time in her life she had ever consciously given herself to reading the Bible. But there was a charm about the words that gave them new meaning, the charm of his voice as she heard them in memory and watched again his face change and stir at the words as he read.

The day waned and the train flew on, but the landscape had lost its attraction now for the girl. She pleaded weariness and remained apart from the rest, dreaming over her wonderful experience, and thinking new deep thoughts of wonder, regret, sadness, joy, and when night fell and the great moon rose lighting the world again, she knelt beside her car window, looking long into the wide clear sky, the sky that covered him and herself; the moon that looked down upon them both. Then switching on the electric light over her berth she read the psalm once more, and fell asleep with her cheek upon the little book and in her heart a prayer for him.

John Brownleigh, standing upon the station platform, watching the train disappear behind the foot-hills, experienced, for the first time since his coming to Arizona, a feeling of the utmost desolation. Lonely he had been, and homesick, sometimes, but always with a sense that he was master of it all, and that with the delight of his work it would pass and leave him free and glad in the power wherewith his God had called him to the service. But now he felt that with this train the light of life was going from him, and all the glory of Arizona and the world in which he had loved to be was darkened on her account. For a moment or two his soul cried out that it could not be, that he must mount some winged steed and speed after her whom his heart had enthroned. Then the wall of the inevitable appeared before his eager eyes, and Reason crowded close to bring him to his senses. He turned away to hide the emotion in his face. The stolid Indian boy, who had been holding both horses, received his customary smile and pleasant word, but the missionary gave them more by habit than thought this time. His soul had entered its Gethsemane, and his spirit was bowed within him.

As soon as he could get away from the people about the station who had their little griefs and joys and perplexities to tell him, he mounted Billy, and leading the borrowed pony rode away into the desert, retracing the way they had come together but a short time before.

Billy was tired and walked slowly, drooping his head, and his master was sad at heart, so there was no cheerful converse between them as they travelled along.

It was not far they went, only back to the edge of the corn, where they had made their last stop of the journey together a few short hours before, and here the missionary halted and gave the beasts their freedom for a respite and refreshment. He himself felt too weary of soul to go further.

He took out the ring, the little ring that was too small to go more than half-way on his smallest finger, the ring she had taken warm and flashing from her white hand and laid within his palm!

The sun low down in the west stole into the heart of the jewel and sent its glory in a million multicoloured facets, piercing his soul with the pain and the joy of his love. He cast himself down upon the grass where she had sat, where, with his eyes closed and his lips upon the jewel she had worn, he met his enemy and fought his battle out.

Wearied at last with the contest, he slept. The sun went down, the moon made itself manifest once more, and when the night went coursing down its way of silver, two jewels softly gleamed in its radiance, the one upon his finger where he had pressed her ring, the other from the grass beside him. With a curious wonder he put forth his hand to the second and found it was the topaz set in the handle of her whip which she had dropped and forgotten when they sat together and talked by the way. He seized it eagerly now, and gathered it to him. It seemed almost a message of comfort from her he loved. It was something tangible, this, and the ring, to show him he had not dreamed her coming; she had been real, and she had wanted him to tell her of his love, had said it would make a difference all the rest of her life.

He remembered that somewhere he had read or heard a great man say that to be worthy of a great love one must be able to do without it. Here now, then, he would prove his love by doing without. He stood with uplifted face, transfigured in the light of the brilliant night, with the look of exalted self-surrender, but only his heart communed that night, for there were no words on his dumb lips to express the fullness of his abnegation.

Then forth upon his way he went, his battle fought, the stronger for it, to be a staff for other men to lean upon.

X. HIS MOTHER

Deserts and mountains remain, duties crowd and press, hearts ache but the world rushes on. The weeks that followed showed these two that a great love is eternal.

Brownleigh did not try to put the thought of it out of his life, but rather let it glorify the common round. Day after day passed and he went from post to post, from hogan to mesa, and back to his shanty again, always with the thought of her companionship, and found it sweet. Never had he been less cheery when he met his friends, though there was a quiet dignity, a tender reserve behind it all that a few discerning ones perceived. They said at the Fort that he was losing flesh, but if so, he was gaining muscle. His lean brown arms were never stronger, and his fine strong face was never sad when any one was by. It was only in the night-time alone upon the moonlit desert, or in his little quiet dwelling place when he talked with his Father, and told all the loneliness and heartache. His people found him more sympathetic, more painstaking, more tireless than ever before, and the work prospered under his hand.

The girl in the city deliberately set herself to forget.

The first few days after she left him had been a season of ecstatic joy mingled with deep depression, as she alternately meditated upon the fact of a great love, or faced its impossibility.

She had scorched Milton Hamar with her glance of aversion, and avoided him constantly even in the face of protest from her family, until he had made excuse and left the party at Pasadena. There, too, Aunt Maria had relieved them of her annoying interference, and the return trip taken by the southern route had been an unmolested time for meditation for the girl. She became daily more and more dissatisfied with herself and her useless, ornamental life. Some days she read the little book, and other days she shut it away and tried to get back to her former life, telling herself it was useless to attempt to change herself. She had found that the little book gave her a deep unrest and a sense that life held graver, sweeter things than just living to please one's self. She began to long for home, and the summer round of gaieties, with which to fill the emptiness of her heart.

As the summer advanced there was almost a recklessness sometimes about the way she planned to have a good time every minute; yet in the quiet of her own room there would always come back the yearning that had been awakened in the desert and would not be silenced.

Sometimes when the memory of that great deep love she had heard expressed for herself came over her, the bitter tears would come to her eyes and one thought would throb through her consciousness: "Not worthy! Not worthy!" He had not thought her fit to be his wife. Her father and her world would think it quite otherwise. They would count him unworthy to mate with her, an heiress, the pet of society; he a man who had given up his life for a whim, a fad, a fanatical fancy! But she knew it was not so. She knew him to be a man of all men. She knew it was true that she was not such a woman as a man like that could fitly wed, and the thought galled her constantly.

She tried to accustom herself to think of him as a pleasant experience, a friend who might have been if circumstances with them both had been different; she tried to tell herself that it was a passing fancy with them which both would forget; and she tried with all her heart to forget, even locking away the precious little book and trying to forget it too.

And then, one day in late summer, she went with a motoring party through New England; as frolicsome and giddy a party as could be found among New York society transferred for the summer to the world of Nature. There was to be a dance or a house party or something of the sort at the end of the drive. Hazel scarcely knew, and cared less. She was becoming utterly weary of her butterfly life.

The day was hot and dusty, Indian summer intensified. They had got out of their way through a mistake of the chauffeur, and suddenly just on the edge of a tiny quaint little village the car broke down and refused to go on without a lengthy siege of coaxing and petting.

The members of the party, powdered with dust and in no very pleasant frame of mind from the delay, took refuge at the village inn, an old-time hostelry close to the roadside, with wide, brick-paved, white-pillared piazza across the front, and a mysterious hedged garden at the side. There were many plain wooden rockers neatly adorned with white crash on the piazza, and one or two late summer boarders loitering about with knitting work or book. The landlord brought cool tinkling glasses of water and rich milk from the spring-house, and they dropped into the chairs to wait while the men of the party gave assistance to the chauffeur in patching up the car.

Hazel sank wearily into her chair and sipped the milk unhungrily. She wished she had not come; wished the day were over, and that she might have planned something more interesting; wished she had chosen different people to be of her party; and idly watched a white hen with yellow kid boots and a coral comb in her nicely groomed hair picking daintily about the green under the oak trees that shaded the street. She listened to the drone of the bees in the garden near by, the distant whetting of a scythe, the monotonous whang of a steam thresher not far away, the happy voices of children, and thought how empty a life in this village would be; almost as dreary and uninteresting as living in a desert-and then suddenly she caught a name and the pink flew into her cheeks and memory set her heart athrob.

It was the landlord talking to a lingering summer boarder, a quiet, gray-haired woman who sat reading at the end of the piazza.

"Well, Miss Norton, so you're goin' to leave us next week. Sorry to hear it. Don't seem nat'ral 'thout you clear through October. Ca'c'late you're comin' back to Granville in the spring?"

Granville! Granville! Where had she heard of Granville? Ah! She knew instantly. It was his old home! His mother lived there! But then of course it might have been another Granville. She wasn't even sure what state they were in now, New Hampshire or Vermont. They had been wavering about on the state line several times that day, and she never paid attention to geography.

Then the landlord raised his voice again.

He was gazing across the road where a white colonial house, white-fenced with pickets like clean sugar frosting, nestled in the luscious grass, green and clean and fresh, and seeming utterly apart from the soil and dust of the road, as if nothing wearisome could ever enter there. Brightly there bloomed a border of late flowers, double asters, zinnias, peonies, with a flame of scarlet poppies breaking into the smoke-like blue of larkspurs and bachelor buttons, as it neared the house. Hazel had not noticed it until now and she almost cried out with pleasure over the splendour of colour.

"Wal," said the landlord chinking some loose coins in his capacious pockets, "I reckon Mis' Brownleigh'll miss yeh 'bout as much as enny of us. She lots on your comin' over to read to her. I've heerd her say as how Amelia Ellen is a good nurse, but she never was much on the readin', an' Amelia Ellen knows it too. Mis' Brownleigh she'll be powerful lonesome fer yeh when yeh go. It's not so lively fur her tied to her bed er her chair, even ef John does write to her reg'lur twicet a week."

And now Hazel noticed that on the covered veranda in front of the wing of the house across the way there sat an old lady on a reclining wheeled chair, and that another woman in a plain blue gown hovered near waiting upon her. A luxuriant woodbine partly hid the chair, and the distance was too great to see the face of the woman, but Hazel grew weak with wonder and pleasure. She sat quite still trying to gather her forces while the summer boarder expressed earnest regret at having to leave her chosen summer abiding place so much earlier than usual. At last her friends began to rally Hazel on her silence. She turned away annoyed, and answered them crossly, following the landlord into the house and questioning him eagerly. She had suddenly arrived at the conclusion that she must see Mrs. Brownleigh and know if she looked like her son, and if she was the kind of mother one would expect such a son to have. She felt that in the sight might lie her emancipation from the bewitchment that had bound her in its toils since her Western trip. She also secretly hoped it might justify her dearest dreams of what his mother was like.

"Do you suppose that lady across the street would mind if I went over to look at her beautiful flowers?" she burst in upon the astonished landlord as he tipped his chair back with his feet on another and prepared to browse over yesterday's paper for the third time that day.

He brought his chair down on its four legs with a thump and drew his hat further over his forehead.

"Not a bit, not a bit, young lady. She's proud to show off her flowers. They're one of the sights of Granville. Mis' Brownleigh loves to have comp'ny. Jest go right over an' tell her I sent you. She'll tell you all about 'em, an' like ez not she'll give you a bokay to take 'long. She's real generous with 'em."

He tottered out to the door after her on his stiff rheumatic legs, and suggested that the other young ladies might like to go along, but they one and all declined, to Hazel's intense relief, and called their ridicule after her as she picked her way across the dusty road and opened the white gate into the peaceful scene beyond.

When she drew close to the side piazza she saw one of the most beautiful faces she had ever looked upon. The features were delicate and exquisitely modelled, aged by years and much suffering, yet lovely with a peace that had permitted no fretting. An abundance of waving silken hair white as driven snow was piled high upon her head against the snowy pillow, and soft brown eyes made the girl's heart throb quickly with their likeness to those other eyes that had once looked into hers.

She was dressed in a simple little muslin gown of white and gray with white cloud-like finish at throat and wrists, and across the helpless limbs was flung a light afghan of pink and gray wool. She made a sweet picture as she lay and watched her approaching guest with a smile of interest and welcome.

"The landlord said you would not mind if I came over to see your flowers," Hazel said with a shy, half-frightened catch in her voice. Now that she was here she was almost sorry she had come. It might not be his mother at all, and what could she say anyway? Yet her first glimpse told her that this was a mother to be proud of. "The most beautiful mother in the world" he had called her, and surely this woman could be none other than the one who had mothered such a son. Her highest ideals of motherhood seemed realized as she gazed upon the peaceful face of the invalid.

And then the voice! For the woman was speaking now, holding out a lily-white hand to her and bidding her be seated in the Chinese willow chair that stood close by the wheeled one; a great green silk cushion at the back, and a large palm leaf fan on the table beside it.

"I am so pleased that you came over," Mrs. Brownleigh was saying. "I have been wondering if some one wouldn't come to me. I keep my flowers partly to attract my friends, for I can stand a great deal of company since I'm all alone. You came in the big motor car that broke down, didn't you? I've been watching the pretty girls over there, in their gay ribbons and veils. They look like human flowers. Rest here and tell me where you have come from and where you are going, while Amelia Ellen picks you some flowers to take along. Afterwards you shall go among them and see if there are any you like that she has missed. Amelia Ellen! Get your basket and scissors and pick a great many flowers for this young lady. It is getting late and they have not much longer to blossom. There are three white buds on the rose-bush. Pick them all. I think they fit your face, my dear. Now take off your hat and let me see your pretty hair without its covering. I want to get your picture fixed in my heart so I can look at you after you are gone."

And so quite simply they fell into easy talk about each other, the day, the village, and the flowers.

"You see the little white church down the street? My husband was its pastor for twenty years. I came to this house a bride, and our boy was born here. Afterwards, when his father was taken away, I stayed right here with the people who loved him. The boy was in college then, getting ready to take up his father's work. I've stayed here ever since. I love the people and they love me, and I couldn't very well be moved, you know. My boy is out in Arizona, a home missionary!" She said it as Abraham Lincoln's mother might have said: "My boy is president of the United

States!" Her face wore a kind of glory that bore a startling resemblance to the man of the desert. Hazel marvelled greatly, and understood what had made the son so great.

"I don't see how he could go and leave you alone!" she broke forth almost bitterly. "I should think his duty was here with his mother!"

"Yes, I know," the mother smiled; "they do say that, some of them, but it's because they don't understand. You see we gave John to God when he was born, and it was our hope from the first that he would choose to be a minister and a missionary. Of course John thought at first after his father went away that he could not leave me, but I made him see that I would be happier so. He wanted me to go with him, but I knew I should only be a hindrance to the work, and it came to me that my part in the work was to stay at home and let him go. It was all I had left to do after I became an invalid. And I'm very comfortable. Amelia Ellen takes care of me like a baby, and there are plenty of friends. My boy writes me beautiful letters twice a week, and we have such nice talks about the work. He's very like his father, and growing more so every day. Perhaps," she faltered and fumbled under the pink and silver lap robe, "perhaps you'd like to read a bit of one of his letters. I have it here. It came yesterday and I've only read it twice. I don't let myself read them too often because they have to last three days apiece at least. Perhaps you'd read it aloud to me. I like to hear John's words aloud sometimes and Amelia Ellen has never spent much time reading. She is peculiar in her pronunciation. Do you mind reading it to me?"

She held a letter forth, written in a strong free hand, the same that had signed the name John Chadwick Brownleigh in the little book. Hazel's heart throbbed eagerly and her hand trembled as she reached it shyly towards the letter. What a miracle was this! that his very letter was being put into her hand, her whom he loved—to read! Was it possible? Could there be a mistake? No, surely not. There could not be two John Brownleighs, both missionaries to Arizona.

"Dear little Mother o' Mine:" it began, and plunged at once into the breezy life of the Western country. He had been to a cattle round-up the week before and he described it minutely in terse and vivid language, with many a flash of wit, or graver touch of wisdom, and here and there a boyish expression that showed him young at heart, and devoted to his mother. He told of a visit he had paid to the Hopi Indians, their strange villages, each like a gigantic house with many rooms, called a pueblo, built on the edges of lofty crags or mesas and looking like huge castles five or six hundred feet above the desert floor. He told of Walpi, a village out on the end of a great promontory, its only access a narrow neck of land less than a rod wide, with one little path worn more than a foot deep in the solid rock by the feet of ten generations passing over it, where now live about two hundred and thirty people in one building. There were seven of these villages built on three mesas that reach out from the northern desert like three great fingers, Oraibi, the largest, having over a thousand people. He explained that Spanish explorers found these Hopis in 1540, long before the pilgrims landed at Plymouth Rock, and called the country Tusayan. Then he went on to describe a remarkable meeting that had been held in which the Indians had manifested deep interest in spiritual things, and had asked many curious questions about life, death and the hereafter.

"You see, dear," said the mother, her eyes shining eagerly, "you see how much they need him, and I'm glad I can give him. It makes me have a part in the work."

Hazel turned back to the letter and went on reading to hide the tears that were gathering in her own eyes as she looked upon the exalted face of the mother.

There was a detailed account of a conference of missionaries, to attend which the rider had ridden ninety miles on horseback; and at the close there was an exquisite description of the spot where they had camped the last night of their ride. She knew it from the first word almost, and her heart beat so wildly she could hardly keep her voice steady to read:

"I stopped over night on the way home at a place I dearly love. There is a great rock, shelving and overhanging, for shelter from any passing storm, and quite near a charming green boudoir of cedars on three sides, and rock on the fourth. An abundant water-hole makes camping easy for me and Billy, and the stars overhead are good tapers. Here I build my fire and boil the kettle, read my portion and lie down to watch the heavens. Mother, I wish you knew how near to God one feels out in the desert with the stars. Last night about three o'clock I woke to replenish my fire and watch a while a great comet, the finest one for many years. I would tell you about it but I've already made this letter too long, and it's time Billy and I were on our way again. I love this spot beside the big rock and often come back to it on my journeys; perhaps because here I once camped with a dear friend and we had pleasant converse together around our brushwood fire. It makes the desert seem less lonely because I can sometimes fancy my friend still reclining over on the other side of the fire in the light that plays against the great rock. Well, little mother o' mine, I must close. Cheer up, for it has been intimated to me that I may be sent East to General Assembly in the spring, and then for three whole weeks with you! That will be when the wild strawberries are out, and I shall carry you in my arms and spread a couch for you on the strawberry hill behind the house, and you shall pick some again with your own hands."

With a sudden catch in her throat like a sob the reading came to an end and Hazel, her eyes bright with tears, handed the letter reverently back to the mother whose face was bright with smiles.

"Isn't he a boy worth giving?" she asked as she folded the letter and slipped it back under the pink and gray cover.

"He is a great gift," said Hazel in a low voice.

She was almost glad that Amelia Ellen came up with an armful of flowers just then and she might bury her face in their freshness and hide the tears that would not be stayed, and then before she had half admired their beauty there was a loud "Honk-honk!" from the road, followed by a more impatient one, and Hazel was made aware that she was being waited for.

"I'm sorry you must go, dear," said the gentle woman. "I haven't seen so beautiful a girl in years, and I'm sure you have a lovely heart, too. I wish you could visit me again."

"I will come again some time if you will let me!" said the girl impulsively, and then stooped and kissed the soft rose-leaf cheek, and fled down the path trying to get control of her emotion before meeting her companions.

Hazel was quiet all the rest of the way, and was rallied much upon her solemnity. She pleaded a headache and closed her eyes, while each heart-throb carried her back over the months and brought her again to the little camp under the rock beneath the stars.

"He remembered still! He cared!" This was what her glad thoughts sang as the car whirled on, and her gay companions forgot her and chattered of their frivolities.

"How wonderful that I should find his mother!" she said again and again to herself. Yet it was not so wonderful. He had told her the name of the town, and she might have come here any time of her own accord. But it was strange and beautiful that the accident had brought her straight to the door of the house where he had been born and brought up! What a beautiful, happy boyhood he must have had with a mother like that! Hazel found herself thinking wistfully, out of the emptiness of her own motherless girlhood. Yes, she would go back and see the sweet mother some day; and she fell to planning how it could be.

XI. REFUGE

Milton Hamar had not troubled Hazel all summer. From time to time her father mentioned him as being connected with business enterprises, and it was openly spoken of now that a divorce had been granted him, and his former wife was soon to marry again. All this, however, was most distasteful to the girl to whom the slightest word about the man served to bring up the hateful scene of the desert.

But early in the fall he appeared among them again, assuming his old friendly attitude towards the whole family, dropping in to lunch or dinner whenever it suited his fancy. He seemed to choose to forget what had passed between Hazel and himself, to act as though it had not been, and resumed his former playful attitude of extreme interest in the girl of whom he had always been fond. Hazel, however, found a certain air of proprietorship in his gaze, a too-open expression of his admiration which was offensive. She could not forget, try as hard as she might for her father's sake to forgive. She shrank away from the man's company, avoided him whenever possible, and at last when he seemed to be almost omnipresent, and growing every day more insistent in his attentions, she cast about her for some absorbing interest which would take her out of his sphere.

Then a strange fancy took her in its possession.

It was in the middle of the night when it came to her, where she had been turning her luxurious pillow for two hours trying in vain to tempt a drowsiness that would not come, and she arose at once and wrote a brief and businesslike letter to the landlord of the little New Hampshire inn where she had been delayed for a couple of hours in the fall. In the morning, true to her impulsive nature, she besieged her father until he gave his permission for her to take her maid and a quiet elderly cousin of his and go away for a complete rest before the society season began.

It was a strange whim for his butterfly daughter to take but the busy man saw no harm in it, and was fully convinced that it was merely her way of punishing some over ardent follower for a few days; and feeling sure she would soon return, he let her go. She had had her way all her life, and why should he cross her in so simple a matter as a few days' rest in a country inn with a respectable chaperone?

The letter to the landlord was outtravelled by a telegram whose answer sent Hazel on her way the next morning, thankful that she had been able to get away during a temporary absence of Milton Hamar, and that her father had promised not to let any of her friends know of her whereabouts. His eye had twinkled as he made the promise. He was quite sure which of her many admirers was being punished, but he did not tell her so. He intended to be most judicious with all her young men friends. He so confided his intentions to Milton Hamar that evening, having no thought that Hazel would mind their old friend's knowing.

Two days later Hazel, after establishing her little party comfortably in the best rooms the New Hampshire inn afforded, putting a large box of new novels at their disposal, and another of sweets, and sending orders for new magazines to be forwarded, went over to call on the sweet old lady towards whom her heart had been turning eagerly, with a longing that would not be put away, ever since that first accidental, or providential, meeting.

When she came back, through the first early snow-storm, with her cheeks like winter roses and her furry hat all feathered with great white flakes, she found Milton Hamar seated in front of the open fire in the office making the air heavy with his best tobacco, and frowning impatiently through the small-paned windows.

The bright look faded instantly from her face and the peace which she had almost caught from the woman across the way. Her eyes flashed indignantly, and her whole small frame stiffened for the combat that she knew must come now. There was no mistaking her look. Milton Hamar knew at once that he was not welcome. She stood for an instant with the door wide open, blowing a great gust of biting air across the wide room and into his face. A cloud of smoke sprang out from the fireplace to meet it and the two came together in front of the man, and made a visible wall for a second between him and the girl.

He sprang to his feet, cigar in hand, and an angry exclamation upon his lips. The office, fortunately, was without other occupant.

"Why in the name of all that's unholy did you lead me a race away off to this forsaken little hole in midwinter, Hazel?" he cried.

Hazel drew herself to her full height and with the dignity that well became her, answered him:

"Really, Mr. Hamar, what right have you to speak to me in that way? And what right had you to follow me?"

"The right of the man who is going to marry you!" he answered fiercely; "and I think it's about time this nonsense stopped. It's nothing but coquettish foolishness, your coming here. I hate coquettish fools. I didn't think you had it in you to coquet, but it seems all women are alike."

"Mr. Hamar, you are forgetting yourself," said the girl quietly, turning to shut the door that she might gain time to get control of her shaken nerves. She had a swift vision of what it would be if she were married to a man like that. No wonder his wife was entirely willing to give him a divorce. But she shuddered as she turned back and faced him bravely.

"Well, what did you come here for?" he asked in a less fierce tone.

"I came because I wanted to be quiet," Hazel said trying to steady her voice, "and—I will tell you the whole truth. I came because I wanted to get away from—you! I have not liked the way you acted towards me since—that day—in Arizona."

The man's fierce brows drew together, but a kind of mask of apology overspread his features. He perceived that he had gone too far with the girl whom he had thought scarcely more than a child. He had thought he could mould her like wax, and that his scorn would instantly wither her wiles. He watched her steadily for a full minute; the girl, though trembling in every nerve, sending back a steady, haughty gaze.

"Do you mean that?" he said at last.

"I do!" Her voice was quiet, but she was on the verge of tears.

"Well, perhaps we'd better talk it over. I see I've taken too much for granted. I thought you'd understood for a year or more what was going on—what I was doing it for."

"You thought I understood! You thought I would be willing to be a party to such an awful thing as you have done!" Hazel's eyes were flashing fire now. The tears were scorched away.

"Sit down! We'll talk it over," said the man moving a great summer chair nearer to his own. His eyes were on her face approvingly and he was thinking what a beautiful picture she made in her anger.

"Never!" said the girl quickly. "It is not a thing I could talk over. I do not wish to speak of it again. I wish you to leave this place at once," and she turned with a quick movement and fled up the quaint old staircase.

She stayed in her room until he left, utterly refusing to see him, refusing to answer the long letters he wrote and sent up to her; and finally, after another day, he went away. But he wrote to her several times, and came again twice, each time endeavouring to surprise her into talking with him. The girl grew to watch nervously every approach of the daily stage which brought stray travellers from the station four miles distant, and was actually glad when a heavy snow-storm shut them in and made it unlikely that her unwelcome visitor would venture again into the country.

The last time he came Hazel saw him descending from the coach, and without a word to any one, although it was almost supper time, and the early winter twilight was upon them, she seized her fur cloak and slipped down the back stairs, out through the shadows, across the road, where she surprised good Amelia Ellen by flinging her arms about her neck and bursting into tears right in the dark front hall, for the gust of wintry wind from the open door blew the candle out, and Amelia Ellen stood astonished and bewildered for a moment in the blast of the north wind with the soft arms of the excited girl in her furry wrappings clinging about her unaccustomed shoulders.

Amelia Ellen had never had many beautiful things in her life, the care of her Dresden-china mistress, and her brilliant garden of flowers, having been the crowning of her life hitherto. This beautiful city girl with her exquisite garments and her face like a flower, flung upon her in sudden appeal, drew out all the latent love and pity and sympathy of which Amelia Ellen had a larger store than most, hidden under a simple and severe exterior.

"Fer the land's sake! Whatever ails you!" she exclaimed when she could speak for astonishment, and to her own surprise her arm enclosed the sobbing girl in a warm embrace while with the other hand she reached to close the door. "Come right in to my kitchen and set in the big chair by the cat and let me give you a cup o' tea. Then you can tell Mis' Brownleigh what's troublin' you. She'll know how to talk to you. I'll git you some tea right away."

She drew the shrinking girl into the kitchen and ousting the cat from a patchwork rocker pushed her gently into it. It was characteristic of Amelia Ellen that she had no thought of ministering to her spiritual needs herself, but knew her place was to bring physical comfort.

She spoke no word save to the cat, admonishing him to mend his manners and keep out from under foot, while she hurried to the tea canister, the bread box, the sugar bowl, and the china closet. Soon a cup of fragrant tea was set before the unexpected guest, and a bit of delicate toast browning over the coals, to be buttered and eaten crisp with the tea; and the cat nestled comfortably at Hazel's feet while she drank the tea and wiped away the tears.

"You'll think I'm a big baby, Amelia Ellen!" cried Hazel trying to smile shamedly, "but I'm just so tired of the way things go. You see somebody I don't a bit like has come up from New York on the evening coach, and I've run away for a little while. I don't know what made me cry. I never cry at home, but when I got safely over here a big lump came in my throat and you looked so nice and kind that I couldn't keep the tears back."

From that instant Amelia Ellen, toasting fork in hand, watching the sweet blue eyes and the tear-stained face that resembled a drenched pink bud after a storm, loved Hazel Radcliffe. Come weal, come woe, Amelia Ellen was from henceforth her staunch admirer and defendant.

"Never you mind, honey, you just eat your tea an' run in to Mis' Brownleigh, an' I'll get my hood an' run over to tell your folks you've come to stay all night over here. Then you'll have a cozy evenin' readin' while I sew, an' you can sleep late come mornin', and go back when you're ready. Nobody can't touch you over here. I'm not lettin' in people by night 'thout I know 'em," and she winked knowingly at the girl by way of encouragement. Well she knew who the unwelcome stranger from New York was. She had keen eyes, and had watched the coach from her well-curtained kitchen window as it came in.

That night Hazel told her invalid friend all about Milton Hamar, and slept in the pleasant bed that Amelia Ellen had prepared for her, with sheets of fragrant linen redolent of sweet clover. Her heart was lighter for the simple, kindly advice and the gentle love that had been showered upon her. She wondered, as she lay half dozing in the morning with the faint odour of coffee and muffins penetrating the atmosphere, why it was that she could love this beautiful mother of her hero so much more tenderly than she had ever loved any other woman. Was it because she had never known her own mother and had longed for one all her life, or was it just because she was *his* dear mother? She gave up trying to answer the question and went smiling down to breakfast, and then across the road to face her unwelcome lover, strong in the courage that friendly counsel had given her.

Milton Hamar left before dinner, having been convinced at last of the uselessness of his visit. He hired a man with a horse and cutter to drive him across country to catch the New York evening express, and Hazel drew a breath of relief and began to find new pleasure in life. Her father was off on a business trip for some weeks; her brother had gone abroad for the winter with a party of college friends. There was no real reason why she should return to New York for some time, and she decided to stay and learn of this saintly woman how to look wisely on the things of life. To her own heart she openly acknowledged that there was a deep pleasure in being near one who talked of the man she loved.

So the winter settled down to business, and Hazel spent happy days with her new friends, for Amelia Ellen had become a true friend in the best sense of the word.

The maid had found the country winter too lonely and Hazel had found her useless and sent her back to town. She was learning by association with Amelia Ellen to do a few things for herself. The elderly cousin, whose years had been a long strain of scrimping to present a respectable exterior, was only too happy to have leisure and quiet to read and embroider to her heart's content. So Hazel was free to spend much time with Mrs. Brownleigh.

They read together, at least Hazel did the reading, for the older eyes were growing dim, and had to be guarded to prevent the terrible headaches which came at the slightest provocation and made the days a blank of suffering for the lovely soul where patience was having its perfect work.

The world of literature opened through a new door to the eager young mind now. Books of which she had never heard were at her hand. New thoughts and feelings were stirred by them. A few friends who knew Mrs. Brownleigh through their summer visits, and others who had known her husband, kept her well supplied with the latest and always the best of everything-history, biography, essays and fiction. But there were also books of a deep spiritual character, and magazines that showed a new world, the religious world, to the girl. She read with zest all of them, and enjoyed deeply the pleasant converse concerning each. Her eyes were being opened to new ways of living. She was beginning to know that there was an existence more satisfying than just to go from one round of amusement to another. And always, more than in any other thing she read, she took a most unusual interest in home missionary literature. It was not because it was so new and strange and like a fairy tale, nor because she knew her friend enjoyed hearing all this news so much, but because it held for her the story of the man she now knew she loved, and who had said he loved her. She wanted to put herself into touch with surroundings like his, to understand better what he had to endure, and why he had not dared to ask her to share his life, his hardship-most of all why he had not thought her worthy to suffer with him.

When she grew tired of reading she would go out into the kitchen and help Amelia Ellen. It was her own whim that she should learn how to make some of the good things to eat for which Amelia Ellen was famous. So while her society friends at home went from one gay scene to another, dancing and frivolling through the night and sleeping away the morning, Hazel bared her round white arms, enveloped herself in a clean blue-checked apron, and learned to make bread and pies and gingerbread and puddings and doughnuts and fruit-cake, how to cook meats and vegetables and make delicious broths from odds and ends, and to concoct the most delectable desserts that would tempt the frailest appetite. Real old country things they were-no fancy salads and whips and froths that society has hunted out to tempt its waning taste till everything has palled. She wrote to one of her old friends, who demanded to know what she was doing so long up there in the country in the height of the season, that she was taking a course in Domestic Science and happily recounted her menu of accomplishments. Secretly her heart rejoiced that she was become less and less unworthy of the love of the man in whose home and at whose mother's side she was learning sweet lessons.

There came letters, of course, from the far-away missionary. Hazel stayed later in the kitchen the morning of their arrival, conscious of a kind of extra presence in his mother's room when his letters arrived. She knew the mother liked to be alone with her son's letters, and that she saved her eyes from other reading for them alone. Always the older face wore a kind of glorified look when the girl entered after she had been reading her letter. The letter itself would be hidden away out of sight in the bosom of her soft gray gown, to be read again and again when she was alone, but seldom was it brought out in the presence of the visitor, much as the mother was growing to love this girl. Frequently there were bits of news.

"My son says he is very glad I am having such delightful company this winter, and he wants me to thank you from him for reading to me," she said once, patting Hazel's hand as she tucked the wool robe about her friend's helpless form. And again:

"My son is starting to build a church. He is very happy about it. They have heretofore held worship in a schoolhouse. He has collected a good deal of the money himself, and he will help to put up the building with his own hands. He is going to send me a photograph when it is up. I would like to be present when it is dedicated. It makes me very proud to have my son doing that."

The next letter brought a photograph, a small snapshot of the canyon, tiny, but clear and distinct. Hazel's hand trembled when the mother gave it to her to look at, for she knew the very spot. She fancied it was quite near the place where they had paused for water. She could feel again the cool breath of the canyon, the damp smell of the earth and ferns, and hear the call of the wild bird.

Then one day there came a missionary magazine with a short article on the work of Arizona and a picture of the missionary mounted on Billy, just ready to start from his little shack on a missionary tour.

Hazel, turning the leaves, came upon the picture and held her breath with astonishment and delight; then rapidly glanced over the article, her heart beating wildly as though she had heard his voice suddenly calling to her out of the distances that separated them. She had a beautiful time surprising the proud mother with the picture and reading the article. From that morning they seemed to have a tenderer tie between them, and once, just before Hazel was leaving for the night, the mother reached out a detaining hand and laid it on the girl's arm. "I wish my boy and you were acquainted, dear," she said wistfully. And Hazel, the rich colour flooding her face at once, replied hesitatingly:

"Oh, why —I —feel-almost-as-though-we *were!*" Then she kissed her friend on the soft cheek and hurried back to the inn.

It was that night that the telegram came to say that her father had been seriously injured in a railway accident and would be brought home at once. She had no time to think of anything then but to hurry her belongings together and hasten to New York.

XII. QUALIFYING FOR SERVICE

During the six weeks' lingering suffering that followed the accident Hazel was never far from her father's bedside. It seemed as though a new bond of understanding had come between them.

He was very low and there was little hope from the beginning. As he grew weaker he seemed never to want his daughter out of sight, and once when he woke suddenly to find her close beside him, a smile of relief spread over his face, and he told her in brief words that he had dreamed she was lost again in Arizona, and that he had been searching for her with the wild beasts howling all about and wicked men prowling in dark caves. He told her how during that awful time of her disappearance he had been haunted by her face as she was a tiny baby after her mother died, and it seemed to him he should go mad if he could not find her at once.

Then to soothe him she told him of the missionary, and how gently he had cared for her; told him of all the pleasant little details of the way, though not, of course, of his love for her nor hers for him. Perhaps the father, with eyes keen from their nearness to the other world, discerned something of her interest as she talked, for once he sighed and said, in reference to the life of sacrifice the missionary was leading: "Well, I don't know but such things are more worth while after all."

And then with sudden impulse she told him of her finding his mother, and why she had wanted to go to the country in the middle of the society season, because she wanted to know more of the peaceful life this woman lived.

"Perhaps you will meet him again. Who knows?" said the father, looking wistfully at his lovely daughter, and then he turned his head away and sighed again.

As the confidence grew between them she told him one day of Milton Hamar's unwelcome proposal, and the indignation of the father knew no bounds.

It was after that she ventured to read to him from the little book, and to tell of the worship held out under the stars in the desert. It came to be a habit between them, as the days grew less, that she should read the little book, and afterwards he would always lie still as if he were asleep.

It was on the words of the precious psalm that he closed his eyes for the last time in this world, and it was the psalm that brought comfort to the daughter's heart when she came back to the empty house after the funeral.

Her brother was there, it is true, but he was afraid of death, and wanted to get back to his world again, back to the European trip where he had left his friends, and especially a gay young countess who had smiled upon him. He was impatient of death and sorrow. Hazel saw that he could not comprehend her loneliness, so she bade him go as soon as decency would allow, and he was not long in obeying her. He had had his own way all his life, and even death was not to deny him.

The work of the trained nurses who had cared for her father interested Hazel deeply. She had talked with them about their life and preparation for it, and when she could no longer stand the great empty house with only Aunt Maria for company, who had come back just before Mr. Radcliffe's death, she determined to become a nurse herself.

There was much ado over her decision among her acquaintances, and Aunt Maria thought it was not quite respectable for her to do so eccentric a thing and so soon after her father's death. She would have preferred to have had her run down to Lakewood for a few weeks and then follow her brother across the water for a year or two of travel; but Hazel was quite determined, and before January was over she was established in the hospital, through the influence of their family physician, and undergoing her first initiation.

It was not easy thus to give up her life of doing exactly as she pleased when she pleased, and become a servant under orders. Her back often ached, and her eyes grew heavy with the watching and the ministering, and she would be almost ready to give over. Then the thought of the man of the desert gave her new courage and strength. It came to her that she was partaking with him in the great work of the kingdom, and with this thought she would rise and go about the strange new work again, until her interest in the individuals to whom she ministered grew deep, and she understood in a measure the reason for the glory in the face of the missionary as he spoke in the starlight about his work.

Often her heart went out wistfully towards her invalid friend in New Hampshire, and she would rest herself by writing a long letter, and would cherish the delicately written answers. Now and again there would be some slight reference to "my son" in these letters. As the spring came on they were more frequent, for May would bring the General Assembly, and the son was to be one of the speakers. How her heart throbbed when she read that this was certain now. A few days later when she happened to read in the daily paper some item about Assembly plans and discovered for the first time that it was to meet in New York, she found herself in a flutter of joy. Would it be possible for her to hear him speak? That was the great question that kept coming and going in her mind. Could she arrange it so that she would be sure to be off duty when his time came to speak? How could she find out about it all? Thereafter her interest in the church news of the daily papers became deep.

Then spring came on with its languid air and the hard round of work, with often a call to watch when overcome with weariness, or to do some unaccustomed task that tried her undisciplined soul. But the papers were full of the coming Assembly, and at last the program and his name!

She laid her plans most carefully, but the case she had been put upon that week was very low, dying, and the woman had taken a fancy to her and begged her to stay by her till the end. It was a part of the new Hazel that she stayed, though her heart rose up in protest and tears of disappointment would keep coming to her eyes. The head nurse marked them with disapproval and told the house doctor that Radcliffe would never make much of a nurse; she had no control over her emotions.

Death came, almost too late, and set her free for the afternoon, but it was but half an hour to the time set for his speech, she was three miles from the place of meeting and still in her uniform. It was almost foolish to try. Nevertheless she hurried to her room and slipped into a plain little street suit, the thing that would go on quickest, and was away.

It seemed as though every cab and car and mode of transit had conspired to hinder her, and five minutes before the time set for the next speech she hurried breathless into the dim hallway of a great crowded church, and pressed up the stairs to the gallery, through the silent leather doors that could scarcely swing open for the crowd inside them, and heard at last —*his* voice!

She was away up at the top of the gallery. Men and women were standing close all about her. She could not catch even a glimpse of the platform with its array of noble men whose consecration and power and intellects had made them great religious leaders. She could not see the young commanding figure standing at the edge of the platform, nor catch the flash of his brown eyes as he held the audience in his power while he told the simple story of his Western work; but she could hear the voice, and it went straight to her lonely, sorrowful heart. Straightway the church with its mass of packed humanity, its arched and carven ceiling, its magnificent stained-glass windows, its wonderful organ and costly fittings, faded from her sight, and overhead there arched a dome of dark blue pierced with stars, and mountains in the distance with a canyon opening, and a flickering fire. She heard the voice speak from its natural setting, though her eyes were closed and full of tears.

He finished his story amid a breathless silence on the part of his audience, and then with scarcely a break in his voice spoke to God in one of his uplifting prayers. The girl, trembling, almost sobbing, felt herself included in the prayer, felt again the protection of an unseen Presence, felt the benediction in his voice as he said, "Amen," and echoed its utmost meaning in her soul.

The audience was still hushed as the speaker turned to go to his seat at the back of the platform. A storm of applause had been made impossible by that prayer, for heaven opened with the words and God looked down and had to do with each soul present. But the applause burst forth after all in a moment, for the speaker had whispered a few words to the moderator and was hurrying from the platform. There were cries of, "Don't go! Tell us more! Keep on till six o'clock!" Hazel could not see a thing though she stretched her neck and stood upon the tips of her toes, but she clasped her hands tightly together when the applause came, and her heart echoed every sound.

The clamour ceased a moment as the moderator raised his hand, and explained that the brother to whom they had all been listening with such pleasure would be glad to speak to them longer, but that he was hastening away to take the train to see his invalid mother who had been waiting for two long years for her boy. A pause, a great sigh of sympathy and disappointment, and then the applause burst forth again, and continued till the young missionary had left the church.

Hazel, in bitter disappointment, turned and slipped out. She had not caught a glimpse of his beloved face. She exulted that she had heard the honour given him, been a part of those who rejoiced in his power and consecration, but she could not have him go without having at least one look at him.

She hurried blindly down the stairs, out to the street, and saw a carriage standing before the door. The carriage door had just been closed, but as she gazed he turned and looked out for an instant, lifting his hat in farewell to a group of ministers who stood on the church steps. Then the carriage whirled him away and the world grew suddenly blank.

She had been behind the men on the steps, just within the shadow of the dim doorway. He had not seen her, and of course would not have recognized her if he had; yet now she realized that she had hoped-oh-what had she not hoped from meeting him here!

But he was gone, and it might be years before he came East again. He had utterly put her from his life. He would not think of her again if he did come! Oh, the loneliness of a world like this! Why, oh why, had she ever gone to the desert to learn the emptiness of her life, when there was no other for her anywhere!

The days that followed were very sad and hard. The only thought that helped now was that she too had tried to give her life for something worth while as he had done, and perhaps it might be accepted. But there was a deep unrest in her soul now, a something that she knew she had not got that she longed inexpressibly to have. She had learned to cook and to nurse. She was not nearly so useless as when she rode all care-free upon the desert. She had overcome much of her unworthiness. But there was still one great obstacle which unfitted her for companionship and partnership with the man of the desert. She had not the something in her heart and life that was the source and centre of self-sacrifice. She was still unworthy.

There was a long letter about the first of June from her friend in New Hampshire, more shakily written, she fancied, than those that had come before, and then there came an interval without any reply to hers. She had little time, however, to worry about it, for the weather was unusually warm and the hospital was full. Her strength was taxed to its utmost to fill her round of daily duties. Aunt Maria scolded and insisted on a vacation, and finally in high dudgeon betook herself to Europe for the summer. The few friends with whom Hazel kept up any intercourse hurried away to mountains or sea, and the summer settled down to business.

And now in the hot, hot nights when she lay upon her small bed, too weary almost to sleep, she would fancy she heard again that voice as he spoke in the church, or longer ago in the desert; and sometimes she could think she felt the breeze of the desert night upon her hot forehead.

The head nurse and the house doctor decided Radcliffe needed a change and suggested a few days at the shore with a convalescing patient, but Hazel's heart turned from the thought, and she insisted upon sticking to her post. She clung to the thought that she could at least be faithful. It was what he would do, and in so much she would be like him, and worthy of his love.

It was the last thought in her mind before she fainted on the broad marble staircase with a tiny baby in her arms, and fell to the bottom. The baby was uninjured, but it took a long time to bring the nurse back to consciousness, and still longer to put heart into her again.

"She isn't fit for the work!" she heard the biting tongue of the head nurse declare. "She's too frail and pretty and-emotional. She feels everybody's troubles. Now I never let a case worry me in the least!" And the house doctor eyed her knowingly and said in his heart:

"Any one would know that."

But Hazel, listening, was more disheartened than ever. Then here, too, she was failing and was adjudged unworthy!

The next morning there came a brief, blunt note from Amelia Ellen: "Dear Mis Raclift Ef yore a trainurse why don't yo cum an' take car o' my Mis Brownleigh She aint long fer heer an she's wearyin to see yo She as gotta hev one, a trainurse I mean Yors respectfooly Amelia Ellen Stout."

After an interview with the house doctor and another with her old family physician, Hazel packed up her uniforms and departed for New Hampshire.

It was the evening of her arrival, after the gentle invalid had been prepared for sleep and left in the quiet and dark, that Amelia Ellen told the story:

"She ain't ben the same since John went back. Seems like she sort o' sensed thet he wouldn't come again while she was livin'. She tole me the next day a lot of things she wanted done after she was gone, and she's ben gettin' ready to leave this earth ever since. Not that she's gloomy, oh, my senses no! She's jes' as interested as can be in her flowers, and in folks, an' the church, but she don't want to try to do so many things, and she has them weak, fainty spells oftener, an' more pain in her heart. She sits fer long hours with jest her Bible open now, but land, she don't need to read it! She knows it most by heart-that is the livin' parts, you know. She don't seem to care 'tall fer them magazine articles now any more. I wish t' the land they'd be anuther Gen'l 'Sembly! Thet was the greatest thing fer her. She jest acted like she was tendin' every blessed one o' them meetin's. Why, she couldn't wait fer me t' git done my breakfast dishes. She'd want me t' fix her up fer the day, an' then set down an' read their doin's. 'We kin let things go, you know, 'Meelia Ellen,' she'd say with her sweet little smile, 'just while the meetin's last. Then when it's over they'll be time 'nough fer work-an' rest too, 'Meelia Ellen,' says she. Well, seems like she was just 'tendin' those meetin's herself, same es if she was there. She'd take her nap like it was a pill, er somethin', and then be wide awake an' ready fer her afternoon freshenin', an' then she'd watch fer the stage to bring the evenin' paper. John, he hed a whole cartload o' papers sent, an' the day he spoke they was so many I jes' couldn't get my bread set. I hed to borry a loaf off the inn. First time that's ever happened to me either. I jest hed to set an' read till my back ached, and my eyes swum. I never read so much in my whole borned days t' oncet; an' I've done a good bit o' readin' in my time, too, what with nursin' her an' bein' companion to a perfessor's invaleed daughter one summer.

"Wal, seems like she jest went on an' on, gettin' workeder-up an' workeder-up, till the 'Sembly closed, an' he come; and she was clear to the top o' the heap all them three weeks whilst he was here. Why, I never seen her so bright since when I was a little girl an' went to her Sunday-school class, an' she wore a poke bonnet trimmed with lute-string ribbon an' a rose inside. Talk 'bout roses-they wasn't one in the garden as bright an' pink as her two cheeks, an' her eyes shone jest fer all the world like his. I was terrible troubled lest she'd break down, but she didn't. She got brighter an' brighter. Let him take her out ridin', an' let him carry her into the orchard an' lay her down under the apple boughs where she could reach a wild strawberry herself. Why, she hedn't ben off'n the porch sence he went away two years ago. But every day he stayed she got brighter. The last day 'fore he left she seemed like she wasn't sick at all. She wanted to get up early, an' she wouldn't take no nap, 'cause she said she couldn't waste a minute of the last day. Well, she actu'lly got on her feet oncet an' made him walk her crost the porch. She hedn't ben on her feet fer more'n a minute fer ten months, an' 'twas more'n she could stan'. She was jest as bright an' happy all thet day, an' when he went 'way she waved her hand as happy like an' smiled an' said she was glad to be able to send him back to his work. But she never said a word about his comin' back. He kep' sayin' he would come back next spring, but she only smiled, an' tole him he might not be able to leave his work, an' 'twas all right. She wanted him to be faithful.

"Well, he went, an' the coach hedn't no more'n got down the hill an' up again an' out o' sight behind the bridge 'fore she calls to me an' she says, "Meelia Ellen, I believe I'm tired with all the goin's on there's been, an' if you don't mind I think I'll take a nap.' So I helps her into her room and fixes her into her night things an' thur she's laid ever since, an' it's six whole weeks ef it's a day. Every mornin' fer a spell I'd go in an' say, 'Ain't you ready fer me to fix you fer the day, Mis' Brownleigh?' An' she'd jest smile an' say, 'Well, I b'leeve not just now, 'Meelia Ellen. I think I'll just rest to-day yet. Maybe I'll feel stronger to-morrow'; but to-morrow never comes, an' it's my thinkin' she'll never git up again."

The tears were streaming down the good woman's cheeks now and Hazel's eyes were bright with tears too. She had noticed the transparency of the delicate flesh, the frailness of the wrinkled hands. The woman's words brought conviction to her heart also.

"What does the doctor say?" she asked, catching at a hope.

"Well, he ain't much fer talk," said Amelia Ellen lifting her tear-stained face from her gingham apron where it had been bowed. "It seems like them two hev just got a secret between 'em thet they won't say nothin' 'bout it. Seems like he understands, and knows she don't want folks to talk about it nor worry 'bout her."

"But her son — —" faltered Hazel. "He ought to be told!"

"Yes, but 'tain't no use; she won't let yeh. I ast her oncet didn't she want me to write him to come an' make her a little visit just to chirk her up, and she shook her head and looked real frightened, and she says: ''Meelia Ellen, don't you never go to sendin' fer him 'thout lettin' me know. I should *not* like it 'tall. He's out there doin' his work, an' I'm happier havin' him at it. A missionary can't take time traipsin' round the country every time a relative gets a little down. I'm jest perfectly all right, 'Meelia Ellen, only I went pretty hard durin' 'Sembly week, and when John was here, an' I'm restin' up fer a while. If I want John sent fer I'll tell you, but *don't you go to doin' it 'fore!* An' I really b'leeve she'd be mad at me if I did. She lots a good deal on givin' her son, an' it would sort o' spoil her sakkerfize, I s'pose, to hev him come back every time she hungers fer him. I b'leeve in my heart she's plannin' to slip away quiet and not bother him to say good-bye. It jest looks thet way to me."

But the next few days the invalid brightened perceptibly, and Hazel began to be reassured. Sweet converse they had together, and the girl heard the long pleasant story of the son's visit home as the mother dwelt lovingly upon each detail, telling it over and over, until the listener felt that every spot within sight of the invalid's window was fragrant with his memory. She enjoyed the tale as much as the teller, and knew just how to give the answer that one loving woman wants from another loving woman when they speak of the beloved.

Then when the story all was told over and over and there was nothing more to tell except the pleasant recalling of a funny speech, or some tender happening, Hazel began to ask deeper questions about the things of life and eternity; and step by step the older woman led her in the path she had led her son through all the years of his childhood.

During this time she seemed to grow stronger again. There were days when she sat up for a little while, and let them put the meals on a tiny swinging table by her chair; and she took a deep interest in leading the girl to a heavenly knowledge. Every day she asked for her writing materials and wrote for a little while; yet Hazel noticed that she did not send all that she had written in the envelope of the weekly letters, but laid it away carefully in her writing portfolio as if it were something yet unfinished.

And one evening in late September, when the last rays of the sunset were lying across the foot of the wheeled chair, and Amelia Ellen was building a bit of a fire in the fireplace because it seemed chilly, the mother called Hazel to her and handed her a letter sealed and addressed to her son.

"Dear," she said gently, "I want you to take this letter and put it away carefully and keep it until I am gone, and then I want you to promise that, if possible for you to do it, you will give it to my son with your own hands."

Hazel took the letter reverently, her heart filled with awe and sorrow and stooped anxiously over her friend. "Oh, why" —she cried —"what is the matter? Do you feel worse to-night? You have seemed so bright all day."

"Not a bit," said the invalid cheerily. "But I have been writing this for a long time—a sort of good-bye to my boy-and there is nobody in the world I would like to have give it to him as well as you. Will it trouble you to promise me, my dear?"

Hazel with kisses and tears protested that she would be glad to fulfill the mission, but begged that she might be allowed to send for the beloved son at once, for a sight of his face, she knew, would be good to his mother.

At last her fears were allayed, though she was by no means sure that the son ought not to be sent for, and when the invalid was happily gone to sleep, Hazel went to her room and tried to think how she might write a letter that would not alarm the young man, while yet it would bring him to his mother's side. She planned how she would go away herself for a few days, so that he need not find her here. She wrote several stiff little notes but none of them satisfied her. Her heart longed to write: "Oh, my dear! Come quickly, for your beloved mother needs you. Come, for my heart is crying out for the sight of you! Come at once!" But finally before she slept she sealed and addressed a dignified letter from Miss Radcliffe, his mother's trained nurse, suggesting that he make at least a brief visit at this time as she must be away for a few days, and she felt that his presence would be a wise thing. His mother did not seem so well as when he was with her. Then she lay down comforted to sleep. But the letter was never sent.

In the early dawn of the morning, when the faithful Amelia Ellen slipped from her couch in the alcove just off the invalid's room, and went to touch a match to the carefully laid fire in the fireplace, she passed the bed and, as had been her custom for years, glanced to see if all was well with her patient; at once she knew that the sweet spirit of the mother had fled.

With her face slightly turned away, a smile of good-night upon her lips, and the peace of God upon her brow, the mother had entered into her rest.

XIII. THE CALL OF THE DESERT

Hazel, with her eyes blinded with tears and her heart swelling with the loss of the woman upon whose motherliness she had come to feel a claim, burned the letter she had written the night before, and sent a carefully worded telegram, her heart yearning with sympathy towards the bereaved son.

"Your dear mother has gone home, quietly, in her sleep. She did not seem any worse than usual, and her last words were of you. Let us know at once what plans we shall make. Nurse Radcliffe." That was the telegram she sent.

Poor Amelia Ellen was all broken up. Her practical common sense for once had fled her. She would do nothing but weep and moan for the beloved invalid whom she had served so long and faithfully. It fell to Hazel to make all decisions, though the neighbours and old friends were most kind with offers of help. Hazel waited anxiously for an answer to the telegram, but night fell and no answer had come. There had been a storm and something was wrong with the wires. The next morning, however, she sent another telegram, and about noon still a third, with as yet no response. She thought perhaps he had not waited to telegraph but had started immediately, and might be with them in a few hours. She watched the evening stage, but he did not come; then realized how her heart was in a flutter, and wondered how she would have had strength to meet him had he come. There was the letter from his mother, and her promise. She had that excuse for her presence-of course she could not have left under the circumstances. Yet she shrank from the meeting, for it seemed somehow a breach of etiquette that she should be the one to break the separation that he had chosen should be between them.

However, he did not come, and the third morning, when it became imperative that something definite should be known, a telegram to the station agent in Arizona brought answer that the missionary was away on a long trip among some tribes of Indians; that his exact whereabouts was not known, but messengers had been sent after him, and word would be sent as soon as possible. The minister and the old neighbours advised with Amelia Ellen and Hazel, and made simple plans for the funeral, yet hoped and delayed as long as possible, and when at last after repeated telegrams there still came the answer, "Messenger not yet returned," they bore the worn-out body of the woman to a quiet resting place beside her beloved husband in the churchyard on the hillside where the soft maples scattered bright covering over the new mound, and the sky arched high with a kind of triumphant reminder of where the spirit was gone.

Hazel tried to have every detail just as she thought he would have liked it. The neighbours brought of their homely flowers in great quantities, and some city friends who had been old summer boarders sent hot-house roses. The minister conducted the beautiful service of faith, and the village children sang about the casket of their old friend, who had always loved every one of them, their hands full of the late flowers from her own garden, bright scarlet and blue and gold, as though it were a joyous occasion. Indeed, Hazel had the impression, even as she moved in the hush of the presence of death, that she was helping at some solemn festivity of deep joy instead of a funeral-so glorious had been the hope of the one who was gone, so triumphant her faith in her Saviour.

After the funeral was over Hazel sat down and wrote a letter telling about it all, filling it with sympathy, trying to show their effort to have things as he would have liked them, and expressing deep sorrow that they had been compelled to go on with the service without him.

That night there came a message from the Arizona station agent. The missionary had been found in a distant Indian hogan with a dislocated ankle. He sent word that they must not wait for him; that he would get there in time, if possible. A later message the next day said he was still unable to travel, but would get to the railroad as soon as possible. Then came an interval of several days without any word from Arizona.

Hazel went about with Amelia Ellen, putting the house in order, hearing the beautiful plaint of the loving-hearted, mourning servant as she told little incidents of her mistress. Here was the chair she sat in the last time she went up-stairs to oversee the spring regulating, and that was Mr. John's little baby dress in which he was christened. His mother smoothed it out and told her the story of his baby loveliness one day. She had laid it away herself in the box with the blue shoes and the crocheted cap. It was the last time she ever came up-stairs.

There was the gray silk dress she wore to weddings and dinner parties before her husband died, and beneath it in the trunk was the white embroidered muslin that was her wedding gown. Yellow with age it was, and delicate as a spider's web, with frostwork of yellowed broidery strewn quaintly on its ancient form, and a touch of real lace. Hazel laid a reverent hand on the fine old fabric, and felt, as she looked through the treasures of the old trunk, that an inner sanctuary of sweetness had been opened for her glimpsing.

At last a letter came from the West.

It was addressed to "Miss Radcliffe, Nurse," in Brownleigh's firm, clear hand, and began: "Dear madam." Hazel's hand trembled as she opened it, and the "dear madam" brought the tears to her eyes; but then, of course, he did not know.

He thanked her, with all the kindliness and courtliness of his mother's son, for her attendance on his dear mother, and told her of many pleasant things his mother had written of her ministrations. He spoke briefly of his being laid up lamed in the Indian reservation and his deep grief that he had been unable to come East to be beside his mother during her last hours, but went on to say that it had been his mother's wish, many times expressed, that he should not leave his post to come to her, and that there need be "no sadness of farewell" when she "embarked," and that though it was hard for him he knew it was a fulfillment of his mother's desires. And now that she was gone, and the last look upon her dear face was impossible, he had decided that he could not bear it just yet to come home and see all the dear familiar places with her face gone. He would wait a little while, until he had grown used to the thought of her in heaven, and then it would not be so hard. Perhaps he would not come home until next spring, unless something called him; he could not tell. And in any case, his injured ankle prevented him making the journey at present, no matter how much he may desire to do so. Miss Radcliffe's letter had told him that everything had been done just as he would have had it done. There was nothing further to make it a necessity that he should come. He had written to his mother's lawyer to arrange his mother's few business affairs, and it only remained for him to express his deep gratitude towards those who had stood by his dear mother when it had been made impossible for him to do so. He closed with a request that the nurse would give him her permanent address that he might be sure to find her when he found it possible to come East again, as he would enjoy thanking her face to face for what she had been to his mother.

That was all.

Hazel felt a blank dizziness settle down over her as she finished the letter. It put him miles away from her again, with years perhaps before another sight of him. She suddenly seemed fearfully alone in a world that no longer interested her. Where should she go; what to do with her life now? Back to the hard grind of the hospital with nobody to care, and the heartrending scenes and tragedies that were daily enacted? Somehow her strength seemed to go from her at the thought. Here, too, she had failed. She was not fit for the life, and the hospital people had discovered it and sent her away to nurse her friend and try to get well. They had been kind and talked about when she should return to them, but she knew in her heart they felt her unfit and did not want her back.

Should she go back to her home, summon her brother and aunt, and plunge into society again? The very idea sickened her. Never again would she care for that life, she was certain. As she searched her heart to see what it was she really craved, if anything in the whole wide world, she found her only interest was in the mission field of Arizona, and now that her dear friend was gone she was cut off from knowing anything much about that.

She gathered herself together after a while and told Amelia Ellen of the decision of Mr. Brownleigh, and together they planned how the house should be closed, and everything put in order to await its master's will to return. But that night Hazel could not sleep, for suddenly, in the midst of her sad reflections, came the thought of the letter that was left in her trust.

It had been forgotten during the strenuous days that had followed the death of its writer. Hazel had thought of it only once, and that on the first morning, with a kind of comforting reflection that it would help the son to bear his sorrow, and she was glad that it was her privilege to put it into his hand. Then the perplexities of the occasion had driven it from her thoughts. Now it came back like a swift light in a dark place. There was yet the letter which she must give him. It was a precious bond that would hold him to her for a little while longer. But how should she give it to him?

Should she send it by mail? No, for that would not be fulfilling the letter of her promise. She knew the mother wished her to give it to him herself. Well, then, should she write and summon him to his old home at once, tell him of the letter and yet refuse to send it to him? How strange that would seem! How could she explain it to him? His mother's whim might be sacred to him-would be, of course-but he would think it strange that a young woman should make so much of it as not to trust the letter to the mail now that the circumstances made it impossible for him to come on at once.

Neither would it do for her to keep the letter until such a time as he should see fit to return to the East and look her up. It might be years.

The puzzling question kept whirling itself about in her mind for hours until at last she formulated a plan which seemed to solve the problem.

The plan was this. She would coax Amelia Ellen to take a trip to California with her, and on the way they would stop in Arizona and give the letter into the hands of the young man. By that time no doubt his injured ankle would be sufficiently strong to allow his return from the journey to the Indian reservation. She would say that she was going West and, as she had promised his mother she would put the letter into his hands, she had taken this opportunity to stop off and keep her promise. The trip would be a good thing for Amelia Ellen too, and take her mind off her loneliness for the mistress who was gone.

Eagerly she broached the subject to Amelia Ellen the next morning, and was met with a blank face of dismay.

"I couldn't noways you'd fix it, my dearie," she said sadly shaking her head. "I'd like nuthin' better'n to see them big trees out in Californy I've been hearin' 'bout all my life; an' summer an' winter with snow on the mountains what some of the boarders 't the inn tells 'bout; but I can't bring it 'bout. You see it's this way. Peter Burley 'n' I ben promused fer nigh on to twelve year now, an' when he ast me I said no, I couldn't leave Mis' Brownleigh long's she needed me; an' he sez will I marry him the week after she dies, an' I sez I didn't like no sech dismal way o' puttin' it; an' he sez well, then, will I marry him the week after she don't need me no more; an' I sez yes, I will, an' now I gotta keep my promus! I can't go back on my faithful word. I'd like real well to see them big trees, but I gotta keep my promus! You see he's waited long 'nough, an' he's ben real patient. Not always he cud get to see me every week, an' he might 'a' tuk Delmira that cooked to the inn five year ago. She'd 'a' had him in a minnit, an' she done her best to git him, but he stayed faithful, an' he sez, sez he, 'Meelia El'n, ef you're meanin' to keep your word, I'll wait ef it's a lifetime, but I hope you won't make it any longer'n you need;' an' the night he said that I promused him agin I'd be hisn soon ez ever I was free to do's I pleased. I'd like to see them big trees, but I can't do it. I jes' can't do it."

Now Hazel was not a young woman who was easily balked in her plans when once they were made. She was convinced that the only thing to do was to take this trip and that Amelia Ellen was the only person in the world she wanted for a companion; therefore she made immediate acquaintance with Peter Burley, a heavy-browed, thoughtful, stolid man, who looked his character of patient lover, every inch of him, blue overalls and all. Hazel's heart almost misgave her as she unfolded her plan to his astonished ears, and saw the look of blank dismay that overspread his face. However, he had not waited all these years to refuse his sweetheart anything in reason now. He drew a deep sigh, inquired how long the trip as planned would take, allowed he "could wait another month ef that would suit," and turned patiently to his barn-yard to think his weary thoughts, and set his hopes a little further ahead. Then Hazel's heart misgave her. She called after him and suggested that perhaps he might like to have the marriage first and go with them, taking the excursion as a wedding trip. She would gladly pay all expenses if he would. But the man shook his head.

"I couldn't leave the stock fer that long, ennyhow you fix it. Thur ain't no one would know to take my place. Besides, I never was fer takin' journeys; but 'Meelia Ellen, she's allus ben of a sprightlier disposition, an' ef she hez a hankerin' after Californy, I 'spect she'll be kinder more contented like ef she sees 'em first an' then settles down in Granville. She better go while she's got the chancet."

Amelia Ellen succumbed, albeit with tears. Hazel could not tell whether she was more glad or sad at the prospect before her. Whiles Amelia Ellen wept and bemoaned the fate of poor Burley, and whiles she questioned whether there really were any big trees like what you saw in the geographies with riding parties sitting contentedly in tunnels through their trunks. But at last she consented to go, and with many an injunction from the admiring and envious neighbours who came to see them off, Amelia Ellen bade a sobbing good-bye to her solemn lover in the gray dawn of an October morning, climbed into the stage beside Hazel, and they drove away into the mystery of the great world. As she looked back at her Peter, standing patient, stooped and gray in the familiar village street, looking after his departing sweetheart who was going out sightseeing into the world, Amelia Ellen would almost have jumped out over the wheel and run back if it had not been for what the neighbours would say, for her heart was Burley's; and now that the big trees were actually pulling harder than Burley, and she had decided to go and see them, Burley began by his very acquiescence to pull harder than the big trees. It was a very teary Amelia Ellen who climbed into the train a few hours later, looking back dismally, hopelessly, towards the old stage they had just left, and wondering after all if she ever would get back to Granville safe and alive again. Strange fears visited her of dangers that might come to Burley during her absence, which if they did she would never forgive herself for having left him; strange horrors of the way of things that might hinder her return; and she began to regard her hitherto beloved travelling companion with almost suspicion, as if she were a conspirator against her welfare.

However, as the miles grew and the wonders of the way multiplied, Amelia Ellen began to sit up and take notice, and to have a sort of excited exultance that she had come; for were they not nearing the great famed West now, and would it not soon be time to see the big trees and turn back home again? She was almost glad she had come. She would be wholly glad she had done so when she had got back safely home once more.

And so one evening about sunset they arrived at the little station in Arizona which over a year ago Hazel had left in her father's private car.

XIV. HOME

Amelia Ellen, stiff from the unaccustomed travel, powdered with the dust of the desert, wearied with the excitement of travel and lack of sleep amid her strange surroundings, stepped down upon the wooden platform and surveyed the magnificent distance between herself and anywhere; observed the vast emptiness, with awful purpling mountains and limitless stretches of vari-coloured ground arched by a dome of sky, higher and wider and more dazzling than her stern New Hampshire soul had ever conceived, and turned panic-stricken back to the train which was already moving away from the little station. Her first sensation had been one of relief at feeling solid ground under her feet once more, for this was the first trip into the world Amelia Ellen had ever made, and the cars bewildered her. Her second impulse was to get back into that train as fast as her feet could carry her and get this awful journey done so that she might earn the right to return to her quiet home and her faithful lover.

But the train was well under way. She looked after it half in envy. It could go on with its work and not have to stop in this wild waste.

She gazed about again with the frightened look a child deserted gives before it puckers its lips and screams.

Hazel was talking composedly with the rough-looking man on the platform, who wore a wide felt hat and a pistol in his belt. He didn't look even respectable to Amelia Ellen's provincial eyes. And behind him, horror of horrors! loomed a real live Indian, long hair, high cheek bones, blanket and all, just as she had seen them in the geography! Her blood ran cold! Why, oh why, had she ever been left to do this daring thing-to leave civilization and come away from her good man and the quiet home awaiting her to certain death in the desert. All the stories of horrid scalpings she had ever heard appeared before her excited vision. With a gasp she turned again to the departing train, which had become a mere speck on the desert, and even as she looked vanished around a curve and was lost in the dim foot-hills of a mountain!

Poor Amelia Ellen! Her head reeled and her heart sank. The vast prairie engulfed her, as it were, and she stood trembling and staring in dazed expectancy of an attack from earth or air or sky. The very sky and ground seemed tottering together and threatening to extinguish her, and she closed her eyes, caught her breath and prayed for Peter. It had been her habit always in any emergency to pray for Peter Burley.

It was no better when they took her to the eating-house across the track. She picked her way among the evil-looking men, and surveyed the long dining table with its burden of coarse food and its board seats with disdain, declined to take off her hat when she reached the room to which the slatternly woman showed them because she said there was no place to lay it down that was fit; scorned the simple bed, refused to wash her hands at the basin furnished for all, and made herself more disagreeable than Hazel had dreamed her gentle, serviceable Amelia Ellen ever could have been. No supper would she eat, nor would she remain long at the table after the men began to file in, with curious eyes towards the strangers.

She stalked to the rough, unroofed porch in the front and stared off at the dark vastness, afraid of the wild strangeness, afraid of the looming mountains, afraid of the multitude of stars. She said it was ridiculous to have so many stars. It wasn't natural. It was irreverent. It was like looking too close into heaven when you weren't intended to.

And then a blood-curdling sound arose! It made her very hair stand on end. She turned with wild eyes and grasped Hazel's arm, but she was too frightened to utter a sound. Hazel had just come out to sit with her. The men out of deference to the strangers had withdrawn from their customary smoking place on the porch to the back of the wood-pile behind the house. They were alone-the two women-out there in the dark, with that awful, awful sound!

Amelia Ellen's white lips framed the words "Indians"? "War-whoop"? but her throat refused her sound and her breath came short.

"Coyotes!" laughed Hazel, secure in her wide experience, with almost a joyous ring to her voice. The sound of those distant beasts assured her that she was in the land of her beloved at last and her soul rejoiced.

"Coy-oh — —" but Amelia Ellen's voice was lost in the recesses of her skimpy pillow whither she had fled to bury her startled ears. She had heard of coyotes, but she had never imagined to hear one outside of a zoölogical garden, of which she had read and always hoped one day to visit. There she lay on her hard little bed and quaked until Hazel, laughing still, came to find her; but all she could get from the poor soul was a pitiful plaint about Burley. "And what would he say if I was to be et with one of them creatures? He'd never forgive me, never, never s'long 's I lived! I hadn't ough' to 'a' come. I hadn't ough' to 'a' come!"

Nothing Hazel could say would allay her fears. She listened with horror as the girl attempted to show how harmless the beasts were by telling of her own night ride up the canyon, and how nothing harmed her. Amelia Ellen merely looked at her with frozen glance made fiercer by the flickering candle flare, and answered dully: "An' you knew 'bout 'em all 'long, an' yet you brung me! It ain't what I thought you'd do! Burley, he'll never fergive me s'long 's I live ef I get et up. It ain't ez if I was all alone in the world, you know. I got him to think of an' I can't afford to run no resks of bein' et, *ef you can.*"

Not a wink of sleep did she get that night and when the morning dawned and to the horrors of the night were added a telegram from a neighbour of Burley's saying that Burley had fallen from the haymow and broken his leg, but he sent his respects and hoped they'd have a good journey, Amelia Ellen grew uncontrollable. She declared she would not stay in that awful country another minute. That she would take the first train back-back to her beloved New Hampshire which she never again would leave so long as her life was spared, unless Burley went along. She would not even wait until Hazel had delivered her message. How could two lone women deliver a message in a land like that? Never, *never* would she ride, drive or walk, no, nor even set foot on the sand of the desert. She would sit by the track until a train came along and she would not even look further than she need. The frenzy of fear which sometimes possesses simple people at sight of a great body of water, or a roaring torrent pouring over a precipice, had taken possession of her at sight of the desert. It filled her soul with its immensity, and poor Amelia Ellen had a great desire to sit down on the wooden platform and grasp firm hold of something until a train came to rescue her from this awful emptiness which had tried to swallow her up.

Poor Peter, with his broken leg, was her weird cry! One would think she had broken it with the wheels of the car in which she had travelled away from him by the way she took on about it and blamed herself. The tragedy of a broken vow and its consequences was the subject of her discourse. Hazel laughed, then argued, and finally cried and besought; but nothing could avail. Go she would, and that speedily, back to her home.

When it became evident that arguments and tears were of no use and that Amelia Ellen was determined to go home with or without her, Hazel withdrew to the front porch and took counsel with the desert in its morning brightness, with the purple luring mountains, and the smiling sky. Go back on the train that would stop at the station in half an hour, with the desert there, and the wonderful land, and its strange, wistful people, and not even see a glimpse of him she loved? Go back with the letter still in her possession and her message still ungiven? Never! Surely she was not afraid to stay long enough to send for him. The woman who had fed them and sheltered them for the night would be her protector. She would stay. There must be some woman of refinement and culture somewhere near by to whom she could go for a few days until her errand was performed; and what was her training in the hospital worth if it did not give her some independence? Out here in the wild free West women had to protect themselves. She could surely stay in the uncomfortable quarters where she was for another day until she could get word to the missionary. Then she could decide whether to proceed on her journey alone to California, or to go back home. There was really no reason why she should not travel alone if she chose; plenty of young women did and, anyway, the emergency was not of her choosing. Amelia Ellen would make herself sick fretting over her Burley, that was plain, if she were detained even a few hours. Hazel came back to the nearly demented Amelia Ellen with her chin tilted firmly and a straight little set of her sweet lips which betokened stubbornness. The train came in a brief space of time, and, weeping but firm, Amelia Ellen boarded it, dismayed at the thought of leaving her dear young lady, yet stubbornly determined to go. Hazel gave her the ticket and plenty of money, charged the conductor to look after her, waved a brave farewell and turned back to the desert alone.

A brief conference with the woman who had entertained them, who was also the wife of the station agent, brought out the fact that the missionary was not yet returned from his journey, but a message received from him a few days before spoke of his probable return on the morrow or the day after. The woman advised that the lady go to the fort where visitors were always welcomed and where there were luxuries more fitted to the stranger's habit. She eyed the dainty apparel of her guest enviously as she spoke, and Hazel, keenly alive to the meaning of her look, realized that the woman, like the missionary, had judged her unfit for life in the desert. She was half determined to stay where she was until the missionary's return, and show that she could adapt herself to any surroundings, but she saw that the woman was anxious to have her gone. It probably put her out to have a guest of another world than her own.

The woman told her that a trusty Indian messenger was here from the fort and was riding back soon. If the lady cared she could get a horse and go under his escort. She opened her eyes in wonder when Hazel asked if there was to be a woman in the party, and whether she could not leave her work for a little while and ride over with them if she would pay her well for the service.

"Oh, you needn't bring none o' them fine lady airs out here!" she declared rudely. "We-all ain't got time fer no sech foolery. You needn't be afraid to go back with Joe. He takes care of the women at the fort. He'll look after you fine. You'll mebbe kin hire a horse to ride, an' strop yer baggage on. Yer trunk ye kin leave here."

Hazel, half frightened at the position she had allowed herself to be placed in, considered the woman's words, and when she had looked upon the Indian's stolid countenance decided to accept his escort. He was an old man with furrowed face and sad eyes that looked as if they could tell great secrets, but there was that in his face that made her trust him, she knew not why.

An hour later, her most necessary baggage strapped to the back of the saddle on a wicked-looking little pony, Hazel, with a sense of deep excitement, mounted and rode away behind the solemn, silent Indian. She was going to the fort to ask shelter, until her errand was accomplished, of the only women in that region who would be likely to take her in. She had a feeling that the thing she was doing was a most wild and unconventional proceeding and would come under the grave condemnation of her aunt, and all her New York friends. She was most thankful that they were far away and could not interfere, for somehow she felt that she must do it anyway. She must put that letter, with her own hands, into the possession of its owner.

It was a most glorious morning. The earth and the heavens seemed newly made for the day. Hazel felt a gladness in her soul that would not down, even when she thought of poor Amelia Ellen crouched in her corner of the sleeper, miserable at her desertion, yet determined to go. She thought of the dear mother, and wondered if 'twere given to her to know now how she was trying to fulfill her last wish. It was pleasant to think she knew and was glad, and Hazel felt as though her presence were near and protecting her.

The silent Indian made few remarks. He rode ahead always with a grave, thoughtful expression, like a student whose thoughts are not to be disturbed. He nodded gravely in answer to the questions Hazel asked him whenever they stopped to water the horses, but he volunteered no information beyond calling her attention to a lame foot her pony was developing.

Several times Joe got down and examined the pony's foot, and shook his head, with a grunt of worried disapproval. Presently as the miles went by Hazel began to notice the pony's lameness herself, and became alarmed lest he would break down altogether in the midst of the desert. Then what would the Indian do? Certainly not give her his horse and foot it, as the missionary had done. She could not expect that every man in this desert was like the one who had cared for her before. What a foolish girl she had been to get herself into this fix! And now there was no father to send out search parties for her, and no missionary at home to find her!

The dust, the growing heat of the day, and the anxiety began to wear upon her. She was tired and hungry, and when at noon the Indian dismounted beside a water-hole where the water tasted of sheep who had passed through but a short time before, and handed her a package of corn bread and cold bacon, while he withdrew to the company of the horses for his own siesta, she was feign to put her head down on the coarse grass and weep for her folly in coming out to this wild country alone, or at least in being so headstrong as to stay when Amelia Ellen deserted her. Then the thought suddenly occurred to her: how would Amelia Ellen have figured in this morning's journey on horseback; and instead of weeping she fell to laughing almost hysterically.

She munched the corn bread-the bacon she could not eat-and wondered if the woman at the stopping-place had realized what an impossible lunch she had provided for her guest. However, here was one of the tests. She was not worth much if a little thing like coarse food annoyed her so much. She drank some of the bitter water, and bravely ate a second piece of corn bread and tried to hope her pony would be all right after his rest. But it was evident after they had gone a mile or two further that the pony was growing worse. He lagged, and limped, and stopped, and it seemed almost cruel to urge him further, yet what could be done? The Indian rode behind now, watching him and speaking in low grunts to him occasionally, and finally they came in sight of a speck of a building in the distance. Then the Indian spoke. Pointing towards the distant building, which seemed too tiny for human habitation, he said: "Aneshodi hogan. Him friend me. Lady stay. Me come back good horse. Pony no go more. He bad!"

Dismay filled the heart of the lady. She gathered that her guide wished to leave her by the way while he went on for another horse, and maybe he would return and maybe not. Meantime, what kind of a place was he leaving her in? Would there be a woman there? Even if she were an Indian woman that would not be so bad. "Aneshodi" sounded as if it might be a woman's name.

"Is this Aneshodi a woman?" she questioned.

The Indian shook his head and grunted. "Na, na. Aneshodi, Aneshodi. Him friend me. Him good friend. No woman!" (In scorn.)

"Is there no woman in the house?" she asked anxiously.

"Na! Him heap good man. Good hogan. Lady stay. Rest."

Suddenly her pony stumbled and nearly fell. She saw that she could not depend on him for long now.

"Couldn't I walk with you?" she asked, her eyes pleading. "I would rather walk than stay. Is it far?"

The Indian shook his head vigorously.

"Lady no walk. Many suns lady walk. Great mile. Lady stay. Me ride fast. Back sundown," and he pointed to the sun which was even now beginning its downward course.

Hazel saw there was nothing for it but to do as the Indian said, and indeed his words seemed reasonable, but she was very much frightened. What kind of a place was this in which she was to stay? As they neared it there appeared to be nothing but a little weather-beaten shanty, with a curiously familiar look, as if she had passed that way before. A few chickens were picking about the yard, and a vine grew over the door, but there was no sign of human being about and the desert stretched wide and barren on every side. Her old fear of its vastness returned, and she began to have a fellow feeling with Amelia Ellen. She saw now that she ought to have gone with Amelia Ellen back to civilization and found somebody who would have come with her on her errand. But then the letter would have been longer delayed!

The thought of the letter kept up her courage, and she descended dubiously from her pony's back, and followed the Indian to the door of the shanty. The vine growing luxuriantly over window and casement and door frame reassured her somewhat, she could not tell just why. Perhaps somebody with a sense of beauty lived in the ugly little building, and a man with a sense of beauty could not be wholly bad. But how was she to stay alone in a man's house where no woman lived? Perhaps the man would have a horse to lend or sell them. She would offer any sum he wanted if she only could get to a safe place.

But the Indian did not knock at the door as she had expected he would do. Instead he stooped to the lower step, and putting his hand into a small opening in the woodwork of the step, fumbled there a minute and presently brought out a key which he fitted into the lock and threw the door wide open to her astonished gaze.

"Him friend me!" explained the Indian again.

He walked into the room with the manner of a partial proprietor of the place, looked about, stooped down to the fireplace where a fire was neatly laid, and set it blazing up cheerfully; took the water bucket and filled it, and putting some water into the kettle swung it over the blaze to heat, then turning, he spoke again:

"Lady stay. Me come back-soon. Sun no go down. Me come back; good horse get lady."

"But where is the owner of this house? What will he think of my being here when he comes back?" said Hazel, more frightened than ever at the prospect of being left. She had not expected to stay entirely alone. She had counted on finding some one in the house.

"Aneshodi way off. Not come back one-two-day mebbe! He know me. He me friend. Lady stay! All right!"

Hazel, her eyes large with fear, watched her protector mount and ride away. Almost she called after him that he must not leave her; then she remembered that this was a part of a woman's life in Arizona, and she was being tried. It was just such things as this the missionary had meant when he said she was unfit for life out here. She would stay and bear the loneliness and fright. She would prove, at least to herself, that she had the courage of any missionary. She would not bear the ignominy of weakness and failure. It would be a shame to her all her life to know she had failed in this trying time.

She watched the Indian riding rapidly away as if he were in hot haste. Once the suspicion crossed her mind that perhaps he had lamed her horse on purpose, and left her here just to get rid of her. Perhaps this was the home of some dreadful person who would return soon and do her harm.

She turned quickly, with alarm in her heart, to see what manner of place she was in, for she had been too excited at first over the prospect of being left to notice it much, save to be surprised that there were chairs, a fireplace, and a look of comparative comfort. Now she looked about to find out if possible just what sort of a person the owner might be, and glancing at the table near the fireplace the first object her eye fell upon was an open book, and the words that caught her vision were: "He that dwelleth in the secret place of the Most High shall abide under the shadow of the Almighty!"

With a start she turned the book over and found it was a Bible, bound in plain, strong covers, with large, clear print, and it lay open as if the owner had been reading it but a short time before and had been called suddenly away.

With a sigh of relief she sank down in the big chair by the fire and let the excited tears have their way. Somehow her fear all vanished with that sentence. The owner of the house could not be very bad when he kept his Bible about and open to that psalm, her psalm, her missionary's psalm! And there was assurance in the very words themselves, as if they had been sent to remind her of her new trust in an Unseen Power. If she was making the Most High her dwelling place continually, surely she was under His protection continually, and had no need to be afraid anywhere, for she was abiding in Him. The thought gave her a strange new sense of sweetness and safety.

After a moment she sat up wiping away the tears and began to look around. Perhaps this was the home of some friend of her missionary. She felt comforted about staying here now. She lifted her eyes to the wall above the mantel and lo, there smiled the face of her dear friend, the mother, who had just gone home to heaven, and beneath it-as if that were not enough to bring a throb of understanding and joy to her heart-beneath it hung her own little jewelled riding whip which she had left on the desert a year ago and forgotten.

Suddenly, with a cry of joy, she rose and clasped her hands over her heart, relief and happiness in every line of her face.

"It is his home! I have come to his own house!" she cried and looked about her with the joy of discovery. This then was where he lived-there were his books, here his chair where he sat and rested or studied-his hands had left the Bible open at her psalm, his psalm —*their* psalm! There was his couch over behind the screen, and at the other end the tiny table and the dishes in the closet! Everything was in place, and careful neatness reigned, albeit an air of manlike uncertainty about some things.

She went from one end to the other of the big room and back again, studying every detail, revelling in the thought that now, whatever came to her, she might take back with her a picture of himself in his own quiet room when his work was laid aside for a little, and when, if ever he had time and allowed himself, he perhaps thought of her.

Time flew on winged feet. With the dear face of her old friend smiling down upon her and that psalm open beside her on the table, she never thought of fear. And presently she remembered she was hungry, and went foraging in the cupboard for something to eat. She found plenty of supplies, and after she had satisfied her hunger sat down in the great chair by the fire and looked about her in contentment. With the peace of the room, his room, upon her, and the sweet old face from the picture looking down in benediction as if in welcome, she felt happier than since her father had died.

The quiet of the desert afternoon brooded outside, the fire burned softly lower and lower at her side, the sun bent down to the west, and long rays stole through the window and across at her feet, but the golden head was drooping and the long-lashed eyes were closed. She was asleep in his chair, and the dying firelight played over her face.

Then, quietly, without any warning, the door opened and a man walked into the room!

XV. THE WAY OF THE CROSS

The missionary had been a far journey to an isolated tribe of Indians outside his own reservation. It was his first visit to them since the journey he had taken with his colleague, and of which he had told Hazel during their companionship in the desert. He had thought to go sooner, but matters in his own extended parish, and his trip East, had united to prevent him.

They had lain upon his heart, these lonely, isolated people of another age, living amid the past in their ancient houses high up on the cliffs; a little handful of lonely, primitive children, existing afar; knowing nothing of God and little of man; with their strange, simple ways, and their weird appearance. They had come to him in visions as he prayed, and always with a weight upon his soul as of a message undelivered.

He had taken his first opportunity after his return from the East to go to them; but it had not been as soon as he had hoped. Matters in connection with the new church had demanded his attention, and then when they were arranged satisfactorily one of his flock was smitten with a lingering illness, and so hung upon his friendship and companionship that he could not with a clear conscience go far away. But at last all hindrances subsided and he went forth on his mission.

The Indians had received him gladly, noting his approach from afar and coming down the steep way to meet him, putting their rude best at his disposal, and opening their hearts to him. No white man had visited them since his last coming with his friend, save a trader who had lost his way, and who knew little about the God of whom the missionary had spoken, or the Book of Heaven; at least he had not seemed to understand. Of these things he was as ignorant, perhaps, as they.

The missionary entered into the strange family life of the tribe who inhabited the vast, many-roomed palace of rock carved high at the top of the cliff. He laughed with them, ate with them, slept with them, and in every way gained their full confidence. He played with their little children, teaching them many new games and amusing tricks, and praising the quick wits of the little ones; while their elders stood about, the stolid look of their dusky faces relaxed into smiles of deep interest and admiration.

And then at night he told them of the God who set the stars above them; who made the earth and them, and loved them; and of Jesus, His only Son, who came to die for them and who would not only be their Saviour, but their loving companion by day and by night; unseen, but always at hand, caring for each one of His children individually, knowing their joys and their sorrows. Gradually he made them understand that he was the servant-the messenger-of this Christ, and had come there for the express purpose of helping them to know their unseen Friend. Around the camp-fire, under the starry dome, or on the sunny plain, whenever he taught them they listened, their faces losing the wild, half-animal look of the uncivilized, and taking on the hidden longing that all mortals have in common. He saw the humanity in them looking wistfully through their great eyes, and gave himself to teach them.

Sometimes as he talked he would lift his face to the sky, and close his eyes; and they would listen with awe as he spoke to his Father in heaven. They watched him at first and looked up as if they half expected to see the Unseen World open before their wondering gaze; but gradually the spirit of devotion claimed them, and they closed their eyes with him, and who shall say if the savage prayers within their breasts were not more acceptable to the Father than many a wordy petition put up in the temples of civilization?

Seven days and nights he abode with them, and they fain would have claimed him for their own, and begged him to give up all other places and live there always. They would give him of their best. He would not need to work, for they would give him his portion, and make him a home as he should direct them. In short, they would enshrine him in their hearts as a kind of under-god, representing to their childish minds the true and Only One, the knowledge of whom he had brought to them.

But he told them of his work, of why he must go back to it, and sadly they prepared to bid him good-bye with many an invitation for return. In going down the cliff, where he had gone with them many a time before, he turned to wave another farewell to a little child who had been his special pet, and turning, slipped, and wrenched his ankle so badly that he could not move on.

They carried him up to their home again, half sorrowful, but wholly triumphant. He was theirs for a little longer; and there were more stories he could tell. The Book of Heaven was a large one, and they wanted to hear it all. They spread his couch of their best, and wearied themselves to supply his necessity with all that their ignorance imagined he needed, and then they sat at his feet and listened. The sprain was a troublesome one and painful, and it yielded to treatment but slowly; meanwhile the messenger arrived with the telegram from the East.

They gathered about it, that sheet of yellow paper with its mysterious scratches upon it, which told such volumes to their friend, but gave no semblance to sign language of anything in heaven above or earth beneath. They looked with awe upon their friend as they saw the anguish in his countenance. His mother was dead! This man who had loved her, and had left her to bring them news of salvation, was suffering. It was one more bond between them, one more tie of common humanity. And yet he could look up and smile, and still speak to the invisible Father! They saw his face as it were the face of an angel with the light of the comfort of Christ upon it; and when he read to them and tried to make them understand the majestic words: "O death, where is thy sting? O grave, where is thy victory?" they sat and looked afar off, and thought of the ones that they had lost. This man said they would all live again. His mother would live; the chief they had lost last year, the bravest and youngest chief of all their tribe, he would live too; their little children would live; all they had lost would live again.

So, when he would most have wished to be alone with his God and his sorrow, he must needs lay aside his own bitter grief, and bring these childish people consolation for their griefs, and in doing so the comfort came to him also. For somehow, looking into their longing faces, and seeing their utter need, and how eagerly they hung upon his words, he came to feel the presence of the Comforter standing by his side in the dark cave shadows, whispering to his heart sweet words that he long had known but had not fully comprehended because his need for them had never come before. Somehow time and things of earth receded, and only heaven and immortal souls mattered. He was lifted above his own loss and into the joy of the inheritance of the servant of the Lord.

But the time had come, all too soon for his hosts, when he was able to go on his way; and most anxious he was to be started, longing for further news of the dear one who was gone from him. They followed him in sorrowful procession far into the plain to see him on his way, and then returned to their mesa and their cliff home to talk of it all and wonder.

Alone upon the desert at last, the three great mesas like fingers of a giant hand stretching cloudily behind him; the purpling mountains in the distance; the sunlight shining vividly down over all the bright sands; the full sense of his loss came at last upon him, and his spirit was bowed with the weight of it. The vision of the Mount was passed, and the valley of the shadow of life was upon him. It came to him what it would be to have no more of his mother's letters to cheer his loneliness; no thought of her at home thinking of him; no looking forward to another home-coming.

As he rode he saw none of the changing landscape by the way, but only the Granville orchard with its showering pink and white, and his mother lying happily beside him on the strawberry bank picking the sweet vivid berries, and smiling back to him as if she had been a girl. He was glad, glad he had that memory of her. And she had seemed so well, so very well. He had been thinking that perhaps when there was hope of building a little addition to his shack and making a possible place of comfort for her, that he might venture to propose that she come out to him and stay. It was a wish that had been growing, growing in his lonely heart since that visit home when it seemed as if he could not tear himself away from her and go back; and yet knew that he could not stay-would not want to stay, because of his beloved work. And now it was over forever, his dream! She would never come to cheer his home, and he would always have to live a lonely life-for he knew in his heart there was only one girl in the whole world he would want to ask to come, and her he might not, must not ask.

As endless and as desolate as his desert his future lay stretched out before his mind. For the time his beloved work and the joy of service was sunk out of sight, and he saw only himself, alone, forsaken of all love, walking his sorrowful way apart; and there surged over him a great and deadly weakness as of a spirit in despair.

In this mind he lay down to rest in the shadow of a great rock about the noon hour, too weary in spirit and exhausted in body to go further without a sleep. The faithful Billy dozed and munched his portion not far away; and high overhead a great eagle soared high and far, adding to the wide desolateness of the scene. Here he was alone at last for the first time with his grief, and for a while it had its way, and he faced it; entering into his Gethsemane with bowed spirit and seeing nothing but blackness all about him. It was so, worn with the anguish of his spirit, that he fell asleep.

While he slept there came to him peace; a dream of his mother, smiling, well, and walking with a light free step as he remembered her when he was a little boy; and by her side the girl he loved. How strange, and wonderful, that these two should come to him and bring him rest! And then, as he lay still dreaming, they smiled at him and passed on, hand in hand, the girl turning and waving her hand as if she meant to return; and presently they passed beyond his sight. Then One stood by him, somewhere within the shelter of the rock under which he lay, and spoke; and the Voice thrilled his soul as it had never been thrilled in life before:

"Lo, *I* am with you *alway*, even unto the end of the world."

The Peace of that Invisible Presence descended upon him in full measure, and when he awoke he found himself repeating: "The peace which passeth understanding!" and realizing that for the first time he knew what the words meant.

Some time he lay quietly like a child who had been comforted and cared for, wondering at the burden which had been lifted, glorying in the peace that had come in its place; rejoicing in the Presence that he felt would be with him always, and make it possible for him to bear the loneliness.

At last he turned his head to see if Billy were far away, and was startled to see the shadow of the rock, under which he lay, spread out upon the sand before him, the semblance of a perfect mighty cross. For so the jutting uneven arms of the rock and the position of the sun arranged the shadows before him. "The shadow of a great rock in a weary land." The words came to his memory, and it seemed to be his mother's voice repeating them as she used to do on Sabbath evenings when they sat together in the twilight before his bedtime. A weary land! It *was* a weary land now, and his soul had been parched with the heat and loneliness. He had needed the rock as he had never needed it before, and the Rock, Christ Jesus, had become a rest and a peace to his soul. But there it lay spread out upon the sand beside him, and it was the way of the cross; the Christ way was always the way of the cross. But what was the song they sang at that great meeting he attended in New York? "The way of the cross leads home." Ah, that was it. Some day it would lead him home, but now it was the way of the cross and he must take it with courage, and always with that unseen but close Companion who had promised to be with him even to the end of the world.

Well, he would rise up at once, strong in that blessed companionship. Cheerfully he made his preparations for starting, and now he turned Billy's head a trifle to the south, for he decided to stop over night with his colleague.

When his grief and loneliness were fresh upon him it had seemed that he could not bear this visit. But since peace had come to his soul he changed his course to take in the other mission, which was really on his way, only that he had purposely avoided it.

They made him welcome, those two who had made a little bit of earthly paradise out of their desert shack; and they compelled him to stay with them and rest three days, for he was more worn with the journey and his recent pain and sorrow than he realized. They comforted him with their loving sympathy and gladdened his soul with the sight of their own joy, albeit it gave him a feeling of being set apart from them. He started in the early dawn of the day when the morning star was yet visible, and as he rode through the beryl air of the dawning hour he was uplifted from his sadness by a sense of the near presence of Christ.

He took his way slowly, purposely turning aside three times from the trail to call at the hogans of some of his parishioners; for he dreaded the home-coming as one dreads a blow that is inevitable. His mother's picture awaited him in his own room, smiling down upon his possessions with that dear look upon her face, and to look at it for the first time knowing that she was gone from earth forever was an experience from which he shrank inexpressibly. Thus he gave himself more time, knowing that it was better to go calmly, turning his mind back to his work, and doing what she would have liked him to do.

He camped that night under the sheltered ledge where he and Hazel had been, and as he lay down to sleep he repeated the psalm they had read together that night, and felt a sense of the comfort of abiding under the shadow of the Almighty.

In visions of the night he saw the girl's face once more, and she smiled upon him with that glad welcoming look, as though she had come to be with him always. She did not say anything in the dream, but just put out her hands to him with a motion of surrender.

The vision faded as he opened his eyes, yet so real had it been that it remained with him and thrilled him with the wonder of her look all day. He began to ponder whether he had been right in persistently putting her out of his life as he had done. Bits of her own sentences came to him with new meaning and he wondered after all if he had not been a fool. Perhaps he might have won her. Perhaps God had really sent her to him to be his life companion, and he had been too blind to understand.

He put the idea from him many times with a sigh as he mended the fire and prepared his simple meal, yet always her face lingered sweetly in his thoughts, like balm upon his saddened spirit.

Billy was headed towards home that morning, and seemed eager to get on. He had not understood his master these sad days. Something had come over his spirits. The little horse neighed cheerfully and started on his way with willing gait. However lonely the master might be, home was good, with one's own stall and manger; and who might tell but some presentiment told Billy that the princess was awaiting them?

The missionary endeavoured to keep his thoughts upon his work and plans for the immediate future, but try as he would the face of the girl kept smiling in between; and all the beauties of the way combined to bring back the ride he had taken with her; until finally he let his fancy dwell upon her with pleasant thoughts of how it would be if she were his, and waiting for him at the end of his journey; or better still, riding beside him at this moment, bearing him sweet converse on the way.

The little shack stood silent, familiar, in the setting sunlight, as he rode up to the door, and gravely arranged for Billy's comfort, then with his upward look for comfort he went towards his lonely home and opening the door stood wondering upon the threshold!

XVI. THE LETTER

It was only an instant before she opened her eyes, for that subconscious state, that warns even in sleep of things that are going on outside the world of slumber, told her there was another soul present.

She awakened suddenly and looked up at him, the rosiness of sleep upon her cheeks and the dewiness of it upon her eyelids. She looked most adorable with the long red slant of sunset from the open door at her feet and the wonder of his coming in her face. Their eyes met, and told the story, before brain had time to give warning of danger and need of self-control.

"Oh, my darling!" the man said and took a step towards her, his arms outstretched as if he would clasp her, yet daring hardly to believe that it was really herself in the flesh.

"My darling! Have you really come to me?" He breathed the question as though its answer meant life or death to him.

She arose and stood before him, trembling with joy, abashed now that she was in his presence, in his home, unbidden. Her tongue seemed tied. She had no word with which to explain. But because he saw the love in her eyes and because his own need of her was great, he became bolder, and coming closer he began to tell her earnestly how he had longed and prayed that God would make a way for him to find her again; how he had fancied her here in this room, his own dear companion-his wife!

He breathed the word tenderly, reverently and she felt the blessing and the wonder of the love of this great simple-hearted man.

Then because he saw his answer in her eyes, he came near and took her reverently in his arms, laid his lips upon hers, and thus they stood for a moment together, knowing that after all the sorrow, the longing, the separation, each had come into his own.

It was some time before Hazel could get opportunity to explain how she came all unknowingly to be in his house, and even then he could not understand what joyful circumstance had set her face forward and dropped her at his door. So she had to go back to the letter, the letter which was the cause of it all, and yet for the moment had been forgotten. She brought it forth now, and his face, all tender with the joy of her presence, grew almost glorified when he knew that it was she who had been his mother's tender nurse and beloved friend through the last days of her life.

With clasped hands they talked together of his mother. Hazel told him all: how she had come upon her that summer's day, and her heart had yearned to know her for his sake; and how she had gone back again, and yet again; all the story of her own struggles for a better life. When she told of her cooking lessons he kissed the little white hands he held, and when she spoke of her hospital work he touched his lips to eyes and brow in reverent worshipfulness.

"And you did all that because ——?" he asked and looked deep into her eyes, demanding hungrily his answer.

"Because I wanted to be worthy of your love!" she breathed softly, her eyes down-drooped, her face rosy with her confession.

"Oh, my darling!" he said, and clasped her close once more. Almost the letter itself was forgotten, until it slipped softly to the floor and called attention to itself. There was really after all no need for the letter. It had done its intended work without being read. But they read it together, his arm about her shoulders, and their heads close, each feeling the need of the comforting love of the other because of the bereavement each had suffered.

And thus they read:

"My dear Son:

"I am writing this letter in what I believe to be the last few days of my life. Long ago I made our dear doctor tell me just what would be the signs that preceded the probable culmination of my disease. He knew I would be happier so, for I had some things I wished to accomplish before I went away. I did not tell you, dear son, because I knew it could but distress you and turn your thoughts away from the work to which you belong. I knew when you came home to me for that dear last visit that I had only a little while longer left here, and I need not tell you what those blessed days of your stay were to me. You know without my telling. You perhaps will blame yourself that you did not see how near the end it was and stay beside me; but John, beloved, I would not have been happy to have had it so. It would have brought before you with intensity the parting side of death, and this I wished to avoid. I want you to think of me as gone to be with Jesus and with your dear father. Besides, I wanted the pleasure of giving you back again to your work before I went away.

"It was because I knew the end was near that I dared do a lot of things that I would have been careful about otherwise. It was in the strength of the happiness of your presence that I forced myself to walk again that you might remember your mother once more on her feet. Remember now when you are reading this I shall be walking the golden streets with as strong and free a gait as you walk your desert, dear. So don't regret anything of the good time we had, nor wish you had stayed longer. It was perfect, and the good times are not over for us. We shall have them again on the other side some day when there are no more partings forever.

"But there is just one thing that has troubled me ever since you first went away, and that is that you are alone. God knew it was not good for man to be alone, and He has a helpmeet for my boy somewhere in the world, I am sure. I would be glad if I might go knowing that you had found her and that she loved you as I loved your father when I married him. I have never talked much about these things to you because I do not think mothers should try to influence their children to marry until God sends the right one, and then it is not the mother who should be the judge, of course. But once I spoke to you in a letter. You remember? It was after I had met a sweet girl whose life seemed so fitted to belong to yours. You opened your heart to me then and told me you had found the one you loved and would never love another-but she was not for you. My heart ached for you, laddie, and I prayed much for you then, for it was a sore trial to come to my boy away out there alone with his trouble. I had much ado not to hate that girl to whom you had given your love, and not to fancy her a most disagreeable creature with airs, and no sense, not to recognize the man in my son, and not to know his beautiful soul and the worth of his love. But then I thought perhaps she couldn't help it, poor child, that she didn't know enough to appreciate you; and likely it was God's good leading that kept you from her. But I have kept hoping that some time He would bring you to love another who was more worthy than she could have been.

"Dear, you have never said anything more about that girl, and I hope you have forgotten her, though sometimes when you were at home I noticed that deep, far-away look in your eyes, and a sadness about your lips that made me tremble lest her memory was just as bright as ever. I have wanted you to know the sweet girl Hazel Radcliffe who has been my dear friend and almost daughter-for no daughter could have been dearer than she has been to me, and I believe she loves me too as I love her. If you had been nearer I would have tried to bring you two together, at least for once, that you might judge for yourselves; but I found out that she was shy as a bird about meeting any one-though she has hosts of young men friends in her New York home-and that she would have run away if you had come. Besides, I could not have given you any reason but the truth for sending for you, and I knew God would bring you two together if it was His will. But I could not go happy from this earth without doing something towards helping you just to see her once, and so I have asked her to give you this letter with her own hand, if possible, and she has promised to do so. You will come home when I am gone and she will have to see you, and when you look on her sweet face if you do not feel as your mother does about her, it is all right, dear son; only I wanted you just to see her once because I love her so much, and because I love you. If you could forget the other and love this one it seems as though I should be glad even in heaven, but if you do not feel that way when you see her, John, don't mind my writing this letter, for it pleased me much to play this little trick upon you before I left; and the dear girl must never know-unless indeed you love her-and then I do not care-for I know she will forgive me for writing this silly letter, and love me just the same.

"Dear boy, just as we never liked to say good-bye when you went away to college, but only 'Au revoir,' so there won't be any good-bye now, only I love you.

"Your Mother."

Hazel was weeping softly when they finished the letter, and there were tears in the eyes of the son, though they were glorified by the smile that shone upon the girl as he folded the letter and said:

"Wasn't that a mother for a fellow to have? And could I do anything else than give myself when she gave all she had? And to think she picked out the very one for me that I loved of all the world, and sent her out to me because I was too set in my way to come back after her. It is just as if my mother sent you down as a gift from heaven to me, dear!" and their lips met once more in deep love and understanding.

The sun was almost setting now, and suddenly the two became aware that night was coming on. The Indian would be returning and they must plan what to do.

Brownleigh rose and went to the door to see if the Indian were in sight. He was thinking hard and fast. Then he came back and stood before the girl.

"Dear!" he said, and the tone of his voice brought the quick colour to her cheeks; it was so wonderful, so disconcerting to be looked at and spoken to in that way. She caught her breath and wondered if it were not a dream after all. "Dear," another of those deep, searching looks, "this is a big, primitive country and we do things in a most summary way out here sometimes. You must tell me if I go too fast; but could —*would* you-do you think you love me enough to marry me at once-to-night?"

"Oh!" she breathed, lifting her happy eyes. "It would be beautiful to never have to leave you again-but-you hardly know me. I am not fitted, you know. You are a great, wonderful missionary, and I—I am only a foolish girl who has fallen in love with you and can't ever be happy again without you."

She buried her face in the arm of the chair and cried happy, shamed tears, and he gathered her up in his arms and comforted her, his face shining with a glorified expression.

"Dear," he said when he could speak again, "dear, don't you know that is all I want? And don't ever talk that way again about me. I am no saint, as you'll very well find out, but I'll promise to love and cherish you as long as we both shall live. Will you marry me to-night?"

There was a silence in the little room broken only by the low crackling of the dying fire.

She lifted shy glad eyes to his, and then came and laid her two hands in his.

"If you are quite sure you want me," she breathed softly.

The rapture of his face and the tenderness of his arms assured her on that point.

"There is just one great regret I have," said the young man, lifting his eyes towards his mother's picture. "If she only could have known it was you that I loved. Why didn't I tell her your name? But then — — Why, my dear, I didn't know your name. Do you realize that? I haven't known your name until now."

"I certainly did realize it," said Hazel with rosy cheeks. "It used to hurt dreadfully sometimes to think that even if you wanted to find me you wouldn't know how to go about it."

"You dear! Did you care so much?" His voice was deep and tender and his eyes were upon her.

"So much!" she breathed softly.

But the splash of red light on the floor at their feet warned them of the lateness of the hour and they turned to the immediate business of the moment.

"It is wonderful that things are just as they are to-night," said Brownleigh in his full, joyous tones. "It certainly seems providential. Bishop Vail, my father's old college chum, has been travelling through the West on missionary work for his church, and he is now at the stopping place where you spent last night. He leaves on the midnight train to-night, but we can get there long before that time, and he will marry us. There is no one I would rather have had, though the choice should have been yours. Are you going to mind very much being married in this brief and primitive manner?"

"If I minded those things I should not be worthy of your love," said Hazel softly. "No, I don't mind in the least. Only I've really nothing along to get married in-nothing suitable for a wedding gown. You won't be able to remember me in bridal attire-and there won't be even Amelia Ellen for bridesmaid." She smiled at him mischievously.

"You darling!" he said laying his lips upon hers again. "You need no bridal attire to make you the sweetest bride that ever came to Arizona, and I shall always remember you as you are now, as the most beautiful sight my eyes ever saw. If there was time to get word to some of my colleagues off at their stations we should have a wedding reception that would outrival your New York affairs so far as enthusiasm and genuine hearty good will is concerned, but they are all from forty to a hundred miles away from here and it will be impossible. Are you sure you are not too tired to ride back to the stopping place to-night?" He looked at her anxiously. "We will hitch Billy to the wagon, and the seat has good springs. I will put in plenty of cushions and you can rest on the way, and we will not attempt to come back to-night. It would be too much for you."

She began to protest but he went on:

"No, dear, I don't mean we'll stay in that little hole where you spent last night. That would be awful! But what would you say to camping in the same spot where we had our last talk? I have been there many times since and often spend the night there because of its sweet association with you. It is not far, you know, from the railroad —a matter of a few minutes' ride-and there is good water. We can carry my little tent and trappings, and then take as much of a wedding trip afterwards as you feel you have strength for before we return, though we shall have the rest of our lives to make one dear long wedding trip of, I hope. Will that plan suit you?"

"Oh, it will be beautiful," said Hazel with shining eyes.

"Very well, then. I will get everything ready for our start and you must rest until I call you." With that he stooped and before she realized what he was doing gently lifted her from her feet and laid her down upon his couch over in the corner, spreading a many-coloured Indian blanket over her. Then he deftly stirred up the fire, filled up the kettle, swung it back over the blaze, and with a smile went out to prepare Billy and the wagon.

Hazel lay there looking about her new home with happy eyes, noting each little touch of refinement and beauty that showed the character of the man who had lived his life alone there for three long years, and wondering if it were really herself, the lonely little struggling nurse with the bitter ache in her heart, who was feeling so happy here to-day —Hazel Radcliffe, the former New York society girl, rejoicing ecstatically because she was going to marry a poor home missionary and live in a shanty! How her friends would laugh and sneer, and how Aunt Maria would lift her hands in horror and say the family was disgraced! But it did not matter about Aunt Maria. Poor Aunt Maria! She had never approved of anything that Hazel wanted to do all her life. As for her brother-and here her face took on a shade of sadness-her brother was of another world than hers and always had been. People said he was like his dead mother. Perhaps the grand man of the desert could help her brother to better things. Perhaps he would come out here to visit them and catch a vision of another kind of life and take a longing for it as she had done. He could not fail at least to see the greatness of the man she had chosen.

There was great comfort to her in this hour to remember that her father had been interested in her missionary, and had expressed a hope that she might meet him again some day. She thought her father would have been pleased at the choice she had made, for he had surely seen the vision of what was really worth while in life before he died.

Suddenly her eyes turned to the little square table over by the cupboard. What if she should set it?

She sprang up and suited the action to the thought.

Almost as a child might handle her first pewter set Hazel took the dishes from the shelves and arranged them on the table. They were pretty china dishes, with a fine old sprigged pattern of delicate flowers. She recognized them as belonging to his mother's set, and handled them reverently. It almost seemed as if that mother's presence was with her in the room as she prepared the table for her first meal with the beloved son.

She found a large white towel in the cupboard drawer that she spread on the rough little table, and set the delicate dishes upon it: two plates, two cups and saucers, knives and forks-two of everything! How it thrilled her to think that in a little while she would belong here in this dear house, a part of it, and that they two would have a right to sit together at this table through the years. There might come hardships and disappointments-of course there would. She was no fool! Life was full of disappointments for everybody, as well as of beautiful surprises! But come what would she knew by the thrill in her heart that she would never be sorry for this day in which she had promised to become the wife of the man of the desert, and she would always cherish the memory of this her first setting of the little table, and let it make all future settings of that table a holy ordinance.

She found a can of soup in the cupboard, and made it hot in a small saucepan on the fire, and set forth on the table crackers and cheese, a glass of jelly, a small bottle of stuffed olives and some little cakes she had brought with her in her suit-case. She had thought she might need something of the sort when she landed in Arizona, for there was no telling but she might have to ride across the desert to find her missionary; and sure enough that had been the case.

It looked very cozy when Brownleigh came in to say that the wagon was ready and he thought he saw the Indian in the dusk coming across the plain, but he stopped short without speech, for here before him was the picture which his mind and heart had painted for him many a time: this girl, the one girl in all the earth for him, kneeling beside his hearth and dishing up the steaming soup into the hot dishes, the firelight playing on her sweet face and golden hair, and every line and motion of her graceful body calling for his adoration! So he stood for one long minute and feasted his hungry eyes upon the sight, until she turned and saw his heart in his eyes, and her own face grew rosy with the joy and the meaning of it all.

And so they sat down to their first meal in the little house together, and then having sent the Indian back to the fort with a message, they took their way forth in the starlight together to begin their wedding journey.

XVII. DEDICATION

Billy made good time in spite of the fact that he had been out all day on parishional work, but he knew who he was hauling, and seemed to take deep satisfaction in having Hazel back again, for now and again he would turn back towards the wagon when they stopped for water and whinny happily.

They reached the stopping place about nine o'clock, and the news that the missionary was going to be married spread like wildfire among the men and out to the neighbouring shacks. In no time a small crowd had collected about the place, peering out of the starlit darkness.

Hazel retired to the forlorn little chamber where she had spent the night before and rummaged in her trunk for bridal apparel. In a few minutes she emerged into the long dining-room where the table had been hastily cleared and moved aside, and upon which the boarders were now seated in long rows, watching the proceedings curiously.

She was dressed in a simple white muslin, touched here and there with exquisite hand embroidery and tiny cobwebby edges of real lace. The missionary caught his breath as he saw her come out to him, and the rough faces of the men softened as they watched her.

The white-haired bishop arose to meet her and welcomed her in a fatherly way he had, and the woman who kept the stopping place came following in Hazel's wake, hastily wiping her hands on her apron, and casting it behind her as she entered. She had been preparing an impromptu supper out of any materials that happened to be at hand, but she could not miss the ceremony if the coffee did burn. Weddings did not come her way every day.

In the doorway, his stolid face shining in the glare of many candles, stood the Indian from the fort. He had followed silently behind the couple to witness the proceedings, well knowing he would be forgiven by his mistress at the fort when he told his news. The missionary was well beloved-and the missionary was going to be married!

What would the four hundred of her own select New York circle have said could they have seen Hazel Radcliffe standing serene, in her simple gown, with her undecked golden hair, in the midst of that motley company of men, with only three curious slatternly women in the background to keep her company, giving herself away to a man who had dedicated his life to work in the desert? But Hazel's happy heart was serenely unconscious of the incongruity of her surroundings, and she answered with a clear ring to her voice as the bishop asked her the questions: "I will." She was coming gladly to her new home.

It was her own ring, the ring she had given him, that John Brownleigh put upon her hand in token of his loyalty and love for her, the ring that for a whole year had lain next his own heart and comforted its loneliness because she had given it, and now he gave it back because she had given him herself.

Graciously she placed her small white hand in the rough awkward ones of the men who came to offer her congratulations, half stumbling over their own feet in their awe and wonder at her beauty. It was to them as if an angel from heaven had suddenly dropped down and condescended to walk their daily path in sight of them all.

Cheerfully she swallowed the stale cake and muddy coffee that the slatternly landlady produced, and afterwards, as she was being helped to get back into her riding dress, bestowed upon her a little lilac wool frock from her trunk that the woman admired greatly. From that moment the landlady of the stopping place was a new creature. Missions and missionaries had been nothing to her through the years, but she believed in them forever after, and donned her new lilac gown in token of her faith in Christianity. Thus Hazel won her first convert, who afterwards proved her fidelity in time of great trial, and showed that even a lilac gown may be an instrument of good.

Out into the starlight together again they rode, with the blessing of the bishop upon them, and the cheers of the men still sounding in their ears.

"I wish mother could have known," said the bridegroom as he drew his bride close within his arm and looked down upon her nestling by his side.

"Oh, I think she does!" said Hazel as she dropped a thankful, weary head against his shoulder. Then the missionary stooped and gave his wife a long, tender kiss, and raising his head and lifting his eyes to the starlit sky he said reverently:

"Oh, my Father, I thank Thee for this wonderful gift. Make me worthy of her. Help her never to regret that she has come to me."

Hazel crept her hand into his free one, and laid her lips upon his fingers, and prayed all quietly by herself for gladness. So they rode out to their camp beneath God's sky.

Three days later an Indian on the way to the fort turned aside with a message for Hazel—a telegram. It read:

> "Arrived safe. Married Burley to once so I could see to him. Do come home right away. Burley says come and live with us. Answer right away. I can't enjoy my new home worrying about you.
>
> "Yours respectful,
> "AMELIA ELLEN STOUT BURLEY."

With laughter and tears Hazel read the telegram whose price must have cost the frugal New England conscience a twinge, and after a moment's thought wrote an answer to send back by the messenger.

> "DEAR AMELIA ELLEN: Love and congratulations for you both. I was married to John Brownleigh the night you left. Come out and see us when your husband gets well, and perhaps we'll visit you when we come East. I am very happy.
>
> "HAZEL RADCLIFFE BROWNLEIGH."

When good Amelia Ellen read that telegram she wiped her spectacles a second time and read it over to see that she had made no mistake, and then she set her toil-worn hands upon her hips and surveyed the prone but happy Burley in dazed astonishment, ejaculating:

"Fer the land sake! Now did you ever? Fer the land! Was that what she was up to all the time? I thought she was wonderful set to go, and wonderful set to stay, but I never sensed what was up. Ef I'd 'a' knowed, I suppose I'd 'a' stayed another day. Why didn't she tell me, I wonder! Well, fer the land sake!"

And Burley murmured contentedly:

"Wal, I'm mighty glad you never knowed, Amelia Ellen!"

A VOICE IN THE WILDERNESS

CHAPTER I

With a lurch the train came to a dead stop and Margaret Earle, hastily gathering up her belongings, hurried down the aisle and got out into the night.

It occurred to her, as she swung her heavy suit-case down the rather long step to the ground, and then carefully swung herself after it, that it was strange that neither conductor, brakeman, nor porter had come to help her off the train, when all three had taken the trouble to tell her that hers was the next station; but she could hear voices up ahead. Perhaps something was the matter with the engine that detained them and they had forgotten her for the moment.

The ground was rough where she stood, and there seemed no sign of a platform. Did they not have platforms in this wild Western land, or was the train so long that her car had stopped before reaching it?

She strained her eyes into the darkness, and tried to make out things from the two or three specks of light that danced about like fireflies in the distance. She could dimly see moving figures away up near the engine, and each one evidently carried a lantern. The train was tremendously long. A sudden feeling of isolation took possession of her. Perhaps she ought not to have got out until some one came to help her. Perhaps the train had not pulled into the station yet and she ought to get back on it and wait. Yet if the train started before she found the conductor she might be carried on somewhere and be justly blame her for a fool.

There did not seem to be any building on that side of the track. It was probably on the other, but she was standing too near the cars to see over. She tried to move back to look, but the ground sloped and she slipped and fell in the cinders, bruising her knee and cutting her wrist.

In sudden panic she arose. She would get back into the train, no matter what the consequences. They had no right to put her out here, away off from the station, at night, in a strange country. If the train started before she could find the conductor she would tell him that he must back it up again and let her off. He certainly could not expect her to get out like this.

She lifted the heavy suit-case up the high step that was even farther from the ground than it had been when she came down, because her fall had loosened some of the earth and caused it to slide away from the track. Then, reaching to the rail of the step, she tried to pull herself up, but as she did so the engine gave a long snort and the whole train, as if it were in league against her, lurched forward crazily, shaking off her hold. She slipped to her knees again, the suit-case, toppled from the lower step, descending upon her, and together they slid and rolled down the short bank, while the train, like an irresponsible nurse who had slapped her charge and left it to its fate, ran giddily off into the night.

The horror of being deserted helped the girl to rise in spite of bruises and shock. She lifted imploring hands to the unresponsive cars as they hurried by her — one, two, three, with bright windows, each showing a passenger, comfortable and safe inside, unconscious of her need.

A moment of useless screaming, running, trying to attract some one's attention, a sickening sense of terror and failure, and the last car slatted itself past with a mocking clatter, as if it enjoyed her discomfort.

Margaret stood dazed, reaching out helpless hands, then dropped them at her sides and gazed after the fast-retreating train, the light on its last car swinging tauntingly, blinking now and then with a leer in its eye, rapidly vanishing from her sight into the depth of the night.

She gasped and looked about her for the station that but a short moment before had been so real to her mind; and, lo! on this side and on that there was none!

The night was wide like a great floor shut in by a low, vast dome of curving blue set with the largest, most wonderful stars she had ever seen. Heavy shadows of purple-green, smoke-like, hovered over earth darker and more intense than the unfathomable blue of the night sky. It seemed like the secret nesting-place of mysteries wherein no human foot might dare intrude. It was incredible that such could be but common sage-brush, sand, and greasewood wrapped about with the beauty of the lonely night.

No building broke the inky outlines of the plain, nor friendly light streamed out to cheer her heart. Not even a tree was in sight, except on the far horizon, where a heavy line of deeper darkness might mean a forest. Nothing, absolutely nothing, in the blue, deep, starry dome above and the bluer darkness of the earth below save one sharp shaft ahead like a black mast throwing out a dark arm across the track.

As soon as she sighted it she picked up her baggage and made her painful way toward it, for her knees and wrist were bruised and her baggage was heavy.

A soft drip, drip greeted her as she drew nearer; something plashing down among the cinders by the track. Then she saw the tall column with its arm outstretched, and looming darker among the sage-brush the outlines of a water-tank. It was so she recognized the engine's drinking-tank, and knew that she had mistaken a pause to water the engine for a regular stop at a station.

Her soul sank within her as she came up to the dripping water and laid her hand upon the dark upright, as if in some way it could help her. She dropped her baggage and stood, trembling, gazing around upon the beautiful, lonely scene in horror; and then, like a mirage against the distance, there melted on her frightened eyes a vision of her father and mother sitting around the library lamp at home, as they sat every evening. They were probably reading and talking at this very minute, and trying not to miss her on this her first venture away from the home into the great world to teach. What would they say if they could see their beloved daughter, whom they had sheltered all these years and let go forth so reluctantly now, in all her confidence of youth, bound by almost absurd promises to be careful and not run any risks.

Yet here she was, standing alone beside a water-tank in the midst of an Arizona plain, no knowing how many miles from anywhere, at somewhere between nine and ten o'clock at night! It seemed incredible that it had really happened! Perhaps she was dreaming! A few moments before in the bright car, surrounded by drowsy fellow-travelers, almost at her journey's end, as she supposed; and now, having merely done as she thought right, she was stranded here!

She rubbed her eyes and looked again up the track, half expecting to see the train come back for her. Surely, surely the conductor, or the porter who had been so kind, would discover that she was gone, and do something about it. They couldn't leave her here alone on the prairie! It would be too dreadful!

That vision of her father and mother off against the purple-green distance, how it shook her! The lamp looked bright and cheerful, and she could see her father's head with its heavy white hair. He turned to look at her mother to tell her of something he read in the paper. They were sitting there, feeling contented and almost happy about her, and she, their little girl — all her dignity as school-teacher dropped from her like a garment now — she was standing in this empty space alone, with only an engine's water-tank to keep her from dying, and only the barren, desolate track to connect her with the world of men and women. She dropped her head upon her breast and the tears came, sobbing, choking, raining down. Then off in the distance she heard a low, rising howl of some snarling, angry beast, and she lifted her head and stood in trembling terror, clinging to the tank.

That sound was coyotes or wolves howling. She had read about them, but had not expected to experience them in such a situation. How confidently had she accepted the position which offered her the opening she had sought for the splendid career that she hoped was to follow! How fearless had she been! Coyotes, nor Indians, nor wild cowboy students — nothing had daunted her courage. Besides, she told her mother it was very different going to a town from what it would be if she were a missionary going to the wilds. It was an important school she was to teach, where her Latin and German and mathematical achievements had won her the place above several other applicants, and where her well-known tact was expected to work wonders. But what were Latin and German and mathematics now? Could they show her how to climb a water-tank? Would tact avail with a hungry wolf?

The howl in the distance seemed to come nearer. She cast frightened eyes to the unresponsive water-tank looming high and dark above her. She must get up there somehow. It was not safe to stand here a minute. Besides, from that height she might be able to see farther, and perhaps there would be a light somewhere and she might cry for help.

Investigation showed a set of rude spikes by which the trainmen were wont to climb up, and Margaret prepared to ascend them. She set her suit-case dubiously down at the foot. Would it be safe to leave it there? She had read how coyotes carried off a hatchet from a camping-party, just to get the leather thong which was bound about the handle. She could not afford to lose her things. Yet how could she climb and carry that heavy burden with her? A sudden thought came.

Her simple traveling-gown was finished with a silken girdle, soft and long, wound twice about her waist and falling in tasseled ends. Swiftly she untied it and knotted one end firmly to the handle of her suit-case, tying the other end securely to her wrist. Then slowly, cautiously, with many a look upward, she began to climb.

It seemed miles, though in reality it was but a short distance. The howling beasts in the distance sounded nearer now and continually, making her heart beat wildly. She was stiff and bruised from her falls, and weak with fright. The spikes were far apart, and each step of progress was painful and difficult. It was good at last to rise high enough to see over the water-tank and feel a certain confidence in her defense.

But she had risen already beyond the short length of her silken tether, and the suit-case was dragging painfully on her arm. She was obliged to steady herself where she stood and pull it up before she could go on. Then she managed to get it swung up to the top of the tank in a comparatively safe place. One more long spike step and she was beside it.

The tank was partly roofed over, so that she had room enough to sit on the edge without danger of falling in and drowning. For a few minutes she could only sit still and be thankful and try to get her breath back again after the climb; but presently the beauty of the night began to cast its spell over her. That wonderful blue of the sky! It hadn't ever before impressed her that skies were blue at night. She would have said they were black or gray. As a matter of fact, she didn't remember to have ever seen so much sky at once before, nor to have noticed skies in general until now.

This sky was so deeply, wonderfully blue, the stars so real, alive and sparkling, that all other stars she had ever seen paled before them into mere imitations. The spot looked like one of Taylor's pictures of the Holy Land. She half expected to see a shepherd with his crook and sheep approaching her out of the dim shadows, or a turbaned, white-robed David with his lifted hands of prayer standing off among the depths of purple darkness. It would not have been out of keeping if a walled city with housetops should be hidden behind the clumps of sage-brush farther on. 'Twas such a night and such a scene as this, perhaps, when the wise men started to follow the star!

But one cannot sit on the edge of a water-tank in the desert night alone and muse long on art and history. It was cold up there, and the howling seemed nearer than before. There was no sign of a light or a house anywhere, and not even a freight-train sent its welcome clatter down the track. All was still and wide and lonely, save that terrifying sound of the beasts; such stillness as she had not ever thought could be — a fearful silence as a setting for the awful voices of the wilds.

The bruises and scratches she had acquired set up a fine stinging, and the cold seemed to sweep down and take possession of her on her high, narrow seat. She was growing stiff and cramped, yet dared not move much. Would there be no train, nor any help? Would she have to sit there all night? It looked so very near to the ground now. Could wild beasts climb, she wondered?

Then in the interval of silence that came between the calling of those wild creatures there stole a sound. She could not tell at first what it was. A slow, regular, plodding sound, and quite far away. She looked to find it, and thought she saw a shape move out of the sage-brush on the other side of the track, but she could not be sure. It might be but a figment of her brain, a foolish fancy from looking so long at the huddled bushes on the dark plain. Yet something prompted her to cry out, and when she heard her own voice she cried again and louder, wondering why she had not cried before.

"Help! Help!" she called; and again: "Help! Help!"

The dark shape paused and turned toward her. She was sure now. What if it were a beast instead of a human! Terrible fear took possession of her; then, to her infinite relief, a nasal voice sounded out:

"Who's thar?"

But when she opened her lips to answer, nothing but a sob would come to them for a minute, and then she could only cry, pitifully:

"Help! Help!"

"Whar be you?" twanged the voice; and now she could see a horse and rider like a shadow moving toward her down the track.

CHAPTER II

The horse came to a standstill a little way from the track, and his rider let forth a stream of strange profanity. The girl shuddered and began to think a wild beast might be preferable to some men. However, these remarks seemed to be a mere formality. He paused and addressed her:

"Heow'd yeh git up thar? D'j'yeh drap er climb?"

He was a little, wiry man with a bristly, protruding chin. She could see that, even in the starlight. There was something about the point of that stubby chin that she shrank from inexpressibly. He was not a pleasant man to look upon, and even his voice was unprepossessing. She began to think that even the night with its loneliness and unknown perils was preferable to this man's company.

"I got off the train by mistake, thinking it was my station, and before I discovered it the train had gone and left me," Margaret explained, with dignity.

"Yeh didn't 'xpect it t' sit round on th' plain while you was gallivantin' up water-tanks, did yeh?"

Cold horror froze Margaret's veins. She was dumb for a second. "I am on my way to Ashland station. Can you tell me how far it is from here and how I can get there?" Her tone was like icicles.

"It's a little matter o' twenty miles, more 'r less," said the man protruding his offensive chin. "The walkin's good. I don't know no other way from this p'int at this time o' night. Yeh might set still till th' mornin' freight goes by an' drap atop o' one of the kyars."

"Sir!" said Margaret, remembering her dignity as a teacher.

The man wheeled his horse clear around and looked up at her impudently. She could smell bad whisky on his breath.

"Say, you must be some young highbrow, ain't yeh? Is thet all yeh want o' me? 'Cause ef 'tis I got t' git on t' camp. It's a good five mile yet, an' I 'ain't hed no grub sence noon."

The tears suddenly rushed to the girl's eyes as the horror of being alone in the night again took possession of her. This dreadful man frightened her, but the thought of the loneliness filled her with dismay.

"Oh!" she cried, forgetting her insulted dignity, "you're not going to leave me up here alone, are you? Isn't there some place near here where I could stay overnight?"

"Thur ain't no palace hotel round these diggin's, ef that's what you mean," the man leered at her. "You c'n come along t' camp 'ith me ef you ain't too stuck up."

"To camp!" faltered Margaret in dismay, wondering what her mother would say. "Are there any ladies there?"

A loud guffaw greeted her question. "Wal, my woman's thar, sech es she is; but she ain't no highflier like you. We mostly don't hev ladies to camp, But I got t' git on. Ef you want to go too, you better light down pretty speedy, fer I can't wait."

In fear and trembling Margaret descended her rude ladder step by step, primitive man seated calmly on his horse, making no attempt whatever to assist her.

"This ain't no baggage-car," he grumbled, as he saw the suit-case in her hand. "Well, h'ist yerself up thar; I reckon we c'n pull through somehow. Gimme the luggage."

Margaret stood appalled beside the bony horse and his uncouth rider. Did he actually expect her to ride with him? "Couldn't I walk?" she faltered, hoping he would offer to do so.

"'T's up t' you," the man replied, indifferently. "Try 't an' see!"

He spoke to the horse, and it started forward eagerly, while the girl in horror struggled on behind. Over rough, uneven ground, between greasewood, sage-brush, and cactus, back into the trail. The man, oblivious of her presence, rode contentedly on, a silent shadow on a dark horse wending a silent way between the purple-green clumps of other shadows, until, bewildered, the girl almost lost sight of them. Her breath came short, her ankle turned, and she fell with both hands in a stinging bed of cactus. She cried out then and begged him to stop.

"L'arned yer lesson, hev yeh, sweety?" he jeered at her, foolishly. "Well, get in yer box, then."

He let her struggle up to a seat behind himself with very little assistance, but when she was seated and started on her way she began to wish she had stayed behind and taken any perils of the way rather than trust herself in proximity to this creature.

From time to time he took a bottle from his pocket and swallowed a portion of its contents, becoming fluent in his language as they proceeded on their way. Margaret remained silent, growing more and more frightened every time the bottle came out. At last he offered it to her. She declined it with cold politeness, which seemed to irritate the little man, for he turned suddenly fierce.

"Oh, yer too fine to take a drap fer good comp'ny, are yeh? Wal, I'll show yeh a thing er two, my pretty lady. You'll give me a kiss with yer two cherry lips before we go another step. D'yeh hear, my sweetie?" And he turned with a silly leer to enforce his command; but with a cry of horror Margaret slid to the ground and ran back down the trail as hard as she could go, till she stumbled and fell in the shelter of a great sage-bush, and lay sobbing on the sand.

The man turned bleared eyes toward her and watched until she disappeared. Then sticking his chin out wickedly, he slung her suit-case after her and called:

"All right, my pretty lady; go yer own gait an' l'arn yer own lesson." He started on again, singing a drunken song.

Under the blue, starry dome alone sat Margaret again, this time with no friendly water-tank for her defense, and took counsel with herself. The howling coyotes seemed to be silenced for the time; at least they had become a minor quantity in her equation of troubles. She felt now that man was her greatest menace, and to get away safely from him back to that friendly water-tank and the dear old railroad track she would have pledged her next year's salary. She stole softly to the place where she had heard the suit-case fall, and, picking it up, started on the weary road back to the tank. Could she ever find the way? The trail seemed so intangible a thing, her sense of direction so confused. Yet there was nothing else to do. She shuddered whenever she thought of the man who had been her companion on horseback.

When the man reached camp he set his horse loose and stumbled into the door of the log bunk-house, calling loudly for something to eat.

The men were sitting around the room on the rough benches and bunks, smoking their pipes or stolidly staring into the dying fire. Two smoky kerosene-lanterns that hung from spikes driven high in the logs cast a weird light over the company, eight men in all, rough and hardened with exposure to stormy life and weather. They were men with unkempt beards and uncombed hair, their coarse cotton shirts open at the neck, their brawny arms bare above the elbow, with crimes and sorrows and hard living written large across their faces.

There was one, a boy in looks, with smooth face and white skin healthily flushed in places like a baby's. His face, too, was hard and set in sternness like a mask, as if life had used him badly; but behind it was a fineness of feature and spirit that could not be utterly hidden. They called him the Kid, and thought it was his youth that made him different from them all, for he was only twenty-four, and not one of the rest was under forty. They were doing their best to help him get over that innate fineness that was his natural inheritance, but although he stopped at nothing, and played his part always with the ease of one old in the ways of the world, yet he kept a quiet reserve about him, a kind of charm beyond which they had not been able to go.

He was playing cards with three others at the table when the man came in, and did not look up at the entrance.

The woman, white and hopeless, appeared at the door of the shed-room when the man came, and obediently set about getting his supper; but her lifeless face never changed expression.

"Brung a gal 'long of me part way," boasted the man, as he flung himself into a seat by the table. "Thought you fellers might like t' see 'er, but she got too high an' mighty fer me, wouldn't take a pull at th' bottle 'ith me, 'n' shrieked like a catamount when I kissed 'er. Found 'er hangin' on th' water-tank. Got off 't th' wrong place. One o' yer highbrows out o' th' parlor car! Good lesson fer 'er!"

The Boy looked up from his cards sternly, his keen eyes boring through the man. "Where is she now?" he asked, quietly; and all the men in the room looked up uneasily. There was that tone and accent again that made the Boy alien from them. What was it?

The man felt it and snarled his answer angrily. "Dropped 'er on th' trail, an' threw her fine-lady b'longin's after 'er. 'Ain't got no use fer thet kind. Wonder what they was created fer? Ain't no good to nobody, not even 'emselves." And he laughed a harsh cackle that was not pleasant to hear.

The Boy threw down his cards and went out, shutting the door. In a few minutes the men heard two horses pass the end of the bunk-house toward the trail, but no one looked up nor spoke. You could not have told by the flicker of an eyelash that they knew where the Boy had gone.

She was sitting in the deep shadow of a sage-bush that lay on the edge of the trail like a great blot, her suit-case beside her, her breath coming short with exertion and excitement, when she heard a cheery whistle in the distance. Just an old love-song dating back some years and discarded now as hackneyed even by the street pianos at home; but oh, how good it sounded!

> From the desert I come to thee!

The ground was cold, and struck a chill through her garments as she sat there alone in the night. On came the clear, musical whistle, and she peered out of the shadow with eager eyes and frightened heart. Dared she risk it again? Should she call, or should she hold her breath and keep still, hoping he would pass her by unnoticed? Before she could decide two horses stopped almost in front of her and a rider swung himself down. He stood before her as if it were day and he could see her quite plainly.

"You needn't be afraid," he explained, calmly. "I thought I had better look you up after the old man got home and gave his report. He was pretty well tanked up and not exactly a fit escort for ladies. What's the trouble?"

Like an angel of deliverance he looked to her as he stood in the starlight, outlined in silhouette against the wide, wonderful sky: broad shoulders, well-set head, close-cropped curls, handsome contour even in the darkness. There was about him an air of quiet strength which gave her confidence.

"Oh, thank you!" she gasped, with a quick little relieved sob in her voice. "I am so glad you have come. I was — just a little — frightened, I think." She attempted to rise, but her foot caught in her skirt and she sank wearily back to the sand again.

The Boy stooped over and lifted her to her feet. "You certainly are some plucky girl!" he commented, looking down at her slender height as she stood beside him. "A 'little frightened,' were you? Well, I should say you had a right to be."

"Well, not exactly frightened, you know," said Margaret, taking a deep breath and trying to steady her voice. "I think perhaps I was more mortified than frightened, to think I made such a blunder as to get off the train before I reached my station. You see, I'd made up my mind not to be frightened, but when I heard that awful howl of some beast — And then that terrible man!" She shuddered and put her hands suddenly over her eyes as if to shut out all memory of it.

"More than one kind of beasts!" commented the Boy, briefly. "Well, you needn't worry about him; he's having his supper and he'll be sound asleep by the time we get back."

"Oh, have we got to go where he is?" gasped Margaret. "Isn't there some other place? Is Ashland very far away? That is where I am going."

"No other place where you could go to-night. Ashland's a good twenty-five miles from here. But you'll be all right. Mom Wallis 'll look out for you. She isn't much of a looker, but she has a kind heart. She pulled me through once when I was just about flickering out. Come on. You'll be pretty tired. We better be getting back. Mom Wallis 'll make you comfortable, and then you can get off good and early in the morning."

Without an apology, and as if it were the common courtesy of the desert, he stooped and lifted her easily to the saddle of the second horse, placed the bridle in her hands, then swung the suit-case up on his own horse and sprang into the saddle.

CHAPTER III

He turned the horses about and took charge of her just as if he were accustomed to managing stray ladies in the wilderness every day of his life and understood the situation perfectly; and Margaret settled wearily into her saddle and looked about her with content.

Suddenly, again, the wide wonder of the night possessed her. Involuntarily she breathed a soft little exclamation of awe and delight. Her companion turned to her questioningly:

"Does it always seem so big here — so — limitless?" she asked in explanation. "It is so far to everywhere it takes one's breath away, and yet the stars hang close, like a protection. It gives one the feeling of being alone in the great universe with God. Does it always seem so out here?"

He looked at her curiously, her pure profile turned up to the wide dome of luminous blue above. His voice was strangely low and wondering as he answered, after a moment's silence:

"No, it is not always so," he said. "I have seen it when it was more like being alone in the great universe with the devil."

There was a tremendous earnestness in his tone that the girl felt meant more than was on the surface. She turned to look at the fine young face beside her. In the starlight she could not make out the bitter hardness of lines that were beginning to be carved about his sensitive mouth. But there was so much sadness in his voice that her heart went out to him in pity.

"Oh," she said, gently, "it would be awful that way. Yes, I can understand. I felt so, a little, while that terrible man was with me." And she shuddered again at the remembrance.

Again he gave her that curious look. "There are worse things than Pop Wallis out here," he said, gravely. "But I'll grant you there's some class to the skies. It's a case of 'Where every prospect pleases and only man is vile.'" And with the words his tone grew almost flippant. It hurt her sensitive nature, and without knowing it she half drew away a little farther from him and murmured, sadly:

"Oh!" as if he had classed himself with the "man" he had been describing. Instantly he felt her withdrawal and grew grave again, as if he would atone.

"Wait till you see this sky at the dawn," he said. "It will burn red fire off there in the east like a hearth in a palace, and all this dome will glow like a great pink jewel set in gold. If you want a classy sky, there you have it! Nothing like it in the East!"

There was a strange mingling of culture and roughness in his speech. The girl could not make him out; yet there had been a palpitating earnestness in his description that showed he had felt the dawn in his very soul.

"You are — a — poet, perhaps?" she asked, half shyly. "Or an artist?" she hazarded.

He laughed roughly and seemed embarrassed. "No, I'm just a — bum! A sort of roughneck out of a job."

She was silent, watching him against the starlight, a kind of embarrassment upon her after his last remark. "You — have been here long?" she asked, at last.

"Three years." He said it almost curtly and turned his head away, as if there were something in his face he would hide.

She knew there was something unhappy in his life. Unconsciously her tone took on a sympathetic sound. "And do you get homesick and want to go back, ever?" she asked.

His tone was fairly savage now. "No!"

The silence which followed became almost oppressive before the Boy finally turned and in his kindly tone began to question her about the happenings which had stranded her in the desert alone at night.

So she came to tell him briefly and frankly about herself, as he questioned — how she came to be in Arizona all alone.

"My father is a minister in a small town in New York State. When I finished college I had to do something, and I had an offer of this Ashland school through a friend of ours who had a brother out here. Father and mother would rather have kept me nearer home, of course, but everybody says the best opportunities are in the West, and this was a good opening, so they finally consented. They would send post-haste for me to come back if they knew what a mess I have made of things right at the start — getting out of the train in the desert."

"But you're not discouraged?" said her companion, half wonderingly. "Some nerve you have with you. I guess you'll manage to hit it off in Ashland. It's the limit as far as discipline is concerned, I understand, but I guess you'll put one over on them. I'll bank on you after to-night, sure thing!"

She turned a laughing face toward him. "Thank you!" she said. "But I don't see how you know all that. I'm sure I didn't do anything particularly nervy. There wasn't anything else to do but what I did, if I'd tried."

"Most girls would have fainted and screamed, and fainted again when they were rescued," stated the Boy, out of a vast experience.

"I never fainted in my life," said Margaret Earle, with disdain. "I don't think I should care to faint out in the vast universe like this. It would be rather inopportune, I should think."

Then, because she suddenly realized that she was growing very chummy with this stranger in the dark, she asked the first question that came into her head.

"What was your college?"

That he had not been to college never entered her head. There was something in his speech and manner that made it a foregone conclusion.

It was as if she had struck him forcibly in his face, so sudden and sharp a silence ensued for a second. Then he answered, gruffly, "Yale," and plunged into an elaborate account of Arizona in its early ages, including a detailed description of the cliff-dwellers and their homes, which were still to be seen high in the rocks of the cañons not many miles to the west of where they were riding.

Margaret was keen to hear it all, and asked many questions, declaring her intention of visiting those cliff-caves at her earliest opportunity. It was so wonderful to her to be actually out here where were all sorts of queer things about which she had read and wondered. It did not occur to her, until the next day, to realize that her companion had of intention led her off the topic of himself and kept her from asking any more personal questions.

He told her of the petrified forest just over some low hills off to the left; acres and acres of agatized chips and trunks of great trees all turned to eternal stone, called by the Indians "Yeitso's bones," after the great giant of that name whom an ancient Indian hero killed. He described the coloring of the brilliant days in Arizona, where you stand on the edge of some flat-topped mesa and look off through the clear air to mountains that seem quite near by, but are in reality more than two hundred miles away. He pictured the strange colors and lights of the place; ledges of rock, yellow, white and green, drab and maroon, and tumbled piles of red boulders, shadowy buttes in the distance, serrated cliffs against the horizon, not blue, but rosy pink in the heated haze of the air, and perhaps a great, lonely eagle poised above the silent, brilliant waste.

He told it not in book language, with turn of phrase and smoothly flowing sentences, but in simple, frank words, as a boy might describe a picture to one he knew would appreciate it — for her sake, and not because he loved to put it into words; but in a new, stumbling way letting out the beauty that had somehow crept into his heart in spite of all the rough attempts to keep all gentle things out of his nature.

The girl, as she listened, marveled more and more what manner of youth this might be who had come to her out of the desert night.

She forgot her weariness as she listened, in the thrill of wonder over the new mysterious country to which she had come. She forgot that she was riding through the great darkness with an utter stranger, to a place she knew not, and to experiences most dubious. Her fears had fled and she was actually enjoying herself, and responding to the wonderful story of the place with soft-murmured exclamations of delight and wonder.

From time to time in the distance there sounded forth those awful blood-curdling howls of wild beasts that she had heard when she sat alone by the water-tank, and each time she heard a shudder passed through her and instinctively she swerved a trifle toward her companion, then straightened up again and tried to seem not to notice. The Boy saw and watched her brave attempts at self-control with deep appreciation. But suddenly, as they rode and talked, a dark form appeared across their way a little ahead, lithe and stealthy and furry, and two awful eyes like green lamps glared for an instant, then disappeared silently among the mesquite bushes.

She did not cry out nor start. Her very veins seemed frozen with horror, and she could not have spoken if she tried. It was all over in a second and the creature gone, so that she almost doubted her senses and wondered if she had seen aright. Then one hand went swiftly to her throat and she shrank toward her companion.

"There is nothing to fear," he said, reassuringly, and laid a strong hand comfortingly across the neck of her horse. "The pussy-cat was as unwilling for our company as we for hers. Besides, look here!" — and he raised his hand and shot into the air. "She'll not come near us now."

"I am not afraid!" said the girl, bravely. "At least, I don't think I am — very! But it's all so new and unexpected, you know. Do people around here always shoot in that — well — unpremeditated fashion?"

They laughed together.

"Excuse me," he said. "I didn't realize the shot might startle you even more than the wildcat. It seems I'm not fit to have charge of a lady. I told you I was a roughneck."

"You're taking care of me beautifully," said Margaret Earle, loyally, "and I'm glad to get used to shots if that's the thing to be expected often."

Just then they came to the top of the low, rolling hill, and ahead in the darkness there gleamed a tiny, wizened light set in a blotch of blackness. Under the great white stars it burned a sickly red and seemed out of harmony with the night.

"There we are!" said the Boy, pointing toward it. "That's the bunk-house. You needn't be afraid. Pop Wallis 'll be snoring by this time, and we'll come away before he's about in the morning. He always sleeps late after he's been off on a bout. He's been gone three days, selling some cattle, and he'll have a pretty good top on."

The girl caught her breath, gave one wistful look up at the wide, starry sky, a furtive glance at the strong face of her protector, and submitted to being lifted down to the ground.

Before her loomed the bunk-house, small and mean, built of logs, with only one window in which the flicker of the lanterns menaced, with unknown trials and possible perils for her to meet.

CHAPTER IV

When Margaret Earle dawned upon that bunk-room the men sat up with one accord, ran their rough, red hands through their rough, tousled hair, smoothed their beards, took down their feet from the benches where they were resting. That was as far as their etiquette led them. Most of them continued to smoke their pipes, and all of them stared at her unreservedly. Such a sight of exquisite feminine beauty had not come to their eyes in many a long day. Even in the dim light of the smoky lanterns, and with the dust and weariness of travel upon her, Margaret Earle was a beautiful girl.

"That's what's the matter, father," said her mother, when the subject of Margaret's going West to teach had first been mentioned. "She's too beautiful. Far too beautiful to go among savages! If she were homely and old, now, she might be safe. That would be a different matter."

Yet Margaret had prevailed, and was here in the wild country. Now, standing on the threshold of the log cabin, she read, in the unveiled admiration that startled from the eyes of the men, the meaning of her mother's fears.

Yet withal it was a kindly admiration not unmixed with awe. For there was about her beauty a touch of the spiritual which set her above the common run of women, making men feel her purity and sweetness, and inclining their hearts to worship rather than be bold.

The Boy had been right. Pop Wallis was asleep and out of the way. From a little shed room at one end his snoring marked time in the silence that the advent of the girl made in the place.

In the doorway of the kitchen offset Mom Wallis stood with her passionless face — a face from which all emotions had long ago been burned by cruel fires — and looked at the girl, whose expression was vivid with her opening life all haloed in a rosy glow.

A kind of wistful contortion passed over Mom Wallis's hopeless countenance, as if she saw before her in all its possibility of perfection the life that she herself had lost. Perhaps it was no longer possible for her features to show tenderness, but a glow of something like it burned in her eyes, though she only turned away with the same old apathetic air, and without a word went about preparing a meal for the stranger.

Margaret looked wildly, fearfully, around the rough assemblage when she first entered the long, low room, but instantly the boy introduced her as "the new teacher for the Ridge School beyond the Junction," and these were Long Bill, Big Jim, the Fiddling Boss, Jasper Kemp, Fade-away Forbes, Stocky, Croaker, and Fudge. An inspiration fell upon the frightened girl, and she acknowledged the introduction by a radiant smile, followed by the offering of her small gloved hand. Each man in dumb bewilderment instantly became her slave, and accepted the offered hand with more or less pleasure and embarrassment. The girl proved her right to be called tactful, and, seeing her advantage, followed it up quickly by a few bright words. These men were of an utterly different type from any she had ever met before, but they had in their eyes a kind of homage which Pop Wallis had not shown and they were not repulsive to her. Besides, the Boy was in the background, and her nerve had returned. The Boy knew how a lady should be treated. She was quite ready to "play up" to his lead.

It was the Boy who brought the only chair the bunk-house afforded, a rude, home-made affair, and helped her off with her coat and hat in his easy, friendly way, as if he had known her all his life; while the men, to whom such gallant ways were foreign, sat awkwardly by and watched in wonder and amaze.

Most of all they were astonished at "the Kid," that he could fall so naturally into intimate talk with this delicate, beautiful woman. She was another of his kind, a creature not made in the same mold as theirs. They saw it now, and watched the fairy play with almost childish interest. Just to hear her call him "Mr. Gardley"! — Lance Gardley, that was what he had told them was his name the day he came among them. They had not heard it since. The Kid! Mr. Gardley!

There it was, the difference between them! They looked at the girl half jealously, yet proudly at the Boy. He was theirs — yes, in a way he was theirs — had they not found him in the wilderness, sick and nigh to death, and nursed him back to life again? He was theirs; but he knew how to drop into her world, too, and not be ashamed. They were glad that he could, even while it struck them with a pang that some day he would go back to the world to which he belonged — and where they could never be at home.

It was a marvel to watch her eat the coarse corn-bread and pork that Mom Wallis brought her. It might have been a banquet, the pleasant way she seemed to look at it. Just like a bird she tasted it daintily, and smiled, showing her white teeth. There was nothing of the idea of greediness that each man knew he himself felt after a fast. It was all beautiful, the way she handled the two-tined fork and the old steel knife. They watched and dropped their eyes abashed as at a lovely sacrament. They had not felt before that eating could be an art. They did not know what art meant.

Such strange talk, too! But the Kid seemed to understand. About the sky — their old, common sky, with stars that they saw every night — making such a fuss about that, with words like "wide," "infinite," "azure," and "gems." Each man went furtively out that night before he slept and took a new look at the sky to see if he could understand.

The Boy was planning so the night would be but brief. He knew the girl was afraid. He kept the talk going enthusiastically, drawing in one or two of the men now and again. Long Bill forgot himself and laughed out a hoarse guffaw, then stopped as if he had been choked. Stocky, red in the face, told a funny story when commanded by the Boy, and then dissolved in mortification over his blunders. The Fiddling Boss obediently got down his fiddle from the smoky corner beside the fireplace and played a weird old tune or two, and then they sang. First the men, with hoarse, quavering approach and final roar of wild sweetness; then Margaret and the Boy in duet, and finally Margaret alone, with a few bashful chords on the fiddle, feeling their way as accompaniment.

Mom Wallis had long ago stopped her work and was sitting huddled in the doorway on a nail-keg with weary, folded hands and a strange wistfulness on her apathetic face. A fine silence had settled over the group as the girl, recognizing her power, and the pleasure she was giving, sang on. Now and then the Boy, when he knew the song, would join in with his rich tenor.

It was a strange night, and when she finally lay down to rest on a hard cot with a questionable-looking blanket for covering and Mom Wallis as her room-mate, Margaret Earle could not help wondering what her mother and father would think now if they could see her. Would they not, perhaps, almost prefer the water-tank and the lonely desert for her to her present surroundings?

Nevertheless, she slept soundly after her terrible excitement, and woke with a start of wonder in the early morning, to hear the men outside splashing water and humming or whistling bits of the tunes she had sung to them the night before.

Mom Wallis was standing over her, looking down with a hunger in her eyes at the bright waves of Margaret's hair and the soft, sleep-flushed cheeks.

"You got dretful purty hair," said Mom Wallis, wistfully.

Margaret looked up and smiled in acknowledgment of the compliment.

"You wouldn't b'lieve it, but I was young an' purty oncet. Beats all how much it counts to be young — an' purty! But land! It don't last long. Make the most of it while you got it."

Browning's immortal words came to Margaret's lips —

> Grow old along with me,
> The best is yet to be,
> The last of life for which the first was made —

but she checked them just in time and could only smile mutely. How could she speak such thoughts amid these intolerable surroundings? Then with sudden impulse she reached up to the astonished woman and, drawing her down, kissed her sallow cheek.

"Oh!" said Mom Wallis, starting back and laying her bony hands upon the place where she had been kissed, as if it hurt her, while a dull red stole up from her neck over her cheeks and high forehead to the roots of her hay-colored hair. All at once she turned her back upon her visitor and the tears of the years streamed down her impassive face.

"Don't mind me," she choked, after a minute. "I liked it real good, only it kind of give me a turn." Then, after a second: "It's time t' eat. You c'n wash outside after the men is done."

That, thought Margaret, had been the scheme of this woman's whole life — "After the men is done!"

So, after all, the night was passed in safety, and a wonderful dawning had come. The blue of the morning, so different from the blue of the night sky, was, nevertheless, just as unfathomable; the air seemed filled with straying star-beams, so sparkling was the clearness of the light.

But now a mountain rose in the distance with heliotrope-and-purple bounds to stand across the vision and dispel the illusion of the night that the sky came down to the earth all around like a close-fitting dome. There were mountains on all sides, and a slender, dark line of mesquite set off the more delicate colorings of the plain.

Into the morning they rode, Margaret and the Boy, before Pop Wallis was yet awake, while all the other men stood round and watched, eager, jealous for the handshake and the parting smile. They told her they hoped she would come again and sing for them, and each one had an awkward word of parting. Whatever Margaret Earle might do with her school, she had won seven loyal friends in the camp, and she rode away amid their admiring glances, which lingered, too, on the broad shoulders and wide sombrero of her escort riding by her side.

"Wal, that's the end o' him, I 'spose," drawled Long Bill, with a deep sigh, as the riders passed into the valley out of their sight.

"H'm!" said Jasper Kemp, hungrily. "I reck'n *he* thinks it's jes' th' beginnin'!"

"Maybe so! Maybe so!" said Big Jim, dreamily.

The morning was full of wonder for the girl who had come straight from an Eastern city. The view from the top of the mesa, or the cool, dim entrance of a cañon where great ferns fringed and feathered its walls, and strange caves hollowed out in the rocks far above, made real the stories she had read of the cave-dwellers. It was a new world.

The Boy was charming. She could not have picked out among her city acquaintances a man who would have done the honors of the desert more delightfully than he. She had thought him handsome in the starlight and in the lantern-light the night before, but now that the morning shone upon him she could not keep from looking at him. His fresh color, which no wind and weather could quite subdue, his gray-blue eyes with that mixture of thoughtfulness and reverence and daring, his crisp, brown curls glinting with gold in the sunlight — all made him good to look upon. There was something about the firm set of his lips and chin that made her feel a hidden strength about him.

When they camped a little while for lunch he showed the thoughtfulness and care for her comfort that many an older man might not have had. Even his talk was a mixture of boyishness and experience and he seemed to know her thoughts before she had them fully spoken.

"I do not understand it," she said, looking him frankly in the eyes at last. "How ever in the world did one like *you* get landed among all those dreadful men! Of course, in their way, some of them are not so bad; but they are not like you, not in the least, and never could be."

They were riding out upon the plain now in the full afternoon light, and a short time would bring them to her destination.

A sad, set look came quickly into the Boy's eyes and his face grew almost hard.

"It's an old story. I suppose you've heard it before," he said, and his voice tried to take on a careless note, but failed. "I didn't make good back there" — he waved his hand sharply toward the East — "so I came out here to begin again. But I guess I haven't made good here, either — not in the way I meant when I came."

"You can't, you know," said Margaret. "Not here."

"Why?" He looked at her earnestly, as if he felt the answer might help him.

"Because you have to go back where you didn't make good and pick up the lost opportunities. You can't really make good till you do that *right where you left off.*"

"But suppose it's too late?"

"It's never too late if we're in earnest and not too proud."

There was a long silence then, while the Boy looked thoughtfully off at the mountains, and when he spoke again it was to call attention to the beauty of a silver cloud that floated lazily on the horizon. But Margaret Earle had seen the look in his gray eyes and was not deceived.

A few minutes later they crossed another mesa and descended to the enterprising little town where the girl was to begin her winter's work. The very houses and streets seemed to rise briskly and hasten to meet them those last few minutes of their ride.

Now that the experience was almost over, the girl realized that she had enjoyed it intensely, and that she dreaded inexpressibly that she must bid good-by to this friend of a few hours and face an unknown world. It had been a wonderful day, and now it was almost done. The two looked at each other and realized that their meeting had been an epoch in their lives that neither would soon forget — that neither wanted to forget.

CHAPTER V

Slower the horses walked, and slower. The voices of the Boy and girl were low when they spoke about the common things by the wayside. Once their eyes met, and they smiled with something both sad and glad in them.

Margaret was watching the young man by her side and wondering at herself. He was different from any man whose life had come near to hers before. He was wild and worldly, she could see that, and unrestrained by many of the things that were vital principles with her, and yet she felt strangely drawn to him and wonderfully at home in his company. She could not understand herself nor him. It was as if his real soul had looked out of his eyes and spoken, untrammeled by the circumstances of birth or breeding or habit, and she knew him for a kindred spirit. And yet he was far from being one in whom she would have expected even to find a friend. Where was her confidence of yesterday? Why was it that she dreaded to have this strong young protector leave her to meet alone a world of strangers, whom yesterday at this time she would have gladly welcomed?

Now, when his face grew thoughtful and sad, she saw the hard, bitter lines that were beginning to be graven about his lips, and her heart ached over what he had said about not making good. She wondered if there was anything else she could say to help him, but no words came to her, and the sad, set look about his lips warned her that perhaps she had said enough. He was not one who needed a long dissertation to bring a thought home to his consciousness.

Gravely they rode to the station to see about Margaret's trunks and make inquiries for the school and the house where she had arranged to board. Then Margaret sent a telegram to her mother to say that she had arrived safely, and so, when all was done and there was no longer an excuse for lingering, the Boy realized that he must leave her.

They stood alone for just a moment while the voluble landlady went to attend to something that was boiling over on the stove. It was an ugly little parlor that was to be her reception-room for the next year at least, with red-and-green ingrain carpet of ancient pattern, hideous chromos on the walls, and frantically common furniture setting up in its shining varnish to be pretentious; but the girl had not seen it yet. She was filled with a great homesickness that had not possessed her even when she said good-by to her dear ones at home. She suddenly realized that the people with whom she was to be thrown were of another world from hers, and this one friend whom she had found in the desert was leaving her.

She tried to shake hands formally and tell him how grateful she was to him for rescuing her from the perils of the night, but somehow words seemed so inadequate, and tears kept crowding their way into her throat and eyes. Absurd it was, and he a stranger twenty hours before, and a man of other ways than hers, besides. Yet he was her friend and rescuer.

She spoke her thanks as well as she could, and then looked up, a swift, timid glance, and found his eyes upon her earnestly and troubled.

"Don't thank me," he said, huskily. "I guess it was the best thing I ever did, finding you. I sha'n't forget, even if you never let me see you again — and — I hope you will." His eyes searched hers wistfully.

"Of course," she said. "Why not?"

"I thank you," he said in quaint, courtly fashion, bending low over her hand. "I shall try to be worthy of the honor."

And so saying, he left her and, mounting his horse, rode away into the lengthening shadows of the afternoon.

She stood in the forlorn little room staring out of the window after her late companion, a sense of utter desolation upon her. For the moment all her brave hopes of the future had fled, and if she could have slipped unobserved out of the front door, down to the station, and boarded some waiting express to her home, she would gladly have done it then and there.

Try as she would to summon her former reasons for coming to this wild, she could not think of one of them, and her eyes were very near to tears.

But Margaret Earle was not given to tears, and as she felt them smart beneath her lids she turned in a panic to prevent them. She could not afford to cry now. Mrs. Tanner would be returning, and she must not find the "new schoolma'am" weeping.

With a glance she swept the meager, pretentious room, and then, suddenly, became aware of other presences. In the doorway stood a man and a dog, both regarding her intently with open surprise, not unmixed with open appraisement and a marked degree of admiration.

The man was of medium height, slight, with a putty complexion; cold, pale-blue eyes; pale, straw-colored hair, and a look of self-indulgence around his rather weak mouth. He was dressed in a city business suit of the latest cut, however, and looked as much out of place in that crude little house as did Margaret Earle herself in her simple gown of dark-blue crêpe and her undeniable air of style and good taste.

His eyes, as they regarded her, had in them a smile that the girl instinctively resented. Was it a shade too possessive and complacently sure for a stranger?

The dog, a large collie, had great, liquid, brown eyes, menacing or loyal, as circumstances dictated, and regarded her with an air of brief indecision. She felt she was being weighed in the balance by both pairs of eyes. Of the two the girl preferred the dog.

Perhaps the dog understood, for he came a pace nearer and waved his plumy tail tentatively. For the dog she felt a glow of friendliness at once, but for the man she suddenly, and most unreasonably, of course, conceived one of her violent and unexpected dislikes.

Into this tableau bustled Mrs. Tanner. "Well, now, I didn't go to leave you by your lonesome all this time," she apologized, wiping her hands on her apron, "but them beans boiled clean over, and I hed to put 'em in a bigger kettle. You see, I put in more beans 'count o' you bein' here, an' I ain't uset to calca'latin' on two extry." She looked happily from the man to the girl and back again.

"Mr. West, I 'spose, o' course, you interjuced yerself? Bein' a preacher, you don't hev to stan' on ceremony like the rest of mankind. You 'ain't? Well, let me hev the pleasure of interjucin' our new school-teacher, Miss Margaret Earle. I 'spect you two 'll be awful chummy right at the start, both bein' from the East that way, an' both hevin' ben to college."

Margaret Earle acknowledged the bow with a cool little inclination of her head. She wondered why she didn't hate the garrulous woman who rattled on in this happy, take-it-for-granted way; but there was something so innocently pleased in her manner that she couldn't help putting all her wrath on the smiling man who came forward instantly with a low bow and a voice of fulsome flattery.

"Indeed, Miss Earle, I assure you I am happily surprised. I am sure Mrs. Tanner's prophecy will come true and we shall be the best of friends. When they told me the new teacher was to board here I really hesitated. I have seen something of these Western teachers in my time, and scarcely thought I should find you congenial; but I can see at a glance that you are the exception to the rule."

He presented a soft, unmanly white hand, and there was nothing to do but take it or seem rude to her hostess; but her manner was like icicles, and she was thankful she had not yet removed her gloves.

If the reverend gentleman thought he was to enjoy a lingering hand-clasp he was mistaken, for the gloved finger-tips merely touched his hand and were withdrawn, and the girl turned to her hostess with a smile of finality as if he were dismissed. He did not seem disposed to take the hint and withdraw, however, until on a sudden the great dog came and stood between them with open-mouthed welcome and joyous greeting in the plumy, wagging tail. He pushed close to her and looked up into her face insistently, his hanging pink tongue and wide, smiling countenance proclaiming that he was satisfied with his investigation.

Margaret looked down at him, and then stooped and put her arms about his neck. Something in his kindly dog expression made her feel suddenly as if she had a real friend.

It seemed the man, however, did not like the situation. He kicked gingerly at the dog's hind legs, and said in a harsh voice:

"Get out of the way, sir. You're annoying the lady. Get out, I say!"

The dog, however, uttered a low growl and merely showed the whites of his menacing eyes at the man, turning his body slightly so that he stood across the lady's way protectingly, as if to keep the man from her.

Margaret smiled at the dog and laid her hand on his head, as if to signify her acceptance of the friendship he had offered her, and he waved his plume once more and attended her from the room, neither of them giving further attention to the man.

"Confound that dog!" said Rev. Frederick West, in a most unpreacher-like tone, as he walked to the window and looked out. Then to himself he mused: "A pretty girl. A *very pretty* girl. I really think it'll be worth my while to stay a month at least."

Up in her room the "very pretty girl" was unpacking her suit-case and struggling with the tears. Not since she was a wee little girl and went to school all alone for the first time had she felt so very forlorn, and it was the little bare bedroom that had done it. At least that had been the final straw that had made too great the burden of keeping down those threatening tears.

It was only a bare, plain room with unfinished walls, rough woodwork, a cheap wooden bed, a bureau with a warped looking-glass, and on the floor was a braided rug of rags. A little wooden rocker, another small, straight wooden chair, a hanging wall-pocket decorated with purple roses, a hanging bookshelf composed of three thin boards strung together with maroon picture cord, a violently colored picture-card of "Moses in the Bulrushes" framed in straws and red worsted, and bright-blue paper shades at the windows. That was the room!

How different from her room at home, simply and sweetly finished anew for her home-coming from college! It rose before her homesick vision now. Soft gray walls, rose-colored ceiling, blended by a wreath of exquisite wild roses, whose pattern was repeated in the border of the simple curtains and chair cushions, white-enamel furniture, pretty brass bed soft as down in its luxurious mattress, spotless and inviting always. She glanced at the humpy bed with its fringed gray spread and lumpy-looking pillows in dismay. She had not thought of little discomforts like that, yet how they loomed upon her weary vision now!

The tiny wooden stand with its thick, white crockery seemed ill substitute for the dainty white bath-room at home. She had known she would not have her home luxuries, of course, but she had not realized until set down amid these barren surroundings what a difference they would make.

Going to the window and looking out, she saw for the first tune the one luxury the little room possessed — a view! And such a view! Wide and wonderful and far it stretched, in colors unmatched by painter's brush, a purple mountain topped by rosy clouds in the distance. For the second time in Arizona her soul was lifted suddenly out of itself and its dismay by a vision of the things that God has made and the largeness of it all.

CHAPTER VI

For some time she stood and gazed, marveling at the beauty and recalling some of the things her companion of the afternoon had said about his impressions of the place; then suddenly there loomed a dark speck in the near foreground of her meditation, and, looking down annoyed, she discovered the minister like a gnat between the eye and a grand spectacle, his face turned admiringly up to her window, his hand lifted in familiar greeting.

Vexed at his familiarity, she turned quickly and jerked down the shade; then throwing herself on the bed, she had a good cry. Her nerves were terribly wrought up. Things seemed twisted in her mind, and she felt that she had reached the limit of her endurance. Here was she, Margaret Earle, newly elected teacher to the Ashland Ridge School, lying on her bed in tears, when she ought to be getting settled and planning her new life; when the situation demanded her best attention she was wrought up over a foolish little personal dislike. Why did she have to dislike a minister, anyway, and then take to a wild young fellow whose life thus far had been anything but satisfactory even to himself? Was it her perverse nature that caused her to remember the look in the eyes of the Boy who had rescued her from a night in the wilderness, and to feel there was far more manliness in his face than in the face of the man whose profession surely would lead one to suppose he was more worthy of her respect and interest? Well, she was tired. Perhaps things would assume their normal relation to one another in the morning. And so, after a few minutes, she bathed her face in the little, heavy, iron-stone wash-bowl, combed her hair, and freshened the collar and ruffles in her sleeves preparatory to going down for the evening meal. Then, with a swift thought, she searched through her suit-case for every available article wherewith to brighten that forlorn room.

The dainty dressing-case of Dresden silk with rosy ribbons that her girl friends at home had given as a parting gift covered a generous portion of the pine bureau, and when she had spread it out and bestowed its silver-mounted brushes, combs, hand-glass, and pretty sachet, things seemed to brighten up a bit. She hung up a cobweb of a lace boudoir cap with its rose-colored ribbons over the bleary mirror, threw her kimono of flowered challis over the back of the rocker, arranged her soap and toothbrush, her own wash-rag and a towel brought from home on the wash-stand, and somehow felt better and more as if she belonged. Last she ranged her precious photographs of father and mother and the dear vine-covered church and manse across in front of the mirror. When her trunks came there would be other things, and she could bear it, perhaps, when she had this room buried deep in the home belongings. But this would have to do for to-night, for the trunk might not come till morning, and, anyhow, she was too weary to unpack.

She ventured one more look out of her window, peering carefully at first to make sure her fellow-boarder was not still standing down below on the grass. A pang of compunction shot through her conscience. What would her dear father think of her feeling this way toward a minister, and before she knew the first thing about him, too? It was dreadful! She must shake it off. Of course he was a good man or he wouldn't be in the ministry, and she had doubtless mistaken mere friendliness for forwardness. She would forget it and try to go down and behave to him the way her father would want her to behave toward a fellow-minister.

Cautiously she raised the shade again and looked out. The mountain was bathed in a wonderful ruby light fading into amethyst, and all the path between was many-colored like a pavement of jewels set in filigree. While she looked the picture changed, glowed, softened, and changed again, making her think of the chapter about the Holy City in Revelation.

She started at last when some one knocked hesitatingly on the door, for the wonderful sunset light had made her forget for the moment where she was, and it seemed a desecration to have mere mortals step in and announce supper, although the odor of pork and cabbage had been proclaiming it dumbly for some time.

She went to the door, and, opening it, found a dark figure standing in the hall. For a minute she half feared it was the minister, until a shy, reluctant backwardness in the whole stocky figure and the stirring of a large furry creature just behind him made her sure it was not.

"Ma says you're to come to supper," said a gruff, untamed voice; and Margaret perceived that the person in the gathering gloom of the hall was a boy.

"Oh!" said Margaret, with relief in her voice. "Thank you for coming to tell me. I meant to come down and not give that trouble, but I got to looking at the wonderful sunset. Have you been watching it?" She pointed across the room to the window. "Look! Isn't that a great color there on the tip of the mountain? I never saw anything like that at home. I suppose you're used to it, though."

The boy came a step nearer the door and looked blankly, half wonderingly, across at the window, as if he expected to see some phenomenon. "Oh! *That!*" he exclaimed, carelessly. "Sure! We have them all the time."

"But that wonderful silver light pouring down just in that one tiny spot!" exclaimed Margaret. "It makes the mountain seem alive and smiling!"

The boy turned and looked at her curiously. "Gee!" said he, "I c'n show you plenty like that!" But he turned and looked at it a long, lingering minute again.

"But we mustn't keep your mother waiting," said Margaret, remembering and turning reluctantly toward the door. "Is this your dog? Isn't he a beauty? He made me feel really as if he were glad to see me." She stooped and laid her hand on the dog's head and smiled brightly up at his master.

The boy's face lit with a smile, and he turned a keen, appreciative look at the new teacher, for the first time genuinely interested in her. "Cap's a good old scout," he admitted.

"So his name is Cap. Is that short for anything?"

"Cap'n."

"Captain. What a good name for him. He looks as if he were a captain, and he waves that tail grandly, almost as if it might be a badge of office. But who are you? You haven't told me your name yet. Are you Mrs. Tanner's son?"

The boy nodded. "I'm just Bud Tanner."

"Then you are one of my pupils, aren't you? We must shake hands on that." She put out her hand, but she was forced to go out after Bud's reluctant red fist, take it by force in a strange grasp, and do all the shaking; for Bud had never had that experience before in his life, and he emerged from it with a very red face and a feeling as if his right arm had been somehow lifted out of the same class with the rest of his body. It was rather awful, too, that it happened just in the open dining-room door, and that "preacher-boarder" watched the whole performance. Bud put on an extra-deep frown and shuffled away from the teacher, making a great show of putting Cap out of the dining-room, though he always sat behind his master's chair at meals, much to the discomfiture of the male boarder, who was slightly in awe of his dogship, not having been admitted into friendship as the lady had been.

Mr. West stood back of his chair, awaiting the arrival of the new boarder, an expectant smile on his face, and rubbing his hands together with much the same effect as a wolf licking his lips in anticipation of a victim. In spite of her resolves to like the man, Margaret was again struck with aversion as she saw him standing there, and was intensely relieved when she found that the seat assigned to her was on the opposite side of the table from him, and beside Bud. West, however, did not seem to be pleased with the arrangement, and, stepping around the table, said to his landlady:

"Did you mean me to sit over here?" and he placed a possessive hand on the back of the chair that was meant for Bud.

"No, Mister West, you jest set where you ben settin'," responded Mrs. Tanner. She had thought the matter all out and decided that the minister could converse with the teacher to the better advantage of the whole table if he sat across from her. Mrs. Tanner was a born match-maker. This she felt was an opportunity not to be despised, even if it sometime robbed the Ridge School of a desirable teacher.

But West did not immediately return to his place at the other side of the table. To Margaret's extreme annoyance he drew her chair and waited for her to sit down. The situation, however, was somewhat relieved of its intimacy by a sudden interference from Cap, who darted away from his frowning master and stepped up authoritatively to the minister's side with a low growl, as if to say:

"Hands off that chair! That doesn't belong to you!"

West suddenly released his hold on the chair without waiting to shove it up to the table, and precipitately retired to his own place. "That dog's a nuisance!" he said, testily, and was answered with a glare from Bud's dark eyes.

Bud came to his seat with his eyes still set savagely on the minister, and Cap settled down protectingly behind Margaret's chair.

Mrs. Tanner bustled in with the coffee-pot, and Mr. Tanner came last, having just finished his rather elaborate hair-comb at the kitchen glass with the kitchen comb, in full view of the assembled multitude. He was a little, thin, wiry, weather-beaten man, with skin like leather and sparse hair. Some of his teeth were missing, leaving deep hollows in his cheeks, and his kindly protruding chin was covered with scraggy gray whiskers, which stuck out ahead of him like a cow-catcher. He was in his shirt-sleeves and collarless, but looked neat and clean, and he greeted the new guest heartily before he sat down, and nodded to the minister:

"Naow, Brother West, I reckon we're ready fer your part o' the performance. You'll please to say grace."

Mr. West bowed his sleek, yellow head and muttered a formal blessing with an offhand manner, as if it were a mere ceremony. Bud stared contemptuously at him the while, and Cap uttered a low rumble as of a distant growl. Margaret felt a sudden desire to laugh, and tried to control herself, wondering what her father would feel about it all.

The genial clatter of knives and forks broke the stiffness after the blessing. Mrs. Tanner bustled back and forth from the stove to the table, talking clamorously the while. Mr. Tanner joined in with his flat, nasal twang, responding, and the minister, with an air of utter contempt for them both, endeavored to set up a separate and altogether private conversation with Margaret across the narrow table; but Margaret innocently had begun a conversation with Bud about the school, and had to be addressed by name each time before Mr. West could get her attention. Bud, with a boy's keenness, noticed her aversion, and put aside his own backwardness, entering into the contest with remarkably voluble replies. The minister, if he would be in the talk at all, was forced to join in with theirs, and found himself worsted and contradicted by the boy at every turn.

Strange to say, however, this state of things only served to make the man more eager to talk with the lady. She was not anxious for his attention. Ah! She was coy, and the acquaintance was to have the zest of being no lightly won friendship. All the better. He watched her as she talked, noted every charm of lash and lid and curving lip; stared so continually that she finally gave up looking his way at all, even when she was obliged to answer his questions.

Thus, at last, the first meal in the new home was concluded, and Margaret, pleading excessive weariness, went to her room. She felt as if she could not endure another half-hour of contact with her present world until she had had some rest. If the world had been just Bud and the dog she could have stayed below stairs and found out a little more about the new life; but with that oily-mouthed minister continually butting in her soul was in a tumult.

When she had prepared for rest she put out her light and drew up the shade. There before her spread the wide wonder of the heavens again, with the soft purple of the mountain under stars; and she was carried back to the experience of the night before with a vivid memory of her companion. Why, just *why* couldn't she be as interested in the minister down there as in the wild young man? Well, she was too tired to-night to analyze it all, and she knelt beside her window in the starlight to pray. As she prayed her thoughts were on Lance Gardley once more, and she felt her heart go out in longing for him, that he might find a way to "make good," whatever his trouble had been.

As she rose to retire she heard a step below, and, looking down, saw the minister stalking back and forth in the yard, his hands clasped behind, his head thrown back raptly. He could not see her in her dark room, but she pulled the shade down softly and fled to her hard little bed. Was that man going to obsess her vision everywhere, and must she try to like him just because he was a minister?

So at last she fell asleep.

CHAPTER VII

The next day was filled with unpacking and with writing letters home. By dint of being very busy Margaret managed to forget the minister, who seemed to obtrude himself at every possible turn of the day, and would have monopolized her if she had given him half a chance.

The trunks, two delightful steamer ones, and a big packing-box with her books, arrived the next morning and caused great excitement in the household. Not since they moved into the new house had they seen so many things arrive. Bud helped carry them up-stairs, while Cap ran wildly back and forth, giving sharp barks, and the minister stood by the front door and gave ineffectual and unpractical advice to the man who had brought them. Margaret heard the man and Bud exchanging their opinion of West in low growls in the hall as they entered her door, and she couldn't help feeling that she agreed with them, though she might not have expressed her opinion in the same terms.

The minister tapped at her door a little later and offered his services in opening her box and unstrapping her trunks; but she told him Bud had already performed that service for her, and thanked him with a finality that forbade him to linger. She half hoped he heard the vicious little click with which she locked the door after him, and then wondered if she were wicked to feel that way. But all such compunctions were presently forgotten in the work of making over her room.

The trunks, after they were unpacked and repacked with the things she would not need at once, were disposed in front of the two windows with which the ugly little room was blessed. She covered them with two Bagdad rugs, relics of her college days, and piled several college pillows from the packing-box on each, which made the room instantly assume a homelike air. Then out of the box came other things. Framed pictures of home scenes, college friends and places, pennants, and flags from football, baseball, and basket-ball games she had attended; photographs; a few prints of rare paintings simply framed; a roll of rose-bordered white scrim like her curtains at home, wherewith she transformed the blue-shaded windows and the stiff little wooden rocker, and even made a valance and bed-cover over pink cambric for her bed. The bureau and wash-stand were given pink and white covers, and the ugly walls literally disappeared beneath pictures, pennants, banners, and symbols.

When Bud came up to call her to dinner she flung the door open, and he paused in wide-eyed amazement over the transformation. His eyes kindled at a pair of golf-sticks, a hockey-stick, a tennis-racket, and a big basket-ball in the corner; and his whole look of surprise was so ridiculous that she had to laugh. He looked as if a miracle had been performed on the room, and actually stepped back into the hall to get his breath and be sure he was still in his father's house.

"I want you to come in and see all my pictures and get acquainted with my friends when you have time," she said. "I wonder if you could make some more shelves for my books and help me unpack and set them up?"

"Sure!" gasped Bud, heartily, albeit with awe. She hadn't asked the minister; she had asked *him* — *Bud!* Just a boy! He looked around the room with anticipation. What wonder and delight he would have looking at all those things!

Then Cap stepped into the middle of the room as if he belonged, mouth open, tongue lolling, smiling and panting a hearty approval, as he looked about at the strangeness for all the world as a human being might have done. It was plain he was pleased with the change.

There was a proprietary air about Bud during dinner that was pleasant to Margaret and most annoying to West. It was plain that West looked on the boy as an upstart whom Miss Earle was using for the present to block his approach, and he was growing most impatient over the delay. He suggested that perhaps she would like his escort to see something of her surroundings that afternoon; but she smilingly told him that she would be very busy all the afternoon getting settled, and when he offered again to help her she cast a dazzling smile on Bud and said she didn't think she would need any more help, that Bud was going to do a few things for her, and that was all that was necessary.

Bud straightened up and became two inches taller. He passed the bread, suggested two pieces of pie, and filled her glass of water as if she were his partner. Mr. Tanner beamed to see his son in high favor, but Mrs. Tanner looked a little troubled for the minister. She thought things weren't just progressing as fast as they ought to between him and the teacher.

Bud, with Margaret's instructions, managed to make a very creditable bookcase out of the packing-box sawed in half, the pieces set side by side. She covered them deftly with green burlap left over from college days, like her other supplies, and then the two arranged the books. Bud was delighted over the prospect of reading some of the books, for they were not all school-books, by any means, and she had brought plenty of them to keep her from being lonesome on days when she longed to fly back to her home.

At last the work was done, and they stood back to survey it. The books filled up every speck of space and overflowed to the three little hanging shelves over them; but they were all squeezed in at last except a pile of school-books that were saved out to take to the school-house. Margaret set a tiny vase on the top of one part of the packing-case and a small brass bowl on the top of the other, and Bud, after a knowing glance, scurried away for a few minutes and brought back a handful of gorgeous cactus blossoms to give the final touch.

"Gee!" he said, admiringly, looking around the room. "Gee! You wouldn't know it fer the same place!"

That evening after supper Margaret sat down to write a long letter home. She had written a brief letter, of course, the night before, but had been too weary to go into detail. The letter read:

DEAR MOTHER AND FATHER, — I'm unpacked and settled at last in my room, and now I can't stand it another minute till I talk to you.

Last night, of course, I was pretty homesick, things all looked so strange and new and different. I had known they would, but then I didn't realize at all how different they would be. But I'm not getting homesick already; don't think it. I'm not a bit sorry I came, or at least I sha'n't be when I get started in school. One of the scholars is Mrs. Tanner's son, and I like him. He's crude, of course, but he has a brain, and he's been helping me this afternoon. We made a bookcase for my books, and it looks fine. I wish you could see it. I covered it with the green burlap, and the books look real happy in smiling rows over on the other side of the room. Bud Tanner got me some wonderful cactus blossoms for my brass bowl. I wish I could send you some. They are gorgeous!

But you will want me to tell about my arrival. Well, to begin with, I was late getting here [Margaret had decided to leave out the incident of the desert altogether, for she knew by experience that her mother would suffer terrors all during her absence if she once heard of that wild adventure], which accounts for the lateness of the telegram I sent you. I hope its delay didn't make you worry any.

A very nice young man named Mr. Gardley piloted me to Mrs. Tanner's house and looked after my trunks for me. He is from the East. It was fortunate for me that he happened along, for he was most kind and gentlemanly and helpful. Tell Jane not to worry lest I'll fall in love with him; he doesn't live here. He belongs to a ranch or camp or something twenty-five miles away. She was so afraid I'd fall in love with an Arizona man and not come back home.

Mrs. Tanner is very kind and motherly according to her lights. She has given me the best room in the house, and she talks a blue streak. She has thin, brown hair turning gray, and she wears it in a funny little knob on the tip-top of her round head to correspond with the funny little tuft of hair on her husband's protruding chin. Her head is set on her neck like a clothes-pin, only she is squattier than a clothes-pin. She always wears her sleeves rolled up (at least so far she has) and she always bustles around noisily and apologizes for everything in the jolliest sort of way. I would like her, I guess, if it wasn't for the other boarder; but she has quite made up her mind that I shall like him, and I don't, of course, so she is a bit disappointed in me so far.

Mr. Tanner is very kind and funny, and looks something like a jack-knife with the blades half-open. He never disagrees with Mrs. Tanner, and I really believe he's in love with her yet, though they must have been married a good while. He calls her "Ma," and seems restless unless she's in the room. When she goes out to the kitchen to get some more soup or hash or bring in the pie, he shouts remarks at her all the time she's gone, and she answers, utterly regardless of the conversation the rest of the family are carrying on. It's like a phonograph wound up for the day.

Bud Tanner is about fourteen, and I like him. He's well developed, strong, and almost handsome; at least he would be if he were fixed up a little. He has fine, dark eyes and a great shock of dark hair. He and I are friends already. And so is the dog. The dog is a peach! Excuse me, mother, but I just must use a little of the dear old college slang somewhere, and your letters are the only safety-valve, for I'm a schoolmarm now and must talk "good and proper" all the time, you know.

The dog's name is Captain, and he looks the part. He has constituted himself my bodyguard, and it's going to be very nice having him. He's perfectly devoted already. He's a great, big, fluffy fellow with keen, intelligent eyes, sensitive ears, and a tail like a spreading plume. You'd love him, I know. He has a smile like the morning sunshine.

And now I come to the only other member of the family, the boarder, and I hesitate to approach the topic, because I have taken one of my violent and naughty dislikes to him, and — awful thought — mother! father! *he's a minister!* Yes, he's a *Presbyterian minister*! I know it will make you feel dreadfully, and I thought some of not telling you, but my conscience hurt me so I had to. I just can't *bear* him, so there! Of course, I may get over it, but I don't see how ever, for I can't think of anything that's more like him than *soft soap*! Oh yes, there is one other word. Grandmother used to use it about men she hadn't any use for, and that was "squash." Mother, I can't help it, but he does seem something like a squash. One of that crook-necked, yellow kind with warts all over it, and a great, big, splurgy vine behind it to account for its being there at all. Insipid and thready when it's cooked, you know, and has to have a lot of salt and pepper and butter to make it go down at all. Now I've told you the worst, and I'll try to describe him and see what you think I'd better do about it. Oh, he isn't the regular minister here, or missionary — I guess they call him. He's located quite a distance off, and only comes once a month to preach here, and, anyhow, *he's* gone East now to take his wife to a hospital for an operation, and won't be back for a couple of months, perhaps, and this man isn't even taking his place. He's just here for his health or for fun or something, I guess. He says he had a large suburban church near New York, and had a nervous breakdown; but I've been wondering if he didn't make a mistake, and it wasn't the church had the nervous breakdown instead. He isn't very big nor very little; he's just insignificant. His hair is like wet straw, and his eyes like a fish's. His hand feels like a dead toad when you have to shake hands, which I'm thankful doesn't have to be done but once. He looks at you with a flat, sickening grin. He has an acquired double chin, acquired to make him look pompous, and he dresses stylishly and speaks of the inhabitants of this country with contempt. He wants to be very affable, and offers to take me to all sorts of places, but so far I've avoided him. I can't think how they ever came to let him be a minister — I really can't! And yet, I suppose it's all my horrid old prejudice, and father will be grieved and you will think I am perverse. But, really, I'm sure he's not one bit like father was when he was young. I never saw a minister like him. Perhaps I'll get over it. I do sometimes, you know, so don't begin to worry yet. I'll try real hard. I suppose he'll preach Sunday, and then, perhaps, his sermon will be grand and I'll forget how soft-soapy he looks and think only of his great thoughts.

But I know it will be a sort of comfort to you to know that there is a Presbyterian minister in the house with me, and I'll really try to like him if I can.

There's nothing to complain of in the board. It isn't luxurious, of course, but I didn't expect that. Everything is very plain, but Mrs. Tanner manages to make it taste good. She makes fine corn-bread, almost as good as yours — not quite.

My room is all lovely, now that I have covered its bareness with my own things, but it has one great thing that can't compare with anything at home, and that is its view. It is wonderful!

I wish I could make you see it. There is a mountain at the end of it that has as many different garments as a queen. To-night, when sunset came, it grew filmy as if a gauze of many colors had dropped upon it and melted into it, and glowed and melted until it turned to slate blue under the wide, starred blue of the wonderful night sky, and all the dark about was velvet. Last night my mountain was all pink and silver, and I have seen it purple and rose. But you can't think the wideness of the sky, and I couldn't paint it for you with words. You must see it to understand. A great, wide, dark sapphire floor just simply ravished with stars like big jewels!

But I must stop and go to bed, for I find the air of this country makes me very sleepy, and my wicked little kerosene-lamp is smoking. I guess you would better send me my student-lamp, after all, for I'm surely going to need it.

Now I must turn out the light and say good night to my mountain, and then I will go to sleep thinking of you. Don't worry about the minister. I'm very polite to him, but I shall never — *no, never* — fall in love with *him* — tell Jane.

Your loving little girl,
MARGARET

CHAPTER VIII

Margaret had arranged with Bud to take her to the school-house the next morning, and he had promised to have a horse hitched up and ready at ten o'clock, as it seemed the school was a magnificent distance from her boarding-place. In fact, everything seemed to be located with a view to being as far from everywhere else as possible. Even the town was scattering and widespread and sparse.

When she came down to breakfast she was disappointed to find that Bud was not there, and she was obliged to suffer a breakfast tête-à-tête with West. By dint, however, of asking him questions instead of allowing him to take the initiative, she hurried through her breakfast quite successfully, acquiring a superficial knowledge of her fellow-boarder quite distant and satisfactory. She knew where he spent his college days and at what theological seminary he had prepared for the ministry. He had served three years in a prosperous church of a fat little suburb of New York, and was taking a winter off from his severe, strenuous pastoral labors to recuperate his strength, get a new stock of sermons ready, and possibly to write a book of some of his experiences. He flattened his weak, pink chin learnedly as he said this, and tried to look at her impressively. He said that he should probably take a large city church as his next pastorate when his health was fully recuperated. He had come out to study the West and enjoy its freedom, as he understood it was a good place to rest and do as you please unhampered by what people thought. He wanted to get as far away from churches and things clerical as possible. He felt it was due himself and his work that he should. He spoke of the people he had met in Arizona as a kind of tamed savages, and Mrs. Tanner, sitting behind her coffee-pot for a moment between bustles, heard his comments meekly and looked at him with awe. What a great man he must be, and how fortunate for the new teacher that he should be there when she came!

Margaret drew a breath of relief as she hurried away from the breakfast-table to her room. She was really anticipating the ride to the school with Bud. She liked boys, and Bud had taken her fancy. But when she came down-stairs with her hat and sweater on she found West standing out in front, holding the horse.

"Bud had to go in another direction, Miss Earle," he said, touching his hat gracefully, "and he has delegated to me the pleasant task of driving you to the school."

Dismay filled Margaret's soul, and rage with young Bud. He had deserted her and left her in the hands of the enemy! And she had thought he understood! Well, there was nothing for it but to go with this man, much as she disliked it. Her father's daughter could not be rude to a minister.

She climbed into the buckboard quickly to get the ceremony over, for her escort was inclined to be too officious about helping her in, and somehow she couldn't bear to have him touch her. Why was it that she felt so about him? Of course he must be a good man.

West made a serious mistake at the very outset of that ride. He took it for granted that all girls like flattery, and he proceeded to try it on Margaret. But Margaret did not enjoy being told how delighted he was to find that instead of the loud, bold "old maid" he had expected, she had turned out to be "so beautiful and young and altogether congenial"; and, coolly ignoring his compliments, she began a fire of questions again.

She asked about the country, because that was the most obvious topic of conversation. What plants were those that grew by the wayside? She found he knew greasewood from sage-brush, and that was about all. To some of her questions he hazarded answers that were absurd in the light of the explanations given her by Gardley two days before. However, she reflected that he had been in the country but a short time, and that he was by nature a man not interested in such topics. She tried religious matters, thinking that here at least they must have common interests. She asked him what he thought of Christianity in the West as compared with the East. Did he find these Western people more alive and awake to the things of the Kingdom?

West gave a startled look at the clear profile of the young woman beside him, thought he perceived that she was testing him on his clerical side, flattened his chin in his most learned, self-conscious manner, cleared his throat, and put on wisdom.

"Well, now, Miss Earle," he began, condescendingly, "I really don't know that I have thought much about the matter. Ah — you know I have been resting absolutely, and I really haven't had opportunity to study the situation out here in detail; but, on the whole, I should say that everything was decidedly primitive; yes — ah — I might say — ah — well, crude. Yes, *crude* in the extreme! Why, take it in this mission district. The missionary who is in charge seems to be teaching the most absurd of the old dogmas such as our forefathers used to teach. I haven't met him, of course. He is in the East with his wife for a time. I am told she had to go under some kind of an operation. I have never met him, and really don't care to do so; but to judge from all I hear, he is a most unfit man for a position of the kind. For example, he is teaching such exploded doctrines as the old view of the atonement, the infallibility of the Scriptures, the deity of Christ, belief in miracles, and the like. Of course, in one sense it really matters very little what the poor Indians believe, or what such people as the Tanners are taught. They have but little mind, and would scarcely know the difference; but you can readily see that with such a primitive, unenlightened man at the head of religious affairs, there could scarcely be much broadening and real religious growth. Ignorance, of course, holds sway out here. I fancy you will find that to be the case soon enough. What in the world ever led you to come to a field like this to labor? Surely there must have been many more congenial places open to such as you." He leaned forward and cast a sentimental glance at her, his eyes looking more "fishy" than ever.

"I came out here because I wanted to get acquainted with this great country, and because I thought there was an opportunity to do good," said Margaret, coldly. She did not care to discuss her own affairs with this man. "But, Mr. West, I don't know that I altogether understand you. Didn't you tell me that you were a Presbyterian minister?"

"I certainly did," he answered, complacently, as though he were honoring the whole great body of Presbyterians by making the statement.

"Well, then, what in the world did you mean? All Presbyterians, of course, believe in the infallibility of the Scriptures and the deity of Jesus — and the atonement!"

"Not necessarily," answered the young man, loftily. "You will find, my dear young lady, that there is a wide, growing feeling in our church in favor of a broader view. The younger men, and the great student body of our church, have thrown to the winds all their former beliefs and are ready to accept new light with open minds. The findings of science have opened up a vast store of knowledge, and all thinking men must acknowledge that the old dogmas are rapidly vanishing away. Your father doubtless still holds to the old faith, perhaps, and we must be lenient with the older men who have done the best they could with the light they had; but all younger, broad-minded men are coming to the new way of looking at things. We have had enough of the days of preaching hell-fire and damnation. We need a religion of love to man, and good works. You should read some of the books that have been written on this subject if you care to understand. I really think it would be worth your while. You look to me like a young woman with a mind. I have a few of the latest with me. I shall be glad to read and discuss them with you if you are interested."

"Thank you, Mr. West," said Margaret, coolly, though her eyes burned with battle. "I think I have probably read most of those books and discussed them with my father. He may be old, but he is not without 'light,' as you call it, and he always believed in knowing all that the other side was saying. He brought me up to look into these things for myself. And, anyhow, I should not care to read and discuss any of these subjects with a man who denies the deity of my Saviour and does not believe in the infallibility of the Bible. It seems to me you have nothing left — "

"Ah! Well — now — my dear young lady — you mustn't misjudge me! I should be sorry indeed to shake your faith, for an innocent faith is, of course, a most beautiful thing, even though it may be unfounded."

"Indeed, Mr. West, that would not be possible. You could not shake my faith in my Christ, because *I know Him*. If I had not ever felt His presence, nor been guided by His leading, such words might possibly trouble me, but having seen 'Him that is invisible,' *I know*." Margaret's voice was steady and gentle. It was impossible for even that man not to be impressed by her words.

"Well, let us not quarrel about it," he said, indulgently, as to a little child. "I'm sure you have a very charming way of stating it, and I'm not sure that it is not a relief to find a woman of the old-fashioned type now and then. It really is man's place to look into these deeper questions, anyway. It is woman's sphere to live and love and make a happy home — "

His voice took on a sentimental purr, and Margaret was fairly boiling with rage at him; but she would not let her temper give way, especially when she was talking on the sacred theme of the Christ. She felt as if she must scream or jump out over the wheel and run away from this obnoxious man, but she knew she would do neither. She knew she would sit calmly through the expedition and somehow control that conversation. There was one relief, anyway. Her father would no longer expect respect and honor and liking toward a minister who denied the very life and foundation of his faith.

"It can't be possible that the school-house is so far from the town," she said, suddenly looking around at the widening desert in front of them. "Haven't you made some mistake?"

"Why, I thought we should have the pleasure of a little drive first," said West, with a cunning smile. "I was sure you would enjoy seeing the country before you get down to work, and I was not averse myself to a drive in such delightful company."

"I would like to go back to the school-house at once, please," said Margaret, decidedly, and there was that in her voice that caused the man to turn the horse around and head it toward the village.

"Why, yes, of course, if you prefer to see the school-house first, we can go back and look it over, and then, perhaps, you will like to ride a little farther," he said. "We have plenty of time. In fact, Mrs. Tanner told me she would not expect us home to dinner, and she put a very promising-looking basket of lunch under the seat for us in case we got hungry before we came back."

"Thank you," said Margaret, quite freezingly now. "I really do not care to drive this morning. I would like to see the school-house, and then I must return to the house at once. I have a great many things to do this morning."

Her manner at last penetrated even the thick skin of the self-centered man, and he realized that he had gone a step too far in his attentions. He set himself to undo the mischief, hoping perhaps to melt her yet to take the all-day drive with him. But she sat silent during the return to the village, answering his volubility only by yes or no when absolutely necessary. She let him babble away about college life and tell incidents of his late pastorate, at some of which he laughed immoderately; but he could not even bring a smile to her dignified lips.

He hoped she would change her mind when they got to the school building, and he even stooped to praise it in a kind of contemptuous way as they drew up in front of the large adobe building.

"I suppose you will want to go through the building," he said, affably, producing the key from his pocket and putting on a pleasant anticipatory smile, but Margaret shook her head. She simply would not go into the building with that man.

"It is not necessary," she said again, coldly. "I think I will go home now, please." And he was forced to turn the horse toward the Tanner house, crestfallen, and wonder why this beautiful girl was so extremely hard to win. He flattered himself that he had always been able to interest any girl he chose. It was really quite a bewildering type. But he would win her yet.

He set her down silently at the Tanner door and drove off, lunch-basket and all, into the wilderness, vexed that she was so stubbornly unfriendly, and pondering how he might break down the dignity wherewith she had surrounded herself. There would be a way and he would find it. There was a stubbornness about that weak chin of his, when one observed it, and an ugliness in his pale-blue eye; or perhaps you would call it a hardness.

CHAPTER IX

She watched him furtively from her bedroom window, whither she had fled from Mrs. Tanner's exclamations. He wore his stylish derby tilted down over his left eye and slightly to one side in a most unministerial manner, showing too much of his straw-colored back hair, which rose in a cowlick at the point of contact with the hat, and he looked a small, mean creature as he drove off into the vast beauty of the plain. Margaret, in her indignation, could not help comparing him with the young man who had ridden away from the house two days before.

And he to set up to be a minister of Christ's gospel and talk like that about the Bible and Christ! Oh, what was the church of Christ coming to, to have ministers like that? How ever did he get into the ministry, anyway? Of course, she knew there were young men with honest doubts who sometimes slid through nowadays, but a mean little silly man like that? How ever did he get in? What a lot of ridiculous things he had said! He was one of those described in the Bible who "darken counsel with words." He was not worth noticing. And yet, what a lot of harm he could do in an unlearned community. Just see how Mrs. Tanner hung upon his words, as though they were law and gospel! How *could* she?

Margaret found herself trembling yet over the words he had spoken about Christ, the atonement, and the faith. They meant so much to her and to her mother and father. They were not mere empty words of tradition that she believed because she had been taught. She had lived her faith and proved it; and she could not help feeling it like a personal insult to have him speak so of her Saviour. She turned away and took her Bible to try and get a bit of calmness.

She fluttered the leaves for something — she could not just tell what — and her eye caught some of the verses that her father had marked for her before she left home for college, in the days when he was troubled for her going forth into the world of unbelief.

> As ye have therefore received Christ Jesus the Lord, so walk ye in him: Rooted and built up in him, and established in the faith, as ye have been taught, abounding therein with thanksgiving. Beware lest any man spoil you through philosophy and vain deceit, after the tradition of men, after the rudiments of the world, and not after Christ. For in him dwelleth all the fullness of the Godhead bodily....

How the verses crowded upon one another, standing out clearly from the pages as she turned them, marked with her father's own hand in clear ink underlinings. It almost seemed as if God had looked ahead to these times and set these words down just for the encouragement of his troubled servants who couldn't understand why faith was growing dim. God knew about it, had known it would be, all this doubt, and had put words here just for troubled hearts to be comforted thereby.

> For I know whom I have believed [How her heart echoed to that statement!], and am persuaded that he is able to keep that which I have committed unto him against that day.

And on a little further:

> Nevertheless the foundation of God standeth sure, having this seal, The Lord knoweth them that are his.

There was a triumphant look to the words as she read them.

Then over in Ephesians her eye caught a verse that just seemed to fit that poor blind minister:

> Having the understanding darkened, being alienated from the life of God through the ignorance that is in them, because of the blindness of their heart.

And yet he was set to guide the feet of the blind into the way of life! And he had looked on her as one of the ignorant. Poor fellow! He couldn't know the Christ who was her Saviour or he never would have spoken in that way about Him. What could such a man preach? What was there left to preach, but empty words, when one rejected all these doctrines? Would she have to listen to a man like that Sunday after Sunday? Did the scholars in her school, and their parents, and the young man out at the camp, and his rough, simple-hearted companions have to listen to preaching from that man, when they listened to any? Her heart grew sick within her, and she knelt beside her bed for a strengthening word with the Christ who since her little childhood had been a very real presence in her life.

When she arose from her knees she heard the kitchen door slam down-stairs and the voice of Bud calling his mother. She went to her door and opened it, listening a moment, and then called the boy.

There was a dead silence for an instant after her voice was heard, and then Bud appeared at the foot of the stairs, very frowning as to brow, and very surly as to tone:

"What d'ye want?"

It was plain that Bud was "sore."

"Bud," — Margaret's voice was sweet and a bit cool as she leaned over the railing and surveyed the boy; she hadn't yet got over her compulsory ride with that minister — "I wanted to ask you, please, next time you can't keep an appointment with me don't ask anybody else to take your place. I prefer to pick out my own companions. It was all right, of course, if you had to go somewhere else, but I could easily have gone alone or waited until another time. I'd rather not have you ask Mr. West to go anywhere with me again."

Bud's face was a study. It cleared suddenly and his jaw dropped in surprise; his eyes fairly danced with dawning comprehension and pleasure, and then his brow drew down ominously.

"I never ast him," he declared, vehemently. "He told me you wanted him to go, and fer me to get out of the way 'cause you didn't want to hurt my feelings. Didn't you say nothing to him about it at all this morning?"

"No, indeed!" said Margaret, with flashing eyes.

"Well, I just thought he was that kind of a guy. I told ma he was lying, but she said I didn't understand young ladies, and, of course, you didn't want me when there was a man, and especially a preacher, round. Some preacher he is! This 's the second time I've caught him lying. I think he's the limit. I just wish you'd see our missionary. If he was here he'd beat the dust out o' that poor stew. *He's* some man, he is. He's a regular white man, *our missionary*! Just you wait till *he* gets back."

Margaret drew a breath of relief. Then the missionary was a real man, after all. Oh, for his return!

"Well, I'm certainly very glad it wasn't your fault, Bud. I didn't feel very happy to be turned off that way," said the teacher, smiling down upon the rough head of the boy.

"You bet it wasn't my fault!" said the boy, vigorously. "I was sore's a pup at you, after you'd made a date and all, to do like that; but I thought if you wanted to go with that guy it was up to you."

"Well, I didn't and I don't. You'll please understand hereafter that I'd always rather have your company than his. How about going down to the school-house some time to-day? Have you time?"

"Didn't you go yet?" The boy's face looked as if he had received a kingdom, and his voice had a ring of triumph.

"We drove down there, but I didn't care to go in without you, so we came back."

"Wanta go now?" The boy's face fairly shone.

"I'd love to. I'll be ready in three minutes. Could we carry some books down?"

"Sure! Oh — gee! That guy's got the buckboard. We'll have to walk. Doggone him!"

"I shall enjoy a walk. I want to find out just how far it is, for I shall have to walk every day, you know."

"No, you won't, neither, 'nless you wanta. I c'n always hitch up."

"That'll be very nice sometimes, but I'm afraid I'd get spoiled if you babied me all the time that way. I'll be right down."

They went out together into the sunshine and wideness of the morning, and it seemed a new day had been created since she got back from her ride with the minister. She looked at the sturdy, honest-eyed boy beside her, and was glad to have him for a companion.

Just in front of the school-house Margaret paused. "Oh, I forgot! The key! Mr. West has the key in his pocket! We can't get in, can we?"

"Aw, we don't need a key," said her escort. "Just you wait!" And he whisked around to the back of the building, and in about three minutes his shock head appeared at the window. He threw the sash open and dropped out a wooden box. "There!" he said, triumphantly, "you c'n climb up on that, cantcha? Here, I'll holdya steady. Take holta my hand."

And so it was through the front window that the new teacher of the Ridge School first appeared on her future scene of action and surveyed her little kingdom.

Bud threw open the shutters, letting the view of the plains and the sunshine into the big, dusty room, and showed her the new blackboard with great pride.

"There's a whole box o' chalk up on the desk, too; 'ain't never been opened yet. Dad said that was your property. Want I should open it?"

"Why, yes, you might, and then we'll try the blackboard, won't we?"

Bud went to work gravely opening the chalk-box as if it were a small treasure-chest, and finally produced a long, smooth stick of chalk and handed it to her with shining eyes.

"You try it first, Bud," said the teacher, seeing his eagerness; and the boy went forward awesomely, as if it were a sacred precinct and he unworthy to intrude.

Shyly, awkwardly, with infinite painstaking, he wrote in a cramped hand, "William Budlong Tanner," and then, growing bolder, "Ashland, Arizona," with a big flourish underneath.

"Some class!" he said, standing back and regarding his handiwork with pride. "Say, I like the sound the chalk makes on it, don't you?"

"Yes, I do," said Margaret, heartily, "so smooth and business-like, isn't it? You'll enjoy doing examples in algebra on it, won't you?"

"Good night! Algebra! Me? No chance. I can't never get through the arithmetic. The last teacher said if he'd come back twenty years from now he'd still find me working compound interest."

"Well, we'll prove to that man that he wasn't much of a judge of boys," said Margaret, with a tilt of her chin and a glint of her teacher-mettle showing in her eyes. "If you're not in algebra before two months are over I'll miss my guess. We'll get at it right away and show him."

Bud watched her, charmed. He was beginning to believe that almost anything she tried would come true.

"Now, Bud, suppose we get to work. I'd like to get acquainted with my class a little before Monday. Isn't it Monday school opens? I thought so. Well, suppose you give me the names of the scholars and I'll write them down, and that will help me to remember them. Where will you begin? Here, suppose you sit down in the front seat and tell me who sits there and a little bit about him, and I'll write the name down; and then you move to the next seat and tell me about the next one, and so on. Will you?"

"Sure!" said Bud, entering into the new game. "But it ain't a 'he' sits there. It's Susie Johnson. She's Bill Johnson's smallest girl. She has to sit front 'cause she giggles so much. She has yellow curls and she ducks her head down and snickers right out this way when anything funny happens in school." And Bud proceeded to duck and wriggle in perfect imitation of the small Susie.

Margaret saw the boy's power of imitation was remarkable, and laughed heartily at his burlesque. Then she turned and wrote "Susie Johnson" on the board in beautiful script.

Bud watched with admiration, saying softly under his breath; "Gee! that's great, that blackboard, ain't it?"

Amelia Schwartz came next. She was long and lank, with the buttons off the back of her dress, and hands and feet too large for her garments. Margaret could not help but see her in the clever pantomime the boy carried on. Next was Rosa Rogers, daughter of a wealthy cattleman, the pink-cheeked, blue-eyed beauty of the school, with all the boys at her feet and a perfect knowledge of her power over them. Bud didn't, of course, state it that way, but Margaret gathered as much from his simpering smile and the coy way he looked out of the corner of his eyes as he described her.

Down the long list of scholars he went, row after row, and when he came to the seats where the boys sat his tone changed. She could tell by the shading of his voice which boys were the ones to look out for.

Jed Brower, it appeared, was a name to conjure with. He could ride any horse that ever stood on four legs, he could outshoot most of the boys in the neighborhood, and he never allowed any teacher to tell him what to do. He was Texas Brower's only boy, and always had his own way. His father was on the school board. Jed Brower was held in awe, even while his methods were despised, by some of the younger boys. He was big and powerful, and nobody dared fool with him. Bud did not exactly warn Margaret that she must keep on the right side of Jed Brower, but he conveyed that impression without words. Margaret understood. She knew also that Tad Brooks, Larry Parker, Jim Long, and Dake Foster were merely henchmen of the worthy Jed, and not negligible quantities when taken by themselves. But over the name of Timothy Forbes — "Delicate Forbes," Bud explained was his nickname — the boy lingered with that loving inflection of admiration that a younger boy will sometimes have for a husky, courageous older lad. The second time Bud spoke of him he called him "Forbeszy," and Margaret perceived that here was Bud's model of manhood. Delicate Forbes could outshoot and outride even Jed Brower when he chose, and his courage with cattle was that of a man. Moreover, he was good to the younger boys and wasn't above pitching baseball with them when he had nothing better afoot. It became evident from the general description that Delicate Forbes was not called so from any lack of inches to his stature. He had a record of having licked every man teacher in the school, and beaten by guile every woman teacher they had had in six years. Bud was loyal to his admiration, yet it could be plainly seen that he felt Margaret's greatest hindrance in the school would be Delicate Forbes.

Margaret mentally underlined the names in her memory that belonged to the back seats in the first and second rows of desks, and went home praying that she might have wisdom and patience to deal with Jed Brower and Timothy Forbes, and through them to manage the rest of her school.

She surprised Bud at the dinner-table by handing him a neat diagram of the school-room desks with the correct names of all but three or four of the scholars written on them. Such a feat of memory raised her several notches in his estimation.

"Say, that's going some! Guess you won't forget nothing, no matter how much they try to make you."

CHAPTER X

The minister did not appear until late in the evening, after Margaret had gone to her room, for which she was sincerely thankful. She could hear his voice, fretful and complaining, as he called loudly for Bud to take the horse. It appeared he had lost his way and wandered many miles out of the trail. He blamed the country for having no better trails, and the horse for not being able to find his way better. Mr. Tanner had gone to bed, but Mrs. Tanner bustled about and tried to comfort him.

"Now that's too bad! Dearie me! Bud oughta hev gone with you, so he ought. Bud! *Oh*, Bud, you 'ain't gonta sleep yet, hev you? Wake up and come down and take this horse to the barn."

But Bud declined to descend. He shouted some sleepy directions from his loft where he slept, and said the minister could look after his own horse, he "wasn'ta gonta!" There was "plentya corn in the bin."

The minister grumbled his way to the barn, highly incensed at Bud, and disturbed the calm of the evening view of Margaret's mountain by his complaints when he returned. He wasn't accustomed to handling horses, and he thought Bud might have stayed up and attended to it himself. Bud chuckled in his loft and stole down the back kitchen roof while the minister ate his late supper. Bud would never leave the old horse to that amateur's tender mercies, but he didn't intend to make it easy for the amateur. Margaret, from her window-seat watching the night in the darkness, saw Bud slip off the kitchen roof and run to the barn, and she smiled to herself. She liked that boy. He was going to be a good comrade.

The Sabbath morning dawned brilliantly, and to the homesick girl there suddenly came a sense of desolation on waking. A strange land was this, without church-bells or sense of Sabbath fitness. The mountain, it is true, greeted her with a holy light of gladness, but mountains are not dependent upon humankind for being in the spirit on the Lord's day. They are "continually praising Him." Margaret wondered how she was to get through this day, this dreary first Sabbath away from her home and her Sabbath-school class, and her dear old church with father preaching. She had been away, of course, a great many times before, but never to a churchless community. It was beginning to dawn upon her that that was what Ashland was — a churchless community. As she recalled the walk to the school and the ride through the village she had seen nothing that looked like a church, and all the talk had been of the missionary. They must have services of some sort, of course, and probably that flabby, fish-eyed man, her fellow-boarder, was to preach; but her heart turned sick at thought of listening to a man who had confessed to the unbeliefs that he had. Of course, he would likely know enough to keep such doubts to himself; but he had told her, and nothing he could say now would help or uplift her in the least.

She drew a deep sigh and looked at her watch. It was late. At home the early Sabbath-school bells would be ringing, and little girls in white, with bunches of late fall flowers for their teachers, and holding hands with their little brothers, would be hurrying down the street. Father was in his study, going over his morning sermon, and mother putting her little pearl pin in her collar, getting ready to go to her Bible class. Margaret decided it was time to get up and stop thinking of it all.

She put on a little white dress that she wore to church at home and hurried down to discover what the family plans were for the day, but found, to her dismay, that the atmosphere belowstairs was just like that of other days. Mr. Tanner sat tilted back in a dining-room chair, reading the weekly paper, Mrs. Tanner was bustling in with hot corn-bread, Bud was on the front-door steps teasing the dog, and the minister came in with an air of weariness upon him, as if he quite intended taking it out on his companions that he had experienced a trying time on Saturday. He did not look in the least like a man who expected to preach in a few minutes. He declined to eat his egg because it was cooked too hard, and poor Mrs. Tanner had to try it twice before she succeeded in producing a soft-boiled egg to suit him. Only the radiant outline of the great mountain, which Margaret could see over the minister's head, looked peaceful and Sabbath-like.

"What time do you have service?" Margaret asked, as she rose from the table.

"Service?" It was Mr. Tanner who echoed her question as if he did not quite know what she meant.

Mrs. Tanner raised her eyes from her belated breakfast with a worried look, like a hen stretching her neck about to see what she ought to do next for the comfort of the chickens under her care. It was apparent that she had no comprehension of what the question meant. It was the minister who answered, condescendingly:

"Um! Ah! There is no church edifice here, you know, Miss Earle. The mission station is located some miles distant."

"I know," said Margaret, "but they surely have some religious service?"

"I really don't know," said the minister, loftily, as if it were something wholly beneath his notice.

"Then you are not going to preach this morning?" In spite of herself there was relief in her tone.

"Most certainly not," he replied, stiffly. "I came out here to rest, and I selected this place largely because it was so far from a church. I wanted to be where I should not be annoyed by requests to preach. Of course, ministers from the East would be a curiosity in these Western towns, and I should really get no rest at all if I had gone where my services would have been in constant demand. When I came out here I was in much the condition of our friend the minister of whom you have doubtless heard. He was starting on his vacation, and he said to a brother minister, with a smile of joy and relief, 'No preaching, no praying, no reading of the Bible for six whole weeks!'"

"Indeed!" said Margaret, freezingly. "No, I am not familiar with ministers of that sort." She turned with dismissal in her manner and appealed to Mrs. Tanner. "Then you really have no Sabbath service of any sort whatever in town?" There was something almost tragic in her face. She stood aghast at the prospect before her.

Mrs. Tanner's neck stretched up a little longer, and her lips dropped apart in her attempt to understand the situation. One would scarcely have been surprised to hear her say, "Cut-cut-cut-ca-daw-cut?" so fluttered did she seem.

Then up spoke Bud. "We gotta Sunday-school, ma!" There was pride of possession in Bud's tone, and a kind of triumph over the minister, albeit Bud had adjured Sunday-school since his early infancy. He was ready now, however, to be offered on the altar of Sunday-school, even, if that would please the new teacher — and spite the minister. "I'll take you ef you wanta go." He looked defiantly at the minister as he said it.

But at last Mrs. Tanner seemed to grasp what was the matter. "Why! — why! — why! You mean preaching service!" she clucked out. "Why, yes, Mr. West, wouldn't that be fine? You could preach for us. We could have it posted up at the saloon and the crossings, and out a ways on both trails, and you'd have quite a crowd. They'd come from over to the camp, and up the cañon way, and roundabouts. They'd do you credit, they surely would, Mr. West. And you could have the school-house for a meeting-house. Pa, there, is one of the school board. There wouldn't be a bit of trouble —"

"Um! Ah! Mrs. Tanner, I assure you it's quite out of the question. I told you I was here for absolute rest. I couldn't think of preaching. Besides, it's against my principles to preach without remuneration. It's a wrong idea. The workman is worthy of his hire, you know, Mrs. Tanner, the Good Book says." Mr. West's tone took on a self-righteous inflection.

"Oh! Ef that's all, that 'u'd be all right!" she said, with relief. "You could take up a collection. The boys would be real generous. They always are when any show comes along. They'd appreciate it, you know, and I'd like fer Miss Earle here to hear you preach. It 'u'd be a real treat to her, her being a preacher's daughter and all." She turned to Margaret for support, but that young woman was talking to Bud. She had promptly closed with his offer to take her to Sunday-school, and now she hurried away to get ready, leaving Mrs. Tanner to make her clerical arrangements without aid.

The minister, meantime, looked after her doubtfully. Perhaps, after all, it would have been a good move to have preached. He might have impressed that difficult young woman better that way than any other, seeing she posed as being so interested in religious matters. He turned to Mrs. Tanner and began to ask questions about the feasibility of a church service. The word "collection" sounded good to him. He was not averse to replenishing his somewhat depleted treasury if it could be done so easily as that.

Meantime Margaret, up in her room, was wondering again how such a man as Mr. West ever got into the Christian ministry.

West was still endeavoring to impress the Tanners with the importance of his late charge in the East as Margaret came down-stairs. His pompous tones, raised to favor the deafness that he took for granted in Mr. Tanner, easily reached her ears.

"I couldn't, of course, think of doing it every Sunday, you understand. It wouldn't be fair to myself nor my work which I have just left; but, of course, if there were sufficient inducement I might consent to preach some Sunday before I leave."

Mrs. Tanner's little satisfied cluck was quite audible as the girl closed the front door and went out to the waiting Bud.

The Sunday-school was a desolate affair, presided over by an elderly and very illiterate man, who nursed his elbows and rubbed his chin meditatively between the slow questions which he read out of the lesson-leaf. The woman who usually taught the children was called away to nurse a sick neighbor, and the children were huddled together in a restless group. The singing was poor, and the whole of the exercises dreary, including the prayer. The few women present sat and stared in a kind of awe at the visitor, half belligerently, as if she were an intruder. Bud lingered outside the door and finally disappeared altogether, reappearing when the last hymn was sung. Altogether the new teacher felt exceedingly homesick as she wended her way back to the Tanners' beside Bud.

"What do you do with yourself on Sunday afternoons, Bud?" she asked, as soon as they were out of hearing of the rest of the group.

The boy turned wondering eyes toward her. "Do?" he repeated, puzzled. "Why, we pass the time away, like 'most any day. There ain't much difference."

A great desolation possessed her. No church! Worse than no minister! No Sabbath! What kind of a land was this to which she had come?

The boy beside her smelled of tobacco smoke. He had been off somewhere smoking while she was in the dreary little Sunday-school. She looked at his careless boy-face furtively as they walked along. He smoked, of course, like most boys of his age, probably, and he did a lot of other things he ought not to do. He had no interest in God or righteousness, and he did not take it for granted that the Sabbath was different from any other day. A sudden heart-sinking came upon her. What was the use of trying to do anything for such as he? Why not give it up now and go back where there was more promising material to work upon and where she would be welcome indeed? Of course, she had known things would be discouraging, but somehow it had seemed different from a distance. It all looked utterly hopeless now, and herself crazy to have thought she could do any good in a place like this.

And yet the place needed somebody! That pitiful little Sunday-school! How forlorn it all was! She was almost sorry she had gone. It gave her an unhappy feeling for the morrow, which was to be her first day of school.

Then, all suddenly, just as they were nearing the Tanner house, there came one riding down the street with all the glory of the radiant morning in his face, and a light in his eyes at seeing her that lifted away her desolation, for here at last was a friend!

She wondered at herself. An unknown stranger, and a self-confessed failure so far in his young life, and yet he seemed so good a sight to her amid these uncongenial surroundings!

CHAPTER XI

This stranger of royal bearing, riding a rough Western pony as if it were decked with golden trappings, with his bright hair gleaming like Roman gold in the sun, and his blue-gray eyes looking into hers with the gladness of his youth; this one who had come to her out of the night-shadows of the wilderness and led her into safety! Yes, she was glad to see him.

He dismounted and greeted her, his wide hat in his hand, his eyes upon her face, and Bud stepped back, watching them in pleased surprise. This was the man who had shot all the lights out the night of the big riot in the saloon. He had also risked his life in a number of foolish ways at recent festal carouses. Bud would not have been a boy had he not admired the young man beyond measure; and his boy worship of the teacher yielded her to a fitting rival. He stepped behind and walked beside the pony, who was following his master meekly, as though he, too, were under the young man's charm.

"Oh, and this is my friend, William Tanner," spoke Margaret, turning toward the boy loyally, (Whatever good angel made her call him William? Bud's soul swelled with new dignity as he blushed and acknowledged the introduction by a grin.)

"Glad to know you, Will," said the new-comer, extending his hand in a hearty shake that warmed the boy's heart in a trice. "I'm glad Miss Earle has so good a protector. You'll have to look out for her. She's pretty plucky and is apt to stray around the wilderness by herself. It isn't safe, you know, boy, for such as her. Look after her, will you?"

"Right I will," said Bud, accepting the commission as if it were Heaven-sent, and thereafter walked behind the two with his head in the clouds. He felt that he understood this great hero of the plains and was one with him at heart. There could be no higher honor than to be the servitor of this man's lady. Bud did not stop to question how the new teacher became acquainted with the young rider of the plains. It was enough that both were young and handsome and seemed to belong together. He felt they were fitting friends.

The little procession walked down the road slowly, glad to prolong the way. The young man had brought her handkerchief, a filmy trifle of an excuse that she had dropped behind her chair at the bunk-house, where it had lain unnoticed till she was gone. He produced it from his inner pocket, as though it had been too precious to carry anywhere but over his heart, yet there was in his manner nothing presuming, not a hint of any intimacy other than their chance acquaintance of the wilderness would warrant. He did not look at her with any such look as West had given every time he spoke to her. She felt no desire to resent his glance when it rested upon her almost worshipfully, for there was respect and utmost humility in his look.

The men had sent gifts: some arrow-heads and a curiously fashioned vessel from the cañon of the cave-dwellers; some chips from the petrified forest; a fern with wonderful fronds, root and all; and a sheaf of strange, beautiful blossoms carefully wrapped in wet paper, and all fastened to the saddle.

Margaret's face kindled with interest as he showed them to her one by one, and told her the history of each and a little message from the man who had sent it. Mom Wallis, too, had baked a queer little cake and sent it. The young man's face was tender as he spoke of it. The girl saw that he knew what her coming had meant to Mom Wallis. Her memory went quickly back to those few words the morning she had wakened in the bunk-house and found the withered old woman watching her with tears in her eyes. Poor Mom Wallis, with her pretty girlhood all behind her and such a blank, dull future ahead! Poor, tired, ill-used, worn-out Mom Wallis! Margaret's heart went out to her.

"They want to know," said the young man, half hesitatingly, "if some time, when you get settled and have time, you would come to them again and sing? I tried to make them understand, of course, that you would be busy, your time taken with other friends and your work, and you would not want to come; but they wanted me to tell you they never enjoyed anything so much in years as your singing. Why, I heard Long Jim singing 'Old Folks at Home' this morning when he was saddling his horse. And it's made a difference. The men sort of want to straighten up the bunk-room. Jasper made a new chair yesterday. He said it would do when you came again." Gardley laughed diffidently, as if he knew their hopes were all in vain.

But Margaret looked up with sympathy in her face, "I'll come! Of course I'll come some time," she said, eagerly. "I'll come as soon as I can arrange it. You tell them we'll have more than one concert yet."

The young man's face lit up with a quick appreciation, and the flash of his eyes as he looked at her would have told any onlooker that he felt here was a girl in a thousand, a girl with an angel spirit, if ever such a one walked the earth.

Now it happened that Rev. Frederick West was walking impatiently up and down in front of the Tanner residence, looking down the road about that time. He had spent the morning in looking over the small bundle of "show sermons" he had brought with him in case of emergency, and had about decided to accede to Mrs. Tanner's request and preach in Ashland before he left. This decision had put him in so self-satisfied a mood that he was eager to announce it before his fellow-boarder. Moreover, he was hungry, and he could not understand why that impudent boy and that coquettish young woman should remain away at Sunday-school such an interminable time.

Mrs. Tanner was frying chicken. He could smell it every time he took a turn toward the house. It really was ridiculous that they should keep dinner waiting this way. He took one more turn and began to think over the sermon he had decided to preach. He was just recalling a particularly eloquent passage when he happened to look down the road once more, and there they were, almost upon him! But Bud was no longer walking with the maiden. She had acquired a new escort, a man of broad shoulders and fine height. Where had he seen that fellow before? He watched them as they came up, his small, pale eyes narrowing under their yellow lashes with a glint of slyness, like some mean little animal that meant to take advantage of its prey. It was wonderful how many different things that man could look like for a person as insignificant as he really was!

Well, he saw the look between the man and maiden; the look of sympathy and admiration and a fine kind of trust that is not founded on mere outward show, but has found some hidden fineness of the soul. Not that the reverend gentleman understood that, however. He had no fineness of soul himself. His mind had been too thoroughly taken up with himself all his life for him to have cultivated any.

Simultaneous with the look came his recognition of the man or, at least, of where he had last seen him, and his little soul rejoiced at the advantage he instantly recognized.

He drew himself up importantly, flattened his chin upward until his lower lip protruded in a pink roll across his mouth, drew down his yellow brows in a frown of displeasure, and came forward mentor-like to meet the little party as it neared the house. He had the air of coming to investigate and possibly oust the stranger, and he looked at him keenly, critically, offensively, as if he had the right to protect the lady. They might have been a pair of naughty children come back from a forbidden frolic, from the way he surveyed them. But the beauty of it was that neither of them saw him, being occupied with each other, until they were fairly upon him. Then, there he stood offensively, as if he were a great power to be reckoned with.

"Well, well, well, Miss Margaret, you have got home at last!" he said, pompously and condescendingly, and then he looked into the eyes of her companion as if demanding an explanation of *his* presence there.

Margaret drew herself up haughtily. His use of her Christian name in that familiar tone annoyed her exceedingly. Her eyes flashed indignantly, but the whole of it was lost unless Bud saw it, for Gardley had faced his would-be adversary with a keen, surprised scrutiny, and was looking him over coolly. There was that in the young man's eye that made the eye of Frederick West quail before him. It was only an instant the two stood challenging each other, but in that short time each knew and marked the other for an enemy. Only a brief instant and then Gardley turned to Margaret, and before she had time to think what to say, he asked:

"Is this man a friend of yours, Miss *Earle?*" with marked emphasis on the last word.

"No," said Margaret, coolly, "not a friend — a boarder in the house." Then most formally, "Mr. West, my *friend* Mr. Gardley."

If the minister had not been possessed of the skin of a rhinoceros he would have understood himself to be dismissed at that; but he was not a man accustomed to accepting dismissal, as his recent church in New York State might have testified. He stood his ground, his chin flatter than ever, his little eyes mere slits of condemnation. He did not acknowledge the introduction by so much as the inclination of his head. His hands were clasped behind his back, and his whole attitude was one of righteous belligerence.

Gardley gazed steadily at him for a moment, a look of mingled contempt and amusement gradually growing upon his face. Then he turned away as if the man were too small to notice.

"You will come in and take dinner with me?" asked Margaret, eagerly. "I want to send a small package to Mrs. Wallis if you will be so good as to take it with you."

"I'm sorry I can't stay to dinner, but I have an errand in another direction and at some distance. I am returning this way, however, and, if I may, will call and get the package toward evening."

Margaret's eyes spoke her welcome, and with a few formal words the young man sprang on his horse, said, "So long, Will!" to Bud, and, ignoring the minister, rode away.

They watched him for an instant, for, indeed, he was a goodly sight upon a horse, riding as if he and the horse were utterly one in spirit; then Margaret turned quickly to go into the house.

"Um! Ah! Miss Margaret!" began the minister, with a commandatory gesture for her to stop.

Margaret was the picture of haughtiness as she turned and said, "Miss *Earle*, if you please!"

"Um! Ah! Why, certainly, Miss — ah — *Earle*, if you wish it. Will you kindly remain here for a moment? I wish to speak with you. Bud, you may go on."

"I'll go when I like, and it's none of your business!" muttered Bud, ominously, under his breath. He looked at Margaret to see if she wished him to go. He had an idea that this might be one of the times when he was to look after her.

She smiled at him understandingly. "William may remain, Mr. West," she said, sweetly. "Anything you have to say to me can surely be said in his presence," and she laid her hand lightly on Bud's sleeve.

Bud looked down at the hand proudly and grew inches taller enjoying the minister's frown.

"Um! Ah!" said West, unabashed. "Well, I merely wished to warn you concerning the character of that person who has just left us. He is really not a proper companion for you. Indeed, I may say he is quite the contrary, and that to my personal knowledge — "

"He's as good as you are and better!" growled Bud, ominously.

"Be quiet, boy! I wasn't speaking to you!" said West, as if he were addressing a slave. "If I hear another word from your lips I shall report it to your father!"

"Go 's far 's you like and see how much I care!" taunted Bud, but was stopped by Margaret's gentle pressure on his arm.

"Mr. West, I thought I made you understand that Mr. Gardley is my friend."

"Um! Ah! Miss Earle, then all I have to say is that you have formed a most unwise friendship, and should let it proceed no further. Why, my dear young lady, if you knew all there is to know about him you would not think of speaking to that young man."

"Indeed! Mr. West, I suppose that might be true of a good many people, might it not, *if we knew all there is to know about them*? Nobody but God could very well get along with some of us."

"But, my dear young lady, you don't understand. This young person is nothing but a common ruffian, a gambler, in fact, and an habitué at the saloons. I have seen him myself sitting in a saloon at a very late hour playing with a vile, dirty pack of cards, and in the company of a lot of low-down creatures — "

"May I ask how you came to be in a saloon at that hour, Mr. West?" There was a gleam of mischief in the girl's eyes, and her mouth looked as if she were going to laugh, but she controlled it.

The minister turned very red indeed. "Well, I — ah — I had been called from my bed by shouts and the report of a pistol. There was a fight going on in the room adjoining the bar, and I didn't know but my assistance might be needed!" (At this juncture Bud uttered a sort of snort and, placing his hands over his heart, ducked down as if a sudden pain had seized him.) "But imagine my pain and astonishment when I was informed that the drunken brawl I was witnessing was but a nightly and common occurrence. I may say I remained for a few minutes, partly out of curiosity, as I wished to see all kinds of life in this new world for the sake of a book I am thinking of writing. I therefore took careful note of the persons present, and was thus able to identify the person who has just ridden away as one of the chief factors in that evening's entertainment. He was, in fact, the man who, when he had pocketed all the money on the gaming-table, arose and, taking out his pistol, shot out the lights in the room, a most dangerous and irregular proceeding —"

"Yes, and you came within an ace of being shot, pa says. The Kid's a dead shot, he is, and you were right in the way. Served you right for going where you had no business!"

"I did not remain longer in that place, as you may imagine," went on West, ignoring Bud, "for I found it was no place for a — for — a — ah — minister of the gospel; but I remained long enough to hear from the lips of this person with whom you have just been walking some of the most terrible language my ears have ever been permitted to — ah — witness!"

But Margaret had heard all that she intended to listen to on that subject. With decided tone she interrupted the voluble speaker, who was evidently enjoying his own eloquence.

"Mr. West, I think you have said all that it is necessary to say. There are still some things about Mr. Gardley that you evidently do not know, but I think you are in a fair way to learn them if you stay in this part of the country long. William, isn't that your mother calling us to dinner? Let us go in; I'm hungry."

Bud followed her up the walk with a triumphant wink at the discomfited minister, and they disappeared into the house; but when Margaret went up to her room and took off her hat in front of the little warped looking-glass there were angry tears in her eyes. She never felt more like crying in her life. Chagrin and anger and disappointment were all struggling in her soul, yet she must not cry, for dinner would be ready and she must go down. Never should that mean little meddling man see that his words had pierced her soul.

For, angry as she was at the minister, much as she loathed his petty, jealous nature and saw through his tale-bearing, something yet told her that his picture of young Gardley's wildness was probably true, and her soul sank within her at the thought. It was just what had come in shadowy, instinctive fear to her heart when he had hinted at his being a "roughneck," yet to have it put baldly into words by an enemy hurt her deeply, and she looked at herself in the glass half frightened. "Margaret Earle, have you come out to the wilderness to lose your heart to the first handsome sower of wild oats that you meet?" her true eyes asked her face in the glass, and Margaret Earle's heart turned sad at the question and shrank back. Then she dropped upon her knees beside her gay little rocking-chair and buried her face in its flowered cushions and cried to her Father in heaven:

"Oh, my Father, let me not be weak, but with all my heart I cry to Thee to save this young, strong, courageous life and not let it be a failure. Help him to find Thee and serve Thee, and if his life has been all wrong — and I suppose it has — oh, make it right for Jesus' sake! If there is anything that I can do to help, show me how, and don't let me make mistakes. Oh, Jesus, Thy power is great. Let this young man feel it and yield himself to it."

She remained silently praying for a moment more, putting her whole soul into the prayer and knowing that she had been called thus to pray for him until her prayer was answered.

She came down to dinner a few minutes later with a calm, serene face, on which was no hint of her recent emotion, and she managed to keep the table conversation wholly in her own hands, telling Mr. Tanner about her home town and her father and mother. When the meal was finished the minister had no excuse to think that the new teacher was careless about her friends and associates, and he was well informed about the high principles of her family.

But West had retired into a sulky mood and uttered not a word except to ask for more chicken and coffee and a second helping of pie. It was, perhaps, during that dinner that he decided it would be best for him to preach in Ashland on the following Sunday. The young lady could be properly impressed with his dignity in no other way.

CHAPTER XII

When Lance Gardley came back to the Tanners' the sun was preparing the glory of its evening setting, and the mountain was robed in all its rosiest veils.

Margaret was waiting for him, with the dog Captain beside her, wandering back and forth in the unfenced dooryard and watching her mountain. It was a relief to her to find that the minister occupied a room on the first floor in a kind of ell on the opposite side of the house from her own room and her mountain. He had not been visible that afternoon, and with Captain by her side and Bud on the front-door step reading *The Sky Pilot* she felt comparatively safe. She had read to Bud for an hour and a half, and he was thoroughly interested in the story; but she was sure he would keep the minister away at all costs. As for Captain, he and the minister were sworn enemies by this time. He growled every time West came near or spoke to her.

She made a picture standing with her hand on Captain's shaggy, noble head, the lace of her sleeve falling back from the white arm, her other hand raised to shade her face as she looked away to the glorified mountain, a slim, white figure looking wistfully off at the sunset. The young man took off his hat and rode his horse more softly, as if in the presence of the holy.

The dog lifted one ear, and a tremor passed through his frame as the rider drew near; otherwise he did not stir from his position; but it was enough. The girl turned, on the alert at once, and met him with a smile, and the young man looked at her as if an angel had deigned to smile upon him. There was a humility in his fine face that sat well with the courage written there, and smoothed away all hardness for the time, so that the girl, looking at him in the light of the revelations of the morning, could hardly believe it had been true, yet an inner fineness of perception taught her that it was.

The young man dismounted and left his horse standing quietly by the roadside. He would not stay, he said, yet lingered by her side, talking for a few minutes, watching the sunset and pointing out its changes.

She gave him the little package for Mom Wallis. There was a simple lace collar in a little white box, and a tiny leather-bound book done in russet suède with gold lettering.

"Tell her to wear the collar and think of me whenever she dresses up."

"I'm afraid that'll never be, then," said the young man, with a pitying smile. "Mom Wallis never dresses up."

"Tell her I said she must dress up evenings for supper, and I'll make her another one to change with that and bring it when I come."

He smiled upon her again, that wondering, almost worshipful smile, as if he wondered if she were real, after all, so different did she seem from his idea of girls.

"And the little book," she went on, apologetically; "I suppose it was foolish to send it, but something she said made me think of some of the lines in the poem. I've marked them for her. She reads, doesn't she?"

"A little, I think. I see her now and then read the papers that Pop brings home with him. I don't fancy her literary range is very wide, however."

"Of course, I suppose it is ridiculous! And maybe she'll not understand any of it; but tell her I sent her a message. She must see if she can find it in the poem. Perhaps you can explain it to her. It's Browning's 'Rabbi Ben Ezra.' You know it, don't you?"

"I'm afraid not. I was intent on other things about the time when I was supposed to be giving my attention to Browning, or I wouldn't be what I am to-day, I suppose. But I'll do my best with what wits I have. What's it about? Couldn't you give me a pointer or two?"

"It's the one beginning:

>"Grow old along with me!
>The best is yet to be,
>The last of life, for which the first was made:
>Our times are in His hand

> Who saith, 'A whole I planned,
> Youth shows but half; trust God: see all, nor be afraid!'"

He looked down at her still with that wondering smile. "Grow old along with you!" he said, gravely, and then sighed. "You don't look as if you ever would grow old."

"That's it," she said, eagerly. "That's the whole idea. We don't ever grow old and get done with it all, we just go on to bigger things, wiser and better and more beautiful, till we come to understand and be a part of the whole great plan of God!"

He did not attempt an answer, nor did he smile now, but just looked at her with that deeply quizzical, grave look as if his soul were turning over the matter seriously. She held her peace and waited, unable to find the right word to speak. Then he turned and looked off, an infinite regret growing in his face.

"That makes living a different thing from the way most people take it," he said, at last, and his tone showed that he was considering it deeply.

"Does it?" she said, softly, and looked with him toward the sunset, still half seeing his quiet profile against the light. At last it came to her that she must speak. Half fearfully she began: "I've been thinking about what you said on the ride. You said you didn't make good. I — wish you would. I — I'm sure you could — "

She looked up wistfully and saw the gentleness come into his face as if the fountain of his soul, long sealed, had broken up, and as if he saw a possibility before him for the first time through the words she had spoken.

At last he turned to her with that wondering smile again. "Why should you care?" he asked. The words would have sounded harsh if his tone had not been so gentle.

Margaret hesitated for an answer. "I don't know how to tell it," she said, slowly. "There's another verse, a few lines more in that poem, perhaps you know them? —

> 'All I never could be, All, men ignored in me,
> This I was worth to God, whose wheel the pitcher shaped.'

I want it because — well, perhaps because I feel you are worth all that to God. I would like to see you be that."

He looked down at her again, and was still so long that she felt she had failed miserably.

"I hope you will excuse my speaking," she added. "I — It seems there are so many grand possibilities in life, and for you — I couldn't bear to have you say you hadn't made good, as if it were all over."

"I'm glad you spoke," he said, quickly. "I guess perhaps I have been all kinds of a fool. You have made me feel how many kinds I have been."

"Oh no!" she protested.

"You don't know what I have been," he said, sadly, and then with sudden conviction, as if he read her thoughts: "You *do* know! That prig of a parson has told you! Well, it's just as well you should know. It's right!"

A wave of misery passed over his face and erased all its brightness and hope. Even the gentleness was gone. He looked haggard and drawn with hopelessness all in a moment.

"Do you think it would matter to me — *anything* that man would say?" she protested, all her woman's heart going out in pity.

"But it was true, all he said, probably, and more — "

"It doesn't matter," she said, eagerly. "The other is true, too. Just as the poem says, 'All that man ignores in you, just that you are worth to God!' And you *can* be what He meant you to be. I have been praying all the afternoon that He would help you to be."

"Have you?" he said, and his eyes lit up again as if the altar-fires of hope were burning once more. "Have you? I thank you."

"You came to me when I was lost in the wilderness," she said, shyly. "I wanted to help *you* back — if — I might."

"You will help — you have!" he said, earnestly. "And I was far enough off the trail, too, but if there's any way to get back I'll get there." He grasped her hand and held it for a second. "Keep up that praying," he said. "I'll see what can be done."

Margaret looked up. "Oh, I'm so glad, so glad!"

He looked reverently into her eyes, all the manhood in him stirred to higher, better things. Then, suddenly, as they stood together, a sound smote their ears as from another world.

"Um! Ah! — "

The minister stood within the doorway, barred by Bud in scowling defiance, and guarded by Cap, who gave an answering growl.

Gardley and Margaret looked at each other and smiled, then turned and walked slowly down to where the pony stood. They did not wish to talk here in that alien presence. Indeed, it seemed that more words were not needed — they would be a desecration.

So he rode away into the sunset once more with just another look and a hand-clasp, and she turned, strangely happy at heart, to go back to her dull surroundings and her uncongenial company.

"Come, William, let's have a praise service," she said, brightly, pausing at the doorway, but ignoring the scowling minister.

"A praise service! What's a praise service?" asked the wondering Bud, shoving over to let her sit down beside him.

She sat with her back to West, and Cap came and lay at her feet with the white of one eye on the minister and a growl ready to gleam between his teeth any minute. There was just no way for the minister to get out unless he jumped over them or went out the back door; but the people in the doorway had the advantage of not having to look at him, and he couldn't very well dominate the conversation standing so behind them.

"Why, a praise service is a service of song and gladness, of course. You sing, don't you? Of course. Well, what shall we sing? Do you know this?" And she broke softly into song:

> "When peace like a river attendeth my way;
> When sorrows like sea-billows roll;
> Whatever my lot Thou hast taught me to say,
> It is well, it is well with my soul."

Bud did not know the song, but he did not intend to be balked with the minister standing right behind him, ready, no doubt, to jump in and take the precedence; so he growled away at a note in the bass, turning it over and over and trying to make it fit, like a dog gnawing at a bare bone; but he managed to keep time and make it sound a little like singing.

The dusk was falling fast as they finished the last verse, Margaret singing the words clear and distinct, Bud growling unintelligibly and snatching at words he had never heard before. Once more Margaret sang:

> "Abide with me; fast falls the eventide;
> The darkness deepens; Lord, with me abide!
> When other refuge fails and comforts flee,
> Help of the helpless, oh, abide with me!"

Out on the lonely trail wending his way toward the purple mountain — the silent way to the bunk-house at the camp — in that clear air where sound travels a long distance the traveler heard the song, and something thrilled his soul. A chord that never had been touched in him before was vibrating, and its echoes would be heard through all his life.

On and on sang Margaret, just because she could not bear to stop and hear the commonplace talk which would be about her. Song after song thrilled through the night's wideness. The stars came out in thick clusters. Father Tanner had long ago dropped his weekly paper and tilted his chair back against the wall, with his eyes half closed to listen, and his wife had settled down comfortably on the carpet sofa, with her hands nicely folded in her lap, as if she were at church. The minister, after silently surveying the situation for a song or two, attempted to join his voice to the chorus. He had a voice like a cross-cut saw, but he didn't do much harm in the background that way, though Cap did growl now and then, as if it put his nerves on edge. And by and by Mr. Tanner quavered in with a note or two.

Finally Margaret sang:

> "Sun of my soul, Thou Saviour dear,
> It is not night if Thou art near,
> Oh, may no earth-born cloud arise
> To hide Thee from Thy servant's eyes."

During this hymn the minister had slipped out the back door and gone around to the front of the house. He could not stand being in the background any longer; but as the last note died away Margaret arose and, bidding Bud good night, slipped up to her room.

There, presently, beside her darkened window, with her face toward the mountain, she knelt to pray for the wanderer who was trying to find his way out of the wilderness.

CHAPTER XIII

Monday morning found Margaret at the school-house nerved for her new task.

One by one the scholars trooped in, shyly or half defiantly, hung their hats on the hooks, put their dinner-pails on the shelf, looked furtively at her, and sank into their accustomed seats; that is, the seats they had occupied during the last term of school. The big boys remained outside until Bud, acting under instructions from Margaret — after she had been carefully taught the ways of the school by Bud himself — rang the big bell. Even then they entered reluctantly and as if it were a great condescension that they came at all, Jed and "Delicate" coming in last, with scarcely a casual glance toward the teacher's desk, as if she were a mere fraction in the scheme of the school. She did not need to be told which was Timothy and which was Jed. Bud's description had been perfect. Her heart, by the way, instantly went out to Timothy. Jed was another proposition. He had thick, overhanging eyebrows, and a mouth that loved to make trouble and laugh over it. He was going to be hard to conquer. She wasn't sure the conquering would be interesting, either.

Margaret stood by the desk, watching them all with a pleasant smile. She did not frown at the unnecessary shuffling of feet nor the loud remarks of the boys as they settled into their seats. She just stood and watched them interestedly, as though her time had not yet come.

Jed and Timothy were carrying on a rumbling conversation. Even after they took their seats they kept it up. It was no part of their plan to let the teacher suppose they saw her or minded her in the least. They were the dominating influences in that school, and they wanted her to know it, right at the start; then a lot of trouble would be saved. If they didn't like her and couldn't manage her they didn't intend she should stay, and she might as well understand that at once.

Margaret understood it fully. Yet she stood quietly and watched them with a look of deep interest on her face and a light almost of mischief in her eyes, while Bud grew redder and redder over the way his two idols were treating the new teacher. One by one the school became aware of the twinkle in the teacher's eyes, and grew silent to watch, and one by one they began to smile over the coming scene when Jed and Timothy should discover it, and, worst of all, find out that it was actually directed against them. They would expect severity, or fear, or a desire to placate; but a twinkle — it was more than the school could decide what would happen under such circumstances. No one in that room would ever dare to laugh at either of those two boys. But the teacher was almost laughing now, and the twinkle had taken the rest of the room into the secret, while she waited amusedly until the two should finish the conversation.

The room grew suddenly deathly still, except for the whispered growls of Jed and Timothy, and still the silence deepened, until the two young giants themselves perceived that it was time to look up and take account of stock.

The perspiration by this time was rolling down the back of Bud's neck. He was about the only one in the room who was not on a broad grin, and he was wretched. What a fearful mistake the new teacher was making right at the start! She was antagonizing the two boys who held the whole school in their hands. There was no telling what they wouldn't do to her now. And he would have to stand up for her. Yes, no matter what they did, he would stand up for her! Even though he lost his best friends, he must be loyal to her; but the strain was terrible! He did not dare to look at them, but fastened his eyes upon Margaret, as if keeping them glued there was his only hope. Then suddenly he saw her face break into one of the sweetest, merriest smiles he ever witnessed, with not one single hint of reproach or offended dignity in it, just a smile of comradeship, understanding, and pleasure in the meeting; and it was directed to the two seats where Jed and Timothy sat.

With wonder he turned toward the two big boys, and saw, to his amazement, an answering smile upon their faces; reluctant, 'tis true, half sheepish at first, but a smile with lifted eyebrows of astonishment and real enjoyment of the joke.

A little ripple of approval went round in half-breathed syllables, but Margaret gave no time for any restlessness to start. She spoke at once, in her pleasantest partnership tone, such as she had used to Bud when she asked him to help her build her bookcase. So she spoke now to that school, and each one felt she was speaking just to him especially, and felt a leaping response in his soul. Here, at least, was something new and interesting, a new kind of teacher. They kept silence to listen.

"Oh, I'm not going to make a speech now," she said, and her voice sounded glad to them all. "I'll wait till we know one another before I do that. I just want to say how do you do to you, and tell you how glad I am to be here. I hope we shall like one another immensely and have a great many good times together. But we've got to get acquainted first, of course, and perhaps we'd better give most of the time to that to-day. First, suppose we sing something. What shall it be? What do you sing?"

Little Susan Johnson, by virtue of having seen the teacher at Sunday-school, made bold to raise her hand and suggest, "Thar-thpangle Banner, pleath!" And so they tried it; but when Margaret found that only a few seemed to know the words, she said, "Wait!" Lifting her arm with a pretty, imperative gesture, and taking a piece of chalk from the box on her desk, she went to the new blackboard that stretched its shining black length around the room.

The school was breathlessly watching the graceful movement of the beautiful hand and arm over the smooth surface, leaving behind it the clear, perfect script. Such wonderful writing they had never seen; such perfect, easy curves and twirls. Every eye in the room was fastened on her, every breath was held as they watched and spelled out the words one by one. "Gee!" said Bud, softly, under his breath, nor knew that he had spoken, but no one else moved.

"Now," she said, "let us sing," and when they started off again Margaret's strong, clear soprano leading, every voice in the room growled out the words and tried to get in step with the tune.

They had gone thus through two verses when Jed seemed to think it was about time to start something. Things were going altogether too smoothly for an untried teacher, if she *was* handsome and unabashed. If they went on like this the scholars would lose all respect for him. So, being quite able to sing a clear tenor, he nevertheless puckered his lips impertinently, drew his brows in an ominous frown, and began to whistle a somewhat erratic accompaniment to the song. He watched the teacher closely, expecting to see the color flame in her cheeks, the anger flash in her eyes; he had tried this trick on other teachers and it always worked. He gave the wink to Timothy, and he too left off his glorious bass and began to whistle.

But instead of the anger and annoyance they expected, Margaret turned appreciative eyes toward the two back seats, nodding her head a trifle and smiling with her eyes as she sang; and when the verse was done she held up her hand for silence and said:

"Why, boys, that's beautiful! Let's try that verse once more, and you two whistle the accompaniment a little stronger in the chorus; or how would it do if you just came in on the chorus? I believe that would be more effective. Let's try the first verse that way; you boys sing during the verse and then whistle the chorus just as you did now. We really need your voices in the verse part, they are so strong and splendid. Let's try it now." And she started off again, the two big astonished fellows meekly doing as they were told, and really the effect was beautiful. What was their surprise when the whole song was finished to have her say, "Now everybody whistle the chorus softly," and then pucker up her own soft lips to join in. That completely finished the whistling stunt. Jed realized that it would never work again, not while she was here, for she had turned the joke into beauty and made them all enjoy it. It hadn't annoyed her in the least.

Somehow by that time they were all ready for anything she had to suggest, and they watched again breathlessly as she wrote another song on the blackboard, taking the other side of the room for it, and this time a hymn — "I Need Thee Every Hour."

When they began to sing it, however, Margaret found the tune went slowly, uncertainly.

"Oh, how we need a piano!" she exclaimed. "I wonder if we can't get up an entertainment and raise money to buy one. How many will help?"

Every hand in the place went up, Jed's and Timothy's last and only a little way, but she noted with triumph that they went up.

"All right; we'll do it! Now let's sing that verse correctly." And she began to sing again, while they all joined anxiously in, really trying to do their best.

The instant the last verse died away, Margaret's voice took their attention.

"Two years ago in Boston two young men, who belonged to a little group of Christian workers who were going around from place to place holding meetings, sat talking together in their room in the hotel one evening."

There was instant quiet, a kind of a breathless quiet. This was not like the beginning of any lesson any other teacher had ever given them. Every eye was fixed on her.

"They had been talking over the work of the day, and finally one of them suggested that they choose a Bible verse for the whole year — "

There was a movement of impatience from one back seat, as if Jed had scented an incipient sermon, but the teacher's voice went steadily on:

"They talked it over, and at last they settled on II Timothy ii:15. They made up their minds to use it on every possible occasion. It was time to go to bed, so the man whose room adjoined got up and, instead of saying good night, he said, 'Well, II Timothy ii:15,' and went to his room. Pretty soon, when he put out his light, he knocked on the wall and shouted 'II Timothy ii:15,' and the other man responded, heartily, 'All right, II Timothy ii:15.' The next morning when they wrote their letters each of them wrote 'II Timothy ii:15' on the lower left-hand corner of the envelope, and sent out a great handful of letters to all parts of the world. Those letters passed through the Boston post-office, and some of the clerks who sorted them saw that queer legend written down in the lower left-hand corner of the envelope, and they wondered at it, and one or two wrote it down, to look it up afterward. The letters reached other cities and were put into the hands of mail-carriers to distribute, and they saw the queer little sentence, 'II Timothy ii:15,' and they wondered, and some of them looked it up."

By this time the entire attention of the school was upon the story, for they perceived that it was a story.

"The men left Boston and went across the ocean to hold meetings in other cities, and one day at a little railway station in Europe a group of people were gathered, waiting for a train, and those two men were among them. Pretty soon the train came, and one of the men got on the back end of the last car, while the other stayed on the platform, and as the train moved off the man on the last car took off his hat and said, in a good, loud, clear tone, 'Well, take care of yourself, II Timothy ii:15,' and the other one smiled and waved his hat and answered, 'Yes, II Timothy ii:15.' The man on the train, which was moving fast now, shouted back, 'II Timothy ii:15,' and the man on the platform responded still louder, waving his hat, 'II Timothy ii:15,' and back and forth the queer sentence was flung until the train was too far away for them to hear each other's voices. In the mean time all the people on the platform had been standing there listening and wondering what in the world such a strange salutation could mean. Some of them recognized what it was, but many did not know, and yet the sentence was said over so many times that they could not help remembering it; and some went away to recall it and ask their friends what it meant. A young man from America was on that platform and heard it, and he knew it stood for a passage in the Bible, and his curiosity was so great that he went back to his boarding-house and hunted up the Bible his mother had packed in his trunk when he came away from home, and he hunted through the Bible until he found the place, 'II Timothy ii:15,' and read it; and it made him think about his life and decide that he wasn't doing as he ought to do. I can't tell you all the story about that queer Bible verse, how it went here and there and what a great work it did in people's hearts; but one day those Christian workers went to Australia to hold some meetings, and one night, when the great auditorium was crowded, a man who was leading the meeting got up and told the story of this verse, how it had been chosen, and how it had gone over the world in strange ways, even told about the morning at the little railway station when the two men said good-by. Just as he got to that place in his story a man in the audience stood up and said: 'Brother, just let me say a word, please. I never knew anything about all this before, but I was at that railway station, and I heard those two men shout that strange good-by, and I went home and read that verse, and it's made a great difference in my life.'

"There was a great deal more to the story, how some Chicago policemen got to be good men through reading that verse, and how the story of the Australia meetings was printed in an Australian paper and sent to a lady in America who sent it to a friend in England to read about the meetings. And this friend in England had a son in the army in India, to whom she was sending a package, and she wrapped it around something in that package, and the young man read all about it, and it helped to change his life. Well, I thought of that story this morning when I was trying to decide what to read for our opening chapter, and it occurred to me that perhaps you would be interested to take that verse for our school verse this term, and so if you would like it I will put it on the blackboard. Would you like it, I wonder?"

She paused wistfully, as if she expected an answer, and there was a low, almost inaudible growl of assent; a keen listener might almost have said it had an impatient quality in it, as if they were in a hurry to find out what the verse was that had made such a stir in the world.

"Very well," said Margaret, turning to the board; "then I'll put it where we all can see it, and while I write it will you please say over where it is, so that you will remember it and hunt it up for yourselves in your Bibles at home?"

There was a sort of snicker at that, for there were probably not half a dozen Bibles, if there were so many, represented in that school; but they took her hint as she wrote, and chanted, "II Timothy ii:15, II Timothy ii:15," and then spelled out after her rapid crayon, "Study to show thyself approved unto God, a workman that needeth not to be ashamed."

They read it together at her bidding, with a wondering, half-serious look in their faces, and then she said, "Now, shall we pray?"

The former teacher had not opened her school with prayer. It had never been even suggested in that school. It might have been a dangerous experiment if Margaret had attempted it sooner in her program. As it was, there was a shuffling of feet in the back seats at her first word; but the room, grew quiet again, perhaps out of curiosity to hear a woman's voice in prayer:

"Our Heavenly Father, we want to ask Thee to bless us in our work together, and to help us to be such workmen that we shall not need to be ashamed to show our work to Thee at the close of the day. For Christ's sake we ask it. Amen."

They did not have time to resent that prayer before she had them interested in something else. In fact, she had planned her whole first day out so that there should not be a minute for misbehavior. She had argued that if she could just get time to become acquainted with them she might prevent a lot of trouble before it ever started. Her first business was to win her scholars. After that she could teach them easily if they were once willing to learn.

She had a set of mental arithmetic problems ready which she propounded to them next, some of them difficult and some easy enough for the youngest child who could think, and she timed their answers and wrote on the board the names of those who raised their hands first and had the correct answers. The questions were put in a fascinating way, many of them having curious little catches in them for the scholars who were not on the alert, and Timothy presently discovered this and set himself to get every one, coming off victorious at the end. Even Jed roused himself and was interested, and some of the girls quite distinguished themselves.

When a half-hour of this was over she put the word "TRANSFIGURATION" on the blackboard, and set them to playing a regular game out of it. If some of the school-board had come in just then they might have lifted up hands of horror at the idea of the new teacher setting the whole school to playing a game. But they certainly would have been delightfully surprised to see a quiet and orderly room with bent heads and knit brows, all intent upon papers and pencils. Never before in the annals of that school had the first day held a full period of quiet or orderliness. It was expected to be a day of battle; a day of trying out the soul of the teacher and proving whether he or she were worthy to cope with the active minds and bodies of the young bullies of Ashland. But the expected battle had been forgotten. Every mind was busy with the matter in hand.

Margaret had given them three minutes to write as many words as they could think of, of three letters or more, beginning with T, and using only the letters in the word she had put on the board. When time was called there was a breathless rush to write a last word, and then each scholar had to tell how many words he had, and each was called upon to read his list. Some had only two or three, some had ten or eleven. They were allowed to mark their words, counting one for each person present who did not have that word and doubling if it were two syllables, and so on. Excitement ran high when it was discovered that some had actually made a count of thirty or forty, and when they started writing words beginning with R every head was bent intently from the minute time was started.

Never had three minutes seemed so short to those unused brains, and Jed yelled out: "Aw, gee! I only got three!" when time was called next.

It was recess-time when they finally finished every letter in that word, and, adding all up, found that Timothy had won the game. Was that school? Why, a barbecue couldn't be named beside it for fun! They rushed out to the school-yard with a shout, and the boys played leap-frog loudly for the first few minutes. Margaret, leaning her tired head in her hands, elbows on the window-seat, closing her eyes and gathering strength for the after-recess session, heard one boy say: "Wal, how d'ye like 'er?" And the answer came: "Gee! I didn't think she'd be that kind of a guy! I thought she'd be some stiff old Ike! Ain't she a peach, though?" She lifted up her head and laughed triumphantly to herself, her eyes alight, herself now strengthened for the fray. She wasn't wholly failing, then?

After recess there was a spelling-match, choosing sides, of course, "Because this is only the first day, and we must get acquainted before we can do real work, you know," she explained.

The spelling-match proved an exciting affair also, with new features that Ashland had never seen before. Here the girls began to shine into prominence, but there were very few good spellers, and they were presently reduced to two girls — Rosa Rogers, the beauty of the school, and Amanda Bounds, a stolid, homely girl with deep eyes and a broad brow.

"I'm going to give this as a prize to the one who stands up the longest," said Margaret, with sudden inspiration as she saw the boys in their seats getting restless; and she unpinned a tiny blue-silk bow that fastened her white collar.

The girls all said "Oh-h-h!" and immediately every one in the room straightened up. The next few minutes those two girls spelled for dear life, each with her eye fixed upon the tiny blue bow in the teacher's white hands. To own that bow, that wonderful, strange bow of the heavenly blue, with the graceful twist to the tie! What delight! The girl who won that would be the admired of all the school. Even the boys sat up and took notice, each secretly thinking that Rosa, the beauty, would get it, of course.

But she didn't; she slipped up on the word "receive," after all, putting the i before the e; and her stolid companion, catching her breath awesomely, slowly spelled it right and received the blue prize, pinned gracefully at the throat of her old brown gingham by the teacher's own soft, white fingers, while the school looked on admiringly and the blood rolled hotly up the back of her neck and spread over her face and forehead. Rosa, the beauty, went crestfallen to her seat.

It was at noon, while they ate their lunch, that Margaret tried to get acquainted with the girls, calling most of them by name, to their great surprise, and hinting of delightful possibilities in the winter's work. Then she slipped out among the boys and watched their sports, laughing and applauding when some one made a particularly fine play, as if she thoroughly understood and appreciated.

She managed to stand near Jed and Timothy just before Bud rang the bell. "I've heard you are great sportsmen," she said to them, confidingly. "And I've been wondering if you'll teach me some things I want to learn? I want to know how to ride and shoot. Do you suppose I could learn?"

"Sure!" they chorused, eagerly, their embarrassment forgotten. "Sure, you could learn fine! Sure, *we'll learn* you!"

And then the bell rang and they all went in.

The afternoon was a rather informal arrangement of classes and schedule for the next day, Margaret giving out slips of paper with questions for each to answer, that she might find out just where to place them; and while they wrote she went from one to another, getting acquainted, advising, and suggesting about what they wanted to study. It was all so new and wonderful to them! They had not been used to caring what they were to study. Now it almost seemed interesting.

But when the day was done, the school-house locked, and Bud and Margaret started for home, she realized that she was weary. Yet it was a weariness of success and not of failure, and she felt happy in looking forward to the morrow.

CHAPTER XIV

The minister had decided to preach in Ashland, and on the following Sabbath. It became apparent that if he wished to have any notice at all from the haughty new teacher he must do something at once to establish his superiority in her eyes. He had carefully gone over his store of sermons that he always carried with him, and decided to preach on "The Dynamics of Altruism."

Notices had been posted up in saloons and stores and post-office. He had made them himself after completely tabooing Mr. Tanner's kindly and blundering attempt, and they gave full information concerning "the Rev. Frederick West, Ph.D., of the vicinity of New York City, who had kindly consented to preach in the school-house on 'The Dynamics of Altruism.'"

Several of these elaborately printed announcements had been posted up on big trees along the trails, and in other conspicuous places, and there was no doubt but that the coming Sabbath services were more talked of than anything else in that neighborhood for miles around, except the new teacher and her extraordinary way of making all the scholars fall in love with her. It is quite possible that the Reverend Frederick might not have been so flattered at the size of his audience when the day came if he could have known how many of them came principally because they thought it would be a good opportunity to see the new teacher.

However, the announcements were read, and the preacher became an object of deep interest to the community when he went abroad. Under this attention he swelled, grew pleased, bland, and condescending, wearing an oily smile and bowing most conceitedly whenever anybody noticed him. He even began to drop his severity and silence at the table, toward the end of the week, and expanded into dignified conversation, mainly addressed to Mr. Tanner about the political situation in the State of Arizona. He was trying to impress the teacher with the fact that he looked upon her as a most insignificant mortal who had forfeited her right to his smiles by her headstrong and unseemly conduct when he had warned her about "that young ruffian."

Out on the trail Long Bill and Jasper Kemp paused before a tree that bore the Reverend Frederick's church notice, and read in silence while the wide wonder of the desert spread about them.

"What d'ye make out o' them cuss words, Jap?" asked Long Bill, at length. "D'ye figger the parson's goin' to preach on swearin' ur gunpowder?"

"Blowed ef I know," answered Jasper, eying the sign ungraciously; "but by the looks of him he can't say much to suit me on neither one. He resembles a yaller cactus bloom out in a rain-storm as to head, an' his smile is like some of them prickles on the plant. He can't be no 'sky-pilot' to me, not just yet."

"You don't allow he b'longs in any way to *her*?" asked Long Bill, anxiously, after they had been on their way for a half-hour.

"B'long to *her*? Meanin' the schoolmarm?"

"Yes; he ain't sweet on her nor nothin'?"

"Wal, I guess not," said Jasper, contentedly. "She's got eyes sharp's a needle. You don't size her up so small she's goin' to take to a sickly parson with yaller hair an' sleek ways when she's seen the Kid, do you?"

"Wal, no, it don't seem noways reasonable, but you never can tell. Women gets notions."

"She ain't that kind! You mark my words, *she ain't that kind*. I'd lay she'd punch the breeze like a coyote ef he'd make up to her. Just you wait till you see him. He's the most no-'count, measleyest little thing that ever called himself a man. My word! I'd like to see him try to ride that colt o' mine. I really would. It would be some sight for sore eyes, it sure would."

"Mebbe he's got a intellec'," suggested Long Bill, after another mile. "That goes a long ways with women-folks with a education."

"No chance!" said Jasper, confidently. "'Ain't got room fer one under his yaller thatch. You wait till you set your lamps on him once before you go to gettin' excited. Why, he ain't one-two-three with our missionary! Gosh! I wish *he'd* come back an' see to such goin's-on — I certainly do."

"Was you figgerin' to go to that gatherin' Sunday?"

"I sure was," said Jasper. "I want to see the show, an', besides, we might be needed ef things got too high-soundin'. It ain't good to have a creature at large that thinks he knows all there is to know. I heard him talk down to the post-office the day after that little party we had when the Kid shot out the lights to save Bunchy from killin' Crapster, an' it's my opinion he needs a good spankin'; but I'm agoin' to give him a fair show. I ain't much on religion myself, but I do like to see a square deal, especially in a parson. I've sized it up he needs a lesson."

"I'm with ye, Jap," said Long Bill, and the two rode on their way in silence.

Margaret was so busy and so happy with her school all the week that she quite forgot her annoyance at the minister. She really saw very little of him, for he was always late to breakfast, and she took hers early. She went to her room immediately after supper, and he had little opportunity for pursuing her acquaintance. Perhaps he judged that it would be wise to let her alone until after he had made his grand impression on Sunday, and let her "make up" to him.

It was not until Sunday morning that she suddenly recalled that he was to preach that day. She had indeed seen the notices, for a very large and elaborate one was posted in front of the school-house, and some anonymous artist had produced a fine caricature of the preacher in red clay underneath his name. Margaret had been obliged to remain after school Friday and remove as much of this portrait as she was able, not having been willing to make it a matter of discipline to discover the artist. In fact, it was so true to the model that the young teacher felt a growing sympathy for the one who had perpetrated it.

Margaret started to the school-house early Sunday morning, attended by the faithful Bud. Not that he had any more intention of going to Sunday-school than he had the week before, but it was pleasant to be the chosen escort of so popular a teacher. Even Jed and Timothy had walked home with her twice during the week. He did not intend to lose his place as nearest to her. There was only one to whom he would surrender that, and he was too far away to claim it often.

Margaret had promised to help in the Sunday-school that morning, for the woman who taught the little ones was still away with her sick neighbor, and on the way she persuaded Bud to help her.

"You'll be secretary for me, won't you, William?" she asked, brightly. "I'm going to take the left-front corner of the room for the children, and seat them on the recitation-benches, and that will leave all the back part of the room for the older people. Then I can use the blackboard and not disturb the rest."

"Secretary?" asked the astonished Bud. He was, so to speak, growing accustomed to surprises. "Secretary" did not sound like being "a nice little Sunday-school boy."

"Why, yes! take up the collection, and see who is absent, and so on. I don't know all the names, perhaps, and, anyhow, I don't like to do that when I have to teach!"

Artful Margaret! She had no mind to leave Bud floating around outside the school-house, and though she had ostensibly prepared her lesson and her blackboard illustration for the little children, she had hidden in it a truth for Bud — poor, neglected, devoted Bud!

The inefficient old man who taught the older people that day gathered his forces together and, seated with his back to the platform, his spectacles extended upon his long nose, he proceeded with the questions on the lesson-leaf, as usual, being more than ordinarily unfamiliar with them; but before he was half through he perceived by the long pauses between the questions and answers that he did not have the attention of his class. He turned slowly around to see what they were all looking at, and became so engaged in listening to the lesson the new teacher was drawing on the blackboard that he completely forgot to go on, until Bud, very important in his new position, rang the tiny desk-bell for the close of school, and Margaret, looking up, saw in dismay that she had been teaching the whole school.

While they were singing a closing hymn the room began to fill up, and presently came the minister, walking importantly beside Mr. Tanner, his chin flattened upward as usual, but bent in till it made a double roll over his collar, his eyes rolling importantly, showing much of their whites, his sermon, in an elaborate leather cover, carried conspicuously under his arm, and the severest of clerical coats and collars setting out his insignificant face.

Walking behind him in single file, measured step, just so far apart, came the eight men from the bunk-house — Long Bill, Big Jim, Fiddling Boss, Jasper Kemp, Fade-away Forbes, Stocky, Croaker, and Fudge; and behind them, looking like a scared rabbit, Mom Wallis scuttled into the back seat and sank out of sight. The eight men, however, ranged themselves across the front of the room on the recitation-bench, directly in front of the platform, removing a few small children for that purpose.

They had been lined up in a scowling row along the path as the minister entered, looking at them askance under his aristocratic yellow eyebrows, and as he neared the door the last man followed in his wake, then the next, and so on.

Margaret, in her seat half-way back at the side of the school-house near a window, saw through the trees a wide sombrero over a pair of broad shoulders; but, though she kept close watch, she did not see her friend of the wilderness enter the school-house. If he had really come to meeting, he was staying outside.

The minister was rather nonplussed at first that there were no hymn-books. It almost seemed that he did not know how to go on with divine service without hymn-books, but at last he compromised on the long-meter Doxology, pronounced with deliberate unction. Then, looking about for a possible pipe-organ and choir, he finally started it himself; but it is doubtful whether any one would have recognized the tune enough to help it on if Margaret had not for very shame's sake taken it up and carried it along, and so they came to the prayer and Bible-reading.

These were performed with a formal, perfunctory style calculated to impress the audience with the importance of the preacher rather than the words he was speaking. The audience was very quiet, having the air of reserving judgment for the sermon.

Margaret could not just remember afterward how it was she missed the text. She had turned her eyes away from the minister, because it somehow made her feel homesick to compare him with her dear, dignified father. Her mind had wandered, perhaps, to the sombrero she had glimpsed outside, and she was wondering how its owner was coming on with his resolves, and just what change they would mean in his life, anyway. Then suddenly she awoke to the fact that the sermon had begun.

CHAPTER XV

"Considered in the world of physics," began the lordly tones of the Reverend Frederick, "dynamics is that branch of mechanics that treats of the effects of forces in producing motion, and of the laws of motion thus produced; sometimes called kinetics, opposed to statics. It is the science that treats of the laws of force, whether producing equilibrium or motion; in this sense including both statics and kinetics. It is also applied to the forces producing or governing activity or movement of any kind; also the methods of such activity."

The big words rolled out magnificently over the awed gathering, and the minister flattened his chin and rolled his eyes up at the people in his most impressive way.

Margaret's gaze hastily sought the row of rough men on the front seat, sitting with folded arms in an attitude of attention, each man with a pair of intelligent eyes under his shaggy brows regarding the preacher as they might have regarded an animal in a zoo. Did they understand what had been said? It was impossible to tell from their serious faces.

"Philanthropy has been called the dynamics of Christianity; that is to say, it is Christianity in action," went on the preacher. "It is my purpose this morning to speak upon the dynamics of altruism. Now altruism is the theory that inculcates benevolence to others in subordination to self-interest; interested benevolence as opposed to disinterested; also, the practice of this theory."

He lifted his eyes to the audience once more and nodded his head slightly, as if to emphasize the deep truth he had just given them, and the battery of keen eyes before him never flinched from his face. They were searching him through and through. Margaret wondered if he had no sense of the ridiculous, that he could, to such an audience, pour forth such a string of technical definitions. They sounded strangely like dictionary language. She wondered if anybody present besides herself knew what the man meant or got any inkling of what his subject was. Surely he would drop to simpler language, now that he had laid out his plan.

It never occurred to her that the man was trying to impress *her* with his wonderful fluency of language and his marvelous store of wisdom. On and on he went in much the same trend he had begun, with now and then a flowery sentence or whole paragraph of meaningless eloquence about the "brotherhood of man" — with a roll to the r's in brotherhood.

Fifteen minutes of this profitless oratory those men of the wilderness endured, stolidly and with fixed attention; then, suddenly, a sentence of unusual simplicity struck them and an almost visible thrill went down the front seat.

"For years the church has preached a dead faith, without works, my friends, and the time has come to stop preaching faith! I repeat it — fellow-men. I repeat it. The time has come *to stop preaching faith* and begin to do good works!" He thumped the desk vehemently. "Men don't need a superstitious belief in a Saviour to save them from their sins; they need to go to work and save themselves! As if a man dying two thousand years ago on a cross could do any good to you and me to-day!"

It was then that the thrill passed down that front line, and Long Bill, sitting at their head, leaned slightly forward and looked full and frowning into the face of Jasper Kemp; and the latter, frowning back, solemnly winked one eye. Margaret sat where she could see the whole thing.

Immediately, still with studied gravity, Long Bill cleared his throat impressively, arose, and, giving the minister a full look in the eye, of the nature almost of a challenge, he turned and walked slowly, noisily down the aisle and out the front door.

The minister was visibly annoyed, and for the moment a trifle flustered; but, concluding his remarks had been too deep for the rough creature, he gathered up the thread of his argument and proceeded:

"We need to get to work at our duty toward our fellow-men. We need to down trusts and give the laboring-man a chance. We need to stop insisting that men shall believe in the inspiration of the entire Bible and get to work at something practical!"

The impressive pause after this sentence was interrupted by a sharp, rasping sound of Big Jim clearing his throat and shuffling to his feet. He, too, looked the minister full in the face with a searching gaze, shook his head sadly, and walked leisurely down the aisle and out of the door. The minister paused again and frowned. This was becoming annoying.

Margaret sat in startled wonder. Could it be possible that these rough men were objecting to the sermon from a theological point of view, or was it just a happening that they had gone out at such pointed moments. She sat back after a minute, telling herself that of course the men must just have been weary of the long sentences, which no doubt they could not understand. She began to hope that Gardley was not within hearing. It was not probable that many others understood enough to get harm from the sermon, but her soul boiled with indignation that a man could go forth and call himself a minister of an evangelical church and yet talk such terrible heresy.

Big Jim's steps died slowly away on the clay path outside, and the preacher resumed his discourse.

"We have preached long enough of hell and torment. It is time for a gospel of love to our brothers. Hell is a superstition of the Dark Ages. *There is no hell!*"

Fiddling Boss turned sharply toward Jasper Kemp, as if waiting for a signal, and Jasper gave a slight, almost imperceptible nod. Whereupon Fiddling Boss cleared his throat loudly and arose, faced the minister, and marched down the aisle, while Jasper Kemp remained quietly seated as if nothing had happened, a vacancy each side of him.

By this time the color began to rise in the minister's cheeks. He looked at the retreating back of Fiddling Boss, and then suspiciously down at the row of men, but every one of them sat with folded arms and eyes intent upon the sermon, as if their comrades had not left them. The minister thought he must have been mistaken and took up the broken thread once more, or tried to, but he had hopelessly lost the place in his manuscript, and the only clue that offered was a quotation of a poem about the devil; to be sure, the connection was somewhat abrupt, but he clutched it with his eye gratefully and began reading it dramatically:

> "'Men don't believe in the devil now
> As their fathers used to do —'"

But he had got no further when a whole clearing-house of throats sounded, and Fade-away Forbes stumbled to his feet frantically, bolting down the aisle as if he had been sent for. He had not quite reached the door when Stocky clumped after him, followed at intervals by Croaker and Fudge, and each just as the minister had begun:

"Um! Ah! To resume —"

And now only Jasper Kemp remained of the front-seaters, his fine gray eyes boring through and through the minister as he floundered through the remaining portion of his manuscript up to the point where it began, "And finally — " which opened with another poem:

> "'I need no Christ to die for me.'"

The sturdy, gray-haired Scotchman suddenly lowered his folded arms, slapping a hand resoundingly on each knee, bent his shoulders the better to pull himself to his feet, pressing his weight on his hands till his elbows were akimbo, uttered a deep sigh and a, "Yes — well — *ah!*"

With that he got to his feet and dragged them slowly out of the school-house.

By this time the minister was ready to burst with indignation. Never before in all the bombastic days of his egotism had he been so grossly insulted, and by such rude creatures! And yet there was really nothing that could be said or done. These men appeared to be simple creatures who had wandered in idly, perhaps for a few moments' amusement, and, finding the discourse above their caliber, had innocently wandered out again. That was the way it had been made to appear. But his plans had been cruelly upset by such actions, and he was mortified in the extreme. His face was purple with his emotions, and he struggled and spluttered for a way out of his trying dilemma. At last he spoke, and his voice was absurdly dignified:

"Is there — ah — any other — ah — auditor — ah — who is desirous of withdrawing before the close of service? If so he may do so now, or — ah — " He paused for a suitable ending, and familiar words rushed to his lips without consciousness for the moment of their meaning — "or forever after hold their peace — ah!"

There was a deathly silence in the school-house. No one offered to go out, and Margaret suddenly turned her head and looked out of the window. Her emotions were almost beyond her control.

Thus the closing eloquence proceeded to its finish, and at last the service was over. Margaret looked about for Mom Wallis, but she had disappeared. She signed to Bud, and together they hastened out; but a quiet Sabbath peace reigned about the door of the school-house, and not a man from the camp was in sight; no, nor even the horses upon which they had come.

And yet, when the minister had finished shaking hands with the worshipful women and a few men and children, and came with Mr. Tanner to the door of the school-house, those eight men stood in a solemn row, four on each side of the walk, each holding his chin in his right hand, his right elbow in his left hand, and all eyes on Jasper Kemp, who kept his eyes thoughtfully up in the sky.

"H'w aire yeh, Tanner? Pleasant 'casion. Mind steppin' on a bit? We men wanta have a word with the parson."

Mr. Tanner stepped on hurriedly, and the minister was left standing nonplussed and alone in the doorway of the school-house.

CHAPTER XVI

"Um! Ah!" began the minister, trying to summon his best clerical manner to meet — what? He did not know. It was best to assume they were a penitent band of inquirers for the truth. But the memory of their recent exodus from the service was rather too clearly in his mind for his pleasantest expression to be uppermost toward these rough creatures. Insolent fellows! He ought to give them a good lesson in behavior!

"Um! Ah!" he began again, but found to his surprise that his remarks thus far had had no effect whatever on the eight stolid countenances before him. In fact, they seemed to have grown grim and menacing even in their quiet attitude, and their eyes were fulfilling the promise of the look they had given him when they left the service.

"What does all this mean, anyway?" he burst forth, suddenly.

"Calm yourself, elder! Calm yourself," spoke up Long Bill. "There ain't any occasion to get excited."

"I'm not an elder; I'm a minister of the gospel," exploded West, in his most pompous tones. "I should like to know who you are and what all this means?"

"Yes, parson, we understand who you are. We understand quite well, an' we're agoin' to tell you who we are. We're a band of al-tru-ists! That's what we are. We're *altruists*!" It was Jasper Kemp of the keen eyes and sturdy countenance who spoke. "And we've come here in brotherly love to exercise a little of that dynamic force of altruism you was talkin' about. We just thought we'd begin on you so's you could see that we got some works to go 'long with our faith."

"What do you mean, sir?" said West, looking from one grim countenance to another. "I — I don't quite understand." The minister was beginning to be frightened, he couldn't exactly tell why. He wished he had kept Brother Tanner with him. It was the first time he had ever thought of Mr. Tanner as "brother."

"We mean just this, parson; you been talkin' a lot of lies in there about there bein' no Saviour an' no hell, ner no devil, an' while we ain't much credit to God ourselves, bein' just common men, we know all that stuff you said ain't true about the Bible an' the devil bein' superstitions, an' we thought we better exercise a little of that there altruism you was talkin' about an' teach you better. You see, it's real brotherly kindness, parson. An' now we're goin' to give you a sample of that dynamics you spoke about. Are you ready, boys?"

"All ready," they cried as one man.

There seemed to be no concerted motion, nor was there warning. Swifter than the weaver's shuttle, sudden as the lightning's flash, the minister was caught from where he stood pompously in that doorway, hat in hand, all grandly as he was attired, and hurled from man to man. Across the walk and back; across and back; across and back; until it seemed to him it was a thousand miles all in a minute of time. He had no opportunity to prepare for the onslaught. He jammed his high silk hat, wherewith he had thought to overawe the community, upon his sleek head, and grasped his precious sermon-case to his breast; the sermon, as it well deserved, was flung to the four winds of heaven and fortunately was no more — that is, existing as a whole. The time came when each of those eight men recovered and retained a portion of that learned oration, and Mom Wallis, not quite understanding, pinned up and used as a sort of shrine the portion about doubting the devil; but as a sermon the parts were never assembled on this earth, nor could be, for some of it was ground to powder under eight pairs of ponderous heels. But the minister at that trying moment was too much otherwise engaged to notice that the child of his brain lay scattered on the ground.

Seven times he made the round up and down, up and down that merciless group, tossed like a thistle-down from man to man. And at last, when his breath was gone, when the world had grown black before him, and he felt smaller and more inadequate than he had ever felt in his whole conceited life before, he found himself bound, helplessly bound, and cast ignominiously into a wagon. And it was a strange thing that, though seemingly but five short minutes before the place had been swarming with worshipful admirers thanking him for his sermon, now there did not seem to be a creature within hearing, for he called and cried aloud and roared with his raucous voice until it would seem that all the surrounding States might have heard that cry from Arizona, yet none came to his relief.

They carried him away somewhere, he did not know where; it was a lonely spot and near a water-hole. When he protested and loudly blamed them, threatening all the law in the land upon them, they regarded him as one might a naughty child who needed chastisement, leniently and with sorrow, but also with determination.

They took him down by the water's side and stood him up among them. He began to tremble with fear as he looked from one to another, for he was not a man of courage, and he had heard strange tales of this wild, free land, where every man was a law unto himself. Were they going to drown him then and there? Then up spoke Jasper Kemp:

"Mr. Parson," he said, and his voice was kind but firm; one might almost say there was a hint of humor in it, and there surely was a twinkle in his eye; but the sternness of his lips belied it, and the minister was in no state to appreciate humor — "Mr. Parson, we've brought you here to do you good, an' you oughtn't to complain. This is altruism, an' we're but actin' out what you been preachin'. You're our brother an' we're tryin' to do you good; an' now we're about to show you what a dynamic force we are. You see, Mr. Parson, I was brought up by a good Scotch grandmother, an' I know a lie when I hear it, an' when I hear a man preach error I know it's time to set him straight; so now we're agoin' to set you straight. I don't know where you come from, nor who brang you up, nor what church set you afloat, but I know enough by all my grandmother taught me — even if I hadn't been a-listenin' off and on for two years back to Mr. Brownleigh, our missionary — to know you're a dangerous man to have at large. I'd as soon have a mad dog let loose. Why, what you preach ain't the gospel, an' it ain't the truth, and the time has come for you to know it, an' own it and recant. Recant! That's what they call it. That's what we're here to see 't you do, or we'll know the reason why. That's the *dynamics* of it. See?"

The minister saw. He saw the deep, muddy water-hole. He saw nothing more.

"Folks are all too ready to believe them there things you was gettin' off without havin' 'em *preached* to justify 'em in their evil ways. We gotta think of those poor ignorant brothers of ours that might listen to you. See? That's the *altruism* of it!"

"What do you want me to do?" The wretched man's tone was not merely humble — it was abject. His grand Prince Albert coat was torn in three places; one tail hung down dejectedly over his hip; one sleeve was ripped half-way out. His collar was unbuttoned and the ends rode up hilariously over his cheeks. His necktie was gone. His sleek hair stuck out in damp wisps about his frightened eyes, and his hat had been "stove in" and jammed down as far as it would go until his ample ears stuck out like sails at half-mast. His feet were imbedded in the heavy mud on the margin of the water-hole, and his fine silk socks, which had showed at one time above the erstwhile neat tyings, were torn and covered with mud.

"Well, in the first place," said Jasper Kemp, with a slow wink around at the company, "that little matter about hell needs adjustin'. Hell ain't no superstition. I ain't dictatin' what kind of a hell there is; you can make it fire or water or anything else you like, but *there is a hell*, an' *you believe in it*. D'ye understand? We'd just like to have you make that statement publicly right here an' now."

"But how can I say what I don't believe?" whined West, almost ready to cry. He had come proudly through a trial by Presbytery on these very same points, and had posed as being a man who had the courage of his convictions. He could not thus easily surrender his pride of original thought and broad-mindedness. He had received congratulations from a number of noble martyrs who had left their chosen church for just such reasons, congratulating him on his brave stand. It had been the first notice from big men he had ever been able to attract to himself, and it had gone to his head like wine. Give that up for a few miserable cowboys! It might get into the papers and go back East. He must think of his reputation.

"That's just where the dynamics of the thing comes in, brother," said Jasper Kemp, patronizingly. "We're here to *make* you believe in a hell. We're the force that will bring you back into the right way of thinkin' again. Are you ready, boys?"

The quiet utterance brought goose-flesh up to West's very ears, and his eyes bulged with horror.

"Oh, that isn't necessary! I believe — yes, I believe in hell!" he shouted, as they seized him.

But it was too late. The Rev. Frederick West was plunged into the water-hole, from whose sheep-muddied waters he came up spluttering, "Yes, I believe in *hell!*" and for the first time in his life, perhaps, he really did believe in it, and thought that he was in it.

The men were standing knee-deep in the water and holding their captive lightly by his arms and legs, their eyes upon their leader, waiting now.

Jasper Kemp stood in the water, also, looking down benevolently upon his victim, his chin in his hand, his elbow in his other hand, an attitude which carried a feeling of hopelessness to the frightened minister.

"An' now there's that little matter of the devil," said Jasper Kemp, reflectively. "We'll just fix that up next while we're near his place of residence. You believe in the devil, Mr. Parson, from now on? If you'd ever tried resistin' him I figger you'd have b'lieved in him long ago. But *you believe in him* from *now on,* an' you *don't preach against him any more!* We're not goin' to have our Arizona men gettin' off their guard an' thinkin' their enemy is dead. There *is* a devil, parson, and you believe in him! Duck him, boys!"

Down went the minister into the water again, and came up spluttering, "Yes, I — I — I — believe — in-the — devil." Even in this strait he was loath to surrender his pet theme — no devil.

"Very well, so far as it goes," said Jasper Kemp, thoughtfully. "But now, boys, we're comin' to the most important of all, and you better put him under about three times, for there mustn't be no mistake about this matter. You believe in the Bible, parson — *the whole Bible?*"

"Yes!" gasped West, as he went down the first time and got a mouthful of the bitter water, "I believe — " The voice was fairly anguished. Down he went again. Another mouthful of water. "*I believe in the whole Bible!*" he screamed, and went down the third time. His voice was growing weaker, but he came up and reiterated it without request, and was lifted out upon the mud for a brief respite. The men of the bunk-house were succeeding better than the Presbytery back in the East had been able to do. The conceit was no longer visible in the face of the Reverend Frederick. His teeth were chattering, and he was beginning to see one really needed to believe in something when one came as near to his end as this.

"There's just one more thing to reckon with," said Jasper Kemp, thoughtfully. "That line of talk you was handin' out about a man dyin' on a cross two thousand years ago bein' nothin' to you. You said you *an' me,* but you can speak for *yourself.* We may not be much to look at, but we ain't goin' to stand for no such slander as that. Our missionary preaches all about that Man on the Cross, an' if you don't need Him before you get through this little campaign of life I'll miss my guess. Mebbe we haven't been all we might have been, but we ain't agoin' to let you ner no one else go back on that there Cross!"

Jasper Kemp's tone was tender and solemn. As the minister lay panting upon his back in the mud he was forced to acknowledge that at only two other times in his life had a tone of voice so arrested his attention and filled him with awe; once when as a boy he had been caught copying off another's paper at examination-time, and he had been sent to the principal's office; and again on the occasion of his mother's funeral, as he sat in the dim church a few years ago and listened to the old minister. For a moment now he was impressed with the wonder of the Cross, and it suddenly seemed as if he were being arraigned before the eyes of Him with Whom we all have to do. A kind of shame stole into his pale, flabby face, all the smugness and complacence gone, and he a poor wretch in the hands of his accusers. Jasper Kemp, standing over him on the bank, looking down grimly upon him, seemed like the emissary of God sent to condemn him, and his little, self-centered soul quailed within him.

"Along near the end of that discourse of yours you mentioned that sin was only misplaced energy. Well, if that's so there's a heap of your energy gone astray this mornin', an' the time has come for you to pay up. Speak up now an' say what you believe or whether you want another duckin' — an' it'll be seven times this time!"

The man on the ground shut his eyes and gasped. The silence was very solemn. There seemed no hint of the ridiculous in the situation. It was serious business now to all those men. Their eyes were on their leader.

"Do you solemnly declare before God — I s'pose you still believe in a God, as you didn't say nothin' to the contrary — that from now on you'll stand for that there Cross and for Him that hung on it?"

The minister opened his eyes and looked up into the wide brightness of the sky, as if he half expected to see horses and chariots of fire standing about to do battle with him then and there, and his voice was awed and frightened as he said:

"I do!"

There was silence, and the men stood with half-bowed heads, as if some solemn service were being performed that they did not quite understand, but in which they fully sympathized. Then Jasper Kemp said, softly:

"Amen!" And after a pause: "I ain't any sort of a Christian myself, but I just can't stand it to see a parson floatin' round that don't even know the name of the firm he's workin' for. Now, parson, there's just one more requirement, an' then you can go home."

The minister opened his eyes and looked around with a frightened appeal, but no one moved, and Jasper Kemp went on:

"You say you had a church in New York. What was the name and address of your workin'-boss up there?"

"What do you mean? I hadn't any boss."

"Why, him that hired you an' paid you. The chief elder or whatever you called him."

"Oh!" The minister's tone expressed lack of interest in the subject, but he answered, languidly, "Ezekiel Newbold, Hazelton."

"Very good. Now, parson, you'll just kindly write two copies of a letter to Mr. Ezekiel Newbold statin' what you've just said to us concernin' your change of faith, sign your name, address one to Mr. Newbold, an' give the duplicate to me. We just want this little matter put on record so you can't change your mind any in future. Do you get my idea?"

"Yes," said the minister, dispiritedly.

"Will you do it?"

"Yes," apathetically.

"Well, now I got a piece of advice for you. It would be just as well for your health for you to leave Arizona about as quick as you can find it convenient to pack, but you won't be allowed to leave this town, day or night, cars or afoot, until them there letters are all O.K. Do you get me?"

"Yes," pathetically.

"I might add, by way of explainin', that if you had come to Arizona an' minded your own business you wouldn't have been interfered with. You mighta preached whatever bosh you darned pleased so far as we was concerned, only you wouldn't have had no sorta audience after the first try of that stuff you give to-day. But when you come to Arizona an' put your fingers in other folks' pie, when you tried to 'squeal' on the young gentleman who was keen enough to shoot out the lights to save a man's life, why, we 'ain't no further use for you. In the first place, you was all wrong. You thought the Kid shot out the lights to steal the gamin'-money; but he didn't. He put it all in the hands of the sheriff some hours before your 'private information' reached him through the mail. You thought you were awful sharp, you little sneak! But I wasn't the only man present who saw you put your foot out an' cover a gold piece that rolled on the floor just when the fight began. You thought nobody was a-lookin', but you'll favor us, please, with that identical gold piece along with the letter before you leave. Well, boys, that'll be about all, then. Untie him!"

In silence and with a kind of contemptuous pity in their faces the strong men stooped and unbound him; then, without another word, they left him, tramping solemnly away single file to their horses, standing at a little distance.

Jasper Kemp lingered for a moment, looking down at the wretched man. "Would you care to have us carry you back to the house?" he asked, reflectively.

"No!" said the minister, bitterly. "No!" And without another word Jasper Kemp left him.

Into the mesquite-bushes crept the minister, his glory all departed, and hid his misery from the light, groaning in bitterness of spirit. He who had made the hearts of a score of old ministers to sorrow for Zion, who had split in two a pleasantly united congregation, disrupted a session, and brought about a scandalous trial in Presbytery was at last conquered. The Rev. Frederick West had recanted!

CHAPTER XVII

When Margaret left the school-house with Bud she had walked but a few steps when she remembered Mom Wallis and turned back to search for her; but nowhere could she find a trace of her, and the front of the school-house was as empty of any people from the camp as if they had not been there that morning. The curtain had not yet risen for the scene of the undoing of West.

"I suppose she must have gone home with them," said the girl, wistfully. "I'm sorry not to have spoken with her. She was good to me."

"You mean Mom Wallis?" said the boy. "No, she ain't gone home. She's hiking 'long to our house to see you. The Kid went along of her. See, there — down by those cottonwood-trees? That's them."

Margaret turned with eagerness and hurried along with Bud now. She knew who it was they called the Kid in that tone of voice. It was the way the men had spoken of and to him, a mingling of respect and gentling that showed how much beloved he was. Her cheeks wore a heightened color, and her heart gave a pleasant flutter of interest.

They walked rapidly and caught up with their guests before they had reached the Tanner house, and Margaret had the pleasure of seeing Mom Wallis's face flush with shy delight when she caught her softly round the waist, stealing quietly up behind, and greeted her with a kiss. There had not been many kisses for Mom Wallis in the later years, and the two that were to Margaret Earle's account seemed very sweet to her. Mom Wallis's eyes shone as if she had been a young girl as she turned with a smothered "Oh!" She was a woman not given to expressing herself; indeed, it might be said that the last twenty years of her life had been mainly of self-repression. She gave that one little gasp of recognition and pleasure, and then she relapsed into embarrassed silence beside the two young people who found pleasure in their own greetings. Bud, boy-like, was after a cottontail, along with Cap, who had appeared from no one knew where and was attending the party joyously.

Mom Wallis, in her big, rough shoes, on the heels of which her scant brown calico gown was lifted as she walked, trudged shyly along between the two young people, as carefully watched and helped over the humps and bumps of the way as if she had been a princess. Margaret noticed with a happy approval how Gardley's hand was ready under the old woman's elbow to assist her as politely as he might have done for her own mother had she been walking by his side.

Presently Bud and Cap returned, and Bud, with observant eye, soon timed his step to Margaret's on her other side and touched her elbow lightly to help her over the next rut. This was his second lesson in manners from Gardley. He had his first the Sunday before, watching the two while he and Cap walked behind. Bud was learning. He had keen eyes and an alert brain. Margaret smiled understandingly at him, and his face grew deep red with pleasure.

"He was bringin' me to see where you was livin'," explained Mom Wallis, suddenly, nodding toward Gardley as if he had been a king. "We wasn't hopin' to see you, except mebbe just as you come by goin' in."

"Oh, then I'm so glad I caught up with you in time. I wouldn't have missed you for anything. I went back to look for you. Now you're coming in to dinner with me, both of you," declared Margaret, joyfully. "William, your mother will have enough dinner for us all, won't she?"

"Sure!" said Bud, with that assurance born of his life acquaintance with his mother, who had never failed him in a trying situation so far as things to eat were concerned.

Margaret looked happily from one of her invited guests to the other, and Gardley forgot to answer for himself in watching the brightness of her face, and wondering why it was so different from the faces of all other girls he knew anywhere.

But Mom Wallis was overwhelmed. A wave of red rolled dully up from her withered neck in its gala collar over her leathery face to the roots of her thin, gray hair.

"Me! Stay to dinner! Oh, I couldn't do that nohow! Not in these here clo'es. 'Course I got that pretty collar you give me, but I couldn't never go out to dinner in this old dress an' these shoes. I know what folks ought to look like an' I ain't goin' to shame you."

"Shame me? Nonsense! Your dress is all right, and who is going to see your shoes? Besides, I've just set my heart on it. I want to take you up to my room and show you the pictures of my father and mother and home and the church where I was christened, and everything."

Mom Wallis looked at her with wistful eyes, but still shook her head. "Oh, I'd like to mighty well. It's good of you to ast me. But I couldn't. I just couldn't. 'Sides, I gotta go home an' git the men's grub ready."

"Oh, can't she stay this time, Mr. Gardley?" appealed Margaret. "The men won't mind for once, will they?"

Gardley looked into her true eyes and saw she really meant the invitation. He turned to the withered old woman by his side. "Mom, we're going to stay," he declared, joyously. "She wants us, and we have to do whatever she says. The men will rub along. They all know how to cook. Mom, *we're going to stay*."

"That's beautiful!" declared Margaret. "It's so nice to have some company of my own." Then her face suddenly sobered. "Mr. Wallis won't mind, will he?" And she looked with troubled eyes from one of her guests to the other. She did not want to prepare trouble for poor Mom Wallis when she went back.

Mom Wallis turned startled eyes toward her. There was contempt in her face and outraged womanhood. "Pop's gone off," she said, significantly. "He went yist'day. But he 'ain't got no call t' mind. I ben waitin' on Pop nigh on to twenty year, an' I guess I'm goin' to a dinner-party, now 't I'm invited. Pop 'd better *not* mind, I guess!"

And Margaret suddenly saw how much, how very much, her invitation had been to the starved old soul. Margaret took her guests into the stiff little parlor and slipped out to interview her landlady. She found Mrs. Tanner, as she had expected, a large-minded woman who was quite pleased to have more guests to sit down to her generous dinner, particularly as her delightful boarder had hinted of ample recompense in the way of board money; and she fluttered about, sending Tanner after another jar of pickles, some more apple-butter, and added another pie to the menu.

Well pleased, Margaret left Mrs. Tanner and slipped back to her guests. She found Gardley making arrangements with Bud to run back to the church and tell the men to leave the buckboard for them, as they would not be home for dinner. While this was going on she took Mom Wallis up to her room to remove her bonnet and smooth her hair.

It is doubtful whether Mom Wallis ever did see such a room in her life; for when Margaret swung open the door the poor little woman stopped short on the threshold, abashed, and caught her breath, looking around with wondering eyes and putting out a trembling hand to steady herself against the door-frame. She wasn't quite sure whether things in that room were real, or whether she might not by chance have caught a glimpse into heaven, so beautiful did it seem to her. It was not till her eyes, in the roving, suddenly rested on the great mountain framed in the open window that she felt anchored and sure that this was a tangible place. Then she ventured to step her heavy shoe inside the door. Even then she drew her ugly calico back apologetically, as if it were a desecration to the lovely room.

But Margaret seized her and drew her into the room, placing her gently in the rose-ruffled rocking-chair as if it were a throne and she a queen, and the poor little woman sat entranced, with tears springing to her eyes and trickling down her cheeks.

Perhaps it was an impossibility for Margaret to conceive what the vision of that room meant to Mom Wallis. The realization of all the dreams of a starved soul concentrated into a small space; the actual, tangible proof that there might be a heaven some day — who knew? — since beauties and comforts like these could be real in Arizona.

Margaret brought the pictures of her father and mother, of her dear home and the dear old church. She took her about the room and showed her the various pictures and reminders of her college days, and when she saw that the poor creature was overwhelmed and speechless she turned her about and showed her the great mountain again, like an anchorage for her soul.

Mom Wallis looked at everything speechlessly, gasping as her attention was turned from one object to another, as if she were unable to rise beyond her excitement; but when she saw the mountain again her tongue was loosed, and she turned and looked back at the girl wonderingly.

"Now, ain't it strange! Even that old mounting looks diffrunt — it do look diffrunt from a room like this. Why, it looks like it got its hair combed an' its best collar on!" And Mom Wallis looked down with pride and patted the simple net ruffle about her withered throat. "Why, it looks like a picter painted an' hung up on this yere wall, that's what that mounting looks like! It kinda ain't no mounting any more; it's jest a picter in your room!"

Margaret smiled. "It is a picture, isn't it? Just look at that silver light over the purple place. Isn't it wonderful? I like to think it's mine — my mountain. And yet the beautiful thing about it is that it's just as much yours, too. It will make a picture of itself framed in your bunk-house window if you let it. Try it. You just need to let it."

Mom Wallis looked at her wonderingly. "Do you mean," she said, studying the girl's lovely face, "that ef I should wash them there bunk-house winders, an' string up some posy caliker, an' stuff a chair, an' have a pin-cushion, I could make that there mounting come in an' set fer me like a picter the way it does here fer you?"

"Yes, that's what I mean," said Margaret, softly, marveling how the uncouth woman had caught the thought. "That's exactly what I mean. God's gifts will be as much to us as we will let them, always. Try it and see."

Mom Wallis stood for some minutes looking out reflectively at the mountain. "Wal, mebbe I'll try it!" she said, and turned back to survey the room again.

And now the mirror caught her eye, and she saw herself, a strange self in a soft white collar, and went up to get a nearer view, laying a toil-worn finger on the lace and looking half embarrassed at sight of her own face.

"It's a real purty collar," she said, softly, with a choke in her voice. "It's too purty fer me. I told him so, but he said as how you wanted I should dress up every night fer supper in it. It's 'most as strange as havin' a mounting come an' live with you, to wear a collar like that — me!"

Margaret's eyes were suddenly bright with tears. Who would have suspected Mom Wallis of having poetry in her nature? Then, as if her thoughts anticipated the question in Margaret's mind, Mom Wallis went on:

"He brang me your little book," she said. "I ain't goin' to say thank yeh, it ain't a big-'nuf word. An' he read me the poetry words it says. I got it wropped in a hankercher on the top o' the beam over my bed. I'm goin' to have it buried with me when I die. Oh, I *read* it. I couldn't make much out of it, but I read the words thorough. An' then *he* read 'em — the Kid did. He reads just beautiful. He's got education, he has. He read it, and he talked a lot about it. Was this what you mean? Was it that we ain't really growin' old at all, we're jest goin' on, *gettin'* there, if we go right? Did you mean you think Him as planned it all wanted some old woman right thar in the bunk-house, an' it's *me*? Did you mean there was agoin' to be a chanct fer me to be young an' beautiful somewheres in creation yit, 'fore I git through?"

The old woman had turned around from looking into the mirror and was facing her hostess. Her eyes were very bright; her cheeks had taken on an excited flush, and her knotted hands were clutching the bureau. She looked into Margaret's eyes earnestly, as though her very life depended upon the answer; and Margaret, with a great leap of her heart, smiled and answered:

"Yes, Mrs. Wallis, yes, that is just what I meant. Listen, these are God's own words about it: 'For I reckon that the sufferings of this present time are not worthy to be compared with the glory that shall be revealed in us.'"

A kind of glory shone in the withered old face now. "Did you say them was God's words?" she asked in an awed voice.

"Yes," said Margaret; "they are in the Bible."

"But you couldn't be sure it meant *me*?" she asked, eagerly. "They wouldn't go to put *me* in the Bible, o' course."

"Oh yes, you could be quite sure, Mrs. Wallis," said Margaret, gently. "Because if God was making you and had a plan for you, as the poem says, He would be sure to put down something in His book about it, don't you think? He would want you to know."

"It does sound reasonable-like now, don't it?" said the woman, wistfully. "Say them glory words again, won't you?"

Margaret repeated the text slowly and distinctly.

"Glory!" repeated Mom Wallis, wonderingly. "Glory! Me!" and turned incredulously toward the glass. She looked a long tune wistfully at herself, as if she could not believe it, and pulled reproachfully at the tight hair drawn away from her weather-beaten face. "I useta have purty hair onct," she said, sadly.

"Why, you have pretty hair now!" said Margaret, eagerly. "It just wants a chance to show its beauty, Here, let me fix it for dinner, will you?"

She whisked the bewildered old woman into a chair and began unwinding the hard, tight knot of hair at the back of her head and shaking it out. The hair was thin and gray now, but it showed signs of having been fine and thick once.

"It's easy to keep your hair looking pretty," said the girl, as she worked. "I'm going to give you a little box of my nice sweet-smelling soap-powder that I use to shampoo my hair. You take it home and wash your hair with it every two or three weeks and you'll see it will make a difference in a little while. You just haven't taken time to take care of it, that's all. Do you mind if I wave the front here a little? I'd like to fix your hair the way my mother wears hers."

Now nothing could have been further apart than this little weather-beaten old woman and Margaret's gentle, dove-like mother, with her abundant soft gray hair, her cameo features, and her pretty, gray dresses; but Margaret had a vision of what glory might bring to Mom Wallis, and she wanted to help it along. She believed that heavenly glory can be hastened a good deal on earth if one only tries, and so she set to work. Glancing out the window, she saw with relief that Gardley was talking interestedly with Mr. Tanner and seemed entirely content with their absence.

Mom Wallis hadn't any idea what "waving" her hair meant, but she readily consented to anything this wonderful girl proposed, and she sat entranced, looking at her mountain and thrilling with every touch of Margaret's satin fingers against her leathery old temples. And so, Sunday though it was, Margaret lighted her little alcohol-lamp and heated a tiny curling-iron which she kept for emergencies. In a few minutes' time Mom Wallis's astonished old gray locks lay soft and fluffy about her face, and pinned in a smooth coil behind, instead of the tight knot, making the most wonderful difference in the world in her old, tired face.

"Now look!" said Margaret, and turned her about to the mirror. "If there's anything at all you don't like about it I can change it, you know. You don't have to wear it so if you don't like it."

The old woman looked, and then looked back at Margaret with frightened eyes, and back to the vision in the mirror again.

"My soul!" she exclaimed in an awed voice. "My soul! It's come a'ready! Glory! I didn't think I could look like that! I wonder what Pop 'd say! My land! Would you mind ef I kep' it on a while an' wore it back to camp this way? Pop might uv come home an' I'd like to see ef he'd take notice to it. I used to be purty onct, but I never expected no sech thing like this again on earth. Glory! Glory! Mebbe I *could* get some glory, *too*."

"'The glory that shall be revealed' is a great deal more wonderful than this," said Margaret, gently. "This was here all the time, only you didn't let it come out. Wear it home that way, of course, and wear it so all the time. It's very little trouble, and you'll find your family will like it. Men always like to see a woman looking her best, even when she's working. It helps to make them good. Before you go home I'll show you how to fix it. It's quite simple. Come, now, shall we go down-stairs? We don't want to leave Mr. Gardley alone too long, and, besides, I smell the dinner. I think they'll be waiting for us pretty soon. I'm going to take a few of these pictures down to show Mr. Gardley."

She hastily gathered a few photographs together and led the bewildered little woman downstairs again, and out in the yard, where Gardley was walking up and down now, looking off at the mountain. It came to Margaret, suddenly, that the minister would be returning to the house soon, and she wished he wouldn't come. He would be a false note in the pleasant harmony of the little company. He would be disagreeable to manage, and perhaps hurt poor Mom Wallis's feelings. Perhaps he had already come. She looked furtively around as she came out the door, but no minister was in sight, and then she forgot him utterly in the look of bewildered astonishment with which Gardley was regarding Mom Wallis.

He had stopped short in his walk across the little yard, and was staring at Mom Wallis, recognition gradually growing in his gaze. When he was fully convinced he turned his eyes to Margaret, as if to ask: "How did you do it? Wonderful woman!" and a look of deep reverence for her came over his face.

Then suddenly he noticed the shy embarrassment on the old woman's face, and swiftly came toward her, his hands outstretched, and, taking her bony hands in his, bowed low over them as a courtier might do.

"Mom Wallis, you are beautiful. Did you know it?" he said, gently, and led her to a little stumpy rocking-chair with a gay red-and-blue rag cushion that Mrs. Tanner always kept sitting by the front door in pleasant weather. Then he stood off and surveyed her, while the red stole into her cheeks becomingly. "What has Miss Earle been doing to glorify you?" he asked, again looking at her earnestly.

The old woman looked at him in awed silence. There was that word again — glory! He had said the girl had glorified her. There was then some glory in her, and it had been brought out by so simple a thing as the arrangement of her hair. It frightened her, and tears came and stood in her tired old eyes.

It was well for Mom Wallis's equilibrium that Mr. Tanner came out just then with the paper he had gone after, for the stolidity of her lifetime was about breaking up. But, as he turned, Gardley gave her one of the rarest smiles of sympathy and understanding that a young man can give to an old woman; and Margaret, watching, loved him for it. It seemed to her one of the most beautiful things a young man had ever done.

They had discussed the article in the paper thoroughly, and had looked at the photographs that Margaret had brought down; and Mrs. Tanner had come to the door numberless times, looking out in a troubled way down the road, only to trot back again, look in the oven, peep in the kettle, sigh, and trot out to the door again. At last she came and stood, arms akimbo, and looked down the road once more.

"Pa, I don't just see how I can keep the dinner waitin' a minute longer, The potatoes 'll be sp'iled. I don't see what's keepin' that preacher-man. He musta been invited out, though I don't see why he didn't send me word."

"That's it, likely, Ma," said Tanner. He was growing hungry. "I saw Mis' Bacon talkin' to him. She's likely invited him there. She's always tryin' to get ahead o' you, Ma, you know, 'cause you got the prize fer your marble cake."

Mrs. Tanner blushed and looked down apologetically at her guests. "Well, then, ef you'll just come in and set down, I'll dish up. My land! Ain't that Bud comin' down the road, Pa? He's likely sent word by Bud. I'll hurry in an' dish up."

Bud slid into his seat hurriedly after a brief ablution in the kitchen, and his mother questioned him sharply.

"Bud, wher you be'n? Did the minister get invited out?"

The boy grinned and slowly winked one eye at Gardley. "Yes, he's invited out, all right," he said, meaningly. "You don't need to wait fer him. He won't be home fer some time, I don't reckon."

Gardley looked keenly, steadily, at the boy's dancing eyes, and resolved to have a fuller understanding later, and his own eyes met the boy's in a gleam of mischief and sympathy.

It was the first time in twenty years that Mom Wallis had eaten anything which she had not prepared herself, and now, with fried chicken and company preserves before her, she could scarcely swallow a mouthful. To be seated beside Gardley and waited on like a queen! To be smiled at by the beautiful young girl across the table, and deferred to by Mr. and Mrs. Tanner as "Mrs. Wallis," and asked to have more pickles and another helping of jelly, and did she take cream and sugar in her coffee! It was too much, and Mom Wallis was struggling with the tears. Even Bud's round, blue eyes regarded her with approval and interest. She couldn't help thinking, if her own baby boy had lived, would he ever have been like Bud? And once she smiled at him, and Bud smiled back, a real boy-like, frank, hearty grin. It was all like taking dinner in the Kingdom of Heaven to Mom Wallis, and getting glory aforetime.

It was a wonderful afternoon, and seemed to go on swift wings. Gardley went back to the school-house, where the horses had been left, and Bud went with him to give further particulars about that wink at the dinner-table. Mom Wallis went up to the rose-garlanded room and learned how to wash her hair, and received a roll of flowered scrim wherewith to make curtains for the bunk-house. Margaret had originally intended it for the school-house windows in case it proved necessary to make that place habitable, but the school-room could wait.

And there in the rose-room, with the new curtains in her trembling hands, and the great old mountain in full view, Mom Wallis knelt beside the little gay rocking-chair, while Margaret knelt beside her and prayed that the Heavenly Father would show Mom Wallis how to let the glory be revealed in her now on the earth.

Then Mom Wallis wiped the furtive tears away with her calico sleeve, tied on her funny old bonnet, and rode away with her handsome young escort into the silence of the desert, with the glory beginning to be revealed already in her countenance.

Quite late that evening the minister returned.

He came in slowly and wearily, as if every step were a pain to him, and he avoided the light. His coat was torn and his garments were mud-covered. He murmured of a "slight accident" to Mrs. Tanner, who met him solicitously in a flowered dressing-gown with a candle in her hand. He accepted greedily the half a pie, with cheese and cold chicken and other articles, she proffered on a plate at his door, and in the reply to her query as to where he had been for dinner, and if he had a pleasant time, he said:

"Very pleasant, indeed, thank you! The name? Um — ah — I disremember! I really didn't ask — That is — "

The minister did not get up to breakfast, In fact, he remained in bed for several days, professing to be suffering with an attack of rheumatism. He was solicitously watched over and fed by the anxious Mrs. Tanner, who was much disconcerted at the state of affairs, and couldn't understand why she could not get the school-teacher more interested in the invalid.

On the fourth day, however, the Reverend Frederick crept forth, white and shaken, with his sleek hair elaborately combed to cover a long scratch on his forehead, and announced his intention of departing from the State of Arizona that evening.

He crept forth cautiously to the station as the shades of evening drew on, but found Long Bill awaiting him, and Jasper Kemp not far away. He had the two letters ready in his pocket, with the gold piece, though he had entertained hopes of escaping without forfeiting them, but he was obliged to wait patiently until Jasper Kemp had read both letters through twice, with the train in momentary danger of departing without him, before he was finally allowed to get on board. Jasper Kemp's parting word to him was:

"Watch your steps spry, parson. I'm agoin' to see that you're shadowed wherever you go. You needn't think you can get shy on the Bible again. It won't pay."

There was menace in the dry remark, and the Reverend Frederick's professional egotism withered before it. He bowed his head, climbed on board the train, and vanished from the scene of his recent discomfiture. But the bitterest thing about it all was that he had gone without capturing the heart or even the attention of that haughty little school-teacher. "And she was such a pretty girl," he said, regretfully, to himself. "Such a *very* pretty girl!" He sighed deeply to himself as he watched Arizona speed by the window. "Still," he reflected, comfortably, after a moment, "there are always plenty more! What was that remarkably witty saying I heard just before I left home? 'Never run after a street-car or a woman. There'll be another one along in a minute.' Um — ah — yes — very true — there'll be another one along in a minute."

CHAPTER XVIII

School had settled down to real work by the opening of the new week. Margaret knew her scholars and had gained a personal hold on most of them already. There was enough novelty in her teaching to keep the entire school in a pleasant state of excitement and wonder as to what she would do next, and the word had gone out through all the country round about that the new teacher had taken the school by storm. It was not infrequent for men to turn out of their way on the trail to get a glimpse of the school as they were passing, just to make sure the reports were true. Rumor stated that the teacher was exceedingly pretty; that she would take no nonsense, not even from the big boys; that she never threatened nor punished, but that every one of the boys was her devoted slave. There had been no uprising, and it almost seemed as if that popular excitement was to be omitted this season, and school was to sail along in an orderly and proper manner. In fact, the entire school as well as the surrounding population were eagerly talking about the new piano, which seemed really to be a coming fact. Not that there had been anything done toward it yet, but the teacher had promised that just as soon as every one was really studying hard and doing his best, she was going to begin to get them ready for an entertainment to raise money for that piano. They couldn't begin until everybody was in good working order, because they didn't want to take the interest away from the real business of school; but it was going to be a Shakespeare play, whatever that was, and therefore of grave import. Some people talked learnedly about Shakespeare and hinted of poetry; but the main part of the community spoke the name joyously and familiarly and without awe, as if it were milk and honey in their mouths. Why should they reverence Shakespeare more than any one else?

Margaret had grown used to seeing a head appear suddenly at one of the school-room windows and look long and frowningly first at her, then at the school, and then back to her again, as if it were a nine days' wonder. Whoever the visitor was, he would stand quietly, watching the process of the hour as if he were at a play, and Margaret would turn and smile pleasantly, then go right on with her work. The visitor would generally take off a wide hat and wave it cordially, smile back a curious, softened smile, and by and by he would mount his horse and pass on reflectively down the trail, wishing he could be a boy and go back again to school — such a school!

Oh, it was not all smooth, the way that Margaret walked. There were hitches, and unpleasant days when nothing went right, and when some of the girls got silly and rebellious, and the boys followed in their lead. She had her trials like any teacher, skilful as she was, and not the least of them became Rosa Rogers, the petted beauty, who presently manifested a childish jealousy of her in her influence over the boys. Noting this, Margaret went out of her way to win Rosa, but found it a difficult matter.

Rosa was proud, selfish, and unprincipled. She never forgave any one who frustrated her plans. She resented being made to study like the rest. She had always compelled the teacher to let her do as she pleased and still give her a good report. This she found she could not do with Margaret, and for the first time in her career she was compelled to work or fall behind. It presently became not a question of how the new teacher was to manage the big boys and the bad boys of the Ashland Ridge School, but how she was to prevent Rosa Rogers and a few girls who followed her from upsetting all her plans. The trouble was, Rosa was pretty and knew her power over the boys. If she chose she could put them all in a state of insubordination, and this she chose very often during those first few weeks.

But there was one visitor who did not confine himself to looking in at the window.

One morning a fine black horse came galloping up to the school-house at recess-time, and a well-set-up young man in wide sombrero and jaunty leather trappings sprang off and came into the building. His shining spurs caught the sunlight and flashed as he moved. He walked with the air of one who regards himself of far more importance than all who may be watching him. The boys in the yard stopped their ball-game, and the girls huddled close in whispering groups and drew near to the door. He was a young man from a ranch near the fort some thirty miles away, and he had brought an invitation for the new school-teacher to come over to dinner on Friday evening and stay until the following Monday morning. The invitation was from his sister, the wife of a wealthy cattleman whose home and hospitality were noted for miles around. She had heard of the coming of the beautiful young teacher, and wanted to attach her to her social circle.

The young man was deference itself to Margaret, openly admiring her as he talked, and said the most gracious things to her; and then, while she was answering the note, he smiled over at Rosa Rogers, who had slipped into her seat and was studiously preparing her algebra with the book upside down.

Margaret, looking up, caught Rosa's smiling glance and the tail end of a look from the young man's eyes, and felt a passing wonder whether he had ever met the girl before. Something in the boldness of his look made her feel that he had not. Yet he was all smiles and deference to herself, and his open admiration and pleasure that she was to come to help brighten this lonely country, and that she was going to accept the invitation, was really pleasant to the girl, for it was desolate being tied down to only the Tanner household and the school, and she welcomed any bit of social life.

The young man had light hair, combed very smooth, and light-blue eyes. They were bolder and handsomer than the minister's, but the girl had a feeling that they were the very same cold color. She wondered at her comparison, for she liked the handsome young man, and in spite of herself was a little flattered at the nice things he had said to her. Nevertheless, when she remembered him afterward it was always with that uncomfortable feeling that if he hadn't been so handsome and polished in his appearance he would have seemed just a little bit like that minister, and she couldn't for the life of her tell why.

After he was gone she looked back at Rosa, and there was a narrowing of the girl's eyes and a frown of hate on her brows. Margaret turned with a sigh back to her school problem — what to do with Rosa Rogers?

But Rosa did not stay in the school-house. She slipped out and walked arm in arm with Amanda Bounds down the road.

Margaret went to the door and watched. Presently she saw the rider wheel and come galloping back to the door. He had forgotten to tell her that an escort would be sent to bring her as early on Friday afternoon as she would be ready to leave the school, and he intimated that he hoped he might be detailed for that pleasant duty.

Margaret looked into his face and warmed to his pleasant smile. How could she have thought him like West? He touched his hat and rode away, and a moment later she saw him draw rein beside Rosa and Amanda, and presently dismount.

Bud rang the bell just then, and Margaret went back to her desk with a lingering look at the three figures in the distance. It was full half an hour before Rosa came in, with Amanda looking scared behind her; and troubled Margaret watched the sly look in the girl's eyes and wondered what she ought to do about it. As Rosa was passing out of the door after school she called her to the desk.

"You were late in coming in after recess, Rosa," said Margaret, gently. "Have you any excuse?"

"I was talking to a friend," said Rosa, with a toss of her head which said, as plainly as words could have done, "I don't intend to give an excuse."

"Were you talking to the gentleman who was here?"

"Well, if I was, what is that to you, Miss Earle?" said Rosa, haughtily. "Did you think you could have all the men and boys to yourself?"

"Rosa," said Margaret, trying to speak calmly, but her voice trembling with suppressed indignation, "don't talk that way to me. Child, did you ever meet Mr. Forsythe before?"

"I'm not a child, and it's none of your business!" flouted Rosa, angrily, and she twitched away and flung herself out of the school-house.

Margaret, trembling from the disagreeable encounter, stood at the window and watched the girl going down the road, and felt for the moment that she would rather give up her school and go back home than face the situation. She knew in her heart that this girl, once an enemy, would be a bitter one, and this her last move had been a most unfortunate one, coming out, as it did, with Rosa in the lead. She could, of course, complain to Rosa's family, or to the school-board, but such was not the policy she had chosen. She wanted to be able to settle her own difficulties. It seemed strange that she could not reach this one girl — who was in a way the key to the situation. Perhaps the play would be able to help her. She spent a long time that evening going over the different plays in her library, and finally, with a look of apology toward a little photographed head of Shakespeare, she decided on "Midsummer-Night's Dream." What if it was away above the heads of them all, wouldn't a few get something from it? And wasn't it better to take a great thing and try to make her scholars and a few of the community understand it, rather than to take a silly little play that would not amount to anything in the end? Of course, they couldn't do it well; that went without saying. Of course it would be away beyond them all, but at least it would be a study of something great for her pupils, and she could meantime teach them a little about Shakespeare and perhaps help some of them to learn to love his plays and study them.

The play she had selected was one in which she herself had acted the part of Puck, and she knew it by heart. She felt reasonably sure that she could help some of the more adaptable scholars to interpret their parts, and, at least, it would be good for them just as a study in literature. As for the audience, they would not be critics. Perhaps they would not even be able to comprehend the meaning of the play, but they would come and they would listen, and the experiment was one worth trying.

Carefully she went over the parts, trying to find the one which she thought would best fit Rosa Rogers, and please her as well, because it gave her opportunity to display her beauty and charm. She really was a pretty girl, and would do well. Margaret wondered whether she were altogether right in attempting to win the girl through her vanity, and yet what other weak place was there in which to storm the silly little citadel of her soul?

And so the work of assigning parts and learning them began that very week, though no one was allowed a part until his work for the day had all been handed in.

At noon Margaret made one more attempt with Rosa Rogers. She drew her to a seat beside her and put aside as much as possible her own remembrance of the girl's disagreeable actions and impudent words.

"Rosa," she said, and her voice was very gentle, "I want to have a little talk with you. You seem to feel that you and I are enemies, and I don't want you to have that attitude. I hoped we'd be the best of friends. You see, there isn't any other way for us to work well together. And I want to explain why I spoke to you as I did yesterday. It was not, as you hinted, that I want to keep all my acquaintances to myself. I have no desire to do that. It was because I feel responsible for the girls and boys in my care, and I was troubled lest perhaps you had been foolish — "

Margaret paused. She could see by the bright hardness of the girl's eyes that she was accomplishing nothing. Rosa evidently did not believe her.

"Well, Rosa," she said, suddenly, putting an impulsive, kindly hand on the girl's arm, "suppose we forget it this time, put it all away, and be friends. Let's learn to understand each other if we can, but in the mean time I want to talk to you about the play."

And then, indeed, Rosa's hard manner broke, and she looked up with interest, albeit there was some suspicion in the glance. She wanted to be in that play with all her heart; she wanted the very showiest part in it, too; and she meant to have it, although she had a strong suspicion that the teacher would want to keep that part for herself, whatever it was.

But Margaret had been wise. She had decided to take time and explain the play to her, and then let her choose her own part. She wisely judged that Rosa would do better in the part in which her interest centered, and perhaps the choice would help her to understand her pupil better.

And so for an hour she patiently stayed after school and went over the play, explaining it carefully, and it seemed at one time as though Rosa was about to choose to be Puck, because with quick perception she caught the importance of that character; but when she learned that the costume must be a quiet hood and skirt of green and brown she scorned it, and chose, at last, to be Titania, queen of the fairies. So, with a sigh of relief, and a keen insight into the shallow nature, Margaret began to teach the girl some of the fairy steps, and found her quick and eager to learn. In the first lesson Rosa forgot for a little while her animosity and became almost as one of the other pupils. The play was going to prove a great means of bringing them all together.

Before Friday afternoon came the parts had all been assigned and the plans for the entertainment were well under way.

Jed and Timothy had been as good as their word about giving the teacher riding-lessons, each vying with the other to bring a horse and make her ride at noon hour, and she had already had several good lessons and a long ride or two in company with both her teachers.

The thirty-mile ride for Friday, then, was not such an undertaking as it might otherwise have been, and Margaret looked forward to it with eagerness.

CHAPTER XIX

The little party of escort arrived before school was closed on Friday afternoon, and came down to the school-house in full force to take her away with them. The young man Forsythe, with his sister, the hostess herself, and a young army officer from the fort, comprised the party. Margaret dismissed school ten minutes early and went back with them to the Tanners' to make a hurried change in her dress and pick up her suit-case, which was already packed. As they rode away from the school-house Margaret looked back and saw Rosa Rogers posing in one of her sprite dances in the school-yard, saw her kiss her hand laughingly toward their party, and saw the flutter of a handkerchief in young Forsythe's hand. It was all very general and elusive, a passing bit of fun, but it left an uncomfortable impression on the teacher's mind. She looked keenly at the young man as he rode up smiling beside her, and once more experienced that strange, sudden change of feeling about him.

She took opportunity during that long ride to find out if the young man had known Rosa Rogers before; but he frankly told her that he had just come West to visit his sister, was bored to death because he didn't know a soul in the whole State, and until he had seen her had not laid eyes on one whom he cared to know. Yet while she could not help enjoying the gay badinage, she carried a sense of uneasiness whenever she thought of the young girl Rosa in her pretty fairy pose, with her fluttering pink fingers and her saucy, smiling eyes. There was something untrustworthy, too, in the handsome face of the man beside her.

There was just one shadow over this bit of a holiday. Margaret had a little feeling that possibly some one from the camp might come down on Saturday or Sunday, and she would miss him. Yet nothing had been said about it, and she had no way of sending word that she would be away. She had meant to send Mom Wallis a letter by the next messenger that came that way. It was all written and lying on her bureau, but no one had been down all the week. She was, therefore, greatly pleased when an approaching rider in the distance proved to be Gardley, and with a joyful little greeting she drew rein and hailed him, giving him a message for Mom Wallis.

Only Gardley's eyes told what this meeting was to him. His demeanor was grave and dignified. He acknowledged the introductions to the rest of the party gracefully, touched his hat with the ease of one to the manner born, and rode away, flashing her one gleam of a smile that told her he was glad of the meeting; but throughout the brief interview there had been an air of question and hostility between the two men, Forsythe and Gardley. Forsythe surveyed Gardley rudely, almost insolently, as if his position beside the lady gave him rights beyond the other, and he resented the coming of the stranger. Gardley's gaze was cold, too, as he met the look, and his eyes searched Forsythe's face keenly, as though they would find out what manner of man was riding with his friend.

When he was gone Margaret had the feeling that he was somehow disappointed, and once she turned in the saddle and looked wistfully after him; but he was riding furiously into the distance, sitting his horse as straight as an arrow and already far away upon the desert.

"Your friend is a reckless rider," said Forsythe, with a sneer in his voice that Margaret did not like, as they watched the speck in the distance clear a steep descent from the mesa at a bound and disappear from sight in the mesquite beyond.

"Isn't he fine-looking? Where did you find him, Miss Earle?" asked Mrs. Temple, eagerly. "I wish I'd asked him to join us. He left so suddenly I didn't realize he was going."

Margaret felt a wondering and pleasant sense of possession and pride in Gardley as she watched, but she quietly explained that the young stranger was from the East, and that he was engaged in some kind of cattle business at a distance from Ashland. Her manner was reserved, and the matter dropped. She naturally felt a reluctance to tell how her acquaintance with Gardley began. It seemed something between themselves. She could fancy the gushing Mrs. Temple saying, "How romantic!" She was that kind of a woman. It was evident that she was romantically inclined herself, for she used her fine eyes with effect on the young officer who rode with her, and Margaret found herself wondering what kind of a husband she had and what her mother would think of a woman like this.

There was no denying that the luxury of the ranch was a happy relief from the simplicity of life at the Tanners'. Iced drinks and cushions and easy-chairs, feasting and music and laughter! There were books, too, and magazines, and all the little things that go to make up a cultured life; and yet they were not people of Margaret's world, and when Saturday evening was over she sat alone in the room they had given her and, facing herself in the glass, confessed to herself that she looked back with more pleasure to the Sabbath spent with Mom Wallis than she could look forward to a Sabbath here. The morning proved her forebodings well founded.

Breakfast was a late, informal affair, filled with hilarious gaiety. There was no mention of any church service, and Margaret found it was quite too late to suggest such a thing when breakfast was over, even if she had been sure there was any service.

After breakfast was over there were various forms of amusement proposed for her pleasure, and she really felt very much embarrassed for a few moments to know how to avoid what to her was pure Sabbath-breaking. Yet she did not wish to be rude to these people who were really trying to be kind to her. She managed at last to get them interested in music, and, grouping them around the piano after a few preliminary performances by herself at their earnest solicitation, coaxed them into singing hymns.

After all, they really seemed to enjoy it, though they had to get along with one hymn-book for the whole company; but Margaret knew how to make hymn-singing interesting, and her exquisite voice was never more at its best than when she led off with "My Jesus, as Thou Wilt," or "Jesus, Saviour, Pilot Me."

"You would be the delight of Mr. Brownleigh's heart," said the hostess, gushingly, at last, after Margaret had finished singing "Abide With Me" with wonderful feeling.

"And who is Mr. Brownleigh?" asked Margaret. "Why should I delight his heart?"

"Why, he is our missionary — that is, the missionary for this region — and you would delight his heart because you are so religious and sing so well," said the superficial little woman. "Mr. Brownleigh is really a very cultured man. Of course, he's narrow. All clergymen are narrow, don't you think? They have to be to a certain extent. He's really *quite* narrow. Why, he believes in the Bible *literally*, the whale and Jonah, and the Flood, and making bread out of stones, and all that sort of thing, you know. Imagine it! But he does. He's sincere! Perfectly sincere. I suppose he has to be. It's his business. But sometimes one feels it a pity that he can't relax a little, just among us here, you know. We'd never tell. Why, he won't even play a little game of poker! And he doesn't smoke! *Imagine* it — *not even when he's by himself*, and *no one would know*! Isn't that odd? But he can preach. He's really very interesting; only a little too Utopian in his ideas. He thinks everybody ought to be good, you know, and all that sort of thing. He really thinks it's possible, and he lives that way himself. He really does. But he is a wonderful person; only I feel sorry for his wife sometimes. She's quite a cultured person. Has been wealthy, you know. She was a New York society girl. Just imagine it; out in these wilds taking gruel to the dirty little Indians! How she ever came to do it! Of course she adores him, but I can't really believe she is happy. No woman could be quite blind enough to give up everything in the world for one man, no matter how good he was. Do you think she could? It wasn't as if she didn't have plenty of other chances. She gave them all up to come out and marry him. She's a pretty good sport, too; she never lets you know she isn't perfectly happy."

"She *is* happy; mother, she's happier than *anybody* I ever saw," declared the fourteen-year-old daughter of the house, who was home from boarding-school for a brief visit during an epidemic of measles in the school.

"Oh yes, she manages to make people think she's happy," said her mother, indulgently; "but you can't make me believe she's satisfied to give up her house on Fifth Avenue and live in a two-roomed log cabin in the desert, with no society."

"Mother, you don't know! Why, *any* woman would be satisfied if her husband adored her the way Mr. Brownleigh does her."

"Well, Ada, you're a romantic girl, and Mr. Brownleigh is a handsome man. You've got a few things to learn yet. Mark my words, I don't believe you'll see Mrs. Brownleigh coming back next month with her husband. This operation was all well enough to talk about, but I'll not be surprised to hear that he has come back alone or else that he has accepted a call to some big city church. And he's equal to the city church, too; that's the wonder of it. He comes of a fine family himself, I've heard. Oh, people can't keep up the pose of saints forever, even though they do adore each other. But Mr. Brownleigh *certainly is* a good man!"

The vapid little woman sat looking reflectively out of the window for a whole minute after this deliverance. Yes, certainly Mr. Brownleigh was a good man. He was the one man of culture, education, refinement, who had come her way in many a year who had patiently and persistently and gloriously refused her advances at a mild flirtation, and refused to understand them, yet remained her friend and reverenced hero. He was a good man, and she knew it, for she was a very pretty woman and understood her art well.

Before the day was over Margaret had reason to feel that a Sabbath in Arizona was a very hard thing to find. The singing could not last all day, and her friends seemed to find more amusements on Sunday that did not come into Margaret's code of Sabbath-keeping than one knew how to say no to. Neither could they understand her feeling, and she found it hard not to be rude in gently declining one plan after another.

She drew the children into a wide, cozy corner after dinner and began a Bible story in the guise of a fairy-tale, while the hostess slipped away to take a nap. However, several other guests lingered about, and Mr. Temple strayed in. They sat with newspapers before their faces and got into the story, too, seeming to be deeply interested, so that, after all, Margaret did not have an unprofitable Sabbath.

But altogether, though she had a gay and somewhat frivolous time, a good deal of admiration and many invitations to return as often as possible, Margaret was not sorry when she said good night to know that she was to return in the early morning to her work.

Mr. Temple himself was going part way with them, accompanied by his niece, Forsythe, and the young officer who came over with them. Margaret rode beside Mr. Temple until his way parted from theirs, and had a delightful talk about Arizona. He was a kindly old fellow who adored his frivolous little wife and let her go her own gait, seeming not to mind how much she flirted.

The morning was pink and silver, gold and azure, a wonderful specimen of an Arizona sunrise for Margaret's benefit, and a glorious beginning for her day's work in spite of the extremely early hour. The company was gay and blithe, and the Eastern girl felt as if she were passing through a wonderful experience.

They loitered a little on the way to show Margaret the wonders of a fern-plumed cañon, and it was almost school-time when they came up the street, so that Margaret rode straight to the school-house instead of stopping at Tanners'. On the way to the school they passed a group of girls, of whom Rosa Rogers was the center. A certain something in Rosa's narrowed eyelids as she said good morning caused Margaret to look back uneasily, and she distinctly saw the girl give a signal to young Forsythe, who, for answer, only tipped his hat and gave her a peculiar smile.

In a moment more they had said good-by, and Margaret was left at the school-house door with a cluster of eager children about her, and several shy boys in the background, ready to welcome her back as if she had been gone a month.

In the flutter of opening school Margaret failed to notice that Rosa Rogers did not appear. It was not until the roll was called that she noticed her absence, and she looked uneasily toward the door many times during the morning, but Rosa did not come until after recess, when she stole smilingly in, as if it were quite the thing to come to school late. When questioned about her tardiness she said she had torn her dress and had to go home and change it. Margaret knew by the look in her eyes that the girl was not telling the truth, but what was she to do? It troubled her all the morning and went with her to a sleepless pillow that night. She was beginning to see that life as a school-teacher in the far West was not all she had imagined it to be. Her father had been right. There would likely be more thorns than roses on her way.

CHAPTER XX

The first time Lance Gardley met Rosa Rogers riding with Archie Forsythe he thought little of it. He knew the girl by sight, because he knew her father in a business way. That she was very young and one of Margaret's pupils was all he knew about her. For the young man he had conceived a strong dislike, but as there was no reason whatever for it he put it out of his mind as quickly as possible.

The second time he met them it was toward evening and they were so wholly absorbed in each other's society that they did not see him until he was close upon them. Forsythe looked up with a frown and a quick hand to his hip, where gleamed a weapon.

He scarcely returned the slight salute given by Gardley, and the two young people touched up their horses and were soon out of sight in the mesquite. But something in the frightened look of the girl's eyes caused Gardley to turn and look after the two.

Where could they be going at that hour of the evening? It was not a trail usually chosen for rides. It was lonely and unfrequented, and led out of the way of travelers. Gardley himself had been a far errand for Jasper Kemp, and had taken this short trail back because it cut off several miles and he was weary. Also, he was anxious to stop in Ashland and leave Mom Wallis's request that Margaret would spend the next Sabbath at the camp and see the new curtains. He was thinking what he should say to her when he saw her in a little while now, and this interruption to his thoughts was unwelcome. Nevertheless, he could not get away from that frightened look in the girl's eyes. Where could they have been going? That fellow was a new-comer in the region; perhaps he had lost his way. Perhaps he did not know that the road he was taking the girl led into a region of outlaws, and that the only habitation along the way was a cabin belonging to an old woman of weird reputation, where wild orgies were sometimes celebrated, and where men went who loved darkness rather than light, because their deeds were evil.

Twice Gardley turned in his saddle and scanned the desert. The sky was darkening, and one or two pale stars were impatiently shadowing forth their presence. And now he could see the two riders again. They had come up out of the mesquite to the top of the mesa, and were outlined against the sky sharply. They were still on the trail to old Ouida's cabin!

With a quick jerk Gardley reined in his horse and wheeled about, watching the riders for a moment; and then, setting spurs to his beast, he was off down the trail after them on one of his wild, reckless rides. Down through the mesquite he plunged, through the darkening grove, out, and up to the top of the mesa. He had lost sight of his quarry for the time, but now he could see them again riding more slowly in the valley below, their horses close together, and even as he watched the sky took on its wide night look and the stars blazed forth.

Suddenly Gardley turned sharply from the trail and made a detour through a grove of trees, riding with reckless speed, his head down to escape low branches; and in a minute or two he came with unerring instinct back to the trail some distance ahead of Forsythe and Rosa. Then he wheeled his horse and stopped stock-still, awaiting their coming.

By this time the great full moon was risen and, strangely enough, was at Gardley's back, making a silhouette of man and horse as the two riders came on toward him.

They rode out from the cover of the grove, and there he was across their path. Rosa gave a scream, drawing nearer her companion, and her horse swerved and reared; but Gardley's black stood like an image carved in ebony against the silver of the moon, and Gardley's quiet voice was in strong contrast to the quick, unguarded exclamation of Forsythe, as he sharply drew rein and put his hand hastily to his hip for his weapon.

"I beg your pardon, Mr. Forsythe" — Gardley had an excellent memory for names — "but I thought you might not be aware, being a new-comer in these parts, that the trail you are taking leads to a place where ladies do not like to go."

"Really! You don't say so!" answered the young man, insolently. "It is very kind of you, I'm sure, but you might have saved yourself the trouble. I know perfectly where I am going, and so does the lady, and we choose to go this way. Move out of the way, please. You are detaining us."

But Gardley did not move out of the way. "I am sure the lady does not know where she is going," he said, firmly. "I am sure that she does not know that it is a place of bad reputation, even in this unconventional land. At least, if she knows, I am sure that *her father* does not know, and I am well acquainted with her father."

"Get out of the way, sir," said Forsythe, hotly. "It certainly is none of your business, anyway, whoever knows what. Get out of the way or I shall shoot. This lady and I intend to ride where we please."

"Then I shall have to say you *cannot*," said Gardley; and his voice still had that calm that made his opponent think him easy to conquer.

"Just how do you propose to stop us?" sneered Forsythe, pulling out his pistol.

"This way," said Gardley, lifting a tiny silver whistle to his lips and sending forth a peculiar, shrilling blast. "And this way," went on Gardley, calmly lifting both hands and showing a weapon in each, wherewith he covered the two.

Rosa screamed and covered her face with her hands, cowering in her saddle.

Forsythe lifted his weapon, but looked around nervously. "Dead men tell no tales," he said, angrily.

"It depends upon the man," said Gardley, meaningly, "especially if he were found on this road. I fancy a few tales could be told if you happened to be the man. Turn your horses around at once and take this lady back to her home. My men are not far off, and if you do not wish the whole story to be known among your friends and hers you would better make haste."

Forsythe dropped his weapon and obeyed. He decidedly did not wish his escapade to be known among his friends. There were financial reasons why he did not care to have it come to the ears of his brother-in-law just now.

Silently in the moonlight the little procession took its way down the trail, the girl and the man side by side, their captor close behind, and when the girl summoned courage to glance fearsomely behind her she saw three more men riding like three grim shadows yet behind. They had fallen into the trail so quietly that she had not heard them when they came. They were Jasper Kemp, Long Bill, and Big Jim. They had been out for other purposes, but without question followed the call of the signal.

It was a long ride back to Rogers's ranch, and Forsythe glanced nervously behind now and then. It seemed to him that the company was growing larger all the time. He half expected to see a regiment each time he turned. He tried hurrying his horse, but when he did so the followers were just as close without any seeming effort. He tried to laugh it all off.

Once he turned and tried to placate Gardley with a few shakily jovial words:

"Look here, old fellow, aren't you the man I met on the trail the day Miss Earle went over to the fort? I guess you've made a mistake in your calculations. I was merely out on a pleasure ride with Miss Rogers. We weren't going anywhere in particular, you know. Miss Rogers chose this way, and I wanted to please her. No man likes to have his pleasure interfered with, you know. I guess you didn't recognize me?"

"I recognized you," said Gardley. "It would be well for you to be careful where you ride with ladies, especially at night. The matter, however, is one that you would better settle with Mr. Rogers. My duty will be done when I have put it into his hands."

"Now, my good fellow," said Forsythe, patronizingly, "you surely don't intend to make a great fuss about this and go telling tales to Mr. Rogers about a trifling matter — "

"I intend to do my duty, Mr. Forsythe," said Gardley; and Forsythe noticed that the young man still held his weapons. "I was set this night to guard Mr. Rogers's property. That I did not expect his daughter would be a part of the evening's guarding has nothing to do with the matter. I shall certainly put the matter into Mr. Rogers's hands."

Rosa began to cry softly.

"Well, if you want to be a fool, of course," laughed Forsythe, disagreeably; "but you will soon see Mr. Rogers will accept my explanation."

"That is for Mr. Rogers to decide," answered Gardley, and said no more.

The reflections of Forsythe during the rest of that silent ride were not pleasant, and Rosa's intermittent crying did not tend to make him more comfortable.

The silent procession at last turned in at the great ranch gate and rode up to the house. Just as they stopped and the door of the house swung open, letting out a flood of light, Rosa leaned toward Gardley and whispered:

"Please, Mr. Gardley, don't tell papa. I'll do *anything* in the world for you if you won't tell papa."

He looked at the pretty, pitiful child in the moonlight. "I'm sorry, Miss Rosa," he said, firmly. "But you don't understand. I must do my duty."

"Then I shall hate you!" she hissed. "Do you hear? I shall *hate* you forever, and you don't know what that means. It means I'll take my *revenge* on you and on *everybody you like*."

He looked at her half pityingly as he swung off his horse and went up the steps to meet Mr. Rogers, who had come out and was standing on the top step of the ranch-house in the square of light that flickered from a great fire on the hearth of the wide fireplace. He was looking from one to another of the silent group, and as his eyes rested on his daughter he said, sternly:

"Why, Rosa, what does this mean? You told me you were going to bed with a headache!"

Gardley drew his employer aside and told what had happened in a few low-toned sentences; and then stepped down and back into the shadow, his horse by his side, the three men from the camp grouped behind him. He had the delicacy to withdraw after his duty was done.

Mr. Rogers, his face stern with sudden anger and alarm, stepped down and stood beside his daughter. "Rosa, you may get down and go into the house to your own room. I will talk with you later," he said. And then to the young man, "You, sir, will step into my office. I wish to have a plain talk with you."

A half-hour later Forsythe came out of the Rogers house and mounted his horse, while Mr. Rogers stood silently and watched him.

"I will bid you good evening, sir," he said, formally, as the young man mounted his horse and silently rode away. His back had a defiant look in the moonlight as he passed the group of men in the shadow; but they did not turn to watch him.

"That will be all to-night, Gardley, and I thank you very much," called the clear voice of Mr. Rogers from his front steps.

The four men mounted their horses silently and rode down a little distance behind the young man, who wondered in his heart just how much or how little Gardley had told Rosa's father.

The interview to which young Forsythe had just been subjected had been chastening in character, of a kind to baffle curiosity concerning the father's knowledge of details, and to discourage any further romantic rides with Miss Rosa. It had been left in abeyance whether or not the Temples should be made acquainted with the episode, dependent upon the future conduct of both young people. It had not been satisfactory from Forsythe's point of view; that is, he had not been so easily able to disabuse the father's mind of suspicion, nor to establish his own guileless character as he had hoped; and some of the remarks Rogers made led Forsythe to think that the father understood just how unpleasant it might become for him if his brother-in-law found out about the escapade.

This is why Archie Forsythe feared Lance Gardley, although there was nothing in the least triumphant about the set of that young man's shoulders as he rode away in the moonlight on the trail toward Ashland. And this is how it came about that Rosa Rogers hated Lance Gardley, handsome and daring though he was; and because of him hated her teacher, Margaret Earle.

An hour later Lance Gardley stood in the little dim Tanner parlor, talking to Margaret.

"You look tired," said the girl, compassionately, as she saw the haggard shadows on the young face, showing in spite of the light of pleasure in his eyes. "You look *very* tired. What in the world have you been doing?"

"I went out to catch cattle-thieves," he said, with a sigh, "but I found there were other kinds of thieves abroad. It's all in the day's work. I'm not tired now." And he smiled at her with beautiful reverence.

Margaret, as she watched him, could not help thinking that the lines in his face had softened and strengthened since she had first seen him, and her eyes let him know that she was glad he had come.

"And so you will really come to us, and it isn't going to be asking too much?" he said, wistfully. "You can't think what it's going to be to the men — to *us*! And Mom Wallis is so excited she can hardly get her work done. If you had said no I would be almost afraid to go back." He laughed, but she could see there was deep earnestness under his tone.

"Indeed I will come," said Margaret. "I'm just looking forward to it. I'm going to bring Mom Wallis a new bonnet like one I made for mother; and I'm going to teach her how to make corn gems and steamed apple dumplings. I'm bringing some songs and some music for the violin; and I've got something for you to help me do, too, if you will?"

He smiled tenderly down on her. What a wonderful girl she was, to be willing to come out to the old shack among a lot of rough men and one uncultured old woman and make them happy, when she was fit for the finest in the land!

"You're *wonderful*!" he said, taking her hand with a quick pressure for good-by. "You make every one want to do his best."

He hurried out to his horse and rode away in the moonlight. Margaret went up to her "mountain window" and watched him far out on the trail, her heart swelling with an unnamed gladness over his last words.

"Oh, God, keep him, and help him to make good!" she prayed.

CHAPTER XXI

The visit to the camp was a time to be remembered long by all the inhabitants of the bunk-house, and even by Margaret herself. Margaret wondered Friday evening, as she sat up late, working away braiding a lovely gray bonnet out of folds of malines, and fashioning it into form for Mom Wallis, why she was looking forward to the visit with so much more real pleasure than she had done to the one the week before at the Temples'. And so subtle is the heart of a maid that she never fathomed the real reason.

The Temples', of course, was interesting and delightful as being something utterly new in her experience. It was comparatively luxurious, and there were pleasant, cultured people there, more from her own social class in life. But it was going to be such fun to surprise Mom Wallis with that bonnet and see her old face light up when she saw herself in the little folding three-leaved mirror she was taking along with her and meant to leave for Mom Wallis's log boudoir. She was quite excited over selecting some little thing for each one of the men — books, pictures, a piece of music, a bright cushion, and a pile of picture magazines. It made a big bundle when she had them together, and she was dubious if she ought to try to carry them all; but Bud, whom she consulted on the subject, said, loftily, it "wasn't a flea-bite for the Kid; he could carry anything on a horse."

Bud was just a little jealous to have his beloved teacher away from home so much, and rejoiced greatly when Gardley, Friday afternoon, suggested that he come along, too. He made quick time to his home, and secured a hasty permission and wardrobe, appearing like a footman on his father's old horse when they were half a mile down the trail.

Mom Wallis was out at the door to greet her guest when she arrived, for Margaret had chosen to make her visit last from Friday afternoon after school, until Monday morning. It was the generosity of her nature that she gave to her utmost when she gave.

The one fear she had entertained about coming had been set at rest on the way when Gardley told her that Pop Wallis was off on one of his long trips, selling cattle, and would probably not return for a week. Margaret, much as she trusted Gardley and the men, could not help dreading to meet Pop Wallis again.

There was a new trimness about the old bunk-house. The clearing had been cleaned up and made neat, the grass cut, some vines set out and trained up limply about the door, and the windows shone with Mom Wallis's washing.

Mom Wallis herself was wearing her best white apron, stiff with starch, her lace collar, and her hair in her best imitation of the way Margaret had fixed it, although it must be confessed she hadn't quite caught the knack of arrangement yet. But the one great difference Margaret noticed in the old woman was the illuminating smile on her face. Mom Wallis had learned how to let the glory gleam through all the hard sordidness of her life, and make earth brighter for those about her.

The curtains certainly made a great difference in the looks of the bunk-house, together with a few other changes. The men had made some chairs — three of them, one out of a barrel; and together they had upholstered them roughly. The cots around the walls were blazing with their red blankets folded smoothly and neatly over them, and on the floor in front of the hearth, which had been scrubbed, Gardley had spread a Navajo blanket he had bought of an Indian.

The fireplace was piled with logs ready for the lighting at night, and from somewhere a lamp had been rigged up and polished till it shone in the setting sun that slanted long rays in at the shining windows.

The men were washed and combed, and had been huddled at the back of the bunk-house for an hour, watching the road, and now they came forward awkwardly to greet their guest, their horny hands scrubbed to an unbelievable whiteness. They did not say much, but they looked their pleasure, and Margaret greeted every one as if he were an old friend, the charming part about it all to the men being that she remembered every one's name and used it.

Bud hovered in the background and watched with starry eyes. Bud was having the time of his life. He preferred the teacher's visiting the camp rather than the fort. The "Howdy, sonny!" which he had received from the men, and the "Make yourself at home, Bill" from Gardley, had given him great joy; and the whole thing seemed somehow to link him to the teacher in a most distinguishing manner.

Supper was ready almost immediately, and Mom Wallis had done her best to make it appetizing. There was a lamb stew with potatoes, and fresh corn bread with coffee. The men ate with relish, and watched their guest of honor as if she had been an angel come down to abide with them for a season. There was a tablecloth on the old table, too — a *white* tablecloth. It looked remarkably like an old sheet, to be sure, with a seam through the middle where it had been worn and turned and sewed together; but it was a tablecloth now, and a marvel to the men. And the wonder about Margaret was that she could eat at such a table and make it seem as though that tablecloth were the finest damask, and the two-tined forks the heaviest of silver.

After the supper was cleared away and the lamp lighted, the gifts were brought out. A book of Scotch poetry for Jasper Kemp, bound in tartan covers of the Campbell clan; a small illustrated pamphlet of Niagara Falls for Big Jim, because he had said he wanted to see the place and never could manage it; a little pictured folder of Washington City for Big Jim; a book of old ballad music for Fiddling Boss; a book of jokes for Fade-away Forbes; a framed picture of a beautiful shepherd dog for Stocky; a big, red, ruffled denim pillow for Croaker, because when she was there before he was always complaining about the seats being hard; a great blazing crimson pennant bearing the name HARVARD in big letters for Fudge, because she had remembered he was from Boston; and for Mom Wallis a framed text beautifully painted in water-colors, done in rustic letters twined with stray forget-me-nots, the words, "Come unto Me, all ye that labor and are heavy laden, and I will give you rest." Margaret had made that during the week and framed it in a simple raffia braid of brown and green.

It was marvelous how these men liked their presents; and while they were examining them and laughing about them and putting their pictures and Mom Wallis's text on the walls, and the pillow on a bunk, and the pennant over the fireplace, Margaret shyly held out a tiny box to Gardley.

"I thought perhaps you would let me give you this," she said. "It isn't much; it isn't even new, and it has some marks in it; but I thought it might help with your new undertaking."

Gardley took it with a lighting of his face and opened the box. In it was a little, soft, leather-bound Testament, showing the marks of usage, yet not worn. It was a tiny thing, very thin, easily fitting in a vest-pocket, and not a burden to carry. He took the little book in his hand, removed the silken rubber band that bound it, and turned the leaves reverently in his fingers, noting that there were pencil-marks here and there. His face was all emotion as he looked up at the giver.

"I thank you," he said, in a low tone, glancing about to see that no one was noticing them. "I shall prize it greatly. It surely will help. I will read it every day. Was that what you wanted? And I will carry it with me always."

His voice was very earnest, and he looked at her as though she had given him a fortune. With another glance about at the preoccupied room — even Bud was busy studying Jasper Kemp's oldest gun — he snapped the band on the book again and put it carefully in his inner breast-pocket. The book would henceforth travel next his heart and be his guide. She thought he meant her to understand that, as he put out his hand unobtrusively and pressed her fingers gently with a quick, low "Thank you!"

Then Mom Wallis's bonnet was brought out and tied on her, and the poor old woman blushed like a girl when she stood with meek hands folded at her waist and looked primly about on the family for their approval at Margaret's request. But that was nothing to the way she stared when Margaret got out the threefold mirror and showed her herself in the new headgear. She trotted away at last, the wonderful bonnet in one hand, the box in the other, a look of awe on her face, and Margaret heard her murmur as she put it away: "Glory! *Me!* Glory!"

Then Margaret had to read one or two of the poems for Jasper Kemp, while they all sat and listened to her Scotch and marveled at her. A woman like that condescending to come to visit them!

She gave a lesson in note-reading to the Fiddling Boss, pointing one by one with her white fingers to the notes until he was able to creep along and pick out "Suwanee River" and "Old Folks at Home" to the intense delight of the audience.

Margaret never knew just how it was that she came to be telling the men a story, one she had read not long before in a magazine, a story with a thrilling national interest and a keen personal touch that searched the hearts of men; but they listened as they had never listened to anything in their lives before.

And then there was singing, more singing, until it bade fair to be morning before they slept, and the little teacher was weary indeed when she lay down on the cot in Mom Wallis's room, after having knelt beside the old woman and prayed.

The next day there was a wonderful ride with Gardley and Bud to the cañon of the cave-dwellers, and a coming home to the apple dumplings she had taught Mom Wallis to make before she went away. All day Gardley and she, with Bud for delighted audience, had talked over the play she was getting up at the school, Gardley suggesting about costumes and tree boughs for scenery, and promising to help in any way she wanted. Then after supper there were jokes and songs around the big fire, and some popcorn one of the men had gone a long ride that day to get. They called for another story, too, and it was forthcoming.

It was Sunday morning after breakfast, however, that Margaret suddenly wondered how she was going to make the day helpful and different from the other days.

She stood for a moment looking out of the clear little window thoughtfully, with just the shadow of a sigh on her lips, and as she turned back to the room she met Gardley's questioning glance.

"Are you homesick?" he asked, with a sorry smile. "This must all be very different from what you are accustomed to."

"Oh no, it isn't that." She smiled, brightly. "I'm not a baby for home, but I do get a bit homesick about church-time. Sunday is such a strange day to me without a service."

"Why not have one, then?" he suggested, eagerly. "We can sing and — you could — do the rest!"

Her eyes lighted at the suggestion, and she cast a quick glance at the men. Would they stand for that sort of thing?

Gardley followed her glance and caught her meaning. "Let them answer for themselves," he said quickly in a low tone, and then, raising his voice: "Speak up, men. Do you want to have church? Miss Earle here is homesick for a service, and I suggest that we have one, and she conduct it."

"Sure!" said Jasper Kemp, his face lighting. "I'll miss my guess if she can't do better than the parson we had last Sunday. Get into your seats, boys; we're goin' to church."

Margaret's face was a study of embarrassment and delight as she saw the alacrity with which the men moved to get ready for "church." Her quick brain turned over the possibility of what she could read or say to help this strange congregation thus suddenly thrust upon her.

It was a testimony to her upbringing by a father whose great business of life was to preach the gospel that she never thought once of hesitating or declining the opportunity, but welcomed it as an opportunity, and only deprecated her unreadiness for the work.

The men stirred about, donned their coats, furtively brushing their hair, and Long Bill insisted that Mom Wallis put on her new bonnet; which she obligingly did, and sat down carefully in the barrel-chair, her hands neatly crossed in her lap, supremely happy. It really was wonderful what a difference that bonnet made in Mom Wallis.

Gardley arranged a comfortable seat for Margaret at the table and put in front of her one of the hymn-books she had brought. Then, after she was seated, he took the chair beside her and brought out the little Testament from his breast-pocket, gravely laying it on the hymn-book.

Margaret met his eyes with a look of quick appreciation. It was wonderful the way these two were growing to understand each other. It gave the girl a thrill of wonder and delight to have him do this simple little thing for her, and the smile that passed between them was beautiful to see. Long Bill turned away his head and looked out of the window with an improvised sneeze to excuse the sudden mist that came into his eyes.

Margaret chose "My Faith looks up to Thee" for the first hymn, because Fiddling Boss could play it, and while he was tuning up his fiddle she hastily wrote out two more copies of the words. And so the queer service started with a quaver of the old fiddle and the clear, sweet voices of Margaret and Gardley leading off, while the men growled on their way behind, and Mom Wallis, in her new gray bonnet, with her hair all fluffed softly gray under it, sat with eyes shining like a girl's.

So absorbed in the song were they all that they failed to hear the sound of a horse coming into the clearing. But just as the last words of the final verse died away the door of the bunk-house swung open, and there in the doorway stood Pop Wallis!

The men sprang to their feet with one accord, ominous frowns on their brows, and poor old Mom Wallis sat petrified where she was, the smile of relaxation frozen on her face, a look of fear growing in her tired old eyes.

Now Pop Wallis, through an unusual combination of circumstances, had been for some hours without liquor and was comparatively sober. He stood for a moment staring amazedly at the group around his fireside. Perhaps because he had been so long without his usual stimulant his mind was weakened and things appeared as a strange vision to him. At any rate, he stood and stared, and as he looked from one to another of the men, at the beautiful stranger, and across to the strangely unfamiliar face of his wife in her new bonnet, his eyes took on a frightened look. He slowly took his hand from the door-frame and passed it over his eyes, then looked again, from one to another, and back to his glorified wife.

Margaret had half risen at her end of the table, and Gardley stood beside her as if to reassure her; but Pop Wallis was not looking at any of them any more. His eyes were on his wife. He passed his hand once more over his eyes and took one step gropingly into the room, a hand reached out in front of him, as if he were not sure but he might run into something on the way, the other hand on his forehead, a dazed look in his face.

"Why, Mom — that ain't really — *you*, now, *is* it?" he said, in a gentle, insinuating voice like one long unaccustomed making a hasty prayer.

The tone made a swift change in the old woman. She gripped her bony hands tight and a look of beatific joy came into her wrinkled face.

"Yes, it's really *me*, Pop!" she said, with a kind of triumphant ring to her voice.

"But — but — you're right *here*, ain't you? You ain't *dead*, an' — an' — gone to — gl-oo-ry, be you? You're right *here*?"

"Yes, I'm right *here*, Pop. I ain't dead! Pop — glory's *come to me!*"

"Glory?" repeated the man, dazedly. "Glory?" And he gazed around the room and took in the new curtains, the pictures on the wall, the cushions and chairs, and the bright, shining windows. "You don't mean it's *heav'n*, do you, Mom? 'Cause I better go back — *I* don't belong in heav'n. Why, Mom, it can't be glory, 'cause it's the same old bunk-house outside, anyhow."

"Yes, it's the same old bunk-house, and it ain't heaven, but it's *goin'* to be. The glory's come all right. You sit down, Pop; we're goin' to have church, and this is my new bonnet. *She* brang it. This is the new school-teacher, Miss Earle, and she's goin' to have church. She done it *all!* You sit down and listen."

Pop Wallis took a few hesitating steps into the room and dropped into the nearest chair. He looked at Margaret as if she might be an angel holding open the portal to a kingdom in the sky. He looked and wondered and admired, and then he looked back to his glorified old wife again in wonder.

Jasper Kemp shut the door, and the company dropped back into their places. Margaret, because of her deep embarrassment, and a kind of inward trembling that had taken possession of her, announced another hymn.

It was a solemn little service, quite unique, with a brief, simple prayer and an expository reading of the story of the blind man from the sixth chapter of John. The men sat attentively, their eyes upon her face as she read; but Pop Wallis sat staring at his wife, an awed light upon his scared old face, the wickedness and cunning all faded out, and only fear and wonder written there.

In the early dawning of the pink-and-silver morning Margaret went back to her work, Gardley riding by her side, and Bud riding at a discreet distance behind, now and then going off at a tangent after a stray cottontail. It was wonderful what good sense Bud seemed to have on occasion.

The horse that Margaret rode, a sturdy little Western pony, with nerve and grit and a gentle common sense for humans, was to remain with her in Ashland, a gift from the men of the bunk-house. During the week that followed Archie Forsythe came riding over with a beautiful shining saddle-horse for her use during her stay in the West; but when he went riding back to the ranch the shining saddle-horse was still in his train, riderless, for Margaret told him that she already had a horse of her own. Neither had Margaret accepted the invitation to the Temples' for the next week-end. She had other plans for the Sabbath, and that week there appeared on all the trees and posts about the town, and on the trails, a little notice of a Bible class and vesper-service to be held in the school-house on the following Sabbath afternoon; and so Margaret, true daughter of her minister-father, took up her mission in Ashland for the Sabbaths that were to follow; for the school-board had agreed with alacrity to such use of the school-house.

CHAPTER XXII

Now when it became noised abroad that the new teacher wanted above all things to purchase a piano, and that to that end she was getting up a wonderful Shakespeare play in which the scholars were to act upon a stage set with tree boughs after the manner of some new kind of players, the whole community round about began to be excited.

Mrs. Tanner talked much about it. Was not Bud to be a prominent character? Mr. Tanner talked about it everywhere he went. The mothers and fathers and sisters talked about it, and the work of preparing the play went on.

Margaret had discovered that one of the men at the bunk-house played a flute, and she was working hard to teach him and Fiddling Boss and Croaker to play a portion of the elfin dance to accompany the players. The work of making costumes and training the actors became more and more strenuous, and in this Gardley proved a fine assistant. He undertook to train some of the older boys for their parts, and did it so well that he was presently in the forefront of the battle of preparation and working almost as hard as Margaret herself.

The beauty of the whole thing was that every boy in the school adored him, even Jed and Timothy, and life took on a different aspect to them in company with this high-born college-bred, Eastern young man who yet could ride and shoot with the daringest among the Westerners.

Far and wide went forth the fame of the play that was to be. The news of it reached to the fort and the ranches, and brought offers of assistance and costumes and orders for tickets. Margaret purchased a small duplicator and set her school to printing tickets and selling them, and before the play was half ready to be acted tickets enough were sold for two performances, and people were planning to come from fifty miles around. The young teacher began to quake at the thought of her big audience and her poor little amateur players; and yet for children they were doing wonderfully well, and were growing quite Shakespearian in their manner of conversation.

"What say you, sweet Amanda?" would be a form of frequent address to that stolid maiden Amanda Bounds; and Jed, instead of shouting for "Delicate" at recess, as in former times, would say, "My good Timothy, I swear to thee by Cupid's strongest bow; by his best arrow with the golden head" — until all the school-yard rang with classic phrases; and the whole country round was being addressed in phrases of another century by the younger members of their households.

Then Rosa Rogers's father one day stopped at the Tanners' and left a contribution with the teacher of fifty dollars toward the new piano; and after that it was rumored that the teacher said the piano could be sent for in time to be used at the play. Then other contributions of smaller amounts came in, and before the date of the play had been set there was money enough to make a first payment on the piano. That day the English exercise for the whole school was to compose the letter to the Eastern piano firm where the piano was to be purchased, ordering it to be sent on at once. Weeks before this Margaret had sent for a number of piano catalogues beautifully illustrated, showing by cuts how the whole instruments were made, with full illustrations of the factories where they were manufactured, and she had discussed the selection with the scholars, showing them what points were to be considered in selecting a good piano. At last the order was sent out, the actual selection itself to be made by a musical friend of Margaret's in New York, and the school waited in anxious suspense to hear that it had started on its way.

The piano arrived at last, three weeks before the time set for the play, which was coming on finely now and seemed to the eager scholars quite ready for public performance. Not so to Margaret and Gardley, as daily they pruned, trained, and patiently went over and over again each part, drawing all the while nearer to the ideal they had set. It could not be done perfectly, of course, and when they had done all they could there would yet be many crudities; but Margaret's hope was to bring out the meaning of the play and give both audience and performers the true idea of what Shakespeare meant when he wrote it.

The arrival of the piano was naturally a great event in the school. For three days in succession the entire school marched in procession down to the incoming Eastern train to see if their expected treasure had arrived, and when at last it was lifted from the freight-car and set upon the station platform the school stood awe-struck and silent, with half-bowed heads and bated breath, as though at the arrival of some great and honorable guest.

They attended it on the roadside as it was carted by the biggest wagon in town to the school-house door; they stood in silent rows while the great box was peeled off and the instrument taken out and carried into the school-room; then they filed in soulfully and took their accustomed seats without being told, touching shyly the shining case as they passed. By common consent they waited to hear its voice for the first time. Margaret took the little key from the envelope tied to the frame, unlocked the cover, and, sitting down, began to play. The rough men who had brought it stood in awesome adoration around the platform; the silence that spread over that room would have done honor to Paderewski or Josef Hoffman.

Margaret played and played, and they could not hear enough. They would have stayed all night listening, perhaps, so wonderful was it to them. And then the teacher called each one and let him or her touch a few chords, just to say they had played on it. After which she locked the instrument and sent them all home. That was the only afternoon during that term that the play was forgotten for a while.

After the arrival of the piano the play went forward with great strides, for now Margaret accompanied some of the parts with the music, and the flute and violin were also practised in their elfin dance with much better effect. It was about this time that Archie Forsythe discovered the rehearsals and offered his assistance, and, although it was declined, he frequently managed to ride over about rehearsal time, finding ways to make himself useful in spite of Margaret's polite refusals. Margaret always felt annoyed when he came, because Rosa Rogers instantly became another creature on his arrival, and because Gardley simply froze into a polite statue, never speaking except when spoken to. As for Forsythe, his attitude toward Gardley was that of a contemptuous master toward a slave, and yet he took care to cover it always with a form of courtesy, so that Margaret could say or do nothing to show her displeasure, except to be grave and dignified. At such times Rosa Rogers's eyes would be upon her with a gleam of hatred, and the teacher felt that the scholar was taking advantage of the situation. Altogether it was a trying time for Margaret when Forsythe came to the school-house. Also, he discovered to them that he played the violin, and offered to assist in the orchestral parts. Margaret really could think of no reason to decline this offer, but she was sadly upset by the whole thing. His manner to her was too pronounced, and she felt continually uncomfortable under it, what with Rosa Rogers's jealous eyes upon her and Gardley's eyes turned haughtily away.

She planned a number of special rehearsals in the evenings, when it was difficult for Forsythe to get there, and managed in this way to avoid his presence; but the whole matter became a source of much vexation, and Margaret even shed a few tears wearily into her pillow one night when things had gone particularly hard and Forsythe had hurt the feelings of Fiddling Boss with his insolent directions about playing. She could not say or do anything much in the matter, because the Temples had been very kind in helping to get the piano, and Mr. Temple seemed to think he was doing the greatest possible kindness to her in letting Forsythe off duty so much to help with the play. The matter became more and more of a distress to Margaret, and the Sabbath was the only day of real delight.

The first Sunday after the arrival of the piano was a great day. Everybody in the neighborhood turned out to the Sunday-afternoon class and vesper service, which had been growing more and more in popularity, until now the school-room was crowded. Every man from the bunk-house came regularly, often including Pop Wallis, who had not yet recovered fully from the effect of his wife's new bonnet and fluffy arrangement of hair, but treated her like a lady visitor and deferred to her absolutely when he was at home. He wasn't quite sure even yet but he had strayed by mistake into the outermost courts of heaven and ought to get shooed out. He always looked at the rose-wreathed curtains with a mingling of pride and awe.

Margaret had put several hymns on the blackboard in clear, bold printing, and the singing that day was wonderful. Not the least part of the service was her own playing over of the hymns before the singing began, which was listened to with reverence as if it had been the music of an angel playing on a heavenly harp.

Gardley always came to the Sunday services, and helped her with the singing, and often they two sang duets together.

The service was not always of set form. Usually Margaret taught a short Bible lesson, beginning with the general outline of the Bible, its books, their form, substance, authors, etc. — all very brief and exceedingly simple, putting a wide space of music between this and the vesper service, into which she wove songs, bits of poems, passages from the Bible, and often a story which she told dramatically, illustrating the scripture read.

But the very Sunday before the play, just the time Margaret had looked forward to as being her rest from all the perplexities of the week, a company from the fort, including the Temples, arrived at the school-house right in the midst of the Bible lesson.

The ladies were daintily dressed, and settled their frills and ribbons amusedly as they watched the embarrassed young teacher trying to forget that there was company present. They were in a distinct sense "company," for they had the air, as they entered, of having come to look on and be amused, not to partake in the worship with the rest.

Margaret found herself trembling inwardly as she saw the supercilious smile on the lips of Mrs. Temple and the amused stares of the other ladies of the party. They did not take any notice of the other people present any more than if they had been so many puppets set up to show off the teacher; their air of superiority was offensive. Not until Rosa Rogers entered with her father, a little later, did they condescend to bow in recognition, and then with that pretty little atmosphere as if they would say, "Oh, you've come, too, to be amused."

Gardley was sitting up in front, listening to her talk, and she thought he had not noticed the strangers. Suddenly it came to her to try to keep her nerve and let him see that they were nothing to her; and with a strong effort and a swift prayer for help she called for a hymn. She sat coolly down at the piano, touching the keys with a tender chord or two and beginning to sing almost at once. She had sent home for some old hymn-books from the Christian Endeavor Society in her father's church, so the congregation were supplied with the notes and words now, and everybody took part eagerly, even the people from the fort condescendingly joining in.

But Gardley was too much alive to every expression on that vivid face of Margaret's to miss knowing that she was annoyed and upset. He did not need to turn and look back to immediately discover the cause. He was a young person of keen intuition. It suddenly gave him great satisfaction to see that look of consternation on Margaret's face. It settled for him a question he had been in great and anxious doubt about, and his soul was lifted up with peace within him. When, presently, according to arrangement, he rose to sing a duet with Margaret, no one could have possibly told by so much as the lifting of an eyelash that he knew there was an enemy of his in the back of the room. He sang, as did Margaret, to the immediate audience in front of him, those admiring children and adoring men in the forefront who felt the school-house had become for them the gate of heaven for the time being; and he sang with marvelous feeling and sympathy, letting out his voice at its best.

"Really," said Mrs. Temple, in a loud whisper to the wife of one of the officers, "that young man has a fine voice, and he isn't bad-looking, either. I think he'd be worth cultivating. We must have him up and try him out."

But when she repeated this remark in another stage whisper to Forsythe he frowned haughtily.

The one glimpse Margaret caught of Forsythe during that afternoon's service was when he was smiling meaningly at Rosa Rogers; and she had to resolutely put the memory of their look from her mind or the story which she was about to tell would have fled.

It was the hunger in Jasper Kemp's eyes that finally anchored Margaret's thoughts and helped her to forget the company at the back of the room. She told her story, and she told it wonderfully and with power, interpreting it now and then for the row of men who sat in the center of the room drinking in her every word; and when the simple service was concluded with another song, in which Gardley's voice rang forth with peculiar tenderness and strength, the men filed forth silently, solemnly, with bowed heads and thoughtful eyes. But the company from the fort flowed up around Margaret like flood-tide let loose and gushed upon her.

"Oh, my dear!" said Mrs. Temple. "How beautifully you do it! And such attention as they give you! No wonder you are willing to forego all other amusements to stay here and preach! But it was perfectly sweet the way you made them listen and the way you told that story. I don't see how you do it. I'd be scared to death!"

They babbled about her awhile, much to her annoyance, for there were several people to whom she had wanted to speak, who drew away and disappeared when the new-comers took possession of her. At last, however, they mounted and rode away, to her great relief. Forsythe, it is true, tried to make her go home with them; tried to escort her to the Tanners'; tried to remain in the school-house with her awhile when she told him she had something to do there; but she would not let him, and he rode away half sulky at the last, a look of injured pride upon his face.

Margaret went to the door finally, and looked down the road. He was gone, and she was alone. A shade of sadness came over her face. She was sorry that Gardley had not waited. She had wanted to tell him how much she liked his singing, what a pleasure it was to sing with him, and how glad she was that he came up to her need so well with the strangers there and helped to make it easy. But Gardley had melted away as soon as the service was over, and had probably gone home with the rest of the men. It was disappointing, for she had come to consider their little time together on Sunday as a very pleasant hour, this few minutes after the service when they would talk about real living and the vital things of existence. But he was gone!

She turned, and there he was, quite near the door, coming toward her. Her face lighted up with a joy that was unmistakable, and his own smile in answer was a revelation of his deeper self.

"Oh, I'm so glad you are not gone!" she said, eagerly. "I wanted to tell you — " And then she stopped, and the color flooded her face rosily, for she saw in his eyes how glad he was and forgot to finish her sentence.

He came up gravely, after all, and, standing just a minute so beside the door, took both her hands in both his. It was only for a second that he stood so, looking down into her eyes. I doubt if either of them knew till afterward that they had been holding hands. It seemed the right and natural thing to do, and meant so much to each of them. Both were glad beyond their own understanding over that moment and its tenderness.

It was all very decorous, and over in a second, but it meant much to remember afterward, that look and hand-clasp.

"I wanted to tell you," he said, tenderly, "how much that story did for me. It was wonderful, and it helped me to decide something I have been perplexed over — "

"Oh, I am glad!" she said, half breathlessly.

So, talking in low, broken sentences, they went back to the piano and tried over several songs for the next Sunday, lingering together, just happy to be there with each other, and not half knowing the significance of it all. As the purple lights on the school-room wall grew long and rose-edged, they walked slowly to the Tanner house and said good night.

There was a beauty about the young man as he stood for a moment looking down upon the girl in parting, the kind of beauty there is in any strong, wild thing made tame and tender for a great love by a great uplift. Gardley had that look of self-surrender, and power made subservient to right, that crowns a man with strength and more than physical beauty. In his fine face there glowed high purpose, and deep devotion to the one who had taught it to him. Margaret, looking up at him, felt her heart go out with that great love, half maiden, half divine, that comes to some favored women even here on earth, and she watched him down the road toward the mountain in the evening light and marveled how her trust had grown since first she met him; marveled and reflected that she had not told her mother and father much about him yet. It was growing time to do so; yes — *it was growing time*! Her cheeks grew pink in the darkness and she turned and fled to her room.

That was the last time she saw him before the play.

CHAPTER XXIII

The play was set for Tuesday. Monday afternoon and evening were to be the final rehearsals, but Gardley did not come to them. Fiddling Boss came late and said the men had been off all day and had not yet returned. He himself found it hard to come at all. They had important work on. But there was no word from Gardley.

Margaret was disappointed. She couldn't get away from it. Of course they could go on with the rehearsal without him. He had done his work well, and there was no real reason why he had to be there. He knew every part by heart, and could take any boy's place if any one failed in any way. There was nothing further really for him to do until the performance, as far as that was concerned, except be there and encourage her. But she missed him, and an uneasiness grew in her mind. She had so looked forward to seeing him, and now to have no word! He might at least have sent her a note when he found he could not come.

Still she knew this was unreasonable. His work, whatever it was — he had never explained it very thoroughly to her, perhaps because she had never asked — must, of course, have kept him. She must excuse him without question and go on with the business of the hour.

Her hands were full enough, for Forsythe came presently and was more trying than usual. She had to be very decided and put her foot down about one or two things, or some of her actors would have gone home in the sulks, and Fiddling Boss, whose part in the program meant much to him, would have given it up entirely.

She hurried everything through as soon as possible, knowing she was weary, and longing to get to her room and rest. Gardley would come and explain to-morrow, likely in the morning on his way somewhere.

But the morning came and no word. Afternoon came and he had not sent a sign yet. Some of the little things that he had promised to do about the setting of the stage would have to remain undone, for it was too late now to do it herself, and there was no one else to call upon.

Into the midst of her perplexity and anxiety came the news that Jed on his way home had been thrown from his horse, which was a young and vicious one, and had broken his leg. Jed was to act the part of Nick Bottom that evening, and he did it well! Now what in the world was she to do? If only Gardley would come!

Just at this moment Forsythe arrived.

"Oh, it is you, Mr. Forsythe!" And her tone showed plainly her disappointment. "Haven't you seen Mr. Gardley to-day? I don't know what I shall do without him."

"I certainly have seen Gardley," said Forsythe, a spice of vindictiveness and satisfaction in his tone. "I saw him not two hours ago, drunk as a fish, out at a place called Old Ouida's Cabin, as I was passing. He's in for a regular spree. You'll not see him for several days, I fancy. He's utterly helpless for the present, and out of the question. What is there I can do for you? Present your request. It's yours — to the half of my kingdom."

Margaret's heart grew cold as ice and then like fire. Her blood seemed to stop utterly and then to go pounding through her veins in leaps and torrents. Her eyes grew dark, and things swam before her. She reached out to a desk and caught at it for support, and her white face looked at him a moment as if she had not heard. But when in a second she spoke, she said, quite steadily:

"I thank you, Mr. Forsythe; there is nothing just at present — or, yes, there is, if you wouldn't mind helping Timothy put up those curtains. Now, I think I'll go home and rest a few minutes; I am very tired."

It wasn't exactly the job Forsythe coveted, to stay in the school-house and fuss over those curtains; but she made him do it, then disappeared, and he didn't like the memory of her white face. He hadn't thought she would take it that way. He had expected to have her exclaim with horror and disgust. He watched her out of the door, and then turned impatiently to the waiting Timothy.

Margaret went outside the school-house to call Bud, who had been sent to gather sage-brush for filling in the background, but Bud was already out of sight far on the trail toward the camp on Forsythe's horse, riding for dear life. Bud had come near to the school-house door with his armful of sage-brush just in time to hear Forsythe's flippant speech about Gardley and see Margaret's white face. Bud had gone for help!

But Margaret did not go home to rest. She did not even get half-way home. When she had gone a very short distance outside the school-house she saw some one coming toward her, and in her distress of mind she could not tell who it was. Her eyes were blinded with tears, her breath was constricted, and it seemed to her that a demon unseen was gripping her heart. She had not yet taken her bearings to know what she thought. She had only just come dazed from the shock of Forsythe's words, and had not the power to think. Over and over to herself, as she walked along, she kept repeating the words: "I *do not* believe it! It is *not* true!" but her inner consciousness had not had time to analyze her soul and be sure that she believed the words wherewith she was comforting herself.

So now, when she saw some one coming, she felt the necessity of bringing her telltale face to order and getting ready to answer whoever she was to meet. As she drew nearer she became suddenly aware that it was Rosa Rogers coming with her arms full of bundles and more piled up in front of her on her pony. Margaret knew at once that Rosa must have seen Forsythe go by her house, and had returned promptly to the school-house on some pretext or other. It would not do to let her go there alone with the young man; she must go back and stay with them. She could not be sure that if she sent Rosa home with orders to rest she would be obeyed. Doubtless the girl would take another way around and return to the school again. There was nothing for it but to go back and stay as long as Rosa did.

Margaret stooped and, hastily plucking a great armful of sage-brush, turned around and retraced her steps, her heart like lead, her feet suddenly grown heavy. How could she go back and hear them laugh and chatter, answer their many silly, unnecessary questions, and stand it all? How could she, with that great weight at her heart?

She went back with a wonderful self-control. Forsythe's face lighted, and his reluctant hand grew suddenly eager as he worked. Rosa came presently, and others, and the laughing chatter went on quite as Margaret had known it would. And she — so great is the power of human will under pressure — went calmly about and directed here and there; planned and executed; put little, dainty, wholly unnecessary touches to the stage; and never let any one know that her heart was being crushed with the weight of a great, awful fear, and yet steadily upborne by the rising of a great, deep trust. As she worked and smiled and ordered, she was praying: "Oh, God, don't let it be true! Keep him! Save him! Bring him! Make him true! I *know* he is true! Oh, God, bring him safely *soon!*"

Meantime there was nothing she could do. She could not send Forsythe after him. She could not speak of the matter to one of those present, and Bud — where was Bud? It was the first time since she came to Arizona that Bud had failed her. She might not leave the school-house, with Forsythe and Rosa there, to go and find him, and she might not do anything else. There was nothing to do but work on feverishly and pray as she had never prayed before.

By and by one of the smaller boys came, and she sent him back to the Tanners' to find Bud, but he returned with the message that Bud had not been home since morning; and so the last hours before the evening, that would otherwise have been so brief for all there was to be done, dragged their weary length away and Margaret worked on.

She did not even go back for supper at the last, but sent one of the girls to her room for a few things she needed, and declined even the nice little chicken sandwich that thoughtful Mrs. Tanner sent back along with the things. And then, at last, the audience began to gather.

By this time her anxiety was so great for Gardley that all thought of how she was to supply the place of the absent Jed had gone from her mind, which was in a whirl. Gardley! Gardley! If only Gardley would come! That was her one thought. What should she do if he didn't come at all? How should she explain things to herself afterward? What if it had been true? What if he were the kind of man Forsythe had suggested? How terrible life would look to her! But it was not true. No, it was not true! She trusted him! With her soul she trusted him! He would come back some time and he would explain all. She could not remember his last look at her on Sunday and not trust him. He was true! He would come!

Somehow she managed to get through the terrible interval, to slip into the dressing-room and make herself sweet and comely in the little white gown she had sent for, with its delicate blue ribbons and soft lace ruffles. Somehow she managed the expected smiles as one and another of the audience came around to the platform to speak to her. There were dark hollows under her eyes, and her mouth was drawn and weary, but they laid that to the excitement. Two bright-red spots glowed on her cheeks; but she smiled and talked with her usual gaiety. People looked at her and said how beautiful she was, and how bright and untiring; and how wonderful it was that Ashland School had drawn such a prize of a teacher. The seats filled, the noise and the clatter went on. Still no sign of Gardley or any one from the camp, and still Bud had not returned! What could it mean?

But the minutes were rushing rapidly now. It was more than time to begin. The girls were in a flutter in one cloak-room at the right of the stage, asking more questions in a minute than one could answer in an hour; the boys in the other cloak-room wanted all sorts of help; and three or four of the actors were attacked with stage-fright as they peered through a hole in the curtain and saw some friend or relative arrive and sit down in the audience. It was all a mad whirl of seemingly useless noise and excitement, and she could not, no, she *could not*, go on and do the necessary things to start that awful play. Why, oh, *why* had she ever been left to think of getting up a play?

Forsythe, up behind the piano, whispered to her that it was time to begin. The house was full. There was not room for another soul. Margaret explained that Fiddling Boss had not yet arrived, and caught a glimpse of the cunning designs of Forsythe in the shifty turning away of his eyes as he answered that they could not wait all night for him; that if he wanted to get into it he ought to have come early. But even as she turned away she saw the little, bobbing, eager faces of Pop and Mom Wallis away back by the door, and the grim, towering figure of the Boss, his fiddle held high, making his way to the front amid the crowd.

She sat down and touched the keys, her eyes watching eagerly for a chance to speak to the Boss and see if he knew anything of Gardley; but Forsythe was close beside her all the time, and there was no opportunity. She struck the opening chords of the overture they were to attempt to play, and somehow got through it. Of course, the audience was not a critical one, and there were few real judges of music present; but it may be that the truly wonderful effect she produced upon the listeners was due to the fact that she was playing a prayer with her heart as her fingers touched the keys, and that instead of a preliminary to a fairy revel the music told the story of a great soul struggle, and reached hearts as it tinkled and rolled and swelled on to the end. It may be, too, that Fiddling Boss was more in sympathy that night with his accompanist than was the other violinist, and that was why his old fiddle brought forth such weird and tender tones.

Almost to the end, with her heart sobbing its trouble to the keys, Margaret looked up sadly, and there, straight before her through a hole in the curtain made by some rash youth to glimpse the audience, or perhaps even put there by the owner of the nose itself, she saw the little, freckled, turned-up member belonging to Bud's face. A second more and a big, bright eye appeared and solemnly winked at her twice, as if to say, "Don't you worry; it's all right!"

She almost started from the stool, but kept her head enough to finish the chords, and as they died away she heard a hoarse whisper in Bud's familiar voice:

"Whoop her up, Miss Earle. We're all ready. Raise the curtain there, you guy. Let her rip. Everything's O. K."

With a leap of light into her eyes Margaret turned the leaves of the music and went on playing as she should have done if nothing had been the matter. Bud was there, anyway, and that somehow cheered her heart. Perhaps Gardley had come or Bud had heard of him — and yet, Bud didn't know he had been missing, for Bud had been away himself.

Nevertheless, she summoned courage to go on playing. Nick Bottom wasn't in this first scene, anyway, and this would have to be gone through with somehow. By this time she was in a state of daze that only thought from moment to moment. The end of the evening seemed now to her as far off as the end of a hale old age seems at the beginning of a lifetime. Somehow she must walk through it; but she could only see a step at a time.

Once she turned half sideways to the audience and gave a hurried glance about, catching sight of Fudge's round, near-sighted face, and that gave her encouragement. Perhaps the others were somewhere present. If only she could get a chance to whisper to some one from the camp and ask when they had seen Gardley last! But there was no chance, of course!

The curtain was rapidly raised and the opening scene of the play began, the actors going through their parts with marvelous ease and dexterity, and the audience silent and charmed, watching those strangers in queer costumes that were their own children, marching around there at their ease and talking weird language that was not used in any class of society they had ever come across on sea or land before.

But Margaret, watching her music as best she could, and playing mechanically rather than with her mind, could not tell if they were doing well or ill, so loudly did her heart pound out her fears — so stoutly did her heart proclaim her trust.

And thus, without a flaw or mistake in the execution of the work she had struggled so hard to teach them, the first scene of the first act drew to its close, and Margaret struck the final chords of the music and felt that in another minute she must reel and fall from that piano-stool. And yet she sat and watched the curtain fall with a face as controlled as if nothing at all were the matter.

A second later she suddenly knew that to sit in that place calmly another second was a physical impossibility. She must get somewhere to the air at once or her senses would desert her.

With a movement so quick that no one could have anticipated it, she slipped from her piano-stool, under the curtain to the stage, and was gone before the rest of the orchestra had noticed her intention.

CHAPTER XXIV

Since the day that he had given Margaret his promise to make good, Gardley had been regularly employed by Mr. Rogers, looking after important matters of his ranch. Before that he had lived a free and easy life, working a little now and then when it seemed desirable to him, having no set interest in life, and only endeavoring from day to day to put as far as possible from his mind the life he had left behind him. Now, however, all things became different. He brought to his service the keen mind and ready ability that had made him easily a winner at any game, a brave rider, and a never-failing shot. Within a few days Rogers saw what material was in him, and as the weeks went by grew to depend more and more upon his advice in matters.

There had been much trouble with cattle thieves, and so far no method of stopping the loss or catching the thieves had been successful. Rogers finally put the matter into Gardley's hands to carry out his own ideas, with the men of the camp at his command to help him, the camp itself being only a part of Rogers's outlying possessions, one of several such centers from which he worked his growing interests.

Gardley had formulated a scheme by which he hoped eventually to get hold of the thieves and put a stop to the trouble, and he was pretty sure he was on the right track; but his plan required slow and cautious work, that the enemy might not suspect and take to cover. He had for several weeks suspected that the thieves made their headquarters in the region of Old Ouida's Cabin, and made their raids from that direction. It was for this reason that of late the woods and trails in the vicinity of Ouida's had been secretly patrolled day and night, and every passer-by taken note of, until Gardley knew just who were the frequenters of that way and mostly what was their business. This work was done alternately by the men of the Wallis camp and two other camps, Gardley being the head of all and carrying all responsibility; and not the least of that young man's offenses in the eyes of Rosa Rogers was that he was so constantly at her father's house and yet never lifted an eye in admiration of her pretty face. She longed to humiliate him, and through him to humiliate Margaret, who presumed to interfere with her flirtations, for it was a bitter thing to Rosa that Forsythe had no eyes for her when Margaret was about.

When the party from the fort rode homeward that Sunday after the service at the schoolhouse, Forsythe lingered behind to talk to Margaret, and then rode around by the Rogers place, where Rosa and he had long ago established a trysting-place.

Rosa was watching for his passing, and he stopped a half-hour or so to talk to her. During this time she casually disclosed to Forsythe some of the plans she had overheard Gardley laying before her father. Rosa had very little idea of the importance of Gardley's work to her father, or perhaps she would not have so readily prattled of his affairs. Her main idea was to pay back Gardley for his part in her humiliation with Forsythe. She suggested that it would be a great thing if Gardley could be prevented from being at the play Tuesday evening, and told what she had overheard him saying to her father merely to show Forsythe how easy it would be to have Gardley detained on Tuesday. Forsythe questioned Rosa keenly. Did she know whom they suspected? Did she know what they were planning to do to catch them, and when?

Rosa innocently enough disclosed all she knew, little thinking how dishonorable to her father it was, and perhaps caring as little, for Rosa had ever been a spoiled child, accustomed to subordinating everything within reach to her own uses. As for Forsythe, he was nothing loath to get rid of Gardley, and he saw more possibilities in Rosa's suggestion than she had seen herself. When at last he bade Rosa good night and rode unobtrusively back to the trail he was already formulating a plan.

It was, therefore, quite in keeping with his wishes that he should meet a dark-browed rider a few miles farther up the trail whose identity he had happened to learn a few days before.

Now Forsythe would, perhaps, not have dared to enter into any compact against Gardley with men of such ill-repute had it been a matter of money and bribery, but, armed as he was with information valuable to the criminals, he could so word his suggestion about Gardley's detention as to make the hunted men think it to their advantage to catch Gardley some time the next day when he passed their way and imprison him for a while. This would appear to be but a friendly bit of advice from a disinterested party deserving a good turn some time in the future and not get Forsythe into any trouble. As such it was received by the wretch, who clutched at the information with ill-concealed delight and rode away into the twilight like a serpent threading his secret, gliding way among the darkest places, scarcely rippling the air, so stealthily did he pass.

As for Forsythe, he rode blithely to the Temple ranch, with no thought of the forces he had set going, his life as yet one round of trying to please himself at others' expense, if need be, but please himself, *anyway*, with whatever amusement the hour afforded.

At home in the East, where his early life had been spent, a splendid girl awaited his dilatory letters and set herself patiently to endure the months of separation until he should have attained a home and a living and be ready for her to come to him.

In the South, where he had idled six months before he went West, another lovely girl cherished mementoes of his tarrying and wrote him loving letters in reply to his occasional erratic epistles.

Out on the Californian shore a girl with whom he had traveled West in her uncle's luxurious private car, with a gay party of friends and relatives, cherished fond hopes of a visit he had promised to make her during the winter.

Innumerable maidens of this world, wise in the wisdom that crushes hearts, remembered him with a sigh now and then, but held no illusions concerning his kind.

Pretty little Rosa Rogers cried her eyes out every time he cast a languishing look at her teacher, and several of the ladies of the fort sighed that the glance of his eye and the gentle pressure of his hand could only be a passing joy. But the gay Lothario passed on his way as yet without a scratch on the hard enamel of his heart, till one wondered if it were a heart, indeed, or perhaps only a metal imitation. But girls like Margaret Earle, though they sometimes were attracted by him, invariably distrusted him. He was like a beautiful spotted snake that was often caught menacing something precious, but you could put him down anywhere after punishment or imprisonment and he would slide on his same slippery way and still be a spotted, deadly snake.

When Gardley left the camp that Monday morning following the walk home with Margaret from the Sabbath service, he fully intended to be back at the school-house Monday by the time the afternoon rehearsal began. His plans were so laid that he thought relays from other camps were to guard the suspected ground for the next three days and he could be free. It had been a part of the information that Forsythe had given the stranger that Gardley would likely pass a certain lonely crossing of the trail at about three o'clock that afternoon, and, had that arrangement been carried out, the men who lay in wait for him would doubtless have been pleased to have their plans mature so easily; but they would not have been pleased long, for Gardley's men were so near at hand at that time, watching that very spot with eyes and ears and long-distance glasses, that their chief would soon have been rescued and the captors be themselves the captured.

But the men from the farther camp, called "Lone Fox" men, did not arrive on time, perhaps through some misunderstanding, and Gardley and Kemp and their men had to do double time. At last, later in the afternoon, Gardley volunteered to go to Lone Fox and bring back the men.

As he rode his thoughts were of Margaret, and he was seeing again the look of gladness in her eyes when she found he had not gone yesterday; feeling again the thrill of her hands in his, the trust of her smile! It was incredible, wonderful, that God had sent a veritable angel into the wilderness to bring him to himself; and now he was wondering, could it be that there was really hope that he could ever make good enough to dare to ask her to marry him. The sky and the air were rare, but his thoughts were rarer still, and his soul was lifted up with joy. He was earning good wages now. In two more weeks he would have enough to pay back the paltry sum for the lack of which he had fled from his old home and come to the wilderness. He would go back, of course, and straighten out the old score. Then what? Should he stay in the East and go back to the old business wherewith he had hoped to make his name honored and gain wealth, or should he return to this wild, free land again and start anew?

His mother was dead. Perhaps if she had lived and cared he would have made good in the first place. His sisters were both married to wealthy men and not deeply interested in him. He had disappointed and mortified them; their lives were filled with social duties; they had never missed him. His father had been dead many years. As for his uncle, his mother's brother, whose heir he was to have been before he got himself into disgrace, he decided not to go near him. He would stay as long as he must to undo the wrong he had done. He would call on his sisters and then come back; come back and let Margaret decide what she wanted him to do — that is, if she would consent to link her life with one who had been once a failure. Margaret! How wonderful she was! If Margaret said he ought to go back and be a lawyer, he would go — yes, even if he had to enter his uncle's office as an underling to do it. His soul loathed the idea, but he would do it for Margaret, if she thought it best. And so he mused as he rode!

When the Lone Fox camp was reached and the men sent out on their belated task, Gardley decided not to go with them back to meet Kemp and the other men, but sent word to Kemp that he had gone the short cut to Ashland, hoping to get to a part of the evening rehearsal yet.

Now that short cut led him to the lonely crossing of the trail much sooner than Kemp and the others could reach it from the rendezvous; and there in cramped positions, and with much unnecessary cursing and impatience, four strong masked men had been concealed for four long hours.

Through the stillness of the twilight rode Gardley, thinking of Margaret, and for once utterly off his guard. His long day's work was done, and though he had not been able to get back when he planned, he was free now, free until the day after to-morrow. He would go at once to her and see if there was anything she wanted him to do.

Then, as if to help along his enemies, he began to hum a song, his clear, high voice reaching keenly to the ears of the men in ambush:

"'Oh, the time is long, mavourneen,
Till I come again, O mavourneen —'"

"And the toime 'll be longer thun iver, oim thinkin', ma purty little voorneen!" said an unmistakable voice of Erin through the gathering dusk.

Gardley's horse stopped and Gardley's hand went to his revolver, while his other hand lifted the silver whistle to his lips; but four guns bristled at him in the twilight, the whistle was knocked from his lips before his breath had even reached it, some one caught his arms from behind, and his own weapon was wrenched from his hand as it went off. The cry which he at once sent forth was stifled in its first whisper in a great muffling garment flung over his head and drawn tightly about his neck. He was in a fair way to strangle, and his vigorous efforts at escape were useless in the hands of so many. He might have been plunged at once into a great abyss of limitless, soundless depths, so futile did any resistance seem. And so, as it was useless to struggle, he lay like one dead and put all his powers into listening. But neither could he hear much, muffled as he was, and bound hand and foot now, with a gag in his mouth and little care taken whether he could even breathe.

They were leading him off the trail and up over rough ground; so much he knew, for the horse stumbled and jolted and strained to carry him. To keep his whirling senses alive and alert he tried to think where they might be leading him; but the darkness and the suffocation dulled his powers. He wondered idly if his men would miss him and come back when they got home to search for him, and then remembered with a pang that they would think him safely in Ashland, helping Margaret. They would not be alarmed if he did not return that night, for they would suppose he had stopped at Rogers's on the way and perhaps stayed all night, as he had done once or twice before. *Margaret!* When should he see Margaret now? What would she think?

And then he swooned away.

When he came somewhat to himself he was in a close, stifling room where candle-light from a distance threw weird shadows over the adobe walls. The witch-like voices of a woman and a girl in harsh, cackling laughter, half suppressed, were not far away, and some one, whose face was covered, was holding a glass to his lips. The smell was sickening, and he remembered that he hated the thought of liquor. It did not fit with those who companied with Margaret. He had never cared for it, and had resolved never to taste it again. But whether he chose or not, the liquor was poured down his throat. Huge hands held him and forced it, and he was still bound and too weak to resist, even if he had realized the necessity.

The liquid burned its way down his throat and seethed into his brain, and a great darkness, mingled with men's wrangling voices and much cursing, swirled about him like some furious torrent of angry waters that finally submerged his consciousness. Then came deeper darkness and a blank relief from pain.

Hours passed. He heard sounds sometimes, and dreamed dreams which he could not tell from reality. He saw his friends with terror written on their faces, while he lay apathetically and could not stir. He saw tears on Margaret's face; and once he was sure he heard Forsythe's voice in contempt: "Well, he seems to be well occupied for the present! No danger of his waking up for a while!" and then the voices all grew dim and far away again, and only an old crone and the harsh girl's whisper over him; and then Margaret's tears — tears that fell on his heart from far above, and seemed to melt out all his early sins and flood him with their horror. Tears and the consciousness that he ought to be doing something for Margaret now and could not. Tears — and more darkness!

CHAPTER XXV

When Margaret arrived behind the curtain she was aware of many cries and questions hurled at her like an avalanche, but, ignoring them all, she sprang past the noisy, excited group of young people, darted through the dressing-room to the right and out into the night and coolness. Her head was swimming, and things went black before her eyes. She felt that her breath was going, going, and she must get to the air.

But when she passed the hot wave of the school-room, and the sharp air of the night struck her face, consciousness seemed to turn and come back into her again; for there over her head was the wideness of the vast, starry Arizona night, and there, before her, in Nick Bottom's somber costume, eating one of the chicken sandwiches that Mrs. Tanner had sent down to her, stood Gardley! He was pale and shaken from his recent experience; but he was undaunted, and when he saw Margaret coming toward him through the doorway with her soul in her eyes and her spirit all aflame with joy and relief, he came to meet her under the stars, and, forgetting everything else, just folded her gently in his arms!

It was a most astonishing thing to do, of course, right there outside the dressing-room door, with the curtain just about to rise on the scene and Gardley's wig was not on yet. He had not even asked nor obtained permission. But the soul sometimes grows impatient waiting for the lips to speak, and Margaret felt her trust had been justified and her heart had found its home. Right there behind the school-house, out in the great wide night, while the crowded, clamoring audience waited for them, and the young actors grew frantic, they plighted their troth, his lips upon hers, and with not a word spoken.

Voices from the dressing-room roused them. "Come in quick, Mr. Gardley; it's time for the curtain to rise, and everybody is ready. Where on earth has Miss Earle vanished? Miss Earle! Oh, Miss Earle!"

There was a rush to the dressing-room to find the missing ones; but Bud, as ever, present where was the most need, stood with his back to the outside world in the door of the dressing-room and called loudly:

"They're comin', all right. Go on! Get to your places. Miss Earle says to get to your places."

The two in the darkness groped for each other's hands as they stood suddenly apart, and with one quick pressure and a glance hurried in. There was not any need for words. They understood, these two, and trusted.

With her cheeks glowing now, and her eyes like two stars, Margaret fled across the stage and took her place at the piano again, just as the curtain began to be drawn; and Forsythe, who had been slightly uneasy at the look on her face as she left them, wondered now and leaned forward to tell her how well she was looking.

He kept his honeyed phrase to himself, however, for she was not heeding him. Her eyes were on the rising curtain, and Forsythe suddenly remembered that this was the scene in which Jed was to have appeared — and Jed had a broken leg! What had Margaret done about it? It was scarcely a part that could be left out. Why hadn't he thought of it sooner and offered to take it? He could have bluffed it out somehow — he had heard it so much — made up words where he couldn't remember them all, and it would have been a splendid opportunity to do some real love-making with Rosa. Why hadn't he thought of it? Why hadn't Rosa? Perhaps she hadn't heard about Jed soon enough to suggest it.

The curtain was fully open now, and Bud's voice as Peter Quince, a trifle high and cracked with excitement, broke the stillness, while the awed audience gazed upon this new, strange world presented to them.

"Is all our company here?" lilted out Bud, excitedly, and Nick Bottom replied with Gardley's voice:

"You were best to call them generally, man by man, according to the scrip."

Forsythe turned deadly white. Jasper Kemp, whose keen eye was upon him, saw it through the tan, saw his lips go pale and purple points of fear start in his eyes, as he looked and looked again, and could not believe his senses.

Furtively he darted a glance around, like one about to steal away; then, seeing Jasper Kemp's eyes upon him, settled back with a strained look upon his face. Once he stole a look at Margaret and caught her face all transfigured with great joy; looked again and felt rebuked somehow by the pureness of her maiden joy and trust.

Not once had she turned her eyes to his. He was forgotten, and somehow he knew the look he would get if she should see him. It would be contempt and scorn that would burn his very soul. It is only a maid now and then to whom it is given thus to pierce and bruise the soul of a man who plays with love and trust and womanhood for selfishness. Such a woman never knows her power. She punishes all unconscious to herself. It was so that Margaret Earle, without being herself aware, and by her very indifference and contempt, showed the little soul of this puppet man to himself.

He stole away at last when he thought no one was looking, and reached the back of the school-house at the open door of the girls' dressing-room, where he knew Titania would be posing in between the acts. He beckoned her to his side and began to question her in quick, eager, almost angry tones, as if the failure of their plans were her fault. Had her father been at home all day? Had anything happened — any one been there? Did Gardley come? Had there been any report from the men? Had that short, thick-set Scotchman with the ugly grin been there? She must remember that she was the one to suggest the scheme in the first place, and it was her business to keep a watch. There was no telling now what might happen. He turned, and there stood Jasper Kemp close to his elbow, his short stature drawn to its full, his thick-set shoulders squaring themselves, his ugly grin standing out in bold relief, menacingly, in the night.

The young man let forth some words not in a gentleman's code, and turned to leave the frightened girl, who by this time was almost crying; but Jasper Kemp kept pace with Forsythe as he walked.

"Was you addressing me?" he asked, politely; "because I could tell you a few things a sight more appropriate for you than what you just handed to me."

Forsythe hurried around to the front of the school-house, making no reply.

"Nice, pleasant evening to be *free*," went on Jasper Kemp, looking up at the stars. "Rather onpleasant for some folks that have to be shut up in jail."

Forsythe wheeled upon him. "What do you mean?" he demanded, angrily, albeit he was white with fear.

"Oh, nothing much," drawled Jasper, affably. "I was just thinking how much pleasanter it was to be a free man than shut up in prison on a night like this. It's so much healthier, you know."

Forsythe looked at him a moment, a kind of panic of intelligence growing in his face; then he turned and went toward the back of the school-house, where he had left his horse some hours before.

"Where are you going?" demanded Jasper. "It's 'most time you went back to your fiddling, ain't it?"

But Forsythe answered him not a word. He was mounting his horse hurriedly — his horse, which, all unknown to him, had been many miles since he last rode him.

"You think you have to go, then?" said Jasper, deprecatingly. "Well, now, that's a pity, seeing you was fiddling so nice an' all. Shall I tell them you've gone for your health?"

Thus recalled, Forsythe stared at his tormentor wildly for a second. "Tell her — tell her" — he muttered, hoarsely — "tell her I've been taken suddenly ill." And he was off on a wild gallop toward the fort.

"I'll tell her you've gone for your health!" called Jasper Kemp, with his hands to his mouth like a megaphone. "I reckon he won't return again very soon, either," he chuckled. "This country's better off without such pests as him an' that measley parson." Then, turning, he beheld Titania, the queen of the fairies, white and frightened, staring wildly into the starry darkness after the departed rider. "Poor little fool!" he muttered under his breath as he looked at the girl and turned away. "Poor, pretty little fool!" Suddenly he stepped up to her side and touched her white-clad shoulder gently. "Don't you go for to care, lassie," he said in a tender tone. "He ain't worth a tear from your pretty eye. He ain't fit to wipe your feet on — your pretty wee feet!"

But Rosa turned angrily and stamped her foot.

"Go away! You bad old man!" she shrieked. "Go away! I shall tell my father!" And she flouted herself into the school-house.

Jasper stood looking ruefully after her, shaking his head. "The little de'il!" he said aloud; "the poor, pretty little de'il. She'll get her dues aplenty afore she's done." And Jasper went back to the play.

Meantime, inside the school-house, the play went gloriously on to the finish, and Gardley as Nick Bottom took the house by storm. Poor absent Jed's father, sent by the sufferer to report it all, stood at the back of the house while tears of pride and disappointment rolled down his cheeks — pride that Jed had been so well represented, disappointment that it couldn't have been his son up there play-acting like that.

The hour was late when the play was over, and Margaret stood at last in front of the stage to receive the congratulations of the entire countryside, while the young actors posed and laughed and chattered excitedly, then went away by two and threes, their tired, happy voices sounding back along the road. The people from the fort had been the first to surge around Margaret with their eager congratulations and gushing sentiments: "So sweet, my dear! So perfectly wonderful! You really have got some dandy actors!" And, "Why don't you try something lighter — something simpler, don't you know. Something really popular that these poor people could understand and appreciate? A little farce! I could help you pick one out!"

And all the while they gushed Jasper Kemp and his men, grim and forbidding, stood like a cordon drawn about her to protect her, with Gardley in the center, just behind her, as though he had a right there and meant to stay; till at last the fort people hurried away and the school-house grew suddenly empty with just those two and the eight men behind; and by the door Bud, talking to Pop and Mom Wallis in the buckboard outside.

Amid this admiring bodyguard at last Gardley took Margaret home. Perhaps she wondered a little that they all went along, but she laid it to their pride in the play and their desire to talk it over.

They had sent Mom and Pop Wallis home horseback, after all, and put Margaret and Gardley in the buckboard, Margaret never dreaming that it was because Gardley was not fit to walk. Indeed, he did not realize himself why they all stuck so closely to him. He had lived through so much since Jasper and his men had burst into his prison and freed him, bringing him in hot haste to the school-house, with Bud wildly riding ahead. But it was enough for him to sit beside Margaret in the sweet night and remember how she had come out to him under the stars. Her hand lay beside him on the seat, and without intending it his own brushed it. Then he laid his gently, reverently, down upon hers with a quiet pressure, and her smaller fingers thrilled and nestled in his grasp.

In the shadow of a big tree beside the house he bade her good-by, the men busying themselves with turning about the buckboard noisily, and Bud discreetly taking himself to the back door to get one of the men a drink of water.

"You have been suffering in some way," said Margaret, with sudden intuition, as she looked up into Gardley's face. "You have been in peril, somehow — "

"A little," he answered, lightly. "I'll tell you about it to-morrow. I mustn't keep the men waiting now. I shall have a great deal to tell you to-morrow — if you will let me. Good night, *Margaret*!" Their hands lingered in a clasp, and then he rode away with his bodyguard.

But Margaret did not have to wait until the morrow to hear the story, for Bud was just fairly bursting.

Mrs. Tanner had prepared a nice little supper — more cold chicken, pie, doughnuts, coffee, some of her famous marble cake, and preserves — and she insisted on Margaret's coming into the dining-room and eating it, though the girl would much rather have gone with her happy heart up to her own room by herself.

Bud did not wait on ceremony. He began at once when Margaret was seated, even before his mother could get her properly waited on.

"Well, we had *some ride*, we sure did! The Kid's a great old scout."

Margaret perceived that this was a leader. "Why, that's so, what became of you, William? I hunted everywhere for you. Things were pretty strenuous there for a while, and I needed you dreadfully."

"Well, I know," Bud apologized. "I'd oughta let you know before I went, but there wasn't time. You see, I had to pinch that guy's horse to go, and I knew it was just a chance if we could get back, anyway; but I had to take it. You see, if I could 'a' gone right to the cabin it would have been a dead cinch, but I had to ride to camp for the men, and then, taking the short trail across, it was some ride to Ouida's Cabin!"

Mrs. Tanner stepped aghast as she was cutting a piece of dried-apple pie for Margaret. "Now, Buddie — mother's boy — you don't mean to tell me *you* went to *Ouida's Cabin*? Why, sonnie, that's an *awful place*! Don't you know your pa told you he'd whip you if you ever went on that trail?"

"I should worry, Ma! I *had* to go. They had Mr. Gardley tied up there, and we had to go and get him rescued."

"*You* had to go, Buddie — now what could *you* do in that awful place?" Mrs. Tanner was almost reduced to tears. She saw her offspring at the edge of perdition at once.

But Bud ignored his mother and went on with his tale. "You jest oughta seen Jap Kemp's face when I told him what that guy said to you! Some face, b'lieve me! He saw right through the whole thing, too. I could see that! He ner the men hadn't had a bite o' supper yet; they'd just got back from somewheres. They thought the Kid was over here all day helping you. He said yesterday when he left 'em here's where he's a-comin'" — Bud's mouth was so full he could hardly articulate — "an' when I told 'em, he jest blew his little whistle — like what they all carry — three times, and those men every one jest stopped right where they was, whatever they was doin'. Long Bill had the comb in the air gettin' ready to comb his hair, an' he left it there and come away, and Big Jim never stopped to wipe his face on the roller-towel, he just let the wind dry it; and they all hustled on their horses fast as ever they could and beat it after Jap Kemp. Jap, he rode alongside o' me and asked me questions. He made me tell all what the guy from the fort said over again, three or four times, and then he ast what time he got to the school-house, and whether the Kid had been there at all yest'iday ur t'day; and a lot of other questions, and then he rode alongside each man and told him in just a few words where we was goin' and what the guy from the fort had said. Gee! but you'd oughta heard what the men said when he told 'em! Gee! but they was some mad! Bimeby we came to the woods round the cabin, and Jap Kemp made me stick alongside Long Bill, and he sent the men off in different directions all in a *big* circle, and waited till each man was in his place, and then we all rode hard as we could and came softly up round that cabin just as the sun was goin' down. Gee! but you'd oughta seen the scairt look on them women's faces; there was two of 'em — an old un an' a skinny-looking long-drink-o'-pump-water. I guess she was a girl. I don't know. Her eyes looked real old. There was only three men in the cabin; the rest was off somewheres. They wasn't looking for anybody to come that time o' day, I guess. One of the men was sick on a bunk in the corner. He had his head tied up, and his arm, like he'd been shot, and the other two men came jumping up to the door with their guns, but when they saw how many men *we* had they looked awful scairt. *We* all had *our* guns out, too! — Jap Kemp gave me one to carry — " Bud tried not to swagger as he told this, but it was almost too much for him. "Two of our men held the horses, and all the rest of us got down and went into the cabin. Jap Kemp, sounded his whistle and all our men done the same just as they went in the door —

some kind of signals they have for the Lone Fox Camp! The two men in the doorway aimed straight at Jap Kemp and fired, but Jap was onto 'em and jumped one side and our men fired, too, and we soon had 'em tied up and went in — that is, Jap and me and Long Bill went in, the rest stayed by the door — and it wasn't long 'fore their other men came riding back hot haste; they'd heard the shots, you know — and some more of *our* men — why, most twenty or thirty there was, I guess, altogether; some from Lone Fox Camp that was watching off in the woods came and when we got outside again there they all were, like a big army. Most of the men belonging to the cabin was tied and harmless by that time, for our men took 'em one at a time as they came riding in. Two of 'em got away, but Jap Kemp said they couldn't go far without being caught, 'cause there was a watch out for 'em — they'd been stealing cattle long back something terrible. Well, so Jap Kemp and Long Bill and I went into the cabin after the two men that shot was tied with ropes we'd brung along, and handcuffs, and we went hunting for the Kid. At first we couldn't find him at all. Gee! It was something fierce! And the old woman kep' a-crying and saying we'd kill her sick son, and she didn't know nothing about the man we was hunting for. But pretty soon I spied the Kid's foot stickin' out from under the cot where the sick man was, and when I told Jap Kemp that sick man pulled out a gun he had under the blanket and aimed it right at me!"

"Oh, mother's little Buddie!" whimpered Mrs. Tanner, with her apron to her eyes.

"*Aw, Ma*, cut it out! *he* didn't *hurt* me! The gun just went off crooked, and grazed Jap Kemp's hand a little, not much. Jap knocked it out of the sick man's hand just as he was pullin' the trigger. Say, Ma, ain't you got any more of those cucumber pickles? It makes a man mighty hungry to do all that riding and shooting. Well, it certainly was something fierce — Say, Miss Earle, you take that last piece o' pie. Oh, g'wan! *Take* it! *You* worked hard. No, I don't want it, really! Well, if you won't take it *anyway*, I might eat it just to save it. Got any more coffee, Ma?"

But Margaret was not eating. Her face was pale and her eyes were starry with unshed tears, and she waited in patient but breathless suspense for the vagaries of the story to work out to the finish.

"Yes, it certainly was something fierce, that cabin," went on the narrator. "Why, Ma, it looked as if it had never been swept under that cot when we hauled the Kid out. He was tied all up in knots, and great heavy ropes wound tight from his shoulders down to his ankles. Why, they were bound so tight they made great heavy welts in his wrists and shoulders and round his ankles when we took 'em off; and they had a great big rag stuffed into his mouth so he couldn't yell. Gee! It was something fierce! He was 'most dippy, too; but Jap Kemp brought him round pretty quick and got him outside in the air. That was the worst place I ever was in myself. You couldn't breathe, and the dirt was something fierce. It was like a pigpen. I sure was glad to get outdoors again. And then — well, the Kid came around all right and they got him on a horse and gave him something out of a bottle Jap Kemp had, and pretty soon he could ride again. Why, you'd oughta seen his nerve. He just sat up there as straight, his lips all white yet and his eyes looked some queer; but he straightened up and he looked those rascals right in the eye, and told 'em a few things, and he gave orders to the other men from Lone Fox Camp what to do with 'em; and he had the two women disarmed — they had guns, too — and carried away, and the cabin nailed up, and a notice put on the door, and every one of those men were handcuffed — the sick one and all — and he told 'em to bring a wagon and put the sick one's cot in and take 'em over to Ashland to the jail, and he sent word to Mr. Rogers. Then we rode home and got to the school-house just when you was playing the last chords of the ov'rtcher. Gee! It was some fierce ride and some *close shave*! The Kid he hadn't had a thing to eat since Monday noon, and he was some hungry! I found a sandwich on the window of the dressing-room, and he ate it while he got togged up — 'course I told him 'bout Jed soon's we left the cabin, and Jap Kemp said he'd oughta go right home to camp after all he had been through; but he wouldn't; he said he was goin' to *act*. So 'course he had his way! But, gee! You could see it wasn't any cinch game for him! He 'most fell over every time after the curtain fell. You see, they gave him some kind of drugged whisky up there at the cabin that made his head feel queer. Say, he thinks that guy from the fort came in and looked at him once while he was asleep. He says it was only a dream, but I bet he did. Say, Ma, ain't you gonta give me another doughnut?"

In the quiet of her chamber at last, Margaret knelt before her window toward the purple, shadowy mountain under the starry dome, and gave thanks for the deliverance of Gardley; while Bud, in his comfortable loft, lay down to his well-earned rest and dreamed of pirates and angels and a hero who looked like the Kid.

CHAPTER XXVI

The Sunday before Lance Gardley started East on his journey of reparation two strangers slipped quietly into the back of the school-house during the singing of the first hymn and sat down in the shadow by the door.

Margaret was playing the piano when they came in, and did not see them, and when she turned back to her Scripture lesson she had time for but the briefest of glances. She supposed they must be some visitors from the fort, as they were speaking to the captain's wife — — who came over occasionally to the Sunday service, perhaps because it afforded an opportunity for a ride with one of the young officers. These occasional visitors who came for amusement and curiosity had ceased to trouble Margaret. Her real work was with the men and women and children who loved the services for their own sake, and she tried as much as possible to forget outsiders. So, that day everything went on just as usual, Margaret putting her heart into the prayer, the simple, storylike reading of the Scripture, and the other story-sermon which followed it. Gardley sang unusually well at the close, a wonderful bit from an oratorio that he and Margaret had been practising.

But when toward the close of the little vesper service Margaret gave opportunity, as she often did, for others to take part in sentence prayers, one of the strangers from the back of the room stood up and began to pray. And such a prayer! Heaven seemed to bend low, and earth to kneel and beseech as the stranger-man, with a face like an archangel, and a body of an athlete clothed in a brown-flannel shirt and khakis, besought the Lord of heaven for a blessing on this gathering and on the leader of this little company who had so wonderfully led them to see the Christ and their need of salvation through the lesson of the day. And it did not need Bud's low-breathed whisper, "The missionary!" to tell Margaret who he was. His face told her. His prayer thrilled her, and his strong, young, true voice made her sure that here was a man of God in truth.

When the prayer was over and Margaret stood once more shyly facing her audience, she could scarcely keep the tremble out of her voice:

"Oh," said she, casting aside ceremony, "if I had known the missionary was here I should not have dared to try and lead this meeting to-day. Won't you please come up here and talk to us for a little while now, Mr. Brownleigh?"

At once he came forward eagerly, as if each opportunity were a pleasure. "Why, surely, I want to speak a word to you, just to say how glad I am to see you all, and to experience what a wonderful teacher you have found since I went away; but I wouldn't have missed this meeting to-day for all the sermons I ever wrote or preached. You don't need any more sermon than the remarkable story you've just been listening to, and I've only one word to add; and that is, that I've found since I went away that Jesus Christ, the only-begotten Son of God, is just the same Jesus to me to-day that He was the last time I spoke to you. He is just as ready to forgive your sin, to comfort you in sorrow, to help you in temptation, to raise your body in the resurrection, and to take you home to a mansion in His Father's house as He was the day He hung upon the cross to save your soul from death. I've found I can rest just as securely upon the Bible as the word of God as when I first tested its promises. Heaven and earth may pass away, but His word shall *never* pass away."

"*Go to it!*" said Jasper Kemp under his breath in the tone some men say "Amen!" and his brows were drawn as if he were watching a battle. Margaret couldn't help wondering if he were thinking of the Rev. Frederick West just then.

When the service was over the missionary brought his wife forward to Margaret, and they loved each other at once. Just another sweet girl like Margaret. She was lovely, with a delicacy of feature that betokened the high-born and high-bred, but dressed in a dainty khaki riding costume, if that uncompromising fabric could ever be called dainty. Margaret, remembering it afterward, wondered what it had been that gave it that unique individuality, and decided it was perhaps a combination of cut and finish and little dainty accessories. A bit of creamy lace at the throat of the rolling collar, a touch of golden-brown velvet in a golden clasp, the flash of a wonderful jewel on her finger, the modeling of the small, brown cap with its two eagle quills — all set the little woman apart and made her fit to enter any well-dressed company of riders in some great city park or fashionable drive. Yet here in the wilderness she was not overdressed.

The eight men from the camp stood in solemn row, waiting to be recognized, and behind them, abashed and grinning with embarrassment, stood Pop and Mom Wallis, Mom with her new gray bonnet glorifying her old face till the missionary's wife had to look twice to be sure who she was.

"And now, surely, Hazel, we must have these dear people come over and help us with the singing sometimes. Can't we try something right now?" said the missionary, looking first at his wife and then at Margaret and Gardley. "This man is a new-comer since I went away, but I'm mighty sure he is the right kind, and I'm glad to welcome him — or perhaps I would better ask if he will welcome me?" And with his rare smile the missionary put out his hand to Gardley, who took it with an eager grasp. The two men stood looking at each other for a moment, as rare men, rarely met, sometimes do even on a sinful earth; and after that clasp and that look they turned away, brothers for life.

That was a most interesting song rehearsal that followed. It would be rare to find four voices like those even in a cultivated musical center, and they blended as if they had been made for one another. The men from the bunk-house and a lot of other people silently dropped again into their seats to listen as the four sang on. The missionary took the bass, and his wife the alto, and the four made music worth listening to. The rare and lovely thing about it was that they sang to souls, not alone for ears, and so their music, classical though it was and of the highest order, appealed keenly to the hearts of these rough men, and made them feel that heaven had opened for them, as once before for untaught shepherds, and let down a ladder of angelic voices.

"I shall feel better about leaving you out here while I am gone, since they have come," said Gardley that night when he was bidding Margaret good night. "I couldn't bear to think there were none of your own kind about you. The others are devoted and would do for you with their lives if need be, as far as they know; but I like you to have *real friends* — real *Christian* friends. This man is what I call a Christian. I'm not sure but he is the first minister that I have ever come close to who has impressed me as believing what he preaches, and living it. I suppose there are others. I haven't known many. That man West that was here when you came was a mistake!"

"He didn't even preach much," smiled Margaret, "so how could he live it? This man is real. And there are others. Oh, I have known a lot of them that are living lives of sacrifice and loving service and are yet just as strong and happy and delightful as if they were millionaires. But they are the men who have not thrown away their Bibles and their Christ. They believe every promise in God's word, and rest on them day by day, testing them and proving them over and over. I wish you knew my father!"

"I am going to," said Gardley, proudly. "*I* am going to him just as soon as I have finished my business and straightened out my affairs; and I am going to tell him *everything* — with your permission, Margaret!"

"Oh, how beautiful!" cried Margaret, with happy tears in her eyes. "To think you are going to see father and mother. I have wanted them to know the real you. I couldn't half *tell* you, the real you, in a letter!"

"Perhaps they won't look on me with your sweet blindness, dear," he said, smiling tenderly down on her. "Perhaps they will see only my dark, past life — for I mean to tell your father everything. I'm not going to have any skeletons in the closet to cause pain hereafter. Perhaps your father and mother will not feel like giving their daughter to me after they know. Remember, I realize just what a rare prize she is."

"No, father is not like that, Lance," said Margaret, with her rare smile lighting up her happy eyes. "Father and mother will understand."

"But if they should not?" There was the shadow of sadness in Gardley's eyes as he asked the question.

"I belong to you, dear, anyway," she said, with sweet surrender. "I trust you though the whole world were against you!"

For answer Gardley took her in his arms, a look of awe upon his face, and, stooping, laid his lips upon hers in tender reverence.

"Margaret — you wonderful Margaret!" he said. "God has blessed me more than other men in sending you to me! With His help I will be worthy of you!"

Three days more and Margaret was alone with her school work, her two missionary friends thirty miles away, her eager watching for the mail to come, her faithful attendant Bud, and for comfort the purple mountain with its changing glory in the distance.

A few days before Gardley left for the East he had been offered a position by Rogers as general manager of his estate at a fine salary, and after consultation with Margaret he decided to accept it, but the question of their marriage they had left by common consent unsettled until Gardley should return and be able to offer his future wife a record made as fair and clean as human effort could make it after human mistakes had unmade it. As Margaret worked and waited, wrote her charming letters to father and mother and lover, and thought her happy thoughts with only the mountain for confidant, she did not plan for the future except in a dim and dreamy way. She would make those plans with Gardley when he returned. Probably they must wait some time before they could be married. Gardley would have to earn some money, and she must earn, too. She must keep the Ashland School for another year. It had been rather understood, when she came out, that if at all possible she would remain two years at least. It was hard to think of not going home for the summer vacation; but the trip cost a great deal and was not to be thought of. There was already a plan suggested to have a summer session of the school, and if that went through, of course she must stay right in Ashland. It was hard to think of not seeing her father and mother for another long year, but perhaps Gardley would be returning before the summer was over, and then it would not be so hard. However, she tried to put these thoughts out of her mind and do her work happily. It was incredible that Arizona should have become suddenly so blank and uninteresting since the departure of a man whom she had not known a few short months before.

Margaret had long since written to her father and mother about Gardley's first finding her in the desert. The thing had become history and was not likely to alarm them. She had been in Arizona long enough to be acquainted with things, and they would not be always thinking of her as sitting on stray water-tanks in the desert; so she told them about it, for she wanted them to know Gardley as he had been to her. The letters that had traveled back and forth between New York and Arizona had been full of Gardley; and still Margaret had not told her parents how it was between them. Gardley had asked that he might do that. Yet it had been a blind father and mother who had not long ago read between the lines of those letters and understood. Margaret fancied she detected a certain sense of relief in her mother's letters after she knew that Gardley had gone East. Were they worrying about him, she wondered, or was it just the natural dread of a mother to lose her child?

So Margaret settled down to school routine, and more and more made a confidant of Bud concerning little matters of the school. If it had not been for Bud at that time Margaret would have been lonely indeed.

Two or three times since Gardley left, the Brownleighs had ridden over to Sunday service, and once had stopped for a few minutes during the week on their way to visit some distant need. These occasions were a delight to Margaret, for Hazel Brownleigh was a kindred spirit. She was looking forward with pleasure to the visit she was to make them at the mission station as soon as school closed. She had been there once with Gardley before he left, but the ride was too long to go often, and the only escort available was Bud. Besides, she could not get away from school and the Sunday service at present; but it was pleasant to have something to look forward to.

Meantime the spring Commencement was coming on and Margaret had her hands full. She had undertaken to inaugurate a real Commencement with class day and as much form and ceremony as she could introduce in order to create a good school spirit; but such things are not done with the turn of a hand, and the young teacher sadly missed Gardley in all these preparations.

At this time Rosa Rogers was Margaret's particular thorn in the flesh.

Since the night that Forsythe had quit the play and ridden forth into the darkness Rosa had regarded her teacher with baleful eyes. Gardley, too, she hated, and was only waiting with smoldering wrath until her wild, ungoverned soul could take its revenge. She felt that but for those two Forsythe would still have been with her.

Margaret, realizing the passionate, untaught nature of the motherless girl and her great need of a friend to guide her, made attempt after attempt to reach and befriend her; but every attempt was met with repulse and the sharp word of scorn. Rosa had been too long the petted darling of a father who was utterly blind to her faults to be other than spoiled. Her own way was the one thing that ruled her. By her will she had ruled every nurse and servant about the place, and wheedled her father into letting her do anything the whim prompted. Twice her father, through the advice of friends, had tried the experiment of sending her away to school, once to an Eastern finishing school, and once to a convent on the Pacific coast, only to have her return shortly by request of the school, more wilful than when she had gone away. And now she ruled supreme in her father's home, disliked by most of the servants save those whom she chose to favor because they could be made to serve her purposes. Her father, engrossed in his business and away much of the time, was bound up in her and saw few of her faults. It is true that when a fault of hers did come to his notice, however, he dealt with it most severely, and grieved over it in secret, for the girl was much like the mother whose loss had emptied the world of its joy for him. But Rosa knew well how to manage her father and wheedle him, and also how to hide her own doings from his knowledge.

Rosa's eyes, dimples, pink cheeks, and coquettish little mouth were not idle in these days. She knew how to have every pupil at her feet and ready to obey her slightest wish. She wielded her power to its fullest extent as the summer drew near, and day after day saw a slow torture for Margaret. Some days the menacing air of insurrection fairly bristled in the room, and Margaret could not understand how some of her most devoted followers seemed to be in the forefront of battle, until one day she looked up quickly and caught the lynx-eyed glance of Rosa as she turned from smiling at the boys in the back seat. Then she understood. Rosa had cast her spell upon the boys, and they were acting under it and not of their own clear judgment. It was the world-old battle of sex, of woman against woman for the winning of the man to do her will. Margaret, using all the charm of her lovely personality to uphold standards of right, truth, purity, high living, and earnest thinking; Rosa striving with her impish beauty to lure them into *any* mischief so it foiled the other's purposes. And one day Margaret faced the girl alone, looking steadily into her eyes with sad, searching gaze, and almost a yearning to try to lead the pretty child to finer things.

"Rosa, why do you always act as if I were your enemy?" she said, sadly.

"Because you are!" said Rosa, with a toss of her independent head.

"Indeed I'm not, dear child," she said, putting out her hand to lay it on the girl's shoulder kindly. "I want to be your friend."

"I'm not a child!" snapped Rosa, jerking her shoulder angrily away; "and you can *never* be my friend, because I *hate* you!"

"Rosa, look here!" said Margaret, following the girl toward the door, the color rising in her cheeks and a desire growing in her heart to conquer this poor, passionate creature and win her for better things. "Rosa, I cannot have you say such things. Tell me why you hate me? What have I done that you should feel that way? I'm sure if we should talk it over we might come to some better understanding."

Rosa stood defiant in the doorway. "We could never come to any better understanding, Miss Earle," she declared in a cold, hard tone, "because I understand you now and I hate you. You tried your best to get my friend away from me, but you couldn't do it; and you would like to keep me from having any boy friends at all, but you can't do that, either. You think you are very popular, but you'll find out I always do what I like, and you needn't try to stop me. I don't have to come to school unless I choose, and as long as I don't break your rules you have no complaint coming; but you needn't think you can pull the wool over my eyes the way you do the others by pretending to be friends. I won't be friends! I hate you!" And Rosa turned grandly and marched out of the school-house.

Margaret stood gazing sadly after her and wondering if her failure here were her fault — if there was anything else she ought to have done — if she had let her personal dislike of the girl influence her conduct. She sat for some time at her desk, her chin in her hands, her eyes fixed on vacancy with a hopeless, discouraged expression in them, before she became aware of another presence in the room. Looking around quickly, she saw that Bud was sitting motionless at his desk, his forehead wrinkled in a fierce frown, his jaw set belligerently, and a look of such, unutterable pity and devotion in his eyes that her heart warmed to him at once and a smile of comradeship broke over her face.

"Oh, William! Were you here? Did you hear all that? What do you suppose is the matter? Where have I failed?"

"You 'ain't failed anywhere! You should worry 'bout her! She's a nut! If she was a boy I'd punch her head for her! But seeing she's only a girl, *you should worry*! She always was the limit!"

Bud's tone was forcible. He was the only one of all the boys who never yielded to Rosa's charms, but sat in glowering silence when she exercised her powers on the school and created pandemonium for the teacher. Bud's attitude was comforting. It had a touch of manliness and gentleness about it quite unwonted for him. It suggested beautiful possibilities for the future of his character, and Margaret smiled tenderly.

"Thank you, dear boy!" she said, gently. "You certainly are a comfort. If every one was as splendid as you are we should have a model school. But I do wish I could help Rosa. I can't see why she should hate me so! I must have made some big mistake with her in the first place to antagonize her."

"Naw!" said Bud, roughly. "No chance! She's just a *nut*, that's all. She's got a case on that Forsythe guy, the worst kind, and she's afraid somebody 'll get him away from her, the poor stew, as if anybody would get a case on a tough guy like that! Gee! You should worry! Come on, let's take a ride over t' camp!"

With a sigh and a smile Margaret accepted Bud's consolations and went on her way, trying to find some manner of showing Rosa what a real friend she was willing to be. But Rosa continued obdurate and hateful, regarding her teacher with haughty indifference except when she was called upon to recite, which she did sometimes with scornful condescension, sometimes with pert perfection, and sometimes with saucy humor which convulsed the whole room. Margaret's patience was almost ceasing to be a virtue, and she meditated often whether she ought not to request that the girl be withdrawn from the school. Yet she reflected that it was a very short time now until Commencement, and that Rosa had not openly defied any rules. It was merely a personal antagonism. Then, too, if Rosa were taken from the school there was really no other good influence in the girl's life at present. Day by day Margaret prayed about the matter and hoped that something would develop to make plain her way.

After much thought in the matter she decided to go on with her plans, letting Rosa have her place in the Commencement program and her part in the class-day doings as if nothing were the matter. Certainly there was nothing laid down in the rules of a public school that proscribed a scholar who did not love her teacher. Why should the fact that one had incurred the hate of a pupil unfit that pupil for her place in her class so long as she did her duties? And Rosa did hers promptly and deftly, with a certain piquant originality that Margaret could not help but admire.

Sometimes, as the teacher cast a furtive look at the pretty girl working away at her desk, she wondered what was going on behind the lovely mask. But the look in Rosa's eyes, when she raised them, was both deep and sly.

Rosa's hatred was indeed deep rooted. Whatever heart she had not frivoled away in wilfulness had been caught and won by Forsythe, the first grown man who had ever dared to make real love to her. Her jealousy of Margaret was the most intense thing that had ever come into her life. To think of him looking at Margaret, talking to Margaret, smiling at Margaret, walking or riding with Margaret, was enough to send her writhing upon her bed in the darkness of a wakeful night. She would clench her pretty hands until the nails dug into the flesh and brought the blood. She would bite the pillow or the blankets with an almost fiendish clenching of her teeth upon them and mutter, as she did so: "I hate her! I *hate* her! I could *kill* her!"

The day her first letter came from Forsythe, Rosa held her head high and went about the school as if she were a princess royal and Margaret were the dust under her feet. Triumph sat upon her like a crown and looked forth regally from her eyes. She laid her hand upon her heart and felt the crackle of his letter inside her blouse. She dreamed with her eyes upon the distant mountain and thought of the tender names he had called her: "Little wild Rose of his heart," "No rose in all the world until you came," and a lot of other meaningful sentences. A real love-letter all her own! No sharing him with any hateful teachers! He had implied in her letter that she was the only one of all the people in that region to whom he cared to write. He had said he was coming back some day to get her. Her young, wild heart throbbed exultantly, and her eyes looked forth their triumph malignantly. When he did come she would take care that he stayed close by her. No conceited teacher from the East should lure him from her side. She would prepare her guiles and smile her sweetest. She would wear fine garments from abroad, and show him she could far outshine that quiet, common Miss Earle, with all her airs. Yet to this end she studied hard. It was no part of her plan to be left behind at graduating-time. She would please her father by taking a prominent part in things and outdoing all the others. Then he would give her what she liked — jewels and silk dresses, and all the things a girl should have who had won a lover like hers.

The last busy days before Commencement were especially trying for Margaret. It seemed as if the children were possessed with the very spirit of mischief, and she could not help but see that it was Rosa who, sitting demurely in her desk, was the center of it all. Only Bud's steady, frowning countenance of all that rollicking, roistering crowd kept loyalty with the really beloved teacher. For, indeed, they loved her, every one but Rosa, and would have stood by her to a man and girl when it really came to the pinch, but in a matter like a little bit of fun in these last few days of school, and when challenged to it by the school beauty who did not usually condescend to any but a few of the older boys, where was the harm? They were so flattered by Rosa's smiles that they failed to see Margaret's worn, weary wistfulness.

Bud, coming into the school-house late one afternoon in search of her after the other scholars had gone, found Margaret with her head down upon the desk and her shoulders shaken with soundless sobs. He stood for a second silent in the doorway, gazing helplessly at her grief, then with the delicacy of one boy for another he slipped back outside the door and stood in the shadow, grinding his teeth.

"Gee!" he said, under his breath. "Oh, gee! I'd like to punch her fool head. I don't care if she is a girl! She needs it. Gee! if she was a boy wouldn't I settle her, the little darned mean sneak!"

His remarks, it is needless to say, did not have reference to his beloved teacher.

It was in the atmosphere everywhere that something was bound to happen if this strain kept up. Margaret knew it and felt utterly inadequate to meet it. Rosa knew it and was awaiting her opportunity. Bud knew it and could only stand and watch where the blow was to strike first and be ready to ward it off. In these days he wished fervently for Gardley's return. He did not know just what Gardley could do about "that little fool," as he called Rosa, but it would be a relief to be able to tell some one all about it. If he only dared leave he would go over and tell Jasper Kemp about it, just to share his burden with somebody. But as it was he must stick to the job for the present and bear his great responsibility, and so the days hastened by to the last Sunday before Commencement, which was to be on Monday.

CHAPTER XXVII

Margaret had spent Saturday in rehearsals, so that there had been no rest for her. Sunday morning she slept late, and awoke from a troubled dream, unrested. She almost meditated whether she would not ask some one to read a sermon at the afternoon service and let her go on sleeping. Then a memory of the lonely old woman at the camp, and the men, who came so regularly to the service, roused her to effort once more, and she arose and tried to prepare a little something for them.

She came into the school-house at the hour, looking fagged, with dark circles under her eyes; and the loving eyes of Mom Wallis already in her front seat watched her keenly.

"It's time for *him* to come back," she said, in her heart. "She's gettin' peeked! I wisht he'd come!"

Margaret had hoped that Rosa would not come. The girl was not always there, but of late she had been quite regular, coming in late with her father just a little after the story had begun, and attracting attention by her smiles and bows and giggling whispers, which sometimes were so audible as to create quite a diversion from the speaker.

But Rosa came in early to-day and took a seat directly in front of Margaret, in about the middle of the house, fixing her eyes on her teacher with a kind of settled intention that made Margaret shrink as if from a danger she was not able to meet. There was something bright and hard and daring in Rosa's eyes as she stared unwinkingly, as if she had come to search out a weak spot for her evil purposes, and Margaret was so tired she wanted to lay her head down on her desk and cry. She drew some comfort from the reflection that if she should do so childish a thing she would be at once surrounded by a strong battalion of friends from the camp, who would shield her with their lives if necessary.

It was silly, of course, and she must control this choking in her throat, only how was she ever going to talk, with Rosa looking at her that way? It was like a nightmare pursuing her. She turned to the piano and kept them all singing for a while, so that she might pray in her heart and grow calm; and when, after her brief, earnest prayer, she lifted her eyes to the audience, she saw with intense relief that the Brownleighs were in the audience.

She started a hymn that they all knew, and when they were well in the midst of the first verse she slipped from the piano-stool and walked swiftly down the aisle to Brownleigh's side.

"Would you please talk to them a little while?" she pleaded, wistfully. "I am so tired I feel as if I just couldn't, to-day."

Instantly Brownleigh followed her back to the desk and took her place, pulling out his little, worn Bible and opening it with familiar fingers to a beloved passage:

> "'Come unto me, all ye that labor and are heavy laden, and I will give you rest.'"

The words fell on Margaret's tired heart like balm, and she rested her head back against the wall and closed her eyes to listen. Sitting so away from Rosa's stare, she could forget for a while the absurd burdens that had got on her nerves, and could rest down hard upon her Saviour. Every word that the man of God spoke seemed meant just for her, and brought strength, courage, and new trust to her heart. She forgot the little crowd of other listeners and took the message to herself, drinking it in eagerly as one who has been a long time ministering accepts a much-needed ministry. When she moved to the piano again for the closing hymn she felt new strength within her to bear the trials of the week that were before her. She turned, smiling and brave, to speak to those who always crowded around to shake hands and have a word before leaving.

Hazel, putting a loving arm around her as soon as she could get up to the front, began to speak soothingly: "You poor, tired child!" she said; "you are almost worn to a frazzle. You need a big change, and I'm going to plan it for you just as soon as I possibly can. How would you like to go with us on our trip among the Indians? Wouldn't it be great? It'll be several days, depending on how far we go, but John wants to visit the Hopi reservation, if possible, and it'll be so interesting. They are a most strange people. We'll have a delightful trip, sleeping out under the stars, you know. Don't you just love it? I do. I wouldn't miss it for the world. I can't be sure, for a few days yet, when we can go, for John has to make a journey in the other direction first, and he isn't sure when he can return; but it might be this week. How soon can you come to us? How I wish we could take you right home with us to-night. You need to get away and rest. But your Commencement is to-morrow, isn't it? I'm so sorry we can't be here, but this other matter is important, and John has to go early in the morning. Some one very sick who wants to see him before he dies — an old Indian who didn't know a thing about Jesus till John found him one day. I suppose you haven't anybody who could bring you over to us after your work is done here to-morrow night or Tuesday, have you? Well, we'll see if we can't find some one to send for you soon. There's an old Indian who often comes this way, but he's away buying cattle. Maybe John can think of a way we could send for you early in the week. Then you would be ready to go with us on the trip. You would like to go, wouldn't you?"

"Oh, so much!" said Margaret, with a sigh of wistfulness. "I can't think of anything pleasanter!"

Margaret turned suddenly, and there, just behind her, almost touching her, stood Rosa, that strange, baleful gleam in her eyes like a serpent who was biding her time, drawing nearer and nearer, knowing she had her victim where she could not move before she struck.

It was a strange fancy, of course, and one that was caused by sick nerves, but Margaret drew back and almost cried out, as if for some one to protect her. Then her strong common sense came to the rescue and she rallied and smiled at Rosa a faint little sorry smile. It was hard to smile at the bright, baleful face with the menace in the eyes.

Hazel was watching her. "You poor child! You're quite worn out! I'm afraid you're going to be sick."

"Oh no," said Margaret, trying to speak cheerfully; "things have just got on my nerves, that's all. It's been a particularly trying time. I shall be all right when to-morrow night is over."

"Well, we're going to send for you very soon, so be ready!" and Hazel followed her husband, waving her hand in gay parting.

Rosa was still standing just behind her when Margaret turned back to her desk, and the younger girl gave her one last dagger look, a glitter in her eyes so sinister and vindictive that Margaret felt a shudder run through her whole body, and was glad that just then Rosa's father called to her that they must be starting home. Only one more day now of Rosa, and she would be done with her, perhaps forever. The girl was through the school course and was graduating. It was not likely she would return another year. Her opportunity was over to help her. She had failed. Why, she couldn't tell, but she had strangely failed, and all she asked now was not to have to endure the hard, cold, young presence any longer.

"Sick nerves, Margaret!" she said to herself. "Go home and go to bed. You'll be all right to-morrow!" And she locked the school-house door and walked quietly home with the faithful Bud.

The past month had been a trying time also for Rosa. Young, wild, and motherless, passionate, wilful and impetuous, she was finding life tremendously exciting just now. With no one to restrain her or warn her she was playing with forces that she did not understand.

She had subjugated easily all the boys in school, keeping them exactly where she wanted them for her purpose, and using methods that would have done credit to a woman of the world. But by far the greatest force in her life was her infatuation for Forsythe.

The letters had traveled back and forth many times between them since Forsythe wrote that first love-letter. He found a whimsical pleasure in her deep devotion and naïve readiness to follow as far as he cared to lead her. He realized that, young as she was, she was no innocent, which made the acquaintance all the more interesting. He, meantime, idled away a few months on the Pacific coast, making mild love to a rich California girl and considering whether or not he was ready yet to settle down.

In the mean time his correspondence with Rosa took on such a nature that his volatile, impulsive nature was stirred with a desire to see her again. It was not often that once out of sight he looked back to a victim, but Rosa had shown a daring and a spirit in her letters that sent a challenge to his sated senses. Moreover, the California heiress was going on a journey; besides, an old enemy of his who knew altogether too much of his past had appeared on the scene; and as Gardley had been removed from the Ashland vicinity for a time, Forsythe felt it might be safe to venture back again. There was always that pretty, spirited little teacher if Rosa failed to charm. But why should Rosa not charm? And why should he not yield? Rosa's father was a good sort and had all kinds of property. Rosa was her father's only heir. On the whole, Forsythe decided that the best move he could make next would be to return to Arizona. If things turned out well he might even think of marrying Rosa.

This was somewhat the train of thought that led Forsythe at last to write to Rosa that he was coming, throwing Rosa into a panic of joy and alarm. For Rosa's father had been most explicit about her ever going out with Forsythe again. It had been the most relentless command he had ever laid upon her, spoken in a tone she hardly ever disobeyed. Moreover, Rosa was fearfully jealous of Margaret. If Forsythe should come and begin to hang around the teacher Rosa felt she would go wild, or do something terrible, perhaps even kill somebody. She shut her sharp little white teeth fiercely down into her red under lip and vowed with flashing eyes that he should never see Margaret again if power of hers could prevent it.

The letter from Forsythe had reached her on Saturday evening, and she had come to the Sunday service with the distinct idea of trying to plan how she might get rid of Margaret. It would be hard enough to evade her father's vigilance if he once found out the young man had returned; but to have him begin to go and see Margaret again was a thing she could not and would not stand.

The idea obsessed her to the exclusion of all others, and made her watch her teacher as if by her very concentration of thought upon her some way out of the difficulty might be evolved; as if Margaret herself might give forth a hint of weakness somewhere that would show her how to plan.

To that intent she had come close in the group with the others around the teacher at the close of meeting, and, so standing, had overheard all that the Brownleighs had said. The lightning flash of triumph that she cast at Margaret as she left the school-house was her own signal that she had found a way at last. Her opportunity had come, and just in time. Forsythe was to arrive in Arizona some time on Tuesday, and wanted Rosa to meet him at one of their old trysting-places, out some distance from her father's house. He knew that school would just be over, for she had written him about Commencement, and so he understood that she would be free. But he did not know that the place he had selected to meet her was on one of Margaret's favorite trails where she and Bud often rode in the late afternoons, and that above all things Rosa wished to avoid any danger of meeting her teacher; for she not only feared that Forsythe's attention would be drawn away from her, but also that Margaret might feel it her duty to report to her father about her clandestine meeting.

Rosa's heart beat high as she rode demurely home with her father, answering his pleasantries with smiles and dimples and a coaxing word, just as he loved to have her. But she was not thinking of her father, though she kept well her mask of interest in what he had to say. She was trying to plan how she might use what she had heard to get rid of Margaret Earle. If only Mrs. Brownleigh would do as she had hinted and send some one Tuesday morning to escort Miss Earle over to her home, all would be clear sailing for Rosa; but she dared not trust to such a possibility. There were not many escorts coming their way from Ganado, and Rosa happened to know that the old Indian who frequently escorted parties was off in another direction. She could not rest on any such hope. When she reached home she went at once to her room and sat beside her window, gazing off at the purple mountains in deep thought. Then she lighted a candle and went in search of a certain little Testament, long since neglected and covered with dust. She found it at last on the top of a pile of books in a dark closet, and dragged it forth, eagerly turning the pages. Yes, there it was, and in it a small envelope directed to "Miss Rosa Rogers" in a fine angular handwriting. The letter was from the missionary's wife to the little girl who had recited her texts so beautifully as to earn the Testament.

Rosa carried it to her desk, secured a good light, and sat down to read it over carefully.

No thought of her innocent childish exultation over that letter came to her now. She was intent on one thing — the handwriting. Could she seize the secret of it and reproduce it? She had before often done so with great success. She could imitate Miss Earle's writing so perfectly that she often took an impish pleasure in changing words in the questions on the blackboard and making them read absurdly for the benefit of the school. It was such good sport to see the amazement on Margaret's face when her attention would be called to it by a hilarious class, and to watch her troubled brow when she read what she supposed she had written.

When Rosa was but a little child she used to boast that she could write her father's name in perfect imitation of his signature; and often signed some trifling receipt for him just for amusement. A dangerous gift in the hands of a conscienceless girl! Yet this was the first time that Rosa had really planned to use her art in any serious way. Perhaps it never occurred to her that she was doing wrong. At present her heart was too full of hate and fear and jealous love to care for right or wrong or anything else. It is doubtful if she would have hesitated a second even if the thing she was planning had suddenly appeared to her in the light of a great crime. She seemed sometimes almost like a creature without moral sense, so swayed was she by her own desires and feelings. She was blind now to everything but her great desire to get Margaret out of the way and have Forsythe to herself.

Long after her father and the servants were asleep Rosa's light burned while she bent over her desk, writing. Page after page she covered with careful copies of Mrs. Brownleigh's letter written to herself almost three years before. Finally she wrote out the alphabet, bit by bit as she picked it from the words, learning just how each letter was habitually formed, the small letters and the capitals, with the peculiarities of connection and ending. At last, when she lay down to rest, she felt herself capable of writing a pretty fair letter in Mrs. Brownleigh's handwriting. The next thing was to make her plan and compose her letter. She lay staring into the darkness and trying to think just what she could do.

In the first place, she settled it that Margaret must be gotten to Walpi at least. It would not do to send her to Ganado, where the mission station was, for that was a comparatively short journey, and she could easily go in a day. When the fraud was discovered, as of course it would be when Mrs. Brownleigh heard of it, Margaret would perhaps return to find out who had done it. No, she must be sent all the way to Walpi if possible. That would take at least two nights and the most of two days to get there. Forsythe had said his stay was to be short. By the time Margaret got back from Walpi Forsythe would be gone.

But how manage to get her to Walpi without her suspicions being aroused? She might word the note so that Margaret would be told to come half-way, expecting to meet the missionaries, say at Keams. There was a trail straight up from Ashland to Keams, cutting off quite a distance and leaving Ganado off at the right. Keams was nearly forty miles west of Ganado. That would do nicely. Then if she could manage to have another note left at Keams, saying they could not wait and had gone on, Margaret would suspect nothing and go all the way to Walpi. That would be fine and would give the school-teacher an interesting experience which wouldn't hurt her in the least. Rosa thought it might be rather interesting than otherwise. She had no compunctions whatever about how Margaret might feel when she arrived in that strange Indian town and found no friends awaiting her. Her only worry was where she was to find a suitable escort, for she felt assured that Margaret would not start out alone with one man servant on an expedition that would keep her out overnight. And where in all that region could she find a woman whom she could trust to send on the errand? It almost looked as though the thing were an impossibility. She lay tossing and puzzling over it till gray dawn stole into the room. She mentally reviewed every servant on the place on whom she could rely to do her bidding and keep her secret, but there was some reason why each one would not do. She scanned the country, even considering old Ouida, who had been living in a shack over beyond the fort ever since her cabin had been raided; but old Ouida was too notorious. Mrs. Tanner would keep Margaret from going with her, even if Margaret herself did not know the old woman's reputation. Rosa considered if there were any way of wheedling Mom Wallis into the affair, and gave that up, remembering the suspicious little twinkling eyes of Jasper Kemp. At last she fell asleep, with her plan still unformed but her determination to carry it through just as strong as ever. If worst came to worst she would send the half-breed cook from the ranch kitchen and put something in the note about his expecting to meet his sister an hour's ride out on the trail. The half-breed would do anything in the world for money, and Rosa had no trouble in getting all she wanted of that commodity. But the half-breed was an evil-looking fellow, and she feared lest Margaret would not like to go with him. However, he should be a last resort. She would not be balked in her purpose.

CHAPTER XXVIII

Rosa awoke very early, for her sleep had been light and troubled. She dressed hastily and sat down to compose a note which could be altered slightly in case she found some one better than the half-breed; but before she was half through the phrasing she heard a slight disturbance below her window and a muttering in guttural tones from a strange voice. Glancing hastily out, she saw some Indians below, talking with one of the men, who was shaking his head and motioning to them that they must go on, that this was no place for them to stop. The Indian motioned to his squaw, sitting on a dilapidated little moth-eaten burro with a small papoose in her arms and looking both dirty and miserable. He muttered as though he were pleading for something.

We believe that God's angels follow the feet of little children and needy ones to protect them; does the devil also send his angels to lead unwary ones astray, and to protect the plan's of the erring ones? If so then he must have sent these Indians that morning to further Rosa's plans, and instantly she recognized her opportunity. She leaned out of her window and spoke in a clear, reproving voice:

"James, what does he want? Breakfast? You know father wouldn't want any hungry person to be turned away. Let them sit down on the bench there and tell Dorset I said to give them a good hot breakfast, and get some milk for the baby. Be quick about it, too!"

James started and frowned at the clear, commanding voice. The squaw turned grateful animal eyes up to the little beauty in the window, muttering some inarticulate thanks, while the stolid Indian's eyes glittered hopefully, though the muscles of his mask-like countenance changed not an atom.

Rosa smiled radiantly and ran down to see that her orders were obeyed. She tried to talk a little with the squaw, but found she understood very little English. The Indian spoke better and gave her their brief story. They were on their way to the Navajo reservation to the far north. They had been unfortunate enough to lose their last scanty provisions by prowling coyotes during the night, and were in need of food. Rosa gave them a place to sit down and a plentiful breakfast, and ordered that a small store of provisions should be prepared for their journey after they had rested. Then she hurried up to her room to finish her letter. She had her plan well fixed now. These strangers should be her willing messengers. Now and then, as she wrote she lifted her head and gazed out of the window, where she could see the squaw busy with her little one, and her eyes fairly glittered with satisfaction. Nothing could have been better planned than this.

She wrote her note carefully:

> Dear Margaret [she had heard Hazel call Margaret by her first name, and rightly judged that their new friendship was already strong enough to justify this intimacy], — I have found just the opportunity I wanted for you to come to us. These Indians are thoroughly trustworthy and are coming in just the direction to bring you to a point where we will meet you. We have decided to go on to Walpi at once, and will probably meet you near Keams, or a little farther on. The Indian knows the way, and you need not be afraid. I trust him perfectly. Start at once, please, so that you will meet us in time. John has to go on as fast as possible. I know you will enjoy the trip, and am so glad you are coming.
>
> Lovingly,
>
> Hazel Radcliffe Brownleigh.

Rosa read it over, comparing it carefully with the little yellow note from her Testament, and decided that it was a very good imitation. She could almost hear Mrs. Brownleigh saying what she had written. Rosa really was quite clever. She had done it well.

She hastily sealed and addressed her letter, and then hurried down to talk with the Indians again.

The place she had ordered for them to rest was at some distance from the kitchen door, a sort of outshed for the shelter of certain implements used about the ranch. A long bench ran in front of it, and a big tree made a goodly shade. The Indians had found their temporary camp quite inviting.

Rosa made a detour of the shed, satisfied herself that no one was within hearing, and then sat down on the bench, ostensibly playing with the papoose, dangling a red ball on a ribbon before his dazzled, bead-like eyes and bringing forth a gurgle of delight from the dusky little mummy. While she played she talked idly with the Indians. Had they money enough for their journey? Would they like to earn some? Would they act as guide to a lady who wanted to go to Walpi? At least she wanted to go as far as Keams, where she might meet friends, missionaries, who were going on with her to Walpi to visit the Indians. If they didn't meet her she wanted to be guided all the way to Walpi? Would they undertake it? It would pay them well. They would get money enough for their journey and have some left when they got to the reservation. And Rosa displayed two gold pieces temptingly in her small palms.

The Indian uttered a guttural sort of gasp at sight of so much money, and sat upright. He gasped again, indicating by a solemn nod that he was agreeable to the task before him, and the girl went gaily on with her instructions:

"You will have to take some things along to make the lady comfortable. I will see that those are got ready. Then you can have the things for your own when you leave the lady at Walpi. You will have to take a letter to the lady and tell her you are going this afternoon, and she must be ready to start at once or she will not meet the missionary. Tell her you can only wait until three o'clock to start. You will find the lady at the school-house at noon. You must not come till noon — " Rosa pointed to the sun and then straight overhead. The Indian watched her keenly and nodded.

"You must ask for Miss Earle and give her this letter. She is the school-teacher."

The Indian grunted and looked at the white missive in Rosa's hand, noting once more the gleam of the gold pieces.

"You must wait till the teacher goes to her boarding-house and packs her things and eats her dinner. If anybody asks where you came from you must say the missionary's wife from Ganado sent you. Don't tell anybody anything else. Do you understand? More money if you don't say anything?" Rosa clinked the gold pieces softly.

The strange, sphinx-like gaze of the Indian narrowed comprehensively. He understood. His native cunning was being bought for this girl's own purposes. He looked greedily at the money. Rosa had put her hand in her pocket and brought out yet another gold piece.

"See! I give you this one now" — she laid one gold piece in the Indian's hand — "and these two I put in an envelope and pack with some provisions and blankets on another horse. I will leave the horse tied to a tree up where the big trail crosses this big trail out that way. You know?"

Rosa pointed in the direction she meant, and the Indian looked and grunted, his eyes returning to the two gold pieces in her hand. It was a great deal of money for the little lady to give. Was she trying to cheat him? He looked down at the gold he already held. It was good money. He was sure of that. He looked at her keenly.

"I shall be watching and I shall know whether you have the lady or not," went on the girl, sharply. "If you do not bring the lady with you there will be no money and no provisions waiting for you. But if you bring the lady you can untie the horse and take him with you. You will need the horse to carry the things. When you get to Walpi you can set him free. He is branded and he will likely come back. We shall find him. See, I will put the gold pieces in this tin can."

She picked up a sardine-tin that lay at her feet, slipped the gold pieces in an envelope from her pocket, stuffed it in the tin, bent down the cover, and held it up.

"This can will be packed on the top of the other provisions, and you can open it and take the money out when you untie the horse. Then hurry on as fast as you can and get as far along the trail as possible to-night before you camp. Do you understand?"

The Indian nodded once more, and Rosa felt that she had a confederate worthy of her need.

She stayed a few minutes more, going carefully over her directions, telling the Indian to be sure his squaw was kind to the lady, and that on no account he should let the lady get uneasy or have cause to complain of her treatment, or trouble would surely come to him. At last she felt sure she had made him understand, and she hurried away to slip into her pretty white dress and rose-colored ribbons and ride to school. Before she left her room she glanced out of the window at the Indians, and saw them sitting motionless, like a group of bronze. Once the Indian stirred and, putting his hand in his bosom, drew forth the white letter she had given him, gazed at it a moment, and hid it in his breast again. She nodded her satisfaction as she turned from the window. The next thing was to get to school and play her own part in the Commencement exercises.

The morning was bright, and the school-house was already filled to overflowing when Rosa arrived. Her coming, as always, made a little stir among admiring groups, for even those who feared her admired her from afar. She fluttered into the school-house and up the aisle with the air of a princess who knew she had been waited for and was condescending to come at all.

Rosa was in everything — the drills, the march, the choruses, and the crowning oration. She went through it all with the perfection of a bright mind and an adaptable nature. One would never have dreamed, to look at her pretty dimpling face and her sparkling eyes, what diabolical things were moving in her mind, nor how those eyes, lynx-soft with lurking sweetness and treachery, were watching all the time furtively for the appearance of the old Indian.

At last she saw him, standing in a group just outside the window near the platform, his tall form and stern countenance marking him among the crowd of familiar faces. She was receiving her diploma from the hand of Margaret when she caught his eye, and her hand trembled just a quiver as she took the dainty roll tied with blue and white ribbons. That he recognized her she was sure; that he knew she did not wish him to make known his connection with her she felt equally convinced he understood. His eye had that comprehending look of withdrawal. She did not look up directly at him again. Her eyes were daintily downward. Nevertheless, she missed not a turn of his head, not a glance from that stern eye, and she knew the moment when he stood at the front door of the school-house with the letter in his hand, stolid and indifferent, yet a great force to be reckoned with.

Some one looked at the letter, pointed to Margaret, called her, and she came. Rosa was not far away all the time, talking with Jed; her eyes downcast, her cheeks dimpling, missing nothing that could be heard or seen.

Margaret read the letter. Rosa watched her, knew every curve of every letter and syllable as she read, held her breath, and watched Margaret's expression. Did she suspect? No. A look of intense relief and pleasure had come into her eyes. She was glad to have found a way to go. She turned to Mrs. Tanner.

"What do you think of this, Mrs. Tanner? I'm to go with Mrs. Brownleigh on a trip to Walpi. Isn't that delicious? I'm to start at once. Do you suppose I could have a bite to eat? I won't need much. I'm too tired to eat and too anxious to be off. If you give me a cup of tea and a sandwich I'll be all right. I've got things about ready to go, for Mrs. Brownleigh told me she would send some one for me."

"H'm!" said Mrs. Tanner, disapprovingly. "Who you goin' with? Just *him*? I don't much like *his* looks!"

She spoke in a low tone so the Indian would not hear, and it was almost in Rosa's very ear, who stood just behind. Rosa's heart stopped a beat and she frowned at the toe of her slipper. Was this common little Tanner woman going to be the one to balk her plans?

Margaret raised her head now for her first good look at the Indian, and it must be admitted a chill came into her heart. Then, as if he comprehended what was at stake, the Indian turned slightly and pointed down the path toward the road. By common consent the few who were standing about the door stepped back and made a vista for Margaret to see the squaw sitting statue-like on her scraggy little pony, gazing off at the mountain in the distance, as if she were sitting for her picture, her solemn little papoose strapped to her back.

Margaret's troubled eyes cleared. The family aspect made things all right again. "You see, he has his wife and child," she said. "It's all right. Mrs. Brownleigh says she trusts him perfectly, and I'm to meet them on the way. Read the letter."

She thrust the letter into Mrs. Tanner's hand, and Rosa trembled for her scheme once more. Surely, surely Mrs. Tanner would not be able to detect the forgery!

"H'm! Well, I s'pose it's all right if she says so, but I'm sure I don't relish them pesky Injuns, and I don't think that squaw wife of his looks any great shakes, either. They look to me like they needed a good scrub with Bristol brick. But then, if you're set on going, you'll go, 'course. I jest wish Bud hadn't 'a' gone home with that Jasper Kemp. He might 'a' gone along, an' then you'd 'a' had somebody to speak English to."

"Yes, it would have been nice to have William along," said Margaret; "but I think I'll be all right. Mrs. Brownleigh wouldn't send anybody that wasn't nice."

"H'm! I dun'no'! She's an awful crank. She just loves them Injuns, they say. But I, fer one, draw the line at holdin' 'em in my lap. I don't b'lieve in mixin' folks up that way. Preach to 'em if you like, but let 'em keep their distance, I say."

Margaret laughed and went off to pick up her things. Rosa stood smiling and talking to Jed until she saw Margaret and Mrs. Tanner go off together, the Indians riding slowly along behind.

Rosa waited until the Indians had turned off the road down toward the Tanners', and then she mounted her own pony and rode swiftly home.

She rushed up to her room and took off her fine apparel, arraying herself quickly in a plain little gown, and went down to prepare the provisions. There was none too much time, and she must work rapidly. It was well for her plans that she was all-powerful with the servants and could send them about at will to get them out of her way. She invented a duty for each now that would take them for a few minutes well out of sight and sound; then she hurried together the provisions in a basket, making two trips to get them to the shelter where she had told the Indian he would find the horse tied. She had to make a third trip to bring the blankets and a few other things she knew would be indispensable, but the whole outfit was really but carelessly gotten together, and it was just by chance that some things got in at all.

It was not difficult to find the old cayuse she intended using for a pack-horse. He was browsing around in the corral, and she soon had a halter over his head, for she had been quite used to horses from her babyhood.

She packed the canned things, tinned meats, vegetables, and fruit into a couple of large sacks, adding some fodder for the horses, a box of matches, some corn bread, of which there was always plenty on hand in the house, some salt pork, and a few tin dishes. These she slung pack fashion over the old horse, fastened the sardine-tin containing the gold pieces where it would be easily found, tied the horse to a tree, and retired behind a shelter of sage-brush to watch.

It was not long before the little caravan came, the Indians riding ahead single file, like two graven images, moving not a muscle of their faces, and Margaret a little way behind on her own pony, her face as happy and relieved as if she were a child let out from a hard task to play.

The Indian stopped beside the horse, a glitter of satisfaction in his eyes as he saw that the little lady had fulfilled her part of the bargain. He indicated to the squaw and the lady that they might move on down the trail, and he would catch up with them; and then dismounted, pouncing warily upon the sardine-tin at once. He looked furtively about, then took out the money and tested it with his teeth to make sure it was genuine.

He grunted his further satisfaction, looked over the pack-horse, made more secure the fastenings of the load, and, taking the halter, mounted and rode stolidly away toward the north.

Rosa waited in her covert until they were far out of sight, then made her way hurriedly back to the house and climbed to a window where she could watch the trail for several miles. There, with a field-glass, she kept watch until the procession had filed across the plains, down into a valley, up over a hill, and dropped to a farther valley out of sight. She looked at the sun and drew a breath of satisfaction. She had done it at last! She had got Margaret away before Forsythe came! There was no likelihood that the fraud would be discovered until her rival was far enough away to be safe. A kind of reaction came upon Rosa's overwrought nerves. She laughed out harshly, and her voice had a cruel ring to it. Then she threw herself upon the bed and burst into a passionate fit of weeping, and so, by and by, fell asleep. She dreamed that Margaret had returned like a shining, fiery angel, a two-edged sword in her hand and all the Wallis camp at her heels, with vengeance in their wake. That hateful little boy, Bud Tanner, danced around and made faces at her, while Forsythe had forgotten her to gaze at Margaret's face.

CHAPTER XXIX

To Margaret the day was very fair, and the omens all auspicious. She carried with her close to her heart two precious letters received that morning and scarcely glanced at as yet, one from Gardley and one from her mother. She had had only time to open them and be sure that all was well with her dear ones, and had left the rest to read on the way.

She was dressed in the khaki riding-habit she always wore when she went on horseback; and in the bag strapped on behind she carried a couple of fresh white blouses, a thin, white dress, a little soft dark silk gown that folded away almost into a cobweb, and a few other necessities. She had also slipped in a new book her mother had sent her, into which she had had as yet no time to look, and her chessmen and board, besides writing materials. She prided herself on having got so many necessaries into so small a compass. She would need the extra clothing if she stayed at Ganado with the missionaries for a week on her return from the trip, and the book and chessmen would amuse them all by the way. She had heard Brownleigh say he loved to play chess.

Margaret rode on the familiar trail, and for the first hour just let herself be glad that school was over and she could rest and have no responsibility. The sun shimmered down brilliantly on the white, hot sand and gray-green of the greasewood and sage-brush. Tall spikes of cactus like lonely spires shot up now and again to vary the scene. It was all familiar ground to Margaret around here, for she had taken many rides with Gardley and Bud, and for the first part of the way every turn and bit of view was fraught with pleasant memories that brought a smile to her eyes as she recalled some quotation of Gardley's or some prank of Bud's. Here was where they first sighted the little cottontail the day she took her initial ride on her own pony. Off there was the mountain where they saw the sun drawing silver water above a frowning storm. Yonder was the group of cedars where they had stopped to eat their lunch once, and this water-hole they were approaching was the one where Gardley had given her a drink from his hat.

She was almost glad that Bud was not along, for she was too tired to talk and liked to be alone with her thoughts for this few minutes. Poor Bud! He would be disappointed when he got back to find her gone, but then he had expected she was going in a few days, anyway, and she had promised to take long rides with him when she returned. She had left a little note for him, asking him to read a certain book in her bookcase while she was gone, and be ready to discuss it with her when she got back, and Bud would be fascinated with it, she knew. Bud had been dear and faithful, and she would miss him, but just for this little while she was glad to have the great out-of-doors to herself.

She was practically alone. The two sphinx-like figures riding ahead of her made no sign, but stolidly rode on hour after hour, nor turned their heads even to see if she were coming. She knew that Indians were this way; still, as the time went by she began to feel an uneasy sense of being alone in the universe with a couple of bronze statues. Even the papoose had erased itself in sleep, and when it awoke partook so fully of its racial peculiarities as to hold its little peace and make no fuss. Margaret began to feel the baby was hardly human, more like a little brown doll set up in a missionary meeting to teach white children what a papoose was like.

By and by she got out her letters and read them over carefully, dreaming and smiling over them, and getting precious bits by heart. Gardley hinted that he might be able very soon to visit her parents, as it looked as though he might have to make a trip on business in their direction before he could go further with what he was doing in his old home. He gave no hint of soon returning to the West. He said he was awaiting the return of one man who might soon be coming from abroad. Margaret sighed and wondered how many weary months it would be before she would see him. Perhaps, after all, she ought to have gone home and stayed them out with her mother and father. If the school-board could be made to see that it would be better to have no summer session, perhaps she would even yet go when she returned from the Brownleighs'. She would see. She would decide nothing until she was rested.

Suddenly she felt herself overwhelmingly weary, and wished that the Indians would stop and rest for a while; but when she stirred up her sleepy pony and spurred ahead to broach the matter to her guide he shook his solemn head and pointed to the sun:

"No get Keams good time. No meet Aneshodi."

"Aneshodi," she knew, was the Indians' name for the missionary, and she smiled her acquiescence. Of course they must meet the Brownleighs and not detain them. What was it Hazel had said about having to hurry? She searched her pocket for the letter, and then remembered she had left it with Mrs. Tanner. What a pity she had not brought it! Perhaps there was some caution or advice in it that she had not taken note of. But then the Indian likely knew all about it, and she could trust to him. She glanced at his stolid face and wished she could make him smile. She cast a sunny smile at him and said something pleasant about the beautiful day, but he only looked her through as if she were not there, and after one or two more attempts she fell back and tried to talk to the squaw; but the squaw only looked stolid, too, and shook her head. She did not seem friendly. Margaret drew back into her old position and feasted her eyes upon the distant hills.

The road was growing unfamiliar now. They were crossing rough ridges with cliffs of red sandstone, and every step of the way was interesting. Yet Margaret felt more and more how much she wanted to lie down and sleep, and when at last in the dusk the Indians halted not far from a little pool of rainwater and indicated that here they would camp for the night, Margaret was too weary to question the decision. It had not occurred to her that she would be on the way overnight before she met her friends. Her knowledge of the way, and of distances, was but vague. It is doubtful if she would have ventured had she known that she must pass the night thus in the company of two strange savage creatures. Yet, now that she was here and it was inevitable, she would not shrink, but make the best of it. She tried to be friendly once more, and offered to look out for the baby while the squaw gathered wood and made a fire. The Indian was off looking after the horses, evidently expecting his wife to do all the work.

Margaret watched a few minutes, while pretending to play with the baby, who was both sleepy and hungry, yet held his emotions as stolidly as if he were a grown person. Then she decided to take a hand in the supper. She was hungry and could not bear that those dusky, dirty hands should set forth her food, so she went to work cheerfully, giving directions as if the Indian woman understood her, though she very soon discovered that all her talk was as mere babbling to the other, and she might as well hold her peace. The woman set a kettle of water over the fire, and Margaret forestalled her next movement by cutting some pork and putting it to cook in a little skillet she found among the provisions. The woman watched her solemnly, not seeming to care; and so, silently, each went about her own preparations.

The supper was a silent affair, and when it was over the squaw handed Margaret a blanket. Suddenly she understood that this, and this alone, was to be her bed for the night. The earth was there for a mattress, and the sage-brush lent a partial shelter, the canopy of stars was overhead.

A kind of panic took possession of her. She stared at the squaw and found herself longing to cry out for help. It seemed as if she could not bear this awful silence of the mortals who were her only company. Yet her common sense came to her aid, and she realized that there was nothing for it but to make the best of things. So she took the blanket and, spreading it out, sat down upon it and wrapped it about her shoulders and feet. She would not lie down until she saw what the rest did. Somehow she shrank from asking the bronze man how to fold a blanket for a bed on the ground. She tried to remember what Gardley had told her about folding the blanket bed so as best to keep out snakes and ants. She shuddered at the thought of snakes. Would she dare call for help from those stolid companions of hers if a snake should attempt to molest her in the night? And would she ever dare to go to sleep?

She remembered her first night in Arizona out among the stars, alone on the water-tank, and her first frenzy of loneliness. Was this as bad? No, for these Indians were trustworthy and well known by her dear friends. It might be unpleasant, but this, too, would pass and the morrow would soon be here.

The dusk dropped down and the stars loomed out. All the world grew wonderful, like a blue jeweled dome of a palace with the lights turned low. The fire burned brightly as the man threw sticks upon it, and the two Indians moved stealthily about in the darkness, passing silhouetted before the fire this way and that, and then at last lying down wrapped in their blankets to sleep.

It was very quiet about her. The air was so still she could hear the hobbled horses munching away in the distance, and moving now and then with the halting gait a hobble gives a horse. Off in the farther distance the blood-curdling howl of the coyotes rose, but Margaret was used to them, and knew they would not come near a fire.

She was growing very weary, and at last wrapped her blanket closer and lay down, her head pillowed on one corner of it. Committing herself to her Heavenly Father, and breathing a prayer for father, mother, and lover, she fell asleep.

It was still almost dark when she awoke. For a moment she thought it was still night and the sunset was not gone yet, the clouds were so rosy tinted.

The squaw was standing by her, touching her shoulder roughly and grunting something. She perceived, as she rubbed her eyes and tried to summon back her senses, that she was expected to get up and eat breakfast. There was a smell of pork and coffee in the air, and there was scorched corn bread beside the fire on a pan.

Margaret got up quickly and ran down to the water-hole to get some water, dashing it in her face and over her arms and hands, the squaw meanwhile standing at a little distance, watching her curiously, as if she thought this some kind of an oblation paid to the white woman's god before she ate. Margaret pulled the hair-pins out of her hair, letting it down and combing it with one of her side combs; twisted it up again in its soft, fluffy waves; straightened her collar, set on her hat, and was ready for the day. The squaw looked at her with both awe and contempt for a moment, then turned and stalked back to her papoose and began preparing it for the journey.

Margaret made a hurried meal and was scarcely done before she found her guides were waiting like two pillars of the desert, but watching keenly, impatiently, her every mouthful, and anxious to be off.

The sky was still pink-tinted with the semblance of a sunset, and Margaret felt, as she mounted her pony and followed her companions, as if the day was all turned upside down. She almost wondered whether she hadn't slept through a whole twenty-four hours, and it were not, after all, evening again, till by and by the sun rose clear and the wonder of the cloud-tinting melted into day.

The road lay through sage-brush and old barren cedar-trees, with rabbits darting now and then between the rocks. Suddenly from the top of a little hill they came out to a spot where they could see far over the desert. Forty miles away three square, flat hills, or mesas, looked like a gigantic train of cars, and the clear air gave everything a strange vastness. Farther on beyond the mesas dimly dawned the Black Mountains. One could even see the shadowed head of "Round Rock," almost a hundred miles away. Before them and around was a great plain of sage-brush, and here and there was a small bush that the Indians call "the weed that was not scared." Margaret had learned all these things during her winter in Arizona, and keenly enjoyed the vast, splendid view spread before her.

They passed several little mud-plastered hogans that Margaret knew for Indian dwellings. A fine band of ponies off in the distance made an interesting spot on the landscape, and twice they passed bands of sheep. She had a feeling of great isolation from everything she had ever known, and seemed going farther and farther from life and all she loved. Once she ventured to ask the Indian what time he expected to meet her friends, the missionaries, but he only shook his head and murmured something unintelligible about "Keams" and pointed to the sun. She dropped behind again, vaguely uneasy, she could not tell why. There seemed something so altogether sly and wary and unfriendly in the faces of the two that she almost wished she had not come. Yet the way was beautiful enough and nothing very unpleasant was happening to her. Once she dropped the envelope of her mother's letter and was about to dismount and recover it. Then some strange impulse made her leave it on the sand of the desert. What if they should be lost and that paper should guide them back? The notion stayed by her, and once in a while she dropped other bits of paper by the way.

About noon the trail dropped off into a cañon, with high, yellow-rock walls on either side, and stifling heat, so that she felt as if she could scarcely stand it. She was glad when they emerged once more and climbed to higher ground. The noon camp was a hasty affair, for the Indian seemed in a hurry. He scanned the horizon far and wide and seemed searching keenly for some one or something. Once they met a lonely Indian, and he held a muttered conversation with him, pointing off ahead and gesticulating angrily. But the words were unintelligible to Margaret. Her feeling of uneasiness was growing, and yet she could not for the life of her tell why, and laid it down to her tired nerves. She was beginning to think she had been very foolish to start on such a long trip before she had had a chance to get rested from her last days of school. She longed to lie down under a tree and sleep for days.

Toward night they sighted a great blue mesa about fifty miles south, and at sunset they could just see the San Francisco peaks more than a hundred and twenty-five miles away. Margaret, as she stopped her horse and gazed, felt a choking in her heart and throat and a great desire to cry. The glory and awe of the mountains, mingled with her own weariness and nervous fear, were almost too much for her. She was glad to get down and eat a little supper and go to sleep again. As she fell asleep she comforted herself with repeating over a few precious words from her Bible:

> "The angel of the Lord encampeth round about them that fear Him and delivereth them. Thou wilt keep him in perfect peace whose mind is stayed on Thee because he trusteth in Thee. I will both lay me down in peace and sleep, for Thou Lord only makest me to dwell in safety...."

The voice of the coyotes, now far, now near, boomed out on the night; great stars shot dartling pathways across the heavens; the fire snapped and crackled, died down and flickered feebly; but Margaret slept, tired out, and dreamed the angels kept close vigil around her lowly couch.

She did not know what time the stars disappeared and the rain began to fall. She was too tired to notice the drops that fell upon her face. Too tired to hear the coyotes coming nearer, nearer, yet in the morning there lay one dead, stretched not thirty feet from where she lay. The Indian had shot him through the heart.

Somehow things looked very dismal that morning, in spite of the brightness of the sun after the rain. She was stiff and sore with lying in the dampness. Her hair was wet, her blanket was wet, and she woke without feeling rested. Almost the trip seemed more than she could bear. If she could have wished herself back that morning and have stayed at Tanners' all summer she certainly would have done it rather than to be where and how she was.

The Indians seemed excited — the man grim and forbidding, the woman appealing, frightened, anxious. They were near to Keams Cañon. "Aneshodi" would be somewhere about. The Indian hoped to be rid of his burden then and travel on his interrupted journey. He was growing impatient. He felt he had earned his money.

But when they tried to go down Keam's Cañon they found the road all washed away by flood, and must needs go a long way around. This made the Indian surly. His countenance was more forbidding than ever. Margaret, as she watched him with sinking heart, altered her ideas of the Indian as a whole to suit the situation. She had always felt pity for the poor Indian, whose land had been seized and whose kindred had been slaughtered. But this Indian was not an object of pity. He was the most disagreeable, cruel-looking Indian Margaret had ever laid eyes on. She had felt it innately the first time she saw him, but now, as the situation began to bring him out, she knew that she was dreadfully afraid of him. She had a feeling that he might scalp her if he got tired of her. She began to alter her opinion of Hazel Brownleigh's judgment as regarded Indians. She did not feel that she would ever send this Indian to any one for a guide and say he was perfectly trustworthy. He hadn't done anything very dreadful yet, but she felt he was going to.

He had a number of angry confabs with his wife that morning. At least, he did the confabbing and the squaw protested. Margaret gathered after a while that it was something about herself. The furtive, frightened glances that the squaw cast in her direction sometimes, when the man was not looking, made her think so. She tried to say it was all imagination, and that her nerves were getting the upper hand of her, but in spite of her she shuddered sometimes, just as she had done when Rosa looked at her. She decided that she must be going to have a fit of sickness, and that just as soon as she got in the neighborhood of Mrs. Tanner's again she would pack her trunk and go home to her mother. If she was going to be sick she wanted her mother.

About noon things came to a climax. They halted on the top of the mesa, and the Indians had another altercation, which ended in the man descending the trail a fearfully steep way, down four hundred feet to the trading-post in the cañon. Margaret looked down and gasped and thanked a kind Providence that had not made it necessary for her to make that descent; but the squaw stood at the top with her baby and looked down in silent sorrow — agony perhaps would be a better name. Her face was terrible to look upon.

Margaret could not understand it, and she went to the woman and put her hand out sympathetically, asking, gently: "What is the matter, you poor little thing? Oh, what is it?"

Perhaps the woman understood the tenderness in the tone, for she suddenly turned and rested her forehead against Margaret's shoulder, giving one great, gasping sob, then lifted her dry, miserable eyes to the girl's face as if to thank her for her kindness.

Margaret's heart was touched. She threw her arms around the poor woman and drew her, papoose and all, comfortingly toward her, patting her shoulder and saying gentle, soothing words as she would to a little child. And by and by the woman lifted her head again, the tears coursing down her face, and tried to explain, muttering her queer gutturals and making eloquent gestures until Margaret felt she understood. She gathered that the man had gone down to the trading-post to find the "Aneshodi," and that the squaw feared that he would somehow procure firewater either from the trader or from some Indian he might meet, and would come back angrier than he had gone, and without his money.

If Margaret also suspected that the Indian had desired to get rid of her by leaving her at that desolate little trading-station down in the cañon until such time as her friends should call for her, she resolutely put the thought out of her mind and set herself to cheer the poor Indian woman.

She took a bright, soft, rosy silk tie from her own neck and knotted it about the astonished woman's dusky throat, and then she put a silver dollar in her hand, and was thrilled with wonder to see what a change came over the poor, dark face. It reminded her of Mom Wallis when she got on her new bonnet, and once again she felt the thrill of knowing the whole world kin.

The squaw cheered up after a little, got sticks and made a fire, and together they had quite a pleasant meal. Margaret exerted herself to make the poor woman laugh, and finally succeeded by dangling a bright-red knight from her chessmen in front of the delighted baby's eyes till he gurgled out a real baby crow of joy.

It was the middle of the afternoon before the Indian returned, sitting crazily his struggling beast as he climbed the trail once more. Margaret, watching, caught her breath and prayed. Was this the trustworthy man, this drunken, reeling creature, clubbing his horse and pouring forth a torrent of indistinguishable gutturals? It was evident that his wife's worst fears were verified. He had found the firewater.

The frightened squaw set to work putting things together as fast as she could. She well knew what to expect, and when the man reached the top of the mesa he found his party packed and mounted, waiting fearsomely to take the trail.

Silently, timorously, they rode behind him, west across the great wide plain.

In the distance gradually there appeared dim mesas like great fingers stretching out against the sky; miles away they seemed, and nothing intervening but a stretch of varying color where sage-brush melted into sand, and sage-brush and greasewood grew again, with tall cactus startling here and there like bayonets at rest but bristling with menace.

The Indian had grown silent and sullen. His eyes were like deep fires of burning volcanoes. One shrank from looking at them. His massive, cruel profile stood out like bronze against the evening sky. It was growing night again, and still they had not come to anywhere or anything, and still her friends seemed just as far away.

Since they had left the top of Keams Cañon Margaret had been sure all was not right. Aside from the fact that the guide was drunk at present, she was convinced that there had been something wrong with him all along. He did not act like the Indians around Ashland. He did not act like a trusted guide that her friends would send for her. She wished once more that she had kept Hazel Brownleigh's letter. She wondered how her friends would find her if they came after her. It was then she began in earnest to systematically plan to leave a trail behind her all the rest of the way. If she had only done it thoroughly when she first began to be uneasy. But now she was so far away, so many miles from anywhere! Oh, if she had not come at all!

And first she dropped her handkerchief, because she happened to have it in her hand — a dainty thing with lace on the edge and her name written in tiny script by her mother's careful hand on the narrow hem. And then after a little, as soon as she could scrawl it without being noticed, she wrote a note which she twisted around the neck of a red chessman, and left behind her. After that scraps of paper, as she could reach them out of the bag tied on behind her saddle; then a stocking, a bedroom slipper, more chessmen, and so, when they halted at dusk and prepared to strike camp, she had quite a good little trail blazed behind her over that wide, empty plain. She shuddered as she looked into the gathering darkness ahead, where those long, dark lines of mesas looked like barriers in the way. Then, suddenly, the Indian pointed ahead to the first mesa and uttered one word — "Walpi!" So that was the Indian village to which she was bound? What was before her on the morrow? After eating a pretense of supper she lay down. The Indian had more firewater with him. He drank, he uttered cruel gutturals at his squaw, and even kicked the feet of the sleeping papoose as he passed by till it awoke and cried sharply, which made him more angry, so he struck the squaw.

It seemed hours before all was quiet. Margaret's nerves were strained to such a pitch she scarcely dared to breathe, but at last, when the fire had almost died down, the man lay quiet, and she could relax and close her eyes.

Not to sleep. She must not go to sleep. The fire was almost gone and the coyotes would be around. She must wake and watch!

That was the last thought she remembered — that and a prayer that the angels would keep watch once again.

When she awoke it was broad daylight and far into the morning, for the sun was high overhead and the mesas in the distance were clear and distinct against the sky.

She sat up and looked about her, bewildered, not knowing at first where she was. It was so still and wide and lonely.

She turned to find the Indians, but there was no trace of them anywhere. The fire lay smoldering in its place, a thin trickle of smoke curling away from a dying stick, but that was all. A tin cup half full of coffee was beside the stick, and a piece of blackened corn bread. She turned frightened eyes to east, to west, to north, to south, but there was no one in sight, and out over the distant mesa there poised a great eagle alone in the vast sky keeping watch over the brilliant, silent waste.

CHAPTER XXX

When Margaret was a very little girl her father and mother had left her alone for an hour with a stranger while they went out to make a call in a strange city through which they were passing on a summer trip. The stranger was kind, and gave to the child a large green box of bits of old black lace and purple ribbons to play with, but she turned sorrowfully from the somber array of finery, which was the only thing in the way of a plaything the woman had at hand, and stood looking drearily out of the window on the strange, new town, a feeling of utter loneliness upon her. Her little heart was almost choked with the awfulness of the thought that she was a human atom drifted apart from every other atom she had ever known, that she had a personality and a responsibility of her own, and that she must face this thought of herself and her aloneness for evermore. It was the child's first realization that she was a separate being apart from her father and mother, and she was almost consumed with the terror of it.

As she rose now from her bed on the ground and looked out across that vast waste, in which the only other living creature was that sinister, watching eagle, the same feeling returned to her and made her tremble like the little child who had turned from her box of ancient finery to realize her own little self and its terrible aloneness.

For an instant even her realization of God, which had from early childhood been present with her, seemed to have departed. She could not grasp anything save the vast empty silence that loomed about her so awfully. She was alone, and about as far from anywhere or anything as she could possibly be in the State of Arizona. Would she ever get back to human habitations? Would her friends ever be able to find her?

Then her heart flew back to its habitual refuge, and she spoke aloud and said, "God is here!" and the thought seemed to comfort her. She looked about once more on the bright waste, and now it did not seem so dreary.

"God is here!" she repeated, and tried to realize that this was a part of His habitation. She could not be lost where God was. He knew the way out. She had only to trust. So she dropped upon her knees in the sand and prayed for trust and courage.

When she rose again she walked steadily to a height a little above the camp-fire, and, shading her eyes, looked carefully in every direction. No, there was not a sign of her recent companions. They must have stolen away in the night quite soon after she fell asleep, and have gone fast and far, so that they were now beyond the reach of her eyes, and not anywhere was there sign of living thing, save that eagle still sweeping in great curves and poising again above the distant mesa.

Where was her horse? Had the Indians taken that, too? She searched the valley, but saw no horse at first. With sinking heart she went back to where her things were and sat down by the dying fire to think, putting a few loose twigs and sticks together to keep the embers bright while she could. She reflected that she had no matches, and this was probably the last fire she would have until somebody came to her rescue or she got somewhere by herself. What was she to do? Stay right where she was or start out on foot? And should she go backward or forward? Surely, surely the Brownleighs would miss her pretty soon and send out a search-party for her. How could it be that they trusted an Indian who had done such a cruel thing as to leave a woman unprotected in the desert? And yet, perhaps, they did not know his temptation to drink. Perhaps they had thought he could not get any firewater. Perhaps he would return when he came to himself and realized what he had done.

And now she noticed what she had not seen at first — a small bottle of water on a stone beside the blackened bread. Realizing that she was very hungry and that this was the only food at hand, she sat down beside the fire to eat the dry bread and drink the miserable coffee. She must have strength to do whatever was before her. She tried not to think how her mother would feel if she never came back, how anxious they would be as they waited day by day for her letters that did not come. She reflected with a sinking heart that she had, just before leaving, written a hasty note to her mother telling her not to expect anything for several days, perhaps even as much as two weeks, as she was going out of civilization for a little while. How had she unwittingly sealed her fate by that! For now not even by way of her alarmed home could help come to her.

She put the last bit of hard corn bread in her pocket for a further time of need, and began to look about her again. Then she spied with delight a moving object far below her in the valley, and decided it was a horse, perhaps her own. He was a mile away, at least, but he was there, and she cried out with sudden joy and relief.

She went over to her blanket and bags, which had been beside her during the night, and stood a moment trying to think what to do. Should she carry the things to the horse or risk leaving them here while she went after the horse and brought him to the things? No, that would not be safe. Some one might come along and take them, or she might not be able to find her way back again in this strange, wild waste. Besides, she might not get the horse, after all, and would lose everything. She must carry her things to the horse. She stooped to gather them up, and something bright beside her bag attracted her. It was the sun shining on the silver dollar she had given to the Indian woman. A sudden rush of tears came to her eyes. The poor creature had tried to make all the reparation she could for thus hastily leaving the white woman in the desert. She had given back the money — all she had that was valuable! Beside the dollar rippled a little chain of beads curiously wrought, an inanimate appeal for forgiveness and a grateful return for the kindness shown her. Margaret smiled as she stooped again to pick up her things. There had been a heart, after all, behind that stolid countenance, and some sense of righteousness and justice. Margaret decided that Indians were not all treacherous. Poor woman! What a life was hers — to follow her grim lord whither he would lead, even as her white sister must sometimes, sorrowing, rebelling, crying out, but following! She wondered if into the heart of this dark sister there ever crept any of the rebellion which led some of her white sisters to cry aloud for "rights" and "emancipation."

But it was all a passing thought to be remembered and turned over at a more propitious time. Margaret's whole thoughts now were bent on her present predicament.

The packing was short work. She stuffed everything into the two bags that were usually hung across the horse, and settled them carefully across her shoulders. Then she rolled the blanket, took it in her arms, and started. It was a heavy burden to carry, but she could not make up her mind to part with any of her things until she had at least made an effort to save them. If she should be left alone in the desert for the night the blanket was indispensable, and her clothes would at least do to drop as a trail by which her friends might find her. She must carry them as far as possible. So she started.

It was already high day, and the sun was intolerably hot. Her heavy burden was not only cumbersome, but very warm, and she felt her strength going from her as she went; but her nerve was up and her courage was strong. Moreover, she prayed as she walked, and she felt now the presence of her Guide and was not afraid. As she walked she faced a number of possibilities in the immediate future which were startling, and to say the least, undesirable. There were wild animals in this land, not so much in the daylight, but what of the night? She had heard that a woman was always safe in that wild Western land; but what of the prowling Indians? What of a possible exception to the Western rule of chivalry toward a decent woman? One small piece of corn bread and less than a pint of water were small provision on which to withstand a siege. How far was it to anywhere?

It was then she remembered for the first time that one word — "Walpi!" uttered by the Indian as he came to a halt the night before and pointed far to the mesa — "Walpi." She lifted her eyes now and scanned the dark mesa. It loomed like a great battlement of rock against the sky. Could it be possible there were people dwelling there? She had heard, of course, about the curious Hopi villages, each village a gigantic house of many rooms, called pueblos, built upon the lofty crags, sometimes five or six hundred feet above the desert.

Could it be that that great castle-looking outline against the sky before her, standing out on the end of the mesa like a promontory above the sea, was Walpi? And if it was, how was she to get up there? The rock rose sheer and steep from the desert floor. The narrow neck of land behind it looked like a slender thread. Her heart sank at thought of trying to storm and enter, single-handed, such an impregnable fortress. And yet, if her friends were there, perhaps they would see her when she drew near and come to show her the way. Strange that they should have gone on and left her with those treacherous Indians! Strange that they should have trusted them so, in the first place! Her own instincts had been against trusting the man from the beginning. It must be confessed that during her reflections at this point her opinion of the wisdom and judgment of the Brownleighs was lowered several notches. Then she began to berate herself for having so easily been satisfied about her escort. She should have read the letter more carefully. She should have asked the Indians more questions. She should, perhaps, have asked Jasper Kemp's advice, or got him to talk to the Indian. She wished with all her heart for Bud, now. If Bud were along he would be saying some comical boy-thing, and be finding a way out of the difficulty. Dear, faithful Bud!

The sun rose higher and the morning grew hotter. As she descended to the valley her burdens grew intolerable, and several times she almost cast them aside. Once she lost sight of her pony among the sage-brush, and it was two hours before she came to him and was able to capture him and strap on her burdens. She was almost too exhausted to climb into the saddle when all was ready; but she managed to mount at last and started out toward the rugged crag ahead of her.

The pony had a long, hot climb out of the valley to a hill where she could see very far again, but still that vast emptiness reigned. Even the eagle had disappeared, and she fancied he must be resting like a great emblem of freedom on one of the points of the castle-like battlement against the sky. It seemed as if the end of the world had come, and she was the only one left in the universe, forgotten, riding on her weary horse across an endless desert in search of a home she would never see again.

Below the hill there stretched a wide, white strip of sand, perhaps two miles in extent, but shimmering in the sun and seeming to recede ahead of her as she advanced. Beyond was soft greenness — something growing — not near enough to be discerned as cornfields. The girl drooped her tired head upon her horse's mane and wept, her courage going from her with her tears. In all that wide universe there seemed no way to go, and she was so very tired, hungry, hot, and discouraged! There was always that bit of bread in her pocket and that muddy-looking, warm water for a last resort; but she must save them as long as possible, for there was no telling how long it would be before she had more.

There was no trail now to follow. She had started from the spot where she had found the horse, and her inexperienced eyes could not have searched out a trail if she had tried. She was going toward that distant castle on the crag as to a goal, but when she reached it, if she ever did, would she find anything there but crags and lonesomeness and the eagle?

Drying her tears at last, she started the horse on down the hill, and perhaps her tears blinded her, or because she was dizzy with hunger and the long stretch of anxiety and fatigue she was not looking closely. There was a steep place, a sharp falling away of the ground unexpectedly as they emerged from a thicket of sage-brush, and the horse plunged several feet down, striking sharply on some loose rocks, and slipping to his knees; snorting, scrambling, making brave effort, but slipping, half rolling, at last he was brought down with his frightened rider, and lay upon his side with her foot under him and a sensation like a red-hot knife running through her ankle.

Margaret caught her breath in quick gasps as they fell, lifting a prayer in her heart for help. Then came the crash and the sharp pain, and with a quick conviction that all was over she dropped back unconscious on the sand, a blessed oblivion of darkness rushing over her.

When she came to herself once more the hot sun was pouring down upon her unprotected face, and she was conscious of intense pain and suffering in every part of her body. She opened her eyes wildly and looked around. There was sage-brush up above, waving over the crag down which they had fallen, its gray-greenness shimmering hotly in the sun; the sky was mercilessly blue without a cloud. The great beast, heavy and quivering, lay solidly against her, half pinning her to earth, and the helplessness of her position was like an awful nightmare from which she felt she might waken if she could only cry out. But when at last she raised her voice its empty echo frightened her, and there, above her, with wide-spread wings, circling for an instant, then poised in motionless survey of her, with cruel eyes upon her, loomed that eagle — so large, so fearful, so suggestive in its curious stare, the monarch of the desert come to see who had invaded his precincts and fallen into one of his snares.

With sudden frenzy burning in her veins Margaret struggled and tried to get free, but she could only move the slightest bit each time, and every motion was an agony to the hurt ankle.

It seemed hours before she writhed herself free from that great, motionless horse, whose labored breath only showed that he was still alive. Something terrible must have happened to the horse or he would have tried to rise, for she had coaxed, patted, cajoled, tried in every way to rouse him. When at last she crawled free from the hot, horrible body and crept with pained progress around in front of him, she saw that both his forelegs lay limp and helpless. He must have broken them in falling. Poor fellow! He, too, was suffering and she had nothing to give him! There was nothing she could do for him!

Then she thought of the bottle of water, but, searching for it, found that her good intention of dividing it with him was useless, for the bottle was broken and the water already soaked into the sand. Only a damp spot on the saddle-bag showed where it had departed.

Then indeed did Margaret sink down in the sand in despair and begin to pray as she had never prayed before.

CHAPTER XXXI

The morning after Margaret's departure Rosa awoke with no feelings of self-reproach, but rather a great exultation at the way in which she had been able to get rid of her rival.

She lay for a few minutes thinking of Forsythe, and trying to decide what she would wear when she went forth to meet him, for she wanted to charm him as she had never charmed any one before.

She spent some time arraying herself in different costumes, but at last decided on her Commencement gown of fine white organdie, hand-embroidered and frilled with filmy lace, the product of a famous house of gowns in the Eastern city where she had attended school for a while and acquired expensive tastes.

Daintily slippered, beribboned with coral-silk girdle, and with a rose from the vine over her window in her hair, she sallied forth at last to the trysting-place.

Forsythe was a whole hour late, as became a languid gentleman who had traveled the day before and idled at his sister's house over a late breakfast until nearly noon. Already his fluttering fancy was apathetic about Rosa, and he wondered, as he rode along, what had become of the interesting young teacher who had charmed him for more than a passing moment. Would he dare to call upon her, now that Gardley was out of the way? Was she still in Ashland or had she gone home for vacation? He must ask Rosa about her.

Then he came in sight of Rosa sitting picturesquely in the shade of an old cedar, reading poetry, a little lady in the wilderness, and he forgot everything else in his delight over the change in her. For Rosa had changed. There was no mistake about it. She had bloomed out into maturity in those few short months of his absence. Her soft figure had rounded and developed, her bewitching curls were put up on her head, with only a stray tendril here and there to emphasize a dainty ear or call attention to a smooth, round neck; and when she raised her lovely head and lifted limpid eyes to his there was about her a demureness, a coolness and charm that he had fancied only ladies of the city could attain. Oh, Rosa knew her charms, and had practised many a day before her mirror till she had appraised the value of every curving eyelash, every hidden dimple, every cupid's curve of lip. Rosa had watched well and learned from all with whom she had come in contact. No woman's guile was left untried by her.

And Rosa was very sweet and charming. She knew just when to lift up innocent eyes of wonder; when to not understand suggestions; when to exclaim softly with delight or shrink with shyness that nevertheless did not repulse.

Forsythe studied her with wonder and delight. No maiden of the city had ever charmed him more, and withal she seemed so innocent and young, so altogether pliable in his hands. His pulses beat high, his heart was inflamed, and passion came and sat within his handsome eyes.

It was easy to persuade her, after her first seemingly shy reserve was overcome, and before an hour was passed she had promised to go away with him. He had very little money, but what of that? When he spoke of that feature Rosa declared she could easily get some. Her father gave her free access to his safe, and kept her plentifully supplied for the household use. It was nothing to her — a passing incident. What should it matter whose money took them on their way?

When she went demurely back to the ranch a little before sunset she thought she was very happy, poor little silly sinner! She met her father with her most alluring but most furtive smile. She was charming at supper, and blushed as her mother used to do when he praised her new gown and told her how well she looked in it. But she professed to be weary yet from the last days of school — to have a headache — and so she went early to her room and asked that the servants keep the house quiet in the morning, that she might sleep late and get really rested. Her father kissed her tenderly and thought what a dear child she was and what a comfort to his ripening years; and the house settled down into quiet.

Rosa packed a bag with some of her most elaborate garments, arrayed herself in a charming little outfit of silk for the journey, dropped her baggage out of the window; and when the moon rose and the household were quietly sleeping she paid a visit to her father's safe, and then stole forth, taking her shadowy way to the trail by a winding route known well to herself and secure from the watch of vigilant servants who were ever on the lookout for cattle thieves.

Thus she left her father's house and went forth to put her trust in a man whose promises were as ropes of sand and whose fancy was like a wave of the sea, tossed to and fro by every breath that blew. Long ere the sun rose the next morning the guarded, beloved child was as far from her safe home and her father's sheltering love as if alone she had started for the mouth of the bottomless pit. Two days later, while Margaret lay unconscious beneath the sage-brush, with a hovering eagle for watch, Rosa in the streets of a great city suddenly realized that she was more alone in the universe than ever she could have been in a wide desert, and her plight was far worse than the girl's with whose fate she had so lightly played.

Quite early on the morning after Rosa left, while the household was still keeping quiet for the supposed sleeper, Gardley rode into the inclosure about the house and asked for Rogers.

Gardley had been traveling night and day to get back. Matters had suddenly arranged themselves so that he could finish up his business at his old home and go on to see Margaret's father and mother, and he had made his visit there and hurried back to Arizona, hoping to reach Ashland in time for Commencement. A delay on account of a washout on the road had brought him back two days late for Commencement. He had ridden to camp from a junction forty miles away to get there the sooner, and this morning had ridden straight to the Tanners' to surprise Margaret. It was, therefore, a deep disappointment to find her gone and only Mrs. Tanner's voluble explanations for comfort. Mrs. Tanner exhausted her vocabulary in trying to describe the "Injuns," her own feeling of protest against them, and Mrs. Brownleigh's foolishness in making so much of them; and then she bustled in to the old pine desk in the dining-room and produced the letter that had started Margaret off as soon as commencement was over.

Gardley took the letter eagerly, as though it were something to connect him with Margaret, and read it through carefully to make sure just how matters stood. He had looked troubled when Mrs. Tanner told how tired Margaret was, and how worried she seemed about her school and glad to get away from it all; and he agreed that the trip was probably a good thing.

"I wish Bud could have gone along, though," he said, thoughtfully, as he turned away from the door. "I don't like her to go with just Indians, though I suppose it is all right. You say he had his wife and child along? Of course Mrs. Brownleigh wouldn't send anybody that wasn't perfectly all right. Well, I suppose the trip will be a rest for her. I'm sorry I didn't get home a few days sooner. I might have looked out for her myself."

He rode away from the Tanners', promising to return later with a gift he had brought for Bud that he wanted to present himself, and Mrs. Tanner bustled back to her work again.

"Well, I'm glad he's got home, anyway," she remarked, aloud, to herself as she hung her dish-cloth tidily over the upturned dish-pan and took up her broom. "I 'ain't felt noways easy 'bout her sence she left, though I do suppose there ain't any sense to it. But I'm *glad he's back*!"

Meantime Gardley was riding toward Rogers's ranch, meditating whether he should venture to follow the expedition and enjoy at least the return trip with Margaret, or whether he ought to remain patiently until she came back and go to work at once. There was nothing really important demanding his attention immediately, for Rogers had arranged to keep the present overseer of affairs until he was ready to undertake the work. He was on his way now to report on a small business matter which he had been attending to in New York for Rogers. When that was over he would be free to do as he pleased for a few days more if he liked, and the temptation was great to go at once to Margaret.

As he stood waiting beside his horse in front of the house while the servant went to call Rogers, he looked about with delight on the beauty of the day. How glad he was to be back in Arizona again! Was it the charm of the place or because Margaret was there, he wondered, that he felt so happy? By all means he must follow her. Why should he not?

He looked at the clambering rose-vine that covered one end of the house, and noticed how it crept close to the window casement and caressed the white curtain as it blew. Margaret must have such a vine at her window in the house he would build for her. It might be but a modest house that he could give her now, but it should have a rose-vine just like that; and he would train it round her window where she could smell the fragrance from it every morning when she awoke, and where it would breathe upon her as she slept.

Margaret! How impatient he was to see her again! To look upon her dear face and know that she was his! That her father and mother had been satisfied about him and sent their blessing, and he might tell her so. It was wonderful! His heart thrilled with the thought of it. Of course he would go to her at once. He would start as soon as Rogers was through with him. He would go to Ganado. No, Keams. Which was it? He drew the letter out of his pocket and read it again, then replaced it.

The fluttering curtain up at the window blew out and in, and when it blew out again it brought with it a flurry of papers like white leaves. The curtain had knocked over a paper-weight or vase or something that held them and set the papers free. The breeze caught them and flung them about erratically, tossing one almost at his feet. He stooped to pick it up, thinking it might be of value to some one, and caught the name "Margaret" and "Dear Margaret" written several times on the sheet, with "Walpi, Walpi, Walpi," filling the lower half of the page, as if some one had been practising it.

And because these two words were just now keenly in his mind he reached for the second paper just a foot or two away and found more sentences and words. A third paper contained an exact reproduction of the letter which Mrs. Tanner had given him purporting to come from Mrs. Brownleigh to Margaret. What could it possibly mean?

In great astonishment he pulled out the other letter and compared them. They were almost identical save for a word here and there crossed out and rewritten. He stood looking mutely at the papers and then up at the window, as though an explanation might somehow be wafted down to him, not knowing what to think, his mind filled with vague alarm.

Just at that moment the servant appeared.

"Mr. Rogers says would you mind coming down to the corral. Miss Rosa has a headache, and we're keeping the house still for her to sleep. That's her window up there — " And he indicated the rose-bowered window with the fluttering curtain.

Dazed and half suspicious of something, Gardley folded the two letters together and crushed them into his pocket, wondering what he ought to do about it. The thought of it troubled him so that he only half gave attention to the business in hand; but he gave his report and handed over certain documents. He was thinking that perhaps he ought to see Miss Rosa and find out what she knew of Margaret's going and ask how she came in possession of this other letter.

"Now," said Rogers, as the matter was concluded, "I owe you some money. If you'll just step up to the house with me I'll give it to you. I'd like to settle matters up at once."

"Oh, let it go till I come again," said Gardley, impatient to be off. He wanted to get by himself and think out a solution of the two letters. He was more than uneasy about Margaret without being able to give any suitable explanation of why he should be. His main desire now was to ride to Ganado and find out if the missionaries had left home, which way they had gone, and whether they had met Margaret as planned.

"No, step right up to the house with me," insisted Rogers. "It won't take long, and I have the money in my safe."

Gardley saw that the quickest way was to please Rogers, and he did not wish to arouse any questions, because he supposed, of course, his alarm was mere foolishness. So they went together into Rogers's private office, where his desk and safe were the principal furniture, and where no servants ventured to come without orders.

Rogers shoved a chair for Gardley and went over to his safe, turning the little nickel knob this way and that with the skill of one long accustomed, and in a moment the thick door swung open and Rogers drew out a japanned cash-box and unlocked it. But when he threw the cover back he uttered an exclamation of angry surprise. The box was empty!

CHAPTER XXXII

Mr. Rogers strode to the door, forgetful of his sleeping daughter overhead, and thundered out his call for James. The servant appeared at once, but he knew nothing about the safe, and had not been in the office that morning. Other servants were summoned and put through a rigid examination. Then Rogers turned to the woman who had answered the door for Gardley and sent her up to call Rosa.

But the woman returned presently with word that Miss Rosa was not in her room, and there was no sign that her bed had been slept in during the night. The woman's face was sullen. She did not like Rosa, but was afraid of her. This to her was only another of Miss Rosa's pranks, and very likely her doting father would manage to blame the servants with the affair.

Mr. Rogers's face grew stern. His eyes flashed angrily as he turned and strode up the stairs to his daughter's room, but when he came down again he was holding a note in his trembling hand and his face was ashen white.

"Read that, Gardley," he said, thrusting the note into Gardley's hands and motioning at the same time for the servants to go away.

Gardley took the note, yet even as he read he noticed that the paper was the same as those he carried in his pocket. There was a peculiar watermark that made it noticeable.

The note was a flippant little affair from Rosa, telling her father she had gone away to be married and that she would let him know where she was as soon as they were located. She added that he had forced her to this step by being so severe with her and not allowing her lover to come to see her. If he had been reasonable she would have stayed at home and let him give her a grand wedding; but as it was she had only this way of seeking her happiness. She added that she knew he would forgive her, and she hoped he would come to see that her way had been best, and Forsythe was all that he could desire as a son-in-law.

Gardley uttered an exclamation of dismay as he read, and, looking up, found the miserable eyes of the stricken father upon him. For the moment his own alarm concerning Margaret and his perplexity about the letters was forgotten in the grief of the man who had been his friend.

"When did she go?" asked Gardley, quickly looking up.

"She took supper with me and then went to her room, complaining of a headache," said the father, his voice showing his utter hopelessness. "She may have gone early in the evening, perhaps, for we all turned in about nine o'clock to keep the house quiet on her account."

"Have you any idea which way they went, east or west?" Gardley was the keen adviser in a crisis now, his every sense on the alert.

The old man shook his head. "It is too late now," he said, still in that colorless voice. "They will have reached the railroad somewhere. They will have been married by this time. See, it is after ten o'clock!"

"Yes, if he marries her," said Gardley, fiercely. He had no faith in Forsythe.

"You think — you don't think he would *dare*!" The old man straightened up and fairly blazed in his righteous wrath.

"I think he would dare anything if he thought he would not be caught. He is a coward, of course."

"What can we do?"

"Telegraph to detectives at all points where they would be likely to arrive and have them shadowed. Come, we will ride to the station at once; but, first, could I go up in her room and look around? There might be some clue."

"Certainly," said Rogers, pointing hopelessly up the stairs; "the first door to the left. But you'll find nothing. I looked everywhere. She wouldn't have left a clue. While you're up there I'll interview the servants. Then we'll go."

As he went up-stairs Gardley was wondering whether he ought to tell Rogers of the circumstance of the two letters. What possible connection could there be between Margaret Earle's trip to Walpi with the Brownleighs and Rosa Rogers's elopement? When you come to think of it, what possible explanation was there for a copy of Mrs. Brownleigh's letter to blow out of Rosa Rogers's bedroom window? How could it have got there?

Rosa's room was in beautiful order, the roses nodding in at the window, the curtain blowing back and forth in the breeze and rippling open the leaves of a tiny Testament lying on her desk, as if it had been recently read. There was nothing to show that the owner of the room had taken a hasty flight. On the desk lay several sheets of note-paper with the peculiar watermark. These caught his attention, and he took them up and compared them with the papers in his pocket. It was a strange thing that that letter which had sent Margaret off into the wilderness with an unknown Indian should be written on the same kind of paper as this; and yet, perhaps, it was not so strange, after all. It probably was the only note-paper to be had in that region, and must all have been purchased at the same place.

The rippling leaves of the Testament fluttered open at the fly-leaf and revealed Rosa's name and a date with Mrs. Brownleigh's name written below, and Gardley took it up, startled again to find Hazel Brownleigh mixed up with the Rogers. He had not known that they had anything to do with each other. And yet, of course, they would, being the missionaries of the region.

The almost empty waste-basket next caught his eye, and here again were several sheets of paper written over with words and phrases, words which at once he recognized as part of the letter Mrs. Tanner had given him. He emptied the waste-basket out on the desk, thinking perhaps there might be something there that would give a clue to where the elopers had gone; but there was not much else in it except a little yellowed note with the signature "Hazel Brownleigh" at the bottom. He glanced through the brief note, gathered its purport, and then spread it out deliberately on the desk and compared the writing with the others, a wild fear clutching at his heart. Yet he could not in any way explain why he was so uneasy. What possible reason could Rosa Rogers have for forging a letter to Margaret from Hazel Brownleigh?

Suddenly Rogers stood behind him looking over his shoulder. "What is it, Gardley? What have you found? Any clue?"

"No clue," said Gardley, uneasily, "but something strange I cannot understand. I don't suppose it can possibly have anything to do with your daughter, and yet it seems almost uncanny. This morning I stopped at the Tanners' to let Miss Earle know I had returned, and was told she had gone yesterday with a couple of Indians as guide to meet the Brownleighs at Keams or somewhere near there, and take a trip with them to Walpi to see the Hopi Indians. Mrs. Tanner gave me this letter from Mrs. Brownleigh, which Miss Earle had left behind. But when I reached here and was waiting for you some papers blew out of your daughter's window. When I picked them up I was startled to find that one of them was an exact copy of the letter I had in my pocket. See! Here they are! I don't suppose there is anything to it, but in spite of me I am a trifle uneasy about Miss Earle. I just can't understand how that copy of the letter came to be here."

Rogers was leaning over, looking at the papers. "What's this?" he asked, picking up the note that came with the Testament. He read each paper carefully, took in the little Testament with its fluttering fly-leaf and inscription, studied the pages of words and alphabet, then suddenly turned away and groaned, hiding his face in his hands.

"What is it?" asked Gardley, awed with the awful sorrow in the strong man's attitude.

"My poor baby!" groaned the father. "My poor little baby girl! I've always been afraid of that fatal gift of hers. Gardley, she could copy any handwriting in the world perfectly. She could write my name so it could not be told from my own signature. She's evidently written that letter. Why, I don't know, unless she wanted to get Miss Earle out of the way so it would be easier for her to carry out her plans."

"It can't be!" said Gardley, shaking his head. "I can't see what her object would be. Besides, where would she find the Indians? Mrs. Tanner saw the Indians. They came to the school after her with the letter, and waited for her. Mrs. Tanner saw them ride off together."

"There were a couple of strange Indians here yesterday, begging something to eat," said Rogers, settling down on a chair and resting his head against the desk as if he had suddenly lost the strength to stand.

"This won't do!" said Gardley. "We've got to get down to the telegraph-office, you and I. Now try to brace up. Are the horses ready? Then we'll go right away."

"You better question the servants about those Indians first," said Rogers; and Gardley, as he hurried down the stairs, heard groan after groan from Rosa's room, where her father lingered in agony.

Gardley got all the information he could about the Indians, and then the two men started away on a gallop to the station. As they passed the Tanner house Gardley drew rein to call to Bud, who hurried out joyfully to greet his friend, his face lighting with pleasure.

"Bill, get on your horse in double-quick time and beat it out to camp for me, will you?" said Gardley, as he reached down and gripped Bud's rough young paw. "Tell Jasper Kemp to come back with you and meet me at the station as quick as he can. Tell him to have the men where he can signal them. We may have to hustle out on a long hunt; and, Bill, keep your head steady and get back yourself right away. Perhaps I'll want you to help me. I'm a little anxious about Miss Earle, but you needn't tell anybody that but old Jasper. Tell him to hurry for all he's worth."

Bud, with his eyes large with loyalty and trouble, nodded understandingly, returned the grip of the young man's hand with a clumsy squeeze, and sprang away to get his horse and do Gardley's bidding. Gardley knew he would ride as for his life, now that he knew Margaret's safety was at stake.

Then Gardley rode on to the station and was indefatigable for two hours hunting out addresses, writing telegrams, and calling up long-distance telephones.

When all had been done that was possible Rogers turned a haggard face to the young man. "I've been thinking, Gardley, that rash little girl of mine may have got Miss Earle into some kind of a dangerous position. You ought to look after her. What can we do?"

"I'm going to, sir," said Gardley, "just as soon as I've done everything I can for you. I've already sent for Jasper Kemp, and we'll make a plan between us and find out if Miss Earle is all right. Can you spare Jasper or will you need him?"

"By all means! Take all the men you need. I sha'n't rest easy till I know Miss Earle is safe."

He sank down on a truck that stood on the station platform, his shoulders slumping, his whole attitude as of one who was fatally stricken. It came over Gardley how suddenly old he looked, and haggard and gray! What a thing for the selfish child to have done to her father! Poor, silly child, whose fate with Forsythe would in all probability be anything but enviable!

But there was no time for sorrowful reflections. Jasper Kemp, stern, alert, anxious, came riding furiously down the street, Bud keeping even pace with him.

CHAPTER XXXIII

While Gardley briefly told his tale to Jasper Kemp, and the Scotchman was hastily scanning the papers with his keen, bright eyes, Bud stood frowning and listening intently.

"Gee!" he burst forth. "That girl's a mess! 'Course she did it! You oughta seen what all she didn't do the last six weeks of school. Miss Mar'get got so she shivered every time that girl came near her or looked at her. She sure had her goat! Some nights after school, when she thought she's all alone, she just cried, she did. Why, Rosa had every one of those guys in the back seat acting like the devil, and nobody knew what was the matter. She wrote things on the blackboard right in the questions, so's it looked like Miss Mar'get's writing; fierce things, sometimes; and Miss Mar'get didn't know who did it. And she was as jealous as a cat of Miss Mar'get. You all know what a case she had on that guy from over by the fort; and she didn't like to have him even look at Miss Mar'get. Well, she didn't forget how he went away that night of the play. I caught her looking at her like she would like to murder her. *Good night!* Some look! The guy had a case on Miss Mar'get, all right, too, only she was onto him and wouldn't look at him nor let him spoon nor nothing. But Rosa saw it all, and she just hated Miss Mar'get. Then once Miss Mar'get stopped her from going out to meet that guy, too. Oh, she hated her, all right! And you can bet she wrote the letter! Sure she did! She wanted to get her away when that guy came back. He was back yesterday. I saw him over by the run on that trail that crosses the trail to the old cabin. He didn't see me. I got my eye on him first, and I chucked behind some sage-brush, but he was here, all right, and he didn't mean any good. I follahed him awhile till he stopped and fixed up a place to camp. I guess he must 'a' stayed out last night —"

A heavy hand was suddenly laid from behind on Bud's shoulder, and Rogers stood over him, his dark eyes on fire, his lips trembling.

"Boy, can you show me where that was?" he asked, and there was an intensity in his voice that showed Bud that something serious was the matter. Boylike he dropped his eyes indifferently before this great emotion.

"Sure!"

"Best take Long Bill with you, Mr. Rogers," advised Jasper Kemp, keenly alive to the whole situation. "I reckon we'll all have to work together. My men ain't far off," and he lifted his whistle to his lips and blew the signal blasts. "The Kid here 'll want to ride to Keams to see if the lady is all safe and has met her friends. I reckon mebbe I better go straight to Ganado and find out if them mission folks really got started, and put 'em wise to what's been going on. They'll mebbe know who them Injuns was. I have my suspicions they weren't any friendlies. I didn't like that Injun the minute I set eyes on him hanging round the school-house, but I wouldn't have stirred a step toward camp if I'd 'a' suspected he was come fur the lady. 'Spose you take Bud and Long Bill and go find that camping-place and see if you find any trail showing which way they took. If you do, you fire three shots, and the men 'll be with you. If you want the Kid, fire four shots. He can't be so fur away by that time that he can't hear. He's got to get provisioned 'fore he starts. Lead him out, Bud. We 'ain't got no time to lose."

Bud gave one despairing look at Gardley and turned to obey.

"That's all right, Bud," said Gardley, with an understanding glance. "You tell Mr. Rogers all you know and show him the place, and then when Long Bill comes you can take the cross-cut to the Long Trail and go with me. I'll just stop at the house as I go by and tell your mother I need you."

Bud gave one radiant, grateful look and sprang upon his horse, and Rogers had hard work to keep up with him at first, till Bud got interested in giving him a detailed account of Forsythe's looks and acts.

In less than an hour the relief expedition had started. Before night had fallen Jasper Kemp, riding hard, arrived at the mission, told his story, procured a fresh horse, and after a couple of hours, rest started with Brownleigh and his wife for Keams Cañon.

326

Gardley and Bud, riding for all they were worth, said little by the way. Now and then the boy stole glances at the man's face, and the dead weight of sorrow settled like lead, the heavier, upon his heart. Too well he knew the dangers of the desert. He could almost read Gardley's fears in the white, drawn look about his lips, the ashen circles under his eyes, the tense, strained pose of his whole figure. Gardley's mind was urging ahead of his steed, and his body could not relax. He was anxious to go a little faster, yet his judgment knew it would not do, for his horse would play out before he could get another. They ate their corn bread in the saddle, and only turned aside from the trail once to drink at a water-hole and fill their cans. They rode late into the night, with only the stars and their wits to guide them. When they stopped to rest they did not wait to make a fire, but hobbled the horses where they might feed, and, rolling quickly in their blankets, lay down upon the ground.

Bud, with the fatigue of healthy youth, would have slept till morning in spite of his fears, but Gardley woke him in a couple of hours, made him drink some water and eat a bite of food, and they went on their way again. When morning broke they were almost to the entrance of Keams Cañon and both looked haggard and worn. Bud seemed to have aged in the night, and Gardley looked at him almost tenderly.

"Are you all in, kid?" he asked.

"Naw!" answered Bud, promptly, with an assumed cheerfulness. "Feeling like a four-year-old. Get on to that sky? Guess we're going to have some day! Pretty as a red wagon!"

Gardley smiled sadly. What would that day bring forth for the two who went in search of her they loved? His great anxiety was to get to Keams Cañon and inquire. They would surely know at the trading-post whether the missionary and his party had gone that way.

The road was still almost impassable from the flood; the two dauntless riders picked their way slowly down the trail to the post.

But the trader could tell them nothing comforting. The missionary had not been that way in two months, and there had been no party and no lady there that week. A single strange Indian had come down the trail above the day before, stayed awhile, picked a quarrel with some men who were there, and then ridden back up the steep trail again. He might have had a party with him up on the mesa, waiting. He had said something about his squaw. The trader admitted that he might have been drunk, but he frowned as he spoke of him. He called him a "bad Indian." Something unpleasant had evidently happened.

The trader gave them a good, hot dinner, of which they stood sorely in need, and because they realized that they must keep up their strength they took the time to eat it. Then, procuring fresh horses, they climbed the steep trail in the direction the trader said the Indian had taken. It was a slender clue, but it was all they had, and they must follow it. And now the travelers were very silent, as if they felt they were drawing near to some knowledge that would settle the question for them one way or the other. As they reached the top at last, where they could see out across the plain, each drew a long breath like a gasp and looked about, half fearing what he might see.

Yes, there was the sign of a recent camp-fire, and a few tin cans and bits of refuse, nothing more. Gardley got down and searched carefully. Bud even crept about upon his hands and knees, but a single tiny blue bead like a grain of sand was all that rewarded his efforts. Some Indian had doubtless camped here. That was all the evidence. Standing thus in hopeless uncertainty what to do next, they suddenly heard voices. Something familiar once or twice made Gardley lift his whistle and blow a blast. Instantly a silvery answer came ringing from the mesa a mile or so away and woke the echoes in the cañon. Jasper Kemp and his party had taken the longer way around instead of going down the cañon, and were just arriving at the spot where Margaret and the squaw had waited two days before for their drunken guide. But Jasper Kemp's whistle rang out again, and he shot three times into the air, their signal to wait for some important news.

Breathlessly and in silence the two waited till the coming of the rest of the party, and cast themselves down on the ground, feeling the sudden need of support. Now that there was a possibility of some news, they felt hardly able to bear it, and the waiting for it was intolerable, to such a point of anxious tension were they strained.

But when the party from Ganado came in sight their faces wore no brightness of good news. Their greetings were quiet, sad, anxious, and Jasper Kemp held out to Gardley an envelope. It was the one from Margaret's mother's letter that she had dropped upon the trail.

"We found it on the way from Ganado, just as we entered Steamboat Cañon," explained Jasper.

"And didn't you search for a trail off in any other direction?" asked Gardley, almost sharply. "They have not been here. At least only one Indian has been down to the trader's."

"There was no other trail. We looked," said Jasper, sadly. "There was a camp-fire twice, and signs of a camp. We felt sure they had come this way."

Gardley shook his head and a look of abject despair came over his face. "There is no sign here," he said. "They must have gone some other way. Perhaps the Indian has carried her off. Are the other men following?"

"No, Rogers sent them in the other direction after his girl. They found the camp all right. Bud tell you? We made sure we had found our trail and would not need them."

Gardley dropped his head and almost groaned.

Meanwhile the missionary had been riding around in radiating circles from the dead camp-fire, searching every step of the way; and Bud, taking his cue from him, looked off toward the mesa a minute, then struck out in a straight line for it and rode off like mad. Suddenly there was heard a shout loud and long, and Bud came riding back, waving something small and white above his head.

They gathered in a little knot, waiting for the boy, not speaking; and when he halted in their midst he fluttered down the handkerchief to Gardley.

"It's hers, all right. Gotter name all written out on the edge!" he declared, radiantly.

The sky grew brighter to them all now. Eagerly Gardley sprang into his saddle, no longer weary, but alert and eager for the trail.

"You folks better go down to the trader's and get some dinner. You'll need it! Bud and I'll go on. Mrs. Brownleigh looks all in."

"No," declared Hazel, decidedly. "We'll just snatch a bite here and follow you at once. I couldn't enjoy a dinner till I know she is safe." And so, though both Jasper Kemp and her husband urged her otherwise, she would take a hasty meal by the way and hurry on.

But Bud and Gardley waited not for others. They plunged wildly ahead.

It seemed a long way to the eager hunters, from the place where Bud had found the handkerchief to the little note twisted around the red chessman. It was perhaps nearly a mile, and both the riders had searched in all directions for some time before Gardley spied it. Eagerly he seized upon the note, recognizing the little red manikin with which he had whiled away an hour with Margaret during one of her visits at the camp.

The note was written large and clear upon a sheet of writing-paper:

"I am Margaret Earle, school-teacher at Ashland. I am supposed to be traveling to Walpi, by way of Keams, to meet Mr. and Mrs. Brownleigh of Ganado. I am with an Indian, his squaw and papoose. The Indian said he was sent to guide me, but he is drunk now and I am frightened. He has acted strangely all the way. I do not know where I am. Please come and help me."

Bud, sitting anxious like a statue upon his horse, read Gardley's face as Gardley read the note. Then Gardley read it aloud to Bud, and before the last word was fairly out of his mouth both man and boy started as if they had heard Margaret's beloved voice calling them. It was not long before Bud found another scrap of paper a half-mile farther on, and then another and another, scattered at great distances along the way. The only way they had of being sure she had dropped them was that they seemed to be the same kind of paper as that upon which the note was written.

How that note with its brave, frightened appeal wrung the heart of Gardley as he thought of Margaret, unprotected, in terror and perhaps in peril, riding on she knew not where. What trials and fears had she not already passed through! What might she not be experiencing even now while he searched for her?

It was perhaps two hours before he found the little white stocking dropped where the trail divided, showing which way she had taken. Gardley folded it reverently and put it in his pocket. An hour later Bud pounced upon the bedroom slipper and carried it gleefully to Gardley; and so by slow degrees, finding here and there a chessman or more paper, they came at last to the camp where the Indians had abandoned their trust and fled, leaving Margaret alone in the wilderness.

It was then that Gardley searched in vain for any further clue, and, riding wide in every direction, stopped and called her name again and again, while the sun grew lower and lower and shadows crept in lurking-places waiting for the swift-coming night. It was then that Bud, flying frantically from one spot to another, got down upon his knees behind a sage-bush when Gardley was not looking and mumbled a rough, hasty prayer for help. He felt like the old woman who, on being told that nothing but God could save the ship, exclaimed, "And has it come to that?" Bud had felt all his life that there was a remote time in every life when one might need to believe in prayer. The time had come for Bud.

Margaret, on her knees in the sand of the desert praying for help, remembered the promise, "Before they call I will answer, and while they are yet speaking I will hear," and knew not that her deliverers were on the way.

The sun had been hot as it beat down upon the whiteness of the sand, and the girl had crept under a sage-bush for shelter from it. The pain in her ankle was sickening. She had removed her shoe and bound the ankle about with a handkerchief soaked with half of her bottle of witch-hazel, and so, lying quiet, had fallen asleep, too exhausted with pain and anxiety to stay awake any longer.

When she awoke again the softness of evening was hovering over everything, and she started up and listened. Surely, surely, she had heard a voice calling her! She sat up sharply and listened. Ah! There it was again, a faint echo in the distance. Was it a voice, or was it only her dreams mingling with her fancies?

Travelers in deserts, she had read, took all sorts of fancies, saw mirages, heard sounds that were not. But she had not been out long enough to have caught such a desert fever. Perhaps she was going to be sick. Still that faint echo made her heart beat wildly. She dragged herself to her knees, then to her feet, standing painfully with the weight on her well foot.

The suffering horse turned his anguished eyes and whinnied. Her heart ached for him, yet there was no way she could assuage his pain or put him out of his misery. But she must make sure if she had heard a voice. Could she possibly scale that rock down which she and her horse had fallen? For then she might look out farther and see if there were any one in sight.

Painfully she crawled and crept, up and up, inch by inch, until at last she gained the little height and could look afar.

There was no living thing in sight. The air was very clear. The eagle had found his evening rest somewhere in a quiet crag. The long corn waved on the distant plain, and all was deathly still once more. There was a hint of coming sunset in the sky. Her heart sank, and she was about to give up hope entirely, when, rich and clear, there it came again! A voice in the wilderness calling her name: "Margaret! Margaret!"

The tears rushed to her eyes and crowded in her throat. She could not answer, she was so overwhelmed; and though she tried twice to call out, she could make no sound. But the call kept coming again and again: "Margaret! Margaret!" and it was Gardley's voice. Impossible! For Gardley was far away and could not know her need. Yet it was his voice. Had she died, or was she in delirium that she seemed to hear him calling her name?

But the call came clearer now: "Margaret! Margaret! I am coming!" and like a flash her mind went back to the first night in Arizona when she heard him singing, "From the Desert I Come to Thee!"

Now she struggled to her feet again and shouted, inarticulately and gladly through her tears. She could see him. It was Gardley. He was riding fast toward her, and he shot three shots into the air above him as he rode, and three shrill blasts of his whistle rang out on the still evening air.

She tore the scarf from her neck that she had tied about it to keep the sun from blistering her, and waved it wildly in the air now, shouting in happy, choking sobs.

And so he came to her across the desert!

He sprang down before the horse had fairly reached her side, and, rushing to her, took her in his arms.

"Margaret! My darling! I have found you at last!"

She swayed and would have fallen but for his arms, and then he saw her white face and knew she must be suffering.

"You are hurt!" he cried. "Oh, what have they done to you?" And he laid her gently down upon the sand and dropped on his knees beside her.

"Oh no," she gasped, joyously, with white lips. "I'm all right now. Only my ankle hurts a little. We had a fall, the horse and I. Oh, go to him at once and put him out of his pain. I'm sure his legs are broken."

For answer Gardley put the whistle to his lips and blew a blast. He would not leave her for an instant. He was not sure yet that she was not more hurt than she had said. He set about discovering at once, for he had brought with him supplies for all emergencies.

It was Bud who came riding madly across the mesa in answer to the call, reaching Gardley before any one else. Bud with his eyes shining, his cheeks blazing with excitement, his hair wildly flying in the breeze, his young, boyish face suddenly grown old with lines of anxiety. But you wouldn't have known from his greeting that it was anything more than a pleasure excursion he had been on the past two days.

"Good work, Kid! Whatcha want me t' do?"

It was Bud who arranged the camp and went back to tell the other detachments that Margaret was found; Bud who led the pack-horse up, unpacked the provisions, and gathered wood to start a fire. Bud was everywhere, with a smudged face, a weary, gray look around his eyes, and his hair sticking "seven ways for Sunday." Yet once, when his labors led him near to where Margaret lay weak and happy on a couch of blankets, he gave her an unwonted pat on her shoulder and said in a low tone: "Hello, Gang! See you kept your nerve with you!" and then he gave her a grin all across his dirty, tired face, and moved away as if he were half ashamed of his emotion. But it was Bud again who came and talked with her to divert her so that she wouldn't notice when they shot her horse. He talked loudly about a coyote they shot the night before, and a cottontail they saw at Keams, and when he saw that she understood what the shot meant, and there were tears in her eyes, he gave her hand a rough, bear squeeze and said, gruffly: "You should worry! He's better off now!" And when Gardley came back he took himself thoughtfully to a distance and busied himself opening tins of meat and soup.

In another hour the Brownleighs arrived, having heard the signals, and they had a supper around the camp-fire, everybody so rejoiced that there were still quivers in their voices; and when any one laughed it sounded like the echo of a sob, so great had been the strain of their anxiety.

Gardley, sitting beside Margaret in the starlight afterward, her hand in his, listened to the story of her journey, the strong, tender pressure of his fingers telling her how deeply it affected him to know the peril through which she had passed. Later, when the others were telling gay stories about the fire, and Bud lying full length in their midst had fallen fast asleep, these two, a little apart from the rest, were murmuring their innermost thoughts in low tones to each other, and rejoicing that they were together once more.

CHAPTER XXXIV

They talked it over the next morning at breakfast as they sat around the fire. Jasper Kemp thought he ought to get right back to attend to things. Mr. Rogers was all broken up, and might even need him to search for Rosa if they had not found out her whereabouts yet. He and Fiddling Boss, who had come along, would start back at once. They had had a good night's rest and had found their dear lady. What more did they need? Besides, there were not provisions for an indefinite stay for such a large party, and there were none too many sources of supply in this region.

The missionary thought that, now he was here, he ought to go on to Walpi. It was not more than two hours' ride there, and Hazel could stay with the camp while Margaret's ankle had a chance to rest and let the swelling subside under treatment.

Margaret, however, rebelled. She did not wish to be an invalid, and was very sure she could ride without injury to her ankle. She wanted to see Walpi and the queer Hopi Indians, now she was so near. So a compromise was agreed upon. They would all wait in camp a couple of days, and then if Margaret felt well enough they would go on, visit the Hopis, and so go home together.

Bud pleaded to be allowed to stay with them, and Jasper Kemp promised to make it all right with his parents.

So for two whole, long, lovely days the little party of five camped on the mesa and enjoyed sweet converse. It is safe to say that never in all Bud's life will he forget or get away from the influences of that day in such company.

Gardley and the missionary proved to be the best of physicians, and Margaret's ankle improved hourly under their united treatment of compresses, lotions, and rest. About noon on Saturday they broke camp, mounted their horses, and rode away across the stretch of white sand, through tall cornfields growing right up out of the sand, closer and closer to the great mesa with the castle-like pueblos five hundred feet above them on the top. It seemed to Margaret like suddenly being dropped into Egypt or the Holy Land, or some of the Babylonian excavations, so curious and primitive and altogether different from anything else she had ever seen did it all appear. She listened, fascinated, while Brownleigh told about this strange Hopi land, the strangest spot in America. Spanish explorers found them away back years before the Pilgrims landed, and called the country Tuscayan. They built their homes up high for protection from their enemies. They lived on the corn, pumpkins, peaches, and melons which they raised in the valley, planting the seeds with their hands. It is supposed they got their seeds first from the Spaniards years ago. They make pottery, cloth, and baskets, and are a busy people.

There are seven villages built on three mesas in the northern desert. One of the largest, Orabi, has a thousand inhabitants. Walpi numbers about two hundred and thirty people, all living in this one great building of many rooms. They are divided into brotherhoods, or phratries, and each brotherhood has several large families. They are ruled by a speaker chief and a war chief elected by a council of clan elders.

Margaret learned with wonder that all the water these people used had to be carried by the women in jars on their backs five hundred feet up the steep trail.

Presently, as they drew nearer, a curious man with his hair "banged" like a child's, and garments much like those usually worn by scarecrows — a shapeless kind of shirt and trousers — appeared along the steep and showed them the way up. Margaret and the missionary's wife exclaimed in horror over the little children playing along the very edge of the cliffs above as carelessly as birds in trees.

High up on the mesa at last, how strange and weird it seemed! Far below the yellow sand of the valley; fifteen miles away a second mesa stretching dark; to the southwest, a hundred miles distant, the dim outlines of the San Francisco peaks. Some little children on burros crossing the sand below looked as if they were part of a curious moving-picture, not as if they were little living beings taking life as seriously as other children do. The great, wide desert stretching far!

The bare, solid rocks beneath their feet! The curious houses behind them! It all seemed unreal to Margaret, like a great picture-book spread out for her to see. She turned from gazing and found Gardley's eyes upon her adoringly, a tender understanding of her mood in his glance. She thrilled with pleasure to be here with him; a soft flush spread over her cheeks and a light came into her eyes.

They found the Indians preparing for one of their most famous ceremonies, the snake dance, which was to take place in a few days. For almost a week the snake priests had been busy hunting rattlesnakes, building altars, drawing figures in the sand, and singing weird songs. On the ninth day the snakes are washed in a pool and driven near a pile of sand. The priests, arrayed in paint, feathers, and charms, come out in line and, taking the live snakes in their mouths, parade up and down the rocks, while the people crowd the roofs and terraces of the pueblos to watch. There are helpers to whip the snakes and keep them from biting, and catchers to see that none get away. In a little while the priests take the snakes down on the desert and set them free, sending them north, south, east, and west, where it is supposed they will take the people's prayers for rain to the water serpent in the underworld, who is in some way connected with the god of the rain-clouds.

It was a strange experience, that night in Walpi: the primitive accommodations; the picturesque, uncivilized people; the shy glances from dark, eager eyes. To watch two girls grinding corn between two stones, and a little farther off their mother rolling out her dough with an ear of corn, and cooking over an open fire, her pot slung from a crude crane over the blaze — it was all too unreal to be true.

But the most interesting thing about it was to watch the "Aneshodi" going about among them, his face alight with warm, human love; his hearty laugh ringing out in a joke that the Hopis seemed to understand, making himself one with them. It came to Margaret suddenly to remember the pompous little figure of the Rev. Frederick West, and to fancy him going about among these people and trying to do them good. Before she knew what she was doing she laughed aloud at the thought. Then, of course, she had to explain to Bud and Gardley, who looked at her inquiringly.

"Aw! Gee! *Him? He* wasn't a minister! He was a *mistake*! Fergit him, the poor simp!" growled Bud, sympathetically. Then his eyes softened as he watched Brownleigh playing with three little Indian maids, having a fine romp. "Gee! he certainly is a peach, isn't he?" he murmured, his whole face kindling appreciatively. "Gee! I bet that kid never forgets that!"

The Sunday was a wonderful day, when the missionary gathered the people together and spoke to them in simple words of God — their god who made the sky, the stars, the mountains, and the sun, whom they call by different names, but whom He called God. He spoke of the Book of Heaven that told about God and His great love for men, so great that He sent His son to save them from their sin. It was not a long sermon, but a very beautiful one; and, listening to the simple, wonderful words of life that fell from the missionary's earnest lips and were translated by his faithful Indian interpreter, who always went with him on his expeditions, watching the faces of the dark, strange people as they took in the marvelous meaning, the little company of visitors was strangely moved. Even Bud, awed beyond his wont, said, shyly, to Margaret:

"Gee! It's something fierce not to be born a Christian and know all that, ain't it?"

Margaret and Gardley walked a little way down the narrow path that led out over the neck of rock less than a rod wide that connects the great promontory with the mesa. The sun was setting in majesty over the desert, and the scene was one of breathless beauty. One might fancy it might look so to stand on the hills of God and look out over creation when all things have been made new.

They stood for a while in silence. Then Margaret looked down at the narrow path worn more than a foot deep in the solid rock by the ten generations of feet that had been passing over it.

"Just think," she said, "of all the feet, little and big, that have walked here in all the years, and of all the souls that have stood and looked out over this wonderful sight! It must be that somehow in spite of their darkness they have reached out to the God who made this, and have found a way to His heart. They couldn't look at this and not feel Him, could they? It seems to me that perhaps some of those poor creatures who have stood here and reached up blindly after the Creator of their souls have, perhaps, been as pleasing to Him as those who have known about Him from childhood."

Gardley was used to her talking this way. He had not been in her Sunday meetings for nothing. He understood and sympathized, and now his hand reached softly for hers and held it tenderly. After a moment of silence he said:

"I surely think if God could reach and find me in the desert of my life, He must have found them. I sometimes think I was a greater heathen than all these, because I knew and would not see."

Margaret nestled her hand in his and looked up joyfully into his face. "I'm so glad you know Him now!" she murmured, happily.

They stood for some time looking out over the changing scene, till the crimson faded into rose, the silver into gray; till the stars bloomed out one by one, and down in the valley across the desert a light twinkled faintly here and there from the camps of the Hopi shepherds.

They started home at daybreak the next morning, the whole company of Indians standing on the rocks to send them royally on their way, pressing simple, homely gifts upon them and begging them to return soon again and tell the blessed story.

A wonderful ride they had back to Ganado, where Gardley left Margaret for a short visit, promising to return for her in a few days when she was rested, and hastened back to Ashland to his work; for his soul was happy now and at ease, and he felt he must get to work at once. Rogers would need him. Poor Rogers! Had he found his daughter yet? Poor, silly child-prodigal!

But when Gardley reached Ashland he found among his mail awaiting him a telegram. His uncle was dead, and the fortune which he had been brought up to believe was his, and which he had idly tossed away in a moment of recklessness, had been restored to him by the uncle's last will, made since Gardley's recent visit home. The fortune was his again!

Gardley sat in his office on the Rogers ranch and stared hard at the adobe wall opposite his desk. That fortune would be great! He could do such wonderful things for Margaret now. They could work out their dreams together for the people they loved. He could see the shadows of those dreams — a beautiful home for Margaret out on the trail she loved, where wildness and beauty and the mountain she called hers were not far away; horses in plenty and a luxurious car when they wanted to take a trip; journeys East as often as they wished; some of the ideal appliances for the school that Margaret loved; a church for the missionary and convenient halls where he could speak at his outlying districts; a trip to the city for Mom Wallis, where she might see a real picture-gallery, her one expressed desire this side of heaven, now that she had taken to reading Browning and had some of it explained to her. Oh, and a lot of wonderful things! These all hung in the dream-picture before Gardley's eyes as he sat at his desk with that bit of yellow paper in his hand.

He thought of what that money had represented to him in the past. Reckless days and nights of folly as a boy and young man at college; ruthless waste of time, money, youth; shriveling of soul, till Margaret came and found and rescued him! How wonderful that he had been rescued! That he had come to his senses at last, and was here in a man's position, doing a man's work in the world! Now, with all that money, there was no need for him to work and earn more. He could live idly all his days and just have a good time — make others happy, too. But still he would not have this exhilarating feeling that he was supplying his own and Margaret's necessities by the labor of hand and brain. The little telegram in his hand seemed somehow to be trying to snatch from him all this material prosperity that was the symbol of that spiritual regeneration which had become so dear to him.

He put his head down on his clasped hands upon the desk then and prayed. Perhaps it was the first great prayer of his life.

"O God, let me be strong enough to stand this that has come upon me. Help me to be a man in spite of money! Don't let me lose my manhood and my right to work. Help me to use the money in the right way and not to dwarf myself, nor spoil our lives with it." It was a great prayer for a man such as Gardley had been, and the answer came swiftly in his conviction.

He lifted up his head with purpose in his expression, and, folding the telegram, put it safely back into his pocket. He would not tell Margaret of it — not just yet. He would think it out — just the right way — and he did not believe he meant to give up his position with Rogers. He had accepted it for a year in good faith, and it was his business to fulfil the contract. Meantime, this money would perhaps make possible his marriage with Margaret sooner than he had hoped.

Five minutes later Rogers telephoned to the office.

"I've decided to take that shipment of cattle and try that new stock, provided you will go out and look at them and see that everything is all O. K. I couldn't go myself now. Don't feel like going anywhere, you know. You wouldn't need to go for a couple of weeks. I've just had a letter from the man, and he says he won't be ready sooner. Say, why don't you and Miss Earle get married and make this a wedding-trip? She could go to the Pacific coast with you. It would be a nice trip. Then I could spare you for a month or six weeks when you got back if you wanted to take her East for a little visit."

Why not? Gardley stumbled out his thanks and hung up the receiver, his face full of the light of a great joy. How were the blessings pouring down upon his head these days? Was it a sign that God was pleased with his action in making good what he could where he had failed? And Rogers! How kind he was! Poor Rogers, with his broken heart and his stricken home! For Rosa had come home again a sadder, wiser child; and her father seemed crushed with the disgrace of it all.

Gardley went to Margaret that very afternoon. He told her only that he had had some money left him by his uncle, which would make it possible for him to marry at once and keep her comfortably now. He was to be sent to California on a business trip. Would she be married and go with him?

Margaret studied the telegram in wonder. She had never asked Gardley much about his circumstances. The telegram merely stated that his uncle's estate was left to him. To her simple mind an estate might be a few hundred dollars, enough to furnish a plain little home; and her face lighted with joy over it. She asked no questions, and Gardley said no more about the money. He had forgotten that question, comparatively, in the greater possibility of joy.

Would she be married in ten days and go with him?

Her eyes met his with an answering joy, and yet he could see that there was a trouble hiding somewhere. He presently saw what it was without needing to be told. Her father and mother! Of course, they would be disappointed! They would want her to be married at home!

"But Rogers said we could go and visit them for several weeks on our return," he said; and Margaret's face lighted up.

"Oh, that would be beautiful," she said, wistfully; "and perhaps they won't mind so much — though I always expected father would marry me if I was ever married; still, if we can go home so soon and for so long — and Mr. Brownleigh would be next best, of course."

"But, of course, your father must marry you," said Gardley, determinedly. "Perhaps we could persuade him to come, and your mother, too."

"Oh no, they couldn't possibly," said Margaret, quickly, a shade of sadness in her eyes. "You know it costs a lot to come out here, and ministers are never rich."

It was then that Gardley's eyes lighted with joy. His money could take this bugbear away, at least. However, he said nothing about the money.

"Suppose we write to your father and mother and put the matter before them. See what they say. We'll send the letters to-night. You write your mother and I'll write your father."

Margaret agreed and sat down at once to write her letter, while Gardley, on the other side of the room, wrote his, scratching away contentedly with his fountain-pen and looking furtively now and then toward the bowed head over at the desk.

Gardley did not read his letter to Margaret. She wondered a little at this, but did not ask, and the letters were mailed, with special-delivery stamps on them. Gardley awaited their replies with great impatience.

He filled in the days of waiting with business. There were letters to write connected with his fortune, and there were arrangements to be made for his trip. But the thing that occupied the most of his time and thought was the purchase and refitting of a roomy old ranch-house in a charming location, not more than three miles from Ashland, on the road to the camp.

It had been vacant for a couple of years past, the owner having gone abroad permanently and the place having been offered for sale. Margaret had often admired it in her trips to and from the camp, and Gardley thought of it at once when it became possible for him to think of purchasing a home in the West.

There was a great stone fireplace, and the beams of the ceilings and pillars of the porch and wide, hospitable rooms were of tree-trunks with the bark on them. With a little work it could be made roughly but artistically habitable. Gardley had it cleaned up, not disturbing the tangle of vines and shrubbery that had had their way since the last owner had left them and which had made a perfect screen from the road for the house.

Behind this screen the men worked — most of them the men from the bunk-house, whom Gardley took into his confidence.

The floors were carefully scrubbed under the direction of Mom Wallis, and the windows made shining. Then the men spent a day bringing great loads of tree-boughs and filling the place with green fragrance, until the big living-room looked like a woodland bower. Gardley made a raid upon some Indian friends of his and came back with several fine Navajo rugs and blankets, which he spread about the room luxuriously on the floor and over the rude benches which the men had constructed. They piled the fireplace with big logs, and Gardley took over some of his own personal possessions that he had brought back from the East with him to give the place a livable look. Then he stood back satisfied. The place was fit to bring his bride and her friends to. Not that it was as it should be. That would be for Margaret to do, but it would serve as a temporary stopping-place if there came need. If no need came, why, the place was there, anyway, hers and his. A tender light grew in his eyes as he looked it over in the dying light of the afternoon. Then he went out and rode swiftly to the telegraph-office and found these two telegrams, according to the request in his own letter to Mr. Earle.

Gardley's telegram read:

> Congratulations. Will come as you desire. We await your advice. Have written. — FATHER.

He saddled his horse and hurried to Margaret with hers, and together they read:

> Dear child! So glad for you. Of course you will go. I am sending you some things. Don't take a thought for us. We shall look forward to your visit. Our love to you both. — MOTHER.

Margaret, folded in her lover's arms, cried out her sorrow and her joy, and lifted up her face with happiness. Then Gardley, with great joy, thought of the surprise he had in store for her and laid his face against hers to hide the telltale smile in his eyes.

For Gardley, in his letter to his future father-in-law, had written of his newly inherited fortune, and had not only inclosed a check for a good sum to cover all extra expense of the journey, but had said that a private car would be at their disposal, not only for themselves, but for any of Margaret's friends and relatives whom they might choose to invite. As he had written this letter he was filled with deep thanksgiving that it was in his power to do this thing for his dear girl-bride.

The morning after the telegrams arrived Gardley spent several hours writing telegrams and receiving them from a big department store in the nearest great city, and before noon a big shipment of goods was on its way to Ashland. Beds, bureaus, wash-stands, chairs, tables, dishes, kitchen utensils, and all kinds of bedding, even to sheets and pillow-cases, he ordered with lavish hand. After all, he must furnish the house himself, and let Margaret weed it out or give it away afterward, if she did not like it. He was going to have a house party and he must be ready. When all was done and he was just about to mount his horse again he turned back and sent another message, ordering a piano.

"Why, it's *great!*" he said to himself, as he rode back to his office. "It's simply great to be able to do things just when I need them! I never knew what fun money was before. But then I never had Margaret to spend it for, and she's worth the whole of it at once!"

The next thing he ordered was a great easy carriage with plenty of room to convey Mother Earle and her friends from the train to the house.

The days went by rapidly enough, and Margaret was so busy that she had little time to wonder and worry why her mother did not write her the long, loving, motherly good-by letter to her little girlhood that she had expected to get. Not until three days before the wedding did it come over her that she had had but three brief, scrappy letters from her mother, and they not a whole page apiece. What could be the matter with mother? She was almost on the point of panic when Gardley came and bundled her on to her horse for a ride.

Strangely enough, he directed their way through Ashland and down to the station, and it was just about the time of the arrival of the evening train.

Gardley excused himself for a moment, saying something about an errand, and went into the station. Margaret sat on her horse, watching the oncoming train, the great connecting link between East and West, and wondered if it would bring a letter from mother.

The train rushed to a halt, and behold some passengers were getting off from a private car! Margaret watched them idly, thinking more about an expected letter than about the people. Then suddenly she awoke to the fact that Gardley was greeting them. Who could they be?

There were five of them, and one of them looked like Jane! Dear Jane! She had forgotten to write her about this hurried wedding. How different it all was going to be from what she and Jane had planned for each other in their dear old school-day dreams! And that young man that Gardley was shaking hands with now looked like Cousin Dick! She hadn't seen him for three years, but he must look like that now; and the younger girl beside him might be Cousin Emily! But, oh, who were the others? *Father!* And MOTHER!

Margaret sprang from her horse with a bound and rushed into her mother's arms. The interested passengers craned their necks and looked their fill with smiles of appreciation as the train took up its way again, having dropped the private car on the side track.

Dick and Emily rode the ponies to the house, while Margaret nestled in the back seat of the carriage between her father and mother, and Jane got acquainted with Gardley in the front seat of the carriage. Margaret never even noticed where they were going until the carriage turned in and stopped before the door of the new house, and Mrs. Tanner, furtively casting behind her the checked apron she had worn, came out to shake hands with the company and tell them supper was all ready, before she went back to her deserted boarding-house. Even Bud was going to stay at the new house that night, in some cooked-up capacity or other, and all the men from the bunk-house were hiding out among the trees to see Margaret's father and mother and shake hands if the opportunity offered.

The wonder and delight of Margaret when she saw the house inside and knew that it was hers, the tears she shed and smiles that grew almost into hysterics when she saw some of the incongruous furnishings, are all past describing. Margaret was too happy to think. She rushed from one room to another. She hugged her mother and linked her arm in her father's for a walk across the long piazza; she talked to Emily and Dick and Jane; and then rushed out to find Gardley and thank him again. And all this time she could not understand how Gardley had done it, for she had not yet comprehended his fortune.

Gardley had asked his sisters to come to the wedding, not much expecting they would accept, but they had telegraphed at the last minute they would be there. They arrived an hour or so before the ceremony; gushed over Margaret; told Gardley she was a "sweet thing"; said the house was "dandy for a house party if one had plenty of servants, but they should think it would be dull in winter"; gave Margaret a diamond sunburst pin, a string of pearls, and an emerald bracelet set in diamond chips; and departed immediately after the ceremony. They had thought they were the chief guests, but the relief that overspread the faces of those guests who were best beloved by both bride and groom was at once visible on their departure. Jasper Kemp drew a long breath and declared to Long Bill that he was glad the air was growing pure again. Then all those old friends from the bunk-house filed in to the great tables heavily loaded with good things, the abundant gift of the neighborhood, and sat down to the wedding supper, heartily glad that the "city lady and her gals" — as Mom Wallis called them in a suppressed whisper — had chosen not to stay over a train.

The wedding had been in the school-house, embowered in foliage and all the flowers the land afforded, decorated by the loving hands of Margaret's pupils, old and young. She was attended by the entire school marching double file before her, strewing flowers in her way. The missionary's wife played the wedding-march, and the missionary assisted the bride's father with the ceremony. Margaret's dress was a simple white muslin, with a little real lace and embroidery handed down from former generations, the whole called into being by Margaret's mother. Even Gardley's sisters had said it was "perfectly dear." The whole neighborhood was at the wedding.

And when the bountiful wedding-supper was eaten the entire company of favored guests stood about the new piano and sang "Blest Be the Tie that Binds" — with Margaret playing for them.

Then there was a little hurry at the last, Margaret getting into the pretty traveling dress and hat her mother had brought, and kissing her mother good-by — though happily not for long this time.

Mother and father and the rest of the home party were to wait until morning, and the missionary and his wife were to stay with them that night and see them to their car the next day.

So, waving and throwing kisses back to the others, they rode away to the station, Bud pridefully driving the team from the front seat.

Gardley had arranged for a private apartment on the train, and nothing could have been more luxurious in traveling than the place where he led his bride. Bud, scuttling behind with a suit-case, looked around him with all his eyes before he said a hurried good-by, and murmured under his breath: "Gee! Wisht I was goin' all the way!"

Bud hustled off as the train got under way, and Margaret and Gardley went out to the observation platform to wave a last farewell.

The few little blurring lights of Ashland died soon in the distance, and the desert took on its vast wideness beneath a starry dome; but off in the East a purple shadow loomed, mighty and majestic, and rising slowly over its crest a great silver disk appeared, brightening as it came and pouring a silver mist over the purple peak.

"My mountain!" said Margaret, softly.

And Gardley, drawing her close to him, stooped to lay his lips upon hers.

"My darling!" he answered.

www.ingramcontent.com/pod-product-compliance
Lightning Source LLC
LaVergne TN
LVHW011928070526
838202LV00054B/4533